DATE DUE

"Not since T   light-
fully on the   first
page to last   ver a
marvelous 1-   ould
be proud of.'

                                    HOLS

"Piercy's cha   dom
and intimacy   . . . .
Characteristi   der-
stand the dyr   ow a
needy damse   cuer
like David. If   vays
seem to get sr   ercy
exposes the c

                                    iew

"A seamless   his
past, his ener   n finally settle in   ing,
of men and w

                                    ews

"[A] perceptiv

                                    kly

BOOKS BY MARGE PIERCY

POETRY
Breaking Camp
Hard Loving
4-Telling
To Be of Use
Living in the Open
The Twelve-spoked Wheel Flashing
The Moon Is Always Female
Circles on the Water
Stone, Paper, Knife
My Mother's Body
Available Light
Mars and Her Children
What Are Big Girls Made Of?

FICTION
Going Down Fast
Dance the Eagle to Sleep
Small Changes
Woman on the Edge of Time
The High Cost of Living
Vida
Braided Lives
Fly Away Home
Gone to Soldiers
Summer People
He, She and It
The Longings of Women
City of Darkness, City of Light

ESSAYS
Parti-colored Blocks for a Quilt

ANTHOLOGY
Early Ripening: American Women's Poetry Now

BOOKS BY IRA WOOD

NOVELS
The Kitchen Man
Going Public

PLAY
The Last White Class

Storm Tide

Marge Piercy and Ira Wood

Fawcett Books
The Ballantine Publishing Group
New York

A Fawcett Book
Published by The Ballantine Publishing Group

www.randomhouse.com/BB/

Library of Congress Catalog Card Number: 99-091089

ISBN 0-449-00157-1

Cover photo © Elie Bernager/Tony Stone Images, NY

Manufactured in the United States of America

First Trade Paperback Edition: December 1999

10 9 8 7 6 5 4 3

Storm Tide

DAVID

When the winter was over and my nightmares had passed, when someone else's mistakes had become the subject of local gossip, I set out for the island. I made my way in increments, although the town was all of eighteen miles square. To the bluff overlooking the tidal flats. Down the broken black road to the water's edge. To the bridge where her car was found, overturned like a turtle and buried in mud.

The color of bleached bones, the shape of a crooked spine, the Squeer Island bridge was a product of willful neglect. Every ten years some town official proposed a new bridge and promptly fell into a hole full of lawyers. The beaches were private, the summer people moneyed, the year-rounders reclusive. No one wanted the sandy ways paved or the hedgerows cut back. Your deed bought more than seclusion on Squeer Island; here life as you knew it ceased to exist.

There had been a family named Squeer, but only Stumpy was left. If you asked how the island got its name, people would say, " 'Cause it's queer over there," and they didn't mean homosexual. They meant queer things happened. Peculiar things. Uncommon for a small town.

During high tide there was no access by land. The road to town flooded. Ducks paddled over the bridge. Fish darted through the guardrails. The summer people stocked their shelves with vodka and paperbacks and waited uneasily for the tide to recede. The residents lived for its return.

I left my car on the island side of the bridge. I slogged along the mud banks of the creek, driving fiddler crabs in front of me like herds of frightened crustacean sheep. The grasses were four feet high at the edge of the bank, an inch wide, sharp as razors. They mentioned lacerations across the palms; one in her right eyeball. I closed one eye. I wondered what it was like to sink in this bottomless liquid clay, this mud the fishermen called black mayonnaise. What did it feel like to die this way? They said her hair was encrusted with seaweed and crabs, that an eel had eaten into the armpit. They say she must have struggled to free herself, that as she grabbed at the grass her efforts only increased the suction of the mud. They still call it an accidental death.

* * *

Saltash, Massachusetts, was founded in 1672 and named for a village in Cornwall, England. Summer population: twenty thousand. Winter population: divide by ten. The economy is eighty percent tourism; the leading economic indicator: the number of pickups idling outside Barstow's Convenience at seven A.M. Like any quaint, postcard-perfect Cape Cod town, there are hundreds of stories to be ashamed of here. Only conscience dictates that I start with my own.

If you lived in Saltash, you'd know that I grew up here and had been famous for something—although you probably wouldn't remember what. You might have heard that I left town at eighteen, after having signed a contract for a small fortune, and returned twelve years later. You'd know that I live in a small white half Cape on Round Pond Road and drive a red pickup; that I run a landscaping business with my sister, which (no one forgets to mention) she owns. You might have voted for me for selectman. Everyone I talked to told me they did. (For the record, I received 578 votes.) You would say I wasn't the type to make promises or suck up to people; you might say I kept to myself. You would excuse me for my private life; 578 people obviously did. According to my backers (twelve old men who fancied themselves Saltash's political kingmakers) I had been drawn in by the Squeer Island crowd—a local epithet implying strange sexual practices and not far from the truth. "Seduced" was the explanation whispered most.

It happened in September, the night of the new moon. A storm was tracking our way. Judith warned me that we were facing one of the highest tides of the year. If I couldn't get over the bridge in time, I wouldn't get through at all. "Gordon expects you. He really wants you there," she said, just so I knew it wasn't her who did.

More than anyone I've ever known, Judith loved rituals. She loved to cook for people. They didn't have to be important people or the best of friends. A festive, well-set table surrounded by guests who weren't watching their weight would do: people who arrived on time and had interests other than themselves and remembered to thank her for her trouble. But tonight was special. There were over thirty guests at the table of Gordon Stone and Judith Silver. It was special because it was Rosh Hashanah, and Judith had instituted the celebrating of the Jewish holidays when she became Gordon's fourth wife thirteen years before I met her. Special because Gordon was dying of lung cancer, and he was saying goodbye.

He looked like a living skeleton. His color was grayish-blue and he could not sit up, but reclined, lying on a couch with heaped-up pillows that had been dragged to the table. Judith was wearing a short red shift tonight and her fine skin and dark hair shone. Her necklace and earrings were silver. Judith did not like gold. She once told me silver was a more human metal because it aged, it changed.

Judith had prepared traditional foods. Buckwheat groats with mushroom gravy and bow-tie noodles, roast chicken, potato kugel, gefilte fish, apples dipped in honey. Those friends who weren't Jewish—including two of Gordon's adult children whose mother wasn't—hummed the songs we taught them and bowed their heads as we blessed the wine, and followed everything we did with the curious respect of anthropologists at an Mbundu marriage ceremony in Angola. What they might have missed, however, was the fact that Judith wouldn't be caught alone in the same room with me, removing herself whenever I tried to pull her aside to talk.

No one on the island asked about Judith and Gordon and me. What was common knowledge was never uttered. What mattered was that Gordon had spent an entire summer vacation helping Stumpy Squeer rebuild his house after a fire; that Judith had had a troubling intuition about a high school girl's painful cramps and drove her through a snowstorm to a good Boston hospital in time to be treated for a tubal pregnancy. There were feuds and there were grudges. But judgments among the year-rounders were limited to practical problems: Whose dog had ripped through whose garden? Who rented to noisy college kids in July?

By the second course, the lights began to flicker. The surf was halfway up the dune. Judith had arranged housing for almost everyone, except of course for me. But after the summer of silence, I was determined to talk to her and, finally, finally caught her alone in the kitchen.

"What do you want with me, David?" She turned her back. "Talk to Crystal. You're going to marry her."

"I don't want to marry Crystal. Can we sit down and talk about this?"

"Not here. Not now. I have thirty people to settle in for the night. If you absolutely insist on talking, wait for me in my shack."

Judith's "shack" was an electronic cottage, part sanctum, part home office. It was fitted out with a computer, two printers, copier, scanner, and fax—as well as the double bed where we had made love many times. I lay back against the headboard, waiting, rehearsing my speech while the three cats who had been locked up there for the evening jumped from the dresser to my stomach and off again, taking out their anger on me. Sand pitted the glass and blew in through gaps in the jambs. You found sand in your shoes after nights like this, a film of sand like dust. Every shelf in the cottage shook. Wind lifted the shingles and smacked the roof. The joists shivered and sawdust trickled over the bed like snow. An hour passed. Water ran in sheets down the windows and poured from the downspout. Judith did not come.

When I heard the sound of a car horn, I knew something was wrong. One long drone, as if the driver was leaning on the wheel, and as it got closer, short blasts of pure panic. I ran for the main house, ran hard through the muddy courtyard in the pelting rain.

What I need to say is that I'm telling all this to get it straight, to reduce a tragedy to its parts and somehow understand. Call it an autopsy. A dissection of something that had once been alive; a determination as to the cause of death.

DAVID

2 I was born with a talent, a peculiar accident of reflex and bone, like an eidetic memory, or the facility to play an instrument by ear, an aptitude as curious as it was admired. I was a phenomenon, a teenage celebrity, for by some fluke of chromosomal alchemy that in no way resembled the physiology of my parents, I could throw a baseball faster, harder and with more accuracy than any other boy in my school, my county, my state. I became the focus of my family, the obsession of the local media and the hope of an entire town.

My abilities revealed themselves accidentally. We were not, except for my uncle Georgie, a family inclined toward sports. My father had been a manufacturer of women's dresses who had lost two businesses on Seventh Avenue before going into debt to buy a curtain factory on Cape Cod. Because of the size of the town and the simplicity of the product, my father assumed he could master the transition with ease. But just as his stitchers had sewn half the collars backwards on a big Christmas order of red velvet dresses for Macy's and his best salesman defected, taking the buyers with him, the crises presented themselves in Massachusetts as frequently as they had in Manhattan. My father had no time for games. Baseball, like poker and local women, were the bad habits of his younger brother Georgie, who worked for my father. Georgie—never George to my father; never "my brother" but "my kid brother"—had followed us north. In charge of maintenance and shipping, he partied with the workers his age and the local fishermen as if he were native born. Up at five A.M., never home at night before eight, my father lived exactly as he had in New York, preoccupied with the business, while Georgie dated girls from town and drank beer in the oyster shacks, cast for bluefish and sea bass on the back shore and learned to bait his hooks by the light of the moon.

My father's factory was the largest business in Saltash and the least solvent. As payroll day came around, my parents' arguments began, the recriminations and slamming doors, the curses. My mom took private piano students and worked when she could as a substitute teacher, but every Sunday night my parents sat at the dining room table, staring into the account books, willing the figures to change with the same concentration and futility as if trying to make the furniture levitate.

My sister Holly was too young for the carping to upset her, but I got out of the house whenever I could. What I didn't hear couldn't bother me. My world was the old wooden bridge at the mouth of the Tamar River (long since replaced by a cement dike). When the tide was low, a steep sandy beach full of shells and crabs and acres of stones glistened in the sunlight. When the tide was coming in, waves rolled under the bridge or crashed against the causeway. During spring and fall, the ale-wives migrated underneath and I tried to catch them in an old wire net. The fact that I was different came up occasionally, as when a girl re-fused to kiss me in a game of spin the bottle or when I was held down and stripped by some older kids who wanted to see a circumcised prick. But the incidents were generally benign. (Soon after we moved to Saltash—I was in first grade—the teacher gave me a generic picture to color, a horse instead of a Santa Claus because, as she announced to the class, Jews don't believe in Christmas.) And the truth is, we were different. We spoke more quickly and with accents that turned heads in the street; we didn't eat shellfish, the one product native to the town, and nobody had ever heard of our holidays. We were stocky, with coarse dark hair and light eyes. My mother asked for books that shocked the li-brarian. If isolation bothered me, I wasn't conscious of it, until the day I snapped.

I was sitting on the old wooden bridge with Corkie Pugh, watching a quahog dragger slowly crisscross the harbor. Corkie was an overfed, freckle-faced boy with a lisp and an inclination to sadism. Corkie so en-joyed dismembering small animals and embarrassing his sister in public that even I, who had no friendships to speak of, shied away from him. But because his sister took piano lessons from my mom, I was stuck with him. Corkie's mother usually stayed for coffee after the lesson, and if my mom hadn't made what she called any "real" friends in Saltash, Lucinda Pugh was the woman she saw most often.

Nobody believed this, but there was no precipitating animosity that day, no shouting. We were tossing rocks at an empty beer can in the sand, watching it jump, when Corkie, as easily as he told me how he watched his sister on the toilet through a hole he had drilled in the bathroom wall, said simply, "Your parenth are gettin' a divorth, y'know."

"No, sir."

"Yes, thir. Your mom tol' mine."

I hopped down. Walked off. Kicked a few stones. Flipped one flat stone side-arm over the water's gray-green surface and watched it hop, once, twice, a third time. Then with no thought whatsoever, I began to hurl stones at Corkie, as quickly as I could pick them up, fast and hard. I had aimed at targets before, but never with such delight in my accu-racy, pinging his elbow, his knee, his left buttock as he ran off threatening me with reform school. I wasn't aware of being angry or frustrated. I had no words with which to explain myself. It was as if everything I needed to say could be expressed through the violent articulation of my arm. I walked home without lifting my eyes from the ground. I blew out our garage windows, one after another at thirty feet. I took aim at my mother's car, smashing the taillights, rattling the hubcaps. I was shaking when they stopped me. I dropped to the ground. I was a human gun, an eleven-year-old catapult of accuracy and rage.

I was taken before the school psychologist and the chief of police, but only Georgie seemed to know what to do with me. He set up beer bottles on a tree trunk and bet me a nickel each I couldn't hit them. I did. He took me to the town dump, gave me rocks and pointed: that rusty old alternator. Plink! The fender of the abandoned truck. The headlamp socket. One Friday after work, Georgie gathered some of the factory guys at the loading dock and took bets on what I could hit. A can at forty feet. A stop sign at fifty. A pinecone on a dead branch. With his winnings he bought me a baseball glove.

Saltash was a town with a grade school, three churches, and a movie theater open on weekends only. Saturday night after the show, teenagers raced cars down Hill Street from the town's only grocery to the harbor, whipped around and started uphill again. The stores closed at six and the churches banned bingo. A Little League pitcher who allowed nine runs all season and could strike out half the junior high school team was something to watch. I took us to the state finals three years running. The local paper printed my stats every week in a sidebar on the sports page headed: SALTASH'S DAVEY GREENE. I started pitching for the high school team in ninth grade. In tenth the bird dogs arrived, retired baseball junkies who traveled all over New England searching out talent, notifying the big league scouts who showed up the following year smoking cigars, sitting in their own aluminum lawn chairs instead of the bleachers and logging every pitch I made on their clipboards.

After school, after work, after the season (he never missed a day), Georgie worked out with me. The next Sandy Koufax, he called me. The little Jew that could. Georgie was a veteran who in his army pictures looked like Elvis Presley: pompadour, pouty eyelids, lips in a smirk. I had once heard my parents whispering about a woman and child in Korea. Georgie lived in an apartment built in the loft of the barn behind my parents' house. His window shades were always drawn. He kept Miles Davis albums in milk crates and his mattress on the bedroom floor. One day, when I reached for a baseball that rolled under the couch, I found his girlfriend's black lace bra. Georgie used to meet me every day at the town field for practice. He had a piece of foam rubber he stuffed into his catcher's mitt so his palm wouldn't sting from my fastball. He taught me how Whitey Ford held a runner on first base, how Bob Feller stared into a batter's eyes with contempt. He taught me how to raise my leg and stretch like Warren Spahn so that my delivery was as swift as the recoil of a bow.

In my junior year, I didn't lose a game. My parents and I were invited to ride in the backseat of a yellow convertible in the Fourth of July parade. My mother was suddenly David Greene's mom to every merchant in town. My father mail-ordered a new baseball glove and a pair of white leather baseball shoes from Herman's Wonderful World of Sports. We were invited to the annual Lynch family barbecue.

Georgie said I had the closest thing to a perfect fastball he had ever seen. He had watched Koufax pitch and Larry Sherry and said I had their speed, their power. He convinced my father that he should be given time off from work at the factory to be my coach. It was an investment, Georgie insisted, because when I graduated, I would get a bonus to sign with a professional team.

Georgie went out drinking with the scouts. He was being wooed by the Cubbies, the Pirates, the Mets, who competed to earn my family's trust. He told me stories about athletes who had been swindled out of every dollar they ever made. Every time my fastball cracked into the catcher's mitt, every time I struck out a batter, I glanced at Georgie in the stands. In my senior year, twelve major league teams had scouts at every game. I was working on a string of shutouts. I was throwing at close to eighty miles an hour, putting batters down in five pitches. As the string grew to four, reporters from the big city newspapers interviewed me in my living room at home. When no team scored off me in six games, the front office men arrived. "You're the man," Georgie whispered, rubbing my shoulder. I didn't think about blowing the string because I had never blown it, because I was the only kid in school who didn't have to take gym. (I could hurt myself.) The only kid from Saltash who had ever been asked to speak in front of the Masons (who recruited my father, their first Jew). The batters had heard of me and swung nervously, trying to kill my pitches, or cowered when I hurled a warning shot near their heads. They weren't facing a pitcher but a legend, a seventeen-year-old who had never fixed himself a meal—"What if you burned yourself?" my mother said—whose arm had been kissed by God.

I signed with the Chicago Cubs for the largest bonus ever paid to a kid from my state. I was assigned to play in Wytheville, in the Appalachian League. I was given a going-away party by the entire town. There were fireworks at the pier. Local restaurants served free franks and potato salad. The bandstand was decorated with streamers and a sign was strung across Commercial Street, DAVEY GREENE SALTASH'S PITCHING MACHINE.

Out of the million and a half guys who graduated high school, I was one of only five hundred signed to a professional contract—and every single one of them was a local legend. I was facing the best athletes in America. Like every other rookie, I had good days and bad. Only, I'd never had bad days before. I was shaken by the crack of bat meeting ball, the sight of the coaches' narrowed eyes on the hitters, not on me, the jeers of the home team crowd when I walked a man after twelve pitches. I felt every hit off me as a whiplash across my back, a stinging pain that left me waiting for another. One night, after walking the streets of some town whose name I couldn't even remember, I called Georgie from a phone booth, pleading for help. "What's the matter with me?"

"Nothing's the matter."

"But I stink."

"Did the coaches say that?"

"No."

"'Course not, 'cause they know it takes time. How long did it take Koufax to find himself?"

"Six years, but—"

"But nothing. What did he lead the league in in 'fifty-eight?"

"Wild pitches."

"Fucking right. He was a maniac out of control. Remember that. You gotta have patience. You've got the best stuff I've ever seen. You're Davey Greene, the Pitching Machine."

But my best was only good, not great. In this league they waited out my pitches. They understood the physics of the game, the slow rising trajectory as the ball picked up steam; they didn't try to crush the pitch before it crossed the plate. At first Georgie was right, the coaches weren't concerned. They'd seen a thousand kids like me. I was just another rookie getting his lumps.

But I wasn't. I was the pitching machine. The kid who got his father invited to be a Mason, who gave his parents a reason not to get divorced. Other guys played cards after the games or picked up girls. I commandeered a catcher and pitched. The harder I worked, the more I tired my arm, but I didn't know what else to do. On my best days, I'd pitch three or four decent innings then walk four men, hit a batter, send a pitch into the dirt before I was pulled. I went back to Saltash in October with a record of two wins, nine losses.

I worked indoors with Georgie all winter, determined to make my reputation come spring. The club liked what they saw and sent me up two notches, to Winston-Salem in the Carolina League, where we took chartered buses to our away games instead of school buses and stayed in motel rooms two to a room instead of four. But as soon as I got behind on the count, I began to panic, to lose control, to throw harder, and harder still, until my arm ached. The coaches assured me that fastball pitchers took time to develop, that more important than strength, every movement of the arms, the kick, the follow-through, had to be in sync. I had to grow into my pitch, they told me. It would take years.

But I couldn't wait years. I needed the applause of the crowd like I needed air. I needed the envy of my teammates, my coach's arm around my shoulder as we walked to the clubhouse, the special wink that set me off from the other players, the fear in the batter's eyes.

When I was sent down to Peoria, my manager swore the club still had confidence in me, that I was a second-year rookie who needed to grow into my pitch, my body; to mature, he kept saying. But all I felt was shame. The Peoria Chiefs were a Single A club; the dung heap of baseball. I imagined my old teammates laughing at me; the Corkie Pughs back in Saltash waiting for me to return a failure. I could not keep on losing.

Working with an old reliever who had spent nine years with the Cubbies, I learned how to throw change of speed pitches, curveballs, sliders. I wouldn't give up. I could still win. I dropped my fastball like an unfaithful lover. Instead of overpowering batters, I would psych them out, use strategy. When I finally won a game, I slept the night through for the first time in a year.

Georgie was disappointed I'd abandoned the fastball; he said I'd had a pure talent for it. But Georgie was a small-town shipping clerk, I told myself. Fine with a high school pitcher, ignorant about the reality of the majors.

The following season I was assigned to the Double A Pittsfield Cubs. We trained in Florida with the big club, played our games on the same field. We stayed in single rooms in a hotel with room service. I took my meals in the same restaurants as Billy Buckner, Bruce Sutter, and Dick Tidrow. But what I'd hoped was a minor problem of timing began to recur. My leg twisted when I started my wind up, my shoulder dropped too soon. My hips and feet could not coordinate. All my old moves, my fastball moves, returned. Ten years of memory encoded in my muscles superimposed itself on my newly learned style.

At away games, the crowds cheered in ecstatic disbelief. At home, the fans booed. I no longer had a fastball or a change of speed. My arm was a slingshot with a mind of its own. My manager winced as he watched me wind up. The simplest rhythms were beyond me. The more I concentrated, the more deliberate my movements became, and the more awkward. I was like a man who had forgotten how to walk.

On the morning after blowing a fourteen inning tie with a wild pitch, I found my name on the barracks pink sheet, unconditionally released. I stuffed my suitcase and talked to no one, drove off in a cloud of shame and stopped at the exit with nowhere to go. I'd been selected to do one thing in this world and failed. In a way, the talent had never belonged to me, but to Georgie; to my father and mother. Without the Pitching Machine, there was no Davey Greene. The sports pages were my mirror: without them I didn't have a face.

On those rare occasions when I attempted to make sense of my baseball career, I wrote it off to being young. I'd destroyed my talent by not staying with it; swapped something difficult for the easy way out. But time would tell that this was a deeper flaw, a thin crack in strong cedar that would widen with age. Fifteen years later I was to repeat the mistake, and ruin more lives than my own.

DAVID

3

I remember my first night in Judith's office. I remember watching her middle finger trace the rim of her wineglass around and around lightly, the way we seemed to be circling each other. It was mid-January and the world outside was brittle as glass. After dark, the streets along the waterfront seemed to radiate a frozen phosphor of road salt and snow. She had invited me over to talk politics, but her questions were all about me.

Most people listened to my story with thinly disguised pleasure. Everyone loves the tale of a hero fallen on hard times. Not Judith. "You must have been so lonely," she said, as if she knew how it felt to lose something you loved.

She had begun by asking me a simple question about growing up in Saltash, and I blurted out the story of my life. "In all those years of baseball, I had never held a real job or written a check or cooked myself a meal. I felt like a released convict."

She held back a smile. "With a sixty thousand dollar bonus."

"By the time I was thirty-two, I had blown every cent, ruined my marriage, lost my son and failed at the one thing I ever wanted to do with my life."

"Precocious, weren't you? Takes most men till forty." She avoided causing me embarrassment by averting her eyes. She fussed with her necklace, resettled herself like a bird on its perch, momentarily fluttering. There was something birdlike about Judith. She was small. She moved quickly. Her almost-black eyes were watchful, alert to trouble. She stopped to think before she laughed. Something most people would regard as funny seemed to cause her concern, as if worried the joke might be on her. She looked my age but acted much older. She wore wool and fine leather; I doubt she owned a pair of sweatpants. She was never Judy, always Judith.

I assumed she came from an affluent family because of her elegance, but the past she told me in snippets was of a hardworking immigrant mother, of growing up in a slum. Most women I knew complained of their mothers. Judith spoke of hers with deep affection and respect.

The wind had picked up. A sheaf of ice slid off the roof to the parking lot below. When I was a kid, this old building near the wharf had been a boathouse and after that a feed store; something called the

Rainbow People's Gallery when the first hippies moved to town, then abandoned for years. Judith had renovated it into an office suite downstairs and one enormous loft-style apartment above, in which we sat, overlooking the harbor, frozen solid since New Year's and dry as a salt flat in the clear light of the moon. Everything in the apartment was the color of fire; the stuffed chairs burnt orange, the walls vermilion, the shaggy wool rug a slash of yellows and reds. I remember three sources of light: a table lamp, a gas fire in the grate, and Judith's face, which seemed to absorb them both and cast a glow of its own.

She was known as one of the best lawyers on the Cape. It was tough luck if she wouldn't represent you; disaster if she was on the other side. She had argued zoning cases before the Supreme Judicial Court and had a loyal clientele among those involved in the drug trade, but the specialty that gave her a demonic aura with the men in town was divorce law and custody cases. She had the reputation of getting a good deal for discarded wives.

I felt large in Judith's presence, which was strange. Despite wide shoulders and a blocky frame, I was small for a pitcher. At five-foot-ten, my nickname was Little Chief. I have some Tartar from my mother's side, causing a slightly Asian cast to my eyes. I have long black hair. In summer, when my skin bronzed, my pitching coach for the Winston-Salem Spirits said I looked like a fair-eyed Indian.

"You're suddenly quiet," she said. "Something the matter?"

"Maybe I'm feeling kind of unsure."

"About what?" She wasn't going to make this easy.

"About what we're doing. How we got here like this."

"You drove here in your big red truck."

"I think you know what I mean."

"We're becoming better friends, David. I assume we are."

For a professional athlete, even at my level, there had always been women. But no one like Judith Silver. No one who studied foreign languages for pleasure or was quoted every week in the paper. No one who was happily married to a man with cancer.

I had first met Judith through my sister Holly. Holly always told people she was my business partner, but it was her husband Marty's money behind the nursery. I didn't know a thing about the landscaping business when I moved back to Saltash. I had no skills, no savings; only an ex-wife in Florida and a child I was permitted to see twice a year.

My brother-in-law Marty was a syndicated humorist whose work hit too close to home to make me laugh. My sister was training as a

geneticist when she married him. Next to science, she'd always loved
the outdoors. She told people that she bought McCullough's Nursery
and Garden Center to keep herself from becoming a mad housewife.
Nobody who knew her husband laughed. Marty's twice-weekly column
appeared in over a hundred newspapers nationwide. He wrote frequently for GQ and two of his books had been best-sellers. His shtick
was a nervous dad's response to a society out of control: there wasn't a
man alive better qualified.

Marty lived with an almost paralyzing fear of everyday life. When the
family had a home in the Boston area, he was afraid of schoolyard ab-
ductions. He demanded Holly drop their girls at their classroom every
morning and pick them up in the afternoon. He carefully examined all
toys with moving parts and insisted that Holly soak the family's fruits
and vegetables no less than twenty minutes in a soapy solution before
serving. After the random murder of a law professor in their neighborhood, Marty moved the family to Saltash. Doing lectures, promotions
and television, he was on the road part of every week. He installed a fax
machine in the girls' bedroom and corrected their homework assignments from hotels around the country. He bought Holly a cellular
phone for her birthday so he could reach her anywhere, day or night.

I was out of baseball before Marty met my sister, but it pleased him
that I had been a professional athlete. It meant his children would have
strong genes. "We're Jewish," he said. "We need all the help we can
get." Although I had grown up in a rural Christian area where I never
felt more than a grudging tolerance of my religion, it would be accurate
to say that my most intimate contact with anti-Semitism came from my
brother-in-law, who sincerely hated himself.

I arrived at their kitchen door one night to ask Holly to sign some
checks, when Marty summoned me to the dining room. "Sit down,
David. Have you eaten? You have to eat. Hol? I asked your brother to
stay. He can't eat if he doesn't have a plate."

Besides the girls—Kara, eight, and Allison, six and a half—there
were two other people at the table. The man was much older than
Marty and Holly. He had a long rectangular face, folds of skin like
melting candle wax beneath glittering dark blue eyes. His voice was reso-
nant and he had been holding court until I entered the room, interrupting himself with bouts of a frightening cough. The woman I guessed to
be around my age was dark-haired and petite, a reserved Audrey Hep-
burn to his big-voiced John Huston. They were introduced to me as
Gordon, a former professor of Marty's, and Judith.

"I'm sorry," I said. "I can't stay."

Marty insisted, "Have a little something, have a lot of something. Take a doggie bag, back up your truck. Your sister made enough to feed an army. It's her Jewish obsession with food."

"An obsession?" I noticed a tremor in the older man's hand. "Or a survival technique?"

"Here he goes," Marty said excitedly. "I want to start my tape recorder whenever he opens his mouth."

"Before the expulsion from ancient Israel, the Jews were an agrarian people. On sacred holidays, they congregated outside the Temple to offer a ritual portion of their harvest as thanksgiving. When the Temple was destroyed and the Jews dispersed, the rabbis decreed that each family's dinner table represent the altar of the Temple. Food became more than something to eat. It was a ritual connection to history."

"And that," Marty raised his index finger, "is how we became the Chosen. Eleven million people chosen to eat too much."

"Why can't you stay?" Holly said.

"Just need your signature." I held up the check register.

"For your nursery?" Judith seemed interested for the first time.

"You can call it that," Marty said. "I call it my wife's plan to save me from writer's block. She spends everything I make so I have to work harder."

"Don't believe him," Gordon said. "Sounds like a column to me."

"Herr Professor, on the money again." Marty touched his face to the table, as if bowing. When he raised his head, there was a bit of mashed potato on the tip of his nose and the girls burst into uncontrollable giggles. "It'll run next Monday," Marty said.

"Folks." I backed away. "Pleasure to meet you. Holly, sign this, please. And this." I was out of there.

Holly had bought the nursery at auction after the McCullough family lost it to the bank. The place had a reputation for skinny trees at Christmas and spring seedlings that died as soon as they left the greenhouse, but Holly turned it around. In the nursery Holly effervesced confidence. Around Marty she seemed subdued. That had been the case since they were dating. But at work she was my kid sister again: full of energy and attitude, brown hair braided down her back, her face darkly tanned. She set up a farmer's market to sell apples and fall produce. She lured customers in with a Thanksgiving turkey raffle. As I was standing up the twenty-foot Scotch pine that arrived from Canada every December, she wondered why we couldn't have a menorah and told me to build one, a big silver and gold painted job made of plywood. Holly and I were on our own turf again; we sang oldies in the greenhouse and traded dirty jokes with the McCullough brothers, whom she'd kept on as a landscaping crew. She teased me mercilessly about my sex life.

Two weeks before Christmas, Judith drove up. At five-foot-three, she seemed to peer over the steering wheel of her Jeep. She jumped out in Ferragamo boots, her purse tucked under her arm like a riding crop, and marched through the store back to where I was kneeling by the side of the little pond in the greenhouse. "Where do you keep your Chanukah candles?"

Just the week before, I had released eight more goldfish, large orange carp I'd brought back from Boston. "We don't carry candles."

"But you put up that big menorah out there. No dreydles? No chocolate coins?"

Cheek to the cold black surface of the artificial pond, I peered between the lily pads. "Sorry."

"I had high hopes for you people."

"Christmas trees, wreathes, poinsettias, lights . . ." Even with a flashlight I couldn't see a thing. The goldfish were gone. Not a trace.

She mumbled something and strolled through the greenhouse, then the yard. "David!" she called a few minutes later. I was surprised she remembered my name. "You have broom crowberry. I've been looking for that."

Actually, so had I. I got them from a supplier in New Bedford just the day before, a special order for a good customer and not for sale.

"I'll take both of them," she said.

I assessed her calfskin gloves, her cashmere coat, the scent of lemon and leather when she opened her purse for her checkbook. Judith was miniature perfection. Tiny nose. Pale skin, almost peach. I was trying to guess her age as I led her to the desk. Why was she with the old guy? "I'll have to order them for you," I said.

She wasn't pleased and her attention turned out the window. For a moment, knowing her reputation, I wondered if I could be sued for not selling her the plants. "That's beautiful," she said. "With the lights and all. It's the first time I've ever seen a menorah publicly displayed out here. Believe it or not, it means something to people."

"It was my sister's idea."

"Good for her. I'm tired of passing baby Jesus and the wise men on the highway. I don't begrudge the church their icons but I guess I've always wanted some equal time."

"It's not the church. The town puts it up every year."

"No," she said. "They can't do that. It's a rule of law. There's been a Supreme Court decision."

"They store it in the town garage, they repaint it, they put it up on town time and on town land."

She wanted names and dates, the facts, as if doing whatever they pleased on town time was something new. The guys in the Department of Roads, Bridges and Waterways always served the town while dividing any extras for themselves. One sold firewood cut by his crew, while some used the town equipment to clear new roads for private developments. They did whatever the town boss let them. Judith stared at me. "You know an awful lot about this town."

"It's a short story, really. Just two words."

"Johnny Lynch," she said.

"Love it or leave it, he's Mr. Saltash."

"I don't know too many people who love it."

"That's because you're from away," I said.

She didn't back off. "Aren't you?"

"I'm from here and I'm not," I said.

"You're an interesting man, David Greene. I hope you'll call me." She looked me over one last time. "About the plants."

"Hello. Who is this? What do you want?" were the precise words Gordon used upon answering the telephone.

Had I not convinced myself that my intentions were profit-oriented, I would have had my sister make the call. "You must be Gordon Silver. Your wife stopped into my nursery last week and ordered some broom crowberry."

"There is no Gordon *Silver*. Who the hell is this?"

I introduced myself. "We met at my brother-in-law Marty's."

"You're talking to Gordon Stone. Didn't Marty tell you who I was?" I only knew what her sign read: Judith Silver, Attorney at Law. I apologized.

"Did you go to college?"

I didn't know what business it was of his, but I wasn't going to be put down. "Yes, sir. As a matter of fact."

"Where?"

I knew this game. Your class status in three words or less. I wasn't playing.

He demanded: "What did you read in sociology?"

"Sir, I don't remember. If this is a bad time—"

"You're damned right it is, when supposed college graduates can't even remember the author of a book assigned in almost every college in this country for well over a decade. Why did you call me, then? Why waste my time?"

That evening, just before closing, Judith called. "Hello, David."

In my most professional voice: "I called to tell you your order arrived."

"Thank you. I have to apologize for Gordon. I hope you weren't insulted. From what I understand, he was less than gracious on the phone."

"Well, maybe we should forget it. Maybe it's too late for this season."

"No, David. It's a very good time. The ground here isn't frozen yet."

It wasn't that I didn't think about Judith. The steam escaping her lips in the yard. The way her eyes held mine, like a cat's: eyelids slowly lowering to withhold what seemed offered only a moment before. But she was married to what sounded like a nasty and possessive man. What was the point?

On New Year's Eve, I made an obligatory stop at the party of a good customer. Perched on top of a sand dune overlooking the Atlantic, the house was barely livable in winter. Blowing sand pitted the mammoth windows and shrouded the work I had done on the gardens—which would guarantee another fine contract when the owners returned in spring. I did not intend to stay. This wasn't my crowd.

For as long as Saltash has attracted summer visitors, it has had a taxpaying population of painters and writers, ex-commies and anarchists, and dating back at least to the early 1950s a colony of old Time-Life people. They had retired to vacation homes bought decades ago or spent long summers here, sometimes eight months long, May through December, before going south for the winter or returning to an apartment in New York. I did landscape work for a Professor Emeritus from Yale; an ex-commissar in the Abraham Lincoln Brigade; a researcher who claimed to have written much of John Hersey's war reportage. Some of them had been around for my glory days in Little League. They were friendly, but they weren't my friends. They were articulate and glib, fond of whiskey and wisecracks I didn't always understand. The truth is, they liked having a local guy to talk to, but I wasn't quick enough to interest them in conversation. Moreover, this being the holidays, many of their children were at the party, ex-prep-schoolers who'd summered together since they were kids and whose conversations bragged about their accomplishments since. Backed into a pissing contest between a foreign correspondent covering China and a playwright whose agent at

William Morris said Swoozie and Olympia were dying to star in her new play, I excused my way to the buffet table for one more sandwich before going home. As I reached for the roast beef I overheard someone say, "So you and Gordon are a childless couple?"

"Is that like a burpless cucumber?" Judith smiled, but her stare was as sharp as cut glass.

"But you don't have any children?"

"We thought about it," Judith said. "But decided on a sex life instead. Actually we have five children and six grandchildren. Hello, David." Judith turned her back on the other woman. "I'm glad you're here. I want to ask you something."

She was wearing a black velvet dress, a slender string of natural pearls like baby teeth across her bare upper breast. I followed her to a dimly lit corner near the huge bay windows, and in the glass reflection, instinctively tried to catch sight of her husband.

"I couldn't really ask you on the phone," she said, so softly I had to lean close to hear. "I was afraid you'd say no. Promise you won't say no until you think about it."

I was about to touch her. I was about to make a fool of myself, when she said: "There are a number of people in town who say you'd make a good selectman."

Talk about a cold shower. "Me?" Ridiculous. I wasn't sure how long she'd been living in this town, but people like me didn't run for selectman. Businessmen, professionals, developers: always older, often retired, and until only recently, very connected to Johnny Lynch. "I don't think so."

"Why not? You know a lot of people and everybody knows you. You're the closest this town ever had to a hero, David Greene." I liked hearing her say my name, I liked the attention; *her* attention. As I was about to respond, she touched her finger to my lip. "Remember, you promised," she said. "You can't say no until you think about it."

Saltash was a town built on a hill. From High Street in town center, every road sloped down to the harbor, a deepwater basin with a sizable fishing fleet and some of the best yachting on the Cape. The Tamar flowed into the bay just east of town. Once a swift moving river with a vast floodplain, it was now a muddy stream, bounded by a marsh of cattail and bramble where Johnny had been slowly filling it in. Separating the harbor from the river was Johnny Lynch's dike—maybe ten feet high, fifty long—and whether you favored tearing it down or keeping it determined who your friends were and who ignored you on the street.

Little Saltash was a town at war. Economics was a part of it, but not the core. Retired bankers linked arms with shellfish scratchers; electricians and roofers attended meetings with the president of the golf course; on both sides were rich and poor. At the heart was a tall and courtly man who wore bow ties and a gray felt fedora; who had read stories to the kindergarten children on the fourth Friday of every month and saw to it that no one born in this town went without shelter or a meal. Johnny Lynch had discovered Saltash on a fishing trip the summer of his last year at Suffolk University Law School. He set up an office on High Street and attracted clients by writing their wills for free. Nor did he ever send a bill for helping people fill out their tax forms. They received nothing in the mail but a postcard, asking that they remember him at the polls. John Mosley Lynch won his first seat on the Board of Selectmen by two votes and ran unopposed for the next twenty-four years. He made sure widows kept their houses and residents received building permits while he quietly searched the tax collector's files after the Town Hall closed. Over time he bought hundreds of properties lost to back taxes. He was elected chairman of the Board of Selectmen and moderator of town meetings. He created a rescue squad. He lobbied his State House friends for the funds to construct a pier and dredge a basin for yachts—and filled in a productive salt marsh with the muck that was removed, building a hundred vacation homes in a development he called Neptune's Garden. Johnny Lynch drifted into a dying fishing village and created a new economy based on tourism and a thriving tax base of second home owners.

But the people who bought those homes had a different agenda. They liked Johnny—most of them had been to his house for drinks—but they didn't think he should handpick the police chief, the fire chief and the Board of Health. They said the builders he had chosen for the new grade school had worked so badly the roof leaked and the walls were cracking. They were opposed to men on the town payroll laying out roads on Johnny's subdivisions on town time, using town equipment. They hated him for the concrete dike he'd forced through a town meeting to replace the old wooden bridge washed away in a hurricane. They remembered the acres of dead shellfish after the dike was completed, the stench that carried for miles, the shellfishermen who wandered around their ruined beds in a state of shock, kicking mounds of dried-up oysters they'd raised from tiny seed. They resented the loss of the most productive estuary in the region, which had once given the town hundreds of species of finfish and mollusks. They mourned the loss of habitat for migrating birds, endangered reptiles, marine and terrestrial mammals—all to keep a golf course from flooding.

The retired population, educated and well-to-do, had made it through the Great Depression and World War II and weren't about to be gaveled to silence by Johnny Lynch. They carried copies of Robert's Rules of Order to town meetings. They understood that protecting the environment meant protecting their property values. It was the retired population that voted in new zoning regulations: one new home per acre instead of four; that supported Audubon and tied Johnny up in court. They had time on their hands and they used it to organize. After twenty-four years they voted Johnny Lynch out of office—but he still controlled three of five seats on the Board of Selectmen at least until the upcoming election.

The Monday after the party, I received four phone calls before noon. From the Committee for Civic Responsibility: "Hello, David. Why don't you come to one of our meetings to talk." From a local reporter: "Is it true you're running for selectman?" From my sister: "What the fuck would you want to do that for?" From Judith: "Have you made up your mind?"

Judith and I spoke every day, on the phone or over coffee. We discussed strategy, the three candidates who had already declared for the one seat up for grabs, some of the issues. But not the real one, not until that night in her office.

"This is insane," I said, watching the fire in her gas grate. "I'm not the kind of person who does this."

"Maybe that's why a lot of people want you to do it."

"What lot of people?"

"Everyone we polled," she said.

The word "poll" made me laugh. We were talking about Saltash, a town with a pharmacy that had to special-order any drug stronger than aspirin, with no place after Labor Day to buy a pair of socks.

"People think you're hardworking and honest, David. They think you listen to them when they talk. They think you're very bright."

"By Saltash standards."

"By any standards. Including my own," Judith said, quashing any doubts I had about why I was considering this at all.

At first I thought it might be revenge. Taking power, sitting in judgment. I thought it might be the idea of becoming an important person again. Even making my mother proud. But it was Judith. It was her attention, my name on her lips.

It was being invited upstairs on a freezing winter night, sitting in a wing chair by her fire. It was books all over the walls and photographs of her in a white sundress in Mexico and Arles. It was her chin in her palm as she waited me out, her eyes lingering on my shoulders and hands. "So what have you been thinking?" she said finally.

"About running?"

She laughed. "Is there something else?"

"I think you know there is."

"And would you like that to happen?"

Neither of us spoke for a long time. "Judith, you have a husband. And from what people say, Gordon is a very nice man."

"You didn't answer my question."

"Yes," I said. "I'd like it to happen. If I didn't feel I was taking you away from someone who's weak, who can't defend himself, who—"

Judith closed her eyes. She held up her palm: stop. When I did, she said this: "David, you can never take me away from Gordon." We both heard the chill in her voice. "There are no models for the way Gordon and I live. We do not fit a mold. We do not ever try to hurt each other. We don't have affairs. We do have close friendships. Do you understand?"

I did not. I said I did because I could not imagine refusing this gift.

"It'll be all right," she said, kneeling on the rug in front of me, laying her cheek on my lap.

She undressed me slowly. She moved her fingertips from my neck to my breast bone to my nipples. She sighed when I touched her. She grabbed my wrists to govern the speed and pressure of my hands. She wanted it to last, she whispered. It had to last all night and all week until the next time. When I touched her between the legs, she arched back reflexively. She seemed to quiver. When I entered her, she gave a short cry. The first time I made love to Judith, I thought I had hurt her, but she explained that great pleasure could almost be a kind of pain. We lay awake in each other's arms, barely moving—estivating, she called it, nearly asleep but fully aware—making it last. "Trust me," she said. "Don't you trust me? Why so glum?"

Because even then I knew, it would not be all right. Even as I traced my fingertips down the bridge of her nose, to her mouth, to her breasts. Even as my cheek touched her naked belly, I knew it was wrong.

JUDITH

Judith had a birthday party the day before, with twelve candles on the chocolate cake. Her mother had given her a new flowered rayon skirt. Her other father, Sandy, had given her a necklace with a golden rose on it. Yirina, her mother, had her call Sandy "Daddy," which was okay with Judith. Sandy's full name was Sanford. He told her New York Jews of his generation all had names like Sanford and Sherwin and Marvin and Walcott. They wanted to be WASPs he said, but of course as soon as Jews used those names, the WASPs dropped them. Sandy had hair like his name, and he was suntanned even in April, her birth month, because he was a painter for real and a housepainter for money. All week he worked, but he spent weekends with them.

Now today, her real birthday, they were having another birthday party with Dr. Silver. She was very careful with Dr. Silver. Her mother's American name was Jerri Silver. She was not married to Dr. Silver, who had another legal family, two daughters and a wife named Sharon, but when Mother had been buying the papers that would let her enter the U.S. as an immigrant, with Dr. Silver's secret sponsorship, she had taken his name. Mother had thought he would marry her, pregnant with his son.

"If you had been born a boy," Yirina said oftener than Judith liked, "he would have married me. All that American wife has given him is two daughters, no better than you." But then ten minutes later Yirina would kiss her and take her on her lap and tell her how precious she was. Judith had only not to cry, not to speak and to wait, and her mother's love would return.

"We're lucky he acknowledges you, think of that, child."

"He doesn't acknowledge me. I have two sisters I've never seen. I know about them but they don't know I exist."

"So it must be," Yirina said. Dr. Silver visited them every Wednesday night and he gave Yirina money. They always needed money. Mother had various jobs. She had met Sandy when she was playing cocktail piano in a restaurant-bar right off Prospect Park. But they had got rid of her a couple of years ago. Mother said she was getting too old for that work, but Judith did not believe it. "You're beautiful," she told Yirina. As with so much else about her mother, it was impossible to know her age, which varied up to fifteen years depending to whom she was speaking and her mood. According to Yirina, she had escaped Czechoslovakia in 1938 when she was fifteen, eighteen, twenty, and once, twenty-three.

Yirina had baked both cakes and decorated them. She had sent Judith into Prospect Park where the daffodils were in bloom, to cut some and hide them in a bag pinned into her old coat that no longer properly buttoned. They looked lovely in the vases Yirina had brought with her from Mexico. Yirina had taken out the good tablecloth she always washed by hand, with fine embroidery of birds and flowers. Yirina had had it since her years in Turkey, during The War. Judith's mother could always make a feast. She could make a celebration out of a chicken, a couple of candles and a bottle of cheap Chianti. She could make a celebration out of a sunny afternoon and tuna fish sandwiches in Prospect Park. For Judith's father, Dr. Silver, she was wearing her best red dress of real silk and the diamond necklace that went in and out of the pawnshop several times a year. It was very important that they please Dr. Silver. Judith wondered if she ever really pleased him. Was he happy she existed? Did he wish she had never been born? She was always covertly staring at his square face, impeccably shaven, and trying to read his feelings for her.

Once again Judith unwrapped the flowered skirt that her mother had wrapped in the same paper, carefully opened the night before. Dr. Silver was a stout man of medium height, a bit stooped. His hair was all white, even the hair that bristled from his nose and ears. His eyes were a pale luminous blue, but Judith had dark eyes like her mother. Sometimes she tried to find herself in her father. She had her mother's dark hair, her mother's pale skin with an olive tint. Dr. Silver was ruddy. She was small like her mother, small for her age. Her mother could pretend she was ten for several years longer, when they occasionally went to the movies. But she had her father's hands, what Yirina proudly called "a surgeon's hands." Long-fingered but quite strong. She had his long narrow feet. Her mother's feet were small but wide. Her mother wore size 5C, a size they looked for in sale bins or rummage sales at the nearby churches of Brooklyn.

"I've brought you something I noticed you need, Judith," Dr. Silver said. "I hope it's the right size."

"I'm sure it is," Yirina said. She had been on the phone with the doctor's secretary, for Judith had listened, pressed against the wall. The doctor's secretary, a formidable woman called Cindy, was the only person in the doctor's world who knew Judith existed, except for Dr. Silver's lawyer. When Judith was little, Cindy would give her lollipops on the rare occasions Judith and Yirina went to Dr. Silver's office. Now that she was older, Cindy gave her magazines from the office. Judith studied them for clues on how an American woman was supposed to be. Cindy did the doctor's shopping for him, for his wife, Yirina, and all three daughters, the legitimate and the illegitimate. That was a word Judith brooded over. People spoke of the legitimate theater. And children. She was a bastard. When Yirina lost her temper, she called her daughter that. To which Judith, if she was furious, would yell back, "Whose fault is that?"

But it was her fault for being born a girl, apparently. Dr. Silver sat at the head of the table, his hands in his lap. They had eaten the cinnamon-flavored chicken. (Her mother cooked Czech; her mother cooked Turkish; her mother cooked Mexican; her mother cooked American. Yirina said proudly that she knew a hundred ways to cook chicken.) They had eaten the lemon poppyseed cake, a particular favorite of Dr. Silver's. When he was in the little three-room apartment, everything swirled around him sitting stiffly until he retired into the bedroom with Yirina and Judith was told to watch television on the set he had bought them five years before. They did not watch it much. Judith had homework every night, which she did passionately. Dr. Silver gave her a dollar for every A she got and fifty cents for every B. She managed to bring in almost all A's. A good report card could feed them for several days. But she also wanted to prove to him she was worthy, of value. She hoped that her grades were better than the grades of his other daughters.

She opened the package carefully, automatically saving the paper and the ribbon. It would all be used again. Sometimes the ribbons turned up in her clothing or Yirina's. Inside was a red spring coat. "It's beautiful!" she said. "Can I put it on?"

It was truly beautiful, and a little big, but she would not say that. She knew Yirina had wanted it that way so that it would last longer. She paraded around the table, as Yirina told her to do. "Doesn't she have fine posture?"

"Like a little princess," Dr. Silver said. "Judith, I hope you are improving your grades in math."

"I like science better," she said. "But I'm working on the math."

She was named after Dr. Silver's grandmother, who had died the year she was born. Who had never known about her. She was a secret child. She kissed Dr. Silver dutifully. She could feel his slight embarrassment. They were both awkward at affection with each other. She felt he liked her but could not love her. Often she wondered if he loved his other daughters. She fantasized sometimes that they all shared some holiday, Passover or an American holiday like Thanksgiving. "I'm going to visit my half-sister Lisa this afternoon," she would say. They would all become friends. She would have a real family as others did, instead of only her mother, old photos and Yirina's shape-shifting memories. If they only could meet her, she knew they would like her. She would please them. She would.

Then it was time for Dr. Silver and Yirina to retire into the bedroom and for Judith to turn on the TV loud until, about an hour later, they emerged. She hated those times but she gave no sign of her feelings, because she understood this was how Yirina kept Dr. Silver coming back. She minded less with Sandy, because he spent the night and she slept on the daybed. Other nights she and her mother shared the double bed. Sandy was almost like a real husband.

They had a small apartment on the top floor of a narrow brownstone in a neighborhood just turning Black. Most of her classmates were Jewish, like her, but not like her. Most had two parents. At school she said her parents were divorced, but that her father came to see her once a week. That was acceptable. She learned what she could say about her family life. She did not bring friends home. She was careful whom she trusted. Dr. Silver paid for her Hebrew lessons at a local synagogue; it was understood she would have a bat mitzvah next year, although Dr. Silver would not be there. Sandy would, if he was still with her mother then. Judith had learned not to take such continuity for granted. But Yirina said of herself, "At least I know how to please a man. That's important, Judith. If he pleases you, that's nice, but it's icing on the cake, you understand me?"

"I won't need to please a man," Judith said, when Yirina was going on about speaking softly and laughing in a pleasant refined manner. "I will work and make money."

"I don't work?" Yirina laughed dramatically, tossing her head with the black hair all teased up in a new style. "I just sit on my fanny all day. Who would have known from the way my back aches?"

"If I go to college—"

"We must get Dr. Silver to help you go. We must!" Yirina's mood changed abruptly. She was wearing her house smock, sitting at the sewing machine with material all over the kitchen. She was making drapes for a lady in the next block. Yirina did alterations and made draperies and slipcovers. She had signs up at all the dry cleaners. "My own mother tried to tell me I should go to college. She was a doctor, Judith, back when there were few women doctors. She had an office on Listopadu." Whenever Yirina used a Czech word, a name from Prague where she had grown up, her face changed. It softened. A nostalgic glow came upon her. "She tried to make me get an education, Judith, but I wouldn't listen. I was a pretty girl, and I thought that was all I needed. I went to university, but my classes meant nothing to me. Only boys mattered. Never be like that, Judith. *They* can take everything from you, your money, your home, every possession, your name, but an education, Judith, you can take that with you wherever you go." Then she leaned forward, staring at Judith, as if to see into her bones. "You must speak properly, not the way they do around here. They talk like hoodlums. You must speak like an educated person. I have an accent. But you have no reason to have one."

Judith usually remembered to speak a different way at school with other kids than at home. Sometimes she forgot.

A week after Judith's bat mitzvah, paid for by Dr. Silver, but attended by Sandy, there was a phone call from Cindy. "Jerri," Cindy said. She always spoke so loud that Judith, sitting next to her mother, could hear both sides of the conversation. Yirina, who had excellent hearing, held the phone away from her ear while Cindy was bellowing. "Jerri, it's Dr. Silver. He's had a heart attack. He's in the hospital."

Dr. Silver never recovered consciousness. Cindy said they should not go to the funeral, but Yirina disobeyed. Yirina got Sandy to drive them (it did not matter anymore if he went with them, since Dr. Silver could no longer ask who he was) to the cemetery, way out on Long Island where they had never been. It was a cemetery in a wilderness of cemeteries. They stood well back. Judith stared at her sisters. They were older. The widow was blond and so was one of the daughters. They were dressed in suits and hats.

She got a much better look at them a couple of days later, when they were called in by Dr. Silver's lawyer, Mr. Vetter, along with the rest of the family. He seemed ironically amused as he introduced them, without explanation. "Jerri Silver," the widow Sharon Silver repeated. "Are you a cousin?"

Yirina shook her head no. She volunteered no information. Judith stared at her sisters. Lisa was pretty, dressed in a pink pants suit with bell bottoms. She must be eighteen, maybe nineteen. Brenda was pregnant. Her husband was addressed as Doctor. They all kept looking at Yirina and Judith. Judith felt frightened. Yirina was wearing black, one of the dresses she used to put on when she was playing piano in the cocktail lounge. She held Judith tightly by the hand and sat upright in one of the chairs.

"I don't understand why they're here," the widow said. "What are they, some obscure relatives?"

"It will all be clear when I read the will," Mr. Vetter said suavely, poking his glasses higher up the bridge of his nose. "Should I commence, then?"

This man was the first lawyer Judith had ever met face-to-face. Judith did not have any desire to be a doctor, although Yirina spoke of it as the highest calling. She hated hospitals and sickbeds and pain. But it looked powerful to be a lawyer. You told people what was what. The law stood behind you. People waited on your words. She felt as if Mr. Vetter did not despise them, but was somehow on their side. He was a slight man, balding with a patch of dark hair over either ear, but he seemed to radiate power and confidence. He had a strong carrying voice like an actor or a rabbi.

Dr. Silver left most of his considerable estate to his wife and his daughters, with a trust for his coming grandchildren. But he also left a trust for Judith, to be applied only to her education. It was not to be touched except for that purpose. If she failed to attend college by age twenty-five, it was to revert to his other daughters. She was so referred to. She was finally spoken for as a daughter. They were his other daughters. Judith began to weep, not from grief or joy, but from the overwhelming sense of no longer being invisible. She hardly listened when the lawyer read the bequest of five thousand dollars to Yirina, to be paid in two installments a year apart. She hardly registered the screams of the widow and the daughters, their ranting, their insults.

"You're telling me my husband was having an affair for the last fourteen years? That's not possible. This is a lie!"

The blond daughter, Lisa, began to sob. "Our daddy wouldn't do something that low! You're trying to tell us that . . . that shabby creature is our sister! She doesn't look anything like us! And her mother can't even speak English."

"I speak six languages," Yirina said coldly. "English, Czech, German, Turkish, Spanish and Yiddish. I also read and write them. If you never have to change countries in your life, you should thank Adonai, rather than insult those who have had to begin again and again."

"I don't know who you are or what kind of hold you had on my husband, but you will not get a penny!" the widow said, shaking her lacquered finger at Yirina. "I see no resemblance between this gawky child and my dear husband."

Mr. Vetter stood. "Dr. Silver has acknowledged his daughter. He wishes to leave her a small remembrance. That was his wish and I doubt if you will find a court in New York to overturn this will, ladies. After all, he left you almost everything."

Yirina stepped forward and smiled at the lawyer. "Thank you, sir. You've been very understanding to a woman who has survived many troubles. Dr. Silver meant a great deal to me. I'm sorry his widow and his other daughters resent his acknowledgment of his second family. But I appreciate your gentlemanly treatment of me and our daughter."

"Five thousand dollars," Yirina said after they left. "He wasn't so generous. I thought he might give me a little house or a trust fund or some stocks. He promised to take care of me. Well, it's better than nothing."

For Judith, the will meant she would go to college; and it meant she was visible, no more a shameful secret. She no longer believed her sisters would be her friends, for they had treated her as if she were a rabid dog. But she still felt better. Mr. Vetter was her new hero.

JUDITH

5 Judith went to NYU on scholarship, majoring in political science and commuting from Brooklyn by subway. In her junior year she had a part-time job typing for a professor. Often she did not get home until ten at night, after studying at the library, working for Professor Jamison, sometimes seeing her boyfriend Mark or working on her column for the school paper.

Mark had an apartment with two other guys in what was beginning to be called the East Village, which sounded better to parents than calling it the Lower East Side. His apartment was dirty and run-down, with what passed for a bath in the kitchen. There was only one bedroom, with bunk beds. The guys took turns sleeping on the fold-out couch at one end of the big room, the kitchen. It was hard to get privacy, but obviously that was the only place they had to make love. They had managed it six times. Judith found it awkward, never knowing if the roommates would walk in, hearing the neighbors through the open barred window. The guys had been robbed once, of the TV and stereo parents had provided. This was the beginning of spring vacation, so both roommates were gone tonight. Mark had decided to stay around, to have time alone with her and to work on a term paper.

They were both earnest skillful students, adept at taking exams and dealing with professors' demands and foibles. She was the more driven, viewing being a student as a job. He did not have to work as hard, since his parents were putting him through. They lived in Fairlawn, New Jersey, where his father owned a men's clothing store. Mark had many clothes and his roommates were always borrowing them. It was part of his capital at college. She thought Mark extremely handsome: he was a full head taller than she was, slender, with a curly dark golden beard that made him look far older than twenty-one. Mark had light brown hair, a shade or two darker than his beard, and medium brown eyes she thought soulful and commanding. He had a fine singing voice. His roommates called him the Lounge Lizard because of his habit of singing show tunes in the tub. He was her first lover: she found everything about him extraordinary.

But when she came home, Yirina was a cold shower. Yirina did not think much of Mark, although she did not dislike him. She simply viewed him as a puppy, with friendly contempt. "He's just a boy," she said to Judith. "You have twice his brains. Don't tie yourself down. He'll do as a boyfriend, but anything more? He's a pastime. You'll forget him."

Sandy had long gone, marrying a woman whose house he had painted, a woman with a steady income and two children. Yirina played out a five-year affair with Dr. Silver's lawyer, but that too was over. She was working in a dry cleaner's, which gave her terrible headaches, but what choice of jobs did she have? She had finally begun to look her age, whatever that was. "I'm tired is all, darling. I'm so tired." They lived in the same apartment. The neighborhood was eighty percent Black now, a lot of Haitians. All summer police helicopters hung over the rooftops, setting their nerves on edge. There was a drug scene on the corner, but Yirina had always got on with her Black neighbors. Many people knew her from the cleaners, owned by a Haitian couple. Yirina's legs kept swelling. "It's from standing so much," she said. "My feet could explode!"

Yirina was nostalgic these days. She did not have many mementos or photographs from her previous lives, but what she had, she cherished more than ever. Often she took down the leather-bound album with its black pages and showed Judith the two photos she had of her parents, the photo of her brother graduating from the lycée, even a photo of her husband, a handsome Turk. In one photo, Yirina, fresh-faced in a flowered dress, was standing in the curve of his arm holding a baby.

"Who is that?" Judith asked.

Yirina's face crumpled. "Don't ask me that."

She wondered if somewhere in Turkey she had a half brother. Her half sisters were both married with children. They pretended she did not exist, but now they knew. They could not undo her existence or their knowledge of her. For that she was grateful. Neither of them had amounted to anything, as Yirina said. "But you, my daughter, you'll be a success! Not just a suburban house biddy."

It was the end of spring vacation and she longed to stay over at Mark's. At ten she called Yirina. There was no answer. She knew Yirina would not be going out. She was too exhausted after work. Judith was afraid her mother had been mugged. Something was wrong. She must go home. "But you can't go! You promised!" Mark insisted, pouting.

"I have to see what's wrong."

When she finally reached the apartment, the lights were on. She called Yirina, hurrying through the rooms. Her mother's purse was on the couch. Yirina lay on the bathroom floor, her face twisted, breathing hoarsely. She was unconscious. Judith could not tell if she had hit her head. She knelt over Yirina, wiping her face with a damp cloth and calling, "Mama! Yirina! Can you hear me?" Judith called an ambulance. It took half an hour to arrive. Ambulance services did not like to go into Black neighborhoods.

Yirina had suffered a massive stroke. In four days, she was dead. Judith hated sleeping in the apartment. She was depressed, lonely, given to weeping half the night. Everything reminded her of her mother, every dish, every chair, the bottles of scent and lotion on Yirina's vanity. They had never been separated. She wandered their rooms, no longer at home in a place that meant only deprivation.

A month later, over the protests of his parents, Mark and Judith were married. Only his roommates and two of her friends from school attended. They could not find a rabbi who would marry them over his parents' objections, so they were married at City Hall. Mark did not want to move to Brooklyn. They found an apartment three blocks from where he'd been living, similar in layout, a bedroom, a bathroom, a big kitchen and a tiny room overlooking the street that became Mark's study. She studied in the kitchen. She brought her desk from Brooklyn, along with the things of Yirina's that were precious to her: a teapot with marvelous curlicue blue and white designs on it, the Mexican vases, some pieces of jewelry (the diamond necklace was long since permanently pawned), some fine Czech glassware. Within a month those were broken. She could not keep Mark from using the goblets for beer and then leaving them in the sink, where other dishes inevitably ended up on top of them. She started out keeping house with zeal, studying recipes, scrubbing the floor, making curtains.

That Friday she roasted a chicken with carrots and potatoes. Mark did not come home when she expected him. An hour later she gave up. Weeping quietly, she lit the Shabbat candles and sat down to supper. When he came in at nine, she was furious.

"Well, who asked you to make a stupid fancy supper? I had a hamburger at the Cedars with guys from my class. Jeez, what is this stuff? We aren't living in Fairlawn. What's got into you? Who needs all this bourgeois fussing?"

She did not do well on her midterms. That frightened her. She stopped cleaning daily and then stopped cleaning weekly. The dirty clothes piled up and the dirty dishes began to swarm with roaches. She studied at the library. Now that she wasn't trying to keep house, she had time. Mark expected her to be there when he got home, and he expected to have sex with her. Weekends they went to movies, danced in a bar, bicycled in Central Park. They went to a lecture on the constitutional implications of Watergate; she went alone to hear Gloria Steinem. She worked for her professor whenever he wanted her to type papers.

Their lives went on as before they were married, except that they fought more. She got her grades back up by finals and finished well. She admitted to herself she was bitterly lonely without Yirina, and that Mark did not make an adequate replacement for her mother. He was a kid, as Yirina had warned her. She did not feel married. He was not her image of a husband. She had never had a father, but she had many fantasies. They were not fulfilled by an adolescent whose idea of a great evening was watching a Knicks game in a bar while eating potato chips or nachos and drinking beer.

They both got summer jobs in New York and went on living in their dirty apartment. In the fall, they were seniors with a full load of classes. They ate most meals in the school cafeteria or in hangouts around the Village. She could not remember why she had married Mark; she was sure he had no clue why he had married her. She felt ashamed. When she met some women who were meeting for consciousness-raising, she joined them every Wednesday night. It was a month before she confessed she was married. She felt it was a fake marriage, a failed improvisation, each of them playing in different stories. His parents finally had them to dinner, but it was painful. Mark disappeared with his brother after supper. She was left to make conversation.

She had never told Mark about her family; she had given him the official story, and by the time they were married, it was too late to tell him the truth. She felt her face turning to brittle lacquer as she answered his mother's questions about her dead father. It was hard to explain why her father had not left her mother better off, considering he was a doctor; she invented an unscrupulous uncle who had obliterated their inheritance in bad investments. Whatever she said sounded hollow to her, and relieved none of their anxieties. She could not cough up a normal family for them. She sat on the beige sofa balancing a cup and a china plate with a slice of cherry cheesecake on it and lied and lied. Finally, unable to eat and half nauseous, she dropped the cheesecake into her lap.

Without telling Mark, she applied to law schools. She went to see Mr. Vetter. He kept repeating how bad he felt about Yirina's death. "She was a lovely woman, an old-fashioned woman. They don't make them like that anymore." For the five years he had his affair with Yirina, he had helped financially. He had been far more generous than Dr. Silver.

"Will my father's trust cover graduate school?"

"The way it's set up, it should. The investments yield a good return. Why do you want to go to graduate school? You're married now."

"I don't know if it's going to last," she said frankly. Mr. Vetter was the first person outside her family to understand her situation, and she was always truthful with him—it was a pleasure. "I want to be a lawyer."

"I suppose you could practice domestic law," he said doubtfully. "Some women do well with that. Or estates and trusts."

"I've wanted to be a lawyer since the first time I came to this office—do you remember?"

He grimaced. "How could I forget such high drama? Well, you have an orderly mind and you're argumentative. Perhaps you can do research or title searches. Divorce law is untidy, but it can be lucrative. . . . Where have you applied? And does your husband know?"

"We haven't discussed life after graduation."

She was accepted to three law schools. The money from the trust would cover only tuition and some expenses. Then, finally, a letter came from Michigan, offering her a scholarship that made the deal sweet. Mark was interviewing with corporations. She was almost terrified. She could go to law school. She could do what she wanted if she dared. If she could admit she had been an idiot and married someone with whom she could share little.

She precipitated the final confrontation by leaving her correspondence with Michigan on the kitchen table when she went off to school. She knew he would see it when he drank his coffee and ate his muffin.

"You bitch!" he screamed when she came home at four. He had cut his late afternoon class to confront her. She refused to be baited. She had done her crying. "You used me!"

"How?" she asked. But he was probably right. She had been lonely and he wanted to screw her. He paid the rent. "I would have made you a good wife if you'd really wanted a wife."

He calmed down by suppertime and they went out to share an Italian meal. "It was a stupid thing to get married," he said. "I'm never doing it again."

"Sure you will. But in a few years, when you really want a home and family."

"Do you think you'll ever get married again?" He studied her face and her hands on the table.

She did not want to hurt his feelings further. "I don't know," she said. "I can't imagine it."

"You really going to be some shyster?"

"I shall fight for the right and the underdog," she said, and got a smile out of him. For a moment they almost liked each other.

That night they had sex as usual. She did not want to, but far more, she did not want to make a scene. She just wanted to detach, quietly. In her head she was figuring out her finances.

There was no property, no alimony, no children, nothing but a few books and records to divide. Mark took his clothes and ski equipment; she packed up her surviving mementos from Yirina. Awkwardly they stepped around each other. He was off to a job in New Jersey. She was bound for Ann Arbor to look for an apartment and a summer job. In the midst of their boxes and trash, they shook hands politely.

She went down the steps first. One of her friends from the women's group was going to store her things until she found a place. She would sleep on her friend's couch tonight and leave for Detroit by bus.

She had to return for the divorce, but it was hardly worth bus fare. Mr. Vetter had arranged for an inexpensive lawyer to file her papers. It was over in ten minutes. She took back her maiden name. The divorce left her feeling vaguely unclean. She seemed no more likely to be a wife permanently than her mother had been. Her marriage was a pile of dirty dishes she had fled.

DAVID

The chief of police salted his fries, knocking the bottom of the white plastic shaker against the heel of his hand. He ate more than any man his size I'd ever known. You were more likely to find Abel Smalley at the Binnacle Cafe than in his office, and in a better mood as well. He spread tartar sauce on a fried fish and melted cheddar sandwich, dropped two pats of butter in his corn chowder and shook his head with a soft but regretful smile, "That's a Department of Roads, Bridges and Waterways issue."

"It's an issue of safety," I said. "The assholes plowed all the snow to the corner and left it there in a mountain ten feet high. My mother can't see around it to leave her driveway until she's in the middle of the street."

Despite the trend in small communities to recruit professionals, Abel was Saltash's first and only chief of police, for decades our only full-time cop. He knew everyone's bad habits and every teenager by name. It was Abel's strategy to ignore trouble until it was impossible, then cover the dirt like a cat. Not too deep, they said about Abel. Just so it didn't smell. "Why not call Donkey Sparks about it?"

"He doesn't return my calls. Chief, you know how fast cars take that corner. Especially now, when it's icy."

He was strong and wiry, no taller than five-eight. His white hair stood up like a bristle brush and his gaze was hard, the clear ice blue of a menthol cough drop. He didn't wear a uniform or a firearm and rarely took a case to court. Years ago, when the local lumberyard caught fire, Abel paid a call on the last worker laid off. No investigation ensued, no charges were filed. The young man enlisted in the army the following week. When Abel received complaints about a gang of kids smoking pot on the town green, he slowly crossed Main Street and invited them to lunch at this same window table. He treated them all to burgers and made his position plain: There were twelve thousand acres in Saltash, and they'd be wise to party on one that wasn't in front of Town Hall. "You plow snow yourself," he said. "Why don't you just remove it?"

"I'm not paid to plow for the town." I had signed up but I'd never been called.

So that was it. When Abel smiled, his eyes narrowed to slits, straight as a ruler. Two years ago a homeless family was discovered squatting in a large vacation home in the woods. The local newspaper carried it as a headline story: CITY PROBLEMS IN SMALL TOWN. A neighbor sent a copy to the owner of the home, a psychiatrist from New Haven, who faxed Abel he'd be up to survey the damage and press charges. By the time he arrived, the homeless family was gone. No one could say where, except the town accountant, who quietly processed a bill for five Greyhound bus tickets to Atlanta, under police budget line item number 762000, Travel/Seminars & Training. If Abel could, he'd put me on a bus. He asked, "You call the town manager?"

"Twice."

"And?"

"And I wouldn't be wasting your time if I wasn't worried about my mother being blindsided one night when she leaves to rehearse the choir."

"I'll drive by this afternoon." He unwrapped a fresh package of Lucky Strikes. "But I'm the wrong person to see." The right person was Johnny Lynch, who'd appointed Abel and every other department head in Saltash. Johnny liked my mother and would probably help if she asked, but he'd been in Florida since his last heart attack. "You gotta go through channels. That's the way things work in this town."

"Thanks, Chief. I know very well how things work in this town."

The Saltash Committee for Civic Responsibility met around a glass-topped liquor cart every other Wednesday night in the parlor of a white Victorian captain's house overlooking the harbor. Twelve regulars, old New Deal Democrats, most approaching eighty, dozed off with drinks in their hands but woke up sputtering fury at the mention of Johnny Lynch. They talked about the need for young blood and looked me over like a steak. They reminded me they made generous campaign contributions and were good for 250 votes. Judith called them the *Alter Kockers* Against Johnny.

"Old cocks?"

"Didn't your parents speak Yiddish? Old shits."

Judith and I had our own line about most groups in town, and nicknames (should I decide to run) for my potential opponents: Blossom End-Rot, Bird Man, Captain Ahab. We met when we could after work, after dark, and the mere sound of tires on my oyster shell driveway, like the tip of her tongue on my nipple, gave me goose bumps. The first time she came over, she stayed the night. There was a new moon tide the next morning that would have kept her from getting to court if she returned to the island. I stopped her in the hallway and kissed her eyes, her lips, her fingers. She whispered, "David, David, David," her cheek against my chest, then took a step back and requested a hanger for her coat.

She walked though the living room, then the kitchen, disappointed. "You haven't made supper?"

It was past eight o'clock. I'd had a sandwich after work. "I can't cook."

"You can't fry an egg?"

"Is that what you want right now? An egg?"

"With a little Parmesan cheese, fresh bread and a decent red wine, why not—as long as you don't burn it."

So saying, she lugged a shopping bag to the kitchen. A bottle of wine. Fresh bread. Parmesan cheese. "You have eggs, don't you?" (I did.) Apricot preserves. Olive oil. Coffee.

"You didn't think I had coffee?"

In weeks to come she'd arrive with casseroles from home, flower bouquets, a reading lamp, fragrant soaps. Beginning with that first night's coat hanger, she commandeered half my hall closet and a dresser drawer for her underthings. She opened the wine with her own corkscrew—the truth is, I was a beer drinker and didn't have one—pulled a wire whisk from the bottom of the bag and started an omelet.

"Not talking?" she said over her shoulder. "What was your day like? What did you do?"

As far as I was concerned we could talk on the telephone but had a very small window of time when she didn't have to go home to her husband, prepare for court, or beat the tide over the bridge back to Squeer Island. I missed her and I wanted to touch her, and I suppose I was hurt that she didn't want me. She didn't say a word as she ate, just watched me as if amused and waited me out.

"I met somebody in the post office who wanted to know my position on school taxes. I don't think she was pleased."

"Why? What did you say?"

"I told her what I thought."

"Wrong. You're supposed to ask her what *she* thinks." Judith cut a slice of bread then dipped it in olive oil and cheese. "You want to leave people with the opinion that you both think the same way."

"Maybe we don't."

"You want the best education for the fairest price, right? Same as the woman in the post office, same as everybody. Just ask her how she believes you can go from here to there." She drew an arrow on my tabletop in bread crumbs. "Nod a lot. Tell her you hear what she's saying."

"Isn't that deceptive?"

"Not if you're listening."

"Judith. I'm not sure about this. I'm no politician."

"That's your strong point. Stand up." She did. "Let's practice."

"Where are you going?"

She dropped her plate in the sink. "To get my mail."

"What do I do?"

"Come up and ask me for my vote."

"Get serious."

"Then I won't vote for you. What are you waiting for? Stand up! I'm going to leave you behind with the junk mail. I don't have all day."

"Hello. I'm David Greene."

"Mmmm." A tip of tongue peaked through her lips.

"What does that mean?"

"I'm summing you up. Most women will." She cocked her head. "Honest face. *Great* shoulders. Very intense eyes. I'm listening."

"Can I have your vote?"

"Just like that? Don't you know women like to talk for a while first?"

"Well, ma'am. I've been thinking that things have been the same around here for a long time. I was thinking you might be ready for some new blood."

"I like that. Very visceral."

"What's *visceral*?"

"You are," she said. I lifted my fingers to her breast. She grabbed my hand. She was fast. Strong. "What are your goals?"

"I'm supposed to ask you that."

She studied my face. She wasn't smiling now. She spoke slowly, forming every word. "I want to be with you, David Greene. I want us to be happy." The game was over. She whispered, "Let's make love now," and led me to my bedroom as if it was her own. She was wearing a little cream-colored camisole through which her nipples stood up hard and brown. She was mine for the night, all night until morning, and I kept myself from sleeping even after we'd made love a second time, after she succumbed to sleep. The scent our bodies made together, the lingering stickiness of her sex on my face: I wanted it to last.

The moonlight overlaying the furniture and our clothes on the floor; her panties where she stepped out of them like a puddle; all mine for one night.

Late the next afternoon, she phoned me from court. Her case wouldn't finish until tomorrow. She would have to work late at the office but she was going to sleep there. Would I like to join her?

The following day at work, my sister seemed preoccupied. I went my own way all morning. By noon she was shoving things around her desk, avoiding me in wide conspicuous arcs.

"Is there something the matter, Holly?"

"Why, David, have you done anything wrong?"

Only one thing I could think of. "Does this have to do with Judith?"

"Are you fucking anyone else?"

"How did you know?"

"David, your own mother knows. She heard it at the beauty shop."

I started to laugh. I was thirty-seven years old. "Am I supposed to care?"

"I think it's a pretty cruel thing you're doing, don't you? Screwing a sick man's wife. Or did you think you could keep it a secret? If so, you shouldn't have parked your bright red truck with the name of my business on it outside her office all night."

"*Your* business." Holly had always treated me as a full partner although I'd had no money to buy in.

She sighed, "Mine and Marty's."

"Is that what this is about? Did he go out for his morning *New York Times* and hear the gossip at the Binnacle? Did he blame you?"

"He's protective of Gordon," she said. "He thinks what you're doing to Gordon is wrong. And so do I. And if you were thinking about anything but getting laid, so would you."

Judith didn't talk a lot about Gordon, but he was a presence, always; a looming figure, like the portrait of a great progenitor. She never acted guilty about sleeping with me, never complained about their marriage. I assumed myself to be a pleasant secret; that however brightly Judith glowed in my dim life, I was only a flicker of warmth in hers. My sister, like her husband and a legion of former students and ex-colleagues, saw the man as a living legend.

Gordon Stone's compound had been notorious for dancing that lasted until daybreak when people coupled off in the dunes or lay in heaps around the fire to sleep. Holly will still talk about the night Gordon's guests, men and women both, came to blows over politics, then tore off their clothes and ran naked into the bay. She'll tell you that

Johnny Lynch wrote the town's antinoise, anticamping, and antinudity bylaws as a response to Gordon's annual summer solstice celebrations; that people still remember the FBI men snooping around and the marijuana bust—a small-scale military operation at four-thirty A.M. that sent one of the summer neighbors to the hospital with a heart attack. Since then, Gordon's botanical projects were legal: He collected hearty succulents, yucca and cactus from all over the world, so that the compound looked like a patch of high desert in the New England sand dunes.

Long before Judith arrived in his life, Gordon had laid out a courtyard with a mosaic of stones and beach glass. He had no vision of a compound when he began, Holly said, but followed his whims. The idea of espaliered peach trees spurred him to build a wall blocking the north wind. The wall reminded him of a cottage in Taos—so he built one. Unable to house all the students like Marty who used to descend on him in summer and the colleagues who managed to appear without their wives, Gordon built a second main house larger than the first. He used massive beams from an abandoned mill in New Bedford which he floated across the inlet because the Squeer Island bridge couldn't bear the weight of big trucks.

Gordon had been fired from three colleges and written fourteen books. (Marty had all of them on a shelf in his study; signed first editions.) He had marched with Martin Luther King in Selma. When he was still healthy, Holly said, you might see him skirting the roof rim of some new building going up—shirtless, a hammer in his hand, a butt in his lips. Or he might be sitting on his deck, naked, in front of his typewriter, inhaling as if ideas could be dragged out of a Marlboro. Holly said that Gordon was still with Judith only because she was wife number four. Like a greyhound, he had needed to sprint for the better part of his life before he was tranquil enough to live with. He was over fifty when they married; she was in her twenties.

Gordon had a reputation as a satyr, an American Picasso—tyrant, genius, egomaniac—an undisciplined savant who could not write in solitude but threw enormous parties in which he talked himself into an intellectual frenzy before stealing off to a shack with a bottle of scotch to pour out his book. Gordon was rumored to have lived with three women at once, and every night to choose the one with whom he shared his bed. Holly knew only that Judith had broken into his life like an ax through a window in a room full of gas. "Judith is not a warm person," Holly said, before leaving me to contemplate my behavior. "But she's been good to Gordon. At least until now."

Later that evening, I called Judith at her office to tell her we'd made the headlines in Donna Marie's Beauty Salon.

I was ready to concede we had to cool it for a while. Instead she said, "Come out to the house Saturday, can you?" Her voice trailed off as she checked the tide chart. "About one? Gordon's been asking to meet you."

DAVID

7

The first thing I noticed was the pistol in Gordon Stone's hand. He approached my car with a steady smile. Although Judith hadn't warned me to expect something like this, I knew I deserved it. Half the town was talking about his wife and me.

Judith protected Gordon. Once I'd asked her: "Do you sleep with your husband?"

She grimaced. "Could you sleep with somebody who snores like a bull moose?"

"But do you sleep in the same bed?"

"How can I sleep if he keeps me awake?"

"Judith, do you have sex with him?"

"Does the idea make you jealous?"

I didn't think I had the right to be jealous. "Do you know that whenever you don't want to answer my questions you ask me another one instead?"

She seemed intrigued. "Does that annoy you?"

"You've just done it again."

It had more to do with how I judged myself than anything I actually knew about Gordon, but I assumed that Judith had turned to me out of desperation. I invented an image of her husband as a man who depended on a regimen of drugs that erased his pain as well as his ability to satisfy his wife. I told myself they lived like dear friends, that affection had replaced passion. I simply had to picture Gordon as more intellect than flesh. I could not imagine him watching her dress, for instance. I refused to believe that any husband, however frail and disinterested, could bear to watch my Judith step into her black silk panties in the morning and know she would slide them to her knees for another man.

I had left my house that afternoon as late as I dared and drove at a coward's pace down the road to the island, only recently emerging from the last high tide. The salt marsh grass was silver in the sun, the creek swollen and meandering. To me, heaven would smell like a salt marsh, fresh and yeasty and sweet with life—a little like a woman. I rolled my window all the way down and inhaled. As my front wheels hit the first loose plank of the bridge, a great blue heron rose from the creek, the scythelike shadow of its wings guiding me like a bat to Nosferatu's castle.

Just beyond the first dune, the road made an abrupt left turn in front of Stumpy Squeer's new house. About a quarter mile up a dirt road I made out the letters on an old driftwood oar, STONE—SILVER. I was hearing loud cracks, five or six in succession, pistol fire. Two men were plinking cans arranged on a picnic table. As I drove into the parking area, the taller man stopped shooting and turned. He was broad from the back but willowy, craning slightly forward at the waist as if nursing a pain in the belly. A baseball cap cast all but his mouth in shade. He moved in a slow straight line to my truck. "David Greene?" Gordon spoke my name like a bailiff in a court of law. I climbed slowly out of the truck. Judith appeared on the deck of the house just above us. Gordon said, "If you're going to be coming to this house, do not be late for lunch again. I am famished. Damned woman wouldn't serve until you got here." He switched the gun to his left hand and extended his right to shake mine.

"That's a nine-millimeter automatic, isn't it?"

He seemed impressed. "A Smith & Wesson. Do you shoot?"

"A little." Before my uncle Georgie married and moved to Hawaii, it was something for us to do together that didn't involve talking.

"Got another shooter here, Stumpy."

Stumpy Squeer was a Saltash legend. Some said he never left the island, but actually he rowed across the harbor to town every couple of weeks for provisions. Stumpy was short and thick, fifty more or less, with barrel-like haunches that made him seem to roll forward as he walked.

Judith stood on the steps. "Let's go, you guys. Gordon? David! Lunch!"

"Will you join us, Stumpy?" Gordon's voice was deep and courtly.

Stumpy shook his head no. People said that he had stopped growing at eleven, on the night his father shot his mother in the face. She had just returned from a party where she danced with another man. Her blood seeped through the floorboards on Stumpy, sleeping in the bedroom below.

"Going to get back to your book?" Gordon asked him. "Stumpy's been working on one for three years now."

"Four," Stumpy said.

"Really?" I loved the idea. Stumpy Squeer, hermit scholar. "What are you writing about?"

"Not writin'. Been readin' it," he said. "Almost finished too."

Judith called again. "I said, let's go!"

The house was situated at the base of a tall clay sea scarp protecting it from the beach on the other side. Gordon climbed the outer stairs with effort. The Smith & Wesson seemed to weigh him down. I wanted to take it, or even grab his elbow to help him make the climb, but I wasn't about to embarrass him.

The deck wrapped around the house and offered a quick view of the compound, six wooden structures of differing colors and sizes and styles, some with porches, one with a cupola, one painted pink, all built in a protected bowl between the dunes. Gordon seemed to stagger as he led me through the kitchen door. Although the afternoon temperature hovered just above freezing, I noticed a few drops of sweat rolling into his collar.

Judith took the gun, ejected the clip, then disappeared with him into one of the back rooms. As my eyes adjusted, I took in a large kitchen of hardwood and tile, mostly in shades of brown and yellow. Baskets were suspended from hooks on the ceiling. Bowls everywhere overflowed with fruit, with dried herbs, with balls of yarn; some filled only with other bowls. Where there weren't windows there were bookshelves and hundreds of cookbooks with broken spines. Judith had referred to this as the Big House. Through an archway and three steps down, a baby grand stood in front of a truly fantastical hearth. As much a sculpture as a fireplace, the bricks flowed and changed directions like brush strokes in an Impressionist landscape.

"Gordon calls it his wailing wall." Judith caught me running my fingers along the grooves between the brick. "Because he groaned and complained the whole time it took him to build it."

She had to call him several times. When he appeared, he was older than the man I had met outside. His skin was gray and his chest looked hollow. Gordon felt stronger or weaker during the day, sometimes energetic, sometimes enervated to near exhaustion. Mornings were good (I was to find out), while by late afternoon his strength ebbed. Judith served a beet and cabbage soup with bread and salad. Gordon stared into his bowl, chewing without interest.

I imagined the man's shame in my presence, the rage he must feel. Although I found the silence intolerable, I couldn't think of a thing to break it. "How's the campaign going?" Judith said finally.

"What campaign?" Only after I spoke did I realize that I'd probably blown the only thing we all had in common. "Well, I was asked to speak to the Saltash Friendship Association."

Gordon lifted his eyes from his bowl. "The old Johnny Lynch clubhouse."

I'd never heard that one before. "I thought it used to be a church."

Gordon seemed livelier. "A church, and then a grange hall and fishermen's co-op and a social club. Used to be a dance there every Saturday night." His eyes narrowed mischievously, "That's where Stumpy's mother was spied in the arms of another man. But for years and years, Johnny's group met there for cocktails before the Board of Selectmen meetings. Johnny used to get to Town Hall so drunk that the minutes of the meetings made no sense. The secretary couldn't understand half what he said, and when she asked him, he couldn't remember."

"Did people know?"

"Everybody knew. But they didn't care. Because he was the nicest, funniest, friendliest guy in the world. They loved Johnny Lynch. Hell, *I* loved Johnny Lynch. He handled all my mortgages and wrote my wills and never charged me a dime—until I spoke against him one night at town meeting. Then I got a bill for fifteen years' worth of work! Johnny never made his money from the law. It was my vote he wanted, and my loyalty. He had to be a town official, you see, that was his access to government contracts, to the pot of gold." Gordon looked at the table as if a mistake had been made. "Judith, where's the wine? Don't we have some cold white wine?"

"For lunch?" she asked, but was quickly on her feet, searching the refrigerator.

"Understand," Gordon said, "and I should never tell this to a politician, but people don't care what you do. It's what you do *for them*. Johnny Lynch took care of people. He saw that every nitwit who couldn't find a trade drove a truck for the town. If you couldn't make your taxes, Johnny had a word with the tax collector. He intervened when you were in trouble with the bank."

"He was Chairman of the Board," I said.

Gordon seemed impressed that I knew. "He took care of your wife if you went to the army."

"That's never been proven." Judith set the glasses and the bottle on the table.

Gordon winked. "Johnny had friends on the Selective Service Board. One of his girlfriends was married to a boy who'd left her. Summer of 'sixty-nine. 'Seventy?" he asked Judith, who shrugged, working on the cork. "When the boy showed up in Saltash again and started making trouble, what do you think happened?"

"He got drafted?"

"Johnny Lynch was King David in this town. And do you know why? Because people wanted a king."

When the wine was gone and the sun filled the space between the clouds like a pink neon fire, Gordon led me outside, literally by the sleeve. "Help me with something, will you?" Four rolls of roofing paper, four pallets of asphalt shingles, were piled at the foot of the drive. Gordon asked me to carry them up the dune. As I lifted the first, he turned his back to the house and slipped a pipe and a pouch of tobacco from his jacket pocket. "Ever do any construction?"

"Some," I said. I had worked for my father-in-law in Florida. Not a period in my life I cared to talk about.

"After you played baseball." He watched my reaction. "Davey Greene, the Pitching Machine. I used to take my son to watch you play." He led me up the slope. "Wind lifts these damned shingles like feathers. Finish one roof, start another. One a year, every year. Used to do it by myself, if you can believe that." He stopped outside a cottage with a peaked roof.

I managed one roll on each shoulder, all four up the dune in two trips. I couldn't carry more than one pallet of shingles at a time. On my last trip up, number six, I was laboring like an old mule. Gordon was waiting for me, smoking his pipe, staring at the purple silhouette of the peaked roof. "Don't mention to Judith I was smoking. She won't let me buy cigarettes, but she doesn't know I have a pipe. So are you going to do it?" There was no question what he meant.

"I don't know."

"There's a line drawn right down the middle of this town."

"If this is about the dike, it's not as simple as that. People stand on both sides," I said.

"And where do you stand? With Johnny Lynch?"

I didn't like him trying to push me. "Why don't you run?"

"I'm an old man."

"So is Johnny."

"But he's desperate now, don't you see? He's fighting for all he's worth. Johnny's been in and out of court for years. He never invested his money. Why bother? Saltash was a money farm. He could always grow more. Now all he's got left are those lots in the river valley. As long as the dike stays closed and the land stays dry, he can build. To make sure it does, he needs the Board of Selectmen. He's got two votes, we've got two. You're the tie breaker."

"That's a lot to drop on my shoulders."

"From what I hear, you've got some pair of shoulders."

What did Judith say about me when they were alone? How much did he know?

"Will you do it?"

Was he making me some kind of deal in exchange for his wife? "Why me?"

"You're bright. Fair-minded. You're perceived as neutral."

"Tell me something, Gordon, have you people asked anybody else?"

"Oh, yes. Maybe twenty people."

"And they said no."

"Every one."

Judith insisted on showing me around. Putting on a goose down parka, she led me down a lowland path through the pines. "He liked you!" She skipped ahead like an excited little girl and drew me into the forest. As the sun disappeared, the scent of pine sap overwhelmed. I walked faster and faster to catch up. "I thought it would work out," she said over her shoulder.

I liked him too, which didn't make screwing his wife any easier.

About fifty yards ahead, I made out a clearing, a gap where the trees opened to the twilight. As we neared it, Judith began to run. She stopped abruptly at the gate to her garden. It was an enormous square, protected by a wood and wire fence. On top of each fence post was a painted wooden finial, some red and white, some yellow, green and red, or orange striped with black like tigers. There were bamboo tripods for growing pole beans, the withered vines now frozen like brown lace; all kinds of structures made out of bicycle spokes and hammered fenders, torn nets salvaged from the sea, a huge scarecrow with a rusted muffler torso and arms of copper pipe. There wasn't a plant left growing and yet it was alive, a frozen circus on the edge of a marsh.

Judith took my hand and led me to a small A-frame beyond the garden, with a double bed inside, a desk, a computer and files. "I work here. I fixed it up when Gordon got sick." The room smelled of her perfume and cedar; it was still warm from an earlier fire. She touched her finger to my cheek. I moved toward the door.

"You don't want to be with me now?" she asked.

"But he's at the house. Suppose he follows us."

"He's taking a nap. He doesn't object."

"I can't believe he doesn't care."

"He loves me, David. He wishes me happiness."

I was not proud of myself. I thought a better person would resist. But as she kissed my eyes, I found her zipper. As she sought my lips, I cupped her buttocks and carried her to the bed. As her husband slept, I licked her sex like an eager puppy.

"It's going to be all right," she whispered. "We won't be like anything you've ever done before. Can you understand that? Can you give up how you think people are supposed to love? How they're supposed to live? Because we're not going to be what people expect. We're not going to live that way." Judith clung to me with a strength that belied her size. "But I'll promise you something. If we're honest with each other and if we have patience and respect, we'll live more happily than anyone you've ever known."

I wanted to believe Judith. I would have conceded anything she asked. But what I thought I was agreeing to, a kind of consensual adultery, fell wide of the mark. I didn't understand what Judith and Gordon had in mind because it was unthinkable.

JUDITH

8

Law school was like camping in a wind tunnel. After the first two weeks, Judith hardly knew who she was. She was no longer Yirina's daughter, she was no longer the child of shame and romantic mystery, whose mother had three different passports in different names hidden in her underwear drawer, kept although they had long expired. Nor was she the adult she had felt herself to be after her divorce. She was a tired cranky frightened child, assigned seats, given hours and hours of unintelligible fudge to learn in minute detail, at the mercy of tyrannical professors, sleeping at first six hours a night, then five, then three and then hardly at all. She felt ugly and drawn thin as paper. Her skin looked sour and blotchy. Her hair was usually dirty. She lived on food that Yirina would not have considered fit for consumption, pizza and bad Chinese takeout. She ate cafeteria food and fast food. She no longer spoke like a human being. When she opened her mouth, legalese came out. All she thought of were torts and contracts, opinions and citations. Her passion was pleasing professors who despised their women students; she loved only her grades. She had no culture. She had no heart. She had only a headache that never went away and fatigue that drained color from the sky.

She lived for the approval of cold distant daddies, the professors who taught enormous classes. The first time she was in the hot seat, called upon to discuss the fine points of a case, her throat closed and her voice emerged squeaking like a mouse in mortal danger. Who was she? She was her grade point average. She was her first brief. She was what her professors pronounced her. What was she doing inside the baroque castle of the law? Like K., she was guilty already. Like K., she would be punished no matter what she did. How could she, the child of illegality and secrecy, make her way in the law? But its very power attracted her. She wanted to live in that castle of power. She wanted to bring that power to those who most needed its help.

Yirina had always been powerless. Judith did not want to be. She saw her classmates in the second year gravitating toward the corporate law firms. That was where money and prestige were. By the time she interviewed for a job for the summer between her second and third years, she looked much like all the other savvy law school women. She wore a gray suit. She had bought that and a navy one at a discount barn in

New York. She had good earrings from Yirina. She put herself together and got a job for the summer in a Boston law firm already looking over students for associates. Prestigious large firms were beginning to court women, under pressure from antidiscrimination legislation. Her grades were as high as any woman in her class. She interned at Tremont, Smith and Cordovan, where there were forty-two partners and a hundred-odd associates. It was an unusual firm, in that there were two women partners. Both were divorced and neither had children. They worked twelve to fourteen hours a day.

All the associates seemed to put in at least a sixteen-hour day. Not infrequently they worked all night, they worked weekends. They dressed well, they made good money, but there was no intimacy in their lives. If they were married, they probably made love twice a month. If a woman had children, sometimes she became part-time; then the others spoke of her as if she had died. "Adrienne was a good lawyer," they said elegiacally. "Too bad."

For what did these people destroy themselves, burn up their years? Money. Not power. She did not see any women with power. Even the two women partners were less powerful than any of the male partners. They were not rainmakers; they did not count. One had created a valuable niche for herself as a specialist in pension funds. Little that happened here seemed useful. She found most of the partners nasty and overbearing.

The summer was no vacation, as much as she loved Boston, and she did. It was less tropical in the summer than New York and somehow more manageable. She had little time to play tourist but knew she wanted to live there. After a couple of years in the Midwest, it felt sunnier, saltier, brisker. She worked as fiercely as she had in school, but in addition, she had to look presentable every day. She had to shine. That summer job between the second and third years was supposed to be the forerunner of the job she would take when she graduated. By the time the summer was over, she knew that she was not going to follow the high path. She would not go into corporate law.

She decided on family law, as Mr. Vetter had long ago recommended, but she was also drawn to criminal law. She could easily identify with people on the fringes of society, with the illegitimate, the poor, even the violent. She went after a job with Legal Aid.

The veteran lawyer who interviewed her asked before the interview was five minutes old, "Do you think you can handle child abuse? Domestic violence? The seamy side of the city the way you can't imagine it."

"I want to do this work. I think it's important."

"Do you have any idea what you'll really be doing? It's not Perry Mason. It's sleaze. You're dealing with the riffraff of the city so they can go back on the streets. You're dealing with crazy old ladies and crack mothers and kids who think cockroaches are decoration. You get all of five minutes to prepare a case and you'll be handling sixty cases at a time."

"I can do it," she said. "I grew up in Bedford-Stuyvesant. Those riffraff were my neighbors. They're human to me and I can talk to them. I can learn quickly."

She was hired, although her interviewer told her he didn't expect her to last eighteen months.

After graduation from law school, Judith received the last of her bequest from her father, Dr. Julian Silver, one thousand dollars upon finishing her schooling successfully. "I thought we might consider that your schooling was successful," Mr. Vetter said. "On the law review. Honors. Your father would be proud of you."

"Would he? I never understood him. I was always a little afraid of him."

"His own daughters were never what he imagined they would be. You are. You're beautiful as your mother and bright and capable. I think you'll go far."

She did, immediately. As a present to herself, she took a charter flight to Europe with two friends from law school, Hannah and Stephanie. Hannah was the real beauty, blond, willowy and well-connected. Her father was a state senator. She would be interning in Washington. Stephanie was going into a big firm in Chicago. She was tall, a little gawky but extremely hard-driving. Judith could not imagine what she would be like on vacation. Hannah, Stephanie and Judith had gone through law school in a study group with two other women off already to their new jobs, dividing up assignments before exams, trying to carry each other through the grind.

Judith was desperate to be done with schooling. She had been deferring her life. She needed a vacation and she needed to see Europe, finally. She had always felt only partly American, with her mother so European, so multilingual. She had a heritage she barely understood, like the legacy of a diary in a language of which she knew just an occasional word. She had only a vague notion of her quest, what she must find to complete herself. She should be studying to pass the Massachusetts bar, but she would do that when she returned.

I did what I set out to do, she thought to herself: I conquered. But there's no *I* left. She had five weeks. She had to be back in Boston by July first to move into the apartment she had rented, to get ready for the bar exam and to begin her new job at poor pay and long hours in Dorchester.

The charter flight put them down in Amsterdam, which was pleasant. She got by on her bad German which was really Yiddish, scanty, rich in curses but poor in daily phrases like "Where is the women's toilet?" They went on to Paris. There, a sublet and a temporary job had been arranged for Hannah. Stephanie and Judith lived in a cheap Latin Quarter hotel, famous for a nineteenth-century French poet Judith had never read. Every day they walked miles. Stephanie was eager to notch every museum, but Judith found she liked best to wander the neighborhoods. To sit in cafés staring at passersby. She felt like someone in a movie, a young woman vacationing in Paris, waiting no doubt for romance. But she did not fall in love with a Frenchman. She fell in love with a village.

It was in the mountains of Provence. Stephanie and she were staying at a small inn set in vineyards belonging to the inn family. The inn had only six guest rooms. In the middle distance were cliffs studded with juniper and pine. The local houses seemed to sprout from rock. Red rocks, beige rocks, gray rocks, black rocks. The sound of goat bells came into her bedroom. Bougainvillea grew up the side wall, spilling its luminescent blossoms everywhere. Doves cooed under the red tile roof.

She was in the middle of a large self-involved family. The wine served was grown in the surrounding vineyards. The food was cooked by Madame, mistress of the house. One of the daughters was pregnant and lay out by the pool like a beached whale, sunning her belly. They were always laughing together, the married and unmarried sisters and a sister-in-law. They all looked somewhat alike, about the size and coloring of Judith, with dark brown eyes and black hair. She had grown up hearing many languages, and she picked them up quickly. Unlike Stephanie, she was not afraid to use her French. The sisters normally ignored the guests as if they were made of glass, but gradually they found her acceptable. They began to include her in their gossip and their games. They had names for all the men who came by. They strolled in the vineyard. They shelled beans. They picked flowers and decorated the inn. They mended, they knitted, they read, they talked, they swam in the pool.

Judith and Stephanie had been supposed to move on in three days. Stephanie did. Judith canceled the rest of her reservations and persuaded the family to let her stay. Gradually she began to do small tasks. Her rent was reduced. She spent the next three weeks as part guest and part servant and almost family, not a daughter certainly, but almost a cousin.

Partly it was a fantasy, a big family in place of the isolation in which she had grown up. A female-dominated family full of singing and laughter and in-jokes, full of grooming and flirting. She was studying something at least as interesting as anything she had learned in law school. What Judith saw that caused her to stay was that these were people who knew truly how to live in a daily, ordinary way. They were rich in small pleasures.

Madame could turn any scrap fish or tough old hen into a sumptuous repast. They worked hard but they also had much time simply to sit and talk, to sip wine and enjoy. There was a casual grace to their lives that was partly the beauty of the sunburnt landscape, partly the closeness to peasant life but with enough money to provide little luxuries, partly the climate and the habits of the place. She did not idealize them. They had no idea she was a Jew, and she was careful not to tell them. She was a spy in the house of comfort. They were parochial people who despised the tourists and vacationers they catered to. Madame would not let any of them near the stove when they were menstruating, since she held as an article of faith that a menstruating woman would curdle milk and spoil wine. Madame believed in sympathetic magic and tried to cure most ailments with herbs and what seemed to Judith voodoo. Gradually Judith learned to cook most of Madame's dishes, from watching, from making notes. She understood that the cooking style of Madame was not so much a matter of recipes as of overriding formulae. Nothing was measured; nothing was ever quite the same twice. But there were general rules and she learned them. She knew what to do with a firm fleshed fish and how to make a marinade or a sauce from olive oil, tomatoes, a few herbs and a little wine or vinegar or lemon.

Stephanie called her from Florence. "I hate traveling alone. Italian men are driving me crazy! What are you doing there? It's not even the beach."

"I'm resting," she said. "I'm exhausted. I never want to move again."

She could not explain her pleasure in scraping carrots and washing rice, watering the kitchen garden, picking caterpillars off the roses: hardly Stephanie's idea of a vacation. Hannah would think she had lost her mind. Yet Judith was almost, almost happy. She had not been happy since Yirina died. Stephanie and Hannah were two women who had been part of her study group all through law school. She was as close to them as she was to anyone, a slightly frightening thought because now they seemed to have nothing in common.

She still did not know who she was, but she had found a part of herself that had been lost, the part that had flavor and a body and tastes and knew, as Yirina would say, how to enjoy an orchard in a flower pot.

She observed how these women dressed, how they laughed, how they held their bodies. Her particular mentor was the sister-in-law, Yvonne, who was a little the outsider too, married to the older son. The younger son was off in Toulouse in hotel school. Soon he would be working in Switzerland for a couple of years. Yvonne cut Judith's hair and restyled it, critiqued her wardrobe, showed her tricks of coddling the skin with strawberries and milk. It astonished Judith how comfortable she felt with the Barbière family. This was not her life, just a pause for healing and rest. Yet she felt more at home here than she ever had with Mark or her various roommates. It was not that she felt truly intimate, for they did not know her and did not even ask the sort of questions that might have led them to understand. She told them her mother was Czech. Czech refugees were not uncommon. They assumed her mother had left her country to escape the Communist regime. For years she had let people make what assumptions they chose about her background.

The younger son was home for a weekend, on his way to Switzerland. He flirted with her. "You're so beautiful," he told her. "You're like a perfectly ripe peach, delicate and suave."

Like all the family, he was handsome. They seemed to radiate a sensual health that was attractive and unrefined, like the coat of a well-groomed, glossy and well-fed horse. He kissed her under the arbor. She did not let it go further. She had had only one affair since her marriage. Men her own age seemed callow to her, a regiment of Marks; she did not believe in getting involved with her professors, although two pursued her mildly. She had had a romance with an older man the summer between her first and second years, where she was interning. He said he was separated from his wife; it turned out he meant, by several miles, from the suburb where he lived. She let it go on in a desultory manner until she returned to school. It was mildly educational and sexually all right. She had backed into it and could not extract herself gracefully.

The son left. An Italian on vacation kissed her under the same arbor. He left and she stayed on. She asked Yvonne if she was beautiful, since Mr. Vetter and the son Armand had both said she was. Yvonne cocked her head. *"Bien sûr,"* Yvonne said, "you're pretty enough . . . *assez jolie.*" She had not classic features, Yvonne explained. Her chin was a trifle sharp. She was short of stature. Her nose was a little long, perhaps. "But," Yvonne said, waving her finger, "what does that matter? You must have confidence that you are quite pretty enough for any man you want. That's what matters. That you feel you are desirable and that you act desirable. A woman does not have to be a classic beauty to get exactly what she wants, little Judith. She just has to act as if she is one."

Finally the pregnant daughter went to the hospital and the tempo of the house increased and withdrew from her. Judith understood it was time to leave. She phoned Stephanie in Athens and said she would meet her in Paris. Her French had vastly improved, even though French vacationers told her she had a Provençal accent. "You must get rid of that!" they said, but she did not want to.

She had a week before she was due in Amsterdam to catch her flight home. She stayed with Hannah in her small flat. She had not spent as much money as she had expected to. She spent it now on clothes, on accessories—exotic panty hose, a stylish bag. She experienced a frantic desire to shop, to bring home souvenirs of what she felt she had learned. I want to live well, she thought to herself. I will work hard but I want something different. I want a graceful life. A life that satisfies the senses and the brain. Yirina would have understood perfectly. She knew she would not be able to put any of her desires into effect for years, since she must establish herself as an attorney. She would be working at least sixty hours a week. But she knew what she wanted, and she would not forget. Eventually, eventually, she would reach that pleasant shore.

JUDITH

Judith thought that the mother or perhaps both parents might come in with her client, but the family group that trekked into her office was larger and noisier than she had expected. There were four other adults and a child. She had one of the smaller offices at Birch and Fogarty, a Boston law firm she had joined after two and a half years at Legal Aid, and she had to borrow chairs from the other associates.

Her eyes went first to her client, looking surly and messy. When it came to court, she would have to make him clean up his act, or the judge would punish him. He was a kid from an affluent respectable family, and he had to look like one, not a bad imitation of a ghetto runner. "In this office, you will remove your hat," she said firmly, not smiling, gesturing at the greasy wool cap he had pulled down almost to his eyes.

"What for?"

"To get used to looking like someone the judge should take pity on. They don't like drug cases. It's going to be a battle to make sure you don't do time. The sooner you get used to taking my advice, the better our odds are."

Larry Stone was pouting, oozing self-pity. He was tall like his father, but looked rather water-softened, slumping in the chair. His attitude was just as it had been the first time she sat down with him, petulant and put upon. Being caught was something he shouldn't have to endure.

"Larry can't go to jail!" That was his mother, now Mrs. Caldwell, talking. She was a well-kept woman with short crisp blond hair and nails that matched her pale blue designer suit. Judith was sure her gold was twenty-four karat and her earrings were real pearls. Her current husband said nothing. He looked extremely bored, glancing at his Rolex every two minutes. He was a Texan in a beige suit who resented every second he spent in her modest office.

Her eyes kept being drawn against her will to her client's father, Gordon Stone. Years ago when she was an undergraduate, she had gone to hear him speak. He was still an impressive presence. So far he was mostly listening, yet the room seemed to revolve around him. He was a tall lean man with dark hard blue eyes, fierce, hawklike, but his mouth was full and sensual. He had what people called good bones, meaning his face would photograph well and his features had an edge, a definition she had to call attractive, charismatic. While she was talking, she caught herself trying to figure out his age. Fifty maybe? No, he had to be older.

She lectured on the seriousness of Larry being caught selling marijuana at B.U. He had done a sloppy job of it and someone who did not like him had reported him to the campus police. It was probable that if Gordon had a better history with the college administration, the matter would have been quietly dropped. But Gordon Stone had always been too famous for his own good, controversial, often being quoted on topics the administration would have preferred he ignore, and he had been fired from B.U. before being hired by Brandeis.

"Larry has to say he's very, very sorry, right?" That was Natasha, eleven and bright. She seemed to be trying to take care of her half brother, who did not even look at her when she spoke. Natasha was a forthright child with whom Judith had immediately fallen a little in love. She could be my child, Judith thought, although of course that was not literally true: she was only sixteen years older than Natasha. But Natasha was the child she could wish for.

"The more persuasively he can apologize and the humbler he seems, the better we're likely to do in court," Judith said.

Larry made a retching sound. "This is just sickening."

"My darling, I feel for you," his mother, Mrs. Caldwell, said. "This is so unfair. They're treating him like a criminal." She glared at Gordon Stone. "I know you could have hushed this up, if you'd tried a little harder."

The current Mrs. Stone, the third one—Judith consulted her notes to discover she was named Fern—sighed heavily. "This is all such a trivial matter clogged in process and meaningless words." Fern had been gazing out the window, as if she could pass through it and escape. She was wearing wide silk pants, an overblouse and various shawls, scarves, draperies. She was so vague and unkempt it was only the third time Judith glanced at her that she noticed how beautiful Fern was. Her hair was long and red-blond; Judith realized where the term strawberry-blond came from. Fern's eyes were large and pale brown against her ivory skin. Her face was oval and her features classic. Vaguely Judith remembered that Larry had described her as an ex–soap opera queen; but then Larry was sarcastic about everyone in his family. Fern did not seek to be the center of attention, as Judith would have expected from an actress. She basically seemed to want quiet. Judith thought of the White Queen in *Through the Looking Glass*. This was a gentle ineffectual woman who appeared to generate centrifugal force that caused her to leak scarves, tissues, sighs.

Gordon sat up and glared. "Why don't you go back to the ashram, Fern. You aren't doing us any good—as usual."

"It isn't an ashram." She wrapped her arms in her shawl. "The center is based on the teachings of Bodhisatva Selena MacDowell, also called—"

"Please, Fern, shut up and leave if you want to."

Smiling slightly for the first time, Fern gathered up her fringed cloth bag and several shawls. "I'm used to operating on a higher plane."

"Mother!" Natasha yelled. "Larry may go to jail. Wake up." She planted herself in front of her mother, frowning.

"It's not the place that defines us, but we define our place. Selena wrote that. . . ." Fern floated out, abandoning them all.

Gordon grinned. "My wife has grown a little weary of the world, defined as me and the family."

"Including me," Natasha said, tugging at her hair.

"No, darling," Gordon said, "nobody ever tires of you. It's the rest of us who bring her down."

Judith tapped on the desk. "Now if we could discuss our strategy in Larry's impending trial, there might be some chance you won't have to traipse off to prison to visit him."

Judith did in fact get Larry a sentence of community service and two years' probation. He barely thanked her, but Gordon paid her bill in full and promptly. He was the family member she had the most contact with, besides her client. He was the one who argued with Larry to obey her. He was the one who listened carefully to her plans. He picked out Larry's clothes for court, with her approval. When she had to consult the family, it was Gordon she called, and she now called him Gordon. She admitted she liked having an excuse to talk with him. Their conversations rarely stayed on the case. She was almost sorry when the trial process ended with her successful plea bargain. She would miss their discussions of the events of the day, politics, the judicial process.

Therefore she was surprised but delighted to be invited out to what Gordon called the Compound for July Fourth. She had no other good invitations and she was curious about him. She threw some clothes in an overnight bag and drove out, following the photocopied directions. They were so precise she assumed Gordon had written them. After a series of turns, she found herself crossing a humpbacked rickety wooden bridge to the island where Gordon had a summer home.

She had imagined a glassy modern house on various levels, nicely landscaped. There was such a house, but there were five other buildings, four of wood and one of stucco, so different one from the other and bizarrely constructed, she assumed Gordon, perhaps with the help of some of his sons and daughters (she knew he had five children ranging in ages from nine years older than her to sixteen years younger), had thrown them up by whim. All this random architecture was built in the lee of a bayside sand dune obviously blowing away. No one had landscaped. Piles of discarded objects lay about, not trash, not bottles and cans, but abandoned projects—a fence that separated nothing from nothing, a shed without a roof, a half-built tower, a flagstone path that led halfway across the courtyard, various pieces of abstract sculpture of rusting metal. She learned that the second wife, Mrs. Caldwell, had dabbled in sculpture.

Gordon greeted her with a kiss on the cheek and a little more body language in the hug than she had expected. "Where's Fern?" she asked, looking around. She saw many people picnicking, sunbathing, sitting in the shade—including a baby in a playpen—but no Fern.

"Fern has filed papers. I told you, she's tired of the noise. I think she imagined that things would quiet down over the years, but they never have." He waved his hands vaguely at the scene. Children in a loose posse were chasing a black Labrador. Another kid was throwing a ball hard against one of the houses. Voices were raised in song somewhere, several radios were playing not only competing stations but wildly incompatible music, opera and rock duking it out in the ears of everyone. Two teenagers were having a fierce argument. Someone had started a fire that was smoking badly. No one was tending it.

She found Natasha in the kitchen trying to make lunch, near tears because she had burnt the tomato soup.

Judith put down her bag on a kitchen chair and took over. She tried to send Natasha off to amuse herself, but the girl begged to stay. "I want to help. I have to learn how to do all this!"

"Won't you go with your mother?"

"To that stupid place where people walk slowly like zombies and sit on the ground with stuck-up smiles? No thank you. I'd rather be with Daddy. Besides, I'm hoping he gets married again real soon."

Gordon had come quietly into the kitchen. She could feel him behind them. She realized she had begun to be aware of him physically. She did not want to turn, but finally she had to.

He was propped against the doorjamb, amused. "You're making order out of chaos. A rare talent. Everyone here seems to have the opposite knack."

"Is that why Fern gave up?"

"Let's talk about that another time." He was wearing a tee and shorts. His body was lean and tightly muscled, a much harder body than his son had. As if he could read her thoughts, she felt her face heat. She turned back to the stove.

It was twilight. A group of them had decided to stroll on the beach. She started off walking with a young woman whose thesis advisor Gordon had been. They talked about the Reagan administration. Gordon appeared at her elbow. Gradually she found herself walking with him instead. He was full of questions. They sat on the beach as the last lavender light drained from the sky, the waves whooshing in over the pebbles to their bare feet.

"So, where do you come from, Miss Judith, lawyer? Not New York or Boston. You have no obvious accent."

"I grew up in Brooklyn."

"So much for my ear. Where in Brooklyn?"

"The corner of Bedford-Stuyvesant that touches Flatbush Avenue and Prospect Park. I am the illegitimate child of a doctor whose name I bear and a mother who was born in Prague, married and divorced in Turkey—I think—and may have had a son there I know nothing about. She met my father in Mexico."

"Why didn't he marry your mother?"

"He was married already. To a very middle-class lady. He had two daughters, both older than me."

She did not know when she decided to tell the truth. She did not know why. Perhaps she felt it did not matter or perhaps she felt it mattered very much. She found herself compelled. His attention was like a drug that loosened her mouth. Suddenly she wanted to be who she was. She had developed a proficiency for obfuscating her past; but now she just wanted to speak of herself. She decided to take that enormous chance for the first time in her life. Her husband, Mark, had known less about her after a year of marriage than this man knew right now.

They spent the evening talking, until the breeze grew cool and she was chilled. Walking back to the compound, he put his arm around her. He led her to a room she assumed was his. She resisted the pressure of his arm and stood flatfooted in the hall. "I don't have casual sex," she said, planting her feet. "It doesn't appeal to me."

"Who says this is casual?"

"I've only been with two men, and one of them I was married to."

He frowned, tilting on the balls of his feet, regarding her. "I must say, I'm disappointed. A lack of curiosity I didn't expect in you."

She turned away. "There are other things to be curious about."

He stepped back. "You're too young for me. Of course."

"I'm not too young for you!" she snapped. "I'm more mature and more capable than either of your wives I've seen so far."

He began to laugh helplessly, sliding down the doorjamb. She gave him a hand and drew him to his feet. He opened the door to his bedroom and bowed her in. She went.

What she had considered satisfactory sex before that night was if the man was not unclean or piggy and did not hurt her, and if she had an orgasm from time to time. Perhaps Gordon was simply more sensual than any man she had been with, perhaps he was simply more patient, perhaps he was simply more experienced with the bodies and needs of women. Whatever it was, she lost control as she never had. By the time he entered her, she was moaning like an animal, grabbing at him, lurching to meet him. When she came, it shook her. She lay afterwards with the feeling of having been dropped from a great height. She fell asleep almost at once.

Natasha was up before her in the morning, waiting impatiently in the kitchen. "You stayed with Daddy. Do you like him?"

"Yes, I like him a lot. You know too damned much for your age, Natasha."

"I have to. I'm the house mother, haven't you noticed? Daddy says Fern started turning things over to me by the time I was seven! I want a stepmother, but I want some choice."

"It's a little early to talk about that."

"It's never too early," Natasha said firmly. "We can't let you get away."

She decided that what she saw around her was a paradise gone to weeds. Sunburned children chased puppies nobody had bothered to housebreak; students camped out on the beach among great mounds of garbage bags and green-headed flies. Gordon had begun building a tower to distance himself from the chaos. He simply could not manage the logistics any longer. He needed help, obviously, and she began slowly to make order.

She did not leave the next day. She did not leave until the morning she was due in court. By the time she drove into the city through the hot gritty morning in rush-hour traffic, she knew she was obsessed with him. That night she called Hannah in Washington. They often spoke at ten at night, about the time they usually got home to their respective tiny apartments from their respective overheated demanding jobs.

"Do you love him?" Hannah asked.

"I don't know . . ." Judith clutched the receiver hard. "I never thought I was capable of falling in love."

"When you look at him, does he make you feel weak?" Hannah asked.

"No! He makes me feel strong." She was going to marry him. She knew it then. Yirina would have loved him too.

DAVID

10

"Let's play home movies," Judith said, curled up with me before the fire. "Tell me about your marriage. I was married before too. I was twenty when I got married and twenty-one when I got divorced."

The image that came to me as she talked was a cartoon of a pimply faced boy from New Jersey; then I added a beard to the pimply faced boy. Ridiculous. But Judith was more interested in questioning me.

"I married the boss's daughter. I was twenty-three, I had forty thousand dollars left of my bonus, every possibility in the world, and I couldn't think of one. I was drifting around Florida, where I felt comfortable because everybody seemed to come from someplace else." I lay on my side staring at the flames in the gas grate. The room was almost tropical. She had turned the heat high when we made love.

One night in the lounge of a seafood restaurant under the bridge to Singer Island, I met a guy who'd seen me pitch. He'd played baseball himself. "But never professionally," he said. Few people knew enough to refer to minor leaguers as professional.

"Jewish kid, aren't you?" Wynn Hardy was the kind of man who thought he could say anything he liked. He was taller than me, lean except for the beer belly he steered like the hood ornament of an expensive car. His lips were always set in a half smile, so everything he said could be taken as a provocation or a joke. "It's a compliment, son. Means you're probably smarter than the average asshole I hire, that you don't stay out drinking till four in the morning when you have to be at work at eight." Wynn described a forty-acre property he'd just bought, only recently an orange grove, six miles from the coast, twenty miles north of Palm Beach. He was putting up a hundred Spanish-style ranches with white plaster arches and wrought-iron grillwork. He offered me a job and I took it.

"I liked working construction," I told Judith. "The same as I like nursery work." I liked swinging a hammer, using the power in my shoulders and upper arms. Most of Wynn's crew were Dominican and Cuban. When it came to keeping records of deliveries and dealing with inspectors, I was important.

"So what was she like, the boss's daughter?" Judith leaned over me, her eyes alight with curiosity. "Did she have a name?"

"Vicki. She loved horses." Had she won the lottery or married a rich man, she might have spent all her time preparing for competition. But she had to work, which left her only mornings, from dawn until about eight, evenings and weekends to exercise her horses and muck out the stables. Vicki Hardy was as strong as most men her size. Her butt was pure muscle and something of a family joke. Her doctor, Wynn Hardy's best friend, once said that giving her a booster shot was like trying to penetrate an orange with a drinking straw.

"What did she look like?"

"She was lean and mean, sort of a boy's body. Blond hair." Short, because she couldn't find the time to fuss with it; bleached by the sun a pale white-yellow. Her eyes were light blue, almost turquoise, and contrasted with her skin, the color of a scuffed penny, to give her face the impression of a tomboy with dirty cheeks. Because she was employed by her father's company, she didn't have to dress for work, but drove from the stable to the office in blue jeans, boots and one of a drawer full of faded chambray shirts from which she carefully removed the sleeves at the shoulder seam with a razor blade. She smelled of leather and cloves and the horses she loved.

Vicki drove out to the site every Thursday afternoon with our paychecks. When she brought me mine, we talked. She told me she'd dropped out of community college. What she really loved was business, her dad's business, making it grow, and her riding. "Nothing else in the world interests me. . . ."

Vicki was twenty and lived with her parents. I always asked about her horses because I liked to watch the sun-gold goddess gush like a little girl. Gallant Prince was a seven-year-old quarterhorse and Arab cross. Sheena was a chestnut mare, with a star and wide-set eyes; her filly's name was Dottie because she was dun color with dapples. At least one weekend a month, Vicki went off to cross-country competitions. I knew nothing about horses and felt like Sancho Panza when I clambered up on one. But I had been a competitor.

"It's almost like I hate it and I love it," Vicki said. "All week and for a month beforehand, all I think about is the course. And then just as our number is called, just as I'm trying to settle Gallant down, I get so nervous I want to cry and run away."

"Sometimes before a game, my stomach would clench so tight I'd get the dry heaves."

She laughed. "I *wish* mine were dry."

"But I felt so alive at that moment. That nothing else in my whole life had ever been or ever would be as intense."

She said shyly, "Do you want to go with me to Bradenton for a show?"

"Where do you stay?"

"We'll get a motel room," she said.

The Monday after Vicki and I returned from Bradenton, I was afraid to face her father, but Wynn dropped his arm on my shoulder and asked me out to the house. From then on I was a regular Sunday guest. Unlike my own family, the Hardys didn't carp at each other, complain about their neighbors or things that might have been, parties they weren't invited to. They *gave* parties, every Sunday for bridge and barbecue around the pool. I got to know Vicki's brothers and their girlfriends; aunts, cousins, all the family friends. I was so in love with the Hardys and grateful for their acceptance that it hadn't occurred to me I might be exactly what they were looking for.

Vicki was still exotic to me. She made love the way she rode, with a fierce, faraway look in her eyes and tough silent concentration. She liked to be fucked hard, ridden high, and thrust herself to meet me with alarming strength. We never spoke in bed. Watching her mouth roll open, her head sway side to side and the shimmer of her tiny breasts, I imagined her riding me in her mind, across fields of new-mown alfalfa. Sex wasn't easy for Vicki, but a matter of concentration and muscle control. Not unlike riding. Or for that matter, pitching. It was usually after sex that I wondered, Who does she think about when she's alone? What does she want? I was afraid of the answer so I didn't ask the question. I was too in love with my place in the family.

"After we got married, Wynn sent me to school. I worked days, took business courses at night. Weekends Vicki and I would go to one of her meets or just hang around the Hardys' pool."

Judith frowned. For a moment I had a sense of the litigator in her. "The woman you describe sounds damaged. As if some early trauma had damped her down and made her cut her losses."

I stared. I could only say, "Nobody mentioned it until we were married and a friend of her mother's started telling me how good she thought I was for 'poor Vicki.' "

Wynn Hardy had caught his daughter with a boy named Mauricio, the son of a Cuban who worked for Wynn laying tile. They were just fifteen and went to school together. Wynn drove to the beach one day and found Vicki topless. He threatened if he ever saw them together again, he'd kill both of them. He sent her to a private school. She phoned her mother in tears every night.

Then Vicki stopped calling. The school called instead. The kids were caught in a bus station in Tampa, waiting for a connection to New Orleans. When Mauricio was returned to his home, his father and two uncles who worked for Wynn had been let go. Wynn never lifted a hand to the boy. His own father beat him half to death.

"What happened to Vicki?"

"Wynn got her an abortion. And her first horse."

We received a three and a half acre lot from Vicki's parents for a wedding present, large enough for a stable and a paddock. I used my bonus money for the down payment on the house, but the truth is, we wouldn't have had a house at all if Wynn hadn't built it. Soon he was talking about kids. We weren't avoiding having kids, we weren't using protection; we just doubted it could happen. Vicki menstruated with comical irregularity. I had a year to go for my degree when Vicki went to the family doctor for digestive problems. It turned out she was in her third month.

Wynn, Mrs. Hardy and I ganged up on Vicki to try to get her to stop riding. She stopped jumping, but that was all. It was a difficult pregnancy. She hated the changes in her body; she hated feeling fat. One Saturday she came back from the stables and her water broke. My son was born prematurely just after midnight Sunday morning. The birth was terrifying. Vicki was home from the hospital after two nights. The baby stayed three weeks. I'd been married to Vicki Hardy for five years and hadn't the faintest idea how she would respond to motherhood. I was secretly afraid she'd just go off riding every day and leave the baby to the maid the Hardys had hired.

My first quarrel with Wynn was over naming the baby. My father had died a few years before, and while I didn't expect them to like the name Sam, I wanted something that started with the letter S, as was the custom among Ashkenazi Jews. Steven or Seth or Stan—I would have been happy with any small honor to my father's name, but the Hardys wanted Wynn the Third. I didn't believe it.

"He'll be called Terry," Vicki said. "Tertius. It means 'the third' in Latin. That's what we do in my family."

"But not in mine, Vicki."

"Why are you doing this to me?" She brought her hands up to hide her face. Arguments with her father could make her physically ill. "Why do you always think about yourself?"

I began losing my son before he was out of the premie ward.

Vicki took a leave of absence. I was at work all day and still finishing up school in the evenings. Vicki spent any time she wasn't with the horses at the Hardy house. Terry was fussed over by his grandparents, by his nursemaid, by his mother and all the family friends. He was a small baby, but by the time he was crawling, he was growing every week. His hair was yellow at first, but gradually began to darken. His eyes were mine; his other features and his long lean body seemed to come from Wynn. He stood up at around eleven months and began to walk soon after that.

"I remember the day I began to feel superfluous," I told Judith, "like a pitcher about to be cut. It was a Sunday at the Hardys' pool. Terry was a year and a half and running around like a little colt. He tripped over a hose and fell on the concrete, banging his knee. He began to wail. I picked him up and kissed him but he wouldn't stop crying—until Wynn lifted him out of my arms."

"What happened to the marriage? Did Mauricio return? Did she have an affair? Did you?"

"It was a matter of business."

Wynn got backing from a local savings and loan for a new development. The land was flat as a soccer field. The nearest town was fifteen miles away and the only view was the interstate. But Wynn had big plans.

He gathered the family around to name the place. Think in the grand Spanish style, he told us. He talked about an Olympic-size pool, a health club, an on-site shopping plaza and a long wide entrance road he called the Boulevard of Palms. Vicki's older brother designed glossy full-color brochures in English and Spanish. I was in charge of sales, Vicki the office, Wynn and Vicki's younger brother, construction. When La Fonda del Sol was featured in the Sunday real estate section, Wynn used the headline in all our ads: DEVELOPED BY THE HARDY FAMILY. Early interest was tremendous. Our clients were largely Spanish speakers buying their first homes outside the Miami area. Wynn had planned 130 four-bedroom homes with red tile roofs. Construction went on six days a week. The development was sixty percent occupied when the complaints began. Where was the swimming pool? The health club complex? Where was the on-site shopping center they had read about in the brochure? The nearest store was a half-hour drive. Trucks stirred up clouds of dust on streets that had yet to be paved; there wasn't a tree planted on the Boulevard of Palms. Residents appeared at my desk every day, and all I could do was beg their patience and their trust, while I was losing my own.

There were things I didn't like about the way Wynn did business. He had a Spanish-speaking salesman but wrote up all the contracts in English. He never told people they'd have to bear the cost of being connected to the local sewer system. Vicki said I didn't understand his financial pressures, the headaches that kept him up at night. But I couldn't keep quiet any longer.

"Wynn, I have a problem," I said one night over a beer.

"You have a problem? Find a place at the back of the line, son, there's a lot of people ahead of you."

"I thought we could talk about some of the promises we made."

"And what promises might they be?" he said tiredly.

"The pool. The health club."

"I know all about it."

"Then what are we waiting for? We made a deal."

"You made a deal? Your name is on that piece of paper with the bank? Do me a favor. Until you have the union and the inspectors and the bank on your fucking back, just sit in your little air-conditioned of-fice, do what you're paid to do and keep your mouth shut."

"Maybe I can't do that." I hadn't meant it as a threat, but these were good people. No, they didn't speak native English but they worked hard for their money, the way my own father had worked, twelve or fourteen hours a day, and it was wrong to make them come begging for the things they'd paid for. "It just doesn't sit right with me."

"And I'm supposed to give a fuck?" Wynn's eyes burned blue fire. "If I was you, I'd watch my own backyard."

"What's that supposed to mean?"

"It means if what I hear about my daughter and her friends down at the stable is true, if I ever see another grandchild it'll probably be brown."

My hand closed around a bottle of beer. I knew Wynn Hardy and I knew his game, insults instead of answers, but he always aimed for the heart and he'd cut me, hard and deep. Vicki and I hadn't made love six times since our son's birth. I felt like one of those horses who stand at stud. I felt, rightly or not, I had been used to produce the next genera-tion of the Hardy family and that everything I had, including my son, belonged to them and not to me.

That night I told Vicki about the unfulfilled contracts, the violations of federal law. I wasn't going to force another family to suffer the same mistake mine had, sinking farther into the hole to salvage what they'd invested. It took my father years to admit he'd been a fool to take on a dying business in a rotten building, but he would have been the first to tell you that it cost him his marriage and everything he had ever been able to save. Finally I think it cost him his life.

"We're leaving here," I said. "It's time to strike out on our own."

"I can't do that, David. Terry loves his family. I can't yank him away from Mom and Dad. And the foal is just at the training level. She's sup-posed to take her first test next month."

"We can't stay here, Vicki. Trust me. We'll make a better life."

"But I like it the way it is." I had never heard that sharp edge on her voice. "I love my family. I thought you were one of us. If my father needs you to stick by him, I don't see why you can't. What's the matter with you, David? Why do you always put yourself first?" That night she packed Terry off to her parents' and never came back.

When I went to see him, he hardly seemed to know me. When I brought him a toy or a book, he didn't need it. He had plenty. Anything I gave him disappeared into the Hardy family and seemed to dissolve. When I tried to take him someplace for a few hours, he cried.

They wanted full custody. I gave Vicki the house (after all, Wynn had built it), and in return she asked minimal child support. I was supposed to have visiting privileges, two weekends a month, but Terry hated it. I was this stranger who came to drag him off to the movies or the beach or McDonald's, away from his grandparents' pool, his cousins, his golden retriever. I was working construction, living in a furnished room on the Gulf coast, and every time I brought him home to my place, he seemed to stare at me with Wynn's own contempt. When Vicki remarried, I moved back up north. I send my monthly check and visit twice a year and try not to think of him every time I see a kid his age.

"Most of us don't seem to get it right the first time," Judith said, taking my face between her palms. "But it might be possible to do something about your custody arrangements. . . . How old is your son now?"

"He was nine last month." I dug in my wallet. "Every year they send a photo after his birthday with a card he signs thanking me."

"Who did you cut out of the photo?"

"Wynn, Vicki and her two new kids."

"Ah . . ." She was silent, staring at the card-sized image of a tanned and healthy little boy beneath a palm tree. Under a shock of dark brown hair, his pale eyes stared into the camera with a big grin—not at me, at whoever was taking the picture. He had broad shoulders and chubby red cheeks; the son I wasn't allowed to name.

"I do a lot of custody law. . . . If you want things changed, we can talk to someone I trust down there. . . ."

"What do I have to give him, Judith?"

She looked at me the way no one else ever had. "I'd say a lot."

"When I get hopeful, I imagine him striking out on his own to find me when he gets to be seventeen or eighteen, being curious, maybe as a kind of rebellion. But none of the Hardy kids ever left home. It's a fantasy."

"Maybe not," she said. "It happens. Think of it this way. If your marriage had worked out, you would never have moved back here. You'll have a house again, and a wife, but more suited to you. More caring."

"I doubt it," I said.

"I don't." She kissed my lips lightly. "Are you hungry?"

JOHNNY

Johnny Lynch was up at four A.M. with a feeling so foreign that he had to talk to himself to understand it,
coax himself down like a cat from a tree, as he'd coaxed
his wife so many times. Although he was no stranger to
the rush of adrenaline and the cold draft of sweat on
his forehead, it wasn't until the drive into work that he
could even name the problem. Fear. Back to his own office for the first
time in eight weeks, at the desk he'd had custom built—thirty-two
inches high to accommodate his knees—and instead of speeding down
the highway, he slowed for every yellow light. He was as scared as he'd
been of the nuns in school, of his father's rage when he couldn't make
good grades. In order to succeed, he had purged himself of fear, learned
to plunge through it, and in so doing understood that the others were
more scared than he was and would fall in behind him once he cleared
the way.

Johnny Lynch was sixty-eight. He'd lived twice the life of most men
his age and felt half the man he used to be. The last time his dog had
flushed a duck from the tall reeds behind the dike, he'd had all he
could do to lift his shotgun and aim; the recoil nearly brought him to
his knees. By the grace of the Lord, or maybe to provide Him with a
good laugh, Johnny had survived this last bypass—if he could call the
list of foods he couldn't eat, the things he couldn't do, surviving.

This was the day he had anticipated for three weeks in bed and another five in a Fort Myers resort that felt like a cemetery with palm
trees. Now, three hours back in his office, the well-wishers dismissed,
the mail stacked in piles of importance, he sat at his big cherry desk
like the ruler of an empty kingdom. The phone didn't ring, the door
didn't open. Maybe he shouldn't have demanded this afternoon's meeting with the bank. A wiser man might have waited; a lesser man wouldn't
push. But finally, he was John Mosley Lynch, and he preferred bad
news to silence.

He used to order his desk blotters thirty at a time. From them, Maria
copied notes he scribbled while on the telephone, the numbers and
contacts he gleaned, the names and the tips and reminders. Now
there were few of those. He still had the real estate business, which
did well despite the competition. (There hadn't been any when he

began because there was no housing market in Saltash. He created it.) But the big deals were few and far between. To develop property you needed major financing now, for the endless surveys and design reviews, the regulatory hearings created to discourage all but the most determined. He had little interest in summer rentals and second home sales and left that to the girls, most of them grandmothers by now. They were demanding a new secretary, a younger girl who understood computers. As for the law practice, the indictment had all but ended that. He'd beaten the bastards, but it cost him a fortune and his reputation. Before he was indicted, even as the rumors swirled and his partners ran scared and the newspapers descended like vultures on a roadkill, there was no other lawyer worth hiring in this town. He had written the damned bylaws: zoning, health, conservation. Only after the case went to court did he find out who his friends were, who gave him their business and who turned their backs. Six years had passed, six long years of damage control. The worst of it fell on his wife, God rest her delicate soul; a finer woman had never lived.

Emily Ann was too good for this earth, and that was the cause of her troubles. This bitter world was hard on everyone's nerves, but that a woman so sensitive and pure, so good to the marrow of her bones, would succumb to its pressures was no surprise. She had everything a woman could ask, as she herself said a thousand times—a fine home, three children, a town in which she was a veritable queen—but what she needed was a world clean of petty rumors and people who lied for the sheer pleasure of causing pain. It was the indictment that claimed his wife of forty years. All those whispers about a mistress and a love nest, as if he was some Turkish pasha with a harem; those charges of sweetheart contracts and that bad business with Kevin, their second-born, Emily Ann had endured; with help from the doctors they'd gotten through her bad spells. But the indictment had been too much. Two months or three, that was all she'd ever needed to be away up in Boston; then she'd come home, how did she put it? Refreshed. But she had never come home again after he'd been hounded into court, and those who had pursued him had killed her as surely as if they'd hammered a stake straight through her heart.

For a long while he thought it was revenge he was after. He would sit in this chair, staring into the marsh as the shadows lengthened. He would watch as the tide receded and the herons returned to feed, imagining the pain he would deal his enemies. But for all that he had endured, he was not a vengeful man. To be sure, he could deliver an eye for an eye, but to waste time brooding about his enemies was only to play into their hands. Time was his real enemy.

Johnny had built this town not by thinking about it but by making the contacts that mattered, by forging alliances with the governor and the legislature. When he had first moved to Saltash, the selectmen saw Boston as the devil; one, Larsen, boasted that he had never in his life had a reason to go over the bridge—and the idiot died of a burst appendix, diagnosed by a local physician as gas. They tried to make Johnny ashamed of where he came from. Washed ashore, they called him, the mick from South Boston. But it was Boston State House money that built the highway to this town and the pier and dredged the harbor deep enough for yachts. It was all his trips to Boston, three and a half hours each way in those days, that made Saltash a place to visit and put its men to work. "John Mosley Lynch," Emily Ann used to say. "Just what do you do from seven in the morning till twelve at night?" What he'd done was build this town.

They tried to push him out. Those who'd moved into the houses he built, on the land he had cleared: in forests so thick the sunlight didn't shine, off roads no wider than wagon trails. First it was counsel to the town. Thank you very much, if you please, we'll find our legal advice elsewhere. Then selectman. Defeated after two decades on the board by fifty-four votes. They wanted him stuck in an office with three yattering women who rented summer cottages. They wanted him dead and buried.

At a quarter before twelve, apologizing lest she make him late for his one o'clock meeting, Maria brought in the new girl. Maria had worked for him for twenty-two years and knew enough about this town to run it. She was a small Portuguese girl, mother of five, and he'd watched her age over the years as if watching his own face in the mirror. Dark, sensual Maria, whose body had moved with the grace of a cat, with black curly hair and a magnificent round rump. Was she really the gray-haired matron who stood before him? She used to leave the office a half hour early and meet him at the cottage by the lake. She liked to be completely naked when he arrived. She never turned the lights on and didn't like to talk. They knew each other's secrets. Her husband, Pepe, was captain of a scallop dragger; a pot smuggler Johnny had bailed out of trouble more times than he cared to remember. His drinking was under control unless the fleet was frozen in, when he got bored and beat his wife. Johnny never told Maria about the warning he gave Pepe, that if he hit his wife again, he'd bill him for every cent he had, including the boat.

"Mr. Lynch, this is Crystal." Maria dropped the girl's résumé on the desk blotter. In twenty-two years she had never touched him in the office. "Crystal Sinclair."

This was a big girl, a head taller than Maria, substantially built, with strong wrists and a fine heavy bosom. Her white blouse was frayed at the collar and cuffs. There was a yellow stain just below the left shoulder. She needed this job. Good. He didn't want a retired woman, back to work after she'd moved down here; he wanted loyalty. Thirty-two years old, according to the résumé. Same age as his son Kevin. Well, they needed youth around here. Strange, the color of her hair, not blond or silver, but something in between. She was a pretty girl. Her smile was confident and she held his eyes. He liked that.

"Sinclair," he said. "You wouldn't have known a Dr. Sinclair?"

"I'm his daughter."

"No, sir! Well sit down, sit down. He did have two daughters," the sorry bastard. "You know we haven't had a dentist in this town since he . . . moved on." Johnny scanned the résumé with interest. It didn't surprise him that she'd been educated out West. "University of Nevada, Las Vegas. Fine school. Fine school." He didn't know a damned thing about it except they had a basketball team. He'd never been to Las Vegas. Never had the time or interest to gamble. There was something (he didn't want to stare) coquettish? made up? about her. The dark lipstick. The perfume. The tight skirt. Nothing that put him off, exactly. It just wasn't Saltash. "I see you've worked in a law office before."

"Well, I'm not really a legal secretary."

"But you've worked with computers. You've got WordPerfect, Word, Excel." None of it meant a thing to him. "And what brings you back here?" He watched her carefully. He listened for the stammer, the hesitation. The eyes flitting to the floor. Her gaze didn't falter. She was sharp, this one. She'd have the other girls eating out of her hand.

"I wanted a good education for my son."

"You have a boy?"

"He's just turned eight. And, well, I know we have a great school here and it would be perfect for him."

"You thought right. What's his name?"

"Laramie."

"After the western town!" What the fuck kind of thing is that to name a child? "Very nice, very nice." He noticed there was no wedding ring. As soon as he saw her address, he knew her story. Four twelve Dock Street. The closest Saltash had to a housing project. But he wasn't a man who judged people by their morals or their circumstances. Frankly, he thought their politics a better gauge of character. Do you believe in caring for the sick and the hungry or do you babble a few words on Sunday morning? That was the test. "Well, Crystal." He rose, offering his hand. "Welcome aboard."

"Then I have the job?"

"You had it before you walked in. I'm just the rubber stamp around here. Maria's the real power behind the throne."

The meeting was two towns over, fifteen miles up the highway, in the bank's main branch. He was five minutes early. Bernice Cady came out to meet him and escort him back. Bernice had polio as a child, and if her bad leg dragged slightly as she walked, she still walked as fast as anyone he knew. Her family had discouraged her from applying to college and assumed that she'd look after her widowed father the rest of her life. Johnny remembered her buck-toothed smile, her bony arms waving, full of questions, whenever he read stories to her class. When she graduated high school, she asked him for a job at the bank, and in spite of the other board members' reluctance and her father's disapproval, Johnny saw to it she became a part-time teller. The kid surprised him, landing the job full-time within a year. Then she became head teller, branch manager when the local bank merged, most recently a loan officer.

"Mr. Lynch, I'm sorry, no one's back yet. They called to say they'd be a few minutes."

They were still at lunch. Years ago this meeting would have been called for lunch and drinks in a private room in the best restaurant in town. Now, he could wait. Bernice couldn't do him any special favors, other than tell him the truth: it was going to be a hard sell. She saw him daub the bead of perspiration from his cheek and she knew what he had left in the world: the house he lived in and 120 acres behind the dike. He had a pain like a burning lump of coal in his chest, and it only got hotter when her bosses walked in. Two boys of forty, one bald with glasses, the other smelling of onions, both in navy suits, Roger and Steve with the power of money.

"We like your plans, Johnny," Roger the bald one said. "The timing is good. There hasn't been a significant development in Saltash in years."

"About twelve," he said. "Since the bottom dropped out. And there won't be another. There's not a more beautiful spot on Old Cape Cod. You have to see those hills in the light of the moon. The dew turns the color of silver."

The two boys exchanged a glance. Bernice looked away. He knew he sounded like a fool. Steve spoke, and the smell of onion was unbearable. "We're worried about the dike, Johnny. There's been a lot of talk about opening it. If that happens, your acreage is cut by seventy-five percent and the rest is soggy ground."

"That talk has been going on for years."

"But times have changed, Johnny. The town has changed. It's full of new voters."

"If the fools vote to open that dike and the river floods the basements and ruins the property values of fifty luxury homes, owned by doctors and lawyers and the kind of people I'm attracting, the town is looking at a lawsuit that can bankrupt it."

The bald man crossed his legs. "If the homes are built and sold first."

"Jesus, Mary, and Joseph, how can I build them until I have the money?" And what'll I do without the money? he thought. He had never been a man to take expensive vacations or wear extravagant clothes. He liked a new car. He liked to help his children. The bills for Kevin alone were as much as a man made at the height of his career. He'd never gambled with stocks and bonds. Land was where the money was—and he'd had to sell most of it to keep himself out of prison.

"Johnny, you know how much we want to help." He knew the smelly little bastard didn't give a shit about anything but covering his own ass. "But how can we commit to this project when we don't know the houses will be built and sold first? We can't afford to be stuck with ninety acres of soggy land."

Bernice shocked them all by speaking up. "What do we need, Roger?"

"Some guarantee that the dike will still be standing and in place until all the houses go up."

"And what guarantee could I give you?" Johnny felt hopeless.

"There's a seat open on the Board of Selectmen this May. As I understand it," Bernice said, "you have two votes for the dike standing and two committed to tearing it down."

Johnny looked straight into her eyes. "And if the swing seat voted to keep the dike in place?"

"I think that would go a long way toward convincing this committee. Roger?" she asked, and the bald man nodded. "Steve?"

Steve cleared his throat. "Yes. Well, as I said. We would like to do business with you."

When Johnny returned from lunch, something lemony, something fresh, lingered in the air around his desk. The new girl's perfume? The room felt brighter somehow. No, he hadn't gotten what he wanted. But

Johnny Lynch had never expected a thing without working for it, nor the rules to be stacked in his favor. What he asked was a shot at the prize. He felt heady. He felt a lightness in his step. Public opinion was against him. He'd have to work behind the scenes. But he liked a vigorous campaign. A good fight alerted his senses. No time to mull over the past. There was too much work to do.

JUDITH

12

Five years after Gordon and Judith were married, when she was thirty-two, Gordon retired from Brandeis and wanted to live on Squeer Island year-round. It was a hard move for Judith, for it meant giving up her chance at partnership in her Boston law firm, fought for grimly year after year. On the other hand, it meant she could approach the image that had remained in her mind since France of a more gracious, sensual life, integrated into a landscape. Saltash was beautiful, sloping down toward the busy harbor, the hills crowded with Victorian captain's houses, older Capes, mostly white, some painted pale blue or green or cobalt or barn red. Town center was a combination of white steepled churches on High Street and the incongruous but handsome redbrick Town Hall built in 1870, to replace a structure destroyed in a hurricane. The aesthetic of the place appealed to her, the famous light, the sea, the dunes, and of course the compound on the island. Here they would change their life. They would spend far more time together than had been available since they married, with her working at least twelve hours a day and often weekends, and Gordon teaching full-time and then flying around to lecture all over the country.

Judith became a partner in a two-person law firm in Saltash, with Austin Bowman, a man older than Gordon. By her fourth year living in Saltash, Gordon and she were fully involved in the effort to defeat the Johnny Lynch machine. Johnny Lynch controlled the entire town government, but they saw a chance to elect at least one selectman who would not be loyal to Johnny: a beginning, anyhow. It would take years to get a majority, they knew. One February morning, when fog lay over the ice in the Bay, her partner Austin called her shack just as she was about to head to town. "This guy Lyle," he said in his raspy voice. "I don't think he can cut it. Johnny is running his man hard and spreading rumors Lyle wants to raise property taxes. For our first real contest with Johnny, we need a stronger candidate."

Austin was close to seventy and on the verge of retirement, or so he said. He had been saying that since she joined his practice. She said, "Lyle makes a decent speech. People seem to trust Lyle."

"Some do, some don't."

"Suppose we get a reporter to interview both candidates about taxes. That will give Lyle a platform to insist he doesn't want to raise them."

"But, Judith, we need to raise taxes for a new water system."

"Austin, even if we win a seat on the board, one selectman out of five can't push that through."

Austin cleared his throat. "I want you to talk to someone. He's thinking of running, and he might be better for us to back. War hero from Vietnam. Lost a foot. Many relatives here."

She agreed to meet with the putative candidate at four-thirty. That would cut it close to get back over the bridge before high tide. The damned rickety bridge that high tides submerged had seemed amusing and romantic when they were summer people. Now that they lived on the island year-round and she had to make a living on the Cape, it was a nuisance to her—but Gordon had a real attachment to the island and its inhabitants and its customs. She had a cot in her law office so she could sleep over when the tides were not cooperating or when she must appear in court. She respected Gordon's attachments. The bridge might infuriate her, but the view from the bridge was one of life's pleasures, the bay full of islands, the great blue herons when the tide was low, the tern acrobats.

Austin did not like her sleeping in the office, considering it unprofessional. When he finally did retire, she was going to move the practice to a better office with a small apartment attached. That would make life easier. By the time she got off the phone, she had twenty minutes to dress and get herself across the bridge to her office to meet a client.

When she ran into the main house, Gordon was at the kitchen table, a cigarette in one hand and a cup of coffee in the other, the telephone clamped between his chin and his shoulder. "So the manuscript is late," he was saying. "The economy won't go into recession because of it. It's taking longer than I estimated, yes, but I'm making a more interesting and comprehensive book than if I hurried. I had a couple of bouts of bronchitis this winter, and it slowed me down." He nodded to her as she passed. Either his agent or his publisher, having fits because his book was not finished by deadline. She was perhaps excessively punctual, someone who did not like to keep anyone waiting, whose life was timed to the minute. Gordon was casual about deadlines whether they were getting to the supper table or showing up to a meeting. To him, time always seemed far more elastic than to her.

Practicing law here was a motley operation, now a drug dealer, now a divorce case, a suit against the town, restraining orders, whatever local life tossed up. She was getting a reputation as a good hard lawyer, the first choice of people in trouble around Saltash. Some of her clients she liked and some she detested, but she gave them all their money's worth, a well-prepared brief and a good fight in court. She was at her best in the courtroom. She thought well on her feet. It was nine-tenths being prepared and one-tenth pure competition. She liked to win as much as she ever had. She would never be done proving herself. Now she had ten minutes to drive the rutted sand road and cross the bridge before the tide rose.

Her biggest case at the moment was a woman suing the local pizza parlor. The woman, a vigorous fifty-year-old who liked to keep in shape, had fallen through a rotten plank on their deck. Her spine had been injured and her arm broken in three places. She had lost some control of her right hand and she had recurring numbness. The problem was that the pizza parlor had been carrying minimal insurance. The insurance company was refusing to pay, claiming the woman had been careless. The owner claimed that the suit was putting him out of business, the only pizza available in winter for five miles around.

When Judith went into town, about one person in four glared at her. "You're the grinch who stole pizza," the fish man roared at her.

Her first two years in town, she had felt invisible. Now that was all changed. She was visible, all right. She liked her client, Enid Corea, a no-nonsense woman who boarded dogs and had served until her accident as the town dog warden and crossing guard. Mrs. Corea smelled of the kennel, was a cheerful woman whose husband had died on the highway and whose children were grown and departed. She needed the money, and Judith meant to get it for her, even if the suit did close down the only pizza parlor for miles.

Since Gordon's retirement, they had created a life she wanted. Life by the sea, with a garden, with friends of all sorts, with an extended family. Most lawyers she knew had friends who were lawyers, perhaps a few other professionals or politicians. Through Gordon she had friends who were oystermen, scallopers, carpenters, plumbers, friends who taught history at Brandeis or Milan, friends who taught sociology in Berkeley or Melbourne, former freedom riders and war protesters, radical rabbis and radical priests and nuns, writers and painters and colorful drinkers who no longer did much of anything but tell tales of what they had done before they drank so much. Some of them she liked, some she tolerated, but theirs was a style of entertaining that was open at the same time that their work was jealously protected.

She saw her clients in town. They could call her at the office only, but she checked her messages compulsively. If one of her regular clients called, no matter from where, if they had been busted in Westfield or Revere, she got in the car and she went. After all, the time driving was billed at the same rate as her time in court. She made a reasonable living. She would never see the income some friends from law school made. But she earned about as much as Hannah, on the staff of a senator whose mistress she was. Hannah was still her confidante, as she was Hannah's. They saw each other perhaps once a year, but talked twice a week, after ten as they always had.

They were both impassioned about the law and totally involved while they were working, but both demanded to have a life besides. Both were involved with men much older than themselves, whom they admired as much as they loved them. The style of Hannah's life was entirely different from her own, but to Hannah too, how she lived was important. Hannah's elegance was closer to the Washington notion of the good life; Judith's had been formed, she was aware, partly by Yirina's fantasies and partly by her European travels, alone and with Gordon. She wanted a life rooted in a local landscape, rooted in the seasons and natural beauty, however little all that had to do with her profession.

Therefore she put up with the tides, with Gordon's children: the one she loved, Natasha; the two she got on with (the older sons Dan and Ben, their wives and children); and the two she had trouble with, Larry, her former client, and Sarah. She had trouble with them for different reasons. Sarah was hostile. She was a divorced mother who ran a travel agency, and she considered it an affront that Gordon should have married a woman so close to her in age. Larry tried to mooch, to lean, to leech. He had to be kept within bounds whether he was calling late at night needing money, or whether he was underfoot, feeling sorry for himself. He was an aspiring filmmaker who worked in a video store in New York—if he still had that job. Yet even the offspring who gave her trouble added to her sense of a rich web of connection. It fed a hunger she had always had. She longed for ever more connection into the community.

After the insurance lawyers (an offer finally, too small, but they had begun to waver), she had a meeting with the possible candidate Austin had touted. If they could get even one selectman elected who wasn't controlled by Johnny Lynch, issues could be raised at the weekly meetings, town government could be rendered more accountable. She was looking this guy over for Gordon and the liberals who often met at their house. If she thought he was for real, she would invite him over and they would interview him as a group, deciding whether to back him. She was the first interrogator. If they did not back him, they would back Lyle.

"What do you think about the dike?"

"The dike . . . Well, the dike is certainly a problem, yes. The dike." He was a slight man with a high-pitched voice and a tendency to stare into corners. "We should do something about it, yes."

After ten minutes she realized he was a lost cause. Public meetings would make a fool of him. He meant well, but he couldn't say what he meant quickly or clearly enough. No go. It would have to be Lyle.

"He won't do," she said to Gordon as they sat down to a supper of broiled salmon, boiled potatoes with herbs, bread from the local bakery, spring salad from the garden and pinot grigio. "We need somebody with more . . . conviction, more energy, more charisma."

"Johnny has enough charisma to pave the highway as far as the bridge," Gordon said wryly.

"I never found him charming," she said, propping her chin on a knuckle. "Are you charmed?"

"Sure I am. He's the last old-fashioned boss in Massachusetts politics. He's the real thing."

"A real crook? A real swindler? A real manipulator? That's like saying, a real pothole. They come by the dozen." She wanted to set Gordon off. After nine years of marriage, she was still fascinated by the way he thought. Many of her best moments in any day were spent arguing, discussing with him, listening to him reminisce, analyzing together.

"A true political boss offers as much as he takes, or almost as much, to be more accurate. He gives you a bargain. Support me and I'll do for you when you need it. Can't get a mortgage? Bank threatening to foreclose? Can't meet your payroll this week? Can't afford an operation for the wife? Need a scholarship for the boy? Just give me leeway to develop all the land I want the way I want to, give me leeway to run the town to my advantage, and your boy will go to a state college, your wife will be off to the county hospital, and your roof will stay over your head. That's the devil's bargain—and it is a bargain. The folks who support him aren't stupid. They want it."

After supper they strolled in the twilight that was beginning to perceptibly lengthen as May began. Gordon had to pause several times as they climbed the dune, shaken by coughing. That nasty bronchitis from February had never really let go. Warm weather would dry it up. He liked to bake in the sun, and she could rarely get him to use sun screen. She was always trying to take care of Gordon, to feed him nutritiously, which was not difficult; to monitor his health; to get him to cut down on his smoking, since she had reluctantly realized she would never get him to stop. He was convinced he would not be able to work if he didn't have a cigarette at hand. "My mind is stimulated by nicotine," he would say blithely. "Caffeine in, nicotine in, words out. That's how the machine works."

"I still think you should see Dr. Garvey about that cough. You've had it since February. And see why your arm has been bothering you."

"It doesn't bother me. Just too much wood chopping. And my cough is just a smoker's cough. We're all a little short of breath as we get on. I don't see it slowing me down."

They walked along the bay, not touching but aware of each other. The waves hissed in, the pebbles rattling. There was only a horizon of greenish light left at water level. Venus was bright already. She thought that by the time they turned for home, both of them knew that as soon as they entered the house, they would head for their bedroom and make love. People sometimes let her know that they assumed hers was a marriage blanc, since Gordon was so much older, but there was nothing blank about it. They turned to each other now almost as frequently as they had in the early days. Oftener now she was the top, the more aggressive, the more vigorous, but Gordon's desire had not diminished, nor his skill. Making love was at the center of their marriage.

DAVID

13

The better part of March passed and I'd done nothing about the election. Judith stopped asking if I'd found someone to be treasurer of my campaign, to write absentee voters or nail up signs.

One night Judith put her hands on both sides of my face and stared into my eyes. "I think I finally understand what's happening with your campaign."

"That I'm not the person you're looking for."

"That you're afraid to ask for help."

Tommy Shalhoub was an old friend and the only phone call I could bring myself to make to prove her wrong. He didn't hesitate when I asked if he'd post election signs along the highway and suggested tearing down my opponents' signs as well.

I'd known Tommy Shalhoub since grade school, when his family moved to Saltash from a Syrian neighborhood in East Boston. He was an outsider, like me, but with coarse black curly hair and olive-brown skin, often lumped with the Portuguese, the bottom of the local pecking order. They called him the Sand Nigger; I was merely the Jew. While I escaped into baseball, Tommy was happiest alone, prowling the ponds for snakes and frogs, sleeping under a blanket in the woods. Just about the time I signed a contract with the Chicago Cubs, he left high school in the eleventh grade, got caught selling pot, and enlisted in the army in lieu of prosecution.

Tommy was the only guy I knew who talked with nostalgia about the military. Upon his return to Saltash, he worked as a house framer. Whenever the opportunity arose, he searched out construction work in disaster areas. Homestead after Hurricane Andrew. North Dakota after the Red River flood. Cheap motels and road food were perks for Tommy Shalhoub. He watched Weather Channel the way most people read the help wanted ads. He was out of town for months at a time. I had chosen Tommy to call because asking for help was as easy for me as taking a knife to my flesh, and I did not expect to find him at home. I was even more surprised when he sought me out at the nursery.

Tommy arrived accompanied by the pounding bass of the tape deck in his pickup, a noise that carried above the wind and the creaking joists of the greenhouse and the water I was draining out of the artificial pond. Tommy marched across the gravel floor. His presence seemed to disturb the air, to cause a sudden vibration of molecules like the rumble of a nearing motorcycle. "Dav-eee, what ch'up to?"

"Every time I put goldfish in this damned pond, they disappear. No floating bodies, not even a skeleton. I don't understand it."

"I mean in your life. I mean tonight. Let's have some fun. I got ideas."

"The last one was Lisa." She was a bank teller in her early thirties, a former girlfriend of Tommy's with a cocaine sniffle and hips that could slide into a child's pair of jeans. I knew she was coming off a bad relationship, and she knew I was on the make. We had sex twice, the way you draw water from an old stone well, trying to get what you need without falling in.

"Yeah, Lisa, Lisa," Tommy said. "What's she doin'?"

"Looking very hard for someone to take care of her."

"Listen t'me, Davey. I gotta ask y'somethin'." Tommy wore a thin leather jacket over a V-neck tee. Thirty-five degrees outside: no muffler, no hat, a blue crucifix tattooed on the back of his right hand. "You know my girlfriend, Michelle?"

"I met her last year at a baseball game." Cape Cod league. Tommy had left us alone in the bleachers for an hour. Wouldn't say where he'd gone.

"I remember that, yeah. You explained all the rules to her. But that was a different Michelle. This one has a friend who just moved back to town."

"Tommy, I'm not looking to be fixed up."

He didn't sound surprised. "If I was seeing a certain lady lawyer, I wouldn't either."

Tommy had been married and divorced twice. For all I knew, Judith might have represented Tommy in a court case or fought him on behalf of one of his ex-wives. I wasn't about to feed him information about Judith's private life. "I don't know what you're talking about."

"Then what's the problem? This girl's name is Crystal. She used to live in town. She just moved into Michelle's with her kid. He loves baseball."

"You've got two women on your hands? Is that it?"

"Hey." He threw up his palms, no contest. "If it doesn't fit in your busy schedule . . ." Tommy brushed past me to kneel at the pond. "What the fuck is that?" A black slime-encrusted lump rose from the murky bottom, projecting its head like a snake.

"A turtle?"

"A snapper!" Tommy said as the thing opened and closed its jaws. It had obviously lived on the bottom for months, dining on goldfish. It scrabbled for purchase, preparing to lunge. Tommy clopped into the pond, sinking to his ankles, and grabbed the thing by the rim of its shell. Flailing its limbs, it pissed like an open drain while Tommy held it at arm's length, staring into its ancient eyes. I told him sure, he could have it. He strolled out like a boy of twelve enchanted with his latest find.

As Passover approached, Judith asked me to join Gordon and her, his daughter Natasha, and a few friends, for a small seder. I was surprised. "Gordon told me he wasn't into that stuff," I told her. He'd been telling me where he grew up: "Jewish Cincinnati," he'd said. "But I was never into *that stuff*."

"He's finding his way back," Judith said. It was obvious why. I wanted to accept her invitation, but Passover was the one religious ritual we observed in my family, and it was always spent at Holly's.

Passover was early that year. It fell the day after Gordon's sixty-ninth birthday, which Judith insisted I come over to celebrate. Judith said she would be cooking for two days, today for his birthday and tomorrow for Passover.

The door was opened by a young woman who looked me up and down with open curiosity. I expected indifference or hostility, but there was something in her glance that spoke of complicity. "You're David Greene? I'm Natasha Stone."

She had red-blond hair and Gordon's eyes in a sharp pointy face. All elbows and knees and attitude, she was grinning like a hungry fox. "Come right in. Judith's finishing up the asparagus soup."

The dining room table was not set. "Do you need some help?"

"We're not eating here." She lowered her voice. "Daddy's having a bad day, so Judith set things up in his bedroom." She read my expression. "Just act like everything's normal."

Judith kissed me briefly on the mouth as I came into the kitchen. Then she handed me a tureen of hot soup.

Gordon was sitting up in his queen-sized bed with bookshelves built into the headboards, wearing a plaid nightshirt and looking gaunt. He was even thinner than the last time I had seen him, and there was a bluish cast to his face. His nose seemed to have lengthened. Across his lap, a wooden tray table squatted. Judith had set up card tables on either side of the bed so that Natasha could eat at one and Judith and I could share the other. With the meal, we drank champagne.

If I stepped back from the scene, it was bizarre, Gordon in bed and us at card tables eating roast lamb with garlic potatoes, baby string beans, and for dessert, a strawberry pie; Gordon, his wife, his wife's lover and his youngest daughter. Gordon rallied and was bawdy and cheerful, holding forth about everything from why asparagus made urine smell weird, to the history of Passover and the birthday customs of different cultures. Natasha was obviously crazy about her father and close to Judith. She kept taking me in with sideways glances, no flirtation but a powerful curiosity. After we cleared the remains of the meal, Natasha said, "I always take a birthday picture of my dad, just like he always takes one of me. He started it when I was a baby. This time, you both get in it." So Judith, in her black velvet dress, and I climbed on the bed. Natasha took several shots before she let us get up: Gordon with his arms around both of us, Judith and I lifting our glasses to her behind the lens. I couldn't remember a livelier dinner party or a better meal, and strangely, it felt natural. I was half sorry to miss Passover with them.

The next night, I was off to Marty and Holly's. No one in the family would ever say it, but the truth is, Holly married above herself. Ever since she had first brought Marty home, I sensed she was a little ashamed of us. Marty's father and mother both taught at Harvard Medical School. Their brick colonial on Commonwealth Avenue outside Boston was the kind of home that made my mother sigh. In my parents' presence, the Doctors Sterling wore the kind of patient smiles you see on politicians touring a public school. At the wedding they stayed long enough for pictures and left before the cake. Since my father's death, they no longer invited my mother for Thanksgiving dinner, and Marty himself ignored her unless she came to babysit.

My mom was referred to as "a big girl" by those who liked her, a full-figured woman. With long legs and large feet, she was taller than my father by three inches, although soft to his rigid, tight-bodied intensity. She spoke in a rich alto (in fact she conducted the local choir), and this almost manly voice, coupled with her size and a strange birthmark on her forehead, the color and shape of a spilled cup of coffee, had set her apart from others all her life. She was impatient with herself, obviously anticipating criticism before she received it, and an embarrassing flirt. She tended to treat me and Holly (and my father when he was alive) like a painting she could never quite get right. Holly was hardworking and cautious to a fault, but my mom usually found one. Marty wrote a column once, comparing my mother to a Mobil Travel Guide Inspector and his house to a hotel that couldn't get more than two diamonds. It was very funny and widely reprinted, and Holly and I hated it. Our mom wasn't easy but we resented her being exposed as a national mother-in-law joke.

At the seder, Holly's food was superb, Marty's ceremony short, and

my mother on her best behavior. She cherished her one formal invitation every year (all other holidays were spent at Marty's parents), her
beautiful granddaughters, her famous son-in-law. She wore her best
blue suit. She complimented Marty's singing voice and insisted on doing the dishes with Holly so the girls could watch TV.

Marty sat glumly all through dinner staring at me. As soon as the
dishes were cleared, he asked me back to his study. He did not pull out
the videotapes of himself on the Letterman show or the photographs of
his junket to Japan, but a bottle of cognac from the cabinet behind his
desk and two glasses. Marty had a strong squarish face made vulnerable
by delicate wire-framed glasses, and a tendency for his cheeks to turn a
deep and glowing pink, a litmus test of his emotions. Strangely, he was
just my size. Neck, sleeve length, chest size, shoe. Once a year he'd
drop a box of his old clothes at my feet and act insulted if I didn't plow
through it with effusive thanks. "Tell me something." Marty poured
himself cognac. I didn't care to drink with him. "The truth, what is this
election shit? You're goofing on everybody, right? You're not serious?"

"I'm thinking about running."

"Hell, maybe I'll get a column out of it. Why not? My brother-in-law,
the small-time pol. The ticket fixer. You can feed me the crazy stuff."

"I don't think so, Marty. It wouldn't be fair."

"To who? The motel owners? The restaurants? Are you kidding? My
column has a circulation of four million. They'll be booked all summer."

"Don't you think Saltash has enough problems without turning the
town into Mayberry?"

"You are serious." He studied me over the rim of his glass. "All right,
so tell me the burning issues." He put his feet up on the desk. "Win my
vote."

"Fuck you."

"Don't be so sensitive. We're family, we can't tease each other? Because we're going to be dragged into it, you know. Holly. The children."

"I don't think so."

"People say you're doing it because you like to get laid."

"That's what *people* say? Or you?"

"Me?" Marty said. "I could care less."

"You don't care that Judith and I are friends?"

"Ooh, I like that. Friends." He pitched forward and refilled his glass.
"By that definition of friendship everybody'd be humping each other all
over this great nation of ours. This is my friend. She sucks my cock.
Next time my kid says she made a friend in school, I'm going to get her
birth control."

"You are one nasty son of a bitch."

"Me? Then what do you call a person who screws a sick man's wife?"

"I've had enough." I stood.

"You're not the only one, you know. Judith has a thing for younger guys."

"What's your problem, Marty? You wanted to be one of them?"

I watched his cheeks light up. "One of them was a buddy of mine."

"I find that hard to believe."

"That her husband's an old man and she likes young meat now and then?"

"That you could have a buddy."

Marty stood, knocking his glass to the floor. Holly heard the crash and came to the office door. "You guys all right? Marty? David, where are you going?"

I told my sister I'd had a lovely evening and would see her in the morning. Marty was close behind me. "You don't believe me, David?" he called from the door. "Ask her! Ask her about Brian. Her *friend* Brian!"

Judith was usually awake before sunrise, but because it was Sunday morning, I waited a few hours to call. I sensed what Marty had told me was an exaggeration. The trouble was that it explained things too well. Why a young woman would have an affair in the face of her husband's illness. Why she might choose someone like me. I had to see Judith right away.

At nine-thirty her line was busy. I called again fifteen minutes later, and once or twice after that. I drove out to the highway to buy the Sunday paper. I tried again from a pay phone, and still unable to get through, made a decision I would regret.

The mainland was clear, but a blue band of fog clung to the treetops over the island. In the distance, soft shell clammers were bent in right angles at the waist, clawing a living from the mud as their wide-bottomed boats drifted on long anchored leads. Although there was a bitter chill on this April morning and the roads were slippery with patches of ice, you could see green shoots growing up under the dead brown stalks; you could smell spring in the funky decay of sea life, salt air and mud.

I pulled up in their drive and hit my horn. Through my own reflection in the glass door I saw Gordon tying the strings of his robe. He waved. He started slowly toward me as Judith appeared behind him. She too was wearing a robe, which she held closed with a fist over her heart. She bolted past him and whipped open the door.

"What are you doing here?" she demanded. I smelled toothpaste and soap and the same perfume she daubed between her thighs in my bed-room. "Don't you call first? Do you just barge in on people?"

"I did call. I've been calling for hours."

Gordon laughed, slowly making his way to the telephone on the kitchen wall, where he replaced the receiver on its hook. He ran water at the sink and filled a kettle. He suggested we have coffee. Judith told me to wait outside and ran upstairs to dress.

I followed her down the path to the garden, through the hollow where pine needles crackled beneath our boots, to the little cottage where we met to make love. But this time she didn't beckon me with a silent smile. This time the garden didn't look like magic, but a trap full of nets and sharp edges. She turned on me as soon as she slammed the door. "Do not ever come over here without calling again."

"Sorry I interrupted whatever it was."

"You know what it was," she said icily.

"So you do sleep with him?"

"He is my husband."

"Fine. But why didn't you *tell* me?"

It was not often that Judith would fumble for words. "Because it's . . . not a regular thing."

"I assumed he was too sick, Judith. I assumed that you didn't have that kind of relationship, that I wasn't in the middle of something."

"Most of the time he is too sick. Sometimes he feels all right. I don't always know." By now she seemed more confused than angry. "It's all new, David. Gordon hadn't been . . . able for a long time."

"How new?"

"I don't know."

"Sure you do. Since you started sleeping with me?" The way Gordon sometimes looked at us. Nothing suggestive. He didn't make innuen-does. He never leered. But I sensed that my presence, a younger man with his wife, excited him. "Does it happen after I visit you here?"

She wouldn't answer. She didn't have to.

"Hell, I'm glad he *can* make love to you."

"I doubt that."

"I am," I said. "I'm glad he's well enough."

"He's not well. Sometimes his body can remember me through the pain. Sometimes he wants to be near me. Since I met you, yes, a door has opened. Gordon senses that I'm happy. He's my friend and my family and my teacher. We talk. And we remember what it used to be like. And we try to plan how things are going to be. And this morn-ing . . . yes." There was no fire in the woodstove. We had not turned on a lamp. A shaft of gray light poured through the skylight like a pillar between us.

"Judith, who is Brian?"

"Brian?" She looked confused. There was nothing in her expression to suggest he meant anything. She had trouble recalling his name. "He did a book with Gordon. A photographer. What's going on here?"

"I'm trying to understand what you want with me, Judith."

"I assume," she moved toward me tentatively through the cold shaft of light, "the same as you want with me."

"But Gordon—"

"Wants us all to be happy."

"You're serious."

"Yes. Yes, why not?" There was pleading in her voice. "Gordon and I have a life together. You and I have a life together. No one has to be deceived or disappointed. What is the problem?"

"Where is this supposed to go? How long can it go on?"

"What's to stop us?"

"Only the opinion of everyone around us," I said.

"Are you under the illusion that they, whoever they are, have perfect little marriages? Above criticism? No dirty secrets?"

"Not at all."

"And do you judge them for the way they look for love?"

"I couldn't care less."

"Then what is the problem? We live our own lives. We do what we want. Everybody's honest. Nobody gets hurt. What is the problem?"

Only my own sense of right and wrong.

JUDITH

14 Two weeks after their ninth wedding anniversary, Judith insisted Gordon go to a doctor in Boston. She was not satisfied with the chronic bronchitis diagnosis, and nothing seemed to be helping. She felt guilty because she should have managed to get him to a good doctor months before. She had nagged him, she had set up an appointment. The first appointment she made, he found an excuse to cancel. He was too busy for that nonsense. He had a cough, big deal. At his age, everybody had something. He had missed his deadline on the new book, he had three speaking engagements. He didn't need an unnecessary trek into Boston, just because she was a worrywart and a control freak and overfond of doctors. But she would not let him cancel the second appointment, when she was able to get another. She want in with him, she marched him into the office, she tried to put a good face on his grumpiness.

The doctor poked and prodded him, particularly in his neck and lymph nodes and over his chest and listened to his breathing. Then he pronounced that Gordon must go to another doctor, an oncologist. He was careful how he phrased his opinion. "To eliminate several possibilities, you need to have some tests. Then if you don't have *that problem*, which is at the moment only a possibility, we need to run more diagnostic tests back here."

Oncologist. The doctor they decided on after consulting friends and acquaintances was associated with the Dana Farber Cancer Institute. There, the word was out in the open at last. The man they saw was the surgeon of a particular team, as he put it. Dr. Edward Barrows was a year or two younger than Judith, a handsome West Indian who spoke with a lilt. He called Gordon by his first name, which made Gordon bristle. His assistant took a complete medical history, so complete that Gordon asked, "Are you sure you don't need to know the last time I cut my toenails?" They took a sample of Gordon's sputum and scheduled an X ray and a CAT scan of the chest.

They both understood the doctor was testing for cancer, but they did not talk about it. She did not want to believe Gordon had cancer; she knew Gordon rejected the idea. They both clung to the hope that Dr. Barrows would clear that possibility.

The X-ray diagnosis appeared to be inconclusive. Gordon celebrated with a bottle of champagne. She was not sure but drank it with him. It turned out Dr. Barrows wanted a tissue sample. "You mean you're going to take out a piece of me," Gordon thundered. He was reluctant, but what choice had he? The tests went on, more and more invasive. Needle aspiration. A tube inserted through an incision in the neck to test a lymph node. The tests went on for over a month, back and forth to Boston or to Hyannis, where the doctor had a satellite office.

Finally Dr. Barrows was ready to give a diagnosis. There was a tumor. Given its size and location, a combination of chemotherapy and radiation therapy was indicated to reduce it. Then they would operate, perhaps in six months if the other therapies were successful. Now they knew. The moment the doctor had told them, she realized she had suspected as much secretly, for a year. Never had she mentioned the word "cancer," but she had always been thinking it, in a locked compartment at the back of her mind which usually contained only a certainty that some yutz she was defending was actually guilty of whatever he had been accused of. Hiding that opinion from herself let her function as she must. Hiding her fear for Gordon had let her get through the months when she could not force him to a doctor. But now they both must live with the fact of cancer. Gordon took it well. "It's like going into a dogfight," he said as she drove them home. "You know you may die, but you plan not to. You figure you have your will to live and your reflexes and your knowledge of the enemy and your own plane. There's terror in facing down death, but there's also a crazy high like nothing else I've known since."

As they returned to the office where Dr. Barrows must have given similar bad news to patients every day, the next stage of the process began. "We must agree on a plan of treatment," said the doctor, and somehow his "we" grated on her all the more because he was young, because he was handsome, because he was radiantly healthy. The oncologist who dealt with radiation therapy, Dr. O'Reilly, was much older, red in the face as if he drank or had high blood pressure or had spent too much time in the sun. Judith and Gordon both liked him at once, perhaps because he seemed vulnerable. He explained how precise the machine was that burned away at the tumor, but could not penetrate it all the way.

The doctor in charge of the chemotherapy was a woman about Judith's age, slightly overweight, her hair straggling out of its do, the air of a worried mother. Dr. Sara Ripkin turned out to be the star, when they eventually came to her office. Besides her diplomas, she had a string of plaques for prizes. She worked with several of the oncologists.

"Chemotherapy is a little like cooking," she said to them, resting her elbows on her desk and her chin in her cupped hands as if her head was heavy. "You try a mix and then you see how it tastes—to the tumor, to the cancer cells. There are a great number of possible chemicals and a great many possible combinations and dosages. If at first we don't succeed, we try a different mix. We keep checking, week to week. It may seem tedious but that's the formula for success."

The first question was how much to tell the children.

"Ben's what? Forty? If he can't deal with it now, when will he be able to?" Gordon scowled.

"Forty-five," she corrected automatically. As a good wife should, she had their birthdays memorized. She bought gifts and cards and sent them to his sons and daughters, his grandchildren. Their spouses. A reminder program on her computer told her when it was time to order a gift. Mostly she mail-ordered, except for Natasha, for whom she shopped personally.

"If we tell any of them, we must tell them all," she said.

"Whatever." He looked exhausted. "Can't we just play it down? I have a touch of cancer." He reached automatically for a cigarette.

Her hand was faster. She grabbed the pack and threw it in the fireplace. "No more. The price has been too high already!"

"Isn't it a little late to worry? I might as well enjoy myself."

"It's never too late to worry. You don't want the cancer to metastasize. What I've read suggests that smoking increases the risk. No more, Gordon. You've bullied me into putting up with it for the nine years we've been married, but guess what? My tolerance ran out yesterday. No more, not one." She went to stand in front of him. "I love you, Gordon. You're precious to me. I refuse, I refuse to give you up. We're going to fight this. People have remissions. Some people are cured. And don't think you can smoke out in your shack and I won't know it. I can always smell it. Your puffing days are past."

That night she called Natasha at school. There had been a price tag on her marriage all along: Gordon had said no more children. He had demanded that pledge from her, and she had given it. But she had a daughter. She had raised Natasha from late childhood, and Natasha was far closer to her than to her biological mother, Fern. Hannah and she had often talked about the advantages and problems of being involved with men so much older than either of them. But this cost was new and far higher.

Natasha was in her senior year at Brown, planning to go on to veterinary school. When Judith told her, Natasha was silent for a full minute.

"Sometimes I hate him!" she burst out. "I've been trying to get him to stop smoking since I was seven. I've heard you trying, again and again over the years. He's so arrogant! He thought it couldn't happen to him!"

"But Natasha, getting angry at him won't help him—or you."

"But I don't want to lose my father!"

"I don't want to lose my husband. He's not dying, Natasha, he hasn't even started treatment. We have to express hope, and to do that we have to feel it. They say that attitude has a lot to do with who survives and for how long. We have to be a cheering section. And for that we have to let go of anger and despair—do you understand?"

Squamous cell carcinoma had spread from the lung to the hilar nodes. Even the name was ugly. She had never heard of a squamous cell. Being married to an invalid was a different marriage. Sometimes Judith felt pushed to the wall. Her work was unremitting, full-time law that was now, besides Gordon's pension and occasional royalties, their sole source of income; now full-time nursing as well. She wished she were a more patient woman. She wished she were a better person. She loved Gordon passionately, but now the major way to express that was through taking care of him. The chemotherapy and the radiation therapy sapped his energy and left him debilitated. He was often nauseous. She cleaned him up and cleaned up after him. Nursing did not come naturally to her. Gordon was cranky. He hated being ill. He was heroic in his own way, stoic, committed to the treatment. He had finally stopped sneaking cigarettes. What drove him crazy was not being able to work. He was simply too weak, too tired. His disease was his new career, he said wryly, but he meant it. He had to be taken to Boston twice every week and once to Hyannis. She could not meet those obligations and continue to practice law, so they found a young man to drive him back and forth on Mondays and a young woman who would do the Hyannis trip every Thursday.

Gordon actually liked having two drivers. He was used to enjoying an intense social life. His illness, at least during chemotherapy, curtailed that. He got involved in the lives and problems of Tim, the son of a fisherman serving time for bringing in marijuana, and Camilla, who had moved into her parents' summer house when she lost her job. He knew all about their loves, their family squabbles, their financial burdens, their fantasies and unlikely plans. Judith listened to his reports with as much interest as she could muster, because she was touched by his involvement and she understood what this was in lieu of: his intellectual, professional, political and social life.

Some of the drugs worked and some didn't. It seemed highly experimental. They were throwing drugs into his system to see what happened. He got very sick from some of them. The doctors monitored his white blood cells, the tumor, his blood chemistry. He was losing weight but his face was somewhat swollen, along with his neck. When he was wrapped up in a tweed jacket or sweaters, for he was often chilled, he could even look as if he had gained weight. But she saw his wasting body. She massaged him. Some days she had to dress and undress him. About two weeks after the radiation therapy stopped, his throat was so painful he could swallow nothing, not even water. His hair came out in handfuls. Soon he was bald, Gordon who had always had a full lush halo.

The doctors threw drugs into him and she threw random food in front of him. Finding food he could endure eating was a constant experiment of another sort. His sense of taste was off. Foods he had always loved tasted burnt or spoiled. Some smells disgusted him. She had to stop wearing perfume. Even her hand lotion irritated him. He was always thinking the milk had turned. He developed a taste for something called junket, an old-fashioned pudding made of rennet and flavored with raspberry. She could only find one mail-order source for the stuff. He also liked vanilla tapioca pudding and chicken soup. Childhood foods, perhaps. She would do anything to make him less miserable. Discomfort, the doctors called it, you'll be experiencing some discomfort. They never said pain. Agony. Terror. He was on the chemotherapy for a week and then off for three weeks. Then just as his weakness was lessening, another cycle began.

She slept badly. Insomnia had never been a problem of hers. In law school she had been constantly exhausted, but that was because she only had three hours to waste in bed every night. Now she lay down beside him but rarely slept. She was secretly relieved when he suggested they have separate bedrooms. He found it painful when she bumped against him or curled into his side during the night. Still, it seemed an ominous change, to move out of the bedroom they had shared. It was a long winter and a slow spring. Fern arrived for a week and tried to teach Gordon visualization. At first he was forbearing and went along with her exercises. It made sense to Judith that the mind should be able to infiltrate the immune systems, but it was too New Age for Gordon. Why had he ever married Fern? Fern was not a difficult guest. She was used to living in group situations, and did not spread out through the house and always cleaned up after herself. Actually, Judith rather liked being able to share some of the nursing chores. She could imagine, briefly, the advantages of polygamy. But Fern and Gordon always ended up arguing, as she was sure they had when they were married to each other. That is, Gordon argued and Fern sighed and looked pained and quoted her experts.

"My good body has betrayed me," he told Judith. "Always I've been vigorous, able to stay up all night and dance and fuck and drink, and still work the next day. It's like a great battle horse that suddenly stumbles, and you wonder if you'll have to shoot it. My body is all I think about now. It's a new kind of narcissism."

"It's not narcissism, Gordon. You're trying to recover from a dangerous illness. It takes all your time and all your energy."

Gordon was sitting in his favorite chair in the living room with Portnoy on his lap, the big gray cat who had become his constant companion. Seven years before, Natasha had found him beside Route 6, a discarded, starving kitten with a broken leg. Now Portnoy had decided to take care of Gordon, according to his lights, washing his hands, cuddling against him, keeping the other cats and dogs away. "It is narcissism, Judith. I'm obsessed with how I feel day and night. I keep a journal about my symptoms and my responses. I go through litanies of my aches and pains. I am obsessed with the chemicals, the poisons they put into me. The idea of taking platinum as a drug is fascinating. My body is becoming this expensive and useless artifact."

"With the end in sight of getting better, of being well again."

"The stupidest thing is, I felt much better before they started on me. I keep thinking—and don't yell at me, I'm not acting on it—that all that was wrong with me was a cough and a little fever and a pain in my shoulder. Now my whole body is screwed up. I can't eat, I can't drink, I can't fuck, I can't climb a flight of steps unassisted. I'm wondering if the cure isn't worse than the disease."

"Gordon, lung cancer kills."

"But Judith, it may do that anyhow. And is this living?"

Finally Dr. Ripkin pronounced the tumor shrunk enough for Dr. Barrows to operate, to remove the tumor, affected lymph nodes and, of course, a good portion of Gordon's left lung. Many new tests irritated Gordon. But he was pleased to hear he had a good heart. They always tested for cardiovascular problems before surgery. It seemed as if there was scarcely an inch of his body they did not test in some way, not a system they left alone. Judith had enough warning so that she put everything on hold, found another lawyer to cover for her and went into Boston with him. The surgery would take place at Dana Farber, where they had done the biopsies on his lungs and lymph nodes. They had friends she could have stayed with, but she preferred a hotel. She did not want to have to chat with anyone. It was easier to be alone. She spoke to Natasha twice a day, to Hannah every night and usually also to her best friend on the Cape, her frequent antagonist in court, the assistant district attorney, Barbara Ashbaum. That was as much contact and conversation as she could endure. Most of the other children called the hospital or the doctor. Ben, the oldest, called her the night of the surgery.

Gordon hated the hospital. He was depressed by patients lined up in corridors waiting for X rays, waiting for scans, waiting for doctors. He found the standard ways that nurses and orderlies addressed him demeaning. He was used to admiration, deference, used to people knowing who he was. Here he was just bald Gordon the patient to whom things were administered and done. "They speak to me as if I had lost my mind with my tumor and had the mental level of a five-year-old. It drives me up the wall. Do you know what you mainly do in the hospital? You wait. You're called a patient because you're required to be endlessly, endlessly patient."

She could not stay in Boston the next two weeks, but commuted when she was able. She could not drop her practice, or they would not survive economically. The nights she spent in the house alone were dreadful. When she was in Boston, Stumpy cared for the cats and dogs and the birds and random other animals Natasha brought home. The six cats and two dogs were some kind of comfort. They were worried. They came to her to give and take reassurance. She could not say that she slept alone, for there were up to five other mammals in her bed on any given night.

She was tremendously glad to bring Gordon back to the Cape. He was not to remain in bed, but to get up every day and walk as far as he could endure. He was to eat as much as he could, to regain lost weight. Gradually he began to regain his strength. They walked, slowly, but they walked together along the sand roads, over the hills, along the beaches on both sides of the island. They walked and sometimes they talked. He was short of breath and had to rest frequently, but he was no longer an invalid. His hair was growing back, all white and finer than it had been, like down. He had an appetite. Sometimes they were even able to make love. They tried new ways of pleasing each other, gentler ways of putting their bodies together.

She studied nutrition. Hidden in her office, she had six different tomes on cancer and cancer therapies. Now Gordon was freed from the doctors for a while. He saw Dr. Barrows once a month. Perhaps he was cured; perhaps their life would really resume. His strength seemed to be seeping back. He was at work on his long overdue manuscript. The family came in bunches, and Gordon began to hold forth, as he always had, the hub of everything. She began cautiously, secretly, to hope. To hope that she would retain this man who was the center of her life, the only man she had ever really loved.

JOHNNY

Johnny Lynch had put back a few drinks after dinner and fallen asleep on the couch when the phone woke him. Twenty past midnight, said the ship's clock in his den. Chief of police Smalley filled him in at once. "It's a tragedy," Johnny said. "Did the boy damage the dike?"

"Only himself."

"Did the parents take it hard?"

Abel said he was about to call them. He was sitting at the accident site, talking to Johnny on his car phone. His men were securing the area, and the rescue squad was taking the kid to the hospital twenty miles away.

"And you think he'll lose the arm?"

"What's left of it," Abel said.

"Jesus, Mary and Joseph." He stood, clutching the phone, and dizziness hit him. He ended the conversation sitting on the floor. "The parents will want to be off to the hospital immediately. I'll call the mother in the morning."

He struggled to his feet and climbed the stairs to his bedroom. Once he'd been able to handle a scotch before supper, a bottle of wine with his meal and a few brandies as he sat down afterwards with the newspaper. But he wasn't drinking alone back then and that made all the difference. There were selectmen's meetings and poker games, cocktails with clients and dinners with the family. He'd lost half the old crowd to illness, and the other half to politics.

The following morning he drove the length of High Street, as he did every day, slowly (he didn't care who was behind him) and took in the inn with its huge porch and columns, the churches, so white and pure in the rosy light of the rising sun, redbrick Town Hall, perfectly restored after that little fire, and the street itself, washed clean every day at dawn—he'd made sure of that, wrote it into the job description of the Department of Roads, Bridges and Waterways twenty years ago after a visit to Paris. Johnny parked in the Town Hall lot, bought his three newspapers, walked to his table in the Binnacle. Conversation dropped to a murmur. Even the rattle of plates in the kitchen stopped, the dishwasher and the cook peering through the pantry window. They all wanted to know what to make of the explosion. Was it a serious crime? A seventeen-year-old boy, no stranger to the police, attempting to make some kind of statement by blowing up public property? Or just mischief? Or was this the beginning of war, neighbor versus neighbor?

Nobody approached his table. These were tough, hardworking people; not shy about demanding their due, but respectful. They were churchgoers, some of them, but they were not moralists. There was a tradition of live and let live in Saltash. This was no small midwestern town with a distrust of what was too different, but a village whose economy had depended on the sea; that had sent its men all over the world and felt damned lucky if they made it home, no matter what their quirks and changes. What these people had always sought from him was a vision of how to proceed politically; how to survive in a state whose legislature saw their home as a playland in July and August and a hinterland from September to June. They looked to Johnny for the way around and through state laws never written for their benefit.

The waitress approached his table with a pot of coffee. "How are you today, Johnny? Two eggs, toast and griddle cakes?" He was Johnny to everyone, young and old, rich and poor, except at the office. He didn't believe in humbling people before him any more than in driving fancy cars. People resented you for it. The greatest man he'd ever known drove a Buick and had people call him Jack, until he was elected president.

"Just coffee, dear. Just coffee this morning." He made his point, saw people beyond this girl's fine broad hips stop their chewing, rethink things in light of the accident.

"You feeling all right, Johnny? There's a stomach flu going around."

"To tell the truth, it's the Compton boy, dear. I can't get him off my mind. Has he truly lost that arm? We'll have to find something for him, won't we? And we will." He lifted his eyes, addressing the other tables. "Once we make sure he gets the best damned care available."

Gary Zora twisted around from the table behind. "What in the hell did the kid think he was doing, Johnny? Dike's been through two hurricanes. And did he think he wouldn't get caught?"

Johnny shook his head sadly. "I don't think the boy himself knows. Only thing I thought about at seventeen was baseball and pretty girls." He winked at Doris Fisher at the table next to Gary's. She blushed and touched her fingertips to her tight gray curls.

"I don't know where they get their ideas," Gary said.

"What I want to know is, where did he get the explosives?"

"It was easy enough." Gary was in the fire department and had either responded to last night's call or listened on the radio. The juicy gossip attached to any rescue operation was one of the perks of a dangerous nonpaying job. "He just stuffed a copper pipe full with black powder from his father's shotgun shells and laced it all through with a candle wick."

"I don't believe it, Gary. Saltash kids don't do that kind of thing," Johnny said.

Gary lowered his voice. "You know his father. The apple don't fall very far."

Johnny said, loud enough to make himself heard, "No parent would put his child up to this. No parent would ever want to see his boy lose his arm. Not over a petty municipal disagreement. Am I right?" he asked Birdie Hogan, watching from a corner table.

"Not here, Johnny. Not since I been." Birdie wore coveralls, summer and winter, stained with motor oil, and was always coated with sawdust shavings. Going on seventy-five, he still worked his gas station and, out back, a firewood business. "Not in this town."

Johnny could feel a consensus building, a general return to normality in the clatter of plates, the rise of cigarette smoke and conversation. He had flushed the issue like a pheasant into the open. People weren't inherently mean-spirited or stupid, but the world was complicated. He left feeling better than he had in hours, knowing that he had set things right, let everyone know where he stood.

Although Abel Smalley assured him the kid had done more damage to himself than to the dike, Johnny asked Petersen, a retired engineer and chairman of the Board of Selectmen, to go down and take a look. He'd go by himself after dark when there wouldn't be too many people around, or he could hear it now: Johnny Lynch was out there checking on his dike; Lynch's dike, some called it.

He used to know all the kids in town when his own were in school, and even after, when he used to read his favorites out loud, *A Child's Christmas in Wales*, *The Legend of Sleepy Hollow*. This Compton boy was a blank. The girls in his office said there was something funny about the kid, always on his bicycle, always by himself, riding up and down High Street as if he never had a friend or a home. The girls said the kid's father was at fault. Palmer Compton was as loud as he was nasty, thought the best way from point A to point B was to run everyone down in between. He had one issue, never gave a lick about anything else in town, and he beat it like a deaf mule, so long and hard that even people prone to agree got mad sometimes and voted the opposite way.

Palmer Compton had always been against the dike. He thought the whole town was out to keep him from making a living, when everyone knew the old days of shellfishing were over. Sure there would always be a living for those who were scientific about it and had their own shellfish grant. But scratching clams from the wild? Trying to feed his family with a pail and rake? That was good for the tourists and picturesque, but the money lay in developing the land, in building. If the dike was gone tomorrow and the whole valley flooded over, there still wouldn't be enough shellfish to support more than a few families. Johnny had done everything he could to bring this town into the future, to open it up to real prosperity, to get it in the Sunday travel sections and the guidebooks. But here was this fool Palmer Compton railing about a dike drying up the shellfish, when the dike kept flood tides out of land that could profit the entire town.

Next, Johnny called Sams, the medical examiner, and asked him to find out about the kid. If God forbid the boy died, there'd be a martyr; as if a one-armed half-wit bicycling back and forth on High Street wasn't symbol enough. He'd have to come up with a job for the kid—quietly. Roads and Bridges was out, obviously. Then an idea struck him: with one arm, the kid might qualify for handicapped. There was a lot of money floating around for the handicapped; state and federal. Johnny was sure he could find a job, maybe for the county: get the kid out of Saltash.

The new secretary rapped on his office door. He liked to keep it open if he wasn't seeing a client, to make everybody feel like family. He'd been watching Crystal and he liked what he saw. The old girls cooed over her, and lately he'd heard giggling in the office, the way it used to be.

"Mr. Lynch? Selectman Petersen's on the line." She was only thirty-odd, but she'd been around the block a few times. She had a fine body, thickening around the waist, although that had never bothered him about a woman. Her skills were rusty; he doubted she had done legal work for years. He didn't hire her for her skills, and certainly not because of her father; he hardly owed any favors to Doc Sinclair. He'd kept the dentist out of jail and got the case of the woman whose tongue he had cut up settled out of court.

Then he'd urged Doc Sinclair, with his shaky hands and his drug habit and his history of trouble, to move on. The man had blown it. Sure it was paradise out here, but you had to know your limits. He'd hired Crystal for the same reason he'd sometimes go fishing instead of the office on the first hot days of June; the same reason he'd once come back from a hunting trip with a pony for his daughter. It was a willful submission to temptation, a vague infrequent admission that there was more to his life than politics and the law. He hired her because it amused and titillated him to have her around. And of course because Maria wanted her. At least she did know something about computers.

He made a point to act businesslike in her presence. He couldn't afford to embarrass himself. But the simple truth was that it had been years since he'd found himself smiling for no reason. "Put him on, please, Miss Sinclair . . . Ralph? What's it look like over there? Give it to me straight."

"Nothing to give," Ralph Petersen said.

Prying information out of Petersen took persistence, but his silence worked both ways. The man was unshakable. Never made promises he couldn't keep or shot his mouth off to the newspapers; never lashed out no matter who attacked him at a meeting. He was bald as an egg, with a straight white mustache that looked glued on. Petersen liked to make you feel as if you could answer your own question if you just thought hard enough. His only gesture was to touch the ends of his mustache, as if to make sure they were still there.

"So the explosion didn't harm anything?"

"Everything looks the way it did yesterday and the day before. There's evidence of a small fire—"

"Where?"

"On the rocks just above the dike's floodgate. There's a little carbon residue, that's all."

"The state will find something," Johnny said. The state had been trying to open the dike for years, along with Audubon and the bird-watchers, the bullies like Palmer Compton and the tree-hugging retirees. They'd commissioned scientists and studies trying to prove the dike was detrimental to the town. Any idiot could tell them that once it was removed, the water would rush right up the valley, flood the golf course and the homes and the best land in this town, destroy the natural habitat of fox and deer and coyote.

Johnny had been fighting them for years. Every time he knocked one enemy out, a new one stood up to take his place.. He needed another year, maybe two, to sell off the remaining lots and see his profits. Until then he was counting on the Board of Selectmen to keep the dike in place. If it came down to a final threat to take the case to court, the board could agree to a compromise, a small opening of the floodgate, a little each year to test the impact of change on the

ecosystem. Both sides could use ecology to their advantage. He'd
worked all that out with Petersen. As long as Johnny managed to
keep the majority of the board loyal to him, he'd be all right. This was
still his town. Nobody was going to take it away without a fight, and
there wasn't anybody out there big enough or smart enough to fight him
and win.

DAVID

16 Saltash wasn't a hard town, but the general consensus was that the Compton kid had it coming. In grade school he used to run people off the sidewalks with his bicycle. When he took up skateboarding, he liked to charge in front of moving cars and dare the drivers to hit him. He was a dangerous combination of a need to be noticed and a complete lack of fear. He'd finally made the local headlines last summer, when he stood up in his flimsy rowboat and harpooned a disoriented dolphin just off the town beach. A hundred sun bathers and the stunned local fishing fleet watched helplessly as the suffering creature towed the kid halfway across the harbor before it bled to death.

The kindest thing I heard was attributed to Johnny Lynch. He was going to see that the boy got the best medical care, physical therapy, and job training. Saltash took care of its own, people said—meaning Johnny Lynch did. Look at Stumpy Squeer. Look at Crazy Jane Villa, who used to pull her dress up to her chin on the town green. Johnny Lynch saw they were never sent away, that they lived in their family houses with fuel for the winter and enough to eat.

Gordon called me the evening after the accident. It had been a little over a week since I'd walked in on him and his wife. I was avoiding the two of them, determined to disentangle myself. "Here's your issue like a Christmas goose," he said. There was genuine glee in his voice.

"The dike thing? Is that what you're talking about?"

My lack of enthusiasm diminished his. "You want to see it opened, don't you?"

I didn't play golf or own land on the river or dig shellfish; I wasn't in the building trades and had nothing to gain either way. "I suppose," I said, mostly in opposition to Johnny Lynch.

"Well, you're the only candidate who feels that way and has a chance to win."

"What about Joe Pound?" Bird Man.

"Joe Pound couldn't win if he gave every voter a five-dollar bill and a ride to the polls."

"Gordon, I'm not sure I'm the guy."

"Not sure? I don't understand."

"I changed my mind. I don't want to run."

"You want to see this town built up like a fucking suburb? You want to see the shellfish industry dry up? What else have we got, goddamn it? Tourists are fickle, they like a place for a few years then flock to another. Look at Atlantic City! Look at Rockaway Beach!" He was rattling off lakes and spa towns, ski resorts I'd never heard of. He was furious.

"I said I'd *think* about running. I never said I was definite."

"Did you tell the Committee for Civic Responsibility? They've been raising money for you, David. They've been making phone calls in your behalf."

"Two hundred votes can't win an election against Johnny Lynch."

"Not if you sit on your ass. You have really screwed us, you know that? We can't find another candidate now—it's too late to file. Don't you care how people live? What do you care about? Why did you start this process, anyway?"

Because I wanted to sleep with his wife.

"Look, David Greene, it's very simple. There are four people on the ballot and only two have a chance to win that open seat. One of them is in John Lynch's pocket and the other one isn't. At least I didn't think so."

The implication was that by pulling out, I was handing the race to Lynch. "I resent that, Gordon."

"Well, fuck your resentment." I had made love to this man's wife and he hadn't said a word. Now, his voice was shaking: "You can't mobilize people behind you, then change your mind overnight. I'm asking you to get yourself straight, goddamn it. People are counting on you."

Tommy's girlfriend Michelle lived with her daughter, Kelly Ann, in the old Endicott house. Once a small hotel, later a rooming house for fishermen, and most recently apartments for young townies with little money, it sat at the top of a hill on Dock Street and seemed to brood over the bustling village the way some of its tenants sat on the front steps mulling over their lost chances in life.

Michelle's apartment was on the third floor. The residents used each landing as suburban families used garages: for storage. There were cribs and barbecue grills, box springs and bicycles. The abiding odor of the stairwell was something like mildew and boiled cabbage. As I climbed, I smelled marijuana and cat litter boxes, diapers and incense. When I reached the third floor I began to sneeze uncontrollably. Before I knocked, the door to Michelle's apartment opened. I heard clashing radios, children running; I smelled perfume and chili. What I remember best was Crystal's face, moonlike in that dingy hall, luminescent and cool. Her platinum hair seemed to absorb the available light. Her head cocked, she was obviously expecting me, inspecting me. Even before she spoke, her slightly ironic smile suggested we both knew why I was here.

"Hello, David. Welcome to the fun house." Her voice was whiskey in a tumbler with ice; hard and scratchy with a tinkle of sarcasm, it brought to mind dark cocktail lounges and cigarette smoke. Crystal wore a black cardigan with rhinestone buttons and western boots. Before I stopped sneezing, a child appeared, a thin little boy with light brown bangs. He pressed his cheek to her hip as she smoothed the hair from his eyes. "Is he sick?" the boy asked.

"Nah, he'll be all right," she said. "I think he'll be just fine."

Tommy and Michelle were sitting at the kitchen table. From the way they were dressed, I knew they were not planning to stay. Michelle had large blue eyes, meticulously lined and shadowed, and a rabbit-like overbite. Her hair was her most striking feature, a butter-yellow architecture of elaborate dips and waves as delicate as puff pastry. I'd never spoken to Michelle but I had seen her around. I judged her to be my sister's age and thought I'd ask Holly if they had gone to school together.

The apartment was jammed. Where laundry wasn't drying lay toys, boxes, piles of towels. Michelle's daughter was stretched to her extended length across Tommy's lap, poking her mother's breast with a big toe. The table was set for dinner with mismatched plates and paper napkins. Crystal served. "She was living out West," Tommy said. "That's why she makes great chili. She's a cowgirl. She even named her kid Laramie."

"It's a stupid name," Kelly Ann said.

"She drove all the way across country," Tommy said. "Her and the kid. Did it in three days like an all-night trucker."

Crystal was broad in the bust, the shoulders and hips, but seemed to diminish in size like a servant in the kitchen. She filled the children's milk glasses, got another beer for Tommy, picked up Kelly Ann's napkin when it slipped to the floor. She ate silently with her eyes focused on her son, whose appetite she coaxed with soft whispers.

"It's like fucking courageous, you know?" Tommy said. "To come all the way back here three thousand miles where you don't know nobody anymore."

Michelle set her glass down heavily. "I'm nobody now?"

"I didn't mean it that way," he said. It was not like Tommy Shalhoub to back off, not from a woman, but as Kelly Ann kept poking her mother, as each addition to the conversation only seemed to stall it further, it was apparent how deeply in trouble Tommy had gotten himself with his girlfriend's roommate and how much he needed me to get him out.

"How long have you two known each other?" I asked Michelle.

She divided her chili into four equilateral triangles so her plate looked like the Confederate flag. "We were friends in school," she said grudgingly.

Crystal began to sing: "You need no introduction to who we really are . . ." Tommy led an imaginary orchestra with his fork. Kelly Ann perked up and sang the words. "This shining star, this precious jewel, our Saltash Elementary School."

"Are you here for good?" I asked Crystal.

"Till I get on my feet."

"She just got a job," Tommy said. "At Johnny Lynch's office."

"Oh, what do you do?" I asked.

"Legal secretary," Crystal said.

"Just like a lawyer," Tommy said. " 'Cept they do all the work."

Michelle took offense. "I don't happen to think it's the same thing at all. A nurse is not the same as a doctor."

Tommy's jaw twitched. His fist clenched, then opened. "I'm trying to introduce two people who don't know each other. Isn't that what we wanted to do here, Michelle?"

"Don't kick me," Michelle exploded at her daughter, pushing away Kelly Ann's foot.

"This is good chili," Tommy said. "There's no beans. You notice that? That's the way they do it out West. You ever hear of chili with no beans?"

Michelle's chair screeched as she pushed away from the table, high heels clopping all the way to the bathroom. Kelly Ann straggled behind. Michelle closed the door. The little girl pounded on it. Tommy sighed and got their coats. When the bathroom door opened, Kelly Ann grabbed her mother's leg and started to wail. "I'll be back." Michelle knelt to hush her. "When you wake up tomorrow morning, I'll be in my bed. You come in and we'll cuddle, okay? Okay?" But Kelly Ann clung to her mother until Crystal pried her away and carried her, screaming, into the children's bedroom.

"Does this happen every night?" I whispered to Tommy.

Michelle, whose blue eyeliner was now streaked with tears, cut me an icy glare. "Not before *she* moved in," Michelle said.

When they left, I wandered into the living room and found myself alone with the little boy. Like me, he didn't seem to know where to sit, to stand, how to make himself small enough to stay out of the way. He

was resting his chin on the back of an old couch, which I assumed from
the suitcase next to it and the alarm clock on the coffee table was
where his mother slept. Since I lived so far from my own son, I tried a
little too hard with my sister's daughters. I sensed that I embarrassed
them, that whatever activities they had on their busy agenda were only
interrupted by my awkward attempts to make them my surrogate kids.
He looked younger than Terry, and I felt for this little boy who held
himself, head down, arms at his side, like a peg to be pounded into a
narrow hole. When I said, "Hi," he almost jumped. "Have you started
school yet?"

"Yeah." He drew his hand across the back of the couch.

"Do you like it?"

He shrugged. "They're putting me back a grade. Tomorrow. They said
I have to repeat third."

"That might not be so bad," I said. "You'll be smarter than everybody
because you already know the stuff."

Hope flickered across his face for a moment then went out.

"You might be the biggest kid too."

"In fourth they made fun of me. They said I have a dumb name."

"I think Laramie is a kick-ass name. Like a movie star or a rock
singer. But if you don't like it, change it."

"You can't just change your name 'cause you want to. They won't let
you."

"Why not? When the new teacher introduces you tomorrow, you say,
'My name is Laramie but in my old school everybody called me Larry.'
You could do that."

He was thinking, hard. This was one serious little boy.

When I looked up, I noticed Crystal had inched her way inside the
door frame. She'd been watching me and the boy, listening. She was a
handsome woman. The confidence with which she moved, beneath the
weariness and the baggy shirt, the way her smile demanded my attention and wouldn't let go, suggested she knew her way around men. We
didn't exchange a word as she gathered Laramie in her arms to bring
him to bed, but the heat with which she looked upon him, that same
bright beam of strength and affection, included me in its widening arc.
It had been decided. I was to stay.

DAVID

"You think you remember me, don't you?" Crystal said. Her smile was half tease, half reproach. As she settled back on the couch after putting her son to bed, her blouse was open by an extra button. She pulled her fingers through her hair and shook her head—as if to toss much longer hair in place. Although it was cut short, I imagined it touching her shoulders and trailing down her back. There was a lot I found myself imagining about Crystal because nothing connected her to the past. The crucifix on the living room wall, the sewing machine, the rock star poster belonged to her roommate. Crystal's turquoise bracelets and her platinum hair, even her little boy's name, didn't seem to issue from the woman whose hand was brushing my knee, but struck me, like her western boots, as something of a pose.

I felt a remarkable ease in her presence, however, a shared sympathy. "I probably know you from high school?" I asked.

"Right," she mocked me. "Saltash's Davey Greene, the Pitching Machine. You didn't know I was alive."

"Were you friends with my sister?"

"I wasn't in the sweater set crowd."

"Tommy said your father was a dentist."

"You didn't go to him." There was a touch of resentment in her voice, but she was right. My mother took us to a guy named Horowitz. He was the only Jewish dentist on the entire Cape at the time, and that seemed reason enough to justify the forty-five-minute drive. "Try again. I like this game."

So did I. More than a game, or even a walk through the past, it was a reality check: a contrast between the way I saw my family and the way we were seen. I remember my parents struggling to pay the mortgage, to meet the payroll. They borrowed constantly. Every unplanned expense was a crisis. But what I knew to be just one more of my father's failed businesses, Crystal saw as the factory we owned. While I overheard my father begging Johnny Lynch to ask the bank manager not to foreclose, Crystal saw only the white full Cape with pink native roses, a half acre of locust trees and lush grass.

Her family had moved to Saltash when she was three, she said. Her father had been working too hard in the city and it was killing him. He was the kind of dentist who couldn't turn people away. Rich or poor, every patient got the best he could give. In Saltash, half the time he came home with a bag of flounder or an oil painting or a promise of a truckload of garden manure instead of his fee. When he did get paid, he never kept track. He wasn't interested in money. "All he cared about was helping people."

When her parents split in Crystal's junior year of high school, her mother moved to Arizona. They lived in a town an hour south of Sedona, a little like Saltash, she said, "Poor, scenic and two blocks long." She started dreaming of water. She hated the desert and only an ocean could quench her thirst. After two years of college she headed for the nearest one.

She ended up in Seattle, met an Irishman with a red beard, a fishing boat and a voice like a lullaby. They moved into a house on a bluff with a distant view of the Sound. He cut his drinking to a six-pack a night and she worked in a law office. Then she got pregnant and he turned mean. She lived with Liam for five years, but the first time he hit her she waited exactly thirteen hours, until the bank opened the following morning, then cut out for good.

Crystal left Seattle with two suitcases and a kid with a temperature of 102. I imagined her speeding to nowhere, as I had after being cut, every exit another disappointment, a place someone else could call home. She telephoned Michelle from a service plaza. First she had to remind her they had been best friends in high school—then explain she had nowhere to go.

Crystal's story filled me with a mixture of admiration and pity, although I didn't offer either and she didn't seem to care. "I guess I was wrong," I said finally. "I don't know you at all."

"But you do. We're the same."

I was a little lost here. "Because we both moved back to Saltash?"

"Because we're both failures."

I must have been embarrassed. I laughed.

"You're not doing what you *really* do, David Greene. Admit it. You're an athlete. Nothing you'll ever do in your life will make you as happy. It's inside you all the time."

"I don't know about that," I said. But I did. I knew that I never looked at a level field without measuring out a diamond, calculating the distance from home plate to the mound. I never held an apple without my fingers closing around it in preparation to throw. When I smelled fresh-mown grass I was aware of an emptiness, the absence of a crowd.

"I believe there are people who are born for something," she said. I noticed the way her breasts pushed against the white satin cups of her bra. "I'm not talking about destiny or religion. It's just that some people are born with abilities, that's all. And if they can't do what they're made to do—" She stopped abruptly. She closed her eyes, as if the conversation had already gone too far. "They're a mess."

"And you think I'm a mess?" I said.

"I know I am."

"You didn't tell me what you were born to do."

"I said *some* people. I'm not one of them."

"I don't believe that."

"Because you're nice. Laramie said you're the nicest man he's ever met."

"I want to know. What were you born to be?"

"Just a mom," she said. "Maybe just an overwrought, overweight mom with six kids and a big barn of a house."

"I doubt that. You work in a law office. Don't you ever think of being a lawyer yourself?"

"About a hundred times a day."

"I think you'd be a good one. You're obviously smart. You're experienced. You're compassionate."

"And thirty-two. And a single mom. Much too old to go back to school. Too busy and too tired." When I challenged her, she placed her fingertips over my mouth to silence me. "I'm doing fine, okay? I don't need any help."

We were sitting in a cold room facing her unpacked boxes in a corner. The only lamp cast a sickly yellow light. Through the floorboards we heard a couple fighting. I said, "Of course you don't," and we both started to laugh.

Looking back on the night I met Crystal, I realize I might have seen her differently. I might have perceived a burden. I might have made her a project or even a friend. If all I had wanted was to distance myself from Judith, I could have simply gotten laid. But on that winter night I was kindled with a more urgent fire, a mother and a child's need for me. I thought my efforts could change everything. I thought I could enter her life like a god. What I imagined as Crystal's weakness, however, proved to be my own.

Sometimes in autumn when the storm tides recede, the soft, placid beaches resemble a killing field. Some claim to know the reason whales strand themselves, wash up to suffocate in the sand, their lungs crushed by the weight of their own bodies, their skin cracking in the sun like the walls of old tires. What faulty inner magnet could draw them to their deaths? The old fishermen say under stress and sickness, they follow a leader with the ancient memory of land in her genes, land as safety, land as home. But what if they were trying to save the leader?

Or maybe, once committed to the wrong course, they were afraid of turning back? Many times I told myself the consequences of leaving Crystal were more dangerous than remaining in her bed. Many times it seemed to me that however damaging I knew our course together to be, that she was what I deserved. On that first cold night I had no idea. Only upon looking back did I realize that to wade into Crystal's shallow life was to drown.

Her back pressed to my chest, entwining her fingers in mine as my arms wound around her waist, she seemed to project her story on the wall. I assumed that not facing me was a way to avoid the pain, but of course I didn't even know Crystal's last name at this point, or that her version of history was only a shadow play.

"Look," I said, "maybe you don't want to talk about this now. But I do think you could become something. You have two years of college? You could go back. Take one course a semester. Your life doesn't end when things don't work out the first time. You just have to start another life."

Before she kissed me, she said, "You're also the nicest man I've ever met." She opened her lips like the mouth of an infant asking to be fed. She suckled my ears, my neck, my lips with ferocious hunger. I was mother, she was child, there is no more accurate way to describe it. She put out the light before she undressed. She had heavy breasts and a soft belly, and when she saw me admiring her in the remaining light, she was ashamed. She took my cock between her breasts, guided my hand to her thighs. She told me lightly, lightly touch the rings in her nipples with my tongue. She placed me inside easily, locked her legs around my hips and rocked. But I tell you I was less a man than a source of warmth, a mass of comfort and kindness. I have never felt as purely needed by any lover nor as willing to be consumed.

JUDITH

18

By her seventh year in Saltash, when Judith was thirty-nine, she was becoming better known as a lawyer, an aggressive defense lawyer who would do a good job for anyone in trouble, a lawyer who would sue any corporation or government entity for a client. She was becoming even better known as a shark of a divorce lawyer who would get for her predominantly women clients a better deal than other lawyers even tried for. People saw her as unscrupulous, hard, even immoral, because she fought to win.

But what could she do against the enemy stealing Gordon from her? The cancer had returned, in the other lung. The cancer had touched his liver. More chemotherapy. Another operation. Sometimes Gordon could work, but not as he had; mostly his profession was his disease. He would not go into a cancer support group. "What am I supposed to do with a bunch of people whose only connection with me is that parts of our bodies are sick or missing?"

Over their years together they had dined out frequently. Now she cooked every night she could, to tempt him to eat, to get good nutrition into him. At night in bed, besides briefs she read cookbooks. She had given up low-fat cooking. Gordon kept losing weight. She was congenitally thin herself. Natasha compared her to a shrew who had to eat every ten minutes or starve. Now she cooked whatever might tempt him to eat. If it was hollandaise sauce, so be it. When she spent the night across the bridge in the loft above her new law office on the harbor, she had arranged for Jana Baer (who lived on the island) to come in to cook him a meal.

Gordon had been her rock. Since the first year of their marriage, she had relied on him as she had relied on no one since the death of her mother. They would fight, they would yell at each other, they would violently disagree about people or the exact interpretation of political events or a movie they had seen, but on the big things they agreed, on values, on their love, on how they should live. Now she would sometimes look at him, his face gaunt and visibly showing his age, and she would feel fear serrated, cold, sawing at her. He was her joy: the center of her life was collapsing.

That spring, she suggested they try to cut back on the number of summer guests, that they simply reduce their entertaining to be less of a strain on him than the usual delirium. She had wanted to cancel the big Fourth of July party too, but Gordon insisted that while he was alive, it continue. He had begun to use that phrase, which angered her.

Tonight she called him on it. "Anyone could say that. A truck could run me off the road tomorrow. I could choke on a chicken bone. I could die of food poisoning from fast food. Some ex-client could shoot me in court. Or somebody who just hates lawyers."

"Judith, you want to avoid thinking about my death. Dr. Barrows says I have two years at the very best, probably less."

"It could go into remission. You're more stubborn than he understands. It's a lottery." She would probably throw herself into the law, continuing the process that had already begun. Because of Gordon's illness, she had become a better lawyer, fiercer, more inventive, because there and only there she could still win.

"And I've never been fool enough to play the lottery. The odds, Judith, you perfectly well understand odds. I'm not sentimental and I'm not delusional. The odds are I'll be dead soon, and we have to think about that together."

"I don't want to think about it! What good does it do?"

"What good does it do to pretend I'll live forever? We have to make plans. I can't stand the pretending. I need to know you're going to be all right."

"Gordon, there's no way I'll be all right without you. But I'll go on. I have my work. I'll just work harder."

"Do you intend to go on living out here?"

"How do I know?" She threw her hands up, furious at him for insisting on talking about something she preferred to think about alone in the middle of the night when no one could see her cry.

"Your practice is here. Your reputation is growing. You have as many cases as you can handle. If you moved back to Boston, you'd have to start over."

"I hardly want to do that. I'm thirty-nine. So I imagine I'll stay."

"I've split the land and buildings between you and Natasha. Nobody else has a claim. I've left a modest bequest to all my children."

"Gordon, you gave me a copy of your will two months ago. Do we have to dwell on this?"

"Judith, you've been the best choice I ever made in my life, because you're bright and level-headed and you've always brought your full intelligence to bear on everything you do, from practicing law to choosing a broom. I love that. But you haven't been willing to bring any intelligence whatsoever to the situation we're in. When you married me, you didn't think I was twenty-seven too. You knew I was much older than

you and the odds were enormous that I'd die first. Now I have lung cancer. You read all the books. You know what the survival rate is for recurrent lung cancer. About a five percent chance of being alive in five
years. When you refuse to be open-minded and clear-eyed about this
event so important to me, then I'm left to face it alone."

"What do you want from me? To sit down with you and plan your
funeral?"

"I'm not into that yet, although given my flair for self-dramatization, I
won't miss that last grand opportunity. What I have to know is how
things will be with you. I have to leave you set up."

"Well, I'll have the house and my practice. That's as much set up as
any person has a right to expect."

"I don't agree. I brought you out here, away from the city. It was to
please me."

"Gordon, I love living here. I probably enjoy the Cape's natural resources more than you do."

"But you're here because I was an old man and I retired. Otherwise we'd both be working in the city. And this land is important to me.
This compound is a crazy but vital creation. It's my monument, if you
like. I hate to think of it going on the market and being dismantled by
somebody who wants to replace it all with one of those millionaire's
atrocities."

"Gordon, I live here. I live with you. Enough!" It was a recurrent
quarrel. She did not know what he wanted from her, that she produce a
projection of her life without him like an entrepreneur drafting a plan
for a new business? It was gruesome.

At last Gordon finally found a project he could immerse himself in. He
began writing a book with a photographer about Saltash, its history, its
sociology. It was a true collaboration, and Brian Peyrera, a photographer
from New York, had moved to Saltash for the duration. Gordon had begun several projects since the onset of cancer, but he had abandoned
them all, losing interest. Working with someone on a project of limited
scope seemed to be exactly what he needed. He began to fight less with
her about the future. She was immensely relieved. The photographer,
just about her age and recently divorced, was a very thin young man
with a dazzling smile and lots of dark brown wavy hair.

"Brian ought to move in here," Gordon said one morning at breakfast. "It'd be much easier for us to work together. He's spending a fortune at the inn."

"Live here?" Judith squeaked. "Couldn't we just find him a rental?"

"In June we're supposed to find him a summer rental? Be real. He could live in the cabin Ben built. He wouldn't be underfoot."

She could not deny Gordon his wishes; she had never been good at that. So Brian moved into one of the cabins in the compound, and he was indeed underfoot. He was a wistful good-natured man, a little sorry for himself, talkative but not much of a physical presence. He did not dominate space the way Gordon always had, which was a plus under the circumstances. He took over making lunch and some of the shopping.

"You have the domestic virtues," Judith said as he was helping her clean up from supper. "I appreciate that."

"My wife didn't."

They had tried very hard to have a baby, but the wife miscarried time after time. Finally they had decided to adopt. They were still waiting for a baby when the marriage came apart.

In some ways having Brian around did make life easier. When she could not make it back to the island because of the tides she did not have to put in a desperate call to Jana Baer. Brian was always there, and he was good company for Gordon. The book was marvelous therapy, aside from whether it would ever be finished. Brian seemed in no hurry to be done. He was happy to live with them. Why not? Saltash sure beat Manhattan in summer. The most awkward times for Judith were the evenings, since Gordon often grew weary and went to bed early, leaving the two of them tête-à-tête for hours. Sometimes they both read. Brian was not musical, and if she put a CD on, he would talk over the Mozart until she gave up trying to listen. The trouble was, he was beginning to stare at her when he thought she would not notice, to dote visibly, to sigh and gaze and otherwise exude a gentle but disconcerting desire.

"Gordon, I think maybe having Brian living here is not a great idea."

"I thought you were getting along splendidly."

"Brian's easy to get along with, unlike myself. But Gordon . . . I think he has a crush on me."

"Of course he does. How could he live with you and not fall in love? He's a sweet young man. He's bright and vulnerable—"

"And as crazy as you are." She stomped out of the room, overwhelmed with the suspicion that Gordon was intentionally throwing them together.

Gordon followed her into her room and shut the door. "You can't live out here alone. It's too difficult."

"So I'll get a roommate."

"Judith, you're still young enough to have a family."

"Gordon, you're way off. And you're a damned control freak, you know that? What are you trying to do, plan out my life for the next twenty years?" She stalked from her own bedroom, slamming the door.

When Natasha came home from vet school, eventually Judith told her. Anger roughened her voice. She could not hold it in. "He's pushing me to have an affair with that Brian, can you believe it? As if I've ever, ever shown interest in another man! It's just sick!"

Natasha had a conversation with Gordon. After that, she saw the situation differently. "He wants to know you'll be all right. And he loves this place. I think he wants to control who lives here, who shares it after he . . . in the future."

"It makes me feel dirty."

"Why?" Natasha propped her sharp chin on her hands. Her hair was her mother's, pale apricot, but her eyes were Gordon's, fiercely blue. "Why does it scare you so much? It would give him a sense of survival, to know who you were with, to know that the family goes on. He wants to have input into the choice of your next husband, Judith. Can't you understand?"

"I can't accept it."

"Even to make him happy? Even to give him some peace about how things may go? Maybe he's right. We all want to know that we can still come here, that we can feel at home here."

"I'm not shopping for a husband. I have one. Can't you just trust me to make the family feel at home?"

"He thinks you don't know much about men. He doesn't want you to get hurt after he's gone."

Judith paced, clutching her arms. "This is unbearable!"

"He wants to have an afterlife in your life. Of course it's weird, Judith, but this family is pretty weird. You play housemother to children older than you are. Gordon tries to stay friendly with all his ex-wives, and mostly he manages, but he doesn't think much of the husbands they acquired after him. You were more like an older sister than a mother to me, but you were the main woman in my life for years and years, and you still are. Listen to me. Don't be conventional about this. You didn't marry conventionally. You didn't live your married life conventionally. Listen to Gordon. If you don't agree with him on the man he chooses, say so. Say you'll pick out your own."

*   *   *

She told Hannah what was going on. Hannah was silent for a while. Then she said, "You know, a minor affair isn't the end of the world. It needn't damage a central and serious relationship."

Hannah had been with the senator for nine years. Judith asked, "Have you been involved with anyone else?"

Another silence. "I don't know if I'd go so far as to say involved."

She wanted to ask Hannah how could she, why would she, but she did not, for she did not want to alienate her closest woman friend (unless she counted Natasha, whom she did think of as her daughter). She did not want to make Hannah defensive, so slowly and carefully she circled toward the questions she wanted to ask. But even as she did so, she realized it was futile. Hannah was not her; the senator was not Gordon.

Finally she spoke to Barbara. "Why a man?" Barbara made a gesture of dismissal. "It's so like a man to discount half the world. I like Gordon, but it never seems to occur to him you have other choices."

"Barbara, I respect your choice, but it isn't for me."

"You've never been involved with a woman. . . . But he's pushing the envelope so hard he could rupture it. Why do you have to torture yourself now? Why can't he let you enjoy the end of his life with him, as much as you can?"

"I wish he would. I feel coerced into a complication I don't need."

"But you don't have to do it, Judith," Barbara said calmly, putting her hands flat on her desk. "He can inflict Brian on you in the house, but he can't make you fall in love with him or even in lust. After a while he'll let it go. It will be too boring to continue."

"Barbara, you're always right, do you know that? Or at least fifty percent of the time."

"Eighty-five."

"Fifty-five."

They grinned at each other. Judith felt as if she had been an idiot. She had always taken Gordon's desires, even his whims, seriously, because she wanted so much to please him. If he saw a shirt he liked as they walked past a clothing store, she would return the next day and buy it. If he dropped a hint he was curious about a show, she would call at once for tickets. Perhaps she had had a lot to prove, being the fourth wife, being the child bride, being the youngest, being . . . the last.

Brian was acceptable as a member of the household. She could think of him as a stepson, like Larry. She could think of him as a family pet.

She could handle him: just never let him declare his feelings. She started watching television in the evenings. Renting videos. Then she began to fix up her office at home so she could escape to it. She mostly hadn't bothered working on the island since Austin retired and she moved her practice to the harbor, but it was time to refurbish her home office. It was a distance from the main house, and she would gradually begin spending evenings there. She could bring the walkie-talkie out with her, and if Gordon needed something, he had only to summon her. She would order a new computer Monday with a fast modem. All right, Gordon wanted Brian, he could have Brian as much as he wanted. But she could erect a few barriers to limit Brian's access to her and keep his yearning safely distanced. She would waste no more of their precious time together arguing with Gordon, but neither would she let herself be pushed.

DAVID

19

Candidates' night was a blood sport in Saltash. Every April, heron stabbed alewives, coyote fattened on nestling rabbits, and the people of this town gathered in the elementary school gymnasium with a similar hunger for flesh. Judith had invited me over to help write a speech, but I felt that as soon as she saw me, she'd know; as if that one night with Crystal could cling to my skin like the odor of sex. When Judith telephoned, I said I didn't need help. "You think I don't know why?" she said.

I felt my body square, as if to defend myself. I'd spent one night with a lonely woman while Judith herself was home with her husband. I was about to say something about our little triangle when she added: "You're determined to lose this election, aren't you?"

The election. My shoulders relaxed. "I'm just doing it my own way."

"Which amounts to the same thing. What are you scared of, David?"

Five meetings a week for three years. Small town newspapers poking into my personal life. Town crazies calling me at all hours. And that was if I was elected. At candidates' night last year, a guy running for selectman had to shout to be heard above the insults of the same block of guys now sitting with their legs outstretched in the first row. Although I was pretty sure none of them were against my stand on the issues (since even I couldn't say what my stand might be), old grudges were seldom buried in this town but polished to a shine like brass. Harlan Silvester. Jimmy Phillips. Their fathers had worked for mine. Tony Brockmann had stripped my sister to her underpants when she was ten years old and tied her to a tree. I beat him until his ears filled with blood and earned the enmity of the largest family in town. A quarter of a century had passed; he had married twice, lost his oldest son, buried his parents. Now Tony Brockmann, in unlaced work boots, legs spread wide, himself a grandfather at thirty-eight, glared at me as if to say my time was finally at hand.

The man we called Ahab smelled of beer and climbed the steps dragging his bad leg. With a permanent squint, his nose and cheeks were a crosshatch of tiny broken blood vessels and his face always seemed to be on fire. He had one issue, fishing, and spent almost all his time on the town pier. I only realized, when he raised his chin to return my hello, that I had observed him for years, hands thrust in pockets, collar upturned against the wind, but I had never heard him utter a word.

In contrast, Birdman was usually the first and last to speak at any event and had run for this office three times before. He was built from the waist up like a stack of tires, one smaller than the other as they progressed from his belly to his head—balding and fringed with wild white hair. He was well known to birders statewide for leading a campaign to save piping plovers who nested on the beach. Instead of the binoculars he always wore, he carried a large rolled-up map, which he tapped nervously against his knee.

I figured I'd make it through my five-minute speech with platitudes about hard work and growing up in this town, but I was worried about the questions and answers. I was going to lose this election. I was eager for the campaign to end, but I didn't want to embarrass myself. I had made a mistake. I had a crush on a woman. She asked me to run. Had she asked me for all the savings I had in the bank, or even to help her rob one, I'd probably have agreed. But I didn't have the mind for budgets or the wit to think on my feet. I had for one sterling period of my life mastered the ability to throw a baseball, but now I moved dirt for a living.

Sitting straight in the chair next to mine, her thin ceramic lips counting her supporters as they filled the room, was the front-runner, Blossom Endicott, whom Judith dubbed Blossom End-Rot. A teacher for many years in the Saltash Elementary School, Mrs. Endicott had so internalized her profession that she viewed the world and addressed everyone in it as if it were the fourth grade. Her hair was the cut and color of a stainless steel mixing bowl. She wore a corduroy jumper and clean white Keds. She walked to the stage with a clutch of official-looking papers, which she used like a cop used a club, to divide crowds and hint at her unleashed power.

I was attempting to look neither at Judith, pacing the aisles in her pin-striped coat dress, nor at Gordon among the *alter kockers*, nor at my mother, who was sending me little waves from the third row. I tried to ignore the stooges in the front row and to look at nothing but the double doors at the back of the gym, propped open for air, the whole time praying not to see Crystal in her fringed jacket and cowboy boots. Just as the house lights dimmed, a big late model Ford pulled up in front of the gym. I watched its headlamps die, saw its ceiling lamp flash on as the door opened. The young duty patrolman, upon spotting the vehicle in the fire lane, immediately ran outside—not to chase the illegally parked car but to escort its driver inside.

Johnny Lynch entered the gym with his hand on the young cop's shoulder. He seemed a pillar of smooth gray stone, with his strong square chin and his cropped hair gone white. He was a head taller than almost everyone around him, and his elbow shot out from his body to shake hands like the piston of a well-oiled machine. When I was a boy, Johnny Lynch used to dress up in his Uncle Sam costume to march in the Fourth of July parade. For every kid in this town, he was the living embodiment of government. I could still feel his hand, sliding along the ridge of my shoulder, locking like a vise on my nape. As he dropped a shiny new quarter in my shirt pocket with one hand, he found a nerve with the other and squeezed until I began to howl. "He likes you," my father insisted, but I had watched him torment other boys, watched his lips hitch up as they dangled in his grip like hanged men and tears moistened their eyes. If he moved more slowly now as a result of a heart operation, he seemed no less powerful. Gordon and the *alter kockers* sneered, but a small crowd sprang from their seats to wish him well. He moved up the center aisle like the father-of-the-bride. When he reached the third row—people stood to let him pass—he made his way to the chair next to my mother.

Birdman spoke first, springing to the podium and attaching his map to an easel. Before retiring to Saltash he had been a professor of Shakespeare in a small Minnesota college. His voice was stage-trained, his language precise, his research unassailable; no one doubted his facts. Even the guys in the front row, hunters and fishermen, couldn't disagree with his passion to restore the river valley, yet they watched him like a target through a rifle sight, waiting their moment to fire.

Birdman's map was a simple blowup of Tamar River, in blue, bordered on one side by the Saltash golf course, shown in green, and sixty lots on the other. Colored white and cut up in grids, they represented all the remaining land in the valley, earmarked for development. Brown arrows were superimposed over the grids, drawn in a wiggle pattern like sperm cells and aimed at the river. The speaker then pointed to the dike, explaining that a vote for him would be a vote for removing the dike and returning the yet-to-be developed land to its natural, semi-underwater state. His voice then deepened as he leaned into the microphone, "Do you know what these brown marks represent?"

"More of your shit!" came Tony Brockmann's answer.

"Well, yes. That's exactly what it is," the speaker said good-naturedly, getting in his last few words before Tony and his friends made it impossible for him to go on. The audience broke into applause. Even Johnny Lynch, the owner of the lots in question, joined in, his broad shoulders and confident smile rising above the crowd like the bust of a warrior in granite.

My mother had always been a woman who appreciated size. She liked high ceilings, big American cars, gilded picture frames heavy enough to rip nails right out of the wall. She had resented being taller than my father, having to wear flats and slouch in the company of friends. But she stood fully erect in the presence of Johnny Lynch.

Johnny had been chairman of the board of the Saltash Savings Bank when we spent two weeks in a cabin here one summer. He owned Saltash Real Properties, Inc. He presented the curtain factory to my father as a native industry lacking only good management to thrive. Later, we learned he was unloading an about-to-be foreclosed property for his bank, through his real estate firm; taking a small personal stake in the business in order to keep the town's only factory in operation. My father didn't consider problems with the building or the work force, or that the market for curtains had been replaced by vertical blinds. He was anxious to start a new life for his family, to put the shame of his last failure behind him. My father thought moving from New York City to what he called "the sticks" afforded him the upper hand. If my father took Johnny Lynch for a courtly lawyer from the boondocks who wore brown suits and wide ties, Johnny Lynch saw my father as a fool.

The consequences of that partnership were played out in my living room. Almost nightly, my father was on the phone, begging Johnny Lynch not to withdraw his profits in cash; not to support the employees' demands for higher wages; not to charge his lunches to the business or to give away merchandise as gifts to clients and friends. Johnny Lynch had promised my father that the factory would turn a profit; two years after my father's death, long after he had sold it back to Johnny, the town took the building by eminent domain for a price of $1.2 million.

Compared to Ahab, who stumbled into the podium and knocked over the water pitcher, my remarks were uneventful. Even the clowns in the front row, having tried the audience's patience heckling Birdman, did little more than make faces through my speech and walk out during the applause. Blossom End-Rot, to no one's surprise, was far and away the favorite. Having packed the hall, her reception was long and loud. Afterwards, what questions came from her camp were designed mostly to embarrass Birdman, considered to be her biggest challenge. I was asked merely to comment on the town's recreation budget. I assumed it was over. Some people were already filing out. There would be an election in five weeks. I would come in third, my brief career in politics put to bed. I did not hear her question at first, or even realize Blossom End-Rot was addressing me.

Her voice was oddly kittenish. She gave the impression, with the flutter of her eyes, of curtsying as she spoke. "I was wondering," she spoke to me through the audience, "if David could comment on the problems at the high school and what if anything he would propose to do about them?"

The question was absurd. The high school was regional, the curriculum controlled by the state. The town had little if any input. "Certainly," I said. The audience remained in their seats. "Uh, could you be more specific?"

"The high incidence of teenage pregnancies, for example. The proliferation of alcohol and drugs."

I said something about drug testing.

"Because David knows how important a good moral example is to the children. Don't you, David? Being an athlete," she said as an afterthought.

Instinctively, I searched out Judith. My gaze escaped no one's attention. "Well, we all try to set a good example," I said.

"Some try harder than others." Mrs. Endicott smiled. "Coming as I do from a family with a two-hundred-year tradition in this town, I feel I must set standards. But of course it might be different for a candidate whose family is foreign born and entered this country through Ellis Island. He really can't be expected to have the same commitment, can he, David?"

At that moment I felt only the hammer of my heart in my mouth, anger rushing through me instead of words. If anything proved me unfit for office, it was this moment, this mute and shameful inability to defend myself in public.

DAVID

Saturday, my sister found me in the greenhouse watering seedlings. The April light that morning, as it had when I was growing up, filled me with anticipation of the season to come. I could smell the yeasty mud of the oyster flats at low tide and, when the wind came up, the tree sap running. In a month we'd have more work than we could handle, the election would be over and with it the embarrassment I felt every time I saw my name in the papers. For weeks I'd heard nothing from Holly but a list of things undone. Now she grinned at me. "Were you expecting visitors, David?" She didn't take her eyes from Crystal or Laramie or let them get in a word. "Where have you been keeping these people? Why didn't you tell me you had new friends?"

My sister's marriage had produced the same effect on her as boot camp on a new recruit: she'd lopped off her hair, lost ten pounds and seemed to be on guard all the time. The lilt in her voice when she got excited and her dimpled smile had disappeared. Even her ample breasts, which had hampered her high school swimming but made her a favorite with the boys on the team, had over time been chiseled to fit the body of a lean and efficient über-mom. But as she dropped to one knee to talk to Laramie, I heard a bit of the old little flirt. "You're a handsome young man. Have we met? I don't think so, and I know all the cute guys in my daughters' school. What's your name?"

"It's Laramie but—" He glanced at his mother for encouragement. "—my friends call me Larry."

"I'd like to be your friend, so I'll call you Larry too."

The boy looked to his mother to confirm his success, but Crystal was beaming at me.

"How old are you, Larry? Let me guess." Holly made a show of sizing him up. Height, weight; she stepped forward and back, squinting, looking behind his ears. "Eight," she announced.

"We didn't mean to interrupt you at work," Crystal said. "But Larry wanted to ask your advice. Guy talk." She winked.

Holly stood, slapping her knees clean. "I didn't know you were in town."

"I just moved back," Crystal said.

"When did you meet my brother? Where did you two—"

"Tommy Shalhoub introduced us," Crystal said.

"David didn't mention it."

Until this moment, nobody but Tommy and Michelle had known anything about Crystal and me. Michelle had made pancakes for us the next morning, apparently content that once Crystal met a guy, she wouldn't be after hers. Certainly Tommy seemed relieved, if a little wistful. Crystal couldn't have been cooler. She was up before me, getting her son ready for school. When we walked out, she kissed my cheek. "That was nice," was all she said. I hadn't seen her since that night.

I felt the little boy looking up at me. "What did you want to ask me, Larry?"

"Liam says he wants to get me something for my birthday, and I want a glove."

"Liam's his dad," Crystal said.

"When's your birthday?"

"Not for a month," he said. "But Mom says I have to tell him now."

"If we wait for Liam to ask, it'll be too late. But we've never had a baseball glove, have we, Larry? We wanted to know what we should ask him for."

"Well, you look like a pretty strong kid to me. Step over here a minute. Make a muscle. Good. Squeeze my hand. Ouch!" I measured his hand by placing his palm in mine. I showed him how to throw a ball, remembering how Georgie had once shown me, guiding my arm, placing his palm in the small of my back. Attention was like food for the starved little boy. When I pronounced him a pitcher, he looked as if he'd had an audience with God.

Holly lagged behind as we all strolled to the parking lot. Crystal fell in next to me. "I've been thinking about you." She was wearing a cowhide jacket and silver earrings. Although her eyes seemed clear and confident, she sounded bashful. "We have to get something clear about the other night."

"Crystal—"

"I'm grateful for your confidence in me. For the way you said you thought I could be something."

"Well, I meant it."

"That's why I had to tell you, I've decided to go back to school. To finish up my B.A. Maybe, eventually," she said shyly, "to apply to law school. And I owe it to you. You're a very special man."

"I'm not special at all," I said, but that was a lie: in her presence I felt wise and powerful.

"I'm not the only one who thinks so." She jutted her chin toward

Laramie. "Larry thinks you're the swellest guy in the world. Look." She stopped abruptly. "You may not want to see me again. I understand that."

"I didn't say that, Crystal."

"Let me finish. Please." She was shorter than I remembered her. Standing close so that her voice wouldn't carry, her forehead only reached my cheek. Her voice seemed to quiver with fragile determination. "If you don't want to see me, that's okay. But just do me a favor, will you? Be a friend to the kid. I've seen the way you talk to him. The way he listens. If you don't think we have anything going, okay. But think about being his friend, will you, David? That's really all I ask."

Holly was waiting for me when I walked back from the parking lot. "Did you tell her?"

"Tell her what?"

"Did you tell her about Judith?"

"We have customers," I said, making my way to the register.

"My money's on Crystal."

"For what?"

"To get rid of Judith. But don't worry, David. If what the boys used to say about her is true, you're going to have a really good time."

JUDITH

21

Stumpy came over just after breakfast to help her with the garden. She had planted the peas on St. Patrick's Day, four weeks before, but digging the entire garden was a task Gordon had always done. Now Gordon sat in a deck chair wrapped in a blanket, overseeing Stumpy's digging and her cultivating and planting. They went along in tandem until half the garden—broccoli, lettuce, beets, carrots, leeks—was put in. The sun warmed her back, even though the air was chilly. This soil was her creation, compost, grass clippings, seaweed added to the sand and decayed into a rich brown soil. She loved the feel of it in her hands, looking almost edible, fudgy. Gnats swirled in the path. A mourning cloak butterfly wandered among the pines. She had never found April cruel, but fecund, full of promises that would eventually be kept, promises of growth and productivity. She thought of David. She had not seen him alone since the morning he had arrived unannounced. Being outdoors made her wish he was with her. She had imagined putting in the garden with him instead of Stumpy.

Stumpy stayed for lunch. After he left, as Gordon was retiring for his afternoon nap, he said, "I thought you'd get your young man to help. I'm sure he has some sort of mechanical cultivator that could turn the whole thing over in half an hour."

"I'd meant to ask him, but he's been avoiding me."

"Did you have a fight?"

"I think he was upset that morning he appeared right after we made love."

"Did he think I was too old or too sick to get it up?"

Actually he usually was, but she simply smiled. "I think he knew in theory we make love, but it caught him by surprise to walk in. He'll get over it. The more serious problem, I suspect, is that after candidates' night, the reality of running for office is scaring him shitless."

"He certainly seems flightier than I expected. Do you think he'll back out?"

She shrugged. "I'll talk to him."

"Is he more afraid of winning or losing? Or is it the public process that scares him? Standing up in front of people he's known all his life and making a fool of himself. I'll really regret it if he blows his chance at the seat. He's the best shot we've ever had."

"I promise, I'll give him a pep talk. I know he can win. He has more support than he realizes. He's seen as honest, hardworking, young—"

"And unknown politically. Meaning he hasn't pissed anyone off yet." Gordon looked totally exhausted. Fatigue overtook him often with the abruptness of a blade dropping. She had to help him to bed. She sat beside him as he lay waiting for sleep. "I'm making a lamb and barley soup," she said softly. "The bakery is open and I got a nice bread. I'm always so glad when they open in the spring. The geese fly overhead, the robins come back, and the bakery opens. . . ." He was asleep, she realized, and slipped out, shutting his door soundlessly.

She decided to go over to David's after supper. She could not allow the unspoken estrangement to persist. She must work through whatever had gone wrong. His car was outside and the light on in his kitchen. He had given her a key and she used it, although once inside, she called to him. "David? David? It's me."

He leapt up from the table, apparently startled. He looked almost afraid. He must have been brooding—probably about the election.

She came to him at once and kissed him lightly. "I know you've been avoiding me."

He looked petrified now. "What do you mean?"

She suspected he was afraid that she would withdraw from him if he chose not to run. For all that she had promised Gordon she would try to get him to commit, it was even more important to her that he not feel their relationship was in any way dependent on the election. She thought it would be good for him to run and to win. It would give him confidence that he had not had since the end of his baseball career. But if he was not ready, she would not coerce him, even to please Gordon. Two relationships could be a lot more complicated than Gordon realized, balancing each of them against the other. Doing justice to both men. "I've been pushing you hard to run, and you're angry."

He scratched his head, still avoiding her gaze. "I'm not angry."

"People will be disappointed if you back out—particularly Gordon. He's sure you can win and it means a lot to him. But I want you to do what you want to do. I want you to do what's best for you, and if that involves withdrawing from the race, then do it."

"That's what you wanted to talk to me about?" Now he looked at her, finally.

He was so tense, she could feel it. She loved him even more than she liked to admit to herself or to Gordon. She was besotted with him, the light eyes in the face already tanned from outdoor work, his shock of black hair, the line of his mouth and chin, the sound of his voice, tentative, always issuing from lower in his chest than she expected. His fine blunt hands were on the table, pressing against it as if to keep the world in place. "I want things to be better between us." David was a good man, and she did not want to make things harder for him.

He sat down slowly at the table, still holding her gaze, and she sank into the chair across from him. She said, "I think it's been tying you in knots. I don't want the election to come between us. You're too important to me."

"You wouldn't hate me if I decided not to run?"

"Hate you? Never. David, you may not believe it right now, but what we have together works for both of us. We have a lot to give each other, a lot to teach each other. It may not be a conventional relationship, but that doesn't mean it can't work for us—and work well."

She could tell he was full of doubts—she could feel them churning just under the surface of his apparent calm—but when she rose and walked over to him, he stood and took her in his arms. Patience, she thought to herself, patience. It's taking him a while to get used to the situation, but he does love me.

"You're so precious to me, David. I've missed you these past two weeks."

"I've missed you too," he said, and began easing her toward his bedroom. Through her body and mentally, she relaxed with a sigh. She would have to tell Gordon she had not persuaded David to make a commitment to run, but with great relief she could feel his focus shifting from whatever had been distressing him at the moment to their bodies pressing together, the sweetness of their mouths joining. It would be all right. It would be good again, she was sure.

DAVID

Between Thanksgiving and Memorial Day there were two restaurants in Saltash open after six P.M. One served steaks and seafood and was favored by the retired crowd. The working people gathered at Penia's. Crystal asked me to meet her and the kids there for dinner on Friday night. She told me she had a surprise. Penia's was noisy and smoke-filled and dark. The beer was warm and the pizza was cold, but you could feed a family of four for under twenty dollars. It was the one place in the entire town I knew I'd never see Judith—she was suing them.

"Crystal, you didn't go and get me anything, did you?"

"As a matter of fact," her voice was all whisper and giggle, "I took something away."

Kids were kicking a soccer ball in the parking lot when I arrived and filling balloons at the men's room sink. As we stood in line for a table, Michelle's daughter, Kelly Ann, met two boys from her class, arms up to the elbows in a tank of tropical fish. No, Laramie mumbled, he did not know them. He would not lift his gaze from the tops of his shoes. After the waitress finally took our order, she slouched to the table behind ours and cleared it, chatted up her two booths and ducked into the ladies' room before entering the kitchen.

"What's the matter?" Crystal said. "You keep checking your watch."

"I'm hungry."

"You look nervous."

"Just because people stare at us when they pass."

"You're running for public office. Think that could be it?"

"I hope not."

"I know, I know. Because the last thing you want to do is win."

Laramie frowned. I didn't know much about little boys, but I had never met one so worried about his mother. He not only watched her, he absorbed her every word. His mood changed with our conversation. Every time I opened my mouth to speak, he seemed to set his jaw and wait for her response. When the waitress brought Crystal's tea, he started playing with the bag, sloshing it up and down.

"Cut it out," Crystal told him.

"It makes faster this way," he said.

I ordered two more cups when the pizza arrived, told Laramie to dip the bag in one and to leave the other alone. I gave him my wristwatch and asked him to time which got darker first. Crystal looked at me as if I was a cross between Piaget and Santa Claus.

If the kid sensed that I was tense, he wasn't far off. Sure, Penia's was cheap and a place where kids could amuse themselves. But eating here on a Friday night with a woman and her children was like an announcement to the town, WE ARE AN ITEM! People weren't looking at some guy running for selectman, they were noting who was screwing who.

"Can I ask you a question?" Her voice was apologetic and she hadn't touched her food. Laramie stopped eating and waited for my answer. Her cheeks were flushed. I imagined them warm against my fingertips. "It's a serious question."

"Ask me anything you want."

"Why don't you want to run?"

Although we could hardly hear each other above the jukebox and the rattle of plates, she seemed to be doing everything in her ability to coax me into a better mood.

"You'd be so good." She slid her hand under mine. Laramie saw the gesture and relaxed. What he did not see was the nail of her middle finger moving in circles around my palm.

"Because everybody in this town would rather hate each other than change anything," I said.

"Is that the real reason?"

"It's easier to fight about the way things used to be than to face up to what really needs fixing."

"You mean my boss?"

"Johnny Lynch got rich off this town. You look around this restaurant. There isn't one local kid here who didn't lose a piece of his family's land to Johnny. But who do they hate? Who do they make jokes about and try to run off the highway? Who do they blame for being poor? The retired people, the city people. Do they remember what school was like here when we went? You know why Tommy Shalhoub dropped out of school? Because he couldn't read. Because we had a teacher who made him read out loud and hit him on the head with a book every time he made a mistake. Guess what? She's still teaching."

Laramie and Kelly Ann fell silent. Crystal withdrew her hand. I assumed the conversation was over. Then she asked, "Is that how your friend Judith feels?"

Laramie's face turned the color of a gravestone. How would he even know her name? I don't believe a muscle moved in his entire body— or mine. Crystal nibbled on her pizza, reached across the table to put another slice on Kelly Ann's plate. "Would you like another soda, you two?" Kelly Ann sucked the air through her straw and nodded. "How about you, Larry Stone Face? Do you want to tell me about her, David?"

"Well, she's a good customer. They have a very big garden. She and her husband, Gordon, have been married for thirteen years. He's got cancer. She nurses him as best she can."

"She sounds much older than you. How many children do they have?"

"Gordon has five by other marriages. But none together."

"Mmmm." Crystal flashed a grimace of pity. "So she became a lawyer." She wiped Laramie's lips with a napkin. "I'd like to meet her."

I laughed, involuntarily. It was unthinkable.

"David, if the two of you like each other, I'm sure she and I will."

"I don't know about that."

"I won't push you. But I think it's the most natural thing in the world. Like meeting your mother or an old family friend. I hope you'll change your mind," she said.

Michelle was spending Friday night at Tommy's, a deal the two mothers had worked out, and a fact that Kelly Ann forgot until she came home. Then she refused to get undressed, to turn off the TV, to brush her teeth or stop crying or get into bed. With every story we read, Kelly Ann demanded another, until we had read four of them and Laramie had fallen asleep. When we turned out the lights, the little girl turned them on again and insisted she didn't have to go to sleep if she didn't want to, Crystal wasn't her mother and this wasn't Crystal's house. I couldn't believe how tired I was, how the effort of staying awake and dealing with Kelly Ann, while attempting to control my temper, was as much work as I did in an eight-hour day. I crawled into bed—on the nights when Michelle slept out, Crystal had a real bed—already half asleep. "Don't you want to turn the light out?"

"Then you won't see my surprise," she said.

"What is it?"

"You have to guess."

"Where is it?"

"Oh, I think you know."

"So I've seen it before?"

"Not as much of it."

"I don't understand. There's more of something?"

"Less. But I think you'll like it more." She peeled off the covers and inched her back up the headboard. Slowly and with great ceremony, as if unveiling a work of art, she drew her night gown over her knees, her thighs. I'd been watching her face, her thick, deliberate smile, when she licked her finger and dragged it down her belly to where she had shaved herself smooth. Her mons was as soft and bare and pink as a child's. "I did it for you," she whispered. "Just for you. Do you like it?"

The truth is I had never seen an adult woman shaved before. I couldn't say that I *liked* it, for it disturbed me. I felt momentarily ashamed. I only knew it excited me, that I was fascinated with the act itself, so bold and spontaneous in its eccentricity.

"But she's so cold." Crystal's voice rose and slowed like a girl child's. "Don't you want to kiss her?"

As I covered her with my mouth, she dug her nails in my shoulders. "I want to know everything you like," she said. "You can ask me for anything and I'll make it come true. Anything, do you understand me?" She lifted my head until my eyes met hers. "There are no private parts. There are no secrets. My body inside and out is yours. You can do anything with me. I'm your anything girl."

DAVID

High Street, Saltash, was two lanes wide. Local guys enjoyed a good conversation in the middle of it— windows rolled down, pickups idling, one facing east, the other west, as traffic and tempers built up in both directions. Sometimes it was a demonstration of local rights, a protest against the out-of-state license plate behind them; sometimes just business, the closest a working man came to a car phone. It was also the fastest way for news to get around, and the afternoon I took on the Department of Roads, Bridges and Waterways, they tell me cars were backed up for a quarter mile.

I'd been working the Carlson job. Bob Carlson was a friend of Marty's and one of our best customers. Like a lot of affluent couples from the city, the Carlsons paid late and changed their minds on a whim. One Monday night, they decided on a party at their country home that weekend, for which they expected their fencing erected and their landscaping complete. I hadn't scheduled the job until the middle of May. Much as I wanted to tell the Carlsons to shove it, we needed the business.

Although it was only mid-April, the air was sweet with narcissus and the acid tang of pine sap. Spring peepers trilled at sundown and clouds of gnats rippled the air like waves of heat. Even after I sent the crew home, even as the sun touched the treetops, I worked without a shirt. The Carlsons' was one of the only houses in Johnny Lynch's new development. When Bob Carlson heard that the lot across the road sold, he wanted a fence. Eight feet high, one hundred long, it had taken us three days to complete.

Just beyond the fence, I heard the growl of truck gears, heavy equipment climbing, and caught a glimpse of a front-end loader, the kind road pavers used, laboring up the hill. It was odd to be starting a job this late in the day. I couldn't see the road crew but heard them horsing around. I didn't think much about it. I was driving spikes in a tier of landscape ties, trying to finish before sundown. The stench of the diesel smoke, the noise of the big machine were unpleasant enough to ruin a mild spring evening, but when the loader's engine started straining, roaring loud enough to explode, when I noticed the big rig rolling over the property line, I ran down the drive to take a look. The driver was forcing the loader's bucket under the root ball of a twenty-foot tree, attempting to lift it. The harder he gunned the engine, the farther forward the vehicle tipped, its rear tires leaving the ground. The light was fading. A thick blue cloud of smoke billowed down the hillside, but the lettering on the equipment was unmistakable. This was no moon-lighting road crew working on Johnny Lynch's road, this was the Saltash Department of Roads, Bridges and Waterways, and the idiots were three feet from my fence.

A couple of guys watched from the edge of the road—Harlan Bowman and Tony Brockmann among them—arms folded, beer bottles in their fists. When they saw me coming, they turned their backs. Tiny Sauvage ran alongside the machine, waving his arms, shouting instructions.

I called, "Hey guys." They ignored me. "This is a private road. What are you doing here?"

Harlan Bowman lifted a baseball cap stained with motor oil and ran his hand through his hair. "Clearing trees."

"It took my crew three days to put up that fence. Don't you think he's awful close?"

Harlan shrugged. "He's a new guy." The machine rocked, forward and back, spewing a shower of pebbles and sand.

I was shouting above the noise, "Well, get him out of there," when the huge yellow rig sprang backwards, hit the ground with its rear wheels spinning, shot through two sections of my new cedar fence, lurched forward and died in the middle of the road.

Tiny Sauvage screamed at the driver, "You fuck, you stupid fuck!" The guys crept up cautiously, as if the big rear tires might suddenly come alive.

"You crushed the fence," I said to Tiny. Didn't seem to bother him a bit.

Harlan took a step backward, considering the twelve-foot gap of dangling staves and splinters. "Took a hit there. Yup."

The door of the loader's cab creaked open. A hand appeared, then a boot, dangling cautiously in search of a step.

"Look!" Tiny shouted, his finger pointing at the driver's pants. "He pissed hisself! Sonofabitch pissed hisself!"

Sheepishly, the driver spread his hand over the wet splotch of his pants. "I had an accident," he said. The collective laughter was uncontrolled.

"Guys. Listen to me." I wasn't trying to pick a fight. "The fence is going to have to be replaced."

Tiny said over his shoulder, "We'll take care of it."

"When?"

"When we get to it."

"When you get to it? Guys, my best customer's coming up here to-morrow night. What am I supposed to tell him?"

Tony Brockmann spit in the dust. "Tell him you had an accident."

"It's dark now," Tiny said. "We can't do nothing in the dark."

As long as I could remember, there were two-hour lunch breaks be-hind the ice skating rink, poker games in the town golf course locker room, municipal trucks cruising the highway with their radios scream-ing heavy metal rock. This was Saltash's archaic welfare system, a sociopathic elite hired by Johnny Lynch and tenured by the town. But I wasn't some teacher from Westchester whose electric line they'd acci-dentally cut. This was my work they'd destroyed and me they were laughing at.

"I want it fixed first thing tomorrow morning," I said. "I mean that. Or I'll have to go over your head."

Tiny looked from me to his men—is this guy an asshole or what?—and left me standing alone in the road.

For all the years I'd lived in Saltash, I could count the times I'd been in Town Hall, the only brick building in town. Its long dark halls, hot in summer and clammy in winter, were bleak and dreary and seemed to discourage invaders. "We are not complainers," my father used to say. He was fond of declaring our standards. We tip well. We pay local tradesmen on time. A pitiful code of conduct to be sure, but one we ad-hered to in lieu of our religion and the customs we'd left where we came from. Throughout my life, in spite of lousy tableside service or a pipe that began leaking as soon as the plumber's truck left the driveway, I tipped twenty percent, I paid my bills the day they arrived. I did not complain.

The town manager did not know me from my glory years. He was a tall soft tired man who listened with an interest that seemed directly calibrated to the amount of trouble I was likely to cause.

"Sir, I just want you to know I'm not a complainer," I began, and out-lined the situation from the misuse of town property to the gaping hole in the fence. Without interrupting, the manager made a phone call. "Could you get right up here?" he said, and five minutes later Donkey Sparks arrived.

"David Greene!" His cheeks were pink, his collar too tight. He wore a tie beneath an old cotton sweater that announced he might be man-agement but still close enough to his rank and file not to betray them by wearing a suit. "Christ, it's been years. Do you know this guy?" he asked the town manager without waiting for a reply. Then to me: "You've been back in town how long? And did you come to see me?"

"I—"

"Best damned high school pitcher I ever saw. Damn, he was good. Went all the way to the Chicago Cubs, did you know that? Davey Greene, the Pitching Machine."

"Mr. Greene was telling me about an incident he encountered up, where?"

"This the fence thing?" Donkey waved it off. "Those assholes. Got to watch them every minute. Don't worry about it. We'll have it all taken care of. So, Davey, what are you doing now? You think you'll do some coaching for the Little League?"

"What do you mean taken care of?" I said.

Donkey was so named for a horsey staccato laugh, almost a bray, which escaped him now. "I mean we'll order some sections of fence for you and as soon as they come we'll get up there and make it good as new."

"It was new. These are important customers to me. They'll be up tomorrow night."

"Hey, Davey. Spring is here, my friend. The whole town's breathing down my neck. I told you. As soon as we can. Is that not reasonable?"

Complainers were people who didn't listen to reason; troubled people who searched out trouble. I knew the more I made of it, the less my chances of the fence ever being fixed. "Look, these are difficult customers I'm talking about. They are going to hold me up for the whole job because of that stretch of fence. I'm not going to be able to pay my crew, okay? And why? Because your guys are out there drinking and operating heavy machinery—"

"Drinking?" Donkey glanced at the town manager.

"Yes, I think they were," I said.

"You think."

"They were holding beer bottles."

"And you know what was in those bottles? You know positively that it was alcoholic beer? Because you're making serious accusations, my friend." The flush of his cheeks intensified; all the blood in his body seemed to collect in his face. His smile turned to warning: back off. "You collected those bottles and had them tested? Is that what you're saying? You have the results?"

I didn't have anything of the kind. "What were they doing up there after work, using town equipment on a private road?"

Donkey grinned. That was easy. "Making access for fire vehicles," he said to the manager. "I asked them to put in a little overtime and they were glad to do it. It's all listed in the work detail." Then, ignoring me, "Is there anything else?" Donkey waited, his short square body tensed for a fight.

When I emerged, the weather had turned. A cold fog settled over Saltash, driven by a northeast wind. I drove eighty-five miles to pick up the replacement sections of fence and worked well past dark cementing the posts.

"It's over," Crystal said, warming the meat loaf in a frying pan. "Don't be so hard on yourself."

I ate because she had cooked, but I had no appetite. With no proof—they had taken their beer bottles with them—no witnesses, there was nothing I could have done. Moreover, the fence was fixed. Did I really want to pursue this further, put five men out of work? It was over, I told myself. Over.

Since I'd started seeing Crystal, I was spending less time with Judith, but Crystal considered herself at war. To the extent that she had studied the enemy, Crystal knew that Judith was well read and interesting to talk to; that she had traveled a good deal; that she had a local reputation as a fabulous cook and hostess; that she was quoted in the newspapers regularly, often saying something witty and outrageous. Moreover, Judith was affluent, genetically thin, and to the extent that it meant anything now, my mentor in local politics. This might have been enough to overwhelm any number of women, if they respected any of Judith's virtues. Crystal did not. To Crystal, Judith was incomplete. "If you haven't had a child," she said more than once, "you're not a real woman."

Crystal had not only managed to neuter her enemy but to employ sex as her most potent weapon. She had asked more than once what Judith was like in bed (I would not talk about it), but was confident she was better. Or at least that she tried harder. For on no occasion that I spent the night with her, or as little as half an hour in a place with a door that closed (including my truck) did we fail to have sex. Crystal felt that an evening was incomplete until she had made me come.

Before we got into bed that night, I had told her honestly, sex was the last thing on my mind. Had I displayed the usual signs of disinterest, she might have believed me, but perversely, I was and remained hard as a pole. I simply could not get off. She squat-fucked me, facing front, then rear (coming twice herself in the process); she greased me with massage oil and pumped me with her fist; she sucked me until her jaw ached, all with no luck. "Where are you?" she said, rising from the bed sheets for air.

The photographs over the years show my father as a man with delicate bones, an ever thinning pompadour, and a thick blue vein that ran from his hairline to the corner of his eye. He had borrowed a small fortune from my grandmother to buy into the curtain factory. He was up at three every morning, often loading the trucks himself. When I was eight years old, he scored the biggest order the company ever had, a thousand gross of gingham curtains for a department store chain in the Midwest. His stitchers worked double time to make the deadline. The order had to be delivered on or before the first of October. But because his truck driver had been drinking and had disappeared with both sets of the keys to the truck, the shipment never made it on time. My father was furious and fired the driver. That night, Johnny Lynch stormed into my living room. As my mother paced the kitchen, he called my father a heartless New York kike.

"I'm not doing it, Johnny, no."

I was hiding in the hallway.

"Call." Johnny's voice carried the authority of law.

"The man's a drunk, Johnny."

"He has a wife and children."

"So do I, Johnny. So do I."

"Call him!" Johnny shouted, and the house shook. "Or the bank calls your loan tomorrow. Tell him you apologize. Tell him you had a talk with me."

I remember the ratchet of the old rotary dial, and my father's forehead in the lamplight, the blue vein throbbing, seventeen years before the stroke that killed him.

"You can't give it up, can you?" Crystal said. But neither could she. Having invested two hours in my satisfaction, she was afraid that she'd be sending me off to Judith in the morning hornier than ever. But all I felt was a weight pressing on my head from the inside, a pounding need for revenge. I had two choices: to back off or go at them, not only the idiots on the crew or Donkey Sparks above them, but Johnny at the top of the pyramid. Johnny Lynch had viewed my father as invisible, the way they all looked through me. I doubt I was the first to decide to run for political office while having sex, but something did happen just then. Something had fallen into place. Compare it to a gear, spinning for years without engaging. Compare it to catching your breath; or to orgasm itself, the explosive fusion of mind and body.

I came in what felt like a torrent of memory and emotion. Crystal swallowed, swinging her head to release the crick in her neck. "Finally," she gasped, for both of us.

JOHNNY

Johnny thought of parking in the woods and walking to the house, like the old days when the whole town knew what he was doing before he had his pants off. Around here, your car told people everything they wanted to know, what you drove and where you parked it. He'd learned that the hard way. He'd lost his first election because of that little red Triumph. It was months later before he'd understood how people here perceived him. Playboy. High roller. You could get away with a lot in this town if you knew the limits. Marry a black girl. Drink yourself pickled. Be a lesbian. But drive around in some fancy Mercedes? People wouldn't put up with it.

Ever since, he'd driven a Ford Crown Vic brown or maroon four-door sedan. The dullest car in town, everybody knew it on sight: his problem today. He didn't want the boy to see it in his mother's driveway and drive off angry. But Johnny no longer had the strength to park the car on a sand road and go on foot the way he used to: half a mile sometimes, through the woods like a tomcat.

Johnny didn't like involving Linda Greene, but what could he do? David Greene avoided him. Never set foot in the office when he picked up Crystal. Never returned Johnny's wave in the parking lot. Something had to be done.

"Hello, dear. How are you?" Johnny kissed her cheek but was careful to thrust his gift between them.

"Roses, Johnny! You didn't have to do that."

"You're putting yourself out for me and I appreciate it."

"Oh, you. Putting myself out. It's just brownies and coffee with David."

Linda Greene was a fine-looking woman still, with a high broad bosom and slender legs. Unlike the others her age, she never let herself go gray. She dressed young; a ribbed cotton sweater over black leggings. He'd watched her walking over the years, sometimes with women friends, sometimes just with her dog, but out there rain or shine on Ocean's Edge Road, keeping up a pace, working on her figure.

Johnny usually avoided being alone with Linda Greene, but thought it best to be seated at the kitchen table when the boy walked in. "You'll want to get those in some water." Linda was a little too passionate. He had his excuse now: he could blame his bad heart and her feelings wouldn't be hurt. She was a needful woman. Emotional. Not emotional like his wife, not delicate but the opposite. Before her husband passed away, she'd made her interest in Johnny plain enough. At curtain factory parties. Good Christ, in the elementary school parking lot one snowy December night after the Christmas play. She practically shoved her tongue down his throat. It wasn't for lack of desire on his part. He could have met her in Florida any number of times, where she visited her sister. But Johnny knew this town well enough to keep his hands off the widow of his ex-partner.

He anticipated her return from the sink, her cool fingertips grazing his skin above the shirt collar. "So young David said he was coming, dear? Just what did you tell him?"

"That I wanted him to see a friend."

"You didn't say who?"

"He doesn't hate you, Johnny. He just doesn't understand."

"But you didn't—"

"No, I just told him somebody he hadn't spoken to in a long time wanted to talk to him about running for selectman."

"That's good. That's very good." He let her fingers drift up to his cheek before he removed himself to the window. He supposed he was no better than any man; he enjoyed being wanted. But the truth was, he'd always liked Linda Greene. Far more than the husband who'd never learned to play the game, she was a practical woman. Sure her feelings were hurt when he ignored her interest in him, but she got more out of him as a friend than she ever would in bed. The son was like the father, looking at the dark side of everything. Sure enough when he rolled into the driveway and saw the Crown Vic, he stormed from his truck like a company of marines, throwing open the kitchen door.

"What's he doing here?" David Greene said, without so much as the courtesy to address Johnny by name. He was small like his father but an outdoor man, well-muscled, a scrapper. For a moment Johnny feared for his safety. He studied the boy's eyes, light gray like storm clouds.

The boy had always been a cold one. He'd never sat at Johnny's knee with the other children for stories but hovered back. Even when Johnny had picked the boy to ride with him in the big parade—two hours in the backseat of a convertible, creeping along Main Street in the scorching July sun—David Greene never spoke a word. "Hello, son. Your mother and I were having coffee and cake. Will you join us?"

"Why didn't you tell me this is the friend you wanted me to see?"

"David—"

"Because I asked her not to," Johnny said. "You wouldn't have come."

"You've got that right."

Linda Greene placed herself between them.

"And why is that?" Johnny asked.

David folded his arms. "Where do you want me to start?"

"By sitting down. Stop embarrassing me," Linda said. "The past is the past. You don't know everything."

"I know he bled my father's business dry."

Linda looked away, as if from a photograph she didn't want to see.

"When I first showed him the factory, I told him there was a good life to be had in this town. The idea was to give people jobs, draw a modest salary, enjoy his life. Your uncle George understood that. I told your father again and again to wait, the factory would pay off eventually."

"David, you were so young." Linda Greene was close to tears. "Your father was a very impatient man. There was only one way, his way."

"Enough of this," Johnny said. "I didn't come to rehash the past. I came to wish you luck in your run for public office and to ask you, man-to-man, if you're planning to turn this election into a referendum against me."

"Is there another issue?"

Johnny caught Linda's wrist. "We need a little time alone, dear, the boy and I. Is that all right with you? If David and I take a ride together?"

"I'm not going anywhere with you."

"Then we'll sit right here and have it out in front of your mother, won't we? Is that what you'd rather?"

"Any closer to that car door, son, you'll be on the sidewalk."

David didn't answer. He sat as far from Johnny as was possible in the front seat. His face was a mask of stone. Only the police scanner broke the silence, spitting out the urgent business of the Saltash P.D. *"Roger. Who has the jug of windshield wiper fluid? Over. I think Duffy had it last. Over."*

Johnny caught the boy smiling. "You've got to love this town," he said.

David, obviously uncomfortable, shifted in his seat, staring front-ways, sideways, anywhere but at Johnny. He looked at the backseat covered with election posters for Blossom Endicott.

"First thing Monday, she'll have these up at every traffic light on the highway, every window in the center of town."

"Why would you tell me that? Why rat out Blossom?"

"Because you might win."

"Where are we going?" David sighed, sounding almost resigned.

Johnny continued through Saltash center and out Dock Street along the harbor, up the state highway ten miles, then into the neighboring town of Sandy Bars. Only when he signaled a left turn toward the bay did he answer, "To what they call their town pier."

"What the hell for? There's nothing there."

Johnny pulled into a cracked asphalt parking lot, a peninsula surrounded on three sides by muddy tidal marsh. A row of dories and small motorboats lay one against the other along the back fence. A couple of old-timers in hip boots hung out on the steps of the Sandy Bars harbormaster's shack. This was a high-tide harbor; boats sat in the mud until the tide came up. Until then, there was no channel, no access to the sea. Johnny nosed the car up to a guardrail and shut the engine. "What do you see here?"

"What am I supposed to see? Nothing."

"How does it compare to Saltash harbor?"

"It doesn't," David said.

Saltash had thirty draggers, ten lobster boats, fifteen sport fishing charters. Johnny knew the numbers by heart. In season there were slips for 215 sailboats, 180 powerboats and a waiting list triple that. There were tackle stores and restaurants; two thriving boatyards, a summer theater, picnic tables, parking for four hundred, a bandstand, public showers and a fish market. Johnny stretched his arm across David's seat, sending him sideways to the door. "Now why the fuck do you think that is?"

The boy hedged. "We have a better natural harbor."

"Study your geography, son. Saltash harbor is a shallow embayment with a tidal amplitude of ten feet, about the same as what you're staring at. Sandy Bars could have had a fine harbor too, but nobody had the brains or the balls to make it happen. Thirty-five years ago I looked at Saltash and saw a town crying for an industry. That's why you're looking at this mud puddle in front of you while ten miles down the coast we have a beautiful working harbor."

"On which you bought up and sold—how many waterfront acres was it? Land you made valuable with public money."

So it was a pissing contest he wanted? "All right, David. Let's say I made a little money in my time. Let's say also that I managed to do something for my people along the way. What have *you* done? What did Gordon and his wealthy retired friends do? They don't give a fuck about who works or who doesn't because they don't have to work. As far as they're concerned, the local women can clean their toilets and the men mow their lawns. Take your best shot, son, go ahead. What else do your fancy backers accuse me of? Keeping the state from turning half of Saltash into a fucking bird sanctuary? Am I supposed to apologize? The land we kept out of the state's hands is what we call the tax base, son.

That's what pays for the police and the rescue squad and the best school system within a hundred miles."

"Isn't the principal of the school your sister, Johnny? Maybe we ought to rename the place Coincidence, Massachusetts. Because we sure have our share." The little prick kept pushing. "And didn't the selectmen happen to buy *your* land to build the school on? And didn't you handpick the contractor so the roof always leaks and the foundation is cracking?"

"The people of Saltash always made out," Johnny said, a little louder than he meant to.

"Is that all you wanted to tell me?"

Johnny sighed. He was tired, as if he could sleep for the rest of the afternoon. "What do you say we have a drink together?"

"Thanks. I don't have the time."

Johnny laughed to himself. "Neither did your father, do you know that? In all the years we did business together, he never once had the time for a drink."

As he drove back, Johnny tried to figure it out, how this cocky little high school pitcher had come back to haunt him. Johnny had heard he was screwing Judith Silver, Gordon's child bride. For all the cheap gossip Johnny himself had generated, this town had never seen anything like Gordon Stone and his drugs and naked orgies and string of women. But the kid had been hanging around his new secretary too. He'd have to find out what was going on.

David Greene was a lightweight; youth and resentment, that's all he had going. So what was so upsetting? Why did Johnny feel like he could pull the covers over his head and sleep the day through until morning? In front of Linda Greene's house, Johnny offered his hand. "Well, son, goodbye and good luck. Tell your mother thanks for putting herself out."

The kid nodded and slammed the car door, never acknowledging Johnny as a man or an adversary with whom he'd have to contend in the future.

And that was it, Johnny understood. That's what was bringing him down. Under this boy's contempt, Johnny was disappearing, shedding his importance. All his talent to move people, gone; his influence and the fear he instilled in men, gone; his eyesight and his stamina; his dear wife and what once seemed a small fortune. He was losing his life in pieces.

History and experience, all his accomplishments meant nothing. They kept coming at him: ambitious young pit bulls, smelling weakness, hungry for a fight. If it was a dogfight David Greene wanted, then a dogfight he'd get. The old schoolteacher wouldn't have been Johnny's first choice, but he'd backed worse and he'd won. Her family had been in the town two hundred years, and if people weren't crazy about her, they remembered her dad or her brother fondly. The Endicott clan alone were worth forty votes. It would be a dirty campaign, but Blossom could lick David Greene, and that was all he needed to get this depression off his back. To win, again. To win.

JUDITH

25 Judith's secretary Mattie told her that David had been seen with a woman who just moved back to town. When her partner Austin retired, Judith had kept Mattie on. Mattie was fourteen years older than Judith and doubted she could have found another job as good. Therefore she offered Judith a fierce loyalty that Judith cherished. Mattie had white hair braided around her head in an old-fashioned style, hair that would come well past her shoulders if loosened. She wore thick glasses and was stooped, but bright and fast. She had made herself comfortable with computers. She kept up, with an edge of desperation, for her divorce had left her with little but her house and debts. Her two sons who lived on the Cape were more a drain than a resource.

Mattie knew who Crystal was: the daughter of a dentist who had left town under a shadow. "His hands used to shake. The story was, he was addicted to painkillers and wrote himself script all the time. He got into trouble in two other states, people said, but his license was still good in Massachusetts. Finally he hurt a woman bad, our kindergarten teacher. A sweet lady. Johnny Lynch hushed it up but made him go."

"So how old was Crystal when her family left town?"

"Most of the way through high school, I'd say. A pretty girl, but her reputation wasn't. The parents split up. The mother went out West, I heard, and the father moved to Troy, New York. He and my ex-husband used to go fishing together and, every year, he sends my husband a Christmas card with a fish or a duck on it. I sent him a postcard years ago that Mick had left, but he just ignores it and sends him a card at my house every Christmas."

Mattie paused for a moment, her mouth dipping down. "I don't know if I should say this. I never cared for Crystal. My boy Cal went out with her in high school, and it made me nervous. She had him twisted around her little finger. I kept finding condoms in his drawer, although he'd deny there was any of that going on. I was terrified she was going to get pregnant and he'd have to marry her. I was so relieved when they left town, I can't tell you. She's a sly one. She used to try to butter me up." Mattie shook her head. "It makes me nervous, just having her back. Even though Cal's married. I'm not even going to mention that she's in town again."

Mattie reported two days later that Crystal was living with another woman, her own boy and a little girl at 114 Dock Street. That meant she had no money. Mattie also reported she was working for Johnny Lynch. Was David consorting with the enemy? To what degree? What was Crystal to him? Probably he knew her from school.

Crystal Sinclair. Now she had a name. Judith sat in her office, a little ashamed of herself for her curiosity. But David had withdrawn from her. Even when she was with him at his place she had the sense of something working against her, besides his squeamishness about the unconventionality of their arrangement. Someone perhaps; perhaps Crystal Sinclair. She had felt a kind of shadow between them that had not been there.

Gordon asked what was troubling her, and she told him, briefly, trying to downplay her anxieties. She disliked keeping anything from him, but she did not want to burden him with her worries. He frowned. "Is she pretty?"

"I have no idea. She's younger than me, of course."

"It seemed to me, the way he looked at you, the way he acted, that he was deeply involved." Gordon muttered something she did not catch. Then he said, "You'll have to fight back."

"Perhaps. How many battles can we fight at one time?" Dr. Barrows had told her there would be no more operations. He could see no point to removing more of Gordon's lungs. "We should make him as comfortable as we can," he said. It sounded like a death sentence. She was sleeping badly again. Gordon was weaker. He was on painkillers, a system that released what he needed when he felt he needed help.

"But couldn't he become addicted?" she asked Dr. Barrows.

"That isn't really a problem at this point."

She sometimes felt as if Gordon were headed out to sea in a kayak, alone, paddling into the distance. He had drawn into himself more than at any time since they had been together. All his attachments seemed at a remove from his passionate concern with his body and his illness. If only David had been willing to run, that would have helped, for the only thing that had seemed to absorb Gordon was the possibility of defeating Johnny Lynch and finally ousting him from power, from control of the town. That snagged his attention, that roused his passion and his remaining energy. Sometimes she had thought that hope was keeping him alive. Johnny Lynch and Gordon had squared off against each other years ago. Gordon was convinced Johnny had been behind the great pot raid on his compound, that he had used his influence to cause trouble. He was also convinced Johnny had pushed through building codes specifically to prevent him from playing with his building projects. Johnny,

Gordon said, had always been sick with jealousy of him, what he imagined as his scads of women, the pleasure and the celebrity he enjoyed. With Judith, it was a purely political animosity; but Johnny had brought the authorities down on Gordon's head, costing him thousands in legal expenses.

She was fighting a child custody case for a lesbian jewelry shop owner. It was being pushed hard by the father and his Boston lawyer. By this time he honestly hated his divorced wife and her new lover. There would be no compromise. Barbara had sent the woman to her.

She found herself sitting in her office brooding about David, lying awake at night thinking of him. She missed him. It was unfortunate that she had fallen in love with him. Had she fooled herself about his feelings? Or was the problem the woman he kept being seen with? Was he in love with Crystal? Perhaps she should simply forget him. Or had he withdrawn from her because he was ashamed of backing out of the election? If only he would open up and talk.

Barbara and she often had lunch together when they were both in court, even when they were on opposite sides of a case. They discussed forming a partnership in a few years when Barbara was ready to leave the district attorney's office. The major pull keeping her there was the hope that her boss would be appointed a judge in the next year or two and she would then run for his office. Barbara would like to be the district attorney.

Judith told Barbara about what was happening with David, or not happening. She repeated what she had learned of the woman who had come to Saltash when she was a little girl, who had lived in Arizona and in Seattle. And Nevada. Mattie knew Marie, who worked for Johnny Lynch; Marie told her that Crystal had gone to college in Las Vegas. A wandering woman looking for a better life? A better man?

Gordon was eating less and less. Occasionally he still had a good day. He rallied when old friends visited or when his children came home, particularly Natasha. "I'll be interning on Sanibel Island, where there's a facility that treats wild birds and animals. I'm excited about it. I was lucky to be accepted." Natasha arrived with an injured crow. He was moved into the shed that was an aviary, with a screened enclosure on the side.

"Can you be here for the summer?"

"I'll stay for June. Then I have to report to Sanibel. It's near Fort Myers. I can fly back, if it's necessary."

Neither of them said aloud why it would be necessary. Judith began to feel an invisible guest at every meal, the Angel of Death.

"Natasha, do you think I made a mistake getting involved with David Greene? Did I see more in him than there is?"

Natasha shrugged. "You know him better than I do. I was surprised by your choosing him. I supposed you'd find an intellectual."

"No one I found could ever compete with your father. But I thought he was a good, solid, kind man. I sensed that he wanted to learn things, to grow. And he's a Jew. I feel more comfortable being involved with a Jewish man. It's one less problem. Besides, he has great physical presence. I guess I like that. And he loves the Cape."

"Good physical presence." Natasha grinned slyly. "In other words, he's a hunk."

"Not that, exactly. He's comfortable in his body. He doesn't sit in a little cab up on the top of the machine." She did not tell Natasha that after several years of nursing Gordon, health itself was a treasure to her, strength and health moved her in and of themselves. "I thought he was as serious about me as I am about him. Now I have doubts."

"Maybe he figures he can have a girl on the side, since you're married to Gordon."

"That may be. But I'd feel much better if I didn't sense him withdrawing. And I'd feel much better if he was talking to me about it. He's never mentioned her. Not once."

"Maybe he's scared to. You know, Daddy had affairs when I was growing up. It wasn't a secret."

"But I never have, until David. Now I feel vulnerable."

"Gordon loves you. I love you. If David doesn't, he's an idiot."

Barbara summoned her for a special breakfast together. "I have information on your friend's friend. You're not going to like this."

When Judith returned to her office at ten, she started a file labeled GLASS and encoded it for herself only. Crystal Sinclair had left no record in Arizona except for her driver's license. After six years in the Seattle area, she had gotten in trouble for bad checks but had made restitution and the case was dropped. She next turned up in Vegas. She appeared in police records because a friend, a prostitute, had reported that Crystal had trashed her apartment and threatened her with a scissors. Apparently Crystal accused the woman of interfering between her and her boyfriend. According to the police report, they had been drinking together when the fight broke out, and Crystal, the other woman alleged, had gone crazy. The case dragged on for a year with many delays. Finally the woman disappeared, Crystal pleaded no contest and began to attend alcohol rehab meetings. Apparently the next year she left Las Vegas.

So that was Crystal Sinclair, David's new friend. Judith did not think David naive enough to have become seriously involved with her. Probably he knew her from school and felt sorry for her. She had had a hard life, obviously, and it could not have been easy for her son. Johnny Lynch had protected her father, the addicted dentist, so perhaps he viewed the daughter as owing him, or as under his protection also. She did not intend to tell David what she had learned. It would be unethical, as well as exposing Barbara. Moreover, if he had slept with the woman, she would come off as jealous. But the woman was trouble. She would keep that history in mind.

DAVID

I'd heard a couple of stories about fistfights, shouting, the time Slow Boat Richardson pissed on a candidate's literature. I'd put it off every day this week, but this much I knew: you could call them, write them, post signs in their faces, get your name in the papers and promise the world, but if you didn't have the nerve to greet people face-to-face in the Saltash post office parking lot and ask them for their vote, you were not going to get it.

Saturday, I got there earlier than the postmaster and sat in my front seat with a stack of six-by-eight cards, my picture on one side, on the other every endorsement for my good character I could come up with. The first to pull up was the Corn Man. White hair in a ponytail, red suspenders. Every August the land surrounding his small gray house, front and side yards, every arable inch down to the road, was crowded with stalks of butter and sugar corn.

When he stepped out of his car, I waved. He looked away. I took a step toward him. He jogged to his left. I stopped in front of him with my hand out. He gave up and waited.

"Good morning." I pushed my literature against his tightly closed fist. "My name is David Greene. I'm running for selectman."

He looked from the picture on the card to me and back to the picture. I was indeed the asshole I said I was. Now what?

"If you have any questions you'd like to ask?"

"No, no." He gazed longingly over my shoulder at the post office door.

"Well, sir, I hope I can count on your vote."

"Yes, yes," he said, brushing past my shoulder and deftly pitching my card in the trash.

As the sun rose and the wet surface of the parking lot shrank to a small dark puddle, I pressed myself on the Passionate Plumber who wore the zipper of his coveralls open to his navel and doused himself in Old Spice; to my ex–sixth-grade teacher, who proofread my literature; an electrician Holly dated in high school; the chief of police; a couple who tried to sell me a water filtration system; and a man who warned me away with open palms, his wrists and arms slathered pink. "Poison ivy! Poison ivy!" he said, slipping past me like a leper into a dark Calcutta alley.

As afraid as I had been, each person was more afraid of me. What did I want from them? Time? Money? What if they snubbed me and I actually went on to win? "Hi, I'm David Greene. I'm running for selectman. Could I ask you for your vote?"

He was bald and stout and wore brown rubber waders up to his chest, which made me think of something half dipped in chocolate. "You want my vote?" He folded his arms. "Where do you stand on the dike?"

"Out of the wind, so I don't fall in."

"So you don't fall in?" His face brightened like a newly polished coin. "I like that." He slapped my shoulder. "So you don't fall in."

"Hi, I'm David Greene. I'm running for selectman."

She was maybe twenty-five, long black hair, sweater tight across her breasts, with a four-year-old trailing behind. She took my card and asked, squinting into the sun, "You the guy who told Donkey Sparks about those guys getting drunk on the job?"

I said proudly, "That was me, yeah."

"You son of a bitch." She ripped my card in pieces and threw it at me. "My boyfriend could have lost his job."

When Blossom End-Rot drove up to get her mail, her face turned the color of boiled meat. "Well. David Greene." She choked on a smile. "I didn't realize you were mounting such a campaign?"

"You never know what to expect from us pushy immigrant types." I left her to approach another voter. "My name's David Greene . . ."

She wanted desperately to see my literature but couldn't bring herself to ask. As soon as she thought I was distracted, she ripped a card from the hand of someone she knew and studied it front and back. She lifted her eyes to the hip boot man, walking to the car with his mail. "Ask him where he stands on the dike!" he said, waving me a victory sign. "God knows we need somebody with a sense of humor in there."

Could I win? I doubted it but it sure felt good to ruin Blossom's day. Of all the cars that pulled up, however, the one I was waiting for did not: Judith's black Jeep Cherokee. I didn't want to *tell* her I was running. I'd already done that and backed out. I wanted her to see me in action. When I left the post office just after noon, I drove by her office. Closed. I headed for Mary's Tea Room. Judith sat at a rear table reading, her back to the door.

"Hi, my name is David Greene. I'm running for selectman." I handed her a card.

"Where have you been?" I didn't know what I was seeing in her expression. Skepticism? Annoyance? Maybe just my own guilt.

"Incredibly busy. It's the big season for landscapers." I sat down. "How's Gordon?"

She shrugged, not wanting to get into a discussion about cancer. "Do you think he'd still be willing to help?"

"You'll have to ask him."

"Would you still be willing to help?"

"Do you really want this?" Her eyes grew darker, somehow more serious, and I wondered if we were talking about the same thing.

She was wearing a blue silk blouse with long French cuffs and a wide collar, through which I imagined the delicate lacework of her underclothes. "Yes, I do very much," I said.

"I'm talking about *this*." She fanned my card in front of my eyes.

"Do I actually want to be a selectman? I won't know until I win. Do I want to make trouble for Johnny Lynch? Big time, I do. Don't you think that'd be fun?"

The meeting took place the next afternoon at Judith and Gordon's. Along with the *alter kockers* for lynching Johnny, they had rounded up twenty people. There was a table of sandwiches and drinks, and street lists with voters' names. This was serious politics, Saltash style.

Gordon set the tone. "No offense to the candidate," although he looked at me as if I was a sorry excuse for one, "but I want to make it clear we're here for one reason. To put the last nail in Johnny Lynch's coffin."

The drinking started just after dark. The tide was low, the beer was cold, and no one seemed in a rush to get home. I milled around the room attempting to ingratiate myself, until Judith motioned me into the kitchen.

She said quietly, "Say goodbye to everyone personally." This struck me as a sensible idea. "Then leave through the side door."

"Now?"

"Now." Her hand grazed mine. "And meet me in my studio around back."

She joined me half an hour later with a satisfied smile. She drew the curtains and stoked the stove, and just when I thought I knew what she was thinking, took a seat in a rocking chair facing me.

From the house we heard singing. "I missed you," she said. "I've been busy. So have you."

"I'm here now."

"Yes, you are. Yes, you are." She took my face in her hands and outlined my lips with her tongue. She was tentative. Do you still want me? her fingers seemed to ask. Temples and earlobes, biceps and belly. My body was a new land she was mapping. When we began, it was cool in the cottage, the little stove working against the evening chill. We dove beneath the covers and clung together, shivering until our bodies warmed to the boiling point and we came up to cool off and breathe.

Judith took a deep breath. Outside, it began to rain and droplets fell from the eaves, drub, drub, drub, to the wooden porch. An offshore buoy clanged in the early spring wind. She lay in my arms playing with my nipple. She sighed, "I missed you so much."

When the phone rang, Judith sprang from the bed. Upon answering, she looked at the receiver incredulously. "It's for you. It's a child."

The phone sat on her desk, plugged into a jack along with the modem, among law books and journals and briefs in towering piles. I crossed the room, naked, to answer it while Judith took my place under the covers. It was Laramie. "My mom said it was okay to call you."

"It is, Laramie. Sure. What can I do for you?"

Judith mouthed, "Who is Laramie?"

"Um. She wondered if you could pick me up from school on Thursday because she has an—" From somewhere behind him I heard Crystal say, "an interview." "—an interview about college."

"Thursday I can't, Laramie. I'm sorry."

"David?" Judith said, but I looked away from her when I heard the boy say, "Oh," like a small puncture in a lifeboat, and I felt him going under.

"But listen, man, we'll get together soon."

He sighed and I heard traces of a whispered discussion. "Uh, my mom says you should call her, okay?"

"Sure. That'll be fine."

"Thanks. 'Bye," he said, and hung up.

Judith watched me return to bed. "Who's Laramie?"

"He's a little boy I know. My sister's crazy about him."

"He sounds very sad."

"He doesn't have any friends. A new kid in town. You know how it is."

The bed was warm and the sheets smelled of perfume and sweat. I wanted the conversation over and done, but Judith was still curious. "You never mentioned him," she said.

"I just met him pretty recently."

"Pretty fast friendship. His parents approve?"

"Approve of what?"

"Don't be naive. It's not easy for adults to be friends with kids these days. You have to be careful. A lot of charges are thrown, a lot of things imagined. I think twice before I befriend a kid. Parents can be suspicious."

"His parents are split up. His mother's all for it. Okay?"

"That's all I wanted to hear," Judith said. She pushed her hair back and frowned at the far wall, looking past me. "Do you know her well?"

"What is this? Do you want to say what the hell it is you're thinking?"

"All of a sudden there's a child who calls you at my house, a little boy whose name you never mentioned. Naturally I'm surprised."

"That's because you don't have children in your life, Judith. You're not used to them."

"Tell me I'm off here, David. But that sounds like an accusation."

"It's not an accusation. There are just things you can't understand."

"David, I don't want to be mean, but I spent far more time raising Natasha than you did your own son. This sounds like you're trying to create a surrogate son for yourself, all of a sudden."

I had to remind myself where I was. In Judith's shack, with a little fire in the stove casting shadows on the walls. In bed, naked, with a woman I was about to make love to. I could still taste the coffee on Judith's mouth. How had this happened?

"Judith, let's start over again. One. He's a kid I feel sorry for. Two. His mother is cool about the whole thing. Three. I did not mean to imply that because you don't have children you don't know anything about . . . about how weird this world is around kids. I'm sorry. Please accept my apology."

As I drew her against me, she turned. I loved the tight and delicate curve of her back, her small sickle-shaped breasts in the crook of my forearms, my sex thrust between her buttocks. But I could feel a taut coil of resistance inside her. I wasn't surprised when she said to the wall, "Who is his mother, David?"

"Somebody I met."

"Obviously." Judith disentangled herself. When her back was flush against the wall behind the bed, when she had covered herself, she dropped her hands in her lap and stared at them. "She has a name."

"Her name is Crystal."

"And you sleep with Crystal."

"Yes. Like you sleep with Gordon." Even as it left my lips, the comparison felt crude. Gordon was a shell of a lover and had been before I met Judith.

"I understand your justification, David." I had heard her use this tone with workmen who failed to live up to their contracts.

"I don't have to justify myself. It doesn't mean anything. It's casual."

"She called my house," Judith said rising. "She knew you were here. Did you give her the number? It's not listed."

"Holly must have given her the number."

"She's a friend of your sister's." Judith nodded as if chipping away at the truth. Everything I said seemed to make it worse. "A single woman with a child. Of all the stupid people to pick."

"What's better, then? A married woman? A young student? A widow? Who? Do you want to set me parameters, Judith? Give me a list?"

Her face seemed to melt. Her lips trembled and when she finally spoke she sounded helpless. "Why did you do it?"

"Because I've never been involved in anything like what we're doing."

"We're just loving each other, David."

"Fifty yards away from where we're sitting, your husband is entertaining friends. And you're in bed with me. Is that any better or worse than a few lonely nights with some secretary who just moved to town? I love you as much as I ever did. I admit I made a mistake. We'll come back from it."

"I hope so, David. But if she thought the relationship was so casual, she wouldn't have tracked you down and called here."

"She didn't call, her kid did."

As she got out of bed, Judith said mockingly, "Right. As if we both believe that."

"Aren't we going to make love?"

"Do you have a condom?"

"What for? We haven't used a condom since the first time."

"Then get used to it, David. You're screwing two women now. That changes things."

DAVID

Some afternoons, between the time school let out and Crystal got off work, Laramie took the school bus to the nursery. It was Holly's idea. She always had a job for him, watering seedlings, bagging wild bird food mix. He could work methodically for hours, seeming to absorb silence the way plants thrived in humidity. Watching him bag one-pound packages of thistle seed—not one-point-one pounds or point-ninety-nine—was like observing a chemist measure acid into a test tube. Holly paid him two dollars an hour. After work he and I drove around town putting up my election signs. Laramie held the wooden stakes in place as I pounded them into the ground.

I knew early on I hadn't the experience or the organization or the base of support; that all I could really hope to do was to raise some questions, kick up a little dirt. But I was a trained competitor. Although speeches and land use policies were a far cry from lobbing baseballs, I couldn't help playing to win. I'd ordered a hundred signs and put up eighty. Like a rancher in his pickup cruising his spread, I was up every morning before sunrise to check on my signs. Once, I'd dreamed of headlining the sports pages, but it was oddly satisfying to see the solitary squares proclaiming my name in block letters, black and white against the wet grass like Holstein cattle. One morning on my patrol, however, three of my signs were missing. Ten of Blossom End-Rot's had sprung up overnight. I replaced the three. That afternoon, with Laramie's help, I pounded in ten more. The following morning twenty more of hers appeared. Four of mine were down. Blossom had six nephews, but I was obsessed. At work that morning I called in an order for fifty more signs.

"What do you think you're doing?" Holly said.

"I can't let them get away with this."

"People already know you're running, David. They're not more likely to vote for you because you fill the roadsides with cardboard."

"Is there a problem, Holly? Let's have it."

"No, there's no problem. You know I want you to win this thing."

"Do you?"

"If that's what you want, but . . ." Here it was. The reason she was not at candidates' night, and why I saw her scowling while I was cutting scrap wood for sign posts. "It can't be good for this business, David.

We've worked so hard to build it up. You know how crazy people in this town are about politics." Our own father, after seeing a Nixon's the One sign on the lawn of a local farm stand, never bought apples there again. "People hold grudges. If you win, they're going to hate you for some stupid decision you'll have to make. Even if you lose, you ran against someone's candidate."

"But you're not talking about people in this town, are you? You're talking about Johnny Lynch."

"He's an old friend of the family, David."

"You think Dad thought so?"

"I think Dad would have been happy to know his wife was taken care of."

"For fuck sake, Holly, that's how half the town thinks. He gives everyone a little piece of something and keeps the rest for himself. Everyone's so damned afraid of losing their little piece."

"Johnny owns the house Mother lives in."

"Our old house?"

"You were away, David. You were having your own problems in Florida. Daddy couldn't pay the mortgage. Johnny bought it, the way he likes to pick up property. He's let mother live there for years for a nominal rent." Holly looked at me with something like pity.

"She never told me."

"Did you ever ask?"

Late one afternoon I met Judith in her office for a quick update on the campaign that turned into drinks as the sun went down and an invitation to the island for dinner. The kitchen smelled of chicken and garlic. Gordon was sitting near the fireplace with a red wool blanket wrapped around him and a glass of scotch in his big hand. "She'll have it all together in half an hour. Now tell me how the campaign is going."

"Well, as I was putting gas in my truck today, who should pull up?"

Judith ran in from the kitchen. "Blossom End-Rot?"

"Go on," Gordon said.

"Did you see the picture in her ad?" Judith perched on the arm of Gordon's couch. "The meanest teacher you ever had."

"Judith, let him tell the story." Gordon settled back.

"She didn't say hello," I said. "She could barely return my smile. She stuck a newspaper article in my face about some proposed antiprofanity bylaw."

"I never heard of it." Gordon asked Judith, "Have you?"

"Neither had I," the chair screeched as I leapt to my feet. "But once

I knew she was for it, I felt the need to oppose it, to draw crowds, to orate, to reorient people's hearts and minds so that we will always and forever have the right to call each other assholes in public."

"He's got the fever," Gordon said. "Blossom's your only real competitor. The professional widow."

"He was a war hero, right?" Blossom invoked his name regularly, and right in the middle of town, on High Street by the Town Hall, was Lieutenant Phillip Endicott Square. Every Memorial Day a wreath was laid against the street sign.

"He was a local boy who went off to Korea. He came home on furlough looking for a good time, and he got hitched to Blossom instead." Gordon shook his head. "In Korea, he lasted two months."

"It's always been my opinion," Judith said, "that she's far happier as a widow than she ever would have been married to Phil Endicott, who liked his bottle and his feet up, or so Mattie tells me. It was a mismatch. She's the matriarch of her clan in spite of not having children. She gives money, advice, whatever, to her eleven nephews and nieces, and she plays them off against each other. The heroic status of her dead husband—and remember, they were only together for two weeks—has grown with every passing year."

"Her signs are everywhere," I said. "They're green and red to my plain little black and white ones. They're wider than mine. I measured. And longer by six inches. I'm developing a case of sign envy."

Gordon liked my joke. But his laughter caused him to cough hard. Throughout dinner he seemed distracted by pain. He would suddenly drop his hands to the table, eyes alert but otherwise motionless, as if listening to something inside himself. Three or four times Judith suggested he lie down, but despite his obvious fatigue, he refused.

I told them what I'd learned from Holly.

Gordon sat back in his chair, his eyes half closed. "He plays fast and loose and he plays hard. If he can't get what he wants one way, he tries another. Remember the Town Hall fire?"

"Sort of. I was in high school. Wasn't it some kind of accident?"

"That's what the fire chief said. But you always have to ask yourself, who won, who lost, who benefited most? All the records were burned. All the titles, all the deeds. All the town correspondence."

"Are you saying he did it?"

"Funny thing. Johnny was under investigation at the time. All the records the state probers wanted were lost."

"What was he being investigated for?"

"Conflict of interest. Obtaining state grants for the town to build roads through land he owned, to dredge the harbor for a fancy new marina built by his friends. The very site selected belonged to his wife. Sweet woman. Spent the better part of every year in a mental hospital." Gordon seemed to drift off into the past. He was silent for several minutes. "Saltash might have had thousands more acres of protected land if it wasn't for old Johnny. Powerful man. His connections ran high up. You didn't fuck with him. He could be very good to you or come down hard. Two sides of the same coin . . ." His voice trailed off.

"How is he?" I asked Judith when Gordon finally went to bed.

"I'm worried," she said.

"For a while he seemed so lively."

"He's getting a lot of pleasure out of your campaign. He's having fun."

"Isn't that odd? Why does this backward little place mean anything to a man as successful as Gordon?"

"Gordon knows that small places are just as real as large ones. Since he's 'succeeded,' as you call it, on a grand scale, he knows what's at stake here: the well-being of the land, the local economy. He has high hopes for you, David. He thinks you're bright. He told me you have a sharp instinctive intelligence."

"That's a very kind thing to say."

She smiled. "Kind? It's something that his graduate students would have killed to hear."

We finished the dishes together quietly. Before things had changed, I would have taken my sweater off, made myself comfortable. Now I felt like a guest. "I forgot to ask about the tide," I said when we finished.

Judith cocked her head, as if to consider an interesting ploy. "Are you asking if you have to stay or if you can?"

"I'd like to."

"Good." She kissed my nose. "What's wrong?"

"Why do you put up with me and her?" I asked.

"You and Crystal? Is she very much on your mind?"

"No," I said quickly. Unless I was in bed with her, no. Even when sex was over, when she'd offered me something I'd never dared ask a woman to do, we lay side by side without a thing to connect us except what we'd just done. So we did it again.

"How well do you really know her, David?"

"Why? Do you think she's hiding something?"

"Most people are, David. Some more than others."

One afternoon, when business was slow and the back lot was alive with insects and wildflowers, I asked Laramie if he wanted to play catch. He was sweeping up the stock room in his quiet, meticulous way, seeming content, but I felt like a sweatshop foreman keeping children from the light. "I thought you liked baseball?"

As if annoyed with the interruption, he continued sweeping. "I don't have a baseball glove."

"Use mine."

"Too big," he said.

"Well, you're going to get one soon, right? For your birthday. Your dad's sending it."

"No, he's not. He never sends me anything."

"He sent you a tape deck last year. I saw it."

"My mom got it."

"That's not what she told me."

"Yeah, she did. Her handwriting was on the box."

"Maybe he sent it to her and she rewrapped it."

Laramie swept the dirt into a perfect conical pile. "She says my dad sends presents, but she does it. 'Cause she wants me to think he loves me."

Most nights, after Crystal left work, she had both kids to care for. She did the shopping and all her other errands, the laundry, gave the kids supper, cleaned up afterwards, supervised their homework and put them to bed. Two nights a week she came straight from work to my house with clothes for the next day. She loved those nights, she told me. She loved having supper on the table in my house with its shabby furniture and cold drafts, because, she said, "I feel like somebody wants us."

That night, as she usually did, she threw the door back and spread her arms wide. "Where's my guys?" I had brought Laramie home with me from the nursery.

She gathered Laramie up in the folds of her coat and kissed his sallow face until he squirmed and turned pink. Me she dragged behind the closet door and shot her tongue into my mouth murmuring, "Thank you, thank you, thank you, for saving my life." Then the kid and I settled down with her at the kitchen table.

"This is great," she said. "What is it?"

"Obviously not too good if you can't tell."

"Beef stew! We made it," Laramie said.

"You two made this? No sir. I don't believe it. It's takeout from a fancy restaurant."

Laramie's laughter was as pure as water splashing on a ledge of slate.

"I really do not believe you made this," she said to me with a wink. "Is there something you want?" Then, sotto voce, "Because I think you're going to get it."

Laramie studied his mother, not quite understanding the sudden huskiness in her voice, the tip of tongue brushing her upper lip, but trying to.

"So what'd you do in school today?" she asked him.

"I don't know. Nothin'."

"And you, Daddy? Nothin'? You guys." She shook her head. "Well, I have good news."

Because she said it quickly, because it blew across the table and was gone, we continued our conversation. Although I played at being Daddy two nights a week; although I was often mistaken for Laramie's father by shopkeepers and placed in that role by school officials beside themselves in the presence of a man of appropriate age, a working man, taking an interest in a child, I was not Laramie's father. In his presence I watched the years I'd lost with my own boy and imagined taking Laramie down to Florida with me the next time I went to see Terry. I cared a lot for Laramie. In my way, I loved him. But every time Crystal cast me as Daddy—and I believe she did it when I wasn't around—she created expectations that could only break his heart.

"There's a party after work on Friday. For Mr. Lynch's birthday. I know. I know." Crystal deepened her voice. "He's the evil Darth Vader. But he asked you especially to come."

"Well, send my regrets."

"Can't you put politics aside? He's been very nice to me, David. He may give me a recommendation to law school."

"Johnny Lynch can be very nice when he wants something."

"Maybe you'll meet some new people. Isn't that what politicians are supposed to do? Show up and mingle?"

"I doubt anyone in his own office would vote against his candidate."

Her voice became liquid sugar. "That's not what the girls say. They've seen you in the parking lot, David. They think you're adorable."

"I'm sorry. I can't make it on Friday."

"No, of course not, that's not my day, is it? It's Judith's."

I looked at the clock, the wall, anything but the little family I could only seem to disappoint. Crystal took a second helping of stew and wiped the gravy up with stale bread. Laramie's eyes moved from one of us to the other. He barely seemed to breathe.

I was in bed pretending sleep when Crystal crept under the covers and kissed my nose. "I want you to know you're the sweetest, most wonderful boyfriend I've ever had."

"Except that I see another woman."

"That does hurt me. But I know you care about me. We have plans together. For me to go to law school. That's what you, and only you, convinced me I could do. And I believed you. I believe in myself because of you." Crystal turned on the beside lamp. She was wearing a black nylon nightgown. Crystal complained about putting on weight since she'd moved East, but if she had, it only made her breasts bigger and more attractive to me. I had no particular reaction to the small roll of flesh that swelled over her skirt waistband. Her face was round and luscious. "Look, David, you don't know where I came from. My ex didn't want Laramie. When I told him I was pregnant, he—" She stopped abruptly.

"He what?"

"He got very angry. I thought I would lose the baby."

"You never told me."

"It's behind me now, and you're the best thing that ever happened to me."

"You can't mean that."

"At least I have you three nights a week. I know where I can call you if I need you. Liam used to go off for weeks at a time. If the baby got sick, I was on my own. Sometimes he'd have wads of money, stacks of bills. But not for me."

"From what?" Dealing drugs? Gambling? Where did a guy get stacks of bills?

"I didn't ask questions. But then it would be gone as fast as it came." She yawned heavily. "You're great, David, for me and for Laramie."

"Compared to Liam."

"Compared to anyone." She yawned again. "We better do it before I fall asleep."

"We don't have to *do it*. Not if you're tired."

"But you want to, don't you?"

"You were up at five this morning. You got two kids off to school, worked a full day and then did the laundry. We can skip a night."

"You really are the best man in the world." She set the alarm and kissed me. "I'll make it up to you."

"You don't have to."

"Yes, I do." She curled into the crook of my arm and fell asleep within seconds.

The alarm rang in what seemed the middle of the night. Crystal ran off to the bathroom. I was still fumbling with the clock when she returned. "We don't have to get up for another hour."

"But you're seeing her today," Crystal said.

"So what?" The room was cold. A sharp light knifed into the room from the hallway we kept lit for Laramie. I smelled perfume and toothpaste as she crept beneath the sheets. "You want to make love? Now?"

"I want to fuck you dry."

I struggled to get to the toilet but she pushed my shoulders back. "You have to piss, don't you?" She squeezed my balls. "You feel like you're going to burst." She knew men's bodies, the pressure of necessity and desire.

"Just stay here," she said, and began licking me, feathering my cock, lips and tongue, drawing the edge of her teeth across the shaft, giving me pleasure to the point of pain. "I'm going to come," I said, at which she tugged my balls and swallowed me down the tunnel of her throat. She threw her leg over my head and buried my face in her crotch. Smelling of piss and sex, night sweat and traces of perfume, she ground herself to the beat of a primal tune. Feeling me shudder, she scuttled off and presented her ass. "Shove it in deep," she said. I fell into her, quivering. I melted. I ran my palms up her thighs, the plane of her back, her nipples, her throat. Her mouth. She bit my fingers and we collapsed, liquid and skin, into the twisted sheets. "Do you want to do it again?" she said.

"Are you crazy?" I was gasping. Breath and strength had left my body. "Do you?"

Her face half in darkness, half light, her voice cool in spite of the sweat that glistened on her breasts and upper lip, she said: "I can't send you to her with anything left."

JOHNNY

28

Through his office window Johnny watched Crystal running out to her car in the rain—a bit of thigh showing as the wind lifted her skirt—settling herself in the driver's seat, fixing her hair in the rearview mirror. He found himself smiling. Women were all the same. As if she wouldn't have to leave the car in the same pouring rain and get mussed up before anyone saw her. He heard her try the engine, try it again and again until the starter motor screeched and she banged the steering wheel with her fist. As she struggled to open the hood, he ran out with his umbrella, blown inside out by the northeast wind. "Come inside! Come inside now!" he shouted.

Crystal hadn't heard him and jumped, startled, when he appeared behind her. "It won't start!"

"Go back inside and we'll call the garage."

"They won't come in a storm like this."

"They will if I call them. Now get under this umbrella." She resisted his grip but gave up and followed him inside. "That's all I need," he said, "you getting sick and nobody knowing how to work the damned computers."

"I have to pick up my son." She shook out her hair.

Johnny was on the phone with the garage. Whatever idiot they'd left in the office had no idea to whom he was speaking. Johnny gave him the address and hoped for the best. "Now sit down next to the radiator and dry off. The office is closed for the day. Relax."

Crystal seemed uneasy, but no more than he was, he supposed. He hadn't spent ten minutes alone with her since the day of the interview. He didn't want to be caught staring, an old man at a pretty girl. But he could enjoy a glimpse of her profile, the little turned-up nose, the lovely shadow of her earrings against her cheek. As her clothing dried, he smelled roses, probably her perfume. "Let's get you something warming to drink. Would you like that? Would you like a scotch?"

"Oh, no," she said, as if frightened. "I can't drink!"

"Tea then. I suppose I can still boil water." As Johnny lumbered around the staff kitchenette, he saw her watching the window. "We'll give the tow truck the time it takes to drink a cup of tea. If they don't show up, I'll give you a ride."

"You're very nice," she said. "Thank you. Every time it rains, my damned old car gives me trouble."

"It's hard, isn't it? My mother worked all her life," Johnny said. "But people had their families around in those days, cousins, grandmothers."

"I get help sometimes," she said. "I have a roommate."

A roommate. She was raising a child, for Christ's sake, and she lived like a stewardess. "And the boy's father?" He set down the cups and searched for the sugar, asking absently, "He doesn't live in the area?"

"Wouldn't much matter if he did," Crystal said, more amused than angry. "Liam might have been a good father, if he had ever grown up himself."

"I see that all too often, I have to say."

"But you would have liked him," she said. "He was born in Ireland."

"Where? Do you know?"

"Dublin. He had an Irish music band. They were really good. We traveled all up and down the coast in a Volkswagen bus. Going to a different coffeehouse every night and just getting by, making friends everywhere we stopped." He heard a wistful, almost songlike quality in her voice, like his own when he was reading to children. "Once in Lake Tahoe we got arrested for camping, and Liam took out his fiddle and got us off."

"Sounds like a charmer."

"Oh, you don't know the half. He sure got everything he wanted from me."

"But not a baby."

"How'd you guess? Once Laramie was born, Liam had to choose between his music and his family."

"But your boyfriend, dear, if you can bear the questions of a nosy old romantic, is there no chance of wedding bells? I see how David looks at you."

She responded with a self-mocking scowl. "Except I'm not the only one he's looking at."

Johnny expected her to turn away again, to bolt, having offered too much of herself. But she sat quietly, staring into her cup. Johnny sighed. "Two paths in a yellow wood. If he's a good man, he'll know which one to take."

"But he is," she insisted. "She just puts ideas in his head." Everyone in this office knew who *she* was.

"Dear, I've fought Judith Silver for a decade." He felt Crystal's attention. "She's the worst kind of adversary. She fights on moral grounds, tries to persuade you you're acting out of selfish motives, when she and her husband are the most corrupt couple this town has ever seen. The drug parties, the sexual display . . . Gordon Stone has an FBI file as thick as a volume of the encyclopedia. It's not hard to imagine a good man getting mixed up with her. We men are all weak. A woman like that comes along and tells us what we want to hear."

"I think it's the election," Crystal said. "He didn't know her before she asked him to run."

"Didn't he?" This was interesting. Johnny hadn't realized they'd actually recruited the boy. He'd thought David one of the pretty young people they were said to share, to pass between them in bed. But this made perfect sense. David Greene. Local hero. Angry young man. Out of town for almost fifteen years. No political history. A clean slate. He had underestimated Gordon. However slow on the uptake and soft-spoken, David was an excellent choice, far better than his own old witch. He was sorry he hadn't gotten to him first. "You see, they simply have no values, these people. David is a man who was trying to do the right thing by a woman and a child, and they lure him away from his family. I bet you don't see enough of him, do you?"

"Two nights a week. David says after the election he'll have more time."

Johnny saw the tow truck circling the parking lot. He had to work fast. "Not if he wins, believe me. Meetings every night, calls about everything from where a yellow line gets painted down Main Street to who gets to be fire chief. You see, people like Gordon and Judith could never get elected themselves . . ."

The tow truck sounded its horn. But Crystal didn't move. "Look at that," he said. "One beaten up Olds with its hood unlatched, one brand-new Ford, and the idiot can't tell which needs help. Hold on, dear." He ran outside to instruct the driver and at the same time take care of the bill.

Back inside, he continued, "Gordon Stone and his people have been waiting for a puppet for years. Once they attach their strings, they own him. Believe me, as much as he might want to, he won't have time for a family. God bless my dear wife, she would tell you I didn't."

"But David doesn't think he has a chance to win."

"That's not what I hear. People like him. The fishermen go for their man, the environmentalists for theirs. It splits the vote. I think he stands a hell of a chance. Come. Get your coat. Looks like our genius out there has your car started. What's the matter, dear?"

"Nothing. I just . . . I was hoping . . . If David heard me say this he'd kill me. I was hoping he'd lose and the thing with her would be over."

Johnny led her to the door, his hand on her shoulder. "If hope is all we've got, we haven't got much, have we?" He opened the umbrella to the rain and urged her close. She leaned into him; she didn't resist. "But if we had something that might help people see things differently, that might change the voter's mind, then . . ."

Crystal stopped in the middle of the parking lot. "Like what?"

"I have no idea, dear. You're the one who knows David. Just something that might tarnish that fresh-faced image for his own damned good. That might save him from falling permanently into the clutches of that woman. If he loses the election, he'll be of little further interest to that pair."

The following morning Crystal wrote him out a check, paying for the tow service. If anything, she seemed more reserved with him. Polite, always; efficient and helpful, but perhaps a little ashamed of what she had revealed. He couldn't blame her, and in truth he was probably lucky. He had crossed the barrier between boss and employee. He was a silly old man. He wouldn't make a fool of himself again.

At Friday noon, just after the other girls went to lunch, Crystal stepped into his office and closed the door firmly behind her. Approaching his desk, she said softly, "Mr. Lynch. I think I found something you can use." She reached into her purse.

JUDITH

Judith studied the flyer Blossom had put out, simple, vulgar and effective. The headline asked WHO BEST REPRESENTS THE PEOPLE OF SALTASH? One photo showed Birdman in a safari jacket peering through binoculars out to sea, gesturing to some unseen audience like a priggish private school science teacher. Ahab clung to the deck of a boat run aground on a sand bar, waving his arms wildly, red-nosed and demented. Judith remembered that little accident. Could happen to anybody, given the way the harbor bottom changed from season to season, but Blossom had come up with a photo. Next, Blossom with her sleeves rolled up collecting trash on Beach Improvement Day. Finally there was David—David and Gordon and herself. They were lying on a bed together, Gordon in his pajamas, his arms around David and her. A bottle of champagne stood on a bed tray as they all toasted Gordon's last birthday for the camera.

"Well, at least we look as if we're having a good time," Judith said mildly, handing the flyer back to David.

"How did they ever get hold of that picture? Natasha took it, right?"

"Of course. But she's at Cornell, and why would she give a copy to anyone? I suppose it could have been someone in the pharmacy, where the film was left. Or someone in Hyannis, where they send it to be developed. But why are you so agitated?"

Gordon was lying on the couch, eating from the coffee table, perhaps one bite to every ten of theirs. "It can't hurt you unless you act guilty."

"I don't know . . . It makes me out to be some kind of playboy."

"David, everybody sees how hard you work at landscaping and nursery." But in the car afterward with the two of them on their way to a small Shabbat service in the Universalist meeting house, Judith felt she could speak more bluntly. "What upsets you? Are you ashamed to be seen with me—in a photo or in person?"

"Of course not. I'm proud to be with you."

"We never go out together."

"Judith, where do I ever go?"

"I assume, wherever young couples with children go. To Little League games. To the movies. Out for pizza at Penia's."

"We were talking about the election."

"Yes, and you told Gordon you see the photo as an attack."

"I was talking about how Blossom got hold of it. I had a copy in my drawer—"

"Where Crystal won't see it?"

"It's not Crystal. I checked this morning, and it's still there. . . . But it makes me look like a drunken bum."

"We both know what the picture is supposed to say, or Gordon and I wouldn't be in it. So what? If there were two people in town who didn't know about us, they just learned. It seems you have two choices. Either you cut off the relationship—"

"I wouldn't do that!" His voice sounded almost panicked.

"Or you start acting proud. This town is too small to hide in. People know if you go skulking around. Believe it or not, I'm a respected person in this town, and so is Gordon."

"You're married."

"And you're my friend. Married ladies are allowed to have friends. I think you're the one who feels married, David. You act as if Crystal is real and I'm not. Because she has a child and you two play mommy and daddy go to market, mommy and daddy take their son to school. Unless you feel like an adulterer, why be ashamed?"

"I'm not ashamed of you. I never have been."

"Then act it. Gordon and I have a lot of friends. I think we can win this election—but not if you hold us back. I'm asking you to say, 'This is my life, take it or leave it.' You have to be willing to fight and you have to be willing to take the consequences."

Judith listened to herself as she lectured David. It was time to cool down. This was not the way to approach Shabbat. But she decided it was past time she took her own advice. Fight and take the consequences. Go public. Act proud.

When David addressed the Taxpayers Association in mid-week, Judith stood against a back wall with her arms folded, keeping her eyes on him, nodding when he made a good point. She had been practicing his delivery with him; his public speaking was improving. He was going door-to-door every evening, talking with a few families. His literature was being churned out, courtesy of the Greene Team, Judith Silver, Chair. She had written most of it.

Sunday at six she had a get-together for all the volunteers she had been able to line up, everyone from friends of Natasha to old clients, the "reform element," women who simply liked her. She laid out a spread in her office, chicken, vegetarian lasagna, snacks, beer and soda, food for thirty-two who had come out for David and for her. She got commitments from people to put bumper stickers on their cars and to stand on the highway Saturday mornings holding signs. She found a finance chair and two people who offered to drive older people to the polls. Judith was at David's elbow: she was the heart of his campaign now that both her crusades, to elect him and to keep him as her lover, were public. She had been told that Crystal clung to him when they went out, hung on his arm, called him Laramie's daddy. That would never be Judith's style. She simply claimed him publicly. She intended to prove herself essential. The Greene Team banner was draped on the outer wall of her office. If Johnny Lynch considered her the opposition, she would be right in his face. She wanted him to know that win or lose this election, she was not going to vanish. She wanted him thinking about her whenever he pulled something under cover of darkness; and she wanted to have the identical effect on Crystal.

DAVID

"Crystal, stop crying."

"Don't tell me what to do! I'm sick of being ordered around."

"I am not ordering you. I'm asking you to calm down so I can hear you." I assumed there'd be a price to pay for Judith's party. When Holly ran into the yard to tell me Crystal was on the telephone, so upset she could barely speak, I knew this was it. "Calm down, please. You're at work. You can't cry like this, you'll get in trouble with your boss."

"I'm in Mr. Lynch's office. He told me to use his phone. I'm in trouble. I'm being kicked out in the street with my kid. I'm going to be homeless."

"Stop right there. What's going on? Start from the beginning."

"It happened last night. I tried to call you. You weren't home."

Because of course I was with Judith and thirty-two of her loyal friends. Holly was watching me from the register, dying to lift the extension.

"When I got up this morning I found the telephone and electric bills on the kitchen table and a note from Michelle that said she wanted the money by tonight or we're out, me and Laramie. Where can we go?" Crystal was about to start crying again.

"So it's just finding the money?"

"No, she's crazy. You don't understand. The money is an excuse. She wants me out. Everything I do is wrong. She likes it well enough when I take care of her kid. And I take care of her kid a hell of a lot better than she does. I never told anyone this, but she hits Kelly Ann. When Michelle gets angry, her hands fly. That's why that little girl is so messed up."

"Please, let me get this straight. Is it or isn't it a matter of money?"

"I won't be treated this way. I won't be accused of something I didn't do."

"Accused of what?"

She sighed deeply. "She says I was playing around with her boyfriend."

"Tommy? Why would she say that?"

"I don't know. She hates me. She's crazy. Don't tell me you don't trust me either."

"I just asked. I'm trying to understand. How could she say something so ridiculous?"

"She came in late last night and he was here, okay? We were watching TV. Is that such a big deal? He was only waiting for her."

"And that's it? Just because he was waiting for her?"

"She says because the lights were off and we were sitting on the couch. Like there's a lot of furniture in her living room, right?"

"So it's all a misunderstanding? Maybe we can talk to her."

"That's what you care about, appeasing her."

"What I care about is that you and Laramie have a place to live."

"What kind of place to live is it with an ax over our heads that could fall any minute? Any time she wants she can march in and say *get out*. I don't have the money for two months' deposit on a new apartment, *if* I could find one, and a month's rent and heat and utilities and a telephone."

"I can lend it to you."

"I won't take money from you. I never take money from guys. I'd rather be on the street. That's just what she wants, the bitch." I could hear her labored breathing, her voice beginning to crack.

"Stop. You won't be on the street."

Holly was listening openly now, standing at my elbow.

"We will. Laramie and me."

"No, you won't. If Michelle throws you out, you can come to my house."

"Oh, that'll be cute. You and me and Judith."

"Judith has her own house. When I see her, I go over there."

"Always?"

"We can work it out. The two of you can move in temporarily. Until you find your own place."

"Temporarily. Of course. Judith would be upset otherwise." Although there was a bitter cast to her voice, she was noticeably calmer. The crying had stopped. A peace settled over the telephone lines like a baby suddenly falling asleep. When she spoke at last, her voice was matter-of-fact. "All right, I'll go back to work now. But you're all wrong about Mr. Lynch. He had Maria make tea, and he gave me a Valium, or I'd be too hysterical to talk. He's like a father to me, David, just like my own father was. I really do feel less scared for Laramie, now that I've settled what to do. You always make things better."

JUDITH

Judith felt cold through and through, although the first Wednesday in May was balmy, the air moist from the Gulf Stream, the buds on the silver maples breaking their seals. She felt cold with desperation. She had called Lynch's law office at ten yesterday and asked for Crystal, suggesting they have lunch today. She selected Mary's Tea Room because the booths offered a little privacy. She often brought clients there, and she had asked Mary to save her the booth at the end.

With Crystal moving in on David, Judith had to put a face on her and try to reach an understanding. Would it be possible? She had to make it possible. If she could reach some sort of rapport with Crystal, they would stop tugging on David like children fighting over a doll. If the situation had an end in sight, she could simply endure it. If it did not, then Crystal and she must work things out. She did not want the subterranean war they had been waging. It made her feel rotten.

She must not make Crystal think she was trying to bribe her, but at the same time she wanted Crystal to understand that she could help. Crystal was a single mother, as Yirina had been. Judith had to make the younger woman see that she was willing to be a friend. Helping raise another woman's child was a familiar role to Judith. If that's what it takes, she thought. It frightened Judith that Crystal had moved in, that David had allowed it, even though he was apologetic, even though he insisted it was an emergency measure. Judith doubted that Crystal would be in any hurry to move out. She was in residence; she was in possession. When Judith told Hannah, Hannah said, "Well, that was fun while it lasted. Wake up and smell the exhaust. He's gone now." But Judith did not want to believe that Crystal had simply taken him over.

She dressed normally, a silk shirt dress, because while she was not in court today, she had a string of clients all morning and all afternoon. Two divorces in progress, a child custody defense, a suit involving an improperly laid roof that never stopped leaking, a defense of a doctor accused by his patient's family of aiding her desire to die. The last was the most interesting case. She took it on with full fervor, because she was terribly aware of the pain of cancer and how ineffective the means to relieve that pain were. Dying took a long time. Not everyone had

Gordon's patience with the process. He claimed to find it interesting. So far, endurable.

As she walked from her office the six blocks to Mary's, she still felt cold, on a sunny day when dogs were trotting in happy packs and in the marina six different boats were waiting to be launched from winter storage. Gordon and she had talked about buying a boat after Natasha was done with her schooling. Now it would never happen.

She walked briskly, afraid she would be late, but she arrived well before Crystal. She had time to order a cup of coffee and drink it before Crystal arrived. When she saw Crystal enter, she stood and waved. She thought Crystal probably recognized her, but after all, they had never officially met. Crystal was got up in a fashion not exactly appropriate for a law office, or for that matter, lunch in this town. She was wearing western boots, a fringed leather skirt cut a little too tight with a turquoise satin blouse. Her dangling earrings were turquoise also—cheap silver, chip-glued turquoise. She wore a black leather belt with silver conchos and much perfume, one of those horrors they sprayed on hapless passersby in department stores. Judith was not sure exactly what this costume was supposed to signify, but it did serve to remind her that Crystal had spent years in Las Vegas.

They shook hands. Crystal's hands were as warm as hers were cold. Different reactions to stress? But she saw no stress in Crystal's face, only a glitter of hostility barely masked by a sweetish smile and a gush of words. "So nice to meet you finally . . . David talks so much about you. It's been really kind of you to take an interest in his campaign. I know you're so much more experienced than he is in politics and everything else. It's been a real boon to him—that you're willing to help a man not only so much younger, but I'm sure David seems very naive to someone like you."

"Someone like me? David's smart, educated. And a ball player sees quite a lot of people on their best and worst behavior."

"I mean someone older, more sophisticated. Married to a famous man. A lawyer everybody's heard of. People just keep telling me stories about what a great time you and your husband had, parties and all those . . . high times."

From the phrase and expression, she assumed the young woman had heard the story of Gordon's great marijuana bust—long before she met him. "Actually we both mostly work. My husband hasn't produced twenty books by dancing all night. I'm afraid you'll find me simply hardworking and involved in my job."

"David has told me how kind you've been to him. How grateful he is. How . . . obligated he feels to you."

She realized Crystal had gone immediately on the attack. But Mary was standing over them now. "We should order."

Crystal ordered the chef's salad. If Crystal had been a friend, Judith would have warned her that the chef's salad was a few cubes of ham and processed cheese in iceburg lettuce with a couple of canned olives. She ordered a hamburger with french fries (which would probably give her heartburn; she never ate french fries). If there had been anything palatable that was even fattier, she would have ordered that also. This was a silly war, but it was obviously war. Time to go on the offensive.

"So you come to us from Las Vegas?" She let her eyes drift over Crystal's outfit. She decided it was supposed to say S-E-X.

"I went there to be a blackjack dealer. I needed to make good money to support my son. I was running away from his father."

"I've been in Las Vegas," Judith thought it only fair to say, in reference to the dealer fairy tale. Larry, Gordon's youngest son, had gotten in trouble there and they had flown out to pay his debts and take him home. "Why were you fleeing Laramie's father?" She dropped the boy's name intentionally. If Crystal wanted to imply that David talked about her, which she doubted, two could play. Crystal waited while Mary set down the pale salad and Judith's sizzling burger. Mary made good meat and seafood dishes. She just had no interest in vegetables. "Do have some of my french fries. Mary gave me a mountain of them."

"I couldn't!"

"Watching your weight? So often it's a matter of watching it steadily rise." Judith ate her fries one at a time, smiling. "You were going to tell me about Laramie's father."

Crystal shuddered and put her hand up to her face as if feeling a bruise. "He started slapping me around when he was drinking. But after Laramie was born, it got worse. One night he beat me unconscious. The next morning I took Laramie and I left, with what I could throw in a suitcase. I left him everything we owned. I drew half the money out of our account and bought a bus ticket to Las Vegas."

Judith had had perhaps fifty battered women as clients. Why didn't she believe Crystal? She was not sure if she was being intuitive or whether she simply wanted to withhold sympathy. Her doubts made her feel guilty. "It's difficult to leave the father of your child, even if he's violent."

"It was hard. But I couldn't wait any longer. He had been hitting Laramie too. . . ." Crystal closed her eyes and sighed heavily.

"But if you had the money in the bank to leave, I don't understand why you got in trouble for bad checks?" High hard line drive to right field. It's going, going, gone.

Crystal stared, her face going blank and tight. "I don't know what you're talking about. Who told you that?"

"I have friends in Seattle," Judith invented. She could hardly say that the assistant district attorney had told her.

"Well, whatever those *friends* told you is a pack of lies. The problem was Liam kept drawing money out of the bank. He had some bad habits. I was trying to pay bills, and he never told me he'd taken money from our account. But the important thing is that I got away from him and I got Laramie away. . . . He's the treasure of my life!" Crystal's voice took on a breathless quality. She reached out and touched Judith's hand. "Is there anything like the bond of giving birth? It's the richest experience we can ever know, isn't it?"

"I've never had a child." As if you didn't bloody well know that.

"Oh! I'm so sorry." Crystal drew her hand back as if burnt. "Are you still trying? It must be a little late."

"I've never tried. I never felt the need."

Crystal's eyes were wide and pitying. "Having Laramie was the best thing in my life. Until I met David." Crystal beamed.

Judith made herself smile. She motioned to Mary. "I'll have a slice of your wonderful blueberry pie. A la mode." She'd probably fall asleep in her office from eating such a pig-out lunch, unless heartburn kept her awake, but it was a small revenge. Crystal had observed every bite of her hamburger and every french fry. "And coffee," she called after Mary. She had to stay awake this afternoon. She'd have Mattie brew her a big pot.

"I'd never be satisfied with one child," Crystal was saying in the same breathless voice. "I couldn't feel fulfilled. And I think only children are at a disadvantage."

"If you're going to law school, believe me, you don't want another baby. Not until you're established in a practice."

"I'm sure you know all about being a lawyer, but I'd never give up bringing life into the world for anything so . . . dry and dull. I see all day what a successful lawyer does. The opposite of motherhood. The opposite of being nurturing and loving."

"David thinks you're planning to go to law school."

"David is my angel, you know that? He saved me from despair. He restored my faith in men. He wants to be the father of my child."

"Does he?" Judith was coldly furious. Either David was lying all of the time to her, or Crystal was lying. Either way, it was ugly. If David had a child with this woman, she would never, never forgive him. Had she made that serious an error about David? Was he as much a liar as she suspected Crystal to be? Had she made David up, or was he trapped, manipulated? If so, how?

"More than anything else, I want to bear his child. That's how much I love him . . . David and I grew up here. I think we're fated for each other. We probably seem like a dull ordinary couple to you, but I think we'll have a good family life together. Because we really love. Don't you think that's the most important thing?"

When Mary brought the check, Judith did not volunteer to pay. She told Crystal she'd pay two thirds, since she'd eaten more, and handed Crystal the check. It took Crystal three tries to figure out her share, and then she was off by a dollar thirty-two. Judith simply made up the difference.

As she walked back, she shook her head. She knew a little about gambling because she had defended a few gamblers. Dealers in casinos were in the direct line of fire. Besides dealing, they sold chips, paid off winners, and collected from losers. Every move they made was watched by the floorwalker, the pit boss, the casino manager. They had to be fast and cool as ice. They had to do sums in their head. Crystal would never have made it onto the floor of the smallest and cheesiest establishment. It was a story, a romance. Crystal the battered woman, Crystal the dealer. Judith had no idea what it all meant. Was Crystal covering up something? Or nothing? Did Crystal herself know the difference? Perhaps she simply wanted to make herself interesting to whoever was before her. Perhaps she needed to make a more compelling story of her life.

Whatever Crystal was or wasn't, there was one truth evident: she was an enemy. She was trouble.

DAVID

32   Getting out of my truck to help Crystal load her things, I'd expected an icy reception from her roommate, but Crystal and Michelle were laughing together. Michelle couldn't seem to help her enough. "Anytime you want me to take Laramie," she said.

Crystal gathered Michelle's little girl into her arms: "Now you *know* I'm not leaving you. I'm just moving in with David not two miles from here."

In fact things proceeded as they had before: except that whenever I came home, Crystal was in my living room, my kitchen, my bathtub, my bed. Crystal found curtains for the second bedroom and the kitchen windows. She covered the old couch with an Indian madras spread. The women in her office gave us a cast-iron frying pan and a set of plates, a bedside lamp, and a coffee table. Although I didn't want her to start paying rent, she insisted. She found an old student's desk in the garage, stripped it and painted it yellow. The more she invested in the house, the more it became hers. I had not asked how long she might be here. I could never ask "the question" in front of Laramie, although he seemed to be waiting for it. Whenever things got quiet between his mother and me, he inched closer or took a seat in a corner, drawing his knees to his chest. Nor did Crystal offer an answer when we were alone. The night she moved in, while I ran out to Penia's for pizza, she started scrubbing the kitchen floor with steel wool. The next night after work, she began on the bathroom, and the next night shampooed the carpet. "David, is there something you wanted to ask me?" she said when she noticed me watching her.

Caught off guard, I muttered, "No. I mean, yes. You don't have to do all this." Or something like that. Anything else just felt plain cruel.

Soon after they moved in, Crystal and Laramie started arguing. Sometimes it was about getting up in the morning or finishing his toast or cleaning up his stuff, it didn't matter. The kind of terrible rows that used to go on between Crystal and Kelly Ann became a commonplace occurrence in our house. I started spending more time with the boy, making him breakfast, getting him off to school, reading his books together.

One day I heard Crystal shriek from the bathroom. Laramie started crying soon after. Crystal's frustration was humiliating and sharp. "What is this? You're going to be eight years old. You can't do this!"

I arrived to find Laramie in tears, his pants and underwear swaddling his shoes. "Look at this!" Crystal stood over a small puddle of urine in front of the toilet bowl.

"It just happens," Laramie said. "I can't help it."

"Well, you better help it, young man. Or we're going to be asked to leave this house, and you know what I mean."

A ripple of guilt tore through my gut. Did I have that kind of power? "Crystal, please," I said. "Leave us alone for a minute."

"You don't have to do this, David. He's old enough to know better."

"Please," I said, and ushered her out. Laramie stood before me with his eyes down, arms folded. I had not seen my own boy naked since he was three years old. I had never taught him anything about his body. And who was going to teach this kid if not for me? "Laramie, what's going on?"

"Sometimes when I sit down on the toilet, it just happens." Fear and shame clotted his voice. "The pee goes all over the floor."

"You know what you have to do? This happened to me when I was a kid."

"It did?"

"Happens to all little boys. You have to hold your penis down so the pee goes into the water, instead of between the bowl and the seat." I didn't touch him; he wasn't mine, after all, but I illustrated what I meant with my hand and he understood. Nothing that I'd ever done before had made me feel as much like a father.

Most nights after work, I attended a meeting, spoke to some group or stood outside the post office during its last hour before closing to shake hands. Half the people I spoke to sought me out with an ax to grind. Some said they admired my drive. "I don't know you from Adam," an old man told me. "But I'm voting for you because you believe in yourself. You must, you're out here every damned night." He didn't realize he was casting his ballot for a guy who was putting off going home.

Thursday nights I had a standing date with Judith, but the week before, the week Crystal moved in, Judith had to take Gordon into the Dana Farber clinic. I was nervous about the following Thursday date that Wednesday night when I took the "family" out to the movies and then to the supermarket. "You okay?" Crystal kept asking me, stroking my thigh in the dark theater, placing her hand on top of mine as I pushed the grocery cart. We talked about getting shelves and painting the living room. Crystal didn't mention my seeing Judith. As we drove back, Laramie asked if he could get a dog, mother and son waiting in reverent silence for me to decide the fate of their lives. It was half past nine when we got home. Another hour passed before we got the food put away and Laramie to sleep. Still, we made love that night. Crystal made love to me every night that week, but Thursday morning she set the alarm a half hour earlier than usual. When she came back to bed, she took me in her mouth. "Shove him all the way in. All the way down my throat."

As Crystal showered, I realized that one difference between Crystal and Judith, between Crystal and any woman I had ever known, was that sex for her had little to do with her own pleasure. She was glad to have an orgasm and sometimes seemed surprised; but her satisfaction derived not from the intensity of her pleasure but mine. I felt no small amount of shame sometimes. I knew, despite her cries of delight, her grunting in my ear, "You stud! Your cock is God!" that the excitement was an act, a sideshow, and that I was the audience. Yet I could not stop myself. Use me, she said, use me, and I did.

When she stepped out of the shower and was toweling her hair dry, she said, "I forgot to tell you, Tommy's coming over with some stuff I forgot at Michelle's."

"When?"

"Tonight. When you're at Judith's."

"Why?"

"I told you. I forgot something. The exercise bike I bought at the flea market."

"I could have picked it up."

"I didn't want to ask you. You've done so much."

"But why tonight?"

"That's when he said he could do it. You won't be here. I'll be all by myself. You said I should make some friends. I thought it would take some pressure off you if I didn't always depend on you. What's the matter? You're going to be doing what you want to. You're going to be with another friend."

A friend? I made love to Judith. What did that say about Crystal and Tommy? What *had* Michelle walked in on that night? Why had they been on the couch in the dark together? There were lights in that room. There were two other chairs. Did she think that because I slept with Judith that she had the right to sleep with Tommy? Did Tommy think he could walk into my house when I wasn't here and make love to the woman I was living with? I left for work that morning with raw intestines and my head on fire. I couldn't accuse her, not when she knew exactly where I would be and what I would be doing. It was a silent threat: be with Judith and I'll be with someone too.

The following night was Friday and Crystal was waiting for me at the door. She ushered me into the kitchen. "Do you like it?" So much seemed to depend on my answer.

"Of course!"

"It's all here, right?" The table was covered with an old lace cloth instead of the usual vinyl. "I did the whole thing like the book said. I got it all, I think."

"I helped with the bread."

"Oh, I know you did, Laramie," I said. "It's beautiful." He was wearing a dress shirt and a Bruins cap. My sister had lent Crystal *The Complete Book of Jewish Observance*. Crystal, doing her best to create a Shabbat meal, had fashioned candle holders from upturned egg cups and baked a braided bread. "They didn't have poppy seeds. Is sesame all right?"

"It's beautiful," I said. "Thank you."

She had located—probably from the back of my sister's liquor cabinet—a bottle of cherry wine labeled Kosher for Passover. She and Laramie stood at something like attention as I recited the blessings. She wore a silk kerchief and a white Greek fisherman's shirt with balloon sleeves. She had roasted a chicken, and instead of the potato kugel in the "Suggested Menus" chapter, served macaroni and cheese. They began to eat only after I did (Laramie watching for the nod from his mother), and sat in dead formal silence, waiting for something to happen. I had never been one to initiate dinner table conversation. Moreover, my father had led the few ritual dinners we had, and after his death, Marty did it. When I shared Shabbat with Judith, she was the source of prayer and song, shadowy memories for me. The truth is, I didn't know much about being a Jew or how to teach anyone else.

Crystal poured me another glass of cherry wine, half cabernet sauvignon, half Robitussen. "Eat slowly," Crystal reminded Laramie. "I know it's not as good as *she* makes it but—"

"It's wonderful," I said automatically. "It's very good. Don't put yourself down."

"—but it's my first time. I wasn't putting myself down. Did you have a good night last night?"

"What do you mean?"

"I haven't seen you since yesterday morning. I just asked if you had a good night."

In fact it had not been good. The question I could not bring up to Crystal was the first thing Judith asked. How long is she going to be there, David? I said I didn't know. Why? she asked. Why can't you set a date, tell Crystal she has two weeks to find a place? That's a little stiff, I said. All right, two months, David, but make a deadline. How long am I supposed to go on like this? You live with her now. So what? I said, you live with your husband. So you see her five nights a week and I see you two, Judith said. So I'm involved with a man whose house is off limits to me. So you're not even with me when you are here.

Because all I could think about was Crystal and Tommy. I had driven past my house on the way to Judith's at seven. Tommy's truck was not there. Which meant he could have come and gone—or that he wasn't coming until after dark.

"Judith and I mostly dealt with the election," I said. "It was business."

She swept crumbs from the table into her palm. "What kind?"

I didn't want Crystal to be jealous of Judith and me, but the fact that she did not show the slightest concern seemed to prove she had gotten even. "Strategy stuff," I said grudgingly. "We decided to send out a last campaign letter to arrive in the voters' mailboxes the morning of the election."

That night I wanted her with a fierceness fueled by pure anxiety. Everything I'd felt a hundred times seemed new: the tickle of her hair as it lay on my inner thigh; her nipples dangling above my lips. Her breath in my ear made me shiver. I came the first time just kissing and again inside her.

We lay together afterwards in a cold sweat, barely able to move. Sex had left us more wounded than satisfied, more exhausted than content. I listened to her breathing as she certainly listened to mine. Neither of us could sleep. "You want me out of here, don't you?" Crystal said in the dark.

"It's just that I'm used to living by myself."

"Tell me the truth. You think I can't feel it? Nothing I do can make you want us. If I wash the floor, you just think I'm doing it so I can stay here. If I try to make the kind of ritual you like, it doesn't compare to the way she does it."

"I never said that."

"I can feel it. You're mad at me all the time." I reached for her and she pulled away. "Do you think I want to impose on you? It's just so hard for me, David. You don't know how much it costs to have a kid."

"I told you I'd help you. I mean it."

"I don't want your money. If you want us out, okay, just say it. If it wasn't for Laramie I wouldn't even be here. His father doesn't help. He never sends anything. Do you know how hard that is? Laramie thinks nobody loves him. I don't want him to grow up like that."

"You're a good mother, Crystal. There's none better."

"I've made such a lousy life for him."

"No, you haven't. He's a good, beautiful kid."

"He really loves you, David."

"And I love him."

She was suddenly still. "You do? You mean that? I don't care how you feel about me. But if you could care for him. He can't take being kicked again and again."

"Nobody's going to hurt him or you."

"We'll move as soon as I get the money together. I promise. I want to pay off my debts. And then I'll work on saving enough to rent a house. I won't be a burden to you."

"You're not a burden." What else could I say? I had the sense if I ever said flat out, *I do wish you would move, I feel crowded out of my own house,* she would utterly collapse. I had to go gently around her. "I know how hard you work to please me. I know I'm not easy. Don't cry, Crystal. You can stay as long as you need to. Why are you crying?"

"I wanted to hear you say that."

DAVID

The only campaign weapon we had left was our letter, secretly typed, copied, stamped and, by arrangement with the postmaster, delivered in time for voters to find it in their boxes the morning of the election. Gordon suspected that people had tuned out the signs and forgotten the issues. They were tired of the election and might not bother to vote. We needed to goose them, he said, at exactly the right time and above all with a light hand. Gordon had three photos of me taken, each one recalling those in Blossom's letter of attack. Under a photograph of me in a pea coat, looking something like Ahab, was the caption: "a sobering choice." Underscoring me in a Birdmanlike safari shirt, a pair of binoculars around my neck, were the words, "Looking to the future of Saltash." Under a picture of me on the beach holding a garbage bag, just as Blossom had posed, were the block letters: "He doesn't have to talk trash." In place of the photo of me and Gordon and Judith, there was a picture of Blossom and Johnny Lynch, above the caption: "David Greene is his own boss."

But upon delivery at exactly five P.M. the night before the election, we were told by the postmaster that Blossom had sent out a second letter at the same time as ours, unheard of in Saltash politics. Gordon's face was all furrows; lips, cheeks, and brow pinched together in a ruminative grin. "Looks like we have ourselves a mole."

"The voters will get two letters and throw away both," I said. "We're finished."

"Maybe. We'll know tomorrow morning."

"The polls don't close until seven."

"We'll do exit polls."

"In Saltash?"

"You'll see."

Meeting that night with our committee, Gordon looked sharp despite his pallor and weakness, like a general on the eve of battle. His gaze, sometimes prone to wander off, was fixed on the registered voters street listing, a pencil steady in his hand. We would have poll watchers keeping track of who had yet to vote, telephone volunteers to remind them and a driver for those who couldn't drive themselves. More than once Judith urged Gordon to rest. He refused more rudely each time.

Gordon's exit poll worked this way: on election morning, the earlier the better, each candidate staked out a corner where the voters had to pass on their way out of the polls. My job was to wave furiously at each and every car. According to Gordon, their vote was apparent on their faces. Those who would not look at you had not voted for you. They were embarrassed. Those who gave you an enthusiastic wave had certainly been in your corner; and a thumb up and a toot of the horn meant they liked you enough to tell their friends. A middle finger in your face didn't matter. The crude ones didn't bother to vote. A middle finger slyly directed at your opposition, however, was good, because it meant they not only liked you and had probably enlisted their friends to the cause, but had some dirt on the other candidate they were spreading.

At six-forty A.M., I claimed the northeast corner in front of Town Hall, beating the opening of the polls by fifteen minutes and the other candidates by an hour. Blossom was next, her mouth twisted into a plastic smile. For the first two hours we were even in the thumbs-and-toot department but I had gotten more enthusiastic waves. At around ten I caught a middle finger and three no-looks in a row and tried to shrug it off. By noon, when Judith stopped to wish me luck, I was waving my sign and enjoying myself. What the hell. It was lunchtime; seven hours till the polls closed. But right behind Judith's Jeep, Crystal pulled up in her Olds. She approached me with a brown bag lunch, just as Judith had. Standing there between them I couldn't think of a single word to say.

"We're going to kick ass!" Crystal said.

"It's looking good," Judith said, nose-to-nose with Crystal.

"People in my office are all coming out!"

Judith smirked. "To vote for Blossom?"

My face was sunburned and desiccated. My lips were parched from calling out to cars. "You've been out since dawn, poor baby," Crystal said. "As soon as you get home, I'm going to give you a hot meal and a bath."

"He can eat at the victory party," Judith said.

"Victory?" I said through a smile as tight as clenched teeth. "Don't jinx me."

"What party?" Crystal stared from Judith to me and back at Judith.

"At my office," Judith said. "There'll be a lovely buffet. We're having David's supporters over to wait for the results."

"You didn't tell me." Crystal turned to me, her eyes enormous.

"I didn't know about child care. I thought it would be a late night for Laramie."

"Too late to see his father win an election? Are you coming home first?" Crystal said.

"I, uh, don't know if I have time."

"Do you want to come to the party, Crystal?" I knew Crystal was the last person Judith wanted to invite, but she was too polite not to ask her. "I'm sure there'll be people you know."

"Sure," Crystal said, backing away, the glint of broken glass in her eyes. "Maybe I'll do that."

They count the votes one by one in Saltash, reading the names from a paper ballot and shouting them out in an open hall. I swung by Town Hall at nine, when the poll counters were breaking for dinner. The town clerk said there had been a near-record turnout and they wouldn't be finished for hours.

I knew I should go home to change and shower, to touch base with Laramie, but if my time belonged to anyone tonight, it was Judith and Gordon. In spite of my tangled sex life, my disappearances and indecision, they wished me well. In ways that surprised me, I was becoming like them. Small things surfaced, like a taste for meat cooked rare instead of overdone, a liking for vegetables as long as they weren't boiled, a belief that olive oil and garlic were part of a good meal. I'd begun to read, for the first time in my life enjoying books—a memoir about Tip O'Neill that Judith had given me. I was thinking differently too, looking at situations in a way Gordon had taught me, not dwelling on how they affected me so much as asking who stood to lose and who to gain. Judith and Gordon had become a part of me and felt, more than friends, like family. What I was with them was better than what I had been or could be without them. With them, I grew.

Mary, from Mary's Tea Room, and her daughter Jo in white shirts and cummerbunds were setting up platters of cold cuts and tubs of shrimp salad in Judith's office. One of the oystermen was shucking oysters and clams on a folding table. The bar was set up by the windows overlooking the harbor. When I walked in, about twenty people were watching the last bright pink light squeezed between clouds and the horizon. Judith's secretary Mattie put a drink in my hand. She was off to take care of somebody else before I could thank her. People pressed close. How did I feel? Did I think we had taken it? I hadn't hugged or shaken hands with so many people since the day I left town for the Cubs.

Judith made her entrance in a red crepe dress, devastating but simple, slit along the side with a U-neck just low enough to show the slightest hint of décolleté. Between her breasts she wore a heavy silver necklace; her earrings were discs of hammered silver. She had changed for the party but also for me. Our eyes met and did not let go. "I called the town clerk. I couldn't wait," she said between gritted teeth. "They're only three-quarters counted." Later, over the dancing, she shouted, "David! I just got word. They'll be finished by eleven."

The music was a mix of sixties rock and big band swing. Mattie was doing a lindy with the passionate plumber, placing her palm over her bosom to cover it whenever she did a dip backwards. The Birdman, with no party of his own, was chewing Gordon's ear off. If Gordon hadn't looked tired during the last week of the campaign, he did now. Judith got him into a comfortable chair. Stumpy Squeer cleared himself a corner of the buffet table; a fork in one hand, a beer in the other, he looked alternately at each as if unable to choose which to place in his mouth. Twice Natasha called from school, and twice Judith told her that they were still counting ballots. Tommy had come in (without Michelle) and was hunched over the bar. Judith looked worried about the election results, about me, about her guests' wine sloshing over the Xerox machine.

At five to eleven I was summoned to the telephone. "Hello, David," a woman said somberly. "It is my sworn duty as clerk of the Town of Saltash to call each of the candidates in descending order of the number of votes they received. . . ." As I waited, I realized the music had stopped. A crowd of perspiring bodies had formed a horseshoe around me. For all that I'd convinced myself I didn't want to run, blood beat against my temples like a rubber mallet. "And I'm calling you first."

"That means I won?"

The cheer was so loud I didn't hear her response. My knees threatened to give. Had Gordon not been the first to shake my hand, had a hundred people not lined up to wish me well, I might have run to Judith's arms. I might have rushed her upstairs to the loft and knelt in front of her to press my cheek to her belly. I wanted to undress her slowly and thank her in the dark. She had given me much more than help; she had given me a new vision of myself, proven to me I could win again. "Thank you so much, thank you," I said, to anyone and everyone, fighting my way to Judith, drawing her into a corner.

"I knew you could do it! I knew you could!" She pressed her lips to my cheek, demurely, for Gordon was here and she would never embarrass him. "My friends!" Suddenly she was addressing everyone in the room. "I know all of you are as proud as I am. Not only of David," she linked her arm tightly in mine, for all to see, "but of yourselves. For what we've accomplished. David Greene is the rallying point for a new kind of politics, an era of open, accessible, democratic government in the life of this town." Over the applause she said only to me, "You came through. You stuck with it." I could barely hear her. "I'm so proud of you."

"Judith, I want you."

Through a smile, just beneath the noise of the crowd, she said, "Can you stay with me tonight? Can you come back to the house?"

"Yes, yes," I said. "Why not?" But followed the doubt in her eyes to the crowd in front of me, parting for a woman in a fringed western skirt and satin blouse, with tears running into her smile and a little boy in pajamas in her arms.

Crystal spoke as if there was a period at the end of every word. "We. Are. So. Proud. Of you. Tell him, Laramie."

"I love you, Daddy!" Laramie jumped into my arms. There was nothing I could do but catch him as the crowd stepped back and sighed. A flashbulb popped. Judith was gone.

The music began again. A new line formed at the buffet table. Cars streamed into the parking lot. Word had gotten out. Even Holly came, leading my mother in her royal-blue suit. The forces of good had won. A new day was dawning in Saltash. I swung around, searching for Judith. Laramie spotted the desserts and asked for a piece of chocolate cake. I lowered him into Crystal's arms.

Judith was not looking for me. She was standing behind Gordon, massaging his shoulders as he held forth in a circle of friends.

"I lost you," I said. "In the crowd."

She smiled coldly. She could hardly say what was on her mind. She could hardly ask, Why, David? Why did you do this to yourself? Why did you sink so deeply, so unnecessarily? Why couldn't you trust me and Gordon? Why couldn't you give us a chance? "Yes, it's gotten very crowded in here."

"Could I see you tomorrow?"

"Tomorrow." For a moment I was sure she'd say no. She seemed taller, harder. There was no trace of emotion on her face. "Yes. That would be a good idea. Call my office. We have a great deal to talk about."

People touched my shoulder. They grabbed my hand. One man said, "You must be exhausted, son. You look ready to keel over."

Crystal had come to stand beside me again, pressed into me as she held Laramie upright. He was falling asleep on his feet.

My mother studied my face. "I thought you'd be happy now that you've won? Aren't you happy?"

"Sure, Mom. Just a little tired, that's all."

"You look as if you're ready to kill somebody, doesn't he, Holly?" She had no idea who. Or why.

JUDITH

34

The morning after the election, Gordon slept until ten. Judith worked at the kitchen table, hoping to have breakfast with him before she took off. He came out grinning with pride after a very personal victory over Johnny Lynch. But he knew what was on her mind. He said, "Look, you don't understand because you aren't susceptible in the same way. You're divinely pragmatic, sane and sensible. But I wasn't. I was as stupid as David with some women I got involved with."

Judith was forcing herself not to pace. It was not fair to Gordon to dump her grief on him. "Never that stupid. She's one of the most blatant manipulators I've ever encountered. I've met murderers I trusted more."

"Judith, isn't it possible she's just desperate? A woman with a family that's apparently of no use to her, a kid to raise alone. Little training or education. The boy's father doesn't help her. She's in that old situation of women, where she needs a man to support her. It's unfortunate for us she picked David."

He was right, of course, about Crystal's desperation, but that didn't excuse David. "But he picked her too! He could have refused to allow her to move in. He never had to get involved in the first place!"

"Remember the second Mrs. Stone? Beverly, now Caldwell. Beverly eats gold. Her proper environment is pure money. She can't breathe without it. Yet it took me ten years and two children to figure out I could never satisfy her. And to bruise my ego further, while I was used to being now and then unfaithful, I was not accustomed to having it done to me. She had an affair with her therapist. She had an affair with Larry's orthodontist. Believe me, I feel for David. I understand. That bimbo had me eaten up with jealousy."

"You call Beverly a bimbo, but you invite her here every summer."

"She was my wife, Judith. She's the mother of two of my children. I have an obligation to get on with her. Besides, I can enjoy her now that I don't have to support her. You have to admit, she can be funny. She knows how to enjoy herself. Dying puts a lot of things into perspective, including exes."

"She drinks like a fish."

"I used to, my Judith. I used to do the same." Gordon sighed, collapsing on the couch. Half an hour later he returned to bed. Every day he had managed to get up, but now that David's campaign was over, he seemed empty. He was supposed to be revising one of his most famous books: *The Sociology of Fantasy: Americans Who Want to Be Somebody Else*. Over the past months, he had made scant progress. She wished she could provide him with an assistant who would keep him interested.

Thursday, Judith was glad her office was air-conditioned. The temperature had risen twenty-five degrees since yesterday. As suddenly as if the heat had hatched them, tourists were everywhere, driving too fast or too slow on every road, standing in clumps staring at buildings as if the town were a museum. She had a court date tomorrow, and the tides were not cooperative, so she was staying in her office. She expected David, but she was feeling anxiety instead of pleasant anticipation. She ran over her memos, her notes and her brief while she waited. The leaking roof case was finally coming up.

Mattie had left for the day. Judith rubbed her temples. A year ago the thought that she could love a man besides Gordon had appeared absurd. She simply did not look at other men as sexual or romantic objects. Gordon had primed her for experiencing a possible attraction, but until David, none had occurred. Then it had happened quickly, without her willing it or even becoming aware until it was there, full grown, in the middle of her consciousness. She had not quite realized until one night in her office when they were sitting before her gas fire discussing his running for selectman, that she was going to become involved with him. She had not considered the possibility. She was used to men looking at her as David had, with evident attraction, but in fourteen years she had not responded.

She wondered sometimes if she had not plunged into this out of her habit of pleasing Gordon. She knew he was worried about his ultimate creation, his menagerie of buildings, as Natasha worried about the animals she had brought home and who now lived with them, cared for by Judith. They were both terrified she would move away.

Now she considered herself a fool. She had fallen hard, seriously, passionately, for a man who seemed to prefer a coarse and manipulative woman—younger, yes, a liar. Who had grown up here. Who had a child for whom David seemed to care a great deal. All those points Judith had gone over with Hannah, with Barbara, with Natasha, and, in a more restrained way, with Gordon. She had found herself distracted in court last week when she should have been paying close attention to a hostile witness's testimony. She had not been so sloppy and absorbed in something irrelevant to a case since Gordon had been diagnosed with cancer. Her intense focus was her best weapon and she had almost lost it. She owed her clients a housecleaning.

David stood in the parking lot, looking weary and uncertain. He could not guess she was observing him. He grimaced, almost a wince, and then came slowly toward the building. Did he dread seeing her? Did he guess how estranged she felt? More likely the latter. He was observant and smart about people; mostly, that is. He had no smarts about Crystal.

She offered him coffee. They sat facing each other. She needed the distance. They spoke for a few minutes about the election. However important that had felt twenty-four hours before, it did not seem to be foremost on either of their minds. "David, don't you find it a little embarrassing to have Laramie, as sweet as he seems to be, call you Daddy? He has a real father, doesn't he?"

"He was abusive. Violent. Maybe dealing drugs . . . I've never told Laramie to call me Daddy. Crystal tells him to. I can't hurt him by telling him not to. I can't, Judith."

"Do you intend to be his father?"

David shrugged, running his hands roughly through his dark coarse hair. He was darkly tanned. His eyes seemed lighter than ever, chips of something luminous and rare. "I don't know what to do."

"Are you going to marry her?"

He gripped the sides of his chair. "No, but what am I supposed to do? I feel trapped. She had no place to go. Laramie has to have a home."

"David, she has a job. She ought to be getting child support from the boy's father. Do you want me to check if Massachusetts has a reciprocal agreement with Washington? I would pursue this for her if you want me to."

"I should try calling him," David said dispiritedly.

She wanted to shake him. He seemed flaccid, without will. "I ask you again, do you want to marry her? You seem bound on that road."

"I can't hurt the boy, Judith."

"Do you think you'd feel this guilty about a boy you met twelve weeks ago if you saw your son on a more regular basis? If you felt truly involved with Terry?"

"I can't deal with that many 'ifs.' Terry's my son, and the more I'm around Laramie, the bigger hole I feel in my life, hardly seeing him. . . ." He shook his head as if he had no hope.

"How long do you intend for her to live with you?"

"Just until she finds a decent place."

"Is she looking?"

"Is this your best courtroom manner?" He tried a grin. It didn't come off.

"I use the tools I have at hand to come at the truth, David." She forced herself to lean back in her chair. "I assume your lack of answer means she is not looking. So you plan to live with her until death do you part?"

"I read the real estate ads to her every week."

"David, we can barely see each other. When we do, I never know when she is going to have the boy call or charge in herself. We can't be together in your place. You're always nervous with me now. If you want to go on seeing me, give her a real honest deadline."

"I'll try to talk to her again. I'll do something. I promise."

"Are you using condoms with her?"

"This is not something I want to talk about. Besides, she's on the pill."

"She told me she intends to have another baby with you. And that you want to have one with her. Those are her plans. Not law school."

He looked as if she had slapped him hard. With a sharp intake of breath, he sat in silence for several moments. "You misunderstood her."

"Not possible. She said she wanted to have your baby. And you wanted to father a child with her. I am quoting."

"I never said that. She never asked me. No, I don't want her to have a child with me. That's all I need!"

"It is one hell of a lot more than I need, David." She folded her arms tight across her chest. "I've told you before, and I meant it, that I would help you with getting a better situation with your son. You need an arrangement where Terry spends part of every year with you here, maybe a month in the summer, or you'll never have a genuine relationship with him. If you really want a child, I would never rule out that possibility. More and more women my age have babies. But not while Gordon's alive. If you want our relationship to continue as more than political allies and somewhat distant friends, then you will change your life. You will get her out of your house or at least begin serious preparations for that happening. And you will straighten things out with her about whether or not the two of you are going to make a baby. Am I getting through?"

"Loud and clear."

"Good, because, David, I mean it all. I really mean it."

DAVID

35

I found Liam's telephone number in Crystal's address book. I copied it while she was sleeping. I did not want to call him but I had no choice. I was not Laramie's father. I loved him but I did not want to live with his mother. I hated feeling that the choice was her becoming homeless or becoming my wife. Everything had moved too fast. It was Judith who said, "Do you realize you're living with a woman and child you only met twelve weeks ago?"

I was going to ask Liam to take some responsibility for his son, to cough up some child support. Fifty dollars a week could go a long way out here, could mean Crystal finding a decent place of her own. If Laramie knew his dad was thinking about him, even enough to write a check once a month, it might give him a little confidence. In Crystal's photograph album, Liam was a slender black-haired Irishman with a clenched smile and an icy stare. He was wearing black slacks, a white shirt, with his feet propped up, drinking a beer. I carried Liam's picture in my mind as I carried his telephone number in my wallet. I enacted threats. Attempts to reason. Warm stories about his son. I don't know how many times I sat behind the wheel of my truck rehearsing. I decided finally that calling him would do no good. Then, one day at work, I picked up the phone and dialed simply because I was afraid to. It was Saturday, one in the afternoon here, ten on the West Coast.

Crystal talked about Liam the way some 'Nam vets remembered the war. With a trembling bitterness, her eyes glazed over in anger and pain. He hit her when she was pregnant and wouldn't look at his child. Finally, I didn't see any point to a soft approach. I wasn't the law, but neither was Laramie just some unpaid debt.

"Hello?" It was not a man's voice. It sounded like a little girl.

"Who's this?" I asked, wondering if his number had changed.

"I'm Molly! It's me . . . Is this Uncle Mike?"

"Is Liam there?"

"Daddy!" she yelled. "Daddy and Sean are washing the car."

"Could you get him please? I'm calling long distance."

"Okay . . ." She let the phone fall with a clatter and I could hear running steps. I could hear some kind of Irish music playing and some appliance running—a mixer? a blender? It stopped. A woman's voice called something. I waited and waited. I was ready to hang up when a man picked up the receiver. "Uncle Mike? Is that yourself, back home safe and sound?"

"No, this is David Greene calling from Massachusetts. I'm a friend of Crystal Sinclair." She had once mentioned that he had not lost his accent. What she hadn't said was that there was music in it, a kind of whimsical, almost poetic rhythm. But as soon as I announced my connection to Crystal, the music turned to sarcasm. "A friend, you say? That kind of woman doesn't have men friends. So you're screwing the little lady, am I right? She's your problem now."

"That may be. But the boy is yours."

"Christ, man, that's a laugh. How do I know he's mine? I wasn't her only one. You should know that by now."

"I think he's yours, Liam. I think you couldn't pass a blood test to prove he wasn't and you know it."

I was bluffing. I didn't know a thing about blood testing, less how you went about forcing him to take one. Nor had Crystal mentioned other boyfriends. I heard a shuffling on the other end of the line and half expected the receiver to slam down on my ear, when Liam let out a long mournful breath. "I told her I'd pay for her not to have it. I begged her not to. I got down on my knees and pleaded. But she was always pushing. First she moved in with some cock and bull excuse. Then she got herself pregnant."

"I don't think she *got herself* pregnant."

"Think what you goddamn want. I kept telling her I didn't want a child with her. I liked to be with her, sure, but not after she did that. Not after she tricked me, told me she was safe and to mind me business then went and got knocked up."

"Look, there's a child. Laramie's yours and he's a good boy."

"Then you raise him. Because if you think I'm sending a dime so you two can live off me, you're wrong. Let me tell you, if I were you I wouldn't be spending me time hounding some poor bloody waiter, I'd be thinking hard about saving me own ass."

"How can you pretend you don't owe anything to your own son?"

"I got two other sons that I know are mine. And my little daughter. My wife works in a hospital. I kill myself lunches and dinners six days a week and we just squeak by. I'm a family man, Greene or whoever you are. I never asked her to have a baby. I begged her not to. If I was a rich man, I'd send her a whopping big check and tell her to go fuck herself—not that she'll ever have to. But I don't have an extra buck to buy a lottery ticket—you get the picture?"

"You know, we could take this to court."

"If I hear you doing that, I'll take hold of me family and move back to

Dublin. I have over two dozen relatives there. Listen, I screwed her maybe twenty times. I moved out and left her me damned apartment. What else could I do? But I won't talk with her and I won't let her near me wife and me kids. She's poison. Now she's your poison. Sure, and she's not a bit of mine, thank the saints and angels on me knees. And 'yes, me good wife does know about her, so don't be trying to blackmail me about that sad old mess." And then he did hang up.

DAVID

36

The wheels of government don't stop long enough for a new official to learn. Elected on Tuesday, you vote on Thursday—on an issue as routine as a business license or important as a man's career. I spent the first day just hanging around Town Hall, trying to read more than I could digest in a year and convince the secretaries I wasn't some clock-watching reformer out to make their lives miserable. The last time I was in this building, I'd stood nervously beside the town manager's desk. Now he ushered me into his office and offered me a padded leather chair. Through the window onto Main Street, I watched the regulars going in and out of the Binnacle, and the Compton kid on his bicycle, a one-armed teenage moron dodging delivery trucks to impress his friends. The town manager was talking policy. "I'm sure you're concerned about our efforts to keep the tax rate steady."

I nodded, lips tight, the way Georgie had taught me twenty years ago: Don't let anyone know what you don't understand. Keep your mouth shut.

"But of course, next year we face a property tax reval."

Whatever the fuck that meant.

He glanced at the clock over my shoulder. "Is there anything in particular you were curious about, Selectman Greene?" Meaning: What kind of an ax is this guy out to grind?

I shrugged. "Not really. Just trying to get the lay of the land."

"Well, then." He needn't waste his time.

"Maybe, if it's not an inconvenience . . . I was wondering if I could take a look at your performance evaluations for each department."

"That could take a while."

"I took off work today."

"What is this for, exactly?"

"My information. Exactly. According to the charter of this town you serve at the pleasure of the Board of Selectmen. I was just elected one."

"Yes, of course. I didn't mean to imply you weren't entitled."

"Glad to hear it."

"I just want you to understand that everything we do is subject to state law. You can't get elected one day and expect me to let good people go the next."

"I'm not talking about good people." I wondered if I was going to have trouble with this guy. He was already having trouble with me.

"Good or bad, Selectman, there's a chain of command that must be followed in this town."

"And we all know who's on top, don't we?"

"Yes, and it can't change overnight."

"I've got three years," I said. "How long do you expect to stay around?"

"Please wait here." The town manager left me alone in his office while he talked with his secretary outside. He came back with an armload of files, explaining, "This isn't all of what you want. But we're looking. I don't want to get off on the wrong foot here. I just want you to understand that the town can get into a great deal of legal trouble unless every case is handled carefully. Regardless of performance, each employee has legal rights."

"I was wondering. Is it true Abel Smalley and Donkey Sparks are up for reappointment?"

"Chief Smalley has done a good job for many years. He may not be up on his computer technology and grant writing, but his people skills are a real asset in a town like this."

"And Donkey Sparks?"

The town manager knew all about my problems with Donkey Sparks. But he didn't leap to defend him. Instead, I felt him taking my measure, studying me, wondering just who he'd have to sacrifice to save his own job. Anyway, that's what I imagined. He may have been planning his next move. He may even have known I was bluffing. Still, I appreciated the key to Town Hall he pressed into my hand; and the little card with his home and his car phone numbers and the stack of files the secretary came in with, especially the ones stamped CONFIDENTIAL.

On the way out I remembered something that Gordon had said the night of the victory party, calling me over with his eyes. I had knelt to hear his whisper. He was right. This was going to be fun.

JOHNNY

37

"It's true!" Crystal was laughing. Her laughter was ticklish, making him smile. "Don't you know guys like that, Mr. Lynch? Ugly guys who walk around like movie stars and really dumb ones who think they're Einstein."

"Too many," Johnny said, watching a slice of roast beef slide out of his sandwich onto the wrapper he balanced on his lap.

"Then there are these really good-looking guys whose self-image sucks. No matter how much somebody loves them, they just don't believe they're good enough. And do you know the reason for that? Mr. Lynch? Are you laughing at me?"

"Well, there is a daub of yogurt right there on your nose."

"Oh, you!" She licked it off with the tip of her tongue.

If any of the boys, Donkey or Abel, saw him eating lunch with a pretty girl in the front seat of his car, they'd never believe it was business. He'd only planned to familiarize Crystal with the river valley and the dike. She'd suggested the picnic. But the wind was up today, blowing sand in their eyes and forcing them back into the car.

"And the reason is the person's mother," she said, oblivious to the grandest view Saltash had to offer, the vast harbor bluer than heaven itself, then narrowing upriver of the dike into a placid stream. Aspen leaves shimmered like silver dollars. Seabirds wheeled overhead while Crystal, God bless her, rattled on about motherhood. "Between the ages of birth and five years old, that's the window. That's where you have your shot. If you really dedicate yourself to making that one little person feel special, then you're giving the gift of lifelong confidence, and that's as important as any college education."

Johnny had hoped she would grasp the beauty of the place. But he might have known, since she'd never hunted or hiked and fished here as he did, that she was simply one of those people for whom the natural world was just scenery. No matter. A little naiveté could work in his favor.

"Mr. Lynch, are you listening to me?"

"Actually, I was applying what you said to my own boys. My wife did just that. Dedicated herself. With Jackie at least. By the time William came along, well, things had changed."

"Parents aren't perfect." Crystal was lecturing him now like a little schoolteacher. Maria said since David's election, she was holding forth on everything from school budgets to dogs on the beaches. "Parents are people first. But no parent ever intentionally does anything to harm their child. Mrs. Lynch was sick. They didn't understand things like depression back then."

Johnny was uncomfortable now. "You don't know what you're talking about." He crumbled the bag on his lap. He'd told Crystal a great deal about himself, but he'd never mentioned Emily Ann. That was Maria's doing. They chattered like hens. "Now for the reason we're here, then." He heard the coldness in his voice. Crystal jerked upright like a child reprimanded. "Do you see how the trees grow right up to the bank of the river? Those are gray birches."

"They're pretty trees," she said. "This valley is beautiful."

"Beautiful to us, dear. Home to countless of God's creatures."

Since the election, Johnny had a new plan to keep the dike in place. He'd give his adversaries a dose of their own medicine, raise a grand and public stink about the environment. There had been a causeway any storm surge could overrun and a rickety wooden bridge constructed forty years before he'd even heard the name of this town. Behind the bridge there had been a salt marsh and a tidal river useful only to a few shellfish scratchers. He had replaced the bridge with a proper dike, able to withstand hurricanes and ice pileup, protecting the new land behind it. There, the old marsh had been drained, filled and had grown up into meadows and woods. Since then an entire new habitat had been formed. He didn't know all the technical details; Crystal had agreed to work overtime to come up with the proper language, interview a few biologists to get it straight. But he knew this much, and this was his line: if the dike was torn down and the saltwater of the harbor allowed to fill the valley, thousands of animals would be flooded out of their homes. Little red foxes. Innocent baby deer. Weasels, voles, opossum. Coyote would lose their food supply and begin gobbling kittens, mauling the family dog. The issue was environmentally arguable, and sentimental as a children's tale. The timing couldn't be better. It was the summer people who had influence with the legislature, over twenty thousand of them, from districts all over the state. If his luck held out, if time was on his side, he would take the issue of the dike right out of the selectmen's hands and turn it over to the media and the State House.

After eating, they returned to the office in silence. He knew the girl's feelings were hurt, but he didn't know how to smooth things over. She had set herself up a desk in a back corner of the office by the copy machine, an area formerly used to store dead files. Only when the file cabinets were moved did he realize they'd been blocking a window. Now there were plants in it. She had three pictures of her son on her desk, and one of David being sworn in by the town clerk. There was a teddy bear and a dish of hard candy, a coffee mug with red hearts. He made a few forays to the copy machine in hopes of thinking of something light to say, but the other girls were always around. As he was heading back to his office the last time, Crystal said, "Mr. Lynch, I finished those letters you asked me to write."

She handed him three, each handwritten in her loopy feminine curlicues, each addressed to the editor of a different local paper and signed in her own name. They were each two paragraphs long, as he'd advised her, and quite good. "David won't mind?"

"I have a right to protest the killing of innocent animals no matter what he thinks. He never asked *me* what to say in the election."

Johnny hoped people would assume her opinions were David's. But her relationship to the new selectman was too valuable to jeopardize. "I don't want to cause any family problems."

"Family . . ." Crystal repeated. She looked pleased at his choice of words. Then she looked down in embarrassment. "Mr. Lynch?"

"Oh, now." He was afraid she was going to cry. Because he'd used the word "family" to describe her arrangement with David Greene?

"I didn't mean to be sticking my nose into your private affairs. I mean about Mrs. Lynch and your children."

"You mean William?" He rarely mentioned his second son to anyone in this town except, on occasion, Abel Smalley, who could obtain information about the California prison system. But Johnny had a hunch. "You're about his age, aren't you?"

"He was a nice boy," Crystal said.

"I doubt if there are many around here who remember him that way, but thank you, dear."

"He was nice to me. He took me to the junior prom, even though I was a sophomore."

William had many girlfriends before he got involved with drugs. Had Crystal been one? He tried to figure out what she would have looked like at age fifteen. William had gone out with many pretty girls, but in Johnny's memory, they blurred.

"Anyway, I'm very sorry."

Those eyes, like an infant's, that was the only way to describe them, so sad and vulnerable. Johnny looked away. "Crystal, you didn't get yourself arrested for armed robbery. My William did."

"I'm sure he just got in with a bad bunch. It happens, especially when you're away from home and off on your own. I understand that, Mr. Lynch."

"We were talking about children. Which you know a great deal about. I only pray to God your boy doesn't end up the way mine did, and that I have the strength to help William when he finally comes home."

"You will," she said, her hand hovering above his but not touching, not yet, he thought. She said "You're the best boss in the world, Mr. Lynch. I see all the time how many people in town you help. People nobody else seems to care about. You don't turn anybody down. You have the biggest, kindest heart in Saltash, Mr. Lynch."

JUDITH

38 Every social worker in the county and every health worker knew Judith would take on those unpleasant cases of abuse, not only unsavory, but sometimes dangerous for the lawyer as well as the client. When a woman left an abusive man—or began to get ready to leave—she was in acute danger. Sometimes her lawyer too could come into the line of fire. But occasionally domestic troubles were plain bizarre.

She had two new cases. One was a bigamist. Betty Clausen and/or Sirucci had married Sirucci without getting divorced from Clausen. "But Sergio was ready to marry me. Dick wasn't paying child support. He never paid his child support after the first two months. What could I do?" Betty was a slender nervous woman with dark brown hair cut very short, who hailed originally from northern Maine. Her children were being entertained in the outer office by Mattie, who was great with kids. She kept a supply of toys and games in a box.

"Divorce would have been a really good idea, Betty."

"But that takes time. And Sergio was ready to marry me right then. How do I know he'd marry me in a year? I have two kids and he was willing to be their father. They never really had a father, not a loving one. Not a good man like Sergio. And I didn't even have a current address for Dick."

To Betty it all seemed logical. Her kids needed a father; here was a father. Ergo she had to marry him immediately. "But you'd told him you were married?"

"He's such a sweetheart. Of course I told him I'd been married. How else did I get two kids? But I said their father was dead. In Sergio's family, there's no divorce. At least I could say I wasn't a divorced woman, because I wasn't. But if a man picks on you all the time and hits you and hits your kids and doesn't pay a penny for them, how can that be marriage? So if you aren't really married—"

"The law doesn't distinguish between a good marriage and a lousy marriage, in that both are equally valid marriages and require a valid divorce to end them. Betty, there are places like the Dominican Republic where you can get a divorce overnight."

"First, I don't have the money to fly to the Caribbean. Second, how would I explain it to Sergio?"

"How are you explaining the situation now?"

"He's very upset with me." She began to cry. "I couldn't take the chance on him not marrying us. We needed him. We were having trouble making it. This is a real marriage, not like my last one."

Betty hoped if she could only explain to the judge how badly she wanted and needed Sergio, the judge would understand she had been obliged to marry him right away, and everything would be all right.

Judith had ten minutes before her next new client to make notes on the interview. Perhaps she should plea bargain and represent Betty as a devoted mother only trying to care for her children. That might go over. Sooner than put herself and her children on welfare, your honor, this mother of two . . .

The other new case was a reasonably straightforward divorce. The only question was why the woman had stayed so long with a man she described as abusive, unfaithful and often drunk. She was four years older than Betty and looked ten years older. "But where would I go?" she asked, as if she had never heard of a rental unit in her life. She had married out of high school, worked as a waitress, a salesperson in a tee-shirt shop, a chambermaid. She had always worked and never made a living.

After that interview, Judith sat in her office feeling overcome with despair. The lives of women were often so grim and desolate and patched together. No wonder a woman like Crystal grabbed at a hardworking and affectionate man. She despised Crystal because Crystal had destroyed her best hope of a good relationship with David; Crystal must hate her for the same reason. They were in each other's way. Pontificating about how good a woman Crystal was or wasn't, was irrelevant.

She was having supper with David on the island, but meeting him here. Natasha was home for the interval between vet school and her summer internship, and tonight she was cooking. Natasha was a good cook, taught by Judith. At seven-thirty oyster stew and corn bread would await them. She needed the time alone with David before the family scene.

"Any progress?" she greeted him.

"I called Laramie's father." He told her the conversation. "I don't know what to believe."

She could not come down unreservedly on the side of Liam, as she would have liked. "You have to understand that his wife no doubt was listening to every word. The truth in these matters usually lies somewhere in the middle. It is likely they did actually live together for some period of time. It is likely that Crystal was more interested than he was, and didn't believe in his attachment to his family. Most probably when he learned she was pregnant and meant to have his child over his protests, he moved out. He may have hit her or just yelled enough to frighten her. We have no witnesses. Certainly he did not exhibit good-will toward her once she announced her pregnancy."

"You sound like a lawyer again."

"I am a lawyer, David. I deal with desperate women every day, women who think they're helpless and some who actually are. I look for remedies. I send them to counselors and social workers, I send them for medical assistance, I send them to safe houses. I go to court for them. But their desperation sometimes causes them to do foolish and self-destructive things. . . . What worries me most is Crystal's penchant for getting pregnant as glue in a relationship. Have you straightened out the matter of a second child?"

"I'm dealing with that," he said, his face and tone warning her, no further trespassing.

"I hope so, David. I hope so."

Although they made love that evening and he spent the night with her, she had to recognize that it was not as it had been. She was more reserved. She could not help it. She needed a sense of commitment to let herself go sexually. She did not feel that commitment from David. She was reluctant to end the sex, for she and Gordon no longer made love. He simply did not have a sex drive, and any brisk physical activity could cause a dangerous coughing fit. But she had to recognize that the intense almost overwhelming pleasure she had felt with David had diminished into something merely pleasant. She had felt for a while that she had two mates. That had been an illusion, for David had not felt mated to her. If Betty was a desperate bigamist, one could say she herself had tried to be a sane and pragmatic bigamist. She had failed as thoroughly as Betty.

Perhaps Crystal's need was greater, and she should simply get out of the way. If David would only fight for his relationship with her, she would persist. But if it did not mean that much to him, then she could not allow it to mean a great deal to her. He seemed to be choosing Crystal, or at the least allowing Crystal to choose him. She did not sleep that night. As she lay beside David, she found herself reluctantly but inevitably beginning to let go.

In the morning after he had left for work, she lingered at the table with Natasha. Her first appointment had canceled; that couple had reconciled. Her next appointment at ten was with the insurance company representatives. She finally had a good deal for Enid from the fall through the planking outside the pizza parlor. "I'm on the verge of giving up on David."

"But why?" Natasha put her sharp chin into the cup of her hand. "Don't you think you're better for him? Don't you think he loves you? I see the way he looks at you."

"Crystal will do anything to keep David. She's a mother alone with her son and little ability to support him. I keep thinking about Yirina. My mother wasn't the world's most honest and truthful woman, but she did really love me, and she did her best. Men were a means."

"But you know you're better for David."

"I don't know if David understands that, and I'm beginning to think what's best for everybody is for me to give up and get out. I can't go on fighting her. It's demeaning. And I can't help knowing how hard it is for her. Like my mother. Like so many of my clients."

"But if you love David, you have to stay in there and fight for him."

"I thought I loved him, but I'm not sure any longer if I ever knew him well enough to love him. I can't go on combating Crystal. She's the wife now. Let her take what she needs. I can survive without David. I don't think she can."

Natasha said, "Or she thinks she can't."

"It amounts to the same thing, in the end." Crystal needed him; he seemed to want Crystal. What room was left for her? Only the way out.

DAVID

I saw a small red car race up the dirt road, stopping just behind my truck. Alan McCullough shouted over the lawn mower, "It's your sister!" and the two of us watched her run up the hill. "David, Mom's had an accident." Holly was gasping. "They've taken her to the hospital. Come on."

My mother volunteered two mornings a week in a day care center in the Universalist Church. Crossing High Street at noon, she was struck by a kid on a bicycle. "Did she break something?" I asked. "Did she hit her head?"

"I don't know." Her nose almost touching the wheel, elbows pinned to her sides, Holly's whole body seemed to be aimed at the hospital, as if steering a bullet through summer traffic.

"Did they catch the kid?"

"How do I know? Crystal was calling from the ambulance."

"Crystal? How the hell—"

"I don't know, David! I just don't know anything."

I left Holly to find a space in the lot and ran to the E.R. entrance. I was halfway to Reception when Crystal called out to me. "We're okay," she said breathlessly. "It's a minor concussion. That's the good news. But she's in X ray now. They think the ankle is fractured. Her kneecap may be cracked. Over here!" Crystal waved to my sister. She draped her arm around Holly and repeated what she'd told me. "I saw a crowd outside my office window. I ran out when I heard the sirens. When I saw who it was, I couldn't believe it. She was so strong, she kept trying to get to her feet. She wanted to kill the kid. He was laughing. I swear they had to hold her down. She kept yelling, 'You little one-armed worm.'"

"It was Jimmy Compton?"

"He thought the whole thing was a joke. The rescue squad was hovering around him as if he was the one who was hurt. But he just got on his bike and rode away. I think we should press charges. I'm going to ask Mr. Lynch. I think we have a case."

My mother's accident was like a reunion for the Greene family, the first time (I'm ashamed to say) since my father's funeral that we spent more than a seder or Thanksgiving meal together under one roof. My mother left the hospital in a cast, making cooking for herself, even showering, difficult. Ten months of the year finding help would not have been an issue. However, in Saltash everyone had a summer job or two or three. In her way, she managed to put a cheerful spin on a bad situation and see herself, after years of living alone, as the matriarch of a small but dutiful clan.

Marty grilled chicken on her first night back, which we ate surrounding her on the screened-in porch. Laramie relished the extended family. He chased my sister's girls through the grove of locust trees, in and out of the barn and Georgie's old apartment upstairs. Although Laramie was between the girls in age, he was more a mascot than a friend. For hours he searched for them in a game of hide and seek. They dressed him in silly costumes. They played fish and giggled constantly, their voices rising in shrieks and then falling in hushed exchanges.

"I'm so lucky." My mother beamed that night. The following morning Holly volunteered for the breakfast shift and I arrived to prepare lunch. Still no luck in finding a caretaker. That evening I made a lasagna and the happy family dined under the mottled shade of the tall black locusts. I volunteered for the morning shift the following day, but my mother looked uneasy. "I'd rather Holly came. I have to wash my hair or I'll look like a scarecrow."

"Sorry I won't be around for dinner," Marty said. "I'll be in Toronto."

"Of course, Marty." The demands of my brother-in-law's schedule were never questioned.

The girls were looking pensive and whispered in Holly's ear. She sighed, "Mom? Do you think David could do the morning? The girls have an ice skating lesson at eight and it's almost an hour away."

"In the summer?"

"We're trying to keep their training consistent."

"I'm learning a double axel," Kara said. "My instructor says I have a good line."

"How wonderful!" my mother said.

"But I'll be here at seven," I said.

"That's not necessary, David."

"But Mom, I want to make you breakfast."

"I said it's not necessary. I need help getting dressed and . . . things a daughter should do. Not you, David. You go to work. It isn't right for a son to be playing nurse. It isn't right."

The happy family sat in stunned silence. Holly was once again in the wrong. I was uncomfortable, but how could I force myself on my mother? I tried to think of some reliable teenager to hire.

"I can come," Crystal said.

My mother protested.

"But I can. I don't have to be at my desk until nine. If I'm a little late, Mr. Lynch will understand. He's the best."

"Are you really all right with this?" Holly was still frowning.

"We'll have fun. Won't we, Laramie?"

Tonight the girls had dressed him up in lipstick and rouge, an old white shirt of my father's and a velvet curtain sash. No, he didn't mind. For Laramie, clearly any attention was better than none. He liked it, he told Holly when she offered to wash him off. He liked having sisters and a grandma.

Johnny Lynch had no problem with Crystal coming in late every other morning after caring for my mother. One day he showed up for lunch. With my mother sitting in a kitchen chair and supervising, her ankle propped on a cushion, Crystal made sandwiches and served iced tea. She'd begun wearing a blouse I remembered as my mother's, blue linen with embroidery. Another day, Holly touched Crystal's rose ceramic earrings. "Mom, I gave you these."

"They were too heavy for me." My mother never seemed to enjoy Holly's presents.

Holly liked Crystal but had always mentioned her to me with a kind of mischief in her voice, as if to suggest sex. Now the two of them conferred about my mother daily. They went over their schedules at the kitchen table, sharing shifts, giving each other a little extra time at work.

In early August a Mrs. Falco, the librarian's mother, called to say she had lost a client and had time to care for my mom. She had a good reputation. I thought we should grab her. Holly agreed. Only Crystal insisted there was no reason to waste the money. She said my mother shouldn't have to depend on strangers.

The evening before Mrs. Falco was to start, I was watching a Red Sox game with Laramie when Crystal came in with a large box. "What's that?" Laramie was intrigued.

"Mom gave it to me," she said. Since the accident, Crystal had begun speaking about my mother as if she'd known her all her life. Like dolls at a tea party, we'd been assigned roles. I was Daddy. My mother was Mom. Laramie and my nieces were the Kids. Nobody questioned it; nobody blinked. Crystal had simply redefined our family with herself in the middle.

Laramie began pulling at the wrapping tape. "Please can I see?"

"No," Crystal said, with a harshness that drew my attention. She wasn't looking at Laramie but straight ahead, almost blindly. Her fingers grazed the edges of the box as if feeling her way through some dark inner landscape. "It's time to go to bed."

But his curiosity only grew. "Please?"

"They're glasses. Blue cobalt glasses. But we can't unpack them now."

"What's cobalt?"

They were dark blue goblets, dessert cups, water glasses. Because my parents rarely entertained, they were arranged for show on a shelf in our dining room. They'd been relegated to the attic when my mother had new wallpaper put up. I hadn't laid eyes on them since.

"Why can't I see one?"

"Because we don't want to open them here. Because we'll just have to pack them again when we move."

Laramie's face turned the color of newspaper, white-gray. I imagined I could feel the blood leaving his lips, but of course it was my own pulse I felt, behind my eyes, in my wrists as I rubbed my hands against my sides.

"Mom said she was saving these for when we were married. But since David found us another place to live, I might as well take them anyway."

"Crystal . . ." I had not found them another place. I had merely asked a friend of my mother's who managed a cottage colony if there wasn't a year-round unit available. The conversation had lasted thirty seconds. I was opening my mail in the post office. The woman was tossing her duplicate catalogues. Although the situation sounded ideal, the woman had not yet gotten back to me. "Laramie, maybe you should go to bed," I said. "Put your pajamas on. I'll bring in the radio and you can listen to the game until you fall asleep."

It was as if I had not spoken. "Are we moving, Ma?"

"You know Aunt Holly always wanted these, Mom said." Her fingers were peeling the stiff brown tape as her face, her eyes, all but her lips remained absolutely still. "Aunt Holly doesn't need them because she has a house and a business and Uncle Marty to take care of her and buy her things. But we don't have any of that, so we get these. Aren't they pretty?" She lifted a blue water goblet to the light. "Aren't we lucky, Laramie? To have such pretty glasses?"

The boy was looking at me, pleading with me to stop something he had obviously witnessed before, when she raised the glass high and brought it down on the table's edge. The glass was thick and did not shatter with the first blow. She brought it down again. Then she grasped one of the jagged blue edges of the goblet and drew it along her arm.

She was not aiming to cut a vein. This was more the work of an artist, a carver to be precise, for as Crystal backed away from me, as she drew the glass across her flesh she seemed to admire the long white striations that swelled to pink and burst into rivulets of blood that flowed one into another.

"Crystal, I never asked you to leave—"

"But you want us to." Her voice sounded distant, controlled. She drew the glass across her arm again.

"I don't want you to go anywhere. I told you you could stay here as long as you need to, as long as you want to. . . ." As I neared his mother, the boy was at my side, watching her face and the pressure of the glass on her arm. Yes, he seemed to tell me, not with words but the subtlest distortion of his features, his teeth on his bottom lip, the movement of his gaze from his mother and back to me. Keep talking to her, he seemed to be saying. Keep telling her what she needs to hear. "Crystal, remember the morning Michelle asked you to leave? Remember you said that you'd be interested in a place that didn't charge two months security deposit?"

Good, Laramie seemed to be saying. This is the way.

"Remember? You said you didn't want to borrow money from me?"

Her grip on the glass seemed to loosen.

"Well, that's when I asked the lady from the cottage colony. Because she was looking for a family to move in as caretakers. For no deposit. That's when I spoke to her."

"That was two months ago," Crystal said.

"That's right. And I haven't spoken to her since."

Go on, the boy seemed to say.

"Because it's just fine for you and Laramie to be here. Because you can stay here as long as you want."

"You mean that?"

"Of course I mean it. This house is your house too."

"Mine and Laramie's."

"I don't know what my mother was talking about. She gets confused. That's why I think it's best that she has a real nurse. That's why we're getting Mrs. Falco to come in. Because Mom needs real care. She's getting older. . . ."

"She is. She forgets things," Crystal said. "Just last week she forgot Laramie's name and ran through all the kid's names before she got to his. It was really funny. She said Kara, Allison, David . . . before she got to Laramie. Remember?"

The little boy nodded.

Crystal looked at the gash on her arm as if it was nothing, an insect sting, a rash. She placed the broken goblet in my outstretched hand. "You really do want us to stay here, don't you?"

"This is your house now. I mean that sincerely," I said. And I did. It was all hers. If she wouldn't move, I would come up with another plan. I looked at Laramie, wondering at his calm. He seemed ashamed for his mother, but not surprised. I could not risk another scene like the one I had just been through. Neither could I stay in this house.

DAVID

The Board of Selectmen was divided. Two men, Ralph Petersen and Fred Fischel, were said to be in Johnny Lynch's pocket, while Sandra Powell and Lyle Upham had been elected with Judith's help. I knew why I couldn't call Judith—I had nothing yet to say. I hadn't moved out yet. I had plans to gradually detach, cut back. But I thought of Judith. I wanted every meeting night for her to show up, hoping to explain afterwards. It was like being in a storm and remembering a quiet clear place. I missed her voice, her intelligence, her body that seemed an extension of her personality and her mind, instead of a sexual morass into which I had sunk almost over my head. But I understood Judith would not be with me while I was living full-time with Crystal. The way things were now, I rarely saw Judith, and never alone.

The hearing before us was a simple conversion of a license, from wine and beer to a full liquor license. Powell and Upham were opposed and presented arguments against drunk driving, teenage alcohol abuse, and high school kids crossing the line from Wiggins Neck, the next town over. Lyle stood up to address the crowd and asked if one more place to buy hard liquor would improve life in this small town. "I don't think there's anyone here tonight who can forget about last year's rape in the parking lot." This was greeted with a loud rumbling in the audience, gaveled down by Chairman Petersen, who recognized Fred Fischel, a retired accountant with delicate, almost paper-white hands that he nervously rubbed together throughout the meeting. "You can't legislate morality," he said. "These people run a good clean business and follow all the rules. An incident like that can happen outside anyone's store, or anyone's home." Petersen voted with Fischel, for the full liquor license; Powell with Upham, against.

"How do you vote, Mr. Greene?"

Gordon told me Upham had contributed to my campaign. I knew he was pro-environment. That he'd voted for a new school. Sandra ran the local day care center. She was a perky five-foot-two who wore enormous red-framed glasses and her hair in bangs. Her youngest daughter, a budding star on the high school track team, had been hit by a truck a few years back and walked with a permanent limp.

"Mr. Greene?"

Didn't Sandra have the kids' interest at heart? Didn't Petersen and Fischel always toe the Johnny Lynch line? "I vote no," I said.

Promising to take us to court, the owners stormed out. Petersen demanded silence. The next order of business was called. I was warmed from the inside with a feeling of having stood up with the forces of good. I acknowledged a demure smile from Sandra Powell.

On the way out that night, Johnny Lynch grabbed my arm. "Tell me something. Did you know Sandra Powell's nephew just married the owner of the liquor store across the highway?"

I continued past him. "Don't know anything about it."

"Got married three weeks ago Sunday." He would not let go of my sleeve. "You gave them some wedding present there, Davey Greene. Took away their only competition. Nice work."

It was Johnny Lynch who made sure I do everything in my power never to be ignorant again; Johnny Lynch, eyeing me from the back row, waiting for me to fail, who unknowingly encouraged me to study the state ethics laws and the statutes concerning conflict of interest, to dedicate my weekends to research at Town Hall. I would not be used again. I would question and dig and ferret out every small connection and innuendo until I had it right. I would not be caught unprepared. I studied policies and labor contracts, reading sentences twice over, repeating them aloud until they made sense, studying half the night through sometimes, hoping Crystal would fall asleep before I got to bed.

We had stopped using condoms three months ago. When I put one on again, Crystal laughed. "What is that for?"

"Just extra protection."

"Against what? I take the pill, David. You know that. Or do you think I'm sleeping with someone else? Is that it?"

"I never said that."

"Did you pick up something from Judith? Some kind of infection?" Crystal said. Then hopefully: "Is she fucking someone else?"

"It's not about Judith. It's me. I don't think we're ready to have a child right now." Liam's voice had never quite left my mind. Beneath the anger, I'd heard a desperate terror. She tricked me, I could still hear him say. She's poison. "I want to use a condom, okay? There's nothing wrong with being safe."

"Fine. Use a condom," she said. "But you won't feel anything." Crystal lay on her back, legs spread, eyes on the ceiling, as still as a frightened bride, determined not to feel anything either. In turn, I moved on top of her with grim determination. "Enjoying yourself?" she asked.

*   *   *

The boat captain wore a sleeveless black tee-shirt and orange rubber boots that squeaked as he entered the hearing room. One infant son in the crook of his arm, his lean cocoa-skinned wife holding the other two boys—Saltash's only triplets—Dominic approached the selectmen like a jungle cat protecting his young. Those of us who weren't moved to sympathy understood his threats. "I got me a lawyer now and I ain't gonna be shoved around no more." He kicked the chair in front of him. "I already been punished for what I done. Fined by a judge. If you people take away my license, that's double jeopardy. It ain't right and it ain't legal."

Dominic Riggs was nineteen. His father had fished in Saltash, and his grandfather before that. Tall and wiry, with a patchy red-blond beard and a long red ponytail trailing from the back of his baseball cap, he had the kind of drive you encounter in young corporate executives who'll do anything to get to the top. But as a dragger captain, the top wasn't high enough to buy a home and support a family. Dominic was often on the wrong side of the shellfish warden: caught scalloping before the official start of the season, caught in areas closed to fishing. The warden warned the kid repeatedly and often looked the other way, but this time he was pissed off. He not only took Dominic to district court, where he'd been fined for possession of twelve bushels of oysters when the legal limit was ten, he was asking the selectmen to suspend Dominic's license.

"That fine was five hundred dollars. And another seven fifty for the lawyer." Dominic stood shoulder-to-shoulder with his wife, Jamaican born and herself the daughter of a fisherman. "You people are killing the working man."

According to the warden, the oyster harvest had been dwindling for the past two years. If some guys took more than the legal limit, there was less chance for the others to survive. Shellfish would go the way of the halibut and the cod; the resource would disappear.

Nonetheless, Sandra Powell said the boy had been punished enough. Who would feed his family if his license was suspended? Weren't we in the business of helping young people? She moved we deny the warden's request.

"Second." Lyle Upham repeated the dangers of opening the town to a law suit. Fred Fischel, facing reelection, was counting votes in the audience, packed with shellfishermen who preferred to curse the selectmen in the lobby, rather than speak their minds in public. Dominic smiled; opinion was moving in his favor.

"Mr. Chairman," I said.

Petersen responded tiredly, "Mr. Greene," as if this was not the first time I'd raised my hand to speak this evening but the fiftieth. Obviously, once was too much.

"Mr. Chairman, I move that we take the shellfish regulations of the Town of Saltash and flush them down the nearest toilet."

"Order." Petersen banged the gavel. "I said order!" He quieted the crowd. "There's a motion on the floor, Mr Greene. I assume that was meant to be a facetious remark."

"No, sir. I'm waiting for a second to my motion," I said. "Everybody in this town knows everybody else. Everybody is somebody's neighbor or daughter or cousin or friend. We try to look the other way when one of us breaks the rules. Okay. But that means we have no rules. Why pretend we do? Let's just flush them away. Now I know Dominic, and I know he works hard to feed his kids, but so do a lot of other guys. If we start ignoring the rules for every one of them, there'll be no harvest at all. Now if that's what we want, fine. But then let's not pretend we have regulations. Let's just flush them down the damned toilet and call it like it is."

Fred Fischel raised his hand. "Mr. Chairman, I move to order the previous question."

"What does that mean?" I asked.

The chairman didn't even look at me. "It means debate is closed, Mr. Greene. Do I hear a second?"

Within minutes the vote was taken. Dominic won.

"You're in the newspaper!" Crystal said, spreading the *Saltash Eagle* on the kitchen table. Laramie propped his chin on his fists to watch. She read: " 'At last Monday night's meeting, Selectman David Greene likened unenforced regulations to that which is commonly flushed down the commode . . .' "

"I didn't say anything like that."

"You know what Mr. Lynch said? He said you had real balls to take on the Riggs family." Crystal dropped her hand in my lap. "And don't I know it."

I was embarrassed in front of Laramie, who just smiled dreamily at his mother and me. Crystal thought that his stock had risen since my election, that kids who'd never been interested before were pursuing him. I thought the few new friends he'd made came from his association with my sister's girls. If anyone's social life had taken a turn for the better, it was Crystal's. Like my mom, whose status had soared when I pitched for the high school team, Crystal imagined herself the First Lady of Saltash. Sometimes people would call the house with questions— When is my road going to be repaved? Is it true they're planning to build a bike path through the woods?—which Crystal would officiously try to answer. Sometimes she came home with advice from Johnny. "He says never tell reporters anything unless you want it published. Don't mistake them for your friends." One night I heard her tell Laramie, "You have to set an example. People are watching us."

Crystal's wound was shallow but wide. It formed a scab quickly but needed to be protected or it opened and bled again. This happened once when we were in bed. Several times I saw Laramie bandaging it for her. She could have done so herself, but it seemed a ritual for them. Seriously and awkwardly he would put far more gauze around the wound than necessary. The oversized bandage served as a warning to all of us.

After the liquor license hearing, I spent almost all my time at home reading, an activity Crystal elevated to the legal ruminations of a Supreme Court justice. As soon as I opened my briefcase, she would deny Laramie access to the TV. She would make me a pot of coffee and clear the kitchen table and tell anyone who telephoned, "David is studying policy," in the same protective voice my uncle Georgie had used to clear kids away from my practice sessions behind the school.

But what Crystal took for diligence was also a way to hide. Friends had warned me during the election, "You'll never have enough time for the nursery or a personal life." That was exactly the point. I belonged to the town now. Not since I played baseball was so much expected of me; or so little. I worked for everyone now, too busy to be touched.

JOHNNY

41

Johnny found it odd that Crystal should sometimes remind him of his dear departed Emily Ann. Crystal was a woman who had been around the block a few times. He suspected it was more her vulnerability that had got her into trouble than wantonness—although there was a kind of perfume of that about her at times. He put it down to her sorry upbringing. Her father had preferred drugs to his family. Her mother was a petulant woman, far more involved with her own disappointments than with her two daughters.

It was Crystal's desire to please that reminded him of his wife. Emily Ann had wanted to make everything better for him, for her sons, for everyone around her. She must feed every hungry bird. She took in any stray that came by. She had raised an orphan girl, Mary Rose, now living in California with her salesman husband. Turned out better than his own son William, although it hurt him to admit it. Crystal was a good mother, as Emily Ann had been, until she could no longer manage.

Watching Crystal with the other girls, he observed her basking in her role as the more-or-less wife of a selectman. But there was the rub. Living with was not marriage, and Crystal knew it. That was where her vulnerability had got her in trouble again. If you could milk the cow free, why own it? There was a slightly broken quality to her, a resonating fragility like a good porcelain set being used for every day, that made him connect her in his mind to Emily Ann.

His wife would have labeled Crystal a bad woman. Emily Ann had a proper upbringing, her uncle a priest, her parents watching over her, and her aunt and her grandparents all protecting her not only from danger in the world, but from knowledge of danger. Her innocence, her purity had touched him from the first time he met her, at a victory dance held in the ward where she lived in Boston. He had been working for the reelection of a city councillor, his apprenticeship in politics. That very purity had broken her over the hard years. He could read faint cracks in Crystal's composure too. But once she was safely married, she would heal. She was not as pure or fine a creature as his Emily Ann, and marriage would not weaken her but make her stronger.

He was used to looking out for his own, and she had proved to be his, loyal to him, openly admiring, trusting him. She was his hidden weapon in this long struggle to hold on to this sleepy village he had made known to the rest of the world. He would reward her.

That afternoon, he called Crystal into his office. "I want you to take another look at those lots along the river. Come on."

He drove her out there again, taking the road across the dike. She perched forward on the car seat chattering about her son, his good teachers and his bad teachers. He nodded and made encouraging noises, planning his approach.

He talked about what the land here meant to him, although he was sure she was only half listening. Then he got to the clincher. He parked the car in a cul-de-sac and went around to her side to open the door for her, with a courtly little nod. "This is a prize piece of land, Crystal. Can you imagine a house here?" It was hot, but a brisk breeze was blowing off the bay. That was lucky, because his pitch wouldn't go so well if they were both slapping mosquitoes. This near the river, some days they hung in the air like a living fog bank.

Obediently she stared around her. "Right at the end of a road so that you wouldn't worry about your kid being run over. And a nice view of the river." She was trying to sound interested, and he appreciated the effort.

"Near the river. It's too shallow here to worry about your son. Wouldn't this be a lovely spot for him to grow up?"

"My son?" She turned to him as if she didn't understand. "I don't even dream about something like this."

"Crystal, you're working so hard to save this land. I want to show my appreciation. I could sell you this lot so cheap that you and David could afford to build on it. I could arrange a mortgage. I could make sure that you can raise your son in a proper house on your own land."

She stared at him, her mouth slightly open. "Would you really do that?"

"Don't you deserve it? Doesn't your boy?"

Tears formed in her eyes and rolled down her cheeks. She hurtled forward and hugged him, raising her face as if to kiss him, then caught herself. She stepped back, embarrassed. "I didn't mean—"

"You were showing your gratitude, child. You make me feel young again. But of course this can only work if we win the battle. If those maniacs open the dike, this land will be waterlogged. It will be wetlands again and nobody can build on it. And I won't be able to sell it to you, because I'll have less than half my lots buildable. . . . But don't fret. We're going to win. For you and your family. For all the young families that deserve a home." On his shirt and linen jacket he could smell the flowery perfume she wore, still clinging. He could feel her soft big body against him. His member rose in his pants. He smiled in surprise. There was a bit of fight in him still, and a bit of life too. It had been four years since the last time he had used his old friend, a quickie with Maria at the cottage.

There were women whose touch could raise the dead. Crystal was one of them. He would see that she got married. There was always time by and by for a little pleasure. She would owe him, and she would know it. He would see to her as he had arranged for so many of his people to get what they really needed. Crystal walked back to the car with him, almost dancing.

"Mr. Lynch," she said softly, "you're like a father to me."

"And you're my good girl, Crystal. The one I count on. And I take care of my own. I always have."

JUDITH

42 It was the sort of weather tourists, summer people and motel owners liked, and regular residents and the keepers of shops and galleries hated. One sun-baked day followed another under an aluminum sky. Every day was a beach day. The grasses parched to brittle straw the color of rabbit fur. Little ponds dried up and bigger ponds were surrounded by a wide margin of heavily trampled beach. Judith had to water constantly. Her tomatoes were half their normal size. All afternoon Trey, the three-legged dog who preferred to be outside, moved from patch to patch of shade around the compound. The cats stretched in the deep cool under the porch, bellies to the earth, all except Io and Portnoy. Io, with long white fur, lay on the bathroom tile. Portnoy spent all of his time in Gordon's bed or on the porch with him, when Gordon could be helped out there. Portnoy had appointed himself a caretaker. He was careful not to sit on Gordon but was never more than a foot from his side. Portnoy was a solid gray cat with a dignified air, a little chubby and extremely affectionate. He had been hit by a car when still a kitten. Natasha had heard about him. Judith paid his bills and Natasha brought him home. His name was Thousand Dollar Bill until Gordon renamed him.

Judith was summoning all the family members and Gordon's closest friends now for Rosh Hashanah. It came early this year—the second week of September. It did not matter if the children were back in school, it did not matter what kind of arrangements each of them must make on the job. They were to come. Gordon was dying and this would be the final gathering. The doctor thought he would last that long but not much past September. So Judith was giving them six weeks notice to make their arrangements.

She suspected it would be her next to last public duty as Gordon's wife; after that would come only the funeral. She lived with death now in a daily, intimate way, something never entirely out of mind no matter what she was doing. She only hoped that the doctor was right and that Gordon would make it through mid-September. She urged him to stay in his room with the air conditioner, as that spared him the heat and filtered the air.

Gordon was sometimes entirely silly and seemed drunk from the painkillers. Sometimes he disappeared into himself and his eyes did not register her presence. Sometimes he was happy as a puppy. Sometimes he was nostalgic about friends long dismissed or dead, epic demonstrations, mythical parties, journeys to Kyoto and Budapest. Sometimes pain took him over and occupied him like a hostile army. Sometimes he was bitter with anger. He would be silent an entire day and then words and stories would bubble from him. Other days he slipped into heavy sleep or unconsciousness and was gone from her. His fever rose and fell. The doctors changed his drug regime constantly. They were just tinkering.

She copped a plea for Betty; she got a divorce for the woman who had been abused and hustled her off to a new life where she hoped the ex would not find her. Preliminary motions were occupying both her and the prosecution in her defense of the doctor who had assisted a suicide. The roof case kept being postponed: the least of her cases would drag on the longest from that batch. She had a new custody case, a drunk driving case, a tenant suing because lead paint poisoned his daughter. There was never an end to human troubles with the law or each other. She kept busy.

Natasha was down in Florida, learning to care for feral birds, pelicans fishermen had maimed out of hostility, tearing off half of their beaks; herons that had taken fish with hooks in them; a gull shot in the wing; a wood stork hit by a car. Judith wondered in trepidation what discarded pet or lame animal Natasha would bring home with her this time. But the animals were company for her this August of Gordon's slow departure. She lavished attention on all of them. Beppo the Crow was healed and ready to depart, and she let him go. He circled her on the dune once, twice, and then beat off steadily to rejoin his tribe. The next day he came back, but only to visit. Then he was gone again. She expected that she might see him in the winter, when rations were scarce. Would she recognize him, seen with his fellows like Hasids dressed all in black? It would be like seeing David in town and remembering intimacy.

They had less company this summer than ever, for she had made clear (without telling Gordon what she was doing) that people were to come for the holiday to say goodbye to Gordon, but not before then. All summer vacations on the compound were canceled. For the first time since she had visited that July fourth weekend when she had connected with her Bashert, her predestined husband, they were alone—except for his nurse, Mrs. Stranahan, and for Jana Baer, who came in to help and cook. The doctor asked if she would not prefer for Gordon to move into the local hospice. She did not even ask Gordon. Anything that could be done for him would be done right here, with her in attendance. Their marriage would end, but it would end with them together.

She spent all the time she could manage in the compound, even if it meant getting up in the middle of the night to beat the tide across the bridge when she had a court date in the morning. She would not lose any of their remaining time together. She would not waste it. She forgave herself for the time she had spent, yes, spent like mad money on David. She had honestly thought it might work for the three of them and later for her and David. She cut her losses, striving to forget him. At least she and Gordon had accomplished something politically—unless Crystal succeeded in subverting David to Johnny Lynch's will. That was a possible outcome, and it would be ironic indeed—but not irony she would appreciate. If David did betray the people who had elected him, she hoped he would wait until Gordon was gone, so her husband would not lose that sense of accomplishment that had so pleased him; the sense that he had finally changed the rules of politics in Saltash and opened up the government. If David took that away from Gordon, she would get even.

Mattie had shown her the letters in the papers from Crystal. By that point they were two weeks old. Mattie was embarrassed to explain how she had noticed them so late. "Well, it's just that I pile up old papers by the toilet . . ." Another month had passed since then. Basically Judith saw almost no one outside her office, except family.

The second week in August, David showed up at her office just as she was about to leave. He stood close to her, his eyes insisting she meet his gaze. She remembered that intensity of desire, from before Crystal. Searching for a way to keep her distance from him, she brought up the dike letters.

"When I confronted her, she said she felt sorry for the animals and birds, and she thought that area where the houses were going up was just beautiful and perfect for families. That's a quote."

"Did you think to point out to her that it is contradictory to save the land for herons and foxes, then destroy it by building houses there?"

He winced. "I asked her as long as she's living in my house please to show me any more letters she writes to the local papers."

"She's working for Mr. Politics and she's living with a selectman. . . . I hope this doesn't mean you've changed your stand on the dike."

"The more I try to understand the dike issue, the more complex it gets. Now the state's involved too."

"David . . ." She risked touching his cheek for a moment. "Don't turn against the people who worked so hard to elect you. Don't turn this town back to business as usual."

"You think Crystal can make me do that?"

"We haven't come to the end of what she can make you do, David Greene." She picked up her purse and her briefcase.

"Are you leaving? I thought we might have tonight."

"David, you're living with Crystal."

"I am at the moment. I'm working on that."

"I'm not someone you can have on the side. I didn't do that to you. I tried to be clear that this was a major commitment for me—not some fling. Would Crystal approve of your spending time with me?"

"She hates it. But she knows I won't give you up."

"David, you already have." She headed for the door and Gordon. If she drove quickly, she could just make it across the bridge before the 6:45 P.M. high tide covered it. When she pulled into the street, she could see him in the rearview mirror standing in the parking lot, handsome and forlorn. Heat touched the back of her eyes as if she would cry, but she had cried too much this summer. She squinted hard and regained control. As she crossed the rickety bridge, she felt safe. This island was where she belonged, with her only love, her husband.

DAVID

Letters from Florida addressed in Vicki's hand had a way of turning my stomach inside out. I usually tore them open immediately, right there in the post office, to get the bad news over with. But this one was from Terry.

Dear Dad,
Mom said to write you to tell you I'm a pitcher now. Not like you were but just in softball. I pitched for the color war in my camp (we were the Blue team) and I won the game. I miss you. I can't wait til November when you come to visit. I still have the books you bought me at Epcot last time. My cownslor's name is Ted and he says if my real father was a baseball pitcher then I have a strong arm in my jeans to be one too. Granpa Wynn died of a heart attack. We were all crying and stuff. Mom had to sell Valiant Prince. She says maybe I can visit with you if you want but school is starting soon and she says your probably busy but I miss you. If you want to write me back we're moving to an apartment. Mom says she doesn't know the address yet. The baby and Suzi cry a lot but mom says the new apartment will have a pool. Please write me back as soon as you can. I miss you and want you to teach me to be a pitcher like you.

Your son,
Terry

I didn't go back to the nursery from the post office. I went straight to my house. Crystal was working and Laramie was at the summer rec program until three. Vicki should have been at work, but I don't why, I had a feeling. I dialed her home number. "It's David," I said when I heard her voice, bracing myself as always for an unpleasant response.

"Oh," she said, more surprised than annoyed. "Hi. You got Terry's letter. That was fast."

"He said your father . . . Wynn . . . I'm sorry, Vic."

"Well, it was his second heart attack. Then he had a third one in the hospital."

"I didn't know."

Silence. How would I?

"Anyway, Terry sounds like he got through it okay."

"Oh, he's great. He told you about his baseball?"

"Is something wrong, Vicki? I don't want to pry into your life or any-thing." The truth is, I never had. The less I asked, the less I got hurt. As the conversation went on, however, Vicki's voice seemed to soften and almost die away. "The letter said you were moving?"

"Well, there's legal stuff. Some bullshit lawsuit. They were hounding Daddy. Anyway, yeah. We're moving. Me and the kids. Mom had to sell the house. She's moving in with my brother, Junior."

I don't know why it was so hard to ask. I thought I'd gotten over Vicki a long time ago. But pain sticks, I guess, like the question itself in my throat. "And your husband, Cesar. How's he taking all this?"

"Cesar and I split up in May." She sounded annoyed, as if I was in-deed interrogating her. "He moved up to Jacksonville."

"I'm sorry."

"Right."

"Listen. Terry said in the letter he might want to visit. That would be great with me. I'll pay the airfare. It wouldn't cost you a thing."

"Not right now. I think the little ones need him around. He's a really good big brother."

"I know he is," I said, but the truth is, I had no idea.

"I think we should make the move," Vicki said. "Get settled. Then we'll see."

"Is he there?"

"He's at camp. They're doing this overnight thing in the Everglades. Him and his cousin Justin are in the same group."

"I bet he loves it."

"I'll tell him you called, David. All right? He'll be excited."

"He can call me anytime."

"I'll tell him."

"Collect!" I said, but Vicki had already hung up.

I didn't go back to work right away. I did something I hadn't done in years: nothing. I simply sat there on the couch. No TV, no radio, no one arguing, no Laramie sprawled in the living room or Crystal rubbing my back. The quiet seemed to wrap around me like a blanket. I read the letter over and then over again. I even laughed: a strong arm in my jeans. I felt so full of hope I actually knocked wood the way my mother did—three knuckles against the coffee table to ward off the evil eye. Ju-dith had said she could help me bring him home. Part-time, vacations, summers, it didn't matter, it was a start. For years Wynn had built a wall around my son and there was no way through. I'd always hoped Terry would reach out to me; and now he had. I wouldn't hound Vicki, but I wanted some real time with my son, finally. But not here, not in this house. I thought I understood what kept me with Crystal: pity, guilt about leaving Laramie, the complete submission of a woman and her body. But I couldn't subject my son to my mistakes, to a woman who used pleasure and pain as hard currency. Not if I ever hoped to have my son with me. If I was going to make a move, it had to be now.

"Please, Crystal, put your clothes on. We have to get Laramie up. You have to get to work."

"What do you care? You're leaving. You don't love me anymore. You think I'm fat, is that it? I disgust you? That's why you don't want to make love to me?"

"That's not true, any of it." It was impossible for me to speak my mind. My eyes kept drifting over her breasts, the little gold rings in her nipples, even her belly, which she hated, the delicate hill of soft flesh. "Just please get dressed."

"Why should I? It's my bedroom. Oh. Sorry. *Your* bedroom. Which I took away."

"No, it's still your bedroom. Our bedroom. I'm only moving over to my mother's for a few nights a week. I'm trying to keep her off her ankle. You know what the doctor said. Until it heals."

"She has help."

"Mrs. Falco is only part-time. She doesn't get there until after nine. My mother wakes up early. Crystal, this is no big deal."

"No big deal? That you don't like to make love to me anymore?"

"I love to make love with you. We made love last night."

"With a condom, David. You could hardly feel me. We have to stop everything to put it on. You think I'm trying to trick you? You think I want a baby with a man who doesn't want it—or me?"

We'd fallen asleep last night after the same argument. This morning I'd awakened at five A.M. in the midst of an erotic dream that turned out to be a very real Crystal between my legs, sucking me. She sensed I was about to come and began to mount me, when I rose and got out of bed. I did not lie. "I want you so much." I did. Even now.

"Then why are you packing? Why are you leaving our home?"

"We talked about this. It's not right the way it is. You work for Johnny Lynch. You write letters to the newspapers for him—"

"I'm too stupid to have my own opinions, so I do it just for him? Is that what you're saying?"

"I'm saying I'm an elected official. I'm saying you are economically dependent on a man who stands to gain by my vote. I need a place for my notes, a private place to do my work."

"I've never looked at your stupid notes."

"What was your little Donkey Sparks speech about last night?"

Crystal covered her face, the way she did when buying time to think. When she dropped her hands, her eyes looked bloodshot and sore. "I said he had his faults, but was a good manager. That he could handle a rough bunch of guys because he'd earned their respect."

"Now where would you hear that?"

"I work in an office. People talk. Don't you come home and tell me what kind of trees you planted? Sorry, didn't you used to come home and tell me things? You don't anymore. You hardly talk." Crystal sighed, crossed the room and scooped a tee-shirt off the floor. Even as she stretched it over her head and shoulders, I glanced at the perfect shaven lips between her thighs.

"Crystal, I don't think you do it purposely, but Johnny's trying to get to me through you."

"I know that, David. I'm not stupid. But we can use him. Don't you see? Why can't you give me credit for anything?" Her voice broke. Tears collected in the corners of her eyes. "You're a good man. The best this town has ever had. You won't let yourself be fooled. So what if he offers us things?"

"Damn it, three-quarters of an acre is a huge bribe. He wants me to have a financial stake in an issue I'll have to vote on. Don't you see what he's doing?"

"You said you weren't sure about voting to open the dike. You said you had a lot of questions."

"Is that what you told Johnny?"

"This is really because of Judith, isn't it? She's the reason why you're leaving me. She tells you not to trust me. Do you honestly think I'm spying on you for Mr. Lynch?"

"I'm not leaving you," I said, even as I threw clothing and books into a cardboard box. "I'm setting up a space for myself with a desk and a mattress. . . . In case I want to work late. Or if my mother needs me. I'm not leaving you."

"You're not?" Crystal said, pulling the hem of her tee-shirt down to cover herself. "Then tell him."

Laramie stood in the doorway. When I lifted him in my arms and touched his cheek to mine, it was utterly cold.

JOHNNY

Johnny laid his hand on Donkey's shoulder. "Don't you worry. The kid isn't going to vote against you out of spite, just because you once had an argument. I'll call out the troops for you. Never doubt it."

Donkey still looked worried, his long face drooping. "I've done a good job, for you and the town, Johnny. I'm not ready to be hung out and dried. Jeez, who'd have expected the little kike to get in. I never did."

"Sit down, Donkey. Have a touch of scotch." He poured them each a shot and sank back in his BarcaLounger. "People like ex-sports heroes. They're heroes, one, and two, they've come down in the world. Makes people feel good. But you have friends here. And so do I." Johnny thought that Donkey always looked as if he had stayed in the sun too long: his face was permanently pink and his eyes popped. Donkey's father had suffered from high blood pressure, and so did Donkey. The whole Sparks family had it. Donkey's father had died of a sudden heart attack at fifty-two, dropping dead right in the middle of Main Street chasing a tourist who had walked out of his shop without paying. Donkey was forty-nine. "Don't get yourself hot under the collar. You'll keep your job."

"I've always come through for you, Johnny, you know I have. What's this town coming to? I grew up here, and so did my dad and my mother and my granddaddy before them. There's been Sparkses in this town since Adam and Eve. We come over from Devon almost two hunnert years and we been here ever since." Donkey was spread across the whole Naugahyde couch, his arms and legs splayed wide. He was not a big man but occupied a lot of space.

"You're a part of this town for sure," Johnny said soothingly. He would like Donkey to calm down and get off his back. He intended to fight for the man's reappointment, not only for Donkey's sake, but because controlling the Department of Roads, Bridges and Waterways was damned useful. Johnny had controlled it for thirty-five years, and he wasn't about to lose his grip on it now.

"This is good whiskey," Donkey said admiringly. "Smooth as a young girl's behind."

"I wouldn't give you less than my best," Johnny said.

When Donkey finally went home, Johnny tilted the BarcaLounger

upright and sat with a big yellow legal pad on his lap planning his campaign. He had two selectmen but he needed a third. He would draw up
a list of people willing to write a letter or make a phone call, put up a
fight for a hardworking local boy. Shouldn't Davey Greene himself be
owing him something? For that lot they'd be building on? Crystal hadn't
got back to him about that. Just what did the boy say? Did he bite like a
fish or was he coy? The latter, most likely, but he'd come around—once
he realized how much his pride would cost him. Johnny would make
sure there was enough public pressure to make it easy for David to vote
for Donkey.

Johnny arrived at the office Monday morning with his lists. Maria
was working on the books, so he had Tina and Crystal start putting in
the calls. He'd take each one, of course, but they could run the people
down first, leave messages, get whoever they could. By noon he had
talked with eleven people. Then he had lunch with Ralph Petersen, but
not at the Binnacle. He ordered up roast beef sandwiches and soup and
a bit of salad—not that the Binnacle normally did takeout, but this was
for him. He'd seen their expansion through the Zoning Board of Ap-
peals; convinced the Board of Health to grant them a variance on their
septic system. And why not? If you wanted an evening meal in this
town after Labor Day, it was the Binnacle or pizza. They ran a necessary
year-round business. Good for the town.

Johnny and Ralph had a private lunch in the office. Johnny liked to
watch Ralph eat. Ralph was what they used to call a string bean, tall
and skinny with a shiny dome and a white mustache, but he ate as
daintily as a fastidious miss in lace gloves. It was his mustache. He was
vain about it (the only hair he had left above his chin) and dreaded getting something caught in it. It had happened to him publicly maybe fifteen years ago. Palmer Compton, it was—the father of that one-armed
idiot—stood up in a selectmen's meeting and said, "You have tomato
sauce for suppah, Chairman Petersen? Or'd you get that punch in the
mouth you deserve?" Ralph's skin was as thin as the finest silk. He
never again appeared in public with a speck of food in his mustache.

"So how is our new kid selectman doing, Ralph?"

Ralph made a noise in his throat. "Going to be trouble."

"He grew up here, Ralph. Not like our ex-professor and Miss Nursery School. I think we can get to him."

"You gonna fight for Donkey?"

Johnny spoke slowly, because he was about to give Ralph his line:
"Donkey Sparks knows the men and they trust him. By the way, we
should call him Sparks from now on, not Donkey when we refer to him.
Sure, Sparks may lack computer skills and the ability to go out and get

grants from the state, but he keeps a firm hand on a difficult department. He's a hands-on manager of the old school."

"Hands-on manager of the old school," Ralph repeated with satisfaction. "That's one I can use."

"Sparks grew up here and he loves this place and is loyal to it, not
some careerist passing through to a bigger town with a bigger budget."

Ralph put up another finger. "Not using us as a stepping-stone."

"A son of this town, Sparks knows the people and the land." Johnny
paused for Ralph's full attention, "Yes, the people and the land of
Saltash."

Ralph nodded sagely. "Remember the last big snowstorm, when the
old people couldn't get out? Donkey Sparks plowed his way into the
back woods with the meals-on-wheels right behind."

"That's it." Johnny nodded. Ralph was a good man if you gave him
some direction. He didn't need everything spelled out, just the outline
and he'd be ready to take on the foe. "Talk to Davey Greene. Try to get
him on our side. Take him under your wing, Ralph. You can do it."

Ralph shrugged. "I'm not so sure of that."

"He's a local boy. What does he have in common with the Gordon
Stone gang? He got recruited in bed. Now that's over and he's going to
wake up and see where his true alliances are. We can get him to come
over. I know it." Johnny opened his office door. "Crystal, dear, could you
put on a pot of coffee for two old gentlemen?" He winked at Ralph.

"You've got his girlfriend in your pocket."

"Just about. And I suspect he'll be marrying her soon enough."

Ralph nodded, seeing which way the land lay.

"He doesn't want to build a house," Crystal said.

He had asked her to stay a little late for one more letter. "Why
wouldn't he jump at the chance?"

"He said it was a bribe. And now he's moving out!" Crystal's face collapsed and two fat tears rolled down her cheek.

He was glad he had waited till the girls left to broach the subject. He
patted her shoulder. "Moving out where?"

"He's staying half the time in that barn behind his mother's."

"Where his uncle Georgie used to live? It's barely an attic. Did he say
why?"

"He said he can't keep his mother off her feet. You know, her ankle
swelled all up. But I was taking care of her fine before he hired Mrs.
Falco. He's moved his selectman papers there. I think he suspects I
told you about the letter—before the election?—and other stuff. I just

tell you what I think you need to know. I know you want what's best for all of us."

"But why does he suspect you? Has he ever tried to get you to quit?"

She shook her head no. "I think he's too glad I'm working to argue about where."

"Well, that's a blessing. You know how the girls and I depend on you in the office. There's not one of us knows those computers the way you do. Nothing would get done around here without you . . ."

She sniffed and he handed her a crisp white handkerchief, the sort he always carried, Irish linen and monogrammed. "You make me feel important. Nobody else does." Crystal rubbed at her eyes. "I just don't know what's happening with him or what he's feeling."

"What does your little boy think of all this?"

"He's scared. He doesn't say anything. But he watches and he listens and he knows that I'm in trouble."

"So Davey Greene doesn't want to build a house. There could be forty reasons for that, dear. Perhaps he doesn't want to go into debt right now with his mother injured and disabled. You mustn't panic."

She had the air of someone about to burst into hysterics, which he definitely did not want. He kept talking in a soothing voice. "He cares for your son, you've seen that, and obviously he cares about you. Give it time. Perhaps things moved too fast and you need to wait for him to settle down and settle in. Men often get balky, take my word for it, when things get serious. A man needs time to get himself around to thinking it's his idea, not the woman's."

"I just can't believe he moved into that drafty barn to get away from me! It's so unfair."

"Do you think something instigated this move? Something triggered it?"

She wiped her face in his handkerchief and sat down, frowning. She was in control again, a fragile patched-together control, but no longer verging on hysteria. "I know he's stewing about that head of the roads and bridges department."

"Donkey Sparks? Stewing about what, exactly?"

"I'm telling you, two things made him run for office. One was that bitch Judith Silver and the other was Donkey Sparks."

"So that's why he ran?"

"I think that had a lot to do with it. He said Donkey made him feel invisible." Crystal shook her head sadly. "He felt like they ran over him instead of just his fence."

Johnny needed time to think about this.

Crystal was still talking, slowly, her brows drawn together in thought. "He says that Judith Silver broke up with him, but I'm sure she has something to do with this. I know he's sneaking in some evenings to see her, I just know it. That's why he moved over there."

"She's a dangerous woman," Johnny said. "The first time I met her was in court. She lost, and I don't think she ever forgave me. That is one lady, if I can still call her that, who does not like to lose, Crystal. I'll keep my ears open. Nobody has any secrets around here, believe me. If he's seeing her, there's always someone who notices." He would do that for Crystal and for himself, to refine his strategy. When Stumpy came by for his monthly check, Johnny would quietly, indirectly, patiently question him.

As Stumpy rowed across the harbor to town, he brought more than an appetite for beer and sausage: he brought news. This would not be the first or the second or the third time Johnny had used Stumpy for intelligence on the doings of the Stones. Who had come by to visit with Gordon? Whose cars were parked overnight? Who came to a particular meeting? Stumpy noticed everything, but he didn't take sides. He would never understand that information had any value. Day after Labor Day, Stumpy would come in for his check. They'd have a nice long conversation.

DAVID

If Johnny Lynch no longer grabbed the headlines, there was no doubt about his ability to draw a crowd. The night of Donkey Sparks's reappointment hearing, Johnny stood at the door shaking hands, guiding people to their seats like a night club maitre d'. He sat Donkey's family in the first three rows, wife, children, grandchildren; Donkey's loyal crew and their families in the rows behind. All three local reporters had been alerted. The cable news people were setting up lights and cameras. When the seats were all taken, the aisles filled; late arrivals were peering through the doors. Since four of the five votes were set in stone, it appeared that Johnny went to all this trouble to influence me.

The hearing was scheduled to begin at seven-thirty, but at seven, during the open session, Johnny Lynch slowly lumbered to the microphone. "I want to know where we stand on the issue of home-based contractors and parking," he demanded. "You people are holding an ax over our heads." Some months ago the legality of local tradesmen working out of their garages had been questioned. It was an emotional issue for them; an equally excitable one for their neighbors, who didn't want their quiet streets turning into little industrial parks. Johnny knew perfectly well the board had no intention of changing the rules. But one after another, carpenters, plumbers, house painters, come directly from their day jobs or the bar at Penia's Pizza, stood up to warn the board not to mess with their rights. This was not the usual crew we saw at selectmen's meetings, not people accustomed to expressing themselves in a public forum. They were here because Johnny had started a rumor they were about to be screwed—and in so doing had filled the hearing room with people most likely to support Donkey Sparks.

Ralph Petersen called the hearing to order. Ralph had asked after my mother's health this evening; only last week he had begun to address me by my first name. Not a forceful chair, he used cold efficiency to bull his agenda through, announcing the issue in a dry monotone, calling for debate and as soon as possible thereafter, the vote. Fred Fischel not only made the motion to reappoint Donkey Sparks, he read a prepared speech. Fred waved his arms as he recounted the heroic exploits of Donkey leading an army of meals-on-wheels volunteers through the frozen tundra of the Saltash winter forests. I glanced over at the progressives on the board, Sandra Powell and Lyle Upham, who were wearing serene and confident smiles, certain we had the votes.

Petersen called on the audience to speak. The people and the land, they kept repeating, as if scripted. "If there's one thing Donkey knows better than the people of this town, it's the land itself." By my second month on the board, I'd perfected the art of looking fascinated while not listening, and the further ability to avoid the stares of those who were obviously contemplating my grisly death. It was clear that the room was packed with Donkey's supporters, and that the only ones who weren't here were those who had elected me to get rid of him. But Johnny Lynch understood that an X on a ballot is dead and gone, while influence lives in the anger of the people who show up.

One after another they made points I couldn't refute. Donkey Sparks did know every road in this town. He was available twenty-four hours a day. He belonged to the Fire Department, which often worked hand in hand with his own. Although he had never graduated college, he knew as much about highway construction as a civil engineer. Moreover, he knew his men. Knew how to keep them from goofing off (when he cared to), how to send them home when they came in drunk and get them to return sober the next day, how to keep them from filing endless petty grievances with the union.

"I'll hear three more speakers," Ralph said to a line that stretched from the microphone out to the lobby.

Nini Sparks, Donkey's wife, had sung in my mother's choir. She was a soft heavy woman who wore sweatpants and tee-shirts emblazoned with the names of places they'd gone on vacation. She stared at me, her jaw locked, doing her best to threaten, absently chewing her stringy brown hair. Everybody knew about Donkey's temper; everybody saw the bruises on her arms. When Donkey lost his job, how much of his anger would fall on her?

Although he never strayed from the square of space in front of his seat, Donkey made me think of an animal pacing his cage. What hair he had left was clipped close to the scalp, the same texture as the stubble on his cheek, so that his whole head looked to be cast in shadow. Inarticulate, uneducated, crude, as my mother had described him, he stared only at me, alternately offering me certain death and sugarcoated favors. What could I expect if I voted his way? Snow plowing up my mother's driveway to her door? A water view lot in Johnny Lynch's development? First dibs on all the hardwood his crews cut down?

Ralph called for the vote. "Fred?"

"I vote for Mr. Sparks and I hope all of you do the same."

"Lyle?"

"No."

"Sandra?"

"No."

Ralph would cast his vote last, but everyone knew what it would be. There wasn't a sound in the hall. "Davey?" The diminutive now; the guy was practically adopting me.

Harlan Bowman in the sixth row back was bent at the waist, appearing ready to sprint up the aisle. He looked to be coaxing me, eyes wide and hopeful and welcoming. If I came through for them this once, he was trying to tell me, I'd be one of them, as good as native born. And why not? I had to ask myself. Did I imagine I had more in common with retired college professors? With the people whose yards I maintained? Why not prove myself to the locals? Donkey wasn't even the problem. He was a puppet. He jumped when Johnny Lynch pulled the strings. How many department heads would I have to cut off before I killed the hydra? Would I have to retire Abel Smalley? And the town manager? And the health inspector? And the harbormaster? Would I have to knock off Johnny's minions one by one and in the process fire every native-born man and woman in town government? Bring in administrators with advanced degrees, people who at best had vacationed in Saltash, who saw the town as a step in their career path? Was that the only way to get to Johnny?

"Davey? The question on the floor is to reappoint Mr. Duncan Sparks as superintendent of Roads, Bridges and Waterways. How do you vote?"

If Gordon or Judith were here, I'd have a moral anchor. I'd know the way I was about to vote was right. So many things about this job reminded me of Judith. I missed her clarity, her tough legal mind. I had never felt so public and at the same time so alone. I looked from Nini Sparks to her husband's fists. From Harlan Bowman back to Johnny Lynch himself, arms folded, rocking back and forth in his seat. Join us. His smile was soothing. Our side is your side. Join us.

But Johnny read my vote in my eyes, and before the word *no* could leave my lips he was out of his seat, striding to the microphone. "Chairman Petersen!"

"We're voting, Mr. Lynch."

"As Mr. Sparks's attorney, sir, I'd like the opportunity to speak." He didn't wait for permission from the chair. "I believe there may be a conflict of interest here. I believe Mr. Greene has had a personal dispute with Mr. Sparks and I question whether he can be fair and impartial. . . ."

Sandra and Lyle looked at me with steely impatience. Didn't I know this was one of Johnny's tricks? Had I expected him to go down quietly?

Answer yes, of course you can be impartial, and then let's cut the bastard's legs off. What are you waiting for?

"Isn't it true, Mr. Greene, that on the afternoon of April six of this year you accused Mr. Sparks of covering over a scandal in his department? The town manager was in the room at the time, Mr. Greene. Isn't it true that you accused Mr. Sparks of impeding your landscape business? As you well know, this is not a court of law. You are not required to answer, but I suggest that if you do not recuse yourself, you are opening this town to legal action."

Before I could form an answer, Fischel's hand shot up. "Mr. Chairman, I move we indefinitely postpone the motion to reappoint."

"I'll second for the purpose of discussion," Petersen said. "The motion is open to debate."

"Mr. Chairman, we obviously need to talk to legal counsel." Fischel glared at Lyle Upham. "Anyone who doesn't support the motion is clearly exposing the town to risk."

Upham glared at me.

No one in the crowd was sure exactly what had transpired, except Johnny Lynch, who seemed to nod, Well done! to Selectman Fischel and to wink at Donkey Sparks.

JUDITH

Judith wondered sometimes if she shouldn't just take a leave of absence from her law practice so she could spend all her time with Gordon these last weeks of his life. But the bills not covered by insurance piled up and piled up. Her clients could not put their lives or their troubles on hold. So she went on, with half her attention always focused on Gordon. Not that he exactly kept track of when she was there and when she wasn't. She knew he drew comfort from her presence, but he drew almost as much from close friends. He was heavily drugged and high, kiting through internal skies on winds she could not perceive. Sometimes he was back in 1952 or 1967. Usually he recognized her, but now and then he confused her with some previous wife or girlfriend, wanting to reminisce with her about events that preceded her birth. She never corrected him; what would have been the point? Occasionally he realized what he had done, and then he told her he simply could not help imagining she had always been with him, that she was his real wife and the others had been mere preparations, false attempts, approximations.

Dr. Barrows told her that Gordon would last at most another month. He did not tell Gordon, but she suspected Gordon knew. It could happen at any time, was the way Dr. Barrows put it. Again the hospice was discussed and dismissed. She wanted Gordon to have the New Year's celebration he had requested. That week she was taking off as best she could, for she would have a full house of guests. His second oldest son, Dan, came with his family over Labor Day, since he could not come for Rosh Hashanah. They had left the day before. Now Judith was beginning preparations for the meals she would be providing the guests, but especially the dinner on the first night of Rosh Hashanah. Gordon scarcely ate, but he enjoyed the sight of food, and this feast was of enormous and terminal importance to him.

Gordon was lying in bed, gray against maroon sheets. "Did you invite David?"

"No, I did not. Have you forgotten I'm no longer seeing him?"

"Don't be bitter. I've made messes every bit as destructive as David has got himself into."

"I'm only bitter because I let myself count on him."

"I pushed you." Gordon fell silent, his eyes closed. After several minutes she thought he had fallen asleep, as he sometimes did in mid-conversation. But when she was halfway to the door she heard his hoarse whisper behind her. "I want him here. No matter how he may have disappointed us personally, politically he's vitally important. We have to stay in touch with him. We have to keep him on our side."

"You really want me to invite him? He probably goes to his sister's, the same as at Pesach."

"No." Gordon had a fit of coughing and they both waited until he could once again gasp out a sentence. "Marty told me he and Holly go to his parents then. Invite David. I want to see him one last time. After all, he's my project as much as yours."

"Your half of the project was far more successful . . . I'll ask him. Do we have to entertain his girlfriend too?"

"I think he would understand a request that he come alone."

David had left two messages for her, but she had not called him back. She knew what he had to tell her. According to Judith's sources, which included Mary and her daughter Jo, Mattie, Enid Corea, and Jana Baer, David had changed his address and phone and was living part-time in his mother's barn. However, he was still spending at least three nights a week with Crystal. Crystal was reported irked at this development and wanted him back living with her. Judith sighed. At least he was trying to disengage. One thing David had never understood was that while Gordon and she were always minor scandals, they were also deeply linked into the town. They had many friends and many supporters, people for whom one of them had done a favor, people she had represented or helped to services they needed. Like Johnny Lynch, they had multitudes of enemies and multitudes of friends. And like Johnny, they knew there were no secrets in this town. There was always an observer, a witness, a leak. If you wanted to know anything, you had only to wait and someone would come and tell it to you; if you were impatient, you just had to know who to ask. She knew, for instance, that Crystal had leaked David's election morning letter to Johnny Lynch and hence to Blossom. She had heard it from Mary who had overheard Johnny's secretary and his bookkeeper talking about it in the tea room. Nonetheless, she had never told David, but only suggested to him he might be wise to remember that Crystal was on Johnny's payroll. When he moved all his files to his mother's barn, Judith guessed he had figured out a few things.

She still wished him well. She had contempt for women who hated men they had been with for no further reason than that they were no longer lovers. It was undignified; it was petty. She had met the other Mrs. Stones; men had erratic tastes in women. She must pick up the phone and call David. She sat at her desk in her office by the harbor and made ugly doodles on a legal pad. Or could she run into him? That would be easier. She had to invite him at once, before the day was out, or he might make other plans and disappoint Gordon. She had never been capable of disappointing Gordon, even in minor things; but now it was passionately important not to fail him.

She picked up her purse, rushing past Mattie, who called after her, "Where are you going? You have an eleven o'clock."

"On an errand. I'll be back in less than half an hour."

She drove straight to the nursery. She would buy two bronze chrysanthemums. She would do it, that is, if she saw his red truck outside. If he was out on a job, she would make a new plan. But she saw the truck and then she saw him, helping Doris Fisher load a birdbath into her station wagon. Judith parked and caught him as he was walking back into the building. She didn't even have to buy the chrysanthemums.

"David, Gordon's dying. He wants to get all his family and friends together for Rosh Hashanah dinner. He views you as a friend. I hope you won't let him down."

He mumbled an answer, caught by surprise, his head bowed, hardly looking at her. Then he finally raised his gaze. "Do you really want me to come?"

"By yourself. Or do you need to bring the family?"

"I'll come alone."

"Good," she said. "Gordon expects you. He really wants you. It's his goodbye."

His sister was standing at the plate-glass window glaring. Marty had detested Judith ever since he had tried to kiss her at a party years ago and she had given him a hard push. Holly should have appreciated Judith's response, but who knows what she thought had happened? Judith turned on her heel to march back to her car.

"Judith!" David called after her. She swung back, waiting. "Is he really dying?"

"Yes. He knows what's happening. I think he's almost ready for it."

"Judith. I want to talk to you about my son. Once you said maybe you could do something about how things are. Well, I think this might be a good time."

"If you want to consult me as a lawyer, you need to make an appointment at my office, David. I'm not taking on any new cases right now—for reasons I hope are obvious." She had given the invitation for Gordon. She would continue to be friendly, remote and untouchable. Her feelings were her own business.

Gordon had many bad nights now, when the pain was uncontrollable, when his fever rose and convulsions took him. Then the demon would withdraw a bit. He would slide into sleep or unconsciousness. It was hard for her to tell the difference.

Fern had come early from the ashram and settled herself into the shack she had painted pink years ago. She began spending afternoons in Gordon's room. "You seem almost ready to pass over."

Judith, standing in the hall, overheard Fern and came in at once, fearful that Fern would upset Gordon.

"I'm not ready to die . . . but it seems I have no choice . . . I'm game for it, but . . . I had so much else I wanted to do and see. I feel as if I'm . . . walking out on a very good show."

To talk with Gordon required great patience, because it could take him up to five minutes to finish a sentence. His mind was quick, but his breathing was labored and his strength failing. However, Fern was nothing if not patient. When she was not with Gordon or helping Judith, Fern would sit with her hands open in her lap. Judith assumed she was meditating. Sometimes she forgot Fern was in the room. She admired Fern for her patience. She herself sometimes finished Gordon's sentences for him, and then felt bitterly ashamed of herself.

"No, I'm not angry," Gordon was saying. "I've . . . lived the life I wanted . . . I've had so much . . . it would be gluttonous . . . not to . . . be satisfied."

But I'm not satisfied, Judith thought, lurking outside their conversation. I have not had enough of him. I will never have enough of him. How am I going to just keep on after he is gone from me? Suppose I was offered a bargain, you can't ever touch him but you can talk with him, you can sit with him just one hour every day. Even that would be something. Even that. I would pay for it in blood. But I am going to lose him altogether. Knowing the pain he suffers and the convulsions and the difficulty of simply surviving by now, how can I argue with death? No one wins that argument, not even a crack lawyer.

She came to the doorway but did not disturb them. Gordon lay back on his pillows with Fern sitting beside him in a straight chair, one hand on his. This was one of the moments when her beauty shone out. Judith stood there unseen and thought about how much Gordon had been loved and still was loved, yet that love was weak against the dissolution taking him.

DAVID

I was at my new place, what Crystal called the barn, when I heard Judith's voice on the answering machine. Ceilings, walls and floor: I had painted the whole place white so that it felt vast and clean and pure. And quiet. I fell in love with the quiet, the padding of my footsteps in socks across the floorboards, the chatter of squirrels in the locust branches, the rain on the high-pitched roof above the loft. My bed was a mattress on the floor. "Like your uncle Georgie," my mother said, when I helped her upstairs. I couldn't bear furniture clogging the place, blocking the light and my ability to glide across the glossy white floor like a skater. I often lay on that floor to read, to write, to do nothing but stare: at the spiders walking the rafters, at Georgie's old stereo speakers, at my life, which seemed as full of possibilities as this fresh wide-open room. I was listening to one of my handful of CDs and reading when I lunged for the phone. "Judith, wait!" I said. "I'm here."

"Oh, David. Good of you to pick up." This was her lawyer voice. I had sat across her desk and heard it. I had heard her switch it on in bed, when she used the telephone after sex. I had seen her features sharpen as she paced the floor naked, trailing the telephone wire behind her tight little buttocks like the tail of a Siamese cat. I had heard her discuss rape and disfigurement and medical malpractice in the same tone she used with me now.

"You'll never guess what I was reading," I said. "Robert's Rules of Order. Since I'm getting clobbered every week I thought I might as well figure out how they do it."

She ignored me. "It's about Rosh Hashanah, David. There's a problem."

"About you and me?"

"David, there is no 'you and me.'"

"Sorry."

"Rosh Hashanah falls on the new moon, one of the highest tides of the year. It's scheduled to peak at about eight-thirty that night."

"Which means trouble getting over the bridge."

"More complications: I just saw on the Weather Channel that they're predicting a cold front coming in tomorrow night, preceded by a big storm. Those will be winds from the west that tend to push the water in early and keep it in. I'm asking everyone to cross the bridge by six at the very latest. So if you're intending to come—"

"I told you. I'm coming."

"Then come early. I don't think the bridge will be passable after six."

"Judith, can I talk to you about something?"

"I really don't have time, David. I only caught the weather report two hours ago and I'm still calling relatives from out of town."

"Judith, I've missed you."

"Tomorrow night, then. Gordon will be happy to see you."

I told Ralph Petersen I'd be absent from the Monday night meeting. He said Fischel would be out of town too. With just three selectmen— meaning two others who would probably vote against him every time— he'd keep the agenda to a few housekeeping items. But if Judith had a storm to worry about, I still had Hurricane Crystal.

How could I announce I was going to Judith's? The mention of her name would cause a fight. I was apologizing all the time for insisting on condoms, for sleeping at my place four nights a week. Reading Crystal and Laramie the letter from Terry had only made things worse. Crystal asked if I was going to stay in my ex-wife's apartment when I went down to Florida. She was now deeply suspicious of Vicki, convincing herself that since Vicki was getting divorced, she would be interested in me. Laramie thought he was being replaced. He sat in the kitchen drawing pictures of houses burning. He slumped on the couch with his knees drawn up staring at the TV, his mouth slightly open. When I turned off the TV, he didn't move.

Crystal would throw a shit fit if she found out I was going to Squeer Island without her; no less for a Jewish holiday. Everything Jewish was associated with Judith. Crystal didn't like Laramie to question me about Jewish holidays, or even why I was circumcised when he wasn't. She got nervous if she heard him asking Holly's daughters what they learned in Hebrew school, or if they showed him how to write his name in Hebrew letters. My religion was a subject off limits, a battlefield on which she couldn't compete. It had been easy to avoid the issue over the summer. But I couldn't tell her I was going to celebrate the Jewish New Year with Gordon and Judith. Without her.

I waited until Sunday night. I told Crystal that after the regular select-men's meeting there would be an executive session with the town coun-sel. I said I wanted to go out for a drink with him afterwards, to pick his brain. I'd sleep at my place Monday because it was going to be a late night.

"And Tuesday?" she said, as if she'd caught me holding something back. "Were you planning on staying away from us Tuesday too? Because I know what Tuesday is."

"Tuesday?"

"I'm not stupid, David. I have a calendar. Tuesday is Rosh Hashanah, isn't it?"

Her calendar was a free gift from the hardware store. It listed the Jewish holidays, but not that they began at sunset the night before. "If that's what the calendar says."

"I'm making a holiday dinner. Don't look so glum."

"Why do you say that?"

"Because we both remember Shabbat. But I've got a cookbook now and I'll do it right." She pulled out an old yellowing paperback, *The Art of Jewish Cooking* by Jennie Grossinger.

"Where'd you get that?"

"I found it at the thrift store. And you'd better be here. Tomorrow I'm seeing Mom and I'm going to invite her."

"Crystal, it's a weekday night. We have to get up so early. Let's put it off till the weekend. Maybe Friday? Mom won't mind. I'd enjoy it more."

She just smiled. "Just leave it up to me. I won't fuck up."

JUDITH

Judith had her lists. She had lists of foods to be purchased, food to be cooked ahead of time on Sunday. Food to be cooked on Monday. Lists of where each of the thirty guests would be lodged, for almost everyone at the dinner must sleep on the island. The September new moon brought very high tides, and the bridge would be underwater by the time the meal started. Most of Gordon's children had their own accustomed places in the compound, but Sarah had stopped visiting when her father married Judith. In fact, Sarah's old shack had been renovated into Judith's home office, so in recompense, Judith put Sarah and her daughter in her own bedroom in the big house. She would sleep in her office.

She had lists of what her lieutenants were each to do: Natasha, her right arm, her comfort and joy; Jana Baer, who would come back for the dinner. The Baers, like the Squeers, had lived on the island for generations. Mattie, her secretary, would be helping all day Monday but would leave before the tide rose.

Sunday had been a reasonably paced day. People were arriving and must be greeted and escorted to their housing, unless it was where they always stayed. A couple of tents were set up as a boys and a girls dormitory, one on the beach and one on the dune. Judith had the keys to the Bechaud house, where she could put two whole families of Gordon's friends. Then Judith discovered a storm was predicted for tomorrow. She cursed.

Monday began at dawn. Judith went flat out all day. Aside from eating her brief meals in his room, she scarcely saw Gordon. The nurse, Mrs. Stranahan, was with him, as was his oldest son, Ben. Others dropped by until sent on their way by Mrs. Stranahan, protective of Gordon's waning energy. This crowd was what he had wanted: she was providing him with a last gathering of those he cared for. She set Ben and Larry to taking down the tents before the wind did it for them; she figured she would put the kids in sleeping bags on the living room floor once the tables were removed. Ben was forty-nine, taller than his father and much broader. He was an academic, a family man, a little stolid, almost professionally dependable and easy to like. She hated pairing him off for chores with Larry, who at thirty-two was still boyish and liable to sulk.

In the afternoon they cleared the furniture from the living room (except for the baby grand they could only push aside) and set up a square of tables. Most were from the various structures in the compound, but she had also borrowed a big table from the Bechaud house and a card table from Stumpy. They were all covered in tablecloths of various colors. Sarah had gotten involved in creating pleasing color contrasts and choosing the napkins; she regarded herself as artistic. Every dish in the cupboards went out, plates dating all the way back to the first Mrs. Stone and each wife since. The Bechaud house was raided for cutlery. Mattie lent her more glasses. There was a kids' table for the five- to eleven-year-olds and an adolescents' table. By three-thirty it was all set up.

Larry was trying to be sardonic. "It's the funeral feast before the fact," he said in her ear. "So macabre. Like a Buñuel flick."

"This is the time of year to reconsider your faults and failures with other people, Larry. Don't you have something to reconsider?" She bared her teeth at him. But nothing could really touch her. She was efficient, she was busy, she was numb. She must hold it all together. There was no time for pain and the anticipation of worse pain. "Your mother and her husband should be here any moment. Why don't you go wait for them?" The sky was gray and low but the storm had not yet hit. The wind was curiously soft and vague, the bay almost glassy, the air heavy as a damp plush curtain.

At four she sent Natasha with two of the more reliable kids to round up all the animals. At 4:45 the dogs were fed and penned up for the evening. At five all the cats were overfed and then distributed where they would be safe and out of the way, all except Portnoy, the big gray who had spent the last six years never more than two feet from Gordon. She left Portnoy on Gordon's bed. She brought Io, Pretty Boy Floyd and Principessa to her shack. They could amuse themselves throwing her briefs around. They all got along and could sleep with her tonight. The two recovering birds in their cages Natasha moved into the garage. The wind had risen sharply. Now the surf was pounding the beach. When she climbed the dune for a moment's respite from the kitchen, the wind had whipped the surf into a lather the color and consistency of steamed milk. She could see the rain coming across the bay toward them. As she walked back into the house, the first drops stung her neck and back. The day was still sickly warm, but the wind felt chilly. Two of Ben's sons and Mark's stepson were shooting baskets in the rain. Sarah's seven-year-old daughter and Ben's youngest were playing fish on the porch, but the wind was beginning to tear the cards away. As she passed, Sarah and Mark were arguing in the living room.

They could not keep away from each other. Nothing had healed in six years of divorce.

First course, gefilte fish. That she had bought along with white and red horseradish. She did not relish making gefilte fish, although Yirina had done so every year. Judith hated the smell and the mess. Then came chopped chicken livers and newly baked round challah. Three enormous bowls of salad. Apples, being sliced by Jana and Mattie. She checked the clock. Mattie had to leave now. She kissed her and took over. Lemon juice to preserve color.

Sarah, curiously subdued, was ladling honey from a huge jar into little bowls for each section of table. Judith had only met Sarah once, when they had flown out to Phoenix—where Gordon was speaking—and visited her for an evening. Since then she had gotten divorced. Sarah had been distinctly unfriendly then and on the phone since, but not this time. She was blond and sharp-featured like her mother, Bev Caldwell, who had just arrived with her Texan husband, Buck. They had made reservations in Provincetown and announced they would leave when the tide went down, no matter what the time. Judith shrugged. Two less to bed down. She could move the teenage girls into that room.

It was the final assault on dinner for thirty-two. A turkey was in the oven at the Bechauds' with Ben's wife delegated to baste it. She had four chickens in her two ovens here. Another turkey and a chicken were at Jana's. There were huge potato kugels baking that should be crisp and brown on the surface and inside, moist and oniony. She had made baba genoush and hummus yesterday, by the vat. The eight vegetarians would have plenty to eat. For fruit, pomegranates and an apple and carrot tsimmes redolent of cinnamon and nutmeg. The tsimmes had been cooked in the morning and would be reheated on the stove. All the umbrellas were lined up by the door for the use of anyone needing to cross the compound. The rain was coming in hard, at a forty-five-degree angle. It drummed on the roof.

The honey cakes had been baked the day before and were laid out under towels on top of the piano. Almost every couple had brought wine, some kosher, some not. She was sure Gordon did not care. Natasha distributed the bottles along the tables. Ben's youngest boy laid the short ritual on every plate. Natasha and Judith had put it together on Friday and Mattie had photocopied it.

When everyone finally came to the table and was sorted out, she felt so taut she could scarcely sit. Natasha, beside her, whispered, "Relax. There's nothing can go wrong now. The food is all cooked. The guests are all here. Everyone's complained about the weather. Now let's get on with it."

David had arrived sometime in the last twenty minutes. She had been too busy to notice. He was sitting between Natasha and Stumpy. All Gordon's ex-wives were there except his first, who had died in an auto accident. His children were present, and his grandchildren, including those not of his blood (ex-husbands and ex-wives who had married and multiplied) but still of his mishpocheh. Only Dan and his family were missing, and they had come the weekend before. Colleagues, comrades from old battles, drinking companions. Only eight invited had failed to show, and five of those had come over Labor Day. Thus Gordon even at the end commanded loyalty and affection from those who had known him, who had put up with him, who had enjoyed him.

Judith and Natasha rose and lit the candles, blessed the wine and the challah, and almost everyone sang the Shechecheyanu, the Blessing for the New Season. She was amused to hear Stumpy's loud uncertain baritone raised in song. He had heard it so many times over the years, he had learned it. Everyone dipped slices of apple in honey for the new year to be abundant and sweet. Then the pomegranates. The younger kids began spitting the seeds at each other and painting themselves scarlet with the juice. Outside, the storm was an audible roar. Occasionally a branch broke with a thump, or something hit the side of the house. Please, please, please don't let the power go out, she prayed each time the lights flickered. There would be no water from the well, no functioning toilets, no way to wash dishes. Please, she begged, keep the power on until the last one of them leaves.

She stood at the midpoint on the table that was raised a little from the others and presided, as she had over so many feasts and rituals since she had come to this house. Gordon had not been observant, but had gone along with her, and then had gradually come to count on the holidays. At first there had been some resistance. Now his older children—older than she—asked her questions about preparing for their children's bar and bat mitzvahs, about how to put on their own holidays when they did not come to hers.

"Gordon wants me to tell you tonight that I will go on living here after he is gone from among us, and that you will always be as welcome in this house and on this land as you have been before I ever came here. We both want you to know that."

Gordon managed to nod.

"It's hard for him to speak now, so I have to speak for both of us."

Once she and Gordon had thought that when the time came to say goodbye to his family, David would stand beside her and they would all meet him as a family member. So they had dreamed, in their arrogant fantasies. She glanced briefly at him where he sat between Natasha and Stumpy. Several at the table were in tears. David was staring at her with his intense gray eyes in his tanned face. People helped themselves to the fish and the chicken livers, and the meal began.

Gordon was propped up in a big chair. He could speak little and simply watched and dozed off, watched and dozed off. He was skeletal by now. His head, too large for his body, lolled on his wasted neck. His skin was gray with a bluish tone. It was impossible to look at him and not think of death. Ben sat on his right side and Larry on his left. Larry looked extremely nervous. Ben was solicitous. His role of the good loyal son was one he had played with comfort for many years. She was grateful to Ben.

She and Natasha went out to the kitchen to start serving the main part of the meal. Gordon used to insist on carving every bird himself. Now Ben had been recruited. David pressed into the kitchen behind him. "I can help carve. I know how."

"Why not?" She was arranging platters that Natasha, Jana and Ben's wife were carrying out. The kugels would be served in their baking dishes and cut up at each table. Ben was carving one turkey as David attacked the other. Ben was faster. In the meantime, she cut up the roasted chickens and set out platters of vegetables that had been cooked with them, carrots and onions and heads of garlic, aromatic and almost caramelized. Sarah appeared, tentative, and Judith gave her the vegetarian dishes to lay out. Ben finished his turkey and went to serve it. At once, David paused in his carving and turned to her.

"Judith, I have to talk to you. You haven't answered my calls."

"Natasha! Take the last platter of chicken out. David, please finish carving. This is no time for talk. Let's get the food on the tables." She didn't feel particularly motivated to hear his explanations. What was, was. But Gordon wanted a friendship, so she would put up with some self-justification—after the meal was over, after all was done and done well.

For the most part, the dinner went smoothly. There was a screaming match between Sarah's daughter and her ex-husband's wife's son; there were wineglasses tipped over and unlikely flirtations. Ben's sixteen-year-old daughter was doting on Larry. Incest aside, their levels of emotional maturity were a match, she thought. Everyone ate too much and seemed relatively content. Gordon lay on the sofa where Ben and Larry had carried him and smiled vaguely around him. He drank some wine and ate a bite of turkey and of kugel. Then he lay back, exhausted. But he was still smiling.

After dinner, people sang around the piano Ben's son was playing while Larry beat congas ineptly. Some sat reminiscing or arguing or boasting. Ben and Mark put the living room back. Breakfast would be a more informal meal, and most of the guests would be leaving throughout the day tomorrow. Judith was overseeing clean-up. David helped, but whenever she let him catch her eye, he projected an urgency she could not manage to ignore much longer.

He finally caught her as she started the dishwasher with the first load. "Judith, I need to talk to you. There's no use saying there isn't any 'us.' For me, there is."

Ben's wife and his son's girlfriend were carrying in plates. "All right. Wait for me in my shack. I'll get away when I can. I don't know when that will be. We can talk *briefly*."

When she had cleaned up as much as she could (she had run the dishwasher through two cycles and would do more in the morning), Judith ran to make sure Gordon was all right. Ben and Stumpy had carried him to his bed. There he lay in the sleep of the heavily drugged. Portnoy was curled around his head like a gray fur cap. The cat blinked at her, but Gordon did not wake. He was exhausted. She hoped this last goodbye had been worth the drain on him.

She came back into the kitchen intending to head for her shack. Sarah was sobbing. Natasha, who had been comforting her, began to cry. Kids were rushing through the kitchen. Jana was looking for her roaster pan. Judith found it and then coaxed Sarah and Natasha into her bedroom and shut the door.

"He's really going to die!" Sarah moaned. "I can't stand it."

Judith stroked her back and held her, but she could think of little to say. For the last thirteen years, Sarah had seen her father exactly twice. She longed to disentangle from Sarah and go to Natasha, whose tears simply would not stop. Judith felt exhausted, but she had to summon the strength to comfort both women. It was her role. She did not know if she hoped David would wait for her or give up. She only wished there were someone who could hold her and comfort her as she was soothing Natasha and Sarah.

JOHNNY

Johnny saw her first in the drop of Ralph Petersen's jaw, the way he strained halfway across the table to get a better look. Johnny had been dozing through the meeting, thinking of leaving, not that he had anywhere to go but home alone. With barely a quorum present, the selectmen were slogging through a utility pole hearing when discussion stopped. Crystal stood in the open door with the boy pressed to her hip, tears mixed with raindrops streaming down her cheeks. Even before he'd followed Petersen's gaze, Johnny had caught the scent of her rose perfume, heard the clack of her boots on the gray tile floor. Crystal didn't see him wave her over, but stared at the table of three selectmen and two empty chairs. The boy saw Johnny and tugged at her, but she wouldn't move.

Johnny read the expression on her face. He'd caught glimpses of it in the office, when Crystal was upset, but he'd seen it in his wife every time she took ill. That's what scared him. That inability to move, the hopeless glaze, the lips forming sentences only the speaker herself could hear. All he needed was one of his girls going batty in the Town Hall assembly room.

"Ah, you made it, dear," Johnny said for the benefit of the curious. "You finished typing up that brief for me, then. Bless you for bringing it in a rain like this." He took her elbow and steered her to the door.

Although the boy was properly dressed in a yellow slicker with a hood, Crystal's denim jacket was soaked through. She hadn't even thought to wear a hat. Her hair dripped in pale strands down her face. He whispered, "What's going on? Do you mind telling me what you're doing here?"

It was the boy who answered. "Looking for David. But he's not here."

"I couldn't find him." She wasn't talking to Johnny or the boy but to herself. "He wasn't at work or the barn or his mother's house. He's not here."

"What's the fuss, dear? You know you can't be a millstone around a young man's neck."

"He's on the island," she said. "With her."

"Well, if that's true, I think there's a good reason for it."

"What do you mean?" she said, meeting his eyes for the first time.

The lobby was empty but voices carried in this old building. Years ago he'd had a conversation in the men's room that was all over Town Hall before he zipped up his fly. "Have you eaten?" Johnny asked, first Crystal, and when he got no response, the boy. "Have you had a good dinner, my friend?"

"French fries and a hamburger."

"Well, that's more than I've had. How about a little dessert? Would you and your mother be my guests?"

The boy shuffled his feet. He was unsure but sensible. Anything that might cheer up his mother. "Can we?"

"I've got some movie videos my grandchildren used to like. I think we can find something." The boy seemed eager. "Why don't you just follow me home. I'll pick up some ice cream. What's your favorite flavor? Let's have a little party."

"A party for what?" Crystal said.

"Just follow me home." Johnny smiled, eager to share the news.

In the past few years of living alone, Johnny made little use of his recreation room, spending his time in his living room between the TV and the mini bar. He'd stopped shooting pool and never looked at the autographed photos of his favorite baseball stars, the big model of the schooner, the basketballs signed by six Celtic championship teams. The little boy followed Johnny downstairs as if entering Santa's workshop. His eyes were wide as quarters as he turned around and around, stepping toward the trophy case and then the ship in full sail.

Johnny took him by the shoulder. "You like it, then?"

The boy nodded, shy but enthusiastic.

"How about I set you up with a bit of ice cream and a good movie while I talk to your mother upstairs?"

"What movie?" Laramie settled himself on the Naugahyde couch.

"Here's a good one," Johnny said. "*Star Wars*, would you like to see that?"

Laramie nodded and nodded. He kept looking around. "Do you have kids?"

"I have two boys and a girl, but they're all grown up and they don't live here any longer."

Laramie stared at him. "You live here by yourself?"

"That's the way it is, son."

He tucked a quilt around the boy's legs before starting back upstairs. The boy gazed at him as if he were an uncle, a family member, a trusted friend. Crystal was pacing before the big windows in the living room, staring at the whitecapped chop of the harbor where the lights from his outdoor floods illuminated the blackness.

"I was going to make a Jewish holiday dinner for him, from the stupid cookbook. But when I went to invite his mother today, she told me it was tonight, not tomorrow night. She said Holly had left already for her in-laws. That's why I asked you to let me off a little early today. I went straight to the nursery. But it was closed."

"Now sit down," he told Crystal. "You're soaked through. I'm going to give you a little something to calm you down."

"I'm sorry, I can't drink. What did you want to tell me?"

"This is fifteen-year-old single malt scotch. It's not a drink, it's an occasion. Now I'm not going to say a word until you sit down and take off that wet jacket and have a little sip." Given no choice, she obeyed. "That's better. Now I'm not happy about what I have to say, because it involves someone's bad fortune," yet he could feel the scotch rise up in his chest like victory. "Gordon Stone is dying. He hasn't got but a week or two to live."

Crystal's face went deadly still. The finger of scotch he'd given her was gone. When he poured another glass for each of them, she didn't resist. "So you see, if he is over there, there's no hanky-panky going on. The whole harem is there, his dozen wives, his children, his grand-children." At the thought of all Gordon's grandchildren surrounding him at his deathbed, Johnny felt a cold pang of jealousy. Where would his own grandchildren be when he was ready to pass on? His two sons and adopted daughter were all on the West Coast—but of course, he couldn't be jealous of Gordon. Gordon was about to die. Johnny had won.

"How do you know this?" Crystal said. Again her drink was gone; again he filled it.

"Gordon may be a socialist and satyr, but he's always been good to Stumpy Squeer. That may be the one thing the two of us have in common." One cold April night the idiot burned his own house down. Having gone through the two cords of wood Johnny had provided him, and too lazy to cut up more, Stumpy dragged an entire log into his living room, stuck the end of it into the fireplace and lit it as if it would just burn like a candle. That summer Johnny had provided the materials, Gordon the labor, and by late fall Stumpy had a new house. Johnny had to admit he'd enjoyed driving over to the island to see the progress of the house: the arguments with Gordon over the Vietnam war, still raging that summer; the beautiful women Gordon always had around the compound. He'd seen that ex-actress, then Gordon's wife, sunbathing once without her top on.

Crystal was on her feet.

"Now where are you going?"

"I don't know," she said, taking two steps forward, then back, clutching herself. "To see if Laramie's okay."

Johnny poured himself another drink. Waves of rain from the west struck the windows like buckshot. He had constructed the government of this little town as carefully as one of his ship's models; glued his people in place with loving care, the selectmen, the Board of Health, every member of every committee, with himself at the helm. He steered this town like the captain of a ship, through budget crises and state land grabs and unfunded mandates from on high that had sunk other towns this size. For thirty-five years he was the captain, until Gordon and his hippie riffraff and his intellectual pretenders rose up to challenge him. Now who was left standing?

When Crystal returned, she strode directly to the bottle and poured herself a glass. "Is he all right, dear?"

"He's asleep. He fell asleep smiling. He hasn't done that in weeks."

"My own children used to fall asleep on that old couch." He noticed her face, all puffy and red. She'd gone downstairs to cry. "What's the matter, dear? I thought you'd take heart in the news. No one's glad to hear of a man's death, but surely you understand why your man went over there. I dare say I'll pay a visit myself, if not before he passes, then certainly afterward. That's the way of politics."

"Don't you understand? Now she's free. Now he can go to her, he can live with her." Crystal's words were tumbling one on top of another. Too much to drink. "Now he doesn't even live with me, doesn't want to live with me, and he'll go to her."

"No, he will not go to her. Sit down, dear. Sit down and no more whiskey." She did sit. She hung her head, then lifted it as he spoke, looking at him as a little girl looks at her father. "You are a warm and beautiful woman."

"He doesn't think I'm beautiful."

"Then he's an idiot. Because you are. And you're young. Too young to have lost anyone close to you. Because when you do, the last thing on your mind is finding another. Believe me. As cold as Judith Silver is, it'll be months before she's ready to think of loving again. Maybe years. I know that because I went through it. During that time, you will have your chance to talk sense into David, and, I truly believe, you'll win him."

Crystal took his hand, dangling at his side, and kissed it, kissed it not like a daughter on the back of his wrist, although it began that way, but like something else. Slowly, lovingly, the way he'd only imagined in his most private thoughts, she touched the tip of her tongue between his fingers. Then she rose and pulled him close.

"No, dear," he said.

"Yes," she whispered, taking his hand and putting it on her breast.

"Yes, Mr. Lynch—Johnny. You've been so good to me. I want to be with you now. I want to be in your bedroom with you."

"But the boy—"

"He's fast asleep under the quilt you threw over him. Where's your bedroom, Johnny?" It was the woman, not the little girl, who spoke now, who led him upstairs and knelt at his feet and unbuckled him, who took him in her mouth, and then inside her body. "You're so good to me, so good to me." She locked her legs around his back and rocked. She cried into his shoulder. He couldn't believe what was happening, really happening, just like something he imagined when he couldn't sleep. Her body was smooth, lush. When he felt her down there, she was hairless. Maybe young women now shaved themselves? Both her nipples had little rings through them. It was all strange. It was as if she had taken him into a strange country, the country of the young where bodies were beautiful and fragrant, smelling of roses and sex, and exotic in ways unlike the bodies of women he had known, pierced and shaven.

"It's so nice to be with you," she murmured. "You make me feel safe. Your wife was a lucky woman. You make me feel beautiful."

He was half asleep when he heard her dressing. He stood at the window and watched her lift the boy like a sack of potatoes—the way he used to lift his own children—and carry him out to her car. Twice she stumbled but kept on going. Then he slipped back into his warm bed. By the clock, it was now only 9:45. If he was a younger man she might have stayed, but of course, she was not about to share his bed. He would not fool himself. This had happened once and would never happen again; or not for a long while, not until she was secure and married to Greene.

But this was more than satisfaction; this was a justice he could never have imagined. As his enemy lay dying across the roiling waters of the harbor, Johnny Lynch took a woman less than half his age. He slid easily into a deep and blissful sleep.

DAVID

50 I must have been dozing when I heard the horn, a long blare as if the driver had fallen into the steering wheel. Three cats leapt to the window. It must have taken me a few minutes to register all this, to shake off the wine and the heavy supper, to run from Judith's shack to the big house. I arrived as the car pulled up and Beverly climbed the stairs.

Rain ran down the woman's face, blurring her makeup, blue liner through rouged cheeks. "There's a car off that little bridge," she sputtered. "The headlights are on. It's just sitting there underwater."

She spoke to relatives grouped around the kitchen table. Judith was not there. "Call the rescue squad," I said, halfway out the door.

The angry son, Larry, ignored me and languidly stretched his neck in Beverly's direction. "A car underwater? Right, Mom. You drink a little too much Manischewitz tonight?"

"Call 911," I said. Gordon's second wife was a pretentious, over-dressed woman who decked herself in gold, but she had summered on Squeer Island for a decade and knew the territory. "Now!" I directed the stupid boy. "You tell them there's a car off the Squeer Island bridge. Tell them Selectman Greene is down there. *Do it now.*"

All that night I'd been expecting trouble—a screaming phone call from Crystal or Gordon's deathbed curse. An accident didn't surprise me. My truck was blocked. I jumped in the waiting car. "Take me to the bridge."

"Where's my wife? Who are you?" His accent was thick west Texas. Buck, they called him. He was drawing the last puff of a cigarette and listening to a baseball game on the radio.

"A friend of the family."

There was sarcasm in the man's laughter. "Some damned family."

"Take me to the bridge." I was prepared to throw him out of the car and I believe he knew it.

The bridge to Squeer Island was a mile from Judith's house. The road was all sand up to the causeway, slow going in good weather, pocked with deep black puddles in tonight's storm. There was no moon. Wind pushed the rain up the windshield, swamping the wipers. I imagined Judith in that car, crouched in the seat well, rationing air. "Do you have to steer around every puddle?" I said.

"I do if I want to have brakes. For Christ's sake, I'm going as fast as I can."

What I knew as silver-green marsh in the daylight was a vast shifting surface, bottomless and black. Up ahead, in the high beams, I caught sight of the causeway, a thin asphalt ribbon just emerging from the sea.

"You know we could have just seen the accident and driven right on," he said, steering hard right to avoid a mudhole. "We could've looked for a phone booth on the other side and not turned back to the house at all."

"You're a model citizen."

The blacktop was slick as ice. It was six feet wide. Whitecaps lapped the tires. What looked ahead like an old gray raft broken free of its mooring was the Squeer Island bridge, the guardrails hanging in splinters off one side. "Stop the car," I told Buck and jumped out. The bridge seemed to ripple underfoot, thrumming with the force of the wind. As I leaned over the splintered rail, I saw two beams of light in black water. The car was upside down.

On the mainland side, vehicles sped down the hill, lights flashing: police cruisers, an ambulance. By my watch, the tide had peaked two hours ago. But even as the water receded, the rain whipped the shoreline, searing my skin with the force of shot. I couldn't open my eyes without squinting. I could barely hear above the wind. A parade of headlights snaked along the water's edge. Car doors slammed. Rescue workers poured out. The force of their boots shook the bridge.

I shouted, "We can get down there. It's not too late. We can get her out." Her. I don't know why I thought I knew, but I felt her down there, cold, alone. "We can," I insisted, tears and raindrops on my tongue.

Abel Smalley did not address me, but neither did he order me off the bridge. I'd be tolerated, I understood, as long as I stayed out of the way. Divers suited up in the mist. Hulks in orange slickers stood at the ready.

"What are we waiting for?"

"We can't do nothing in a current like this," Abel said. "No way in a wind this fierce."

"Bullshit," I said. "We have to move now. We have to do something."

He turned his back. "You know the procedure," was all he said.

The Rescue Squad was as close to a hospital as we had in this town. Their bravery was beyond question. But their first priority was safety. Risk versus benefit; I'd been apprised of their policies from the day I took office. They would be assessing a car off a bridge in a forty-five-mile-per-hour wind. No bodies visible; no one assumed to be alive.

A fire truck rolled slowly to the water line, its floodlights casting the bridge in a stark white light. I heard the crackle of orders over handheld transceivers. When the tide subsided and the current slowed, they'd have an hour before the creek gave way to mud. Black mayonnaise, they called it. Silt and water, a texture like pudding between the toes: a runny voracious mud known to swallow fishermen and suck a man up to his neck in seconds. All Saltash parents told the story of a little boy who wandered away from his family while chasing a crab and disappeared in front of his mother's eyes, simply slid into the mud quick as an oyster down a man's throat.

"We are not going to stand here and do nothing." I felt my throat burning as I imagined hers filling with saltwater. "I order you—" I screamed at the chief of police, just before he thrust me out of the way.

It was past one A.M. when I saw the first diver blow water from his mouthpiece, adjust his mask and plunge. He shifted the searchlight between his hands. I heard bubbles playing on the surface. By this time, the tires of the car were visible, like the paws of a dog on its back. I seemed to have lost the strength to stand. I leaned against what was left of the railing. Island people were huddled along the causeway. Finally the diver broke the surface. "The driver's side window is smashed," he said, swallowing. "No one in the driver's seat. One body in back. Looks to me like a kid."

DAVID

51

Crystal's body was discovered at daybreak the following morning and wrested from the mud by a small hovercraft. Using a canvas winch fastened beneath her arms, the vessel tugged until the vacuum was broken and she was lifted aboard. A Coast Guard helicopter circled above a small army of rescue personnel and their assembled vehicles, news vans and photographers and a hundred onlookers come to gawk behind a yellow cordon strung up by the police. I watched from the bridge. I heard a radio barking orders, trucks spinning tires in the sand, car doors slamming, and above it all voices asking, Who was she? Why did she climb out the window? Why did she leave the little boy?

I tried to call Crystal's mother that day, but I could not find her address or phone number. It was Johnny Lynch who called her father. Far from dead, as she had told me, he was living in New York outside Troy, remarried and raising Airedales. He drove down at once, a heavyset red-faced man with bulging pale blue eyes, a shambling walk and slightly slurred voice. He seemed overcome and kept wiping his forehead and then his eyes. "I gave her that Olds when she was on her way here. She stopped with us for a month. I had it fixed up for her. It's such a big car, I thought it was safe for her and the boy. I gave it to her because the wreck she was driving had bad brakes. I thought it was a safe car. . . ."

He said he would take the bodies back to Troy, after the autopsy was completed. He wrung my hand. "She thought she could get a better job here. We didn't have room for her to stay with us, but there were apartments. She thought she could do better for herself here. Now look what's happened!"

I meant to arrange some kind of memorial for Crystal and Laramie, but the day after the accident my mother informed me there would be a morning service in the Catholic church. Crystal was not Catholic. The service was not held in the sanctuary nor conducted by a priest. Johnny arranged for the basement hall. In Quaker style, all those whose lives had been touched by the deceased would rise and speak their minds.

Laramie's third-grade class attended, and one by one the students stood to say goodbye. The women in the office rose next and then my sister. Michelle sobbed through the entire service. Tommy sat a little apart from her, rubbing his nose as if it itched. Johnny Lynch wore a black pin-striped suit, a gray vest, and strode the stage like a bad Shake-spearean actor. "Lamentation" and "mortal flesh" and "heartache" left his lips.

Beside me, my mother cried. "If only you had told her the truth . . ."

"A tragedy?" he intoned. "Or a tragic allegory?" He brought his hand to his heart. "A young mother wandering in the darkness, searching for help for her child."

Why did I feel Johnny's hand in Crystal's death? Why had Johnny left with her that night? Ten people told me Crystal had gone off with him. Where did they go? What did he tell her? I had no concrete reason to suspect him. Maybe I just needed someone else to blame. But Johnny Lynch had sent her across that bridge.

I delayed dealing with my house for a week, until I could not put it off. An open cookbook on the kitchen counter; a stack of folded laun-dry. Everything seemed to wait for them to return: Laramie's marking pens, Crystal's clothes. Crystal had astonishingly few clothes. Four dresses in the closet, five skirts, five pairs of pants. One drawer of underpants and socks. Another of sweaters and shirts. Laramie's closet was crammed with jeans she had ironed, flannel-lined khakis, cor-duroys; plaid shirts and plain. There were two winter coats. A little blue blazer. He had one drawer for underwear, another for socks, one more for sweaters. I counted three pairs of sneakers, six pairs of shoes, a new pair of winter boots. I had never noticed how very well dressed she had kept him; how little she spent on herself. Really, the only thing she wanted was a father for her child.

I spent the weekend in the house, sitting mostly, walking from room to room. I wrote a letter to Crystal's mother, whose address her father gave me. I attempted to read: minutes of meetings; the *Baseball Al-manac*; Robert's Rules; a tide chart—anything that promised some sem-blance of order. Saturday night I wrote to Liam. Sunday morning I just stared at Laramie's drawings on the refrigerator. The faded ones showed three figures in a house; in the newer ones they were replaced by flames.

Crystal had dragged an old student desk from my garage to use as a vanity. There she sat every morning applying her eye makeup when she came in fresh from the shower, wrapped in a towel. Laramie would be calling for chocolate milk, the TV screaming cartoons, the dryer would buzz or a bowl would break, while Crystal outlined her eyes with the concentration of a master jeweler. Laramie and I lived all over the house. I had weights in the living room, books over the toilet, piles of mail and magazines on the kitchen table. Laramie's space rangers and action toys were on every shelf and chair. But Crystal had one yellow desk in front of a mirror. I never approached it until she was dead, and then, cautiously, as if she'd appear any minute, as if I was spying.

Twenty perfumes, all samples, all recalling the way she used her middle finger to daub a drop between her thighs. Lipsticks, liners, nail polish, deodorant, lotions, face creams, depilatory; boxes of pins; of tweezers. I was ashamed to think this: they're still half full. What a waste to throw them out. Of course I did, quickly into a plastic bag.

In the bottom drawer, blond hair dye and a hair dryer. Tampons and pads and birth control pills. A box of sewing supplies. Some prescription painkillers from Las Vegas. I emptied the drawer and moved on. The next drawer was full of photos and postcards. I recognized a very young Crystal in jeans and tee-shirt with, yes, Billy Lynch, Johnny's second son. I remembered him, all right. A bully, but once I started playing baseball, he left me alone. Crystal in a prom dress in front of a saguaro cactus, a grinning Mexican-looking guy with his arm around her. Crystal with a blond lady who must be her mother. I'm sure I never met her. The woman was wearing a suit a little too tight and a big corsage. Crystal was dressed as a bridesmaid and beside her mother stood the bride, also blond. On the back, Crystal had written "Didi's Wedding" and dated it eight years ago. There was nothing to suggest Crystal had ever seen her mother or her sister since. What had happened at that wedding?

One photo taken in an arcade showed Crystal and a redheaded guy mugging. Another showed pregnant Crystal with a bald biker. Crystal, a baby (Laramie?), and a middle-aged guy. An uncle? Crystal in Disneyland with Laramie, now three or four. Crystal in western gear posed in front of the Mirage volcano in Las Vegas, her boot up on the fence to show her leg. A studio portrait of Laramie looking serious and hopeful. Crystal with her arms around two guys, in a black bat-girl Halloween costume. A page from a magazine: "Six Ways to Firm Your Breasts." Crystal in a nightie, pouting for the camera. Crystal without a shirt on, palms across her nipples. Always her eyes seemed to be asking the camera, am I okay? Am I doing it right? Is this enough?

The one photo I kept was of Crystal holding Laramie, perhaps two, in her lap. For once, she was not looking at the camera at all, but at him with an expression so intense, it almost frightened me. The men in these photos, they appeared and disappeared, but at the center was her son.

A flattened sprig of lavender crumbled in my hand. A wine label. A black elastic garter wrapped around a matchbook: "Congratulations, Robert and Katherine Ann!" Were they good friends or relatives? Who had she gone to their wedding with? Were they still married? I had a hundred questions about every item in the drawer, an almost physical yearning to know her. I had been afraid to probe, to know too much, to be drawn too far in. Now I felt afraid even to turn around. Crystal was in that room with me; over my shoulder; touching my ear, whispering, "Why couldn't you love me enough to ask?"

I had no words to describe the turmoil I felt. Nor was anyone able to say a thing that made sense to me, except, oddly enough, Liam, whose response to my letter arrived with surprising speed.

I'd written him because I thought he should know; because I'd wish to know if a son of mine, however unwanted, had died. Liam was guilty; Liam was innocent. I felt I understood him in a way I never expected anyone to understand me.

Dear David,
I have to admit I was reluctant to reply. I never really knew the boy. I can't say I feel responsible, except for fooling around with his mother, but no one, least of all the innocent himself, deserves a fate such as this. I can't be sending you any money toward the funeral, if that's what you'd be wanting, only my sincere regrets. It was a tragedy for the mother and son, for us all. What you tell me happened doesn't make sense, but I guess there's no understanding something so sad. What can I say but that Crystal was a troubled girl and I was an idiot. May all my sins be forgiven.

At that I said, Amen.

I sat with Liam's note for almost an hour, reading it over and over in the post office parking lot. A single phrase repeated itself to me then and for hours after. "What you tell me happened doesn't make sense . . ."

Later that day, I called the chief of police and asked to see the autopsy report.

JUDITH

52 Gordon died in her arms exactly two weeks after Rosh Hashanah at 3:35 A.M. The last forty-eight hours had been very bad. He went into convulsions, then slipped into unconsciousness. Occasionally he came to, briefly. His breathing was hoarse and loud, then almost inaudible. He moaned and gasped out nonsense. She sat behind him in bed holding him and stroking him, sometimes singing to him, sometimes just talking in a soothing voice about how much she loved him. His agony was protracted and she was torn between wanting him to stay with her and recognizing he could not endure more and must let go. The strength of his will was keeping him alive by the barest thread. Then she felt it snap. His eyes flew open and his body grew rigid, then limp. His eyes were glazed. She could find no pulse.

It was a quiet night and she could hear the surf after she could no longer hear his halting breath. The surf was up because a tropical storm had passed far out to sea, only the waves and the occasional lost pelagic bird marking its power. Almost at once his body began to cool. Entropy. The end of her life as she had known it. Portnoy remained on the bed, and she allowed him to sniff Gordon's face. He knew. He jumped off the bed, his fur on edge, and went straight to the door demanding to go out. She was afraid he would somehow commit feline suicide, get caught by a coyote, fall in the marsh mud. "No," she said quietly. She would keep him in all week, until he had adjusted to Gordon's absence. She was alone here with the animals, and they would need her. And she would need them.

She told everyone she called they did not have to come. Gordon had insisted on cremation, which she regretted. She would be buried, and she had hoped they would have side-by-side graves. She had not been raised to believe in cremation and could not suddenly embrace it. But Gordon had been insistent, and she would honor his wishes. It had all been arranged. It would be done immediately. There would be a brief Jewish service. She would dig the ashes into the patio of the compound, as he had requested, and in spring she would plant a low growing tree the winds would not injure. A dwarf conifer, perhaps. They had discussed everything, endlessly. Nonetheless she experienced a deep shock as the two undertaker's men carried him out to their hearse in a body bag.

There would be a memorial in the spring, but as she told people, Gordon's goodbye had been the dinner. Nonetheless, Ben and his family came and, of course, Natasha. She made the calls, she made the arrangements, she went through with the cremation and brought the ashes home, half dead herself. She put food on the table and prepared to sit shiva. Natasha took Ben and his family to the plane the next day and remained with her for the next three days.

It was not until she woke on the fifth day after the funeral, alone in the house, that she began to weep uncontrollably. She wept on and off all day. She had canceled her appointments, of course, pulled the phone from the wall. Now she wandered the house, lost, without will or hope. It was a large house and a huge compound around her. Never had it felt so big and so desolate, like an abandoned village. She was out to sea, isolated amidst the wind and the rising surf, alone and desperately lonely. If it had not been for the animals in her care, she would have fled anyplace, into Boston, to New York. Portnoy was miserable and mourned with her, looking for Gordon and then asking to go out, then lying with his head on his paws, eyes half closed, not sleeping and not moving. He seemed her grief clad in gray fur.

She thought that in Gordon's long dying, she had practiced at missing him. She had grown used to being celibate over the last few months. She had grown used to not bothering him with problems and details. She had taken over fixing things he had always done, ordering wood and stacking it or getting help with what she could not manage alone. She had thought she was almost prepared for widowhood, but she had been wrong. His presence, however diminished, was nothing like his total absence.

She did not think she could endure it, but there was nothing to do but endure it. It would not go away; she could not go away. She continued. The following Monday she returned to work. She had Mattie reschedule appointments she had canceled and began working a ten-hour day. She could not sleep. She ate little. But she could work. She could write briefs, she could make deals on the phone, she could probe, she could litigate. While she was engaged in the law, her pain was distant: never gone but no longer overwhelming. However, like a visitor hanging around outside the door waiting to catch her alone, the moment she put down her work or turned aside, pain was back with her. At night she could not escape it. She fell asleep after midnight and woke at three. She was always exhausted, her nerves abraded raw, her eyes sore.

The second Friday in October, Natasha came home for the weekend. She drove straight through from Cornell, arriving just after midnight.

They had omelets and the last garden tomatoes. They drank Beaujolais, and Natasha told her stories of her fellow students, her professors and the animals they were learning to treat. That night, Judith slept. She slept and slept. When she woke, it was nine-fifteen—she, who always was up by six. She felt groggy but well. If only she could keep a piece of Natasha with her. They picked grasses and sea lavender in the marsh to make arrangements with chrysanthemums, golden and bronze and musky pink, from her garden. They dug the potatoes she had forgotten.

"I'm so glad you're here." She tried to tell Natasha how she felt, but words were feeble. "I've been lost, except for work."

"Maybe you need a roommate."

"Oh, Natasha, I'm too bossy. Who could I stand to live with?"

They walked by the bay past closed-up houses, some boarded against winter storms. The tide was receding and bits of seaweed, scallop and slipper shells washed up at their feet, rocks and pebbles vivid in color because they were still wet: gold, greenish, slate-gray, pink, shiny black. They saw footprints of a man and a dog, but no people except far, far in the distance two figures like themselves walked. Across the curve of the bay, a distant town glittered in the afternoon sun like a mirage of paradise. Terns were diving into the gentle ebbing waves. An emerging sandbar was studded with gulls resting.

"So, did anyone give you trouble about that woman drowning?"

"Mattie tells me there was talk in town that she committed suicide. Or that David or I plotted her death. It just seems so long ago. Everything before Gordon's death feels that way."

"But why did she have her kid with her? That's so tragic."

"What was she supposed to do with him at nine-thirty at night? Leave him home alone? That's neglect. When she decided to drive out to the island and confront David, she had to bring the boy. It's too bad she didn't get through. She would have found thirty-two people cleaning up a big meal and singing off key. Hardly cause for a jealous rage. I didn't exchange twenty words with David all night. It was desperation pure and simple, the desperation that drives so many women. That's one reason I bailed out."

"David had already moved out on her, right? And you weren't seeing him. So how can anybody blame you?"

"People can always blame a woman who's seen as strong. No matter how weak as a rag I feel. Anyhow, it was a two-week wonder. Then they had Gordon's death to talk about. Now there's a new scandal. Michelle, Crystal's friend, is accusing Tommy Shalhoub of molesting her daughter. Tommy has been calling me, so I have to decide if I'm willing to take on his case."

"It might keep you busy."

"I'm busy already, Natasha. It doesn't seem to help much. I'm alone, and I'm not used to it. The worst thing about a good marriage is after it ends." She sighed.

"I miss him terribly. I keep thinking of things I want to tell him, stories he'd enjoy." Natasha threw up her hands in a gesture of scattering. "Then I realize I can't tell him. I'll never be able to share anything with him again. He's gone, and I can never, never talk to him."

"I think that's what I miss most too. Talking with him. Our life was so examined, Natasha, examined together. It feels incomplete now. Nothing seems important to me. I don't really care about the gossip and it's hard to make myself care about town at all. I feel too sorry for myself. I'm no role model these days."

"Oh, you think you were my role model? Nonsense, Judith. Dr. Doolittle was. The man who talked to the animals."

"Well, you better get busy talking to them. They're like me, they're all lonely and a little crazy."

DAVID

53

Abel Smalley didn't have to say where, just when. Noon always meant the Binnacle. As I approached his table, I noticed his hand drop over a thin manila envelope. "You sure you want to see this?"

"It's more a question of need, to tell you the truth."

He sighed, "It was a terrible accident. There was marsh grass on the bridge. The surface was slippery, the visibility poor—"

"I was there."

"Suit yourself." He pushed the envelope across the table.

He wasn't required by law to provide me with an autopsy report. I could have made a written request of the medical examiner. But since I'd been elected, Abel had offered me any number of courtesies I'd never dreamed of receiving from the police. A license to carry firearms; a permit to park anywhere in town. If I wanted the autopsy of some dead girl I'd been screwing, his practical smile said, Sure. No problem. You sick fuck.

Commonwealth of Massachusetts
Office of the Chief Medical Examiner
Autopsy Report

CAUSE OF DEATH: *Drowning*

MANNER OF DEATH: __ *Natural Causes*
                   x *Accident*
                   __ *Suicide*
                   __ *Homicide*
                   __ *Undetermined*

HISTORY OF TERMINAL EVENT:
The history as known at the time was provided by the Medical Examiner.
Crystal Lee Sinclair was a thirty-two-year-old white female, living in Saltash, Massachusetts. On the evening of September 22 the car in which she was the driver veered off the Squeer Island bridge, overturned, and sank below the surface of the water. The driver's side window smashed on impact. It is presumed Ms. Sinclair climbed out of the window and in a disoriented state wandered in search of help. On Sept. 23 her body was found by State Police helicopter and recovered from the inner breakwater of Squeer Island

Cove. Body was removed and taken to the Josiah Squeer landing in Saltash where it was viewed by this M.E. at 7:10 A.M. She was pronounced dead at 7:13 A.M. on Sept. 23.

AUTOPSY:

The autopsy was performed in the Medical Examiner's Office between the hours of 10:00 A.M. and 1:00 P.M.

Present at Autopsy: *Medical Examiner and Office Technician.*

Clothing: *The clothing is wet and consists of a denim jacket, brown western boots, brown belt, blue jeans, a white blouse, black socks, black bra, black underpants.*

EXTERNAL EXAMINATION:

The nude body is that of a white female who is five feet six inches and weighs approximately 140 pounds. Scalp shows silver-blond hair about nine inches in length. In the center of the scalp in the parietal region there is a red contusion measuring up to one inch in greatest dimension. The eyes are blue-hazel. The pupils are equal. The conjunctivae are injected. The teeth of both upper and lower jaws are in excellent repair.

I suddenly found myself smiling. "The daughter of a dentist," I said. Abel, stirring his coffee, looked up and shrugged.

The lips reveal no injury. Facial abrasions and signs of feeding activity of crustaceans and marine life are consistent with superficial trauma from waves and contact with ocean bottom and force of breakwater on body. The right and left earlobes show signs of cosmetic piercing.

Chest: *The abdomen is slightly protuberant with a nine-inch curved linear scar in the right lower quadrant. There is an absence of hair in the pubic area. Right and left nipples show scar tissue consistent with cosmetic piercing (rings were found in each nipple).*

Again, I glanced at Abel, embarrassed. At some point the waitress had delivered his meat loaf with mashed potatoes, a side of overboiled green peas in a little dish next to the salad. He hummed as he ate and never looked up from his newspaper.

Arms: *The arms are muscular. The hands reveal evidence of injury on the right palm consistent with slashes due to beach grass. There is a one-inch abrasion beneath the right armpit consistent with the feeding activity of an eel.*

Ever since I'd been a boy, I'd heard of bodies washed up in Saltash harbor, crabs that colonized the skull as comfortably as curling into a paper cup; eels that ate their way through human intestines. For the first time in years, I thought of Corkie Pugh and his morbid stories.

> *Upper arms reveal striated abrasions and evidence of injury due to automobile window glass. One shard of glass, approximately one centimeter in diameter, found in upper arm.*
> Legs: *There is scar tissue on the right inner thigh, approximately 4.5 centimeters in diameter, consistent with the surgical removal of a tattoo.*

"It was a butterfly," Crystal told me. A biker boyfriend liked to brag that he didn't eat his women because it was boring, so she got herself tattooed. "As a joke," she insisted. "To give him something to watch. Like TV." I didn't laugh.

"I was drunk," she had said and looked away, ashamed.

INTERNAL EXAMINATION:
> Heart: *The heart weighs 450 grams. The cardiac valves are normal.*
> Stomach: *The stomach contains approximately one ounce of opaque gray liquid. The small bowel contains semiliquid to semisolid fecal material, and in the rectum there are areas of purple-red streaking and dilated internal hemorrhoids, but no primary nor metatastic tumor is identified.*

"Put it in my ass," she had told me. "Come on, I bet you're a virgin. I want to be your first time." When I did, I felt her back muscles constrict. She clenched her jaw. When I removed myself, I saw a tear roll across her cheek. "Did you like that?" She sat up with difficulty. "Did you? You can do anything you want to me. Anything."

> Brain: *The brain weighs 1290 grams.*
> Body Cavities: *The body cavities are open in the usual manner. There is no evidence of blunt force or penetrating injury to the chest or abdominal cavities. The lungs are expanded and the organs are in their usual anatomic locations. Evidence of semen found in the vagina.*

A sound I made, a gasp, attracted Abel's attention. I had not seen Crystal since the Sunday night before she died. I'd used a condom. "Where was she before the accident?" I asked him.

I was sure he expected the question. He drew back his shoulders. He leveled his voice. "I don't have that information."

I didn't need it. I knew. Why had Johnny left Town Hall with her that night? Where did they go? Crystal was Johnny Lynch's lover. Why hadn't I seen it? Because he was an old man? Because the thought of his nakedness was beyond my imagination? I'd expected Crystal to make me pay for Judith. I was certain the price was Tommy. But Johnny Lynch? Did they meet at my house when I was with Judith? How long had it been going on?

The Commonwealth of Massachusetts
Department of Public Safety
Chemical Laboratory

NAME OF VICTIM: *Crystal Lee Sinclair*
RESULTS: *Blood Alcohol: .11% (MKL)*
Urine Barbiturate Screen: negative (WGH)
Cocaine Metabolite Screen: negative (WGH)

"Abel, what does this mean? Blood Alcohol, point-eleven percent. Is that a lot? Does it mean she was drunk?"

"For a girl her size, I'd say so. Legal limit is point oh-eight."

"So you think that explains it?"

"Why she drove off a bridge? Wandered around disoriented? Sounds like drunk to me."

"Abel, she didn't drink."

"All the more reason, if she wasn't used to it."

"I mean she didn't touch it, Abel. Ever. She gave up drinking years ago. I lived with her. I know."

He said, "Believe anything you want."

"What if somebody got her drunk?"

Abel brought his napkin to his lips. His voice was official. "Due process has been followed, Mr. Greene. I suggest you try to put this unfortunate accident out of your mind."

As if that were possible. As if I would ever forget.

"I'm sorry but I've done the best I can. For you and the girl and her family. The law is satisfied."

I was not.

JOHNNY

54 Johnny dialed his daughter's telephone number, slightly ashamed that he had to rely on his address book. What kind of a father didn't memorize his children's phone numbers? What kind of a world was this, in which their numbers were crossed out and replaced, each one farther away than the last? He had no idea where Novato was (a suburb of San Francisco, she'd said), only that it was seven o'clock out there and Mary Rose should be home. He desperately wanted her to pick up. He needed to tell her how much he loved her, and that if there was anything she needed, anything at all, he was here. He needed to hear her talk about the good times—before her mother took ill; before she'd moved in with that bartender twice her age. He needed to hear from her lips that she loved him.

"Hello and have a nice day!" The damn answering machine spoke in the voice of the new husband, the idiot who sold insurance. "If you have called for Rodney, Mary Rose, Emily, Rebecca, or John . . ." Jesus help us, Johnny thought, Rebecca was four years old and John eleven months. Who in blazes was going to leave a message for them on the answering machine? He'd try later.

He'd tried all day after the memorial service and three times today. Seeing Crystal's father confirmed in his heart his love for his own children: whatever the imagined slights between them, whatever their youthful sins. The Lord worked in mysterious ways. He closed one door and opened another. Johnny had never been a religious man; that had been his wife's department. But he'd begun to see patterns now as he entered his old age; he'd begun to wonder if there was a hidden purpose in things.

Perhaps the Lord in His wisdom had brought Crystal into his life for just this reason, to unite him with his children; to soften his heart toward those he loved and to sharpen his resolve. For who were the rightful owners of the land above the dike? "Who stood to gain or lose?" as Gordon Stone used to proclaim at town meetings. Surely not himself, for he was an old man. Surely it was the rightful inheritance of his children and grandchildren he was fighting for.

Little Laramie and Crystal were messengers, he saw that now. A girl like Crystal had been with a hundred men; rough men, hoods, Las Vegas gamblers, men who used her like David Greene. So why had she ended up in Johnny's care except to show him the way back to his own children? He'd provided everything he could for Crystal, a good job and fatherly advice and, God rest her soul, a fitting memorial service. But he was weaker than the forces of evil, weaker than David Greene and Gordon Stone, who had lured her across that bridge to her death. Had David done his part by her, had he married her and cared for his boy, the door would not have been closed on Crystal, nor opened, to show Johnny the way back.

He tried his daughter's number again. Ten o'clock on the West Coast. They had three children: where the hell could they be?

"Yeah, hello?"

"Hello, Rodney? Is that you? I'd nearly given up. I've been trying to get you for hours."

"Uh, yeah. We went out to eat. Who is this?"

The idiot. "It's Johnny. Mary Rose's father. In Massachusetts."

"Right, she's puttin' the kids to sleep. Can you call back?"

"Well, it's one A.M. here. Can you ask her to come to the phone?"

Johnny thought he heard him mumble, "Shit," before the receiver dropped hard.

"Hello, Dad? Is something wrong? I was in with the baby."

"No, no, dear. I was just wanting to hear your voice. Wanting to tell you I love you, that—"

"Hold on, Dad. Okay? Goddamn it, Rodney. Just wait a minute and I'll be right there. Hello, Dad? I'm glad you called."

"You are?"

"The stove is dying. The old gas stove that came with the house."

"Oh, no, dear. Is it dangerous?"

"No, but I'm down to two burners here, for the five of us."

"Do you need something, dear? Would five hundred dollars be of help?"

"A big help."

"I know what a simple thing like a good kitchen stove can mean. The kitchen is the center of a family." He remembered winter evenings, when he came home after work to find his family at the table, the older ones doing their homework, Emily Ann at the stove.

"Hello, John. Rodney, here."

"Where's Mary Rose?"

"With the baby. Listen, thanks for the kind assistance with the stove. I feel like I want to do something for you in return."

"I'm sure that's not necessary."

"John. Tell me something. What kind of a health care plan do you have in your office, John? Because I think I can really help you with your insurance needs—"

"Thank you, we can talk about that next time. Now it's bedtime for me. I'll send the check off tomorrow." Johnny hung up without waiting for a response. One sleazy husband after another; no wonder Mary Rose didn't have a minute for her dad. Rodney was number three. Mary Rose had been adopted after his wife had lost two babies. Poor Mary Rose was always searching for love. What she needed was security; more than he could send her in dribs and drabs, a real nest egg for herself and her babies. Nothing less than their rightful inheritance.

When the summer crowds were finally gone and the rental business slowed, he had another series of meetings with the dolts from the bank. Roger told him that until the question of the dike was settled, and settled favorably, they could not forward him money on his land. "It will be settled," Johnny said. "It'll be settled soon."

"What do you mean, you want the dike on the agenda?" Ralph Petersen said. "I'd think that's the last thing you'd want."

"No, no, it's time," Johnny insisted. There was a buttery softness to the light in late October, a kind of gentle haze that cast the browning marsh grass in a golden glow. He could have been staring through his office window at a field of wheat. The streets were empty of tourists. Neighbors stopped to chat in the long blue shadows of afternoon. When he was a younger man he was up at four A.M. this time of year, duck hunting in the river valley, arriving at the office on a good day with five or six mallards for the girls. God help him if he brought them home to Emily Ann; she didn't even like his shotguns in the house.

"But the vote won't go your way, Johnny. You know that our young friend asked Abel for an autopsy report."

"And I advised Abel to give it to him. Why not? The girl is dead and buried, Lord rest her soul. It's time to move on, Ralph. I suggest you put it to the board this way: the Capital Improvement Plan is due to be updated in December. If there needs to be any work on the dike, it should be discussed now."

"There shouldn't have to be any work to speak of. It'll either be opened or left closed."

"Well, I'm asking you to call for a vote on that, Ralph."

"Put it off, Johnny. You won't get the votes. Sandra and Fred come up for reelection in May. We can win both seats. We can have the majority back if we work for it. I don't see any new David Greenes in the picture."

"Put the dike on the agenda, Ralph. Do this for me."

David Greene. Six months ago the name was no more than the memory of a small intense boy who played high school baseball. Now he'd joined Judith Silver, Palmer Compton and the attorney general himself on Johnny's list of enemies. Davey Greene, the Pitching Machine. Johnny turned away from the marsh. He opened his office door to walk among his staff. Crystal's desk stood in the corner like a shrine. David Greene. The idea that the amoral little prick should judge Johnny Lynch, when the entire town knew why the dear girl crossed that bridge—to confront him and his dirty little triangle, to demand he act like a proper father to her child, to bring the wayward man home.

He felt David Greene's hatred whenever their paths crossed; he could sense those hard gray eyes across a room. Twice Johnny had attempted to approach him—and why not? They'd both lost a dear presence in their lives; why grieve alone when the natural business of this town drew them together? Both times David Greene simply stared at him with silent accusation, as if he himself had anything to feel guilty about.

All this was unfortunate. Johnny had honestly thought he'd won David over to his thinking about the dike. No, David hadn't accepted a water-view lot; he wasn't greedy and he wasn't stupid. But through his observations over time and his conversations with Crystal, Johnny had come to think of David as a realist rather than a knee-jerk environmentalist. Now it seemed the boy's hatred would hold sway. So be it. If David voted to keep the dike closed, the bank would come on board Johnny's project like a shot. If David's vote swayed the majority to open the dike, well then, he was depriving Johnny of the fair use of his land and opening the town to a sizable lawsuit for recompense. Either way, Johnny would win.

Maria had come to him, closing the door behind her. "We have to replace Crystal," she said bluntly. "None of us can work those programs the way she did. We need someone young. And her empty desk is depressing the girls. Everytime they stop and look at it, one of them starts blubbering."

She put on his desk an ad she had drawn up for the local papers, "Wanted, Secretary for Legal Office, Good Benefits, Must Have Computer Skills."

Now, two weeks later, the ad still sat on his desk. Why hadn't he put it in? He was waiting, superstitiously waiting, until the vote on the dike came up. After that, he would fill the position. It would be nice to have another young face around the office, but this one would be more stable, calmer. Pretty but stolid, that was his recipe for peace in the office.

The hearing on the dike was finally scheduled for the week after Thanksgiving. Sandra Powell and Lyle Upham seemed delighted to take up the issue. They were friendly and full of chat before the meeting began, exactly as Johnny would be if he was about to cut someone down with his vote. Ralph and Fred Fischel were uneasy. Fischel hadn't been convinced the hearing was Johnny's idea. Fred called him when the agenda was announced to hear it from Johnny's own lips. David was Mr. Hatchet Face—had been since the girl went off the bridge. Nobody expected so much as a how-do-you-do from Selectman Greene these days.

All the usual nuts filled the seats. Palmer Compton had his boy by his side. Johnny smiled. "Hello, Palmer," he said, and got a grunt in return. There were all the other conspirators from Gordon Stone's group; Dr. Garvey in his natty bow tie and even Judith Silver, looking, he had to say it, delightful in her gray wool coatdress. Word had it David had not been over on the island since Gordon's death; you had to give him that. So what if the opposition far outnumbered Johnny's own troops tonight? He hadn't bothered sounding the alarm. He felt almost serene as he watched the drama unfold, as if he was a visitor from far away, come to observe the curious behavior of the natives. Let them rail against the dike—and rail they did—a full two hours, as Ralph and Fred seemed to shrink in their seats. Johnny yawned.

It was a quarter past ten when Ralph gaveled discussion to a halt, looking at Johnny in the back row as if to say, This wasn't my idea. Johnny responded with a simple smile.

"Mr. Chairman."

"Mrs. Powell."

"I move that this Board of Selectmen do what we rightly should have done many years ago, that is to open the Tamar River dike."

"Second." Lyle Upham beamed at the applauding crowd.

Ralph looked pale and tired. His voice was pure defeat. "The motion on the floor is to open the dike."

"Mr. Chairman, I move to refer the motion to a committee," David Greene said.

Johnny thought he hadn't quite heard him at first. Refer to committee? What was Greene trying to do? Where did he pick that up? "Mr. Chairman," Johnny shouted. "I rise to a point of order!"

"Excuse me, Mr. Chairman." David Greene again. "Mr. Lynch is not a member of this board . . . any longer. He can't call for a point of order." The little prick smiled straight at Johnny.

Above the noise in the hall, Fred Fischel glanced from Petersen to Greene, obviously confused. "I second the motion to refer."

The fool. What did he think he was doing? A referral to committee would delay action either way, the one thing that could hurt Johnny. He couldn't believe where this was going.

"Debate on the motion is allowed." Ralph's voice was lighter, infused with hope. "Mr. Greene."

"I believe this is one of the most controversial issues in the history of the town," David Greene said. "I think it's only prudent to study the matter further. We have approximately $25,000 left in the consultancy line of the budget. I move we form a committee to draw up a request for a proposal to seek an engineering study that might tell us the effects of either opening or closing the dike."

Johnny was on his feet. "That'll take years!" he heard himself shouting.

Ralph banged his gavel. "I believe the floor is Mr. Greene's."

"As Mr. Lynch himself has pointed out many times, Mr. Chairman, the dike has been in place for over twenty years. It would be imprudent and rash of us to eliminate it without study."

"You're stalling, you little bastard!" Johnny felt sweat under his collar. "You think I can't see through your cheap parliamentary tricks." The bank would not wait for a study; studies took years. He'd be stuck with the property until he died. He'd never cash out. "Yes or no, up or down. It's time to decide. We can't have this hanging over us."

"Mr. Lynch!" Petersen was shouting now, glancing worriedly at the reporters in the front row. "Mr. Lynch, sit down."

David Greene continued, "If we make the wrong decision, as Mr. Lynch, an esteemed attorney and former town counsel knows, we could open the town up to a significant lawsuit."

Before Johnny could shoot his hand up to answer the patronizing bastard, a hundred people were clamoring to speak. He couldn't see Ralph through the waving arms, but debate was cut off. They were already voting as he lumbered to the aisle.

"All those in favor of referring the motion to a committee . . ." Three hands flew up. "Those opposed . . ." Two. "The motion passes."

Palmer Compton leapt on a chair and called them all cowards for not opening the dike once and for all. Joe Pound cornered Upham and Palmer. Fischel huddled with Ralph Petersen and a hundred conversations echoed in the room. Johnny couldn't believe what he'd witnessed, what had slipped through his hands. The reality of his situation weighed like sand in his arms and legs. He could not move. Two reporters stood at his shoulder, asking questions. Ralph Petersen said as he brushed past that he would call the office in the morning. But they were all a blur to Johnny. He saw one thing and one thing only: Judith Silver smiling at him. As another lawyer, she understood as well as Johnny did how thoroughly he had just been skewered.

JUDITH

55

It was a late February day of tentative sunshine and low scudding clouds when Judith buried Portnoy under the Sargent's weeping hemlock, where Gordon's ashes were. The gray cat had always been Gordon's. He had died gradually, like Gordon. The vet said kidney failure, but she knew it was a failure of the will to live. The other deserter was Trey, the three-legged dog, who had attached himself to Stumpy. He needed a male pack leader, and Stumpy seemed flattered and willing to take him in. The other cats and the remaining dog, Silkie, were hers.

It was a quiet winter. Only Natasha came to visit. Judith spoke frequently to Hannah, had supper twice a week with Barbara. She spent more time with all her women friends and made herself go to Boston to see an evening of dance or music every month. She did not read much, because she found herself thinking of Gordon instead of paying attention. On television, sitcoms were too concerned with love and domesticity, medical shows were lethal, so she watched cops, science fiction, documentaries about anything—Antarctica, gerbils, any war, the homeless, coal mining. She took to bringing home videos. She played music loudly, to fill the silences in the house. The house was too big for her, but she could scarcely tear down half of it. She simply closed up the rooms she was not using.

At first she spent an occasional hour in Gordon's room, to conjure him up. Natasha put a stop to that. "It's morbid, keeping the room that way. Besides, it stinks. You have to clear it out. It doesn't make me think of how Daddy was. Only how he died. It's just a sickroom."

Together they bundled up Gordon's clothes and took them to Goodwill. "Somebody will like the warm sweaters and good coats and jackets," Judith said, weeping as she put them into boxes. But she would not let Natasha clear out his office. Two of his colleagues had promised to go through his papers next July and decide if there was anything publishable, what should be kept or archived.

Finally she took out his videos from several television appearances, a taped lecture from Capetown, and spent an evening watching them. That night she did not sleep. In the morning she put them away in his office, where she would not be tempted to look at them again for a long,

long time. She felt as if the tentative skin that had grown over her wound had been torn off.

So the winter passed into March. Now the ground was thawed and the first migrating birds were passing overhead, sometimes settling in the compound. Ducks rested overnight in the pitch pines, one roosting over Gordon's grave. She accepted an invitation to dinner from a lawyer who lived two towns farther up the Cape. It was a pleasant enough evening. Timothy was even taller than Gordon had been and thin as a rapier. His hair had receded, leaving the top of his head quite bald, although it was still thick and brown on the sides. His forehead seemed to go on and on, marked only by slight eyebrows perpetually surprised. Timothy had a deep baritone that he could use to fine effect in the courtroom. His skin was tanned even in late March, for he was an avid boater and always took off a couple of weeks during the winter to sail around the Caribbean. He sailed all winter, keeping his boat in a harbor that usually stayed free of ice on the Sound. He offered to take her out, but she said she'd wait for spring. She saw Timothy again the next week. And the next.

She was not immediately drawn to him as she had been to David, but perhaps this was a more intelligent attraction: he was in her field, a professional, divorced with a daughter he seemed reasonably attentive to. He saw his daughter weekends, which slowed down the progress of their relationship. That was good, for she was in no hurry. She knew she had to see men now, to resume her life. At twenty, dating had felt natural; at forty-one, it seemed a foolish and tedious game. The thought of starting from zero with someone and having to explain exactly who she was, to explain her life, exhausted her in anticipation. She was pleased to have found a sensible man with obligations and standing in the community. Since they were both part of the same collegiality of lawyers practicing in the same courts, they knew a certain amount about each other.

She went out with a recently divorced therapist once and once only. He had a condescending attitude she found abrasive. Mattie introduced her to a somewhat younger man, David's age, who had just moved to the Cape and opened a chiropractic office. He was full of didactic advice on what to eat and what she must not eat, to the degree that supper with him was a duel. No, Timothy was the best man she had interviewed, as it were, and if she was in no hurry to rush into an affair, he seemed equally cautious. They settled into a pattern of eating supper together every Thursday and afterward taking in a movie or a play. The first Saturday in April, he introduced her to his ten-year-old daughter, Amy, and they spent the afternoon at an ice-skating rink.

Timothy was astonished that Judith had never before put on a pair of skates. She did her best to remain upright, but the next day she was sore. Her back felt out. If it stayed this way, she might have to see that didactic chiropractor. She had begun tomato and pepper seedlings inside, half her usual number. Natasha came home every three weeks or so. She had a new boyfriend she was considering bringing on spring break. Judith hoped she would like him, but knew herself hard to win over as far as Natasha's boyfriends went. None seemed worthy. She would try to be more tolerant.

"Do you ever see David?" Natasha asked as they were turning over the garden, about to start planting the hardiest crops.

"I've gone to the selectmen's meetings a few times. But you'd be surprised how long you can go without running into someone, even in a town this small. I get my mail delivered. He picks his up at the post office. I shop on Saturdays. I use the Shell station. A few small changes of pattern, and you can avoid almost anyone."

Natasha leaned on her shovel. "Why do you need to avoid him?"

"Why do I need to see him?"

"You don't ever think about getting together with him?"

"Do you think we should plant the bok choi in the row next to the lettuce? Or should we put the leeks there?"

DAVID

56 During Christmas school vacation I flew down to Florida. Since Terry's first letter, we'd exchanged a couple more and talked most Sunday nights on the phone. But a lifetime apart was hard to make up in two weeks, in spite of our best intentions. The weather didn't help. A cold snap froze half the state's citrus crop. We canceled our camping trip and spent two weeks shuttling between theme parks, Epcot, MGM, Busch Gardens, sleeping late, eating pizza, watching TV, playing catch in the parking lots and arguing about all the things I made him do that his mother didn't. Any notions I'd had about him were nothing more than that—notions. He was a sweet and energetic kid and headstrong just like my sister at his age, but Wynn's death and Cesar's departure had left him bitter and scared.

Our arguments spun full-blown out of nothing. Sometimes Terry flailed at me; sometimes he sulked and wouldn't speak. He was pushing, testing my limits. Who was this son of a bitch who showed up and called himself Father Number Three? I'd been a sentimental idiot to imagine Terry would have welcomed Laramie. He was fiercely jealous of his half siblings. He would have torn Laramie apart. I didn't blame myself for Terry's problems, but I wondered what the hell I had thought I was doing: sacrificing my life to one lost little boy, while my own son didn't know who to call Daddy—his grandfather or a stable hand who passed himself off as a trainer.

The night before I left, Terry called me a fucking asshole, then fell asleep in my arms. I knew that I wanted him to start visiting me, but when I brought that up with Vicki, she put me off as always. She was living with the three kids in a garden apartment in West Palm Beach. She was defensive about her plans. I could not get her to talk seriously with me about Terry or anything else.

The winter back home continued to break all records, which seemed to fit my needs. When I ventured out, it was for breakfast or long walks with my new dog. Work was mostly snow plowing. I occupied myself with crises. The pipes freezing in Town Hall. The roof collapsing in the fire station. An age discrimination suit. What I lacked in intimacy, I made up for in meetings.

*   *   *

"I see you got yourself a dog," Judith said. It was early April and three days of rain had all but washed away the last of the winter's ice. She was standing on the Squeer Island bridge, shielding her eyes from the sun. She looked neither happy nor annoyed to see me, but amused, if not at the mud all over my clothes then at Flubber, who kept leaping up the slippery embankment and sliding back down on his belly.

He was a golden retriever puppy, the kind that wiggles all over and runs for a stick before you throw it. "Stay!" she said firmly when he clopped up the embankment, and stay he did in his way, chasing his tail in circles. Her own dog, the shaggy black one, was upon us in seconds. Both of them slid into the muddy creek bottom, sniffing, running toward each other and away, leaving us alone on the bridge to accomplish much the same thing.

I'd seen Gordon's three-legged dog sitting up in the prow of Stumpy's dinghy, following him into town for his beer and sausages, and now a bag of kibble. "Did Judith give him away?" I asked.

"Didn't give nothing away. This 'un picked me out," Stumpy said proudly. "Moved in on me."

I'd watched for Judith at meetings, at the post office, the tea room; collected stray facts and rumors as if amassing a scrapbook. The stories had her moving to New York, sleeping with another lawyer, selling the house, becoming a lesbian, buying a boat, starting a shelter for wounded seabirds. I'd avoided the island for seven months since Crystal's death, but lately I began walking the dog here in hopes of crossing Judith's path. If she still had Silkie, she had to walk her. Her favorite walks were around the island or from her house to the bridge and back.

She looked even thinner, tired around the eyes. I wasn't surprised that she didn't smile at me the way she once had; encouraging, expectant. If anything she seemed to look through me. I'd practiced a hundred different opening lines and promptly forgot every one. "Did you hear about the new candidate Johnny's running for selectman?" I said. "Bernice Cady."

"Are you serious?" Judith stepped toward me, then stopped. "That sweet little girl who used to be a teller at the bank?"

"Loan officer now. Very bright. Native born. Makes perfect sense, if you think about it. Not abrasive, unassuming. Absolutely one hundred percent loyal to Johnny. People miss the old favor machine."

"Sure, the people who got the favors."

"Well, she's very convincing. Didn't you read about last Monday's meeting?"

Judith hugged herself as if against the cold, shaking her head. "Must have missed it."

"She gave a speech about the way Saltash used to be. Neighbors who used to build each other's houses. Flags in every window for the Fourth of July parade. Respect for our elders."

"Sounds like it got to you."

"Might have, if it was anything like the town I grew up in."

"Sorry I wasn't there."

"People loved it. She may win."

Judith looked in my eyes for a moment, then back up the road, as if someone were calling. "It sounds as if you have your hands full," she said. "Come on, Silkie," she walked back the way she had come.

I was surprised to be invited to the *alter kockers'* meeting because none of them had spoken to me since the hearing on the dike. But if we were to keep the wolf at bay, if we were to defeat Johnny Lynch again, we had to do it together. I was sitting behind the glass-topped liquor cart when I met Judith for the second time. She was wearing a cashmere turtleneck, ribbed, blue; silver half-moon earrings and a perfume that brought me back to the day she led me to her shack, let her coat slip to the floor, and slid her cold hands under my shirt.

In the middle of the meeting she turned suddenly and murmured, "Is there something you want?"

"No. Why do you ask?"

"Because you're staring at me."

"Well, there is something."

"Go on," she said. She didn't sound pleased.

"Do you remember that broom crowberry I got for you last year? Is it still alive or did it die over the winter? It's been a very cold winter."

"It's alive. I had a mulch of pine needles on it."

"Because if it's still alive . . . I think I could get some more and we could make a very nice area for it. If you want to."

"I'll think about it." Her eyes took me in.

"Well, if you do want it . . ."

"I know how to get in touch with you," she said. "If I do."

You can go without seeing somebody for months in this town, then suddenly cross paths every day. Or maybe I was trying to bump into Judith, and she stopped avoiding me. I caught sight of her at the grocery, in the street, her car flashing past, her suede jacket disappearing into the library. She was chatting in front of Town Hall. She was buying a Sunday paper at Barstow's Convenience. She had resumed coming to the selectmen's meetings occasionally.

I brought Kara and Allison to a Disney movie. I was taking them to the four o'clock show with a hundred other parents or surrogates and two hundred overexcited kids, then out for pizza. There was Judith with her lawyer, Timothy Worth. I'd seen him argue a case before our zoning board. Bow tie and Brooks Brothers suit; deep voice and little content. With them was a girl about ten. Before I figured out what to do, Kara bounded over. "Judith!" she screeched. "When is Natasha coming to our school again?"

"When she comes home for Passover, maybe then."

"Will she bring a hawk?"

"I never know what Natasha will bring," Judith said with a rueful smile.

Timothy paid little attention to me. Because they were sleeping together? Or because they weren't? I tried to see how she looked at him, to gauge the electricity.

"Who's Natasha?" his daughter asked. If she didn't know, they probably weren't involved. Yet.

I cleared my throat and butted in. "Did you think about that broom crowberry?"

"All the time," she said, and let Timothy Worth draw her away. What did that mean, all the time? Was she being sarcastic? Did she mean she missed me? Judith always meant something.

I should have called first. But I couldn't bring myself to ask. If Timothy Worth's car was in the drive, I would leave. Judith and I would be friends, nothing more; I owed her that much. It was ten-thirty on a Saturday morning—time enough to be up and dressed. I didn't want to embarrass anybody. I hit the horn when I turned up the drive. I could see that about a third of the garden had been planted. The peas were up and rows of tiny seedlings. Something was growing under plastic milk cartons. Judith's was the only car in sight.

Silkie started barking. Flubber spun around in the front seat, whimpering to be let out. Two cats were sunning themselves on the porch railings, one of them the one-eyed Io and the other Principessa, the huge silver tabby who took one look at me and dove under the porch. "Stay!" I said to the dog. I felt enough of an intruder myself.

I was carrying one pot of the broom crowberry with me, as an excuse, an offering, a talisman. Bring me luck. You did before. Judith peered out the window and then disappeared. For a while nothing happened. Finally the door opened.

I held out the pot.

"But I didn't say I wanted it."

"It's yours anyhow."

"For how long?"

"To live and die here."

She studied my face, my eyes, and then finally she smiled and stood aside, letting me in. "That seems a satisfactory guarantee. I guess I'll take it. Welcome back, David. Welcome home."

I put the pot down carefully and took her in my arms.

DAVID

57

I couldn't say I'd ever moved back into my house after Crystal and Laramie died; but now I was moving out. I sold the house quickly. The new owners wanted the couch, the rugs and kitchen appliances, even the sagging queen bed in my room, utensils, plates, the works. They intended to close the place up winters and rent it by the week in the summer. The couple bargained to the last nickel on every item down to the shower curtain, leading me from room to room, taking turns like interrogating cops. If they hadn't made me feel like a mark, I would have given it all away. I didn't want to look at this old stuff. I had to get out of here.

Although I told Judith there was nothing left to move but my clothing—what little wasn't already at her house—she insisted there were objects I'd overlooked. She loaded three boxes with Laramie's toys alone. There were things of Crystal's that I had ignored or simply could not bring myself to touch. The suitcase that had served as a bedside table next to Michelle's old couch. A black silk kimono on a hook behind the bathroom door. Judith arrived with me at seven A.M. on a Saturday morning and packed boxes furiously until noon. It saddened me to see the house with everything pulled out. A stray button under a dresser, a tiny lost horse behind a door. When Judith's car was loaded and each box labeled—Goodwill, Salvation Army, Day Care Center, Church—she touched my shoulder. "Are you all right?"

"Why not? What do you mean?"

She was looking at Crystal's exercise bike, which I'd discovered behind the couch and begun dismantling. Six bolts, twice that many screws. But my palms were moist and the screwdriver kept slipping from my grip. It had taken me the better part of an hour. "Is it hard to leave?" she said.

"This house? With all the work it needs?"

"But I can't help feeling it's what you wanted." She unbuttoned her coat and made a place for herself, not next to me but on the floor, where the apparatus lay between us like Crystal's dismantled life. "A little house. A little family. There's nothing wrong with that, David."

"But it was a life with you that I wanted. I just thought I couldn't have it. Because you loved Gordon. Because you were so much more than I was."

"David."

"I did the same thing I did when I played baseball. I turned my back on what took work and patience, what I couldn't have right away, and did the next easiest thing. What you and Gordon offered was beyond anything I could imagine possible. Living with Crystal felt familiar. Mother. Father. Child. A little house in town. People wanted me to be that person, don't you see? My mom. My sister. They couldn't understand what I was doing with you. But with Crystal, I was just like them. Even people in town. I was one of the guys out with the woman and kids at Penia's on Friday night. I was one of *them*. Finally. Maybe Crystal is what I felt I deserved."

Judith frowned. "Don't imagine you'll be one of them if you're living with me, David. I'm not the kind of woman nice people like. I say what I mean. That's considered bitchy. I never had children. That's considered weird. Your own sister calls me cold. You'll be living in a ten-acre waterfront compound worth well over a million dollars on the market. Don't imagine people aren't counting. That won't make you one of the guys."

"Why would I care?"

"Because you always did. You were an outsider from the day your folks moved here. You married into a family that used you. You were always looking for a way inside."

"Not anymore. I killed a woman and her son doing that. Maybe I can finally be what I choose, no matter how different it is."

Judith kicked aside the tools and piping between us. She touched her fingers to my lips. "You didn't kill anyone."

"Whatever I did or didn't, it's over. You're the one I want."

"I wish I could believe that."

"You will. Over time, you will."

JUDITH

58 Judith was using her shack again to get away from the construction noise. David was having a greenhouse added onto the south side of the house. It would be part working greenhouse and part breakfast room. It was necessary for David to feel it was his house also, and his needs and his aesthetic did not always coincide with what Gordon had built. Her bedroom was to become their bedroom, with some space borrowed from the room where Gordon had spent the last years of his illness and where he had died. What remained of that room would become an additional bath and a hallway to the new greenhouse. The construction was not the most peaceful way to begin and to work out their relationship, but it was essential.

After selling his house, David used the loft in his mother's barn for his office and occasional bedroom in town. They needed to save money. She had taken a mortgage to finance the renovations. On her advice, David had used the money from selling his house to buy into the nursery. Judith had gone over the books with her accountant and set up the deal. She thought it was important that David actually be a partner instead of an employee—for his position in town, his self-esteem, and as an argument when the custody agreement was reopened.

Sometimes it took all her skill as a negotiator to work out their problems. It would not be easy. David was not as verbal as Gordon, nor as confident in setting forth his needs. He kept his thoughts to himself, and a simple discussion could feel like prying. There were compensations.

In the evening after the construction crew left and they had supper, often they went out into the dunes together. It was June, the perfect month before hordes of tourists and summer people clogged town, before the black and greenhead flies came swarming. It was picnic weather. It was beach blanket weather. It was love with the sun setting across his shoulder, the clouds barred orange and fuchsia. Their bodies fit together even better than they had.

The first summer would be ragged, with Gordon's children and grandchildren having to adjust to a new proprietor, a new boss, a new possessor—of her and the land. David had to work out his roles with each of them. Except for Natasha, all Gordon's offspring were perturbed by David's presence. His mother and sister were not overjoyed with her. She had not succeeded in charming them yet, but she had not given up trying. It would be hard for David to feel he was not an impostor assuming Gordon's clothes; but he would find his own way gradually, she was convinced.

She watched his confidence grow with her in bed, in conversation, in meetings with her more established friends and his inherited family; in dealing with the contractors as if this truly was his house. She knew what he wanted. He needed to have a clear position. That was how it was with David. Patiently she waited for him to bring the matter up: sometime this summer they would marry. She could feel it approaching them like a season, something coming into view. If they were married, it would be easier to renegotiate the custody settlement so that David could have his son part of the summer, half the school vacations. She would make the arrangements so she could plead on a *pro hac vice* motion before a Florida court, along with his new lawyer down there. She had spoken to the lawyer a couple of times and they had exchanged more formal letters. David would pay more child support in return for having his son with him part of the year. They would manage.

The sun slipped into the bay and the sky turned to greenish-violet. A breeze played over their bare skin. It was time to get up and go into their changing house.

Afterword

We're talkers. We talk things over endlessly. Not only dinner, often the first subject broached over coffee every morning at dawn, but the garden, the cats, when to paint the bathroom and fix the car, meetings, families, friends, and, of course, our work. In the car, in the living room, in the supermarket, in bed, we discuss. On long walks through the quiet Cape Cod woods, it is not uncommon to hear our voices shouting through the underbrush, each arguing to get a point across. We've ruined the pensive walks of nature-seeking tourists and sent hunters away sputtering. There's a sense in which our life—like that of many tight couples—is a constant collaboration.

The first time we worked together was shortly after we met, when we wrote a play *The Last White Class*. About the busing crisis in Boston, it was written for community theaters, went through a number of productions and was published. Collaborating was a strain, but we survived it.

We did not think of writing together again for twenty years, when Ira had the idea for a novel that Marge found intriguing but felt needed more strands to complete. We began talking about it, just as a fantasy at first. We thought we might invent a whole new persona to author the novel, and even gave our creation a name and a biography. It was still simply a pastime, but as we discussed the novel, we began to be involved imaginatively in it and finally we simply decided to proceed without telling anybody (agents, editors, friends) what we were doing—so that no one could talk us out of it.

We had a rough idea of the shape of the story. Ira began writing David, and Marge began writing Judith and Johnny. We noticed immediately that David was in the first person (which is often how Ira likes to write) and Judith and Johnny were in the third person (which is how Marge usually writes). The logic was clear: the story begins in David's mind. From then on we alternated characters at various points.

When we had completed the first draft, we switched off for long periods, each of us having input into what the other had written throughout the second draft. We argued a lot in that process. What, you want to change that masterful delicious scene? How dare you! But we galloped along, rewriting and cutting and adding and moving scenes around.

Third and fourth drafts we did together, occasionally taking difficult parts off to be chewed on and worked over separately. Always we put it back together, both sitting in the same room, Marge at the computer (she is by far the faster typist) and Ira looking quite literally over her right shoulder. There were a few technical problems in switching from computer to computer, because although they are the same make and have the same software, we configure them differently. But those were minor glitches. We haggled a lot about the shading of the characters, we fought over sentences and paragraphs, we laughed and carried on and finished up. Then we sent off what we had written to New York.

Eventually we decided to scrap our pseudonym and be ourselves. We had learned something since working on the *The Last White Class*. Collaboration requires respect and good communication. It requires being able to detach from your own preconceptions and actually listen to the other person's notions. That means a fair amount of flexibility in an arena where the writer is usually in complete and godlike control of the story and the characters. It means relinquishing that control or at least easing up on it considerably.

Writing together is easier than writing alone. It isn't exactly half the work, but it is about two-thirds of the work of writing a novel by oneself. It is also more fun. Writing is usually a lonely activity, months and years of labor without much feedback. But collaborating is far from lonely. And when you are in a couple, it can be sexy and satisfying. Although there were times when we each wanted to strangle the other for stubborn resistance to our own precious ideas and our own irreplaceable brilliant words, nonetheless most of the time it was highly enjoyable. Marge enjoys the act of writing (usually), but for Ira it was more of a surprise to find writing pleasurable. We have both begun individual projects since completing *Storm Tide*, but some years down the pike, we may well work together again.

ACKNOWLEDGMENTS

A few acknowledgments: in researching minor league baseball, we found *Good Enough to Dream* by Roger Kahn; *False Spring* by Pat Jordan; and *The Boys Who Would Be Cubs* by Joseph Bosco helpful to us. *Women, Animals and Vegetables* by Maxine Kumin put to rest any fantasies we might have had about keeping horses instead of cats as pets; while *The Whole Horse Catalogue*, edited by Steven D. Price, told us more than we ever wanted to know about the sport of dressage. For information on topics as diverse as nipple piercing, lung cancer and land sale scams in Florida, various sites on the World Wide Web were indispensable. Closer to home, the Wellfleet library once again has our deepest thanks for numerous interlibrary loans. Ruthann Robson, terrific novelist and poet and a fine lawyer too, answered some legal questions that came up via Judith's career. *The Fundamentals of Surgical Oncology* edited by Robert J. McKenna and Gerald P. Murphy was invaluable, as was *Understanding Cancer* by Mark Renneker, in dealing with Gordon's illness.

Storm Tide

MARGE PIERCY
IRA WOOD

A Reader's Guide

A Conversation with Marge Piercy and Ira Wood, the Authors of *Storm Tide*

Q: How did you make the time in the rhythms of your individual writing lives to create this novel together? Were you also working on other, separate projects?

Ira: We had talked about writing together again for many years, but we always put it off because we were working on individual projects. Either Marge would be in the middle of something or I would. Sometime in 1997 we found ourselves, oddly, both free at the same time. Marge had just finished *City of Darkness, City of Light*, and I had just finished another novel. For the first time in twenty years we were in sync and could actually consider a joint project. *Storm Tide* thus became the main project we were working on, and we each devoted our full time to it. This meant roughly six hours a day, sometimes together, sometimes at different computers.

Marge: During the era of working on the novel, I did not write any other fiction. I am always writing poetry, and I wrote a fair number of poems during the various drafts of *Storm Tide*. I was also doing research for my next novel, which I wrote alone.

Q: How did the co-authorship affect the daily ebb and flow of your shared domestic life?

Marge: It had little influence on our domestic life. The things that have to be done, get done. We do our work like any other job, and then we do other things—garden, take walks, read, see friends, go to movies, play with the cats, clean the house, shop, whatever.

Q: What did you learn about each other in the process of this co-authorship?

Ira: Piercy is a world-class novelist. I knew this, obviously, and yet, I was her husband and husbands don't always see their wives clearly. A husband, as enlightened a man as he may think he is, is still a man in a very intimate role with a woman and (am I really saying this?) thinks he knows better in many instances. Because we are both writers and because literature is as common a subject with us as cooking or finances, it's easy, as a husband, to assume the same attitudes, i.e., I know more about literature and cooking and finances. Working together renewed my great respect for Piercy. I learned, moreover, to trust her judgment about plot and character.

Marge: The last time we had written together was in the late seventies, on the play *The Last White Class*. Since then, Ira's mastery of fictional form, of dialogue, his discipline, and his seriousness have grown immensely. I knew that, but working with someone, you experience their abilities in a very direct and daily way.

Q: **The theme of erotic love is strong in *Storm Tide* as well as in your other works of fiction and poetry. Readers have celebrated you both for this "earthiness." Why is it important to write about this aspect of life still avoided in many literary works?**

Marge: I find sexuality and emotionality two of the ways I can grasp a character. People are strongly individual and strongly themselves in those aspects of their lives. They may lie about sex. In fact, I think it is an unalienable right of all Americans to lie about sex. We begin to lie in grade school: *I know what that means. I've done that.* Or later, *Oh no, I've never done that. I'd never do that.* Later still, *That was the greatest! That was wonderful.* But in writing about sexuality, we cut to the quick. We can grasp our characters in those moist irrational interstices between intention and act, between pretense and greed and need. It may not be and often isn't the most important part of a character, but it is a portal into that character that I find enormously useful.

Ira: It would be as difficult for me to ignore a character's sexuality as it would his family: two areas completely ignored by writers who have written very fine books. Sexuality interests me; I'm not afraid of it. Who a character may appear to be with his clothes on is often very different from the man with his clothes off. How better to see inside and through a character than to see him in bed, where power relationships often change, where childhood obsessions are very often brought back to life.

Q: **The physical world—nature, bodies, food, houses—figures intensely in your fiction. Beyond the power of sensual description, how do these tangible parts of life function for you as metaphor?**

Ira: We live in a time, in a society, in which people are obsessed with their bodies. How people view themselves, especially young people, is often symptomatic of how they view their bodies. I can't imagine writing about any Americana under thirty for whom physical appearance does not function as a metaphor for how they see themselves fitting into the society. To a lesser extent, a person's possessions define him/her. Crystal's image of herself as fat, unattractive, and therefore undesirable drove her to view sex as her only weapon. Johnny was slender and tall, and always saw himself as towering over the people in town. He was always aware of the power of symbols: careful, for instance, not to let the car he drove set him apart from others. The physical world is often a function of how people view us and how as a result we are forced to view ourselves . . . and then, how we act.

Q: **You have lived on Cape Cod for many years. Its shapes and textures are integral to this novel. Much is said these days about "a sense of place" in an artist's vision. Please talk about how the world immediately around where you write contributes to the worlds of your fiction.**

Marge: I have loved this place since I first saw it, many years before I moved here. Now I have lived on the Cape for close to thirty years. Before the Cape, I had always lived in cities, in the center of cities. The Cape has changed a lot since I moved here. It is more built up, there are more amenities, a lot more traffic, more year-round people, more shops. I think the Cape has influenced my poetry far more than my fiction. I had little sense of nature, of my place in a natural setting, of myself as a natural being, before I had lived here for a few years. I am now ridiculously closely attuned to seasons, tides, weather. We are experiencing a terrible drought this summer, and it affects me strongly. But I have written about the Cape before, especially in *Summer People*. I'm sure I'll do so again.

Ira: I was born in New York City and raised on the south shore of Long Island. My experience of the world, when I first moved to Cape Cod, was of the people, not the natural world that impresses newcomers to the Cape. With all its history of being a haven for people in the arts, the Cape was not an easy place to make friends. Had we had children in the school system, or had I had a job as a builder or a plumber or an electrician, I would have met people in my daily life, but as a writer, stuck behind my typewriter, I found it extremely difficult to make new friends. I felt for many years like an outsider. It was this experience of place that I brought to the character of David—a fellow who was not quite trusted by the locals, who was always on the outside.

Q: **Both of you have spoken and written forcefully and eloquently about the connection between art and politics. How does that connection manifest itself in, and with, *Storm Tide*?**

Marge: I see the politics of the book as partly feminist—different ways of relating to men, to sexuality, to work. I see it as more about the politics of a small town than about larger political issues, which I've dealt with in many other novels and poems. The politics in *Gone to Soldiers* is international. The politics in *Vida* is national. The issues in *Storm Tide* are partly ecological, and how such decisions impact on a local economy. But finally in a novel politics occurs as it is personally experienced by a character or characters. I never use viewpoint characters. No one person ever is my mouthpiece. The truth of a novel—the political truth as well as the psychological or philosophical or spiritual truth—comes together in the reader's mind as she blends the various viewpoints and experiences of the different characters together and finds her own truth for that particular novel.

Ira: Fiction enables me not so much to mirror the political world but to give it a shape; to show actions and consequences over a long span of time, but time greatly condensed. The time span of *Storm Tide* is roughly one year. In that time the political structure of a town changes from one run by a Boss (not unlike Boss Tweed, or Mayor Daley or Pendergast in Missouri or Boston's James Michael Curly) to a government run by a new, more liberal coalition. Fiction allows one not only to speed up the process and see it whole but to add nuance and personal motivations to characters. I see *Storm Tide* as a microcosm of these larger events, similar to New York City or Chicago but in a smaller, graspable frame. Art enables us to grasp the larger world and shrink it—in time, in space—to a size in which a person, in this case a reader, can encompass a real-world event. Of course, art always enables the writer to cast the event in her/his own vision. Another writer, one who believed in, or profited from, the benefits of government run by a boss, would have cast the David/Judith/Gordon coalition into the role of ruining the town.

Q: **So much of Western literature assumes a Christian cultural perspective. Please talk about the centrality of Judaism in *Storm Tide*.**

Ira: Jews have long been written as outsiders and seen themselves as outsiders in literature, and for that reason have interested readers who are not Jewish. There is not a lot about David that is Jewish: he hardly knows any Hebrew; he's indifferent to ritual; his looks are likened to a fair-eyed native American. Readers relate to David less as a Jew growing up in a Christian town than as an outsider. For me, the Jewish aspect of *Storm Tide* is the Jew as outsider.

Marge: Judaism has an aspect of connection to the natural year, as does all of my writing, including this novel. Also, the novel is built in part around Jewish holidays, particularly Rosh haShona, the new year. Judith is a woman for whom the Jewish holidays are meaningful and important, and she has brought that into her husband's life as she brings it into David's. She is strongly identified as a Jew, and she teaches that to people around her. She is not living in a place where there are a lot of Jews, and she has to improvise a lot. I think one of the aspects of Judaism that impacts my writing is my preference for multiple viewpoint. In the Zohar, a kabbalistic text, we learn that all Jews not yet born were present at Sinai for the marriage of the Jewish people and haShem and that every Jew there learned and experienced something slightly different—and the truth is not complete until every bit of the truth that every individual has to offer is finally put together. Judaism is a religion not of the individual so much as of the group.

Q: **Might *Storm Tide* be considered "a marriage of your imaginations"? What does that phrase mean to you?**

Marge: It was a marriage of imagination, of work habits, of vision, of our different conceptions of plot and character. In a true cooperation, a true collaboration, every scene is a blending of the different visions and different talents of the two writers.

Ira: *Storm Tide* was the most fun writing that I've had in twenty years. I had worked in theater before I started fiction writing and adored the experience of "co-laboring" with other people, learning to trust other people to solve problems and more, marveling at what they could come up with that I could not. I left theater when egos began to strike against each other like swords. It was much easier, and much lonelier, to work by myself. *Storm Tide* is a good novel, I think, because it dramatizes the clashing of characters who are so very different—just as Marge and I are so very different and yet able to work and live together. So what you have in the book (what we have in our lives) is a marriage of great differences, enormous contradictions, that somehow complement and respect each other.

Q: **Please talk more about why, as you explain in the Afterword, you have distinctly different preferences for point of view.**

Ira: David is an uncertain character. During the course of the book he grows more sure of himself, but a good deal of the book's suspense is the fact that we wonder if he'll make the right choices. He's immature, much more so than Judith and Johnny. David is written in the first person so that the reader can fumble along with him, wonder if he's really going to screw up again and again. David is not able to distance himself from the world in the same way that Judith and Johnny are. They are experienced attorneys. They are older. Third-person point of view gives the reader a sense of wisdom, of the ability to separate from a situation and think it through, that David simply does not have.

Marge: I am most comfortable in the third person, and I usually work with multiple viewpoints. Occasionally with multiple viewpoints, I will use a first person, as in Jacqueline's diary in *Gone to Soldiers*. I wrote one novel, *Braided Lives*, in the first person, because I wanted the direct address to the reader available in first person. But generally, I find it too loud somehow. I like to work in the third person, in the mental voice of the character rather than in their physical out-loud voice.

Q: **Why did you choose to begin the novel with David looking back in pain, keeping the identity of the dead woman a mystery?**

Ira: We thought it was an interesting variation on the who-done-it: a who-bought-it? Both women were dear to David; he was passionate in different ways about each of them. We realized that either one could have died, and it seemed an intriguing mystery, so we set it up that way. Any reader could have easily flipped forward to solve it, but I think most people thought they knew who died in the beginning and then became gradually unsure.

Marge: Choosing the precise point of entry is the single most crucial choice in a novel. We discussed endlessly where to begin, and that struck us as apt to do what a beginning must, in order to succeed: arouse the reader's curiosity and interest.

Q: **Why did you choose the world of baseball for David's claim to fame?**

Ira: I knew very little about baseball and treated myself to the opportunity to learn more about it. It's one of the perks of the fiction writer that he/she can immerse him/herself in strange things for months, learn something about it, and move on. You would think that would make writers interesting at parties.

Marge: Woody chose that. It was a sport we both knew an equal amount about, probably the only sport besides horseracing and boxing I know much of. I am pretty ignorant of basketball and football, although on occasion when Ira is passionately involved, I will take an interest. I'm not much of a sports fan. He is.

Q: **Which character(s), if any, did either or both of you find most interesting to watch evolve?**

Ira: For me it was Crystal. I simply did not know from day to day how far this woman would go.

Marge: If I couldn't identify with and find interesting any major character, I wouldn't be able to write about that character. We both wrote all the viewpoint characters. In first draft, I wrote Johnny and Judith, and Ira wrote David. In second draft, we switched off. In subsequent drafts, we did it all together at the computer, except for individual sections that one or another volunteered to take away and work on according to agreed-upon criteria and aims.

Q: **Any words of advice for other pairs of writers—whether couples or friends—who might consider co-authorship?**

Marge: A common intention is paramount. You have to be intending to write the same novel and not each lobbying for a different novel. A great deal of serious and honest conversation beforehand and a fair amount of compromising even before you begin is absolutely essential. Respect is the virtue most necessary to successful collaboration—respect and the ability to actually listen to the other person.

Ira: Be prepared to be told that co-authored books will never do as well as those with one author. People look to the novel for a singular vision. But if you're passionate about the project, proceed. You always have the option, later on, to invent a pseudonym.

life? Ira Wood has said that David is an "outsider" in Saltash. Who else is, and why? What does it mean to be "part" of a town, to "belong" there?

10. Compare Saltash to your own town or city. Do the people around you resemble any of the characters? What political issues are alienating and allying members of the community? Can Saltash be considered a microcosm of the human race, or are its stories determined by its being a small New England town?

11. How many—and what kind of—love stories help to shape this book? Compare and contrast: (1) David's love for Judith and his love for Crystal; (2) Judith's love for Gordon and her love for David; (3) Crystal's love for Laramie and her love for David. How much self-love do these characters—and others—have?

12. What is the weight and pull of money in each of the central characters' lives?

13. David does a pretty thorough job of telling us and showing us his weaknesses, while his early assessment of Judith is that she is "miniature perfection." What are Judith's weaknesses? How does David's assessment hold or change as he gets to know her? Given your insights into her through the narrator, what is *your* assessment of her?

14. Could Crystal's death be considered a kind of murder, as David seems to feel? How might her accident be suicide? Might some readers view her fate as a just punishment for immoral behavior? Might others be glad she was put out of her misery as an unenlightened woman? Could some see her as the most virtuous character of all? How do you feel about her and her fate?

15. At one point Crystal calls herself an "anything girl." How might David be an "anything boy"? Could Judith ever be considered an "anything woman"?

16. While visiting France as a young woman, Judith committed herself to work hard to achieve "a graceful life . . . that satisfies the senses and the brain." Did she realize her dream, with

Q: **Please talk more about how you began to invent "a whole new persona to author the novel" before you decided simply to reveal your own names. You say you gave this persona a name and a biography. How did this process compare to the invention of a novel's characters? Might this persona ever emerge as one of your characters in future work?**

Ira: Many writers I've talked to have the fantasy of creating a new persona: a young, fresh voice; a new discovery, wise beyond her years. Never entirely seriously (living, as we do, two hours from the airport and Boston, we do a lot of driving, and have lots of time to talk), we created an amalgam of our names (always different), a sort of demographically perfect generic young writer. God help us if the book did well and she had to tour!

Marge: It was far more perfunctory than the dossier I standardly create for a major character in a novel. I can't imagine using her, but who knows?

Q: **You tell us that as a tight couple you talk to each other "endlessly" about what you are thinking and doing. Did this ease with orality enter into the composition process? Did you read sections aloud to one another?**

Marge: I always read poems aloud and hear them in my head while I'm writing them. I do pay attention to the rhythms of prose, but not in the same primarily oral sense as poetry.

Ira: Mostly we talked about the work when walking or sitting at the computer. I don't believe we ever read it out loud. I read it over and over to see if it has a rhythm for the reader, but never aloud.

Q: **Have you given shared public readings from *Storm Tide*?**

Marge: Yes, we have. A number of them.

Ira: We did a tour when the book came out and did many public readings, alternating David and Judith chapters. It worked out well.

Q: Is there another joint project yet underway? What new titles of yours—individually—should readers be looking for soon?

Marge: We have no joint projects in mind, except for the workshops we teach together in fiction and in personal narrative, and a possible book based on our techniques. I had two books of poetry published in 1999: *The Art of Blessing the Day: Poems with a Jewish Theme*, from Knopf; and *Early Grrrl*—my early, out-of-print, and uncollected poems—published by Leapfrog.

Ira: No joint projects are underway at the moment. Marge's next novel—out from Morrow in October 1999—is entitled *Three Women*. It's an absolutely contemporary saga about the deep complexities of love among three women in the same family. It will break your heart.

About the Interviewer

Katharyn Howd Machan is a poet, fiction writer, and playwright living in Ithaca, New York, where she teaches on the faculty of Ithaca College as an Associate Professor of Writing and Women's Studies. Former director of the national Feminist Women's Writing Workshops, she continues to serve as president of its board of directors. Her most recently published book, from Sometimes Y Publications, is *Delilah's Veils*, a collection of poems celebrating the art of bellydance.

Reading Group Questions and Topics for Discussion

1. Finding just the right title for a work of literature is important. Why *Storm Tide*? How do weather and seasonal changes function as metaphor in this novel?

2. Think about the *places* central to the novel. Which are most significant? Why?

3. Consider the importance of colors and textures in the authors' description of characters and places, including the names given to them.

4. Cooking and eating appear again and again in the novel. How does food help shape our understanding of the characters? Is it at all metaphorical?

5. In chapter 1, David tells us, "More than anyone I've ever known, Judith loved rituals." He's speaking specifically of the traditions of Judaism, but how is this insight into her also key to the novel's intricacies?

6. How does the convoluted time structure of the novel affect our experience of the events? How does the movement between first person and third person affect the flow of the narrative and our identification with the characters?

7. The novel's structure is a dance among the central characters' lives. How does this kind of shifting work for you? How would the book be different if it were David's monologue throughout, or entirely from Judith's point of view? Can you imagine the whole story being told from Crystal's perspective, or Gordon's, or Johnny's, or even Holly's or Laramie's or Mattie's?

8. Chapter 1 ends with David's claim that he is telling this story in order to understand what happened, in order to determine the cause of death for something that had once been alive. To what and whom might he be referring, besides Crystal?

9. Judith felt invisible—"a shameful secret"—when she was a child. David has felt invisible since his glory days as a baseball player. Who else in the novel struggles with invisibility? What does it mean to be acknowledged, accepted, "validated" in

Gordon? Might David have a similar dream? What is your definition of "a graceful life"? Do you long for one? Have you achieved one?

17. Consider the importance of past and present family members to the central characters. What kind of family life can you imagine Judith and David forging, if they do get back—and stay—together? After talking with her dying father, Natasha tells her stepmother that Gordon "wants to have an afterlife" in Judith's life. His hopes for Brian did not work out, but what about his role in bringing Judith and David together? Will his "ghost" always make a ménage à trois in the Compound?

18. Both Marge Piercy and Ira Wood have expressed concern that a co-authored novel is judged as inferior by many because it does not offer a singularity of vision. What has been your experience in reading this book's duality of vision?

© Debbie Milligan

About the Authors

MARGE PIERCY is the author of thirteen previous novels, including *City of Darkness, City of Light*; *The Longings of Women*; *He, She and It* (winner of the prestigious Arthur C. Clarke Award in Great Britain); *Braided Lives*; *Gone to Soldiers*; and *Woman on the Edge of Time*. She has also written thirteen collections of poetry, including *Mars and Her Children* and *What Are Big Girls Made Of?* She lives on Cape Cod with her husband, the novelist Ira Wood. Her work has been translated into sixteen languages. Her website address is http://www.capecod.net/~tmpiercy.

IRA WOOD is the author of two novels, *The Kitchen Man* and *Going Public*, as well as plays and screenplays. His workshops have inspired students all over the country to dig more deeply into their personal lives, to face the barriers of hopelessness and their fear of writing in order to overcome the inner censor. Recently, he and Marge Piercy started a small independent publishing company. Visit them at http://www.leapfrogpress.com.

BONE CHINA

Roma Tearne

BONE CHINA

Europa
editions

Europa Editions
116 East 16th Street
New York, N.Y. 10003
www.europaeditions.com
info@europaeditions.com

Copyright © 2008 by Roma Tearne
First Publication 2009 by Europa Editions

Library of Congress Cataloging in Publication Data is available
ISBN 978-1-933372-75-4

Tearne, Roma
Bone China

Book design by Emanuele Ragnisco
www.mekkanografici.com

Prepress by Plan.ed – Rome

Printed in Canada

CONTENTS

For Barrie,
Oliver, Alistair and Mollie.

And in memory of my parents.

He who never leaves his country is full of prejudices.

—CARLO GOLDONI

SECRETS

1

From the road all that could be seen of the house was its
long red roof. Everything else was screened by the trees.
Occasionally, depending on the direction of the breeze,
children's voices or a piano being played could be heard, but
usually, the only sound was the faint rush of water falling away
farther down the valley. Until this point where the road ended,
the house and all its grandeur remained hidden. Then suddenly
it burst into view. The car, approaching from the south side,
wound slowly up the tea-covered hills. Passing one breathtaking
view after another, it climbed higher and higher until at last it
rolled to a halt. For a moment Aloysius de Silva sat staring out.
The house had been in his wife's family for more than two hundred years. Local people, those who knew of it and knew the
family, called it the House of Many Balconies. All around its
façade were ornate carvings punctuated by small stone balconies
and deep verandas. The gardens were planted with rhododen-
drons and foxgloves, arum lilies and soft, rain-washed flowers.
"Serendipity," the Governor had called it, "somewhere deep in
the Garden of Eden." It was here, in this undisturbed paradise,
viridian green and temperate, that the dark-eyed Grace had
grown up. And it was here that she waited for him now.

Sighing heavily, for he was returning home after an absence
of several days, Aloysius opened the door of the car, nodding to
the driver. He would walk the rest of the way. It was early morning, on the first day of September 1939. Thin patches of mist
drifted in the rarefied air. In his haste to return home he had

caught only a glimpse of the newspaper headlines. They could no longer be ignored. The war in Europe was official, and because the island of Ceylon was still under British Crown Rule he knew it would affect them all. But this morning Aloysius de Silva had other things on his mind. He was the bearer of some rather pressing news of his own. His wife, he remembered with some reluctance, was waiting. The next few hours would not be easy. Aloysius had been playing poker. He had promised her he would not, but he had broken his promise. He had been drinking, so that, as sometimes happened on such occasions, one thing had led seamlessly to another. One minute he had had the chance to win back, at a single blow, the unravelled fortunes of his family, the horses, the estates. But the next it had vanished with an inevitability that had proved hard to anticipate. A queen, a king, an ace; he could see them clearly still. He had staked his life on a hand of cards. And he had lost. Why had he done this? He had no idea how to tell her the last of her tea estates had gone. It had been the thing he dreaded most of all.

"They're crooks," he declared loudly, a bit later on.

No good beating about the bush, he thought. They were sitting in the turquoise drawing room, surrounded by the Dutch colonial furniture, the Italian glass and the exquisite collection of rare bone china that had belonged to Grace's mother. Family portraits lined the walls, bookcases and vitrines filled the rooms, and a huge chandelier hung its droplets above them.

"Rasanayagaim set me up," said Aloysius. "I could tell there was some funny business going on. You know, all the time there was some sort of message being passed between him and that puppy, Chesterton."

His wife said nothing and Aloysius searched around for a match to light his cigar. When he found none he rang the bell and the servant boy appeared.

"Bring some tea," he said irritably after he relit his cigar. "I was set up," he continued, when the servant had left the room.

"As soon as I saw that bastard Rasanayagaim, I knew there'd be trouble. You remember what happened to Harold Fonsaka? And then later on, to that fellow, Sam? I'm telling you, on every single occasion Rasanayagaim was in the room!"

Aloysius blew a ring of cigar smoke and coughed. Still Grace de Silva said nothing. Aloysius could see she had her inscrutable look. This could go on for days, he thought, eyeing her warily. It was a pity really, given how good-looking she still was. Quite my best asset most of the time. He suppressed the desire to laugh. The conversation was liable to get tricky.

"It was just bad luck, darl," he said, trying another tack. "Just wait, men, I'll win it all back at the next game!"

He could see it clearly. The moment he fanned out the cards there had been a constellation of possibilities. A queen, a king, an ace! But then, it hadn't been enough. Too little, too late, he thought, regretfully. All over Europe the lights were going out. As from this moment, Britain was at war with Germany. Bad luck, thought Aloysius, again. She'll be silent for days now, weeks even, he predicted gloomily. She knows how to punish me. Always has.

The servant brought in the tea on a silver tray. The china was exquisite. Blue and white and faded. It had been in the family for years, commissioned by the Queen for the Hyde Park Exhibition. Does it still belong to us? Grace thought furiously, looking at them. Or has he signed them away too? And what about me? she wanted to shout. I'm surprised he hasn't gambled me away. Aloysius watched her. He was well aware that his wife was corseted in good manners, bound up by good breeding, wrapped in the glow of a more elegant world than the one he had been brought up in. But he also knew, underneath, she had a temper. The servant poured the tea. The porcelain teacups were paper-thin. They let in a faint glow of light when she held them up.

"It isn't as bad as you think," he said conversationally. No use encouraging her silence, he decided, briskly. What's done is done. Move forward, he thought. "We'd have had to give up the house anyway. The Governor wants it for the war. It's been on the cards for ages, you know, darl," he told her, not realising what he was saying.

Grace de Silva pursed her lips. The flower in her hair trembled. Her eyes were blue-black like a kingfisher's beak and she wanted to kill Aloysius.

"So you see, sooner or later we'd have to move."

He waved aside his smoke, coughing. The servant, having handed a cup of tea to Mrs. de Silva, left. Dammit, thought Aloysius, again. Why does she have to be so hard on me? It was a mistake, wasn't it? Her silence unnerved him.

"The fact is, I'm no longer necessary to the British. We were useful as sandbags, once," he continued, sounding more confident than he felt. "Those were the days, hah! It was people like me, you know, who kept civil unrest at bay. But now, now they have their damn war looming, they don't need *me*."

Is she ever going to say anything? he wondered. Women were such strange creatures. He moved restlessly. Not having slept he was exhausted. The effort of wanting to give Grace a surprise windfall had tired him out.

"So, it's only the estate we've lost," he repeated uneasily, trying to gauge her mood. "I don't want to be a manager on a plantation that's no longer ours. What's the point in that? I've no intention of being one of their bloody slaves!"

Grace stirred her tea. Aloysius was a Tamil man who had, by some mysterious means, acquired a Sinhalese surname. He had done this long before Grace knew him, having taken a liking to the name de Silva. When he first began working as the estate manager at her father's factory he had been young and very clever in the sharp ways of an educated Tamil. And he had been eager to learn. But most of all he had been musical and full of high spirits, full of effervescent charm. Grace, the only daughter of the planter boss, had fallen in love. In all her life she had never met anyone as intelligent as Aloysius. He was *still* clever, she thought now, but his weaknesses appalled her. Soon after their marriage he had started gambling with the British officers, staying out late, drinking and losing money. Only then did Grace understand her father's warning.

"He will drink your fortune away, Grace," her father had said. "The British will give him special privileges because of his charm, and it will go to his head. He will not be the husband you think."

Her father had not wanted her to marry Aloysius. He had tried to stop her, but Grace had a stubborn streak. In the end, her father, who could deny her nothing, had given in. Now, finally, she saw what she had done.

"The children have been asked to leave Greenwood," she told him, coldly. "Their school fees haven't been paid for a year. A *year!*"

Hearing her own voice rise she stopped talking. She blamed herself. Five children, she thought. I've borne him *five* children. And now this. Her anger was more than she could bear.

"Stanley Simpson wanted me to play," Aloysius was saying. Stanley Simpson was his boss. "It would have been incorrect of me to refuse." He avoided Grace's eye. "I have always been his equal, darl. How could I suddenly refuse to join in? These English fellows have always relied on me to make up the numbers."

"But they know when to stop," Grace said bitterly. "They don't ruin themselves."

Aloysius looked at his feet. "When it's your hands on the wheel it's so much easier to apply the brake," he mumbled.

They were both silent, listening to the ticking of the grandfather clock. Outside, a bird screeched and was answered by another bird.

"Don't worry about the children, darl," Aloysius said soothingly. "We can get Myrtle to tutor them."

Grace started. *Myrtle?* Had Aloysius completely taken leave of his senses? Myrtle was her cousin. She hated Grace.

"We'll start again, move to Colombo. I'll get the estates back somehow, you'll see. And after the war, we'll get the house back too. I promise you. It's just a small inconvenience."

Grace looked at him. I've been a fool, she thought, bitterly. I've no one to blame but myself. And now he wants to bring Myrtle back into our lives. She suppressed a shiver.

Outside, another day on the tea plantation continued, regardless. The early-morning mist had cleared and the coolies had brought in their baskets of leaves to be weighed. Christopher de Silva, youngest son of Grace and Aloysius, was sneaking in through the back of the house. Christopher had brought his mother a present. Well, it wasn't exactly for her, it was his really. But if he gave it to Grace he knew he'd be allowed to keep it. The older children were still at school and no one had seen his father for some time. It was as good a moment as any. He hurried across the kitchen garden and entered the house through the servants' quarters carrying a large cardboard box punctured with holes. The kitchen was full of activity. Lunch was being prepared. A pale cream tureen was being filled with a mound of hot rice. Napkins were pushed into silver rings.

"Aiyo!" said the cook, seeing him. "You can't put your things there. Mr. de Silva's back and we're late with the lunch."

"Christopher, master," said the servant boy who had just served tea for the lady of the house, "your brothers are coming home this afternoon."

"What?" asked Christopher, startled.

The box he was holding wobbled and he put it down hastily. He stared at the servant boy in dismay. Why were his brothers coming home? Just when he had thought he was rid of them too. Disappointment leapt on his back; he felt bowed down by it. He was only ten years old, too young as yet to attend Greenwood College with Jacob and Thornton. And although he longed for the day when, at the age of eleven, he could join them there, life at home without Thornton was very good. Thornton monopolised his mother and Christopher preferred his absence.

"Is Thornton coming too?" he asked in dismay.

"Yes," said the servant boy. "They're *all* coming home. Alicia and Frieda too."

His eyes were shining with excitement. He was the same age as Christopher. They were good friends.

"You're all going to live in Colombo now," he announced. "I'm going to come too!" He waggled his head from side to side.

"Namil, will you never learn to keep your mouth shut?" cried his mother the cook, pulling the boy by the ear. "Here, you nuisance, take these coconuts outside to be scraped. And Christopher, master, please go and wash your hands, lunch is almost ready."

"What's going on?" muttered Christopher. "I'm going to find out."

Then he remembered the cardboard box in the middle of the floor. A muffled miaowing came from within.

"Namil," he said, "can you put this in my room, carefully? Don't let anyone see. It's a present for my mother."

"What is it?" asked the servant boy, but Christopher had gone, unaware of the horrified expression on the cook's face as she watched the cardboard box rocking on her kitchen floor.

Further down the valley Christopher's older brothers waited on the steps of Greenwood College for the buggy to collect them. Jacob de Silva was worried. They had been told to leave their books before returning home. Although the real significance of the message had not fully dawned on him, the vague sense of unease and suspicion that was his constant companion grew stronger with each passing minute.

"Why d'you think we have to go home?" he asked Thornton.

"I thought you said they hadn't paid our school fees," Thornton replied. He was not really interested.

"But why d'you think that is?" insisted Jacob. "Why didn't they pay them?" Thornton did not care. He was only thirteen, the apple of his mother's eyes, a dreamer, a chaser of the cream butterflies that invaded the valley at this time of year. Today merely signalled freedom for him.

"Oh, who knows with grown-ups," he said. "Just think, tomorrow we'll wake up in our own bedroom. We can go out onto the balcony and look at the garden and no one will mind. And we can have egg hoppers and mangoes for breakfast instead of toast and marmalade. So who cares!" He laughed. "I'm glad we're leaving. It's so boring here. We can do what we want at home." A thought struck him. "I wonder if the girls have been sent back too?"

On their last holiday they had climbed down from the bedroom balcony very early one morning and crept through the mist, to the square where the nuns and the monkeys gathered beside the white Portuguese church. They had had breakfast with Father Jeremy who wheezed and coughed and offered them whisky, which they had drunk in one swift gulp. And afterwards they had staggered back home to bed. Thornton giggled at the memory.

Jacob watched him solemnly. He watched him run down the steps of Greenwood College, this privileged seat of learning for the sons of British government officials and the island's elite, his laughter floating on the sunlight.

"I want to stay here," he said softly, stubbornly, under his breath. "We can go home any time. But we can only learn things here."

He frowned. He could see all the plans for his future begin-ning to fade. The headmaster had told him he could have gone to university had he stayed on at school and finished his stud-ies. His Latin teacher had told him he might have done clas-sics. Then his science teacher had told him that in *his* opinion Jacob could have gone to medical school. Jacob had kept these conversations to himself.

"Oh, I can learn things anywhere," Thornton was saying airily. "I'm a poet, remember." He laughed again. "I'm so lucky," he said. And then, in the fleeting manner of sudden childhood insights, he thought, I'm glad I'm not the eldest.

"Come on," he added kindly, sensing some invisible strug-gle, some unspoken battle going on between them. "Race you to the gate."

But Jacob did not move. He stared morosely ahead of him, not speaking. Both boys wore the same ridiculous English public-school uniform, but whereas Thornton wore his with ease, already in possession of the looks that would mark him out for the rest of his life, Jacob simply looked hot and awk-ward. Again, he was aware of some difficulty, some compari-son in his own mind, between himself and his brother. But what this was he could not say. Thornton's voice drifted faint-ly towards him, but still Jacob did not move.

"I can't." His voice sounded strained. "You don't under-stand. Someone must stay here to wait for the buggy."

He was fifteen years old. He had been brought up to believe he was the inheritor of the tea plantations that rose steeply in tiers around him. The responsibilities of being the eldest child rested heavily on his small shoulders. As he stood watching his brother chasing the butterflies that slipped through the trees, he was suddenly aware of wanting to cry. Something inexplicable and infinitely precious seemed to be breaking inside him. Something he loved. And he could do nothing to stop it.

The buggy never arrived. After a while an older boy came out with a message.

"Your parents have rung," the boy said. "Looks like you're going to have to walk. They don't have a buggy anymore. Perhaps it's been sold off to pay your father's debtors," he grinned.

"We have no debtors," muttered Jacob, but the boy had gone.

Eventually the brothers began to walk. Jacob walked slowly. The long fingers of sun shone pink and low in the sky as they left the driveway of Greenwood for the very last time. Rain had fallen earlier, dampening the ground on this ordinary afternoon, one so like the others, in their gentle upcountry childhood. The air across the valley was filled with the pungent scent of tea, rising steeply as far as the eye could see. In the distance the sound of the factory chute rattled on, endlessly processing, mixing and moving in time to the roar of the waterfall. The two boys wandered on, past the lake brimming with an abundance of water lilies, past clouds of cream butterflies, and through the height of the afternoon, their voices echoed far into the distance. Returning to their home nestling in the hills of Little England.

To his dismay, Christopher discovered the servant boy had been right. Jacob and Thornton were coming home. Alicia and Frieda, still stranded at the Carmelite Convent School, were waiting fruitlessly for another buggy to pick them up. In the end the priest, taking pity on them, drove them home and it was teatime before Grace was able to break the news to them all. The servant brought a butter cake and some Bora into the drawing room. She brought in small triangles of bread spread with butter and jaggery. And she brought in king coconut juice for the children and tea for Grace. The servant, knowing how upset Grace was, served it all on Grace's favourite green Hartley china tea service. Alicia opened the beautiful old Bechstein piano and began to play Schubert. The others ate quietly. For a moment Grace was distracted. The mellow tone of this sonata was one she loved and Alicia's light touch never failed to surprise her. She waited until the andante was over.

"That was lovely," she said, putting her hand gently on her daughter's shoulder. "It's come along a lot since I last heard it."

"That's because we've got a new piano teacher. She's wonderful, Mummy!" Alicia said. "She said I must be careful about the phrasing of this last section. Listen," and she played a few bars over again.

"Yes, I see," Grace said. "Good! Now, I want to talk to all of you about something else. So could you leave the piano for a moment, darling?"

Five pairs of eyes watched her solemnly as she spoke.

"We're moving to Colombo," she told them slowly. "We're going to live in our other house by the sea." She took a deep breath. "Because there's going to be a war the British military needs this house, you see." There was a surprised pause.

Alicia was the first to speak. "What about the piano?" she asked anxiously.

"Oh, the piano will come with us, of course. Don't worry, Alicia, nothing like that will change. I promise you."

She smiled shakily. Jacob was watching her in stony silence. He had guessed correctly. The Greenwood days were over.

"Myrtle will live with us," said Grace, carefully. "She'll give you piano lessons, Alicia. And she'll help in the house generally."

No one spoke. Thornton helped himself to another piece of cake.

"There's a war on," Grace reminded them gently. "Everyone has to economise. Even us." She looked pale.

"Good," nodded Thornton, having decided. "I think Colombo will be great. And we'll have the sea, think of that!"

Grace smiled at him with relief. Christopher, noticing this, scowled. But all he said was: "Can I give you your present now?"

The servant boy, who had been hovering in the background, grinned and brought in the cardboard box. The family crowded around and the miaowing inside the box increased.

"What on earth's in there, Christopher?" asked Alicia, astonished.

"It's a cat," guessed Thornton.

"But we've already got one," said Frieda, puzzled. "We can't have another. They'll fight."

"Have you been stealing kittens again?" asked Jacob, frowning.

"Well, well, what's going on now?" asked Aloysius, coming in.

Having left his wife to break the news to his children he was now in the best of humours. A nap had been all he had needed. Glancing at Grace he assessed her mood correctly. There was still some way for them to go. The miaowing inside the box had turned to a growl. Everyone looked mystified and Christopher grinned.

"What is it?" asked Grace faintly, wondering how many more shocks there were in store for her.

Aloysius's news had not come as a surprise. Grace had always known that one day they would have to leave the valley where she had been born. There had been too many rumours, too many hints dropped by the British planters during the past few months. It had all pointed to this. So much of their own land had gradually been sold off. British taxes, unrest among the workers and general mismanagement of the estates had all played a part. Her drunken husband had merely speeded things up. And with the onset of war they would lose the house anyway. She felt unutterably tired. The effort of waiting for something to happen had worn her out. Now, knowing just how bad things were, she could at least try to deal with them.

In Colombo, she would take charge of her life; manage things herself. It should have happened years ago. In Colombo, things would be different, she told herself firmly. And when the war was over they would come back. To the house at any rate. Of that she was certain. Christopher was holding a box out to her. But what on earth had he brought home this time? she wondered, frowning.

"It's for you," Christopher said. "To take to Colombo."

Slowly she opened the box.

"Yes," said a hollow voice from within. "Hello, men."

Then with a sharp rustle a small, bright-eyed mynah bird flew out and around the room, coming to rest on the grandfather clock, from where it surveyed them with interest. There was a shocked silence.

"It's a mynah bird," said Christopher unnecessarily. "And it can talk. We can teach it all kinds of things. It can say lazy boy, and—"

"Lazy bugger," said the mynah bird, gazing at them solemnly.

"Good God, Christopher!" cried Aloysius, recovering first. He burst out laughing. "What a present to give your mother!"

They were all laughing now. The servant boy was grinning, and even Jacob was smiling.

"But he's wonderful," said Grace, laughing the most. "He's a wonderful present!"

Later on she said, to Christopher's intense joy: "I shall call him Jasper! And we'll take him to our new life in Colombo."

It was in this way that Grace de Silva dealt with their reduced family circumstance. Easily, without fuss, without a single word in public of reproach to her husband and with all the serene good manners that were the hallmark of her character. Aloysius breathed a sigh of relief. Whatever she felt, she would now keep to herself he knew. Outwardly, she would appear no different. And so, as the rumours of impending war on the island grew stronger, the house beside the lake with all its balconies and splendid rooms was emptied. Its furniture and chandeliers, its delicate bone china were packed away, and even as they watched, their beloved home was closed forever and given up to the British for their military efforts. In this way the de Silva family, cast out from the cradle where they had lived for so long, moved south to Colombo. To a white house with a sweeping veranda, close by the railway line where the humidity was very often oppressive, but where the sweet, soft sound of the Indian Ocean was never far away.

2.

August was a dangerous month, when the heat, reaching unbearable proportions, created an oasis of stillness. Every flutter, every breeze, vanished, leaving an eerie calm. Nothing moved. Dogs stretched out on the dusty roads panting, too exhausted to move out of the shade, too parched to bark even. Dust lay tiredly on everything, on buildings, on the soles of the feet of the rickshaw men, on the sides of the old London double-decker buses. Disease scurried through the sun-crisped grass; some said there was typhoid in the south, others that the malaria season had begun. No one knew the truth. A pack of rabid dogs moved up the coast at a trot, and elsewhere in the crowds at Galle Face, baby-pink, raw-faced monkeys chattered and sometimes bit a passer-by. But this was August, when sanity was stretched to its limits.

Four years had vanished in the blink of an eye. Swallowed up beneath a peacock sky while the de Silvas grew and expanded into their new life by the sea. Five de Silva childhoods gone in a flash while the war still limped on unnoticed. It existed in places that were merely names on a map. Vichy, Paris, Dresden, Berlin, Vienna, London. But the hardships in these distant lands barely touched the fringes of the coral-ringed island. The war was a muffled drum, beating elsewhere and leaving the island largely untouched and unconcerned. Grace de Silva hurrying home after one of her trips to Colombo heard the familiar strains of piano music drifting through the long French windows that opened out into the garden. The music cascaded out onto the bougainvillea and was absorbed by it. As she slipped in through the front door, escaping the wall of blistering sunlight, the music rose and swelled and fell delicately. Jasper, the mynah bird who sat by the meshed window in the wide cool hallway, watched her beadily. He had grown enormously.

"Hello," he greeted her. "Hello, men," and he shifted on his perch.

Grace, who had been trying to be quiet, giggled.

"Good morning," continued Jasper severely. "Good morning, men."

Having been silent and alone all day he found it difficult to stop talking. Grace looked away, suppressing a smile. She kicked off her shoes, ignoring him. Any attention, she knew, was likely to make him garrulous. She poured a glass of icy water from the fridge, gasping as she drank.

The sound of the piano drifted through the interior of the house. It travelled softly across the shuttered rooms and along the yellow stick of light that escaped through them. Alicia was playing the second movement of a Mozart sonata with startling tenderness in one so young. Grace stood listening, holding her breath, waiting as though hearing it for the first time. On and on and on played her eldest daughter in an unbroken dialogue with the music. The notes ran like quicksilver through her fingers. Grace closed her eyes. Her body ached sweetly. Without a doubt, she thought, distracted by the music, Alicia ought to be studying at the Conservatoire. But she knew discussing the financial implications of this with Aloysius was an impossibility. Better to give a monkey a ladder, thought Grace wryly. All she would do if she voiced her anxieties was provide him with an excuse to start his poker up again. No, she decided closing her eyes, *I* will have to find the money. There was still some of her legacy left that Aloysius knew nothing about. Grace had hoped to keep it for a rainy day. She frowned.

"Perhaps I shall have to sell the land after all," she said out loud.

"Yes," said Jasper as though he understood.

"Do you think so?" asked Grace absentmindedly, forgetting for a moment who he was.

"Hello, yes, yes, men," said Jasper imperiously, preening himself and ignoring Grace's peal of laughter. Then he squawked flatly and turned his back on her.

Outside, the air was heavy with the smells of late afternoon. The servants were cleaning out the clay pots from lunch, laying them out in the sun to dry. The heat flattened the noises all around into slow hollow slaps as the convent clock struck the hour in a strange flat monotone. Grace paused in the darkened room listening to these unfamiliar southern noises, of crows cawing and bicycle bells. She listened to the lilting sound of the Beethoven study Alicia was now playing. It was interspersed with her husband's drunken snores in the next room. While the steady ticking of the metronome drew and fused all of it, weaving this fleeting moment in time forever. Grace sighed with pleasure. In spite of the difficulty, her family had made the transition into their new life with ease. Their circumstances had been reduced, but they were happy. The freedom of the big city and the unbroken views of the sea had made up for a lot. She poured herself another glass of water.

Myrtle Cruz, hearing the front door, sat up in bed. She had been resting. The heat in Colombo was intolerable. She missed the cool greenness of the hill station where she had been a governess to the British family. She missed the order and calm of the English children she had taught.

"This place is a madhouse," muttered Myrtle, switching off the fan and getting out of bed.

The English family had long gone. And this, thought Myrtle, *this* is my karma. She disliked her cousin Grace. It had happened long ago when they had been young, when Myrtle had first met the new estate manager at her uncle's factory. He had been penniless but handsome and ambitious, often invited to dine at the House of Many Balconies. In those distant, halcyon days Myrtle had understood nothing of the world. She had fallen hopelessly in love with the young Aloysius, with his intelligence, and his good looks. It had been an act of transformation, blinding and total. Unthinkingly, assuming his friendliness meant he felt as she did, she had revealed her feelings. She had not known his interests lay elsewhere. All she had seen was her own compulsive need, her own desperation, so that throwing caution to the winds she had declared her passion. The shame was unbearable. Afterwards she felt it was the single worst thing she had ever done in her life. He had looked at her, first with horror, and then with embarrassment. Aloysius had had no idea she felt that way. He had been bewildered but kind. His kindness had been her greatest humiliation and later on, when she saw all those things he had left unsaid, she realised there had never really been a chance. The presence of the wantonly beautiful Grace in the house would have stopped anything. Her hopes had fallen like ashes of roses, at his feet. No amount of visits to the astrologer, no amount of prayers or offerings made at sacred shrines, had altered anything. Karma was karma, Myrtle had realised with bitterness. She fled her uncle's house imagining they were all laughing at her. She had not come back for the wedding; she had not seen Grace for years after that. By the time she finally met them both again, Grace had other things on her mind. All their money had gone, frittered away. Oh the sweet irony of it! Her cousin was still as beautiful, but Myrtle could see she was no longer happy. Five children and a useless marriage, she had thought, with a small glint in her eye, that too was karma. How different life might have been for Aloysius had he married her instead. *She* would never have let him go to the dogs. *She* would have loved him.

Myrtle could hear Grace moving around the house. She glanced at the clock. Then she pulled out her diary.

Two fifteen, she wrote. *This is the second time in a week! So where the devil has she been? She's missed lunch; she's had no breakfast and it's three o'clock. The shops would have shut long ago. So where's she been?*

Myrtle paused, staring out at the plantain tree outside her window. Two bright sunbirds hovered briefly on a bush before disappearing from view.

There are several things that interest me, she continued, writing furiously. *One, why does she have to work with the Irish nuns in Colombo? Why not work in the convent here, why take the train to Colombo all the time? The chauffeur drops her off at the station, he picks her up, she comes in and goes straight to bed. There is something very, very fishy going on. Two, what is this work she's so involved in?*

Myrtle knew it was useless asking the children. Frieda and Alicia had only the vaguest idea of what their mother did and the boys were never home, anyway. *Is she some sort of spy for the British? She certainly knows plenty of them.*

Myrtle stared at what she had written. Like mother like sons, she thought sourly. Then she closed her diary and went off to have a wash.

The truth about Grace was simpler. She had taken a lover. Well, why not? She was still young. Had she not been a good mother, a good wife too? Did she not deserve a little happiness, having remained with the husband who had squandered her inheritance? Well then, thought Grace, who could argue with that? Grace's lover was called Vijay. He worked in Maya's Silk Merchants in Pettah. One day, soon after the de Silvas had arrived in Colombo, she had gone over to buy her daughters some saris and he had served her. She had noticed him even then, a lean, handsome man probably in his mid-thirties, but with the air of someone much older. A few weeks later she had returned for more silk. He had looked at her in the way that she was used to, in the way men had looked at her all her life, but without, she felt, the suggestiveness that usually accompanied such a look. His look had struck her forcefully. Vijay's eyes had been soft and full of exhaustion and something, some long-forgotten emotion, had stirred within Grace. Years of neglect on Aloysius's part had taken its toll. Suddenly, and without warning, she saw that she had grown indifferent without realising it. Her patience had been stretched for too long. Perhaps her marriage had simply reached its outer limits. Perhaps the end had come long ago. Once Aloysius had been her whole world. But no more. So that eventually, after what felt like a moment's blinding desire, before she could consult her better judgement, say a prayer or argue with her conscience, she found she had given herself to Vijay.

On the first occasion it had happened with a swiftness that took them both by surprise. Grace had been ordering silk. Yards and yards of the stuff. For Frieda and for Alicia.

"I have two daughters," she had told Vijay.

"Then you will have to come back often," Vijay told her softly.

He had not smiled. She heard him as though from a great distance. On the second occasion he had brought out a roll of pale, flamingo-pink material, letting it flow through his hands, letting it stream to the floor.

"See," he said. He could not take his eyes off her. "Feel it," he said. "This is pure cashmere."

"Yes," she agreed, feeling a constriction in her chest.

No one noticed. She saw, from this, they already talked a secret language. Her hand brushed the cloth and accidentally touched his. Something happened to her throat, something ancient and familiar, closing it up as though it were a flower. The shop had become stuffy in spite of the ceiling fan. She had felt she might faint. So that, stepping back, she pretended to look at other things while waiting for the room to clear. And afterwards, after she had bought her saris and given her address for them to be delivered, she had gone out into the blazing sun, only to hear a radio playing somewhere in the distance.

Love is the sweetest thing,
What else on earth could ever bring
Such happiness to everything . . .

Even though she continued to walk on, she was struck by the silly coincidence of the words.

Love is the strangest thing . . .
I only hope that fate may bring
Love's story to you.

Grace stood rooted to the spot listening. She was not a superstitious woman. Nor did she believe in fate, but she had left her umbrella in the shop. Turning round, as though there was no time to lose, as though he was calling her, as if she had *promised* him, she ran back. Like a young girl with foolish dreams in her eyes.

By now the shop was half shuttered. It was midday and the heat had spun a glistening, magical net around everything. The street was empty. Grace stopped abruptly. Why had she expected him still to be there? Perhaps, she thought in panic, it was a terrible mistake. He did not want her after all. Uncertain, feeling ridiculous, she looked around her and saw him standing silently in the doorway. Watching her. Relief exploded in her face. Desire rose like a multicoloured fountain. Happiness somersaulted across the sky. In that moment neither gave a thought to the dangers. Vijay simply waited in the shadows. It was beyond him to summon up a smile and Grace saw the time for smiling had not arrived. In spite of the heat she began to shiver, swaying slightly, mesmerised by his eyes.

"Grace?" he said.

He had walked towards her, something seemed to propel him, something he clearly had no control over. How did he know her name? Hearing his voice, Grace felt electric shocks travel through her. Vijay's voice sounded threadbare, as if he had worn it out with too much longing. Like a bird that was parched; like an animal without hope. Seeing this Grace was overcome by sleepy paralysis. So, holding the heavy weight of her heart, with slow inevitability and leaden feet, she went towards him and placed her head against the length of his body. The door closed behind them. Softly, and with great care. Vijay was too frightened to speak. He rocked against her. Then he unravelled her, shedding her sari as though he were peeling ripe fruit, sinking into the moment, tasting her. A first sip of nectar that left him weakened and snared by his own desire. Slowly he removed the pins from her hair. It was as if he was detonating a bomb. His hands caught against her skin, caressing it, tricked into following a path of its own across her body. Digressing. Grace swallowed. She felt the untold disappointments of years loosen and become smooth and clear and very simple. Vijay kissed her. He kissed her neck and her ears. He pulled her gently towards him and somewhere in that moment, in the three or four seconds it took for this to happen, they crossed an invisible point of no return. The clock ticked on like a metronome. Grace waited. Soon he would kiss her in every conceivable place, in every possible way. Her eyes closed of their own accord. Her eyes seemed to have gone down deep into her body, to some watchful place of their own. She felt his ear against her navel as he listened to the hot shuddering sighs within her. He found a cleft of sweetness and felt the room spin. Then he wrapped himself around her in an ever tightening embrace as they rushed headlong into each other. Later on,

exhausted, they slept, half lying, half sitting against each other
and time stood still once again. She awoke to feel his mouth
against her and then, hearing the beat of his heart marking
time like a drum, she knew that he had begun to count the cost
of what they had done. Prejudice, she saw, would march
between them, like death. Uncompromising and grim.
Everything and nothing had changed. She saw without surprise that there was little more she wanted in the world. As he
began again, turning her over, feeling his way back into her,
defiantly and with certainty she knew, no one would ever keep
them apart. Afterwards, he was filled with remorse, so that sitting between the bales of turmeric-coloured silks, surrounded
by the faint perfume of new cloth, she reached out and
touched him. He was from another caste. To love beyond its
boundaries was outside any remit he might have had. He
understood too well the laws that must not be disobeyed. As
did she. They stood in the darkness of the shop, cocooned by
the silk and she read his thoughts for the first of many times.
She felt the fear within him grow and solidify into a hard, dark,
impenetrable thing. The death of a million silkworms surrounded them, stretched out into a myriad of colours. Grace
was unrepentant; she felt as though a terrible fever had just
passed her by and she was safe at last. Stroking the dips and
slopes of his body, seeing only the smooth brownness of muscles, the long dark limbs, unashamed by his caste, or her class,
she smiled. What could Vijay do after that? In the face of such
a smile? He could hardly recognise his own hands, let alone
turn away. His hands belonged to her now. It was an
unplanned passion, swift and carefree, carrying with it the last
glow of youth.

Alicia was playing something new, something she had never
played before. The notes floated hesitantly and with great clarity across the shuttered house. Vijay was a Tamil man and these

days madness shadowed the Tamils. Luck was no longer on their side. Who knew what the future held. In the early days none of this had meant anything. She had gone on unthinkingly, acting on her instincts, a huge euphoria propelling her to his door. The sky had shouted her happiness. But no one heard. She had launched her delight into the air like a white paper kite. But no one saw. It was only lately that she had begun to think of the future.

This morning Maya's Silk Merchants had been closed so Grace had visited Vijay in his lodgings instead. They were towards the east side of Colombo, which was why she had been late getting back. She smiled, remembering the moment, as it rose and fell to the sound of Alicia's music.

"I've just been listening to the radio," Aloysius said, coming in noiselessly, fresh from his afternoon nap. "You know, darl, it really is going to be quite bad for the Tamils when the British leave."

Grace was startled. "Will they really leave, d'you think?" she asked.

Aloysius might be a fool over money, but when it came to the British, he was shrewd.

"Of course they'll go, and sooner than you think. I imagine there'll be some sort of a backlash after that."

Aloysius poured himself some water. He didn't want to frighten Grace but rumours of a different kind of war were circulating. Sinhalese resentment grew daily, a resentment which would demand acknowledgement. Soon, *they* would be the majority, with unstoppable power over the Tamils. Grace shivered. Independence had begun to frighten her. Aloysius opened the shutters and stared out at the sea. He was sober. He did not like the feeling. It forced him to think of their uncertain future.

"Is that Thornton, coming up the hill?" he asked. "Good God, how can he ride his bicycle in this heat?"

Grace did not answer. She had just left Vijay's small airless room, walking away from his rattan mattress back to her marble floors. Leaving some essential part of herself behind, carrying the sound of his voice home with her. Alicia was playing Schubert. Recently Grace had met a British officer she had known long ago, as a young girl. There had been a time when she had thought she might have married him instead of Aloysius. Now she wanted to go to this man, to ask him if the British would really leave. Would there be an independent government at last? And did he think there would be civil war? But the price for such information was too high. The British, she decided, were best at arm's length. For suddenly Grace was beginning to understand, painfully and with fear, just what might happen to her beloved country. Propelled by this late last love, she had wandered towards frontiers not normally reached by women of her class. She was walking a dangerous road. A secret door in her life had swung open. It could not now be easily closed.

"Sweep the devils out, men," Aloysius said, handing his empty glass to the servant who had walked in, "and who knows what others will come in. The Sinhalese won't stay marginalised forever."

Alicia had stopped her practice; the metronome was no longer ticking.

"I'm going to have a shower," Aloysius said, shaking his head. "Too much foreign rule is bound to tamper with the balance of this place." And he went out, bumping into Thornton, who had just come in.

"Ah! The wanderer returns!" Grace heard him say.

Thornton de Silva was seventeen. In the years since they had left their old upcountry home, he had grown tall and very handsome while his smile remained incontestably beautiful. Colombo suited him. He loved its bustle and energy around him. He loved the noise. The British talked of a Japanese invasion, the navy was on constant alert, and the newspapers were full of depressing predictions. But what did Thornton care? Youth held unimaginable promise. Possibilities festooned his days like strings of coloured lights. Earlier this afternoon he had gone to meet his brother Jacob. The harbour had been a tangle of sounds; muffled horns, and shrill whistles, and waves that washed against the jetty. The air was an invisible ocean, salt-fresh and wet, with a breeze that seemed to throb in time to the sound of motor launches. Further along, in the entry-strictly-prohibited parts of the harbour, brass-buttoned British officers revved their jeeps, while stick-thin boys stepped out of rickshaws carrying native food for important personnel, balancing tiffin tins precariously on their heads. Thornton had brought Jacob his lunch. He had been wheeling his bicycle along the seafront watching the frenzy of activity when he had bumped into two English girls, one of whom he vaguely knew. She had called out to him and Thornton had smiled, a beacon of a smile, a searchlight of happiness, making the girl giggle. She was drinking a bright green limeade through a candy-striped straw. Thornton watched her lips wrap themselves around the straw. Then, regretfully, remembering that his brother was waiting for him, he had waved and moved on. But Jacob, when he met him, had been full of his usual gloom. Thornton sighed, only half listening.

"Crown Rule," Jacob declared loftily, following some thread of his own, "my boss says it's a privilege the Indian Empire doesn't have. Which is why they are in such a mess!"

Thornton had not the faintest idea what his brother was talking about. The girl with the candy-striped straw filled his head.

"Crown Rule is what keeps the elephants in the jungle and stops them trampling all over the parks."

Jacob paused, considering his own words. It was true the parks *were* beautiful. And he could see, Crown Rule did keep the grass green with water sprinklers. It gave the island its economy of rubber and tea. So really, he decided, on balance, it was probably a good thing. Thornton remained silent. Personally he didn't care if the elephants walked on the railway lines, or the grass all died, or the rubber trees dried up. He had no idea what went on in Jacob's head.

"Let's go to the Skyline Hotel tonight," he had suggested instead. "There's a jazz band I know playing there."

"I can't," Jacob said shortly. "I've got overtime."

Since leaving their old home, since he had turned sixteen, Jacob had been working for the Ceylon Tea Board. He was almost nineteen now and he detested Colombo. The trees here were dull green and dirty and the air, when it was not filled with water, was choked with the dust from the spice mills. His childhood was finished and the life that he had so loved gone with it. There was nothing more to say on the subject. These days, his only ambition was to leave this wretched place and sail away to the United Kingdom. Life there, so he'd been led to believe, was much better. Just as soon as the war was over, he planned to escape.

"Why don't you get a job instead of loafing around?" he asked, his irritation barely concealed.

Thornton had stared dreamily at the sea. It lay like a ploughed field beyond the harbour wall and the day was thick and dazzling and humid. It was far too hot to argue. The air had compressed and solidified into a block of heat. It pressed against Thornton, reminding him once again of the girl with the limeade drink. Her dress had been made of a semi-transparent material that clung to her as she walked, hinting of other, interesting things. He imagined brushing his hands against her hips. Or maybe even, he thought, maybe, her neck. Thornton had a strong feeling that a poem was just beginning to develop. Something about breasts, he thought, smiling warmly to himself. And soft, rosy lips.

"Thornton." Jacob's irritation had cut across this delicious daydream. "It's no joke, you know. You have to *plan* your future. It won't simply happen. Don't you *want* your own money?"

What? thought Thornton, confused. All around him the heat shimmered with hormonal promise. His brother's voice buzzed like a fly against his ear. I wonder if I'll be allowed to go to the concert on my own, he thought, whistling the snatch of jazz he had heard earlier. No, he decided, that's not quite right. I haven't got the timing right. When I get back, if Alicia has finished on the piano, I'll try to play it by ear.

"Or are you planning on taking up gambling? Carrying on the family tradition, perhaps?" Jacob had continued, unable to let the subject go.

"Oh God, Jacob!" Thornton had laughed, refusing to be drawn. "Life is not simply about making money. I *keep* telling you, I'm a poet."

"What does that mean, apart from loafing around?"

Thornton had done an impromptu tap dance. Sunlight sparkled on the water.

"I'm not loafing around! *This* is how I get my experience," he said, waving his hands at the activity in front of them. "There is a purpose to everything I do. Can't you see?"

"You're getting worse," Jacob had said gloomily, throwing some crumbs at the seagulls.

Thornton, trying not to laugh again, had decided: his brother simply had no soul.

"I've sent another poem to the *Daily News*," he offered. "It's about fishermen. Maybe it will get published. Who knows? Then I'll be rich *and* famous!"

"That proves it," Jacob told him, satisfied. "You're a complete idiot!"

Having finished his lunch, having had enough, he stood up.

"Right," he said briskly, "I must get back to work. You should think about what I said. I could get you a job here, you know."

And he was gone, leaving Thornton to his daydreams.

Having washed her face and feeling a little cooler, Myrtle went to the kitchen in search of a piece of cake. From the sound of the jazz being played she guessed Thornton was back. Myrtle pursed her lips. The boy was always playing jazz, or swimming, or wandering aimlessly around Colombo. In the past, whenever she had tried tackling Grace on the subject of Thornton's laziness, it had had no effect. Grace merely smiled indulgently; Thornton could do no wrong.

"He's still young," was all she said in a voice that brooked no argument.

Myrtle had given up. Thornton would learn a lesson one day. She had seen it in the cards. Her cards never lied.

Myrtle cut herself an enormous slice of cake, ate it, and went looking for Grace. But Grace was nowhere in sight. Thornton was still at the piano, and Jasper, moving restlessly on his perch, eyed her with interest.

"Good evening," he said slowly. "Where've you been?"

Instantly Myrtle averted her eyes, not wishing to provoke him, but Jasper let out a low whistle. Myrtle retreated hastily into her room, closing the door. Then she got out her pack of cards and began to lay them out. It was her daily practice to see what misfortune might befall the family. The jazz had stopped and a door slammed. A shadow fell across her window. She caught a glimpse of Christopher disappearing into the kitchen. Ah! thought Myrtle, alert again. So *he's* back. For some time she had suspected that Christopher was stealing food. It wouldn't have surprised her if he were selling it on the black market. One way or another they were all up to no good. What else could one expect from a family of gamblers and drunks? The cards were dealt. She began to turn them over, one by one. Perhaps they would offer her an explanation.

Christopher left the house through the back with a parcel under his arm. The servants were resting and so, he hoped, was his mother. No one else mattered. No one else took much notice of him. Now fifteen, Christopher found that Colombo had made little difference to the way he lived his life. He still came and went as he pleased and he still loathed Thornton. He would never forgive his father for sending his brothers to Greenwood while he had never even been to school. Rage, never far off, threatened to overtake him whenever he thought of Thornton. To distract himself he remembered his secret. For Christopher had a secret that of late had brought him immense happiness. None of his family knew that he had fallen in love and was conducting the most wonderful romance. The object of his adoration was a little girl called Kamala whose father ran a sherbet and betel *kadé* on Galle Face Green. It was to Kamala, with her emaciated body and her poverty, that he went with the outpouring of all those things he kept hidden from the rest of the de Silvas. With furious energy and great passion Christopher showered her with his stolen presents. He took food, money, books; anything he could think of that might bring her happiness. This afternoon he had found a cardboard box with some silk in it. His mother was always buying saris. Christopher felt sure she would not miss one. Picking up the box and a packet of English biscuits lying on the kitchen table, he hurried out. Jasper, who had moved to his lower perch, watched him leave with narrow-eyed interest.

"Careful, my boy!" he said, copying Aloysius.

But Christopher only grinned and tweaked the bird's tail feathers affectionately before sauntering out into the sun. He crossed the road and headed towards the seafront. To his surprise he saw Thornton hurrying ahead of him. Christopher slowed down. Thornton was the last person he wanted to meet just at this moment. A bus passed and Thornton ducked suddenly, and then vanished. Christopher looked around, puzzled.

There was nowhere Thornton could have gone. He glanced down the road but there was no sign of him. His brother had disappeared. Perhaps he had been mistaken, Christopher thought, continuing on his way. Stepping off the bus on his afternoon off, Jacob looked across the road. He too was certain he had glimpsed Thornton. Heading off furtively in the direction of the Jewish Quarter of the town.

Having decided to do something about Alicia's musical education, Grace went to see the Director of the Conservatoire. She had known his family from many years before, in the days when her mother was alive and used to hold concerts in their house in the hills. All she wanted, she told the Director, was an opinion on Alicia's ability. Then she would sell her land to pay for her daughter's studies.

"Bring her to me, Grace," the Director said, smiling at her. "Let's hear her play, let's see what she can do first."

The Director had a soft spot for Grace. He had never really understood why she had thrown her life away with Aloysius de Silva. Seeing her lovely, anxious face, he was determined to help if he could.

Grace needn't have worried. Three weeks later Alicia was accepted on her own merits, securing a scholarship for the entire three-year diploma. Her daughter's talent would not be wasted and the last of Grace's legacy would remain untouched. Waiting for that rainy day.

When he heard the news Aloysius looked with admiration at his talented daughter. Alicia was sixteen. Her future was bright.

"You see, darl," he said beaming at Grace. "She's got our talent! Thank goodness one of them has, eh?"

"Well, I think we should all thank Myrtle, first," Grace said, handing the letter of acceptance to her cousin. "Without her lessons, Alicia, you would have been nowhere!"

"You'll be able to play on a Steinway, Alicia," Thornton said, pleased for his sister. "And *everything* sounds wonderful on a Steinway!"

"This calls for a celebration, darl," Aloysius decided, much to Grace's alarm. "Our family will be famous yet, you'll see!"

And he went out to play a game of poker, to win some money and buy his clever daughter a present. Or if not a present for Alicia, thought Aloysius unsteadily, moments before he fell into the sea at Galle Face, then at least some whisky.

Myrtle watched him go. Afterwards, she wrote in her diary.

Thursday, September 4. So, my cousin thanks me as though I am her servant. How she loves to play the good mother while neglecting her husband. As for Aloysius he will die of drink.

Towards evening, an Englishman from the Tea Board brought Aloysius home. Grace would not go to the door. She was too ashamed. She sent the servant instead.

"He's had a slight accident," the Englishman said tactfully to the servant, helping Aloysius into the hall.

There was a brief pause.

"Is Grace de Silva at home by any chance?"

Myrtle, hearing the commotion, opened her door stealthily and listened for a moment. Then she went back to her diary.

Four o'clock, she wrote, grimly. *And Aloysius is drunk again. I shall continue to record what goes on in this house. Who knows when it might come in useful? If Grace is doing something illegal, if she is caught, my diary will be useful evidence.*

Grace was furious. She recognised the man's voice. How could Aloysius make such a fool of them both? *He* might not mind being humiliated, but what about her?

"Charming bastards," said Aloysius staggering in, stopping short at the sight of his wife skulking in the doorway. "Why on earth are you hiding, darl?" he asked cheerily. "I know he's *white* but he's not such a bad fellow, you know, underneath. My clothes made rather a mess of his jeep, I'm afraid!"

He laughed. Grace glared at him. She would never raise her voice in front of the servants.

"They don't like me much anymore," continued Aloysius mildly, unaware of her fury. "They think I'm no use with the local idiots." He wagged a finger at her. "They think I don't know what's going on, that I'm a bloody fool! But I know what the British are up to. I know what's going on." He leaned unsteadily against the door. "Divide and rule. That's been their game for years, darl. These fellows don't give a damn about *any* of us." He made a gesture as though he was cutting his throat. "I think I'll have a little lie-down now, if you don't mind, darl."

And off he went, first to wash off the seawater and then to pour out a small hair of the dog, after which, he informed the servant sternly, he would have a late afternoon nap.

All her life, Myrtle wrote, *G has had everything she wanted. The looks, the wealth and the man I wanted. But she'll never be happy. And he has wasted his life because of her.*

In a month from now Alicia would leave for the Conservatoire. She would be a full-time boarder. Myrtle paused, staring out at the bright afternoon garden. That would leave Frieda, she thought.

The shadow, she wrote, *whom no one notices!*

3.

The war ended. in spite of all the predictions, Japan had not invaded. The enemy, it seemed, was within. The writing on the wall was no longer possible to ignore. A hundred and fifty years of British Rule, guided by Lord Soulbury, drew to a close and the island became a self-governing dominion. One day it would no longer be called Ceylon. A few days before independence was announced Aloysius was offered early retirement.

"They want me out of the way," he told Grace, avoiding her eye.

Ostensibly his retirement was due to his ill health. Privately, all of them knew it was a different matter. His drink problem had never gone away, his liver was failing, his eyesight poor. On his last day he came home early.

"Well, that's that," he announced. "The end of my working life!"

There were several vans with loudspeakers parked outside on the streets delivering party political broadcasts.

"Of course I drink too much," Aloysius shouted above the racket, glaring at the servant who handed him a drink. "But they kicked me out for a different reason." He was more subdued than Grace had seen him for a long time. The servants closed the shutters to muffle the noise.

"I'm a Tamil," Aloysius said, to no one in particular. His voice was expressionless. "That's not going to change, is it? They can give their damn job to one of their own, I don't much care anymore." He was beginning to sound cornered. "The old ways are finished. These fellows have no need for courtesy. Or good manners. Life as we have known it will shrink. We've been sucked dry like a mango stone!"

Discarded, thought Grace. That's how we'll be.

"I shall breed Persian cats," declared Aloysius.

He looked with distaste at the cloudy liquid in his glass.

"I've forgotten what decent whisky tastes like," he muttered.

Christopher, standing in the doorway, looked at both his parents in amazement. Why did his mother remain silent, why couldn't she stop his drinking?

"Hah!" Aloysius continued, grimacing as he drank. "The Sinhalese have been waiting years for this. Well, let's see what happens, now they've got the upper hand."

He's like a worn-out gramophone, thought Grace wearily. In all the years of their marriage, she had never told him what he should do. But she was tired. Aloysius switched on the radio and raised his voice.

"It was bound to happen. I told you! Independence will change *everything*." He was getting into his stride. "The Tamils won't be able to keep a single job."

Pausing, he took a quick swig of his drink.

"The English language will become a thing of the past."

"Don't!" Grace said, sharply.

"What d'you expect, men? The minute the *suddhas*, these white fellows, are gone and Sinhalese becomes the official language, what d'you think will happen? They'll forget every bit of English they've learned. In schools, in the offices, all over the bloody place! It's obvious, isn't it? And then"—he gave a short laugh, drained his glass, and poured himself another drink—"not only will the Tamils suffer but we'll be cut off from the rest of the world. Who the bloody hell except the Sinhalese will speak their language?"

He held his glass up to the light and peered at it for a moment.

"Here's to the new and *independent* Ceylon!"

Christopher waited uneasily. He knew the signs. His father would gradually become louder and his arguments more circular. The six o'clock news finished. Evening shadows lengthened in the garden and a small refreshing breeze stirred the trees. Somewhere the liquid, flute-like notes of a black-hooded oriole could be heard calling sweetly to its mate: *ku-kyi-ho*.

"Our Sinhalese peasants will be the new ruling class," Aloysius declared, waving a hand in the direction of the servants' quarters.

Christopher was horrified. Well, *don't*, for God's sake, antagonise them, he wanted to say. Don't just get drunk, *do* something. His father was all talk.

"On the other hand," Aloysius continued, the arrack taking effect, "can one blame these fellows? The British have been snubbing the Sinhalese for a century. Is it surprising they are angry?" He paced the floor with furious energy. "They lost their language and their religion was totally discarded. How d'you think you can suppress a large majority like this without asking for trouble? Huh? Tell me that, men?"

He glared at his wife as though it was her fault. No one spoke. Grace closed her eyes and waited while Aloysius drained the last drop in his glass, triumphantly.

"Having finished playing merry hell, the British fellows are off now, leaving us to pay the price. Is this fair play? Is this cricket?" He was working himself into a frenzy. "Soon we'll all be talking in Sinhalese. Except I can't speak a bloody word, of course."

He belched loudly. Christopher made as if to leave the room, but Aloysius held out his glass absent-mindedly.

"Get me some ice, will you, putha?" he said.

The radio droned on. It was beginning to give Grace a

headache. She went over and switched it off. Then she looked at her watch. Although she knew he was right, Aloysius in this mood was best ignored.

"That's enough," she said finally. "Dinner will be ready in an hour. Myrtle," she smiled at her cousin, "can you tell the others, please?" She would not have talks of politics at the dinner table. "And stop frowning, Christopher," she added. "Tonight we are celebrating your father's retirement."

She spoke firmly, hiding her anxieties. The signs of civil unrest had been growing steadily for months. Two weeks before independence had been declared, a series of riots had broken out in the north of the island. The poorest outcasts, the coolies, had had their vote withdrawn. Predictions of trouble swarmed everywhere with a high-pitched whine. Rumours, like mosquitoes, punctured the very flesh of the island. Discrimination against the Tamils, it was said, had already begun in the north. When she heard the stories, it was always Vijay that Grace thought of.

Their affair had run on for several years. It had exceeded all their expectations. It had proved that rights and wrongs were complicated things with mysterious inner rhythms. It had given them hope when they had expected none. Vijay was the most disturbed by this. Grace, having discovered her conscience was smaller, steadier than his, had never been as frightened as he was. It was Vijay who struggled to accept what had been given to him. He submerged himself in her, making no demands, never probing her on her other life which was so patently different, never questioning her on her sudden long absences. He loved her with a burning intensity, impossible to quench, existing only for her visits, trustingly, utterly faithful. His understanding still astonished Grace. Whenever she appeared at his door, tense and worn, he would unravel her sari and massage her with sandalwood oil, waiting until the strained anxious look left her face before he accepted what she offered. Silently. He did all this silently. Instinct kept him so. Instinct made him give her the passion she seemed so desperately to crave.

Occasionally, when news from his home town could not be ignored, he would talk about his childhood. Grace, unable to help him, listened as his anger burrowed a hole through his life. Vijay had grown up in a smallholding where the red-brick, earth and the parched years of droughts had made it impossible to grow much.

"Our land was always tired," he had said, stroking her hair, lulling her to sleep, his voice husky. Usually it was after they made love that Vijay did most of his talking. "But my parents never stopped working."

After his father died of dysentery, Vijay's older brothers took over the farm. His mother struggled on, and although food was scarce there was always a pot of dhal and some country rice on the fire.

"I couldn't bear to watch my mother and my brothers becoming old before their time."

He was the youngest child. He was bright. The schoolteacher, before he had lost his job, had wanted Vijay to continue with his studies, and maybe one day try for the university.

"I thought if I moved to Colombo, I could find work and send money home. Maybe I could even begin to study again."

But it was not to be. The only work he could find in Colombo was tiring, and difficult to come by, and Vijay soon became dispirited.

"There are too many prejudices towards the Tamils," he said. "And in this country, if you are born into poverty there is no escape."

At first, alone and homesick, all he had been able to do was survive. He had never expected to stumble upon Grace. She had not been part of any plan, he told her, smiling a little.

"I remember exactly how you looked, and where you stood!"

The light slanted down on them through his small window, casting long purple shadows on the ground.

"I saw you first, long before you even noticed me!" he told her, delighting in teasing her.

He had dropped a bale of silk in his astonishment, he remembered. The silk had slipped and poured onto the ground, so that he had to gather up armfuls of it before the manager saw him. He had stood holding the cloth, cool against his face, watching as Grace went out of the shop.

"Do you remember? You had a young girl with you," Vijay told her, smiling. "I could see, one day she would be like you."

Alicia. Grace had been glad that he had seen Alicia. She longed to show him the others, reckless though it was. She wanted him to meet Frieda and Jacob, her solemn son, and fierce, angry Christopher, and beautiful Thornton. But every time she voiced this thought Vijay shook his head.

"It is enough for me to imagine them." Grace felt her heart contract.

Everything about him, his voice, his words, soothed her. Like the coriander tea he made whenever she came to him, exhausted from dealing with Aloysius. She found it unbearable that he asked for so little. It was the hopelessness of their love that hurt her most of all. But when she told him this he dismissed it lightly, with a small shake of his head.

"It's just a dream of ours," he said. "How can a high-caste woman like you make a life with someone like me? Let's just dream!"

It pained her to hear him speak this way, so accepting of his place in society, with no attempt to change his lot. There were no words to express her own feelings. Not since her father had died had she felt so cherished.

"But he loves you, doesn't he?" Vijay asked her once, referring to Aloysius. "How can he *not* love you? He cannot be a bad man, Grace, not if he loves you."

She loved him for his generosity.

"Yes," she had said, Aloysius loved her. It was not Aloysius's love that was the problem any longer.

"We belonged together in another life," Vijay liked to say. "In some other time. In another place. Perhaps you were my child, or my wife. Only the gods will know." Vijay was a Hindu. It was easy for him to think this way. "After you died," he said, his eyes shining as he kissed the hollow in her neck, "my grief was such that the gods told me, Wait, and she will come back to you."

She wanted to believe him. Often, kneeling in the church, she heard his words. But when she looked all she saw was a cross.

"You are such a courageous woman," he would tell her. "D'you know that? You have insights far in advance of these times we live in." He had learned much from watching her. Slowly he had begun to understand the rich Tamils in this country. "This gambling and drinking is just one more sign of what is happening." They had lost their way, he told her, earnestly. In the wake of British rule, they shared a thread of hopelessness with the poor. "Aloysius is no different from the others," Vijay said, in his defence.

When he ran his hands over her fair, unblemished skin he felt as though he touched all the despair of the island, all their collective troubles, their desires, their confusions, here on this lovely, warm and unlined body.

"For all of us," he told Grace, "are doomed in our different ways. Both rich and poor, it makes no difference. We are caught in the wheel of history."

Dinner that night was quieter than usual. For a start, there were only five of them present. Alicia was at the Conservatoire, Jacob was working late and Thornton was out. Christopher and Frieda were silent. Myrtle watched them without comment. She could see Grace was very agitated, while Aloysius was not so much drunk as in a state of rage. The loudspeakers continued to pour out their endless stream of messages in Sinhalese.

"Why can't they move away from this road?" Aloysius said, irritably.

"Take no notice," Grace told him, quietly. And she asked the servant to close the dining-room shutters.

"No!" Aloysius bellowed, flinging his napkin down. "Why should we be stifled inside our own home? Wait, I'm going to have a word with them."

He stood up. But they would not let him go outside.

"What's the point?" said Christopher, unable to keep silent any longer, glaring at his father. "This isn't the way to do it."

"Christopher," Grace said softly, "that's enough."

"Where's Thornton?" asked Myrtle, challengingly, looking at Grace.

Grace continued to eat, her face expressionless. She refused to be needled by her cousin. The servant brought in another jug of iced water and refilled the glasses. The election vans were moving off to another street but the tension remained.

"Thornton's visiting a friend," Frieda said, quickly.

"Who?" Aloysius asked, sharply. "Who is it this time? Some girl, I suppose. Why doesn't he just get a job and make himself useful, for a change?"

"He'll find it harder and harder to get a job, now that we have independence," Christopher reminded them, slyly, helping himself to more swordfish curry.

"Well, that should suit Thornton, then," Myrtle said. She laughed hollowly.

Grace stopped eating. She was no longer hungry.

"He's a poet! He can't do any old job," protested Frieda.

No one seemed to hear her. Frieda felt like crying. She wished Thornton were here; she loved his cheerfulness. She wished her sister weren't at the Conservatoire; she missed her terribly. I hate Myrtle, she thought, glancing at her mother. Grace looked around the table. She too wished Thornton were present, with his uncomplicated cheerfulness and his easy affection.

"We must stay calm," she said at last. "There's no point in letting all this talk of civil trouble upset us. Nothing has happened. It *will* be all right," she added, with a certainty she did not feel.

Later that evening, after the servants had cleared the plates, she went out into the garden. The loudspeakers had stopped spewing out their propaganda and the sound of the sea could be heard again for the first time that day. Across the city, as the Independence Day celebrations began, fountains of fireworks rose and sparkled in the darkening sky. The scent of jasmine drifted towards her on the cool breeze and mingled with the faint smell of the sea. Grace walked to the end of the garden where the coconut trees rustled and whispered in the grove. Vijay was out again tonight. He had gone to a meeting organised by a group of Tamils from Trincomalee. Grace had not wanted him to go, but he had told her, in the future, the Tamils would need to stick together. She heard the sound of *baila* music somewhere in the distance. Small lights twinkled in the trees beyond the coconut grove. The Burgher family were having a party. What was there to celebrate? Grace wondered. She would have liked to slip out, to go and find Vijay, but in the last week she had suddenly become conscious of Myrtle watching her. Every time Grace had come back from the city Myrtle had stared at her, meaningfully.

"I wish she would leave," Grace had told Vijay. "I can't ask her to go but I don't want her living with us anymore. She hates me!"

Vijay had not taken her seriously. He could not imagine anyone hating Grace. Grace, however, remained uneasily watchful.

She had tried talking to Aloysius about Myrtle but he too had dismissed her fears.

"She's harmless, darl. What's the matter with you? Of course she doesn't hate you! That business before we got married was long ago. She's forgotten about it. She wouldn't be here if she hadn't."

But Grace was no longer so sure.

Having retired to her room after dinner, Myrtle took out her diary. Grace had done her disappearing act, and Aloysius would undoubtedly be drinking himself into a stupor. There would be no interruptions.

October 8. Aloysius left work today and the de Silvas will now be in a serious financial mess. So, where has all their privilege got them? It's true they still have some influence, should it be needed, but they're no longer wealthy in the way they once were. When all is said and done, this is a Tamil family. It will take more than a Sinhalese surname to change that! They look Tamil. And the head of the family is a perfect drunk! What a liability. One wrong word and he'll cause trouble. Tonight, Grace managed to stop him making a fool of himself over the election vans, but how long can she go on stopping him? Poor, useless Aloysius can't see beyond his bottle. Perhaps it is time for me to think of leaving, going back to Jaffna? Perhaps it might be safer there?

She paused and gazed grimly out of her window. The stars were out. Once, her cousin had had everything. Now, however, the planets were moving, they were changing houses. Life did not stay the same forever.

Walking back to the house Grace decided she would begin a novena tonight. She had no control over Aloysius, but this did not bother her. It was Vijay she was thinking of. Last week, he had lost his job at the silk merchants'. The manager was new; he was a Sinhalese man. He had told Vijay that, since the war finished, cutbacks were necessary in the silk business.

Naturally he was sorry to lose Vijay, but, he had shrugged, things weren't so good for small businesses anymore. He would not look at Vijay as he spoke. Later on, Vijay told Grace, he found the other staff would be remaining at Maya's. They were all Sinhalese. Grace had been speechless with anger. She had wanted to go to the silk merchant and talk to him. But Vijay would not let her.

"To think of all the business I gave that man," she cried. "I'll never shop there again."

"Forget it," Vijay had said. "I'll find another job."

I will say a novena for him, thought Grace, staring at the sky. I will go to church especially for him, tomorrow.

Somewhere in the distance a train hooted. Grace shivered. She heard the sound of the gate shut behind her. It was Thornton coming home. In a few weeks Alicia would be graduating at the Conservatoire and they would be all together once more. I must not despair, she thought firmly. Faith was what she needed. Turning towards his footsteps, with a small smile of gladness, she waited for her favourite son to walk up the path.

The concert hall, controlled by the last of the Westernised elite, was packed. They arrived late. Heads turned as they took their seats. The de Silva family out in full force for the occasion were very striking. Thornton watched the audience with interest. This is how it will be one day, he thought, going into his favourite daydream, when *I* am famous! This is how they will come to hear me read my poetry. He felt a little nervous on his sister's behalf. Frieda, too, was nervous. She had gone to Mass that morning to pray for Alicia. Frieda had been longing for this evening. Weeks and weeks of longing. A lifetime seemed to have passed since her sister had left home. Frieda had never stopped missing her. Now, at last, Alicia would be returning. We'll be able to be together, thought Frieda happily, her heart beating with joy. We'll be able to talk properly instead of her constant rushing backwards and forwards. Crossing her fingers she watched the stage expectantly, waiting for Alicia to appear.

Christopher moved restlessly in his seat. After the concert, he was going to see Kamala. He had decided to teach her to read in English. It had only just occurred to him to do this and he was looking forward to seeing the expression on her face when he told her. Jacob was deep in a conversation with a man from work. The Tea Board had been taken over by the Sinhalese, it was not run as efficiently as when the English had been there, but Jacob did not mind. His job was secure enough. He spoke Sinhalese and was generally liked. Besides, what did he care? He was still saving up for his passage to England.

"Jacob has lots of friends among the Sinhalese," remarked Aloysius, in a benign mood, watching his eldest son. "How does he do it?"

"Oh look, there's Anton Gunesekera," said Thornton excitedly. "He's from the *Times*. Shall I tell him about my poetry?"

Idiot, thought Christopher.

"There's a girl staring at you, Thornton," Frieda said, giggling.

Happiness bubbled up in her. At last, sang her heart. The three years were over. Hurray! They would all be together again. Forever and ever. Her lovely family.

"She's been looking at you for ages," she told Thornton, happily.

"Well, there's a surprise," said Myrtle. "Let's hope she's rich!" She laughed at her own joke.

The auditorium was buzzing. Proud parents, talent scouts, even the national newspapers were here. Thornton grinned with delight. It was all so thrilling. The Director of the Conservatoire came over to them.

"Welcome, welcome, Grace, Aloysius," he beamed. "How lovely to see all of you here together, supporting Alicia. I promise you there's a wonderful treat in store for you this evening." He rubbed his hands together. "Drinks backstage afterwards, don't forget."

Aloysius hadn't forgotten. He watched the Director's receding back and then, observing Grace's annoyed expression, he burst out laughing.

"That fellow's keen on you, darl!" he told her.

Aloysius, too, was relaxed tonight. Looking around the concert hall with unusual pride, he thought how beautiful his wife looked. They sat for a while longer, fanning themselves with their programmes. Then without warning the lights dimmed and the noise subsided. The first item was a Beethoven trio. Aloysius sat up, instantly alert. He knew the piece well.

"Good!" he said afterwards, above the applause, as the musicians took a bow. "Well, quite good, a difficult choice, really. For their age, I mean. Don't you think, darl? It's a difficult piece."

Grace agreed. Myrtle looked at them, at their bent heads, and felt a knife twist in her. It had been music that had first brought them together, long ago.

"Here we sit waiting for our daughter to appear!" Aloysius remarked, but he was looking at Grace. How radiant she is, he thought, genuinely surprised. "No different than on the day I first set eyes on you!" he told her, loudly.

Myrtle winced. Yes, thought Grace, sadly, aware of the look, you think I'm someone who has everything.

"We should go out more often, darl," Aloysius said. He was in an expansive mood. "Now I've retired, now I've more time. D'you remember the concerts your father used to put on?"

She nodded. All she had wanted then was him, and his children.

"Of course, these Sinhalese philistines might stop the concerts," Aloysius continued, unable to resist the thought. "They're bound to see Western music as part of the British Empire, just like the language!"

Jacob sighed, pointedly. Grace seemed not to hear. She was lost in thought, engulfed by a sudden wave of sadness, an unspeakable loneliness. Vijay would never share this part of her life. Bending her head, she stared with unseeing eyes at her programme.

"Alicia has become more and more like you," Aloysius burbled on.

Myrtle, unable to stand any more of such remarks, turned her head away. Must be the thought of the backstage party, she decided, sourly.

In the end, thought Grace, as she waited for Alicia to appear, I am alone. Perhaps after all the Buddhists were right and, ultimately, one was always alone. But, as she waited, musing over these things, her face softened with longing, the lights dimmed again and there she was, on the stage. Slim, beautiful Alicia. She was poised and very calm, and her long hair was pinned up, making her appear strangely older. A replica of her mother, yet not quite so. The other de Silvas, watching her, gasped. Is this my daughter? thought Grace, shaken, astonished, forgetting everything else. For Alicia was playing Schubert. In a way they had never heard her play before, with an effortless passion they had not known she possessed. Revealing something about herself none of them had noticed. Had it always been present? Perhaps she had always played in this way; maybe it simply had slipped their attention in the bustle of everyday life. The sounds fell perfectly, parting the darkness as though it were a path, pausing, running on, lifted by Alicia's fingers, cascading into the silent hall, until finally they rose and floated to rest, gently, somewhere above them in the darkness. Where had such music come from? Will she live her life as she plays the piano? Grace wondered, transfixed.

She brought the house down. The applause, when it came, flooded the concert hall. Nothing matched her after that.

"*Brava!*" the audience shouted when she reappeared at the end. "*Brava! A star is born!*"

People were staring at the de Silvas. Flashbulbs exploded like flowers.

"Tomorrow," mouthed the music critic Anton Gunesekera, looking at Grace, pointing to his notebook, "buy the papers tomorrow!"

So young, everyone said. Such talent! Astonishing! Aloysius looked at his wife, his eyes shining, visibly moved. They were both speechless. United for once, thought Myrtle, bitterly. Thornton was writing furiously on his programme. Christopher, glancing at him, burst out laughing.

"Not another bloody poem," he said, but the applause drowned his words. His own hands ached with clapping.

"Come on," Aloysius shouted boisterously over the noise. He waved them onwards. It had been so long since they had something to celebrate. "Backstage, everyone. Come on, come on. I *always* knew she was talented. You see, darl," he told his wife, "I always said she should study at the Conservatoire!"

Grace felt laughter explode in her. The tensions of the last few weeks, the new independence, her daughter's music, all of it, gathered in her, making her eyes shine with unshed tears.

Backstage, all was noisy celebration. Alicia stood among a crowd of fellow students holding a spray of orchids. The de Silva children were startled. Was this their sister, this self-assured, beautiful stranger? Shyly they watched. It was in this way that Sunil Pereira first caught sight of her.

"My name is Sunil," he said above the noise, daringly, having fought his way towards her in the crowd. "I sent you those."

He pointed at the flowers she held. Alicia, delighted, took the hand he offered.

"The Schubert was beautiful," Sunil added.

He hesitated, not knowing how to go on. He felt over-whelmed by the sight of this girl, filled with an unaccountable joy. He was unable to do more than hold her hand.

"Hello, Miss de Silva," said another voice. "I am Ranjith Pieris, Sunil's friend."

Ranjith Pieris was older than Sunil. Putting his arm around his friend, he grinned. Then he too shook Alicia's hand.

"Don't believe a word he says, will you? Sunil's a philistine about music. No, really," he added as Alicia laughed. "Truthfully! I'm telling you, he's completely cloth-eared! What he really means is *you* are beautiful. Now, although I would agree with that, *I* thought you played magnificently, as well!"

Ranjith Pieris winked teasingly and Alicia blushed. She opened her mouth to speak but Ranjith continued, making Alicia laugh a little more.

"As you can see, my friend is unable to speak for himself. Fortunately for me he's lost his voice! So, may *I* use this rare opportunity to invite you to the Mount Lavinia dance next week?"

From the corner of her eye Alicia could see Aloysius. But where was her mother? She smiled again, fanning herself, dropping the spray of orchids, which Sunil bent and retrieved for her.

"Why don't you come and meet my family?" she asked him, starry-eyed.

Her mother was deep in conversation with the Director of the Conservatoire. Alicia waved urgently, trying to catch her attention. And that was when she saw Frieda. And Thornton and Jacob and Christopher, all together in an awestruck group, all looking uncomfortable. She burst out laughing. Tonight she felt as though she had wings.

Aloysius advanced towards his daughter, beaming. He had noticed Sunil Pereira when he had first walked in. Why, the boy looked as though he was in a trance. Hmm, thought

Aloysius. A Sinhalese boy! It could have been worse. His eyes narrowed with interest but he kept his thoughts to himself.

"Splendid! Splendid!" he said out loud.

And having kissed and congratulated his daughter, he asked Sunil what he did for a living. Sunil hardly heard him and it was left to Ranjith Pieris to speak to Aloysius.

"We both work for the External Trade Office," Ranjith said.

"How interesting!" Aloysius nodded. Civil servants, he thought, pleased. Well, well, how very interesting. I may be an old dog, but I can still spot a winner when I see one. How fortunate, they were fluent both in Sinhalese and in English.

"So," he asked, casually, "you work in our new government, huh? How d'you find it there? Now that the British have gone?"

Christopher frowned. His father was looking shifty. "What's he up to, now?" he muttered to Jacob.

Aloysius was thinking furiously. Being in the new government meant access to British whisky and British cigarettes. Aloysius was sick of arrack and unfiltered Old Roses. Being in the government meant better rations and a superior quality of rice. With his eyes firmly on the main chance, he watched Sunil talking to Alicia. His daughter, he observed, with a growing sense of well-being, had changed in the last three years. The promise of her childhood good looks appeared to have come to fruition. Until now her life had been filled exclusively with her music. She had spent her days in a dreamworld hardly straying from the confines of her Bechstein. Never mind, thought Aloysius, delightedly, all this was about to change. Tonight had brought the first public recognition of her talent. What else had it brought? Seeing his wife approaching, he waved, excitedly.

"Darl," he cried, "come and meet Sunil Pereira."

And without a moment's hesitation, before his wife could comment, he invited this courteous young man home. The romance, for clearly it was to be just that, was to be encouraged.

"He seems very nice," Grace admitted later, a little doubtfully. Left to herself she would have waited a while before issuing any invitations. "Aren't we being a bit hasty, though?" she ventured. "Perhaps we should find out a bit more about him first? Her future is just beginning and this is only the first one."

"Nonsense, she's the perfect age, darl," said Aloysius, looking sentimentally at her. "The same age as you were when your father gave me your hand."

Yes, thought Grace, sharply, and look what a mess I made. But she kept her thoughts to herself.

"Why do I have to be there when he visits?" complained Jacob, who had planned to work overtime. "I don't have anything to say to him."

"Oh for heaven's sake, Jacob," Aloysius replied, annoyed, "show some family solidarity, will you?"

The day after Alicia's graduation the newspapers were full of reviews of her performance. Her talent, her youth, her future, all these things were suddenly of interest. Already she had been offered two concerts.

"Beethoven *and* Mozart," she said, in a panic, "all in a month. How will I learn them?"

The de Silvas were staggered. Overnight, Alicia had become something of a celebrity. A photographer came to the house and her picture appeared in a music magazine. The family felt as though they were seeing her for the first time. And suddenly there was an admirer as well. Two more weeks went by. Sunil Pereira came to call. He had thought of nothing else but Alicia since the concert. He waited, impatient for the visit, a prey to Ranjith Pieris's teasing. He hardly slept, dreaming constantly about her.

"Go and see them, men," Ranjith teased. "Put yourself out of your misery, or I'll have to!"

So, plucking up his courage, unprepared for his meeting with her, much less her eccentric colonial family, he went.

Let loose at this first encounter, the de Silvas reacted each in their different ways.

"Hello, Sunil," said Thornton, shaking hands with him, smiling in a new and dazzling way. It was clear he needed to do nothing else. "Why don't you come with us to the party at the Skyline Hotel next week? There's supposed to be an extremely good jazz quartet playing."

Ah, yes, why not? thought Myrtle. Why not show off in our usual fashion?

Christopher, resigned and silent as always, saw no point in getting annoyed with his family. They were completely crazy. Any friends of theirs were bound to be crazy too. What *am* I doing here? he thought. I don't belong.

"Where do your parents live, Sunil?" asked Grace tactfully, thinking, first things first. A few discreet enquiries never went amiss. Earlier that day she had discussed Sunil with Vijay. Lying in his arms, she had told Vijay about their first encounter.

"He has an open, friendly face," she had said.

Seeing him again, she felt she had been right. The young man seemed unaffected and honest.

"My father worked for the railways," Sunil told them. "He was killed in the riots of '47. Now my mother lives in Dondra."

He hesitated. Would a family such as this have heard about the riots in '47? Grace nodded, encouragingly. Of course she remembered.

"He was crushed in an accident," Sunil said. His father, he told them, had been working his shift at the time. He had not been part of the riots, but in the skirmish that followed he had been trampled to death. "My mother couldn't get her widow's pension because it was thought my father had taken part in the demonstration. She should have taken the matter to a tribunal but, well . . ." He spread his hands out expressively.

Alicia was listening. There was not a trace of bitterness in Sunil's voice. In the silence that followed, Grace read between the lines. She had heard how terrible things had been, how many people had been killed. Sunil's childhood would have been very hard as a direct result. Being a Sinhalese woman, Sunil's mother would have been ignored by the British. She would have had no idea how to get any compensation. Aloysius nodded. One brown face, he guessed, would have been the same as any other. Aloysius was unusually silent. The talk turned to other things. To Sunil's political ambitions for the new country they were building. Good God, thought Aloysius, astonished, I must be growing old. This boy's optimism is so refreshing.

"Our only way forward is through education," Sunil told Alicia, earnestly. It was a simple thought, he admitted, apologetically, but the discovery was a turning point for him. Christopher, about to leave the room, stopped in surprise.

"All the foreign rule we've been subjected to is bound to affect us as a country," Sunil continued. "We have become a confused nation. What we desperately need now is free state education. For everyone." He was talking to them all, but it was Alicia he was looking at. "Sinhalese, Tamils, everyone," he said.

There was no doubting his sincerity. Ah, thought Jacob, cynically, here we go again, same old story. Well, what does he think he can achieve alone?

"I went from the village school to being a weekly boarder in town," Sunil told them. "Then I took the scholarship exam for Colombo Boys School."

A self-made man, thought Aloysius, impressed. They are the best. It's men like this we need.

"I found it paid off," Sunil smiled at Alicia. "After that, I could send my mother some money."

But he's wonderful, Alicia was thinking. He's so wonderful! Christopher too was listening hungrily. Here at last, in the midst of his idiotic family whose sole interests were concerts and parties, was someone he might talk to. Here at last was a real person. Someone who might care about the state of this place. Suddenly Christopher wanted desperately to have a proper conversation with Sunil. But there were too many de Silvas present. He stood sullen and uncommunicative, hovering uncertainly in the background, not knowing what to do next.

Sunil had no idea of the tensions around him. The family behaved impeccably, plying him with petits fours (where, he wondered fleetingly, did they get *them*?) and tea, served in exquisite white bone-china cups, and love cake on beautiful, green Hartley china plates. Alicia played the piano for him and Jasper watched the proceedings silently, gimlet-eyed and newly awake from his afternoon nap.

The conversation became general. Grace and Aloysius were charming hosts. All those house parties, those weekend tennis events had not taken place for nothing. Even Jacob became cautiously friendly, talking to Sunil about his work exporting tea. Sunil was interested in everything. Aloysius told him about the tea estates that had once belonged to Grace while Thornton showed him some of his poems. But this last proved to be too much for Christopher. Taking the cats with him, he disappeared.

"Thank God, sister!" shouted Jasper, who loathed the cats.

Sunil was enchanted all over again. How could he not be? Jasper alone was a force to be reckoned with.

"Have you ever played poker, Sunil?" asked Aloysius.

"Oh no, please, no!" exclaimed Grace. But she was laughing.

"Wait, wait," Thornton cried. "Let's all play. Come on, Jacob, you too!"

The evening meandered on. The card table was brought out; ice-cold palmyra toddy in etched Venetian glasses appeared as if from nowhere; and, with the unexpected arrival of the aunts, Coco and Valerie, the family launched into a game of Ajoutha. It was a magical starlit evening, effortlessly filled with the possibilities of youth. Alicia was persuaded to play the piano again, this time for Sunil's friend Ranjith Pieris, who arrived just before dinner was served out on the veranda. Sunil could not remember another time as wonderful as this.

"You know, I have Ranjith to thank for meeting you," he told them, beginning slowly to relax, feeling some inexplicable emotion glowing within him each time his eyes alighted on Alicia. For it had been Ranjith, he told them, shyly, who had bought the tickets for the Conservatoire recital. It had been Ranjith who, persuading Sunil to accompany him, had sent him reluctantly out into this bright looking-glass world of elegance, from which there would be no going back.

The wedding was set for December when it would be cooler. The invisible forces of karma worked with effortless ease. Gladness filled the air. Sunil was a Buddhist, but in the face of Alicia's happiness, no one cared much. For Alicia was radiant. Everyone remarked on the change in her. Her career was taking off. Having given two more concert performances in Colombo she was invited to take part in a radio series in the New Year.

"After that, who knows?" said the Director of the Conservatoire. "An international tour perhaps? Grace, your daughter is an extraordinary girl."

"Let's get the wedding over with first, for goodness' sake!" begged Grace. The world seemed to be spinning madly with so many things happening at once.

"Yes, yes," agreed Aloysius joyously, helping himself to the whisky the bridegroom-to-be had just brought him.

The marriage was arranged for the last day in the year, a Poya day, a night of the full moon. An auspicious sign, a good omen.

"Come along, everyone," cried Aloysius with gusto, "let's drink to the wedding of the year!"

It was the first proper whisky he had drunk in months. It was clear he was going to get on with his future son-in-law like a house on fire.

"What we need is a small windfall," he added with a small gleam in his eyes. "A little poker might do the trick, what d'you think, darl? Huh?"

Grace ignored him. She was still ignoring him when, four weeks later, the windfall turned out to be in the form of a broken arm.

"Don't worry," Aloysius told her, finding it hugely funny. "It's only August, after all. By Christmas I will be out of the sling!"

Grace had other things on her mind.

"Father Giovanni wants the bride and groom to attend matrimonial classes together," announced Frieda, who was in charge of helping her mother on all such matters. Frieda was to be the bridesmaid. "Otherwise, there can't be a church wedding, he told me."

"Hindu bastard!" screeched Jasper, not following the story very well. He was feeling the heat.

"Be quiet, Jasper," said Grace absentmindedly.

"Bastard!" said Jasper sourly.

"That bird should be shot. He's a social embarrassment. I'll do it, if you like, darl," offered Aloysius, whose right hand was still capable of pulling a trigger. "This is entirely Christopher's doing, you know. God knows what he'll come out with when the guests start arriving."

But naturally everyone protested and Jasper was spared yet again.

Meanwhile, in all this commotion, no one noticed Thornton's frequent mealtime absences. Jacob, the usual guardian of all the siblings, was preoccupied. In just over a year's time he hoped to secure a passage on one of the Italian ocean liners that crossed and recrossed the seas to England.

He told no one of this plan which had been fermenting quietly for years. His sister's wedding, his brother's whereabouts,
these things had increasingly become less important to Jacob.
If he noticed his family at all these days, it was from a great distance, their chatter muffled by the sound of the ocean, that
heartbeat of all his hopes. So Jacob, the sharpest of them all,
the one who noticed everything, failed to notice that Thornton
was often absent. Which left Thornton free to do just about
whatever he wanted. At last that wonderful smile was paying
off. These days, his dark curly hair shone glossily and his large
eyes were limpid pools of iridescent light. Such was his laughter when he *was* home, planting a kiss on his mother's head,
tweaking his sister's hair, deferential towards his father, that
nobody really registered those times when he was not. Except
Jasper, that is. Jasper was always saying crossly, "You're late!"

"I know," laughed Thornton, coming in with great energy,
sitting down at the piano, playing the snatch of jazz he had
heard only moments before as he walked up to the house. "I've
been looking for a new mynah bird, old thing!"

"Oh Thornton!" exclaimed Alicia, rushing in. Being in love
made her rush. "You are so clever. I wish I could play by ear."

Thornton laughed, delighted. The piano under his fingers
took on the swagger of the dance floor. He would be playing at
his sister's wedding.

"Will you play 'Maybe' and 'An American in Paris' at the
reception?" begged Alicia, her arms around his neck, hugging
him.

"Yes," said Thornton. "Yes, yes, yes!"

And he laughed again with the sheer joy of it all, pushing
his hat down over his eyes, sticking a cigarette in the side of his
mouth Bogart-style, foot pressed down on the loud pedal, until
he deafened them all with the vibrations. Alicia, because she
was happy, assumed naturally that his happiness was due to
her. Naturally, being in love, what else could she assume? But

Thornton was filled with an exuberance, a secret glow that was nothing whatsoever to do with the sunshine outside, or his sister. It was a tingling feeling that made him belt out "As Time Goes By" one minute and "Maple Leaf Rag"the next.

The house was almost continuously filled with activity, music pouring out of its every window. Love was in the air. Even the stifling heat of the dry season could not dispel it. Everyone was completely wrapped up with this, the first marriage in the family. The visitors' list grew daily. Relatives from across the island, from Australia, and from as far away as Canada were coming.

"We mustn't forget Anslem, you know," said Aloysius. "Oh, and that fellow, what's his name, darl, you know, the chap from the hill station?"

"Harrison?" asked Grace. "Yes. He's on my list. What about Dr. Davidson and his wife?"

"Don't forget the Fernandos," Frieda reminded her. "And is Mabel coming?"

"What about Anton?" asked Thornton. "I hope he's coming."

"He is," said Grace, frowning, looking at her list again, harassed. "Alicia, is Ranjith Pieris *definitely* Sunil's best man? I need to know."

"Yes," shouted Alicia from another part of the house.

"Oh good!" said Thornton. "Hey, Jacob, Anton's coming!"

"Good," said Jacob, hurrying out. He was late for work.

Having sold off a piece of her land, Grace prepared to throw open their doors for a party bigger and grander than anything in living memory. Bigger than Grace's own wedding and grander than the party thrown by her father at the birth of Jacob. Grace was orchestrating the whole event, and Aloysius . . . Aloysius could hardly *wait* for the celebrations. A huge wedding cake was being made. As rationing was still in operation this was no easy task, but in this, at least, the bridegroom was able to help. The list of ingredients was frightening.

"Rulang, sugar, raisins," said Frieda importantly, "sultanas, currants, candied peel, cherries, ginger preserve, chow-chow preserve, pumpkin preserve, almonds, Australian butter, brandy, rose water, bees' honey, vanilla essence, almond essence, nutmeg, cloves, cinnamon, one hundred and fifty eggs."

Even Myrtle was drawn in and for once joined forces with the cook to weigh, chop and mix the ingredients, while Sunil was consulted on the little matter of the eggs. His mother in Dondra was instructed to round up all the hens she could find. Sunil volunteered to fetch the eggs, returning with all one hundred and fifty, travelling on the overnight steam train that hugged the coconut-fringed coastline, lit by the light of the phosphorescent moon.

It was hot and airless in the train, and several times during the night Sunil went out into the corridor where the breeze from the open window made it cooler. A huge moon stretched a path across the water. From where he stood it shone like crumpled cloth. Sunil stood watching the catamarans on the motionless sea and the men silhouetted on their stilts, delicate nets fanning like coral around them. It was the landscape of his birth, the place he loved and had grown up with. It was part and parcel of his childhood. Now, with this sudden momentous turn of events, he was leaving it all behind to begin his married life in Colombo. Soon, very soon, he would have a wife to support. And then, he thought with wonder, then, there would be children! In the darkness his face softened at the thought. He had been an only child. He could not imagine children. His and Alicia's. He knew his mother worried about this unexpected match to a Tamil girl. She had said nothing, but he knew what was on her mind. Sunil, however, was certain. He had given his heart, and his certainty was such that nothing would go wrong, he promised her. If the United Ethnic Party came into power, as he fervently hoped, then his political ambitions and all his wishes for unity on the island would be fulfilled at last, and the vague and reckless talk of civil war would be averted. It *will* be averted, thought Sunil determinedly. One day, he had promised his mother, brushing aside her anxieties, climbing aboard the train, with his parcel of eggs, they would build a house in Dondra, at the furthest tip of land by the lighthouse, overlooking the sea. So that she might live at last surrounded by her memories, so that he and Alicia, and all their children could be frequent visitors. Peering out of the carriage window, with the sea rushing past, his thoughts ran on in this way, planning, dreaming, hoping, as the Capital Express sped along the coast, hissing and hooting plaintively into the night. The ships on the horizon looked out from the darkened sea at the delicate necklace of lights on this small blessed island, as Sunil, gazing at the moon, carried one hundred and fifty eggs back for his beloved's wedding cake.

4.

By late October the heat in Colombo had become impossible. There had been no rain for months and the garden that had thrived under Grace's care began to wilt. The air was thick and clammy and humid but still there was no sign of any rain. Every day the sky appeared a cloudless, gemstone blue, joined seamlessly to the sea. One morning, when the preparations for the wedding were fully under way, Grace decided to leave early for Colombo. These days she was always shopping in Colombo. There was Alicia's entire trousseau to buy; there were clothes for the other children. And there were her own saris, too.

"Start lunch without me," she told Frieda, as she waited for the taxi.

"I won't be in either, darl," Aloysius warned her.

He had joined a new club where he could play poker undisturbed. Grace nodded. She had seen to it that Aloysius had only a limited amount of money each month and she was happy for him to spend it as he pleased. Once this allowance was gone, she told him, firmly, there would be nothing more until the next month. Sitting in her taxi, driving across the heat-soaked city, she dismissed him from her mind. It was Vijay who filled her thoughts. She was on her way to visit him. It had become increasingly difficult for Grace to escape, harder to find suitable excuses to leave the house. But although she was aware of an increased risk, she saw Vijay as often as she dared, seldom leaving it longer than a week. After two months of unemployment Vijay had finally got a new job as a cook in a restaurant. It meant he worked late and was only free during the mornings, and although in some ways this made things easier for Grace, she missed seeing him in the evenings.

"I've been longing to see you," she cried breathlessly, coming in quietly, noticing how cool his tiny room was. Noticing the white sheet on his makeshift bed and the spray of jasmine in water on the table. She loved this room with its pristine cleanliness and its sparse austerity. Vijay was looking at her with a tender expression that made her heart turn over.

"I have all morning," she said, sounding like a young girl, feeling the luxury of her words. They had no need to rush.

Afterwards, lying side by side, she saw there were hours left. Vijay lay with one arm around her staring at a patch of light flickering on the ceiling. Grace could see fragments of them both reflected in the mirror that stood beside the door. A leg entwined with a foot, indistinguishable from a smooth hip. Joined as one. Skin to skin. Turning her face towards his, she pulled him gently away from his private reverie, her eyes dark and very beautiful so that, unable to resist her, unable to remain melancholy in the face of her certainty, he buried his face in her. And began to kiss her, slowly and methodically, inch by inch, with an urgency he had not shown before. Outside the morning sun rose higher in the sapphire sky, shortening the shadows, increasing the heat, unnoticed by them. When finally she could speak again Grace told him about a party she had been invited to. She liked to tell him about her days and what the family did. She wanted him to know everything about her life.

"It's being held in the old Governor's House," she said. "Next Saturday."

They washed each other in water Vijay brought up from the well. The water smelt of damp moss. Vijay began preparing a little lunch. He would have to go to work soon.

"You know the place?" Grace said, pinning up her hair. She

leaned over and he fed her some rice. Then he kissed her. "It overlooks Mount Lavinia Bay. You can see this part of town from their garden. I'll stand on the veranda and think of you," she said tenderly.

"You're going *there*?" Vijay asked her in alarm. "On the night before the eclipse?"

"What difference does the eclipse make?" Grace asked him, laughing. She was aware that for Vijay, as for most other Sri Lankans, the eclipse brought insurmountable fears with it. Superstition threaded darkly across the lives of the Buddhists and the Hindus. But Grace had grown up untouched by all these complicated rituals and she found it hard to take him seriously on this subject.

There had not been a total eclipse for eighty-eight years. The island was feverish with excitement. It prepared itself for the event in different ways. The British (those who remained) brought out their telescopes and their encyclopedias. They were interested in the life cycle of the universe. The Roman Catholics ignored all talk of it. The Buddhists, ruled as they were by the light of the moon, were understandably nervous. Unable to move away from the cycle of their own karma, they, like the Hindus, were trapped in darkness, hoping the vibrations of their prayers would protect them. Only Grace remained fearless.

"Oh, you mustn't give in to the ignorance of this place!" she told him, knowing he wasn't listening, hoping to tease him out of this nonsense. She stole up behind him as he prepared the food and put her arms around his waist. "You of all people shouldn't let these old wives' tales rule your life. Vijay, you *know* it's all rubbish!"

Vijay shook his head stubbornly. The old traditions were ingrained in him and he was not prepared to listen. He would have to go to work in an hour; he would not see Grace for another week, perhaps longer. There was no time for arguments.

"Tell me about the wedding," he said, changing the subject.

"Well, the cake is made," Grace said, smiling, not wanting to argue either. "Frieda and Myrtle made it together. With the cook's help."

She hesitated. There was something else, something she could not put her finger on. It was nothing much, but her suspicions about Myrtle were growing. This morning Grace had had a strong sensation of being followed. Could it be possible that her cousin knew?

"What about Alicia?" asked Vijay. He was boiling some water. Grace had given him one of her mother's old teapots and he was making tea in it.

"She's blissfully happy, of course, but ..." Again Grace hesitated. Alicia's future made her uneasy. Out of loyalty to her daughter she had not discussed it, but what would happen when Alicia had children? As a family the de Silvas had their own strong Tamil identity. What would happen to that?

"What will it be like for Alicia's children?" she asked tentatively. "Their father will be a Sinhalese. What problems will this cause?"

Vijay handed her a cup of tea and smiled broadly. It was his turn to tease her.

"Aiyo! So you have fears too," he said. "Are *you* worrying about becoming a grandmother? Even before the wedding?"

"No, no, I—"

"It's a *good* thing," Vijay said earnestly. "Don't you see? You should be *glad*! The only hope this country has is through intermarriage." He paused. "It's too late for us, but for Alicia there is hope."

He smiled and the ever-present sadness lifted from his eyes making her wish her life back, to live it all over again, differently. But then, just before she left him, he brought up the subject of the eclipse again.

"It's not a very good time, you know," he fretted. "Do you have to go to this party?"

"Vijay?" she said.

She had never seen him so worried. She could feel his heart beating. Vijay took her face in his hands, kissing her luminescent eyes. He should have felt dirty beside her, he told her. A scavenger straying out of his domain. But he felt none of these things, such was the healing strength of her love, pouring over the poor soil that was his life, overwhelming him.

"You and your superstitious country ways!" she teased him, hiding an unaccountable heaviness in her heart. She knew he went to watch the many demonstrations springing up in the heart of the city. She knew there was no stopping him, and she, too, was afraid. "I can come back next Saturday morning," was all she said before leaving him. "I shall say I'm visiting the nuns. Will you be here? Will I see you?"

Vijay nodded. He did not want her to leave. A terrible foreboding had overtaken him. Next Saturday was more than a week away.

Sitting in the taxi, going home, she felt the heat spread like an infectious disease. It carried with it an ugly undercurrent of destruction that hovered wherever one went in the capital. It was not good. The British, sidelined by choice, watched silently. Waiting. Those who loved this island, and there were many who did, were saddened by what they saw. But most of them, Grace knew, had predicted the elephants would soon be out of the jungles.

Having finished her chores, having eaten her lunch alone, Frieda decided to go shopping. There was no one to go with her into Colombo. No one was at home, no one cared, but the fact was, she told herself with a trace of resentment, she felt very lonely. She needed to buy a present for the bride. Today was as good a day as any. Alicia's wedding, just two months away, was threatening to give her a permanent headache. Myrtle's constant questions didn't help. Her mother was preoccupied. They were *all* busy with their own things. I might as well go out, thought Frieda, her eyes filling with tears. The sunlight was a blinding curtain, a bright ache of unhappiness thumping against her heart as she walked. Unhappiness shadowed her as she crossed the dusty streets. I am only a year younger, she thought dully, frowning with concentration, but look at the difference in our lives.

Before her sister had gone to the Conservatoire they had been inseparable, sharing bedrooms, clothes, secrets. She had known this would change when Alicia left home but Frieda had been looking forward so much to her return. And then, unexpectedly, hardly had she completed her diploma than she found Sunil. Frieda had not anticipated this. She had certainly not expected such a quick marriage. The last few months had been terrible. Her headache worsened as she walked. A pair of cymbals clashed together in her head. Nothing will ever be the same, she thought, mournfully. Everything has changed. Once I was her only friend but now Alicia belongs to another. The words went round and round, beating into her head, competing with the boiling sun. Alicia has Sunil *and* she has her music. Thornton has his poetry. What do I have? Nothing. Absolutely nothing. So thought Frieda with a drum roll going on in her head as she hurried down the road to Pettah.

On the way, much to her astonishment, she saw various members of her family. First she saw Thornton. He hurried past furtively and jumped onto a number 16 bus heading towards the east side of town. The Jewish Quarter, thought Frieda, puzzled. Who does he know there? Her favourite brother looked harassed. It wasn't like Thornton to scowl. What was the matter with him? Next she saw Myrtle walking towards Mr. Basher's house. Frieda paused, wondering whether to call out to her. Mr. Basher was a palmist. Myrtle avoided the main door. She rang the bell at the side entrance and went in, hurriedly. Why was Myrtle seeing a palmist? Then she saw Christopher.

He rushed past on the other side of the street looking hot and fierce.

"Goodness," muttered Frieda, startled, "we're all out and we're all in a bad mood!"

She felt a little cheered, without quite knowing why. There was nothing very unusual about Christopher's presence in town. Since the age of thirteen he was more out than in. What was more worrying was that he had two large cardboard boxes tucked under his arm.

"Oh no," Frieda exclaimed aloud, suddenly alert, forgetting her woes. "He's stolen some wedding cake!"

Why would he do a thing like that? Making a mental note to count the cake boxes when she got back she continued on her way. A slight breeze had sprung up. She was nearing the waterfront. Frieda entered Harrison's music shop intent on finding a particular gramophone recording for Alicia. She was uncertain of the name. Lost in thought, she wandered around looking at the recordings, humming to herself, unaware of the fair-haired young man who watched her quizzically.

"Can't you find what you want?" the young man asked, eventually.

Frieda, puzzling over the problem, replied unthinkingly, "No, but I can sort of sing it. I think it's a Beethoven piece."

She hummed loudly, marking time with her hands. She did not look up, mistaking him for a sales assistant. The boy laughed, amused.

"At any rate, you can sing," he said. "Although I doubt it's Beethoven."

"Why?" demanded Frieda, without thinking. "What makes you so sure?"

The boy grinned and Frieda looked at him for the first time. But he's *English*, she thought, confusedly. And he's got *golden* hair!

"Well," said the boy, "does it sound like this?"

He sang the opening bars, conducting it with both hands and accidentally knocking a record off the counter. The assistant hurried towards them. The boy was right; it was not Beethoven at all but Smetana with his river. How foolish she felt. And how strange was the quality of the light, she thought faintly, noticing it as it caught the sharp blueness of his eyes. They were dazzling, like the sea at noon. Something constricted in her heart.

"Robert Grant, at your service," the boy said, bowing over her hand as if he was acting in a play.

Suddenly it felt as though a whole orchestra was playing in Frieda's head.

"I'm Frieda de Silva," she said, wondering why it was so hot. "My sister is getting married soon and this is a present for her."

The boy's eyes were hypnotic. Frieda was unable to look away. Never had she seen such eyes.

"She's a concert pianist too," she said, her voice faint.

"Oh? What's her name?"

"Alicia. Alicia de Silva." Then, with a boldness that was to astonish her, afterwards, she added, "Why don't you come to the concert she's playing in, next week?"

Robert Grant grinned again. He had been bored, but now he was less so.

"I'd love to," he said with alacrity. "Where's it on and at what time?"

The assistant, who knew the de Silva family, handed Frieda her gramophone record and smiled.

"Hello, Miss Frieda, I read a very good review about your sister in the *Times* last week."

Frieda nodded. The orchestra in her head was playing a coda.

"Is she famous?" Robert asked as they walked out, and again Frieda nodded.

"Yes. Yes, well, I mean, she's getting famous," she stammered. "Come and meet her, meet my whole family."

Outside, the heat was solid and impenetrable. Robert wrote down the time of the concert and shook hands with her. There was a small flash of startling blue as he glanced at her, then he was gone. It was as though the sea, ultramarine and wonderful, had seeped into her day. Opening her mouth to call after him, watching his receding back, Frieda stopped abruptly, for what on earth did she think she was doing? Turning, quickly, she began to walk home and entirely missed seeing her mother slipping out of a dark unfamiliar alleyway beside the station, into the afternoon sunshine. As she opened her umbrella and lifted her sari off the ground, Grace had the look of a softly bruised and ripened fruit, with a bloom, not usually found on the face of a woman who had borne five children and lived with a man such as Aloysius. She looked like a woman ten years her junior. But Frieda hurrying home in the scorching heat, with her heart on fire, and a set of wings attached to the soles of her feet, her sari sweeping up the dust of all Asia, saw none of this. Her mother's dazed and secret look was entirely lost on her. For now at last, finally, Frieda had a secret all of her own.

"Yes?" asked Jasper as she entered the house stealthily, adding to himself, when she did not reply, "Up to no good."

Frieda, pouring herself a long, cool glass of water, adding many ice cubes to it, ignored him, certain, even as the liquid slipped down her throat, that her world had changed forever since lunchtime.

Myrtle switched on her ceiling fan. Then she unlocked the drawer in her desk and took out her diary. Refilling her fountain pen she began to write.

October 28. A profitable morning. Followed G as far as the Elephant Hotel but then lost her. The taxi driver was exceedingly stupid and did not seem to understand what following a car meant. However, Mr. B was very helpful. I gave him the information about the wedding and he agreed with me that the mar-

riage is not a good one. Time will tell, he kept saying, shaking his head, gloomily. When I asked him how much time, he spread the cards. He is a very thoughtful and clever man and I am inclined to believe him. By the looks of things this marriage is going to be in serious trouble. Mr. B asked me why I wanted to know so badly. There was no point in going into the details, no point in telling him about G and my suspicions about her activities with the British. I simply told him I wanted to save the rest of the family from further harm. Mr. B nodded his head and told me I would not have long to wait. Months, perhaps, he said. But I had the distinct feeling he meant weeks. Then he gave me something else to stop the marriage. He told me what to do. I daren't write the instructions down. All this has cost me a hell of a lot of money.

Myrtle paused. She could hear someone moving about in the hall. Jasper was saying something. She opened her door gently.

"Up to no good," Jasper was saying morosely. "Up to no good!"

Robert Grant could not believe his luck. Having finished his degree at Oxford earlier that summer, he had arrived in Colombo to visit his parents. Sir John Grant had only a few more months as High Commissioner, after which he would return to England. Robert's mother had decided it was a good thing for him to travel across the empire, before following his father into the Foreign Office. To begin with, Robert had been bored. The embassy was filled with stuffy old people and the only locals he met were shopkeepers or servants. Then, just as he began to wish he were back in England again, quite by chance he had met Frieda de Silva. On her invitation he had gone to Alicia's concert the following Monday and met the rest of her family. Mrs. de Silva invited him to have dinner with them afterwards.

"I know your father!" Grace exclaimed when she had discovered who he was. They had finished eating and were now in the drawing room. "We're very old friends. How lovely to meet you at last. I knew you were coming over here, but not when." Grace was delighted. "We used to play together as children, you know. He used to visit us at the House of Many Balconies. Your grandfather and my father were good friends. How funny! We've just had an invitation to your father's farewell party at Mount Lavinia House."

Robert was pleased.

"How long will you be in Colombo?" asked Grace.

"I'm sailing back just before the New Year."

"Oh what a pity. You'll miss Alicia's wedding!"

Robert was startled. And then dismayed. So the girl Alicia was engaged to be married? Gosh! he thought, not knowing what to say. Suddenly Sunil's presence made sense. He felt a sharp sense of something having passed him by. Something irretrievable and very important.

"I forgot," he mumbled. "What a pity."

"Never mind," Grace told him cheerfully, "we'll see you at the party on Saturday."

"Do you have a telescope?" Aloysius asked suddenly. "You know we're having an eclipse soon?"

In spite of herself Grace shivered. Perhaps, she thought, confused, there will be rain soon. Briefly her eyes met Myrtle's.

"I expect my father has," Robert said, distractedly.

He was unable to take his eyes off Alicia, who was laughing with Thornton. Catching sight of him looking at her, Alicia called him over to join them.

"You know, darl," Aloysius said, turning to Grace, "hundreds of staff on the railways walked out today. The factory workers from the rubber plantations are joining them tomorrow. The copra workers will strike next. The Sinhalese are blaming the Tamils for taking their jobs. I heard on the news yesterday, the government expect things to explode around the time of the eclipse."

"I know," said Grace softly. She looked at Sunil.

"Come on, sis," Thornton was saying, "don't be so boring! Let's play a duet. Tell her, will you, Sunil?"

Sunil smiled. They were both such children! He turned to Grace.

"The government told the factory workers to go back to work or lose their jobs," he said, his face serious. He shook his head. It was utterly unbelievable. "Trade in rubber and copra had fallen, you know. There's not much demand for these materials anymore. That's the reason the factories are closing. It's nothing to do with the Tamils."

"Of course, men," Aloysius agreed, joining in and beginning to get agitated. "This is nothing new, we all know this. Of course, of course. The Tamils haven't taken the jobs. There *are* *no* jobs. It's the fault of the war! Why don't the Sinhalese blame it on the war instead?" he asked belligerently.

Thornton and Alicia had begun to play a duet, laughing and stumbling over the notes, pushing each other off the piano stool. Sunil hesitated, his eyes on Alicia. She was so much younger than him. More than anything else in the world he wanted her life to be trouble-free. He wanted her to live a life of peace.

"I was out on the streets all of last week," he said. "Canvassing for the United Ethnic Party." Robert had gone over to the piano and was watching Alicia. Sunil lowered his voice. "It wasn't too good." He shook his head, gesturing helplessly. "There's a lot of ignorance, a lot of aggression."

He stopped, seeing Grace's face. He could not tell her; what he feared the most was a bloodbath.

Christopher scowled at Robert. White fool, he was thinking. Go back to where you belong. You've done enough damage with your empire-building. Christopher edged nearer to the door. He had hoped to visit Kamala tonight but now it didn't look possible. Thornton's laughter drifted towards him. "Oh why don't you shut up!" muttered Christopher, distracted. Looking around at her family, aware of certain tensions, Grace sighed. There was a guest present; she could not let Aloysius start an argument. She could see that Christopher was unhappy about something; she could hear Jasper making barking noises, he was probably thirsty. It was not the time for discussions; she would talk to Sunil later, when they were alone and she would find out what he really thought. But for now she needed to change the subject.

"Christopher," she said, raising her voice, "could you make sure the servant has given Jasper enough water to drink? It's very hot at the moment and he seems restless."

She smiled at him, but Christopher continued to scowl, ignoring his mother.

"Idiot!" screeched Jasper suddenly, breaking a longer than usual silence. "Imbeciles!"

He fluttered somewhere in the darkness above them. Myrtle could hear his unclipped claws scratch, on heaven knows what antique piece of furniture. Myrtle hated the bird most of all.

"Idiot! Bastards!"

"Jasper!" said Grace sharply. "That's enough. Don't be so *rude*." She smiled at Robert, a smile as sweet as Alicia's, adding somewhat unnecessarily, "Jasper is our mynah bird, Robert. Unfortunately he has no manners. We're really not sure what to do about it, but we do think he's a bit of an oracle!"

Everyone laughed, except Myrtle and Aloysius, who looked meaningfully at his wife. Who knows what Jasper might say at the wedding? his look warned. But Robert, like many before him, was entranced. A talking bird, he thought. How exotic! The household, the whole family, everything about the de Silvas, was delightfully eccentric. Why had he ever thought this country boring? England suddenly seemed a very long way away.

On the day of the Prime Minister's party for the High Commissioner Grace brought Vijay a mango freshly picked from a tree in Jaffna. It had been given to her by a servant. No other mango tasted as sweet as those from the north, Vijay told her. But he did not look happy. Carefully he cut into it with his penknife, the juice running down his arm, and all the fragrance of his childhood, all the yearnings of his youth, gathered and fell to the floor. This morning, during their lovemaking, he had hardly looked at her. Sensing some desperation, she tried questioning him afterwards, but he avoided her eye.

"What is it, Vijay?" she asked, frightened suddenly. "Has something happened?" She knew he did not want her to go to the party tonight and meet the Prime Minister. He hated this figurehead in a puppet government. She wondered if this was the problem.

"I had a letter this morning," Vijay said slowly. And then, in a rush of unaccustomed bitterness, he told her about his niece, his brother's daughter. He had often talked about the girl. "You know she was five last month."

Grace nodded. Vijay looked terrible.

"She became ill with diphtheria a few weeks ago. My brother was very worried. He took his bullock cart into the town where the doctor lived. He walked in the burning heat, the road was covered in red dust. My brother took two pots of curd, hoping to find a doctor he could afford. One that would treat a Tamil child." He stopped talking.

"What's happened?" asked Grace.

Vijay was staring at the floor. "They sent me the news, today," he said barely audibly. "They could not find such a doctor. Now they want me to make a *puja* for her."

The child had died. His brother was inconsolable.

"One more Tamil death is not important," he said quietly.

"Oh my God! What kind of people have we become? Where will it end?"

"There is something wrong with a country that will not unite. There is something wrong with a nation that hates its own people."

Grace could see that things were breaking inside him, and would not be easily mended. The night before there had been a police attack on a crowd of Tamil office workers and tonight there was a large demonstration taking place near Galle Face. Vijay would go to it, Grace was certain. What could she do? He was stubborn and angry, he had been hurt for so long, Grace could not stop him. She stayed as late as she dared. Then she left to get ready for the party.

Towards six o'clock, in the sudden darkness that descended, Vijay went out into the city. The talk was that there would be another march followed by anti-government speeches. He felt a desperate need to be part of it. Just now the darkness lent a little substance to the city. There was no twilight in this part of the tropics. The heat had brought out the local families. Small children played on the beach, lovers strolled, young men loitered, buying sweep tickets, hoping to win the money to purchase a dream. All along the roadside were small shanty *kadés* glowing with green and white lights, selling everything from cheap plastic toys and brooches and bangles to multi-coloured drinks and string hoppers, hot sambals and sweetmeats. The betel seller rolled his leaves, red and white goo dribbling from his toothless mouth. He waved at Vijay. But Vijay did not stop to talk tonight. His niece's death had been in his thoughts all day. He was certain: two more deaths would follow. He walked on through the meat market, with its stench of rancid fat and congealed blood. The heat of the day had penetrated even here, even into this subterranean part. There were flies on every surface, on the vaulted ceilings, clinging to the carcasses, their blue wings hanging like drops of moisture. Vijay walked on seeing none of this, his feet picking their way swiftly and fastidiously through the filth. Unseeing, towards the clock tower, a lone figure in a white sarong, trembling into the distance, silhouetted against the darkened sky.

At some point during the evening, out of a sense of nostalgia and probably because he was bored, Aloysius looked around for his wife.

"This is entirely your mother's fault," he told Frieda grumpily. "Why do we have to be here, wearing all this finery, suffering this silly party?"

Frieda was watching Robert. She too wished they were at home. Percussion instruments jarred in her head. *One look at Alicia and I no longer exist. No one cares, he has forgotten about me!* On and on went Frieda's thoughts, round and round. She felt dizzy. Aloysius, thinking his younger daughter seemed a little glum this evening, helped himself to his third whisky and wandered off. Grace was standing on a balcony overhanging the private beach. She could see the top of Mount Lavinia Hill, with its whitewashed houses and its funfair. Someone on the beach below was flying a box kite and its tail flickered lazily in the wind. As always, whenever she was alone, Grace's thoughts strayed back to Vijay. She had told him she would look across the bay and think of him. Tonight the view was hazy and the horizon had become blurred by a storm far out at sea. In the distance, forked lightning speared the water. The sky was heavy and full of menace. Soon the storm would reach the shore.

"I see Thornton has found all the good-looking women again," Aloysius greeted her peevishly, breaking into her thoughts.

Grace laughed lightly and went inside to see for herself.

It was quite true; Thornton was having a wonderful time. He saw no reason to be as morose as his elder brother Jacob, or bad-tempered like his younger brother Christopher. Not, of course, that anyone knew where the devil Christopher was. Gone, no doubt, to some political rally. Thornton could never understand how anyone would deliberately choose a meeting over such a good party. Well, wasn't that Christopher all over. Always making life difficult for himself. Still, Thornton was not one to try to change the world. No, no, he thought, seriously, shaking his head, frowning a little. He did all of that with his poetry. In the new "voice" he was developing.

"Can I read some of your poems, Thorn?" asked the pretty nurse he was chatting to, anxiously seeing his frown. She hoped she wasn't boring him.

Thornton smiled, and the world tilted. Before righting itself again. The girl's knees locked heavily together, making her sway towards him. Thornton did not notice. He had begun to recite one of his poems.

"Oh!" the girl said breathlessly when he had finished. "I think that was wonderful!" She felt that she might, at any moment, swoon with desire.

"Oh please," asked another girl, joining the group belatedly, looking at Thornton's glossy hair. "Please say it again. I missed the first verse."

Jacob, deep in conversation with someone very dull, glanced up just as his brother was tilting the world again. There was nothing new here as far as Jacob could see, nothing suspicious, he thought, satisfied. Although, he paused, frowning, it suddenly occurred to him that lately Thornton had been out rather a lot. Feeling his elder brother's eye on him, Thornton coolly tried tilting the world at him too, with no success. Jacob merely shook his head disapprovingly and went back to his dull conversation. Oh dear, thought Thornton regretfully, no *joie de vivre*. None whatsoever.

The Prime Minister had asked their sister to play the piano. He had made a little speech about the lovely Miss de Silva. He told them all how proud he was of this home-grown talent. Then he led Alicia to the piano. Everyone fell silent as Alicia began to play. She played as though she were alone. As though she were at home and the Prime Minister had not held her hand and smiled at her. She played as though there were no one there at all. Life was like that for her, thought Frieda, standing beside Robert with her breaking heart, watching him watch Alicia. Life was so easy for her sister. On and on went Alicia's fingers, galloping with the notes, crossing boundaries, lifting barriers, drawing everyone in this elegant room together without the slightest effort. Aloysius reached for another drink. No one noticed.

Sunil watched Alicia from the back of the room. Words like "majority language" did not matter to her. Her language was simpler, older, less complicated. If only life could be like Alicia, he wished, filled with tender pride. It had been a useful evening for Sunil, meeting the Prime Minister, being noticed. His hopes for a united country were strengthened in spite of all the talk of civil unrest.

Alicia was playing when a telephone rang for the Prime Minister. She was still playing when he received the news that rioting had broken out all over the city. The police needed the Prime Minister's authorisation to deal with it. She was still playing as he left the party in his dark-tinted limousine with Sir John and the Chief Constable. No one saw them go. Sunil, suspecting an incident, went in search of more information. He learned that the rioting had got out of hand. What had been a slow protest, a silent march, days of handing out leaflets had turned into crowds of angry people, voices on the end of a megaphone. Someone had been injured. Then the number had risen and there had been some fatalities. A petrol bomb had been thrown. It was a night of the full moon, this night before the eclipse. There was a rumour that a Buddhist monk had been involved. An unknown passer-by had seen a young priest running away, a thin smear of saffron in the night. If a Buddhist monk had really been involved Sunil knew it would be bad for everyone. It would only take one single gesture, he thought, one furious shaven head, for centuries of lotus flowers to be wiped out forever.

Alicia had just finished playing when the intruder broke in. Walking swiftly past the guard, past the doorman who tried and failed to stop him and past the servants who then appeared, he burst in, blood clinging to his shirt. His face was streaked with sweat and dirt. He was no more than a boy, his hands were cut and bruised, one eye was swollen and bleeding. There was glass in his hair and he smelt of smoke and something else. Someone screamed. The servants, having caught up with him, twisted his arms behind his back. The boy did not struggle. He stood perfectly still, searching the faces in the room until he found the face he had been looking for, crying out in anguish, "They killed them! They killed them! I saw them burn! Oh Christ! I saw them burn!"

Grace, recognising him before anyone else, stepped forward saying in Sinhalese, in a voice seldom heard in public, coldly, sharply to the servants, "Let him go! He's my son!" And then in English, "Christopher, who has done this to you?"

Outside, the rain they had all longed for began to fall with a thunderous noise, in long beating waves. Drumming on the earth, on the buildings, lashing against the land in great sheets. But no one heard.

5.

The rain descended with a vengeance. It filled the holes in the road, it beat a tattoo on the fallen coconut shells and moved the dirt, transforming it swiftly into mud. It fell on Grace, standing stock-still and statue-like in the coconut grove, sari silk clinging to her, flowers fallen from her hair. There was no escape. The land became a curtain of green water. Pawpaw leaves detached themselves, floating like large athletic spiders to the ground. The rain spared nothing. There were so many rivulets to form, so many surfaces to hammer against. Although it was still quite early, huge black clouds gave the garden an air of darkness. Even the birds, sheltering, waiting patiently, could barely be heard above the chorus of falling water. Earlier on, in the dead of night, a servant swore she had heard the devil-bird scream. It had come out of the forest because of the rain, the servant said, in the hope of escape. But escape was no longer possible.

"Aiyo," wailed the servant, for she knew this was an ill omen.

"You must leave an offering on the roadside," said her friend the cinnamon seller. "If you heard the devil-bird you must pray to God for protection."

So the servant woman took a plantain leaf and some temple flowers. She wrapped a mound of milk rice and rambutans in it, decorated it with fried fish and coconut, and left it outside the gate. She hoped the gods would be pleased. But the gods were not listening. They were too busy with the rains.

Then just as suddenly, without warning, it stopped. The noise and the roar of the water ceased, and the early-morning traffic picked up from where it had been held up. Bicycle bells rang, the rickshaw men ran, and the crows that had been sheltering under the eaves of buildings came out again and continued their scavenging in the rubbish as though they had never left off. The ground steamed. The mud remained on the road of course, and passers-by still held up their umbrellas to catch any stray drop of wetness, but by and large the rain had stopped for the moment. It was as though someone had turned off a tap. What a different the sun made, bringing out all the everyday symphony of sounds, of callings and cawing and whistling and scrapings, and because she had slept in late after last night's event, Alicia's scales and arpeggios, joining in where the rain left off.

The servant, having made her offering to the gods, on this day of total eclipse, brought in the breakfast. It consisted of milk rice, coarse jaggery, seeni sambal and mangoes.

"For the lady," she said, beaming at Grace.

It was meant as a pleasant surprise, but Grace, coming in just then (where had she been at this hour? wondered Myrtle), soaked to the bone and ashen-faced, did not look pleased.

"What is this?" she had shouted. "Who gave you permission to make milk rice? Who *told* you to make this auspicious dish? Do I pay you to make food without instruction?"

Myrtle was astonished. Her cousin seemed beside herself. She was not normally a woman to show her temper in this way. Grace did not look well. She looked on the verge of collapse.

"Where've you been, darl?" Aloysius asked, astonished. "We've been looking for you everywhere. You're soaking. Here, give her a towel, will you, Myrtle? Thornton, pour your mother a drink."

"I have a headache," Grace said abruptly, seeing Myrtle staring at her. "I'm going to bed."

She disappeared to her room.

"What on earth is going on?" asked Myrtle slyly.

Aloysius, ignoring her, walked abruptly out of the room.

"What's wrong with your mother?" Myrtle asked Frieda.

But Frieda did not want to talk either.

"I think I'm coming down with a fever," Frieda mumbled. And she too disappeared into her room.

Some party, no? thought Myrtle. She nodded her head from side to side, as though having a heated conversation. Jasper watched her intensely. He was on his higher perch this morning and felt much better since it had rained. The air had thinned out and it was generally much cooler. He felt his old self again. Almost. He shuffled round and round the perch.

"Hello, bastards," he said, and when Myrtle ignored him he jauntily whistled a snatch of *The Magic Flute*, the bit he knew the best. Then he did his impersonation of the neighbour's dog and for an encore he whistled the Schubert that Alicia always played. Then, when his saw-drill noise had finally driven her from the room, cursing, he began to repeat a new sound he was learning. Softly at first, for Jasper always perfected his repertoire softly, he practised the sound of the devil-bird. Last night he had been woken up several times. First, there had been the sounds of sirens rushing past. Then Christopher had come crashing in.

"Good morning, men!" Jasper had remarked, though, unusually for him, Christopher had not replied.

The rest of the family followed, making no effort at being quiet. And finally, sometime towards the early morning, he had awoken again to a long and awful scream, so long and so strangled that Jasper, lifting his head, sleepily protested.

"Be quiet, men!"

The sound had gone on and on, not waking anyone else, but it had stayed in Jasper's head and he remembered it now with his usual clarity.

During the shocking, hurried journey home, shocking because no one had ever seen Christopher in quite this way before, hurried because of the embarrassment, they had all been subdued.

"It was a good party you missed," said Thornton tentatively, not wanting to upset Christopher any more by questioning him too closely.

What was the matter with him? he wondered uneasily. Had he been in a fight?

"Time we left anyway," Aloysius said by way of comfort. He looked shocked, Thornton noticed, while Grace seemed almost too upset to speak.

"What on earth were you doing at the demonstration?" asked Jacob. The thought of what might have happened frightened him, making him sound furious. "What did you expect, you fool, if you go to dangerous places like that? I told you to keep away from the riots. I told you. You're lucky to have got away with burnt hands!"

"That's enough now, Jacob," Grace said quietly from the back of the old Austin Morris. Her voice was that of a stranger. It was hardly audible. In the darkness her face looked deathly pale.

"I hope Sunil will be all right," Alicia said anxiously, for, in spite of all her pleas, Sunil had gone back to the UEP headquarters to send a telegram.

"Don't worry, darling," Grace said, "he'll be fine."

She sounded as if she was gasping for air. Thornton's unease grew. Christopher too seemed to be struck dumb. His headlong flight to find his mother, his astonishing uncontrollable grief, was followed by silence. As soon as they got back to the house, he disappeared. No one could make any sense of what had happened, no one could work out why he had been anywhere near the riots. Unobserved by any of them, Christopher slipped away and rode his bicycle all the way back to the beach at Galle Face.

It was now almost four o'clock in the morning. The rain had perfumed the air, only the sound of the sea gnawing at the shore remained, a reminder of the storm. Far away on the horizon a streak of lilac struggled to appear against the sky. The boats were coming in with the day's catch. On the quay, seagulls circled around the fishermen, waiting for a pause in the activities, hoping for a morsel of food. Christopher stared at the beach, miraculously ironed smooth with the morning, every blemish swept as though by an unseen hand. Grief, like nothing he had ever felt before, broke, riding roughshod over him. He was distraught.

Last night was a million light years away. Remembering Jacob's foolish questions he began to heave. Jacob, he thought, busy sucking up to the *whites*. And Thornton, the empty-headed beauty, what did *he* care about, except how he looked and what everyone thought of him? Only his mother, thought Christopher, incoherent now, only his mother had understood.

"Come back," he screamed. "Come back!" His voice was whipped by the sea breeze and caught in the roar of the waves. He stood screaming and choking as the seagulls circled the sky. "I'm finished," he cried. "It's over."

He had not gone to watch the riots as Jacob suspected, or to join in the demonstration. His thoughts became disjointed. Everything that had followed was blurred. Racked by sobs, broken, desperate, he fell to his knees on the soft white sand. Raising his face towards the sky, he whispered, "I can't go on."

Only a few hours earlier he had visited Kamala with a heart that brimmed over with hope. Carrying the tenderness that he showed no one else. Kamala had been ill, but seemed to Christopher's anxious eyes to be much better.

"You *are* better," he recalled saying fiercely, willing her to be. And Kamala, laughing (he always made her laugh), agreed.

Her father was at his Galle Face stall, selling plastic jewellery. White butterflies trapped in Perspex, flecked with gold, dozens of bangles, pink, yellow and green. There was to be a demonstration tonight, and a march organised by the railway and factory workers. A peaceful march. Christopher met Kamala at the stall.

"Let's walk along the beach," he had said, for he had brought money with him. "I want to buy you some fried crab and Lanka lime. Then we can be happy."

Yes, that's what he had said. He remembered it very clearly, being happy was something he could only do with Kamala. As they walked he had talked, as he often did, of his passionate desire for free state education. It was his favourite subject, his dream.

"It *must* be offered to everyone," he had said. "Not just the rich but the coolies, the servants. In any case,"—he paused, while Kamala gazed admiringly at him—"why do we need servants anyway?"

Kamala listened not fully understanding, but agreeing with everything. Full of pride. He had told her the Greenwood story again. He was always telling her that story. How many times had she heard it? But on each occasion she listened patiently.

"By the time it was my turn the money had run out. They gave it all to that fool Thornton. And what did he ever do with it?" he had fumed, unable to stop himself. He had known Kamala hated to hear him talk about his brother in this way.

"You mustn't," she had said, earnestly. "You mustn't say these things. Your family is a gift, Chris. It's *bad* for you to talk like this."

It hadn't stopped him, though. He had taken no notice of her. Last night he had begun again, moaning on and on about Thornton and the price of a decent education in this country. Never knowing how he was wasting time. Kamala had pulled his hand and teased him into a better mood.

"Next year, after my sister's wedding," he told her, "we'll

get married. I'll speak to my mother. Just wait," he said, as if it were Kamala and not he who was in a hurry, "you'll see, I *will* become a journalist."

He hated to think of Kamala sleeping in the shack with the *cajan* roof that let in the monsoon.

"Soon," he promised, "you'll sleep on a proper bed in a clean, dry bedroom with a roof made of tiles. Our children will have decent educations. *All* of them, not just a chosen few."

He had said all this. Only last night.

The Galle Face had been crowded with people. But Kamala's father let her take a walk along the beach with Christopher. He knew his daughter's illness was not curable. It was her karma. So he let them walk together along the seafront, letting them enjoy what brief happiness they could. Two young people with no idea of what their future held, but planning it anyway.

After a while they decided to go back up the hill towards the centre. Someone said there was a street fair and Christopher thought they might try the tombola. He had forgotten about the Tamil strikers' demonstration. It was Kamala's father, catching sight of them retracing their footsteps, who remembered. But by the time he had found someone to mind his stall they had vanished from sight. The crowds had grown. Away from the sea breeze the smell of sweaty bodies mixed with the fetid slabs of meat in the market as he hurried through the maze of stalls. An air of nervous tension hung over the neighbourhood. Outside, close to the Fort and behind the market, a few mounted policemen in white uniforms waited expectantly. Most of the shops in this area were shut or closing, there was no sign of the fair, and no sign of Kamala or Christopher. One or two men on bicycles rode by. A few dogs scavenged in the gutters. Kamala's father quickened his pace.

The whole of this part of the city was in darkness. A muffled sound of voices, the faint throb of a loudspeaker could be heard in the distance, but still he could not see anyone. Out of the corner of his eye he thought he saw a movement, but when he turned there was nothing there. He hurried on knowing he could not leave the stall for long. He needed to find Kamala and Christopher, to warn them to keep away from the demonstration. He was now in St. Anthony's Road and in front of him was the great Roman Catholic cathedral. Close by was Temple Tree Square where the bo trees were tied with offerings. Kamala's father breathed more easily, for this was a sacred site with an open aspect and lights. Through the trees, on the other side of the square, he could see the reason for the silence. The demonstrators, with their banners, had gathered together to listen to the speaker. The march had ended peacefully after all and as he approached Kamala's father saw with relief that Christopher and Kamala were on the edge of the crowd.

"Kamala," he had called. "Kamala, Christopher. Come here." He waved urgently, becoming suddenly, unaccountably afraid.

Only then did he see the shadow of a saffron robe. Only then did he smell the petrol and see the ragged flames, one after another, until too late, a circle of fire surrounded him. Drawing closer and closer. A Kathakali dance of death.

"Watch out," he had shouted in vain. "Be careful. Chris, Chris, take her away."

They heard him shout, but the words were indistinct. Kamala turned and ran towards him. For a brief moment, in the flare of the burning rags, Christopher saw them both clearly, her wide bright eyes reflecting the light, her hair aglow. Then he heard only their screams, father and daughter, mixing and blending together with the sound of his own anguish. Flesh against flesh, ashes to ashes.

The night was nearly over now. For Christopher there would never be such a night again. He stared at his hands.

They oozed liquid through the bandages his mother had used. The burns covered both palms, crossing his lifeline, changing it forever. He had heard afterwards, there had been many others. One of them, he had cried, hardly registering the look on his mother's face, had been the man she knew as Vijay.

The dawn rose, the sun came out. Beach sweepers began clearing the debris from the night before, but still Christopher stood motionless, Kamala's name tolling a steady refrain in his head. A newspaper seller shouted out the headlines, riots, petrol bombs, fourteen dead, seven injured. The government was to impose a curfew. But Christopher heard none of this. It was the day of the total eclipse.

They found his bicycle first. It was another four days before they found him. He had wandered for miles along the outskirts of the city, without shoes, his bandages torn off, his hands a mass of sores and infected pus, his face covered in insect bites. He did not see the eclipse as the moon slipped slowly over the sun. Or the many thousand crescent shadows that drained the warmth from the earth. Or hear the birds, whose confused, small roosting sounds filled the sudden night. And, as his family searched frantically for him, Christopher remained oblivious of the darkness that slipped swiftly across the land before sinking at last, gently, into the Bay of Bengal.

6

G race, face down, fists clenched, was lying across the bed. She was trying to control herself. Somewhere far in the distance a train hooted. The sound sliced the air. She shuddered as though she had been hit by it. Aloysius was frightened. Closing the bedroom door, he stood for a moment staring at her in horror.

"What is it, Grace?" he asked in a whisper. "Nothing happened to Christopher in the end. What's wrong?"

Her face was thrown against the pillow and she was shaking. No sound came from her. Nothing. Just the clenching and unclenching of her fists. "Grace," said Aloysius, fearfully. He took a step towards her, the room blurred for a moment. Not even when he had told her they were leaving their home in the hills had he seen her this way.

"Grace," he said again.

His own voice sounded unrecognisable. He hesitated, suddenly terrified. Then he knelt down beside the bed and tried to take her in his arms. Her sari clung to her, dripping wet with filth from the road. She was shivering.

"What is it, Grace?" Aloysius asked again, pleading, half not wanting to know. "It isn't Christopher, is it?"

Something in the tone of his voice made her turn blindly towards him and he caught her as she fell soaked and weeping into his arms. He had no idea how long he stayed in this way, with her cold body and her heart beating against him. Eventually there was a knock on the door. It was Thornton.

"Not now," Aloysius said quickly, before Thornton could see the state his mother was in.

Then Aloysius undressed her, drying her hair, her arms, wiping her face even as she cried, getting her into bed, unquestioning. Concerned only that she would lie down under the mosquito net, with the lights off and the shutters closed.

"I'll call the doctor," he said, when it was clear that her grief would not abate. "Please," he said, huskily. "Please, Grace. Wait, I'll be back."

And he went out, shutting the door softly behind him, to make his phone call and send Thornton and Myrtle away, telling them Grace was ill with stomach cramp and the doctor would be here soon.

Outside the rain increased and thunder beat against the sky. The air had cooled rapidly and small insects invaded the house. Aloysius woke the servant woman and asked her to make some coriander tea for Grace. Then he waited for the doctor to arrive.

Frieda iced the wedding cake while Myrtle read the instructions out loud.

"'To Ornament Your Wedding Cake.'"

With only two months to go, there was still a lot to be done. Frieda's head ached with a fever. It was raining again, heavy rain that vomited out of the sky, thrashing the branches of the coconut trees. Every word Myrtle uttered, every crack of thunder made the veins in Frieda's temples pulsate harder. How her head ached. The rain had brought in several uninvited guests. Large garden spiders thudded against the walls and a rat snake slithered in through the front door, curling up by the open fire in the kitchen. The cook had been blowing into the flames when she saw it.

"Missy, missy," she shouted to Frieda. "We have a visit from the Hindu God. It is good luck, missy. It is a good omen for the wedding."

The cook would not move the snake. In the end it left of its own accord. Grace, had she heard, would have been annoyed by this superstitious nonsense, but Grace was not well. She had seen the doctor repeatedly, because her stomach pains had worsened. Now, almost a month later, although she was over it, she still slept badly. Once she was an early riser, now, everyone noticed, she found it difficult to get up at all. She looked so exhausted that Frieda and Myrtle had taken over the icing of the cake.

"'For the ornamentation, fancy forcing pipes are not absolutely necessary,'" said Myrtle.

It felt as though a thousand steel hammers banged inside Frieda's head. What was Myrtle saying?

"'This piping will not be easy for a beginner, but with patience and practice there is no reason why it should not be mastered.'"

Frieda imagined Robert. She saw his face reflected in the metal icing nozzle. The beautiful white icing reminded her of him. She wanted to write his name all over the cake. She wanted to write her own name next to it.

Soon the cake was finished, three tiers of it, all beautiful and porcelain-white, pristine and bridal. And then, on top of everything else, Frieda had developed another nagging worry. What was wrong with their mother? Was she sick with some terrible disease? In all her life Frieda had never known Grace to be ill.

"Have you noticed how quiet she is?" she asked Thornton, some time later. But Thornton too seemed preoccupied and answered only vaguely. Next, Frieda tried talking to Jacob.

"D'you think what happened to Christopher has upset her?"

"Christopher is an idiot," Jacob said sternly. "You must not encourage him to worry Mummy like this *ever* again. D'you understand?" He almost said, "When I leave for England you will have to watch Christopher," but he stopped himself. It was too soon to tell anyone of *his* plans.

Grace had changed. In the weeks that followed Christopher's escapade, she stopped going into the city to visit the nuns and spent most of her time at home, sleeping. When she was awake, she seemed tired and short-tempered. Aloysius, too, was different. He seemed to have undergone a transformation, as far as Frieda could tell. He had stopped going to the club, played no poker at all and insisted Grace took her meals in bed. Frieda's worry grew.

"Alicia," she said finally, "have you noticed how exhausted Mummy is all the time?"

"Mmm," said Alicia. "How d'you mean?" She had just finished her practice and was staring at her list of things to do.

"Well," Frieda continued, glad to have her sister's attention at last, "yesterday, when Daddy finally went out, she got one of the servants to bring over a huge climbing jasmine. It was in full flower, but someone had pulled it up by the roots. Now isn't that a strange thing to do? When I asked her where she got it from, she looked annoyed. She told me the nuns gave it to her as a present. I had a feeling she didn't want me to ask."

"So?" asked Alicia, looking up briefly. What was Frieda talking about now? Was she wrong, or had her sister become a little dull of late?

"Well, isn't it a strange present to give her?" persisted Frieda. "When we've got three jasmine bushes in the garden!"

Alicia shook her head, not knowing what to say.

"She got Christopher to plant it underneath her bedroom window," Frieda continued. "One of the branches accidentally broke and she started to *cry*! Can you imagine that? Mummy crying over a jasmine plant? And then, Christopher gave her a *hug*!"

Alicia had to admit, *that* was interesting. But, then again, she wasn't all that surprised.

"Weddings are emotional times," she told her sister wisely. "I read it in the *Book of Etiquette*."

"Perhaps," Frieda mused, "the scare of nearly losing Christopher has affected her more than we realised."

As she iced her sister's cake, Frieda went over the sequences of events on that terrible night. Would any of them ever forget it? Even her father, Frieda noticed, had been affected by it. Her father was clearly very worried. At least Mummy has him, thought Frieda, wistfully, remembering again the way in which Robert had looked at Alicia. Lucky Alicia. Lucky everyone. Did no one care that *she* was suffering too? Staring at the expanse of white icing, thinking of her breaking heart, she listened to the rain. No, she reflected mournfully, no one cares. She was unaware that Myrtle watched her.

Myrtle of course, understood what Frieda's headaches were about. She had mentioned it in her diary, that morning.

October 31. Thank God the monsoons are here at last. I have not been able to write through lack of time. There are still two months left before this wretched wedding. G is too weak to be of much help. It looks as though Mr. Basher was right although I had no idea her downfall would be through an illness. Well, it's as good as any other misfortune, if not better! She certainly looks pretty dreadful. A, of course, is full of such concern that it has become quite comical. I'd like to tell him that he should be looking forward to possible widowerhood! After all, I shall be there; I'll look after him. For the last couple of weeks, needless to say, I have been working like a coolie (with no acknowledgement). F remains uselessly slow and a complete misery, while our little Bride has her head in the clouds. Have an interesting theory about F. I have noticed she likes white boys!! If this isn't nipped in the bud soon there'll be trouble from that direction too. Like mother like daughter. Don't I know it! Anyway, G looks pretty terrible at the moment. There has been no need for me to do the thing Mr. B suggested, as yet. Shall save it for the other event. Apparently the doctor thinks G's got dengue fever.

The month of November passed slowly. All across the capital the riots had temporarily destabilised the country. Everyone desperately wished to put it behind them. Christmas was around the corner, to be followed swiftly by the wedding. The cake was ready, the invitations had been sent out. One evening, Grace, appearing to be much better, came out to sit on the veranda. Everyone was pleased. Thornton pulled up a chair under her newly planted jasmine bush. Alicia began to play her mother's favourite piece of Schubert and Frieda went to tell the cook their mother would be joining them for dinner. Grace had been ill for nearly a month. She looked smaller, more delicate, infinitely more lovely, thought Aloysius, watching her, surreptitiously. He had grown cautious. On that first night, when she had been so distraught, turning to him for the first time in many years, Aloysius had not known what to do. She had begun to tell him something incoherently, and Aloysius had been afraid.

"Don't say anything," he had told her. The less he knew the better. "You don't need to tell me, darl."

I don't want to know, he told himself, repeatedly. Whatever it was, it's enough that she's here, with us now. Afterwards, in the days and nights that had followed, when he had shielded her from the children's anxieties and protected her from Myrtle's curiosity, he had regretted stopping her. He had begun to wish she would confide in him. But as the days turned into weeks and Grace became aware once more of the need not to upset her family, Aloysius saw that the moment had passed. She regained control of herself and he intuited she would never turn to him in that way again. So Aloysius watched her struggle, talking with Christopher for long hours, pulling herself back to life, and refrained from comment.

"It's been too much for her," he told Myrtle, fobbing her off, refusing to be drawn by her questions. "What with losing Alicia soon, and Christopher's nonsense on top of that, she's not as strong as she likes to think she is."

Myrtle raised her eyebrows.

"Of course," agreed Frieda wistfully, "it's the thought of losing Alicia that's upsetting Mummy so much! It's about the wedding, isn't it?"

They had all agreed. Then, as the wedding approached, Grace, with an enormous effort, did seem to pull herself together, so some, if not all, of their former pleasure appeared to return. Sunil was so much a part of their lives now it was hard to imagine a time when he was not present. After the riots he had won a small electoral victory with the UEP in the south.

"No one," he told Alicia passionately, "wants a civil war. This island has lived for centuries in perfect harmony, why can it not do so again?"

He had tried talking to Christopher, but here a door slammed heavily in his face. Sunil did not take offence. He continued his work with simple optimism, determined to walk the road of peace. There was still so much work to be done. His wedding was only a few weeks away. Then, after the Roman Catholic Mass, before they went upcountry for their honeymoon, there would be a brief blessing ceremony at the temple in St Andrew's Road. Sunil's mother had arranged it. For an auspicious time of day.

Somehow Jasper had escaped. He had always lived in a little room off the hall where the windows were covered with wire mesh. But at some point, due to the heavy rains, or perhaps his own feverish pecking, the mesh had worn out. Christopher, who in the past would have been the one to notice this, no longer either noticed or cared. Christopher was beyond all such childish interests. Silent and morose, he did not respond to Jasper's greetings. In fact, no one thought about the bird. Even the dog next door had disappeared and no longer provided sport for him. Bored and ignored, Jasper looked elsewhere for entertainment. Nobody bothered. Nobody missed him. The

wedding and other events had more or less taken over the de
Silva family. Several days went by. He flew gloriously out
through one window and onto the jackfruit tree, then further
on into the plantain tree. Swooping silently in through yet
another window, pecking the kittens, who mewed and hid
under the furniture. For four days, Jasper was mute, afraid, no
doubt, of being caught. Then, having picked his victim, he
descended on her.

Myrtle was not expecting this. After her morning ablutions
she usually spent some time in her room. On this particular
morning, she was in her room, a towel wrapped around her
head, her dark body patched with talcum powder, wrapped in
a vast multicoloured housecoat. She was holding a small metal
object in her hand.

"Hello, sister," said Jasper, swooping down on her.

Myrtle jumped. And dropped the metal plate. Startled, she
raised her arms above her face.

"Get out!" she screeched. "Get out! Get out!"

Jasper watched her with interest.

"Atten-tion!" he said solemnly, imitating the army captain
he had once seen.

"No! No!" yelled Myrtle, flaying her arms about in a vain
attempt to drive him away. "Get out! Get out!"

Jasper narrowed his eyes to thin bright slits. He perched on
the top of her wardrobe, leaving a small deposit that ran easily
down the smooth mahogany, landing on the back of the chair,
close to Myrtle's neatly folded sari. He squawked imperfectly
but with some satisfaction. He was still practising his devil-
bird impersonation. Then he belched, as he had often heard
Aloysius do.

"Easy!" he said. "Easy, sister!" and he swooped down
without warning on the metal plate on the floor. The light
glinting on it had caught his attention. He began to peck it,
cooing tenderly.

Myrtle went berserk. She had always hated Grace's pet. Now, confused by its presence in her room, she snatched up the metal plate, advancing towards him with gritted teeth.

"Bloody bastard, bloody nuisance," she screamed. "I'm going to kill you. I've wanted to kill you for a long time. Come here!" She chased him around the room, hitting out, almost catching him.

"Come here, you bugger," she shouted, attempting to grab at his tailfeathers.

Jasper was entranced. Never had he had so much success, so much flattering attention. Retreating to a point above the ceiling fan, he watched Myrtle. He sent down little presents that splattered onto the floor. He gave her his best saw-drill impersonation, he whistled the bit from *The Magic Flute*, he barked once or twice. By now Myrtle was weeping. Her room was wrecked. Grace and Aloysius, hearing the noise, came hurrying to her door. Quickly, hiding the plate, Myrtle let them in. The sight astonished them.

"Hello," said Jasper, looking as pleased to see them as a mynah bird can. "Good morning! Hello?" he asked, and he glided gracefully around the room. Grace, in spite of herself, felt her face twitch slightly.

"Jasper!" she said, adding weakly, in case there was some mistake, "It's Jasper. What's he doing here?"

"Enough!" screamed Myrtle. "I have had enough of this family, *enough* of the way I am treated, enough of being used. Enough, enough, enough!" she shouted, shaking her head so her hair flew all over her face. "Used and abused by everyone," she screamed, unable to stop now, "even the bloody bird. Look at me. *Just look at me!*" And she stood, arms outstretched magnificently, a crucifix with bird shit running down her face.

"The bird's a damn nuisance," agreed Aloysius, wishing he could have a whisky. Life seemed to be one long crisis at the moment. His wife was depressed, his youngest son had almost been killed, his eldest daughter was leaving them, everything was changing. Nobody had any fun anymore. Everyone made such a fuss about trivial things. He could *kill* for a drink. And after that, he would willingly kill Jasper. Grace, however, would have none of it. She soothed her cousin, called for the servant to clean the room, encouraging Myrtle to have another shower, promising to catch Jasper.

"Shiny," said Jasper helpfully. "Hello, Shiny."

"We should have him put down, darl," said Aloysius, who was beginning to think the bloody bird would outwit all of them. Outlive them too, by the looks of it, God, did he need a drink!

"Shiny," said Jasper again. "Hello, Shiny."

"Jasper!" said Grace softly, looking up at him, to Aloysius's utter astonishment, with a curious warmth to her voice, the first he had heard in months. Aloysius stared at her.

"Jasper," she said again. "You're a *very* naughty boy!"

Jasper, hearing the change in her voice, flew experimentally towards her and perched on the foot of Myrtle's bed.

"No," he agreed. And making a whirling sound, like the grandfather clock being rewound, he sailed swiftly out of the window and into the plantain tree outside.

7

They came from afar to the wedding, like wise men bearing gifts. Uncle Innocent and Prayma, Auntie Angel-Face and the girls. Sarath and Mabel, Anthony and Coco with their own little bevy of children. There were others too, from Toronto and Perth, from Calcutta and Lahore, and Grace's old childhood friend from Glasgow. There were the Sisters of St Peter and St Paul who had come all the way from Stratford-upon-Avon, and there were the old white planters on their way to a World Trade Fair in Melbourne, stopping off to have a bit of light entertainment at Aloysius's daughter's wedding.

"Becoming something of a pianist!" they said.

"Quite famous, I hear."

"How did the old boy manage it?"

"Healthy neglect. Or, more probably, it was the doing of that stunning wife of his, what's her name?"

It was worth a detour, they said, pleased to be asked. Aloysius always knew how to throw a party. There were other less colourful, more predictable guests, who came. Local people, neighbours, people who came to settle old scores, wanting to see how the de Silvas were faring. Drinking chums of Aloysius, friends of the children. But the most eccentric, the noisiest came from afar, with their huge suitcases laden with clothes for the big day, presents for the bride and groom, and of course whisky for the father of the bride. Depending on their relationship to the de Silvas they stayed either with them or in guest houses nearby. It was rumoured that the Prime

Minister himself would be at the church service and maybe, for a little while, at the reception too. Aloysius was delighted.

"We'll need to buy much more champagne," he informed Grace. "I'll ask Sunil. He can get it on the black market. It won't be cheap, but only the best will do." Grace did not disagree. Of late, she went along with whatever he said. No one looked closely at Grace; they were all too busy. She seemed her old self at last, worrying about the catering and the guests. Had they *really* invited so many? What had Aloysius been thinking of? The cook was sulking because two new cooks from upcountry had been hired.

"If the Lady Grace wants coolies to cook for her, then I am leaving," she announced.

Myrtle, writing her diary, smirked. She was still smarting after Jasper's attack.

December 21. My best sari is completely ruined. No amount of cleaning can remove the stain of bird shit. Grace thought it was very funny. Oh I knew what she was thinking, she tried to be sympathetic, she tried her sweet voice on me, but I'm not fooled by it. Nor am I fooled by my dear cousin's jollity. I can see what no one else can. I can see that the preparations, the guests, the family, all of it is a huge effort for her. She's trying to hide it but there's no fooling me. I intend to get to the bottom of whatever it is that's the matter. Yesterday I spoke to Mr. Basher who's suggested, as the results of the last card reading were inconclusive, I should get G's horoscope redrawn. Well, we shall see. Meanwhile, I have to suffer all these wretched visitors; relatives I haven't seen for years and can't stand, especially that woman Mabel.

The relatives were not worried. It was true Grace looked a little strained but they agreed this was perfectly understandable.

"She's losing her eldest daughter; she's losing little Alicia," they said affectionately.

"Of course she looks tired," said Prayma. "What d'you expect!"

"Besides, she *still* looks lovely."

Some even thought, people like Uncle Innocent and Auntie Angel-Face and Coco, that Grace actually looked *lovelier* than ever. Yes, they argued, Grace looked more beautiful than on her own wedding day, and they should know, they'd been there! And off they went reminiscing about *that* wedding, "Aloysius so handsome, he hadn't discovered the drink yet," remembered Auntie Angel-Face, screaming with laughter and slapping Uncle Innocent on the back.

"Don't forget Benedict!" Coco remembered, smiling.

Ah, yes! How proud he had been of his motherless girl, cherished for so long, gliding on his arm. A vision, such a vision of loveliness.

"Yes, a *vision*," shouted Prayma, to Uncle Innocent who was getting a little deaf. Those were the days, weren't they? When Benedict's cooks produced the most wonderful Portuguese *broa*, and *pente frito*, the likes of which had never been tasted since.

"Do you remember the shoe-flower sambals?" asked Coco, starting up a whole hour of "do-you-remembers." Then it was time to go to evening Mass. "Did they have a Mass in the evening here, darling?"

The house party to the wedding meandered on. It was close to Christmas, hot but not unbearable. The rains were still falling. The jasmine climber continued to bloom much to Myrtle's amazement, and Jasper still remained at large. Grace had given up trying to get him back into his room off the hallway.

"He has discovered the delights of independence!" said Uncle Innocent.

"With none of the responsibilities," laughed Prayma.

"Well," said Uncle Innocent, "that will only come through a process of evolution and growth."

"No, no, no, Innocent, you are wrong! The people in this country have not evolved for four hundred years. They have forgotten how," said Auntie Angel-Face.

"Come on, Amma!" said Sarath, feigning despair. "Jasper's just a bird, poor bugger."

"But what a bird!" said Sunil, walking in just at that moment, smiling at his new relatives. A cry of delight went up among the aunts.

"Sunil!" shrieked Auntie Angel-Face, beaming at him. "Where's your bride? How is she treating you today? Will she make a good wife? That's the question on all our lips!"

"I say, Sunil," said Anthony seriously, "shall we all go to the Galle Face Hotel tonight? You, me, Jacob, Thornton, Chris? No? What d'you say? Have a few drinks, men, meet some people?"

"Aiyo, yes!" said Auntie Angel-Face. "Good idea. Why don't you boys all go out together? What fun."

"Who are these fellows you are so keen to meet, Anthony?" Uncle Innocent asked.

"Well, who do you think, Innocent? Girls of course! These are Sunil's last days of freedom, aren't they? He's allowed to roam like Jasper."

They all roared with laughter, finding it hugely funny that sweet little Alicia, who they had last seen running around in a sundress and sandals, teasing her brothers, having her face pinched because she looked so delicious, should have gone and grown up and become so talented and now have this fully grown handsome fiancé. Clever, clever little Alicia to get such a handsome beau!

Myrtle watched the relatives from a safe distance. She found it astonishing that they could make such a fuss over the dark polecat Sunil, as she privately called him. She watched them teasing Alicia. Making her play Mozart, making her laugh, dancing around the piano, singing, until she begged for

Thornton to rescue her. Hah! Thornton, thought Myrtle grimly, I'm watching *him*. Thornton, when he was in, became the life and soul of the group. But Thornton had often some mysterious errand, some urgent business that he hurried to attend to. So what was Golden Boy up to? wondered Myrtle.

"He's a busy man, you know," said his cousins.

"Too busy to get a job," said Jacob sarcastically.

Thornton smiled good-humouredly and played rock and roll on the piano. It was clear Mabel was smitten, and Thornton, charming them all as usual, picking up whenever Grace seemed to flag, played on. Even Jacob could see he had his uses on occasions like these. It let everyone else off the hook. The cousins had been away from the island for so long they wanted to do everything. Drink king coconuts, go for a swim, wander about the city having their horoscopes made, look for girls. Thornton was their man. He was their appointed guide, their chief entertainer. When he was there of course.

December 22, wrote Myrtle. *It is very curious that no one comments on Thornton's behaviour of late. I've noticed he makes a great deal of noise when he's in the house in order to cover up the fact that he's often out. I swear he's up to something. Yesterday I noticed he came home in a very great rush. Then he managed to exhaust everyone in ten minutes before he went out again, leaving them in a state of confusion. I've always thought that he's a clever devil underneath all that sweetness that G's so obsessed with. Just like the bloody bird that now flaps against my bedroom window all the time.*

Jasper, of course, was a nightmare. Aloysius had had mesh put up on Myrtle's window to keep him out because, for some unfathomable reason, Jasper was fascinated with her room. Neither Grace nor Thornton nor any of the younger children could get within striking distance of him. Somehow he evaded all attempts at capture.

"He always manages to slither out of trouble," complained Aloysius, loudly, after a particularly difficult chase around the garden. "I always said Jasper possessed native cunning," he added, making Auntie Angel-Face hoot with laughter. "Now you fellows can detect it for yourselves!"

The relatives found all this hugely entertaining. They were here to have a good time and would have been easily pleased no matter what, so Jasper was merely an added bonus.

"I say, Jasper," said Uncle Innocent, "come here, men, I want to tell you a secret."

"No!" said Jasper from the middle of the plantain tree.

"Come on, men!" said Anthony. "Come on, let's take some arrack together, hah?"

Jasper only narrowed his eyes, making his favourite saw-drill sound from the branch above their heads.

"He's a clever fellow, you know," said Uncle Innocent. "A bit like a terrorist. Cunning too."

"Perhaps," said Auntie Angel-Face, "perhaps he is a bird card reader!" And they all dissolved into hysterical laughter.

"Hello, Shiny," said Jasper solemnly, and Grace wondered if perhaps he was in fact disturbed by all the unusual activity.

Aloysius, seeing her smile, was heartened. Grace, though still suffering from frequent headaches, appeared much improved. The headaches, he informed everyone, were merely the aftermath of the dreadful fever she had contracted. Grace did not disagree. She was determined that Alicia's wedding should not be spoiled and whenever her migraines became overwhelming she simply slipped away to her darkened bedroom and waited until they passed. Aloysius made sure she was undisturbed whenever this happened. Everyone noticed with approval how Aloysius ministered to her needs. So that outwardly, at least, Grace was becoming her old self again.

Meanwhile Frieda struggled. It was no good; she would have to go to confession again. Her thoughts were treacherous, her heart was breaking, and nobody cared. She knew it was hopeless, she was wasting her time, but somehow her uncontrollable heart kept on longing. On Christmas Eve, before they went to midnight Mass, Robert had come over for the last time.

"To see you all," he beamed, but Frieda, watching him stealthily, knew it was really Alicia he wanted to see. It was Alicia he wanted to kiss goodbye.

"I'm so sorry," he said, in his soft English voice, making Frieda want to weep. "I'm so sorry not to be here for the wedding." He looked mournfully at Alicia. "We'll be setting sail for England before the New Year, I'm afraid."

Frieda was afraid too. She was afraid of her dark stormy thoughts. Was she turning into a monster? she wondered fearfully. Robert said his goodbyes. He wanted to say goodbye to Frieda too, although having arrived at the house and having met the relatives he was enchanted all over again by the others and did not notice Frieda's heart, lying broken and bleeding, at his feet. So Robert left, kissing the bride, wishing her luck, asking after Christopher who was nowhere to be seen, hurrying into the rain and out through the old part of the city where all the Christmas lights glittered in the trees.

Later, when the rain had stopped, the wedding party walked back from Mass. Everyone was unusually silent.

I will never see him again, thought Frieda sadly.

In a week I will be back here for my wedding, thought Alicia wonderingly.

In the New Year I will at last leave on a ship to England, thought Jacob with a small thrill of delight.

Grace, staring up at the sky, felt the darkness like a tight band around her; Thornton smiled in the darkness, his secret smile, thinking his own thoughts. Above them, huge tropical stars shone unblinking in the wide, night sky and, as they strolled slowly back in the balmy air, not one of them paused to question whether there would ever be another Christmas like this again.

W hen it dawned, the day held all their expectations in its clear unclouded sky. It was Alicia's day really, hers and Sunil's. The others merely had walk-on parts. Frieda awoke and as usual went into her sister's room. Only now it was for the last time.

"Come on," said Alicia, pulling back the mosquito net. "I haven't slept all night, I've been so excited."

Frieda burst into tears. The smell of milk rice drifted across the house. Grace had ordered this most traditional of dishes to begin the day. The aunts, having woken early, were bringing in the flowers from the garden and the smell of jasmine filled the air. Alicia hugged her sister. Suddenly long-forgotten child-hood memories came rushing back to her.

"Oh, Frieda," she said, "do you remember when we climbed in through the window, when we were late for Mass? The day Sister Joan caught us and told Mummy how bad we were!"

But Frieda, ignoring Alicia, was crying in earnest now. For of course she remembered the things they had shared. And now she was crying for other, more complicated reasons, for which there was no name.

Grace, coming in to wake Alicia, stood looking at them, her face unreadable. The recent past trembled before her. Last night she had lain awake looking at the evening star from her bedroom window. The year was nearly over, tomorrow night Alicia would be gone, life would move on. Since her despair-ing flight into Aloysius's arms Grace had not cried. The secret place within her had closed up, so that the shadows that had once been hidden, appeared now as faint lines across her life. She had known it would be so, she had expected it to happen, but the customs and unwritten laws of this place, the reality of living on this island, had at last been brought home to her. Since Vijay's death she saw that almost anything might be possible. Now that the lovely hope of youth had been disturbed, she understood that the dark shadows in her life could only increase. She was ready for anything, she told herself. But all night, in spite of these last two months, perhaps because of it, Grace had looked up at the sky and seen the stars. It was their light she had noticed. I still have my children, she thought. And she turned towards Aloysius, sleeping silently beside her. He had surprised her by his solicitude and his concern, watching over her with a long-forgotten tenderness, never questioning, never intruding. She had forgotten his generosity of spirit. She had been angry for so long that it had slipped her notice. But last night, when they had returned from midnight Mass, he had sat down at the piano.

"No, you fellows," he had said, laughing at the others, "it's my turn for a change. I'm tired of listening to Schubert and Gershwin. This one's for your mother." And he had played "When the Sun Says Goodbye to the Mountains," and sung it for her in his still beautiful tenor voice, in a way she had not heard for many years. Startled, Grace had laughed and applauded along with the others, but something, some particle of pain had shifted in her heart.

In the morning light standing beside Alicia's bed, watching her daughters, she felt a small ray of gladness touch her. The air was fragrant with frangipani and the sounds of preparation filled the air. Somewhere in the distance she heard the sigh of the sea. Sitting down on Alicia's bed, moving aside the mosquito net, Grace hugged both her daughters. Then, in order to distract Frieda, she told them about her own wedding day when, motherless, she had found her father picking her flowers early in the morning.

"He tied them with a piece of string, can you imagine! Auntie Angel-Face was so cross with us both. She had organised a magnificent bouquet and there we were collecting what she considered to be rubbish."

"What did you do then?"

It was an old story but she told it again.

"Well, I couldn't hurt her feelings so I carried Angel-Face's bouquet all the way to the church in the valley." Grace sighed. "It weighed a ton!" she laughed.

They had heard it all before but now it had a new meaning. Grace talked on in this way until all three were laughing and then, hearing their voices, with a little flurry of feathers through the window, Jasper arrived.

"Hello, chaps!" he said.

Grace groaned. "Oh, Jasper, you're not going to cause trouble today, are you?" she pleaded. "I'm far too busy. I'm going to have you caught if you do. And caged!"

But Jasper, looking as though he had a new lease of life, was not listening. "Hello, Shiny," he said.

"What *does* he mean?" asked Grace. "He keeps saying that. What d'you mean, Jasper?"

"Hello," said Jasper, staring at Grace unblinkingly.

The girls laughed.

"Oh Jasper, Jasper, will you marry me?" begged Alicia. "And tell me who Shiny is?"

"Maybe Shiny is his girlfriend," giggled Frieda.

"Hello, Shiny," said Jasper. "Hindu bastards," he added, sending them into peals of laughter.

"What's going on?" asked Mabel, coming in with Auntie Angel-Face. "Is the bride awake? Hello, my darling Jasper."

"Where's the witch?" asked Prayma, who did not like Myrtle.

When she had quietened them all down and sent them off to get ready, Grace went in search of Aloysius. He, like everyone else, needed close watching this morning.

Myrtle was busy writing her diary in her room. She had been up early this morning, before everyone else. With her black umbrella and handbag she had gone stealthily into the oldest part of the city. No one had seen her. No one except Jasper, whose new sleeping patterns remained mysterious. He had called out cheerily to her as she left the house but she had started to run at the sound of his voice. Always interested by her reaction, he flew swiftly from tree to tree whistling. She turned and hissed at him, shaking her umbrella. In any case, she was now beyond his new territory so, losing interest, he went back to his perch on the plantain tree. Myrtle was gone for nearly an hour. On her return, intent on slipping unnoticed into the house, she missed Thornton sliding quickly in through the back door. Jasper swooped down from the branches and gave a low wolf whistle. Thornton chortled joyfully. After the wedding, thought Myrtle, grimly, entering her room, I shall do something about Jasper. The situation was now insufferable. The creature waited constantly outside her room, scratching himself, barking, peering in. Spying on her. Shitting on her windowsill. Tomorrow, she fumed, tomorrow was Jasper's last day.

Inside, the house was humming with activity. Telegrams were arriving from absent well-wishers. The awning in the garden was opened and a servant began spraying the flowers to keep them cool. The catering staff had managed to soothe the cook's ruffled feathers and now food began to emerge slowly from the kitchen. Grace, dressed in a pink-and-gold sari, appeared amid cries of appreciation.

"Oh, just look at your mother," said Auntie Angel-Face with pride.

"Mummy, you look so beautiful!" said Frieda.

"The bride! The bride!" cried Prayma, as Alicia appeared, trembling a little, wearing her mother's veil with small jasmine flowers in her hair.

Aloysius, about to have one for the road, caught sight of his wife and daughter and gave a shout of delight. But where was Thornton, why was he not ready yet? Ah! thought Grace rashly, here he was, the light of her life, the joy in her heart, devastating in morning dress. Thornton smiled at his mother, a sunbeam of a smile, and bells rang in her heart.

"Come on," said Jacob, impatient, the formality of the clothes suiting his solemn air. "We'll be late, better go now, Mummy."

They stood all together for a photograph, her boys, Jacob, Thornton and Christopher, unfamiliar and silent in his new clothes, and Frieda the bridesmaid, trying not to cry again.

"Perfect, my darlings," shouted Uncle Innocent. "You all look perfect!"

So they left for the church, handing their mother carefully into the car, smiling, joking nervously, for this happy moment was the most perfect of all. The de Silva family. If only, thought Frieda later, if only it had stopped there. Could things have been any better than this moment? But had that happened no one would have seen Alicia smile meltingly as she walked up the aisle on the arm of the handsome, dashing, still debonair Aloysius de Silva. And all those future generations, all that life that shifted continents and changed the course of rivers would never have happened. So it was just as well that the momentarily stilled tableau jerked back into time and the car turned on the gravel and sped through the waiting sunshine, carrying Grace and her children to the church.

It was just as well that Aloysius, leading his elder daughter into the arms of Sunil Pereira, before taking his place beside his wife, had indulged in that drink for the road, for there were many people in the cathedral that day, not all of them expected. There was no time to think. Frieda was suddenly calm.

"Joined together in holy matrimony," intoned Father Giovanni and the altar boys swung the censers high into the air, so that the smell of frankincense rose and hung in veils above them. Aloysius took out his handkerchief and blew noisily into it, indicating this to be a significant moment. Thereupon, everyone who wished to do so followed suit. And then it was over and the organist was playing the Bridal March, and Alicia and Sunil walked back down the aisle together, smiling and waving to them all, the relatives wiping their eyes, the friends, their nearest and dearest.

"Who's that woman talking to Thornton?" asked Grace.

The photographs were taken, the Prime Minister, who had come as he said he would, shook hands with the happy couple, and had his picture taken with them before speeding off in his limousine. The family went back to the house to welcome the guests for the reception.

"Now," said Aloysius with a flourish, "it's time for the champagne toast!"

In the square outside the church, not far from the sacred site of the temple trees and the almshouse, there were no glimpses of saffron robes today. All was quiet. The confetti, the rice and a blue ribbon fluttering in the breeze were all that remained of Alicia de Silva's wedding.

"Who's that person with Thornton?" asked Grace.

The reception was in full swing. After the food there had been the speeches and the toasts. The cake had been cut and a wish made by the newlyweds.

"Thornton," whispered Alicia, "come on, play something, quick. You promised!" So Thornton went over to the piano, followed by a round of applause and whistles of encouragement. He looked very handsome.

"This one's for the bride," he announced, grinning. He began to play. It was the signal for everyone to dance. Sunil, unused to the kind of partying the de Silvas went in for, tried and failed to avoid it.

"Oh, no you don't," laughed Alicia, determined that there would be no escape.

So Alicia taught her new husband to waltz, and then to fox-trot, and after that to tango, with many encouraging shouts from their audience. But she was laughing so much that it was an impossible task. Grace, not to be outdone, danced with Aloysius, but he soon lost her to all the others waiting for a turn. After that everyone joined in the dancing, and any barriers there might have been between the different groups of guests broke down.

"Now, let's get down to the real business," said Aloysius, having watched his wife for a while.

The servants set up the card table and whisky and ice were brought out. Aloysius and his cronies retired to the veranda.

Before long it was time for the bride and groom to leave. They would spend the night at a guest house and in the morning would drive up to the tea country, near Alicia's old home. First, Sunil had promised his mother they would visit the temple where they would give alms to the monks and receive a blessing on their marriage. His mother watched them prepare to leave.

"You were right, putha," she whispered to her son, kissing him goodbye. "These people are no different from us." She felt as if she had known the de Silva family all her life.

"You see." Sunil beamed triumphantly. "I told you, didn't I? There was nothing to worry about."

They waved them off, then, with more laughter and shouts and good advice. Auntie Angel-Face threw a handful of rice and Frieda a shower of shoe-flower petals.

"It was perfect, you look beautiful, my darlings," she said.

"No more looking at other girls, Sunil!"

"Don't forget us," called Prayma, hugging Alicia, crying a little, for the moment required it.

"Give my love to the hills," shouted Uncle Innocent, and they all paused for a moment, thinking of the blue-greenness of the slopes, the places where they had played as children, the sounds of the green bee-eater, their youth, *especially* their youth. Alicia and Sunil smiled at them all.

"Quick, someone take a photograph," shouted Coco.

Standing back, fleetingly, Frieda imagined how it must have been, in the House of Many Balconies, their voices trapped forever in those hills. Alicia and Sunil were smiling. They had smiled all day long, thought Frieda. How happy they must be!

"We'll remember you to the hills," they promised. And then, they were gone.

The sun was setting low on the horizon. In a moment it would be dark. It had been an auspicious, radiant day, and now the full moon shone down on them. Tomorrow was New Year's Day.

But the party was not over yet. The fun had only just begun. The air of expectancy that hung over them all day was still present. Like a playful, soft-footed cat it prowled the edges of the day, waiting to pounce. The garden darkened, its murmuring and warnings muffled by the noise of the music. Someone turned up the gramophone and the serious dancing began. Jasper, masquerading as a bird of prey, flew smoothly across the moon.

"Hello, chaps!" he greeted the garden cheerily. "Anyone for cricket?"

No one noticed him. Myrtle, his favourite, was nowhere to be seen. The night jasmine opened, pouring its scent into the darkness, glowing white against the foliage. There were no drums tonight, no police sirens, no screaming nightbirds. Yet the air trembled with expectation. Rushes of small sounds scurried along in the depths of the garden. No, the party was not over yet. It had a long way to go, unravelling itself, joining all the other events that made up the tapestry of their lives, giving it the colour it would otherwise lack. They would not see any of this just yet, but the soft-footed cat, the leopard in their lives, prowled quietly, closer and closer.

"Prayma, who's that woman dancing with Thornton?" asked Grace again.

"I don't know," said Prayma. "D'you know, Mabel?"

"No," said Mabel. "I'll ask Auntie Angel-Face."

Auntie Angel-Face didn't know either. She was getting a little short-sighted, and deaf too if truth were known.

"She was at the church," said one of the cousins.

"Well, let's ask him," said Auntie Angel-Face, boisterously.

Grace would not do that. Her good manners would not allow herself the luxury of curiosity.

"She's white," said Auntie Angel-Face, in a neutral sort of way.

"She's very pretty," said Coco, uncertain.

"*So old*," said the cousins.

"Innocent!" shrieked Auntie Angel-Face, being unable to stand the suspense any longer. "I want to talk to you. Come here."

Thornton was dancing with the So-Old-White-Woman. He was actually jiving. Rather well, so he thought.

"Who," asked Auntie Angel-Face, "who is *that*?" and she pointed a fat, nail-polished finger in the direction of the So-Old-White-Woman who was wriggling her hips and flapping her thighs together, and who suddenly took a leap into Thornton's arms, her bright red court shoes sticking out on either side of his slim hips, her head lower than his crotch, a suspicion of knickers for those who were looking. Uncle Innocent's eyes bulged out of his head. His jaw dropped. Cigar ash fell to his feet unnoticed. A slow, lascivious smile played on his lips. There were other changes too. He stood up straighter, cleared his throat of its customary phlegm, flicked imaginary ash off his shirt when in fact the ash was all over his shoes, and began to perspire heavily. Sensing an audience, Thornton turned, slowly, with a sensuous shake of his hips. The music stopped. He smiled broadly and walked towards them. Towards Uncle Innocent, Auntie Angel-Face, his cousins, his sister, towards his mother. He had been waiting for the right moment and here it was, presenting itself.

"This is Hildegard," he beamed. "Mummy, Hildegard and I were married this morning!"

"Hello, Mrs. de Silva," said Hildegard, holding out her pretty hand, filling the awkwardness of the moment. "I am Hildegard." And then, as there didn't seem to be much response, "May I call you Mother?"

No one spoke. Thornton looked at his mother. He saw with some surprise that the expression on her face was not as he expected. Because his mother, Thornton realised somewhat belatedly, was looking at him, the Light of Her Life, her Boy Who Could Tilt the World With a Smile, in a way that did not bode well for the immediate future. Thornton hesitated. The famous smile faltered. His mother's expression, he saw, would have to be dealt with.

Married this *morning*? thought Grace, disbelievingly.

"How *old* is she?" asked Auntie Angel-Face, and Prayma and Mabel and Uncle Innocent, stalling for time. And that was even before the uproar from Aloysius and Jacob. Jacob had a field day, years of accumulated resentment were aired that night, and the next, and for many nights after. In fact, Jacob had such a time of it that for a while he stopped thinking about his plans for the UK. Such was the disruption caused by that night. Such was the *drama*.

Only Christopher had no comment to make. It was debatable as to whether Christopher even knew what on earth was going on. He hovered on the periphery unnoticed. Alicia had tried dancing with him, the cousins had tried joking with him but Christopher would not be drawn. He had nothing to say. He wandered over to the servants' quarters where the cook's son was rolling betel and squatted down, belching loudly. Close by in the murunga tree Jasper kept watch.

"Here comes another idiot," said Jasper.

"Hello," said Christopher, rather unsteadily. "What are you drinking?"

"Whisky, putha," said Jasper from the depth of the tree, getting it right for once.

"Good idea," muttered Christopher. "That's the best suggestion I've heard all day."

The servant boy offered him a bottle of arrack.

"Listen!" said Christopher, after he had taken a swig. He stabbed at the air and swayed towards the servant boy. "I'm going to overthrow this government."

The servant boy took the bottle back and Christopher glared at him.

"It's no laughing matter," he said loudly. "D'you hear me? You're going to help me."

He belched and Jasper belched back, making him jump. Then he laughed, high-pitched and strained. The servant boy stopped rolling his betel and grinned. He pulled his sarong tighter and nodded his head.

"Hello, Shiny?" asked Jasper suddenly from above.

Christopher collapsed in a fit of hysterics.

"Jasper!" he screeched. "Jasper, I'm trying to organise a coup and all you can do is talk about Shiny!"

The servant boy laughed. He had never seen Master Christopher like this before.

"Bastards!" said Christopher, beginning to weep. The servant boy held out the bottle again, but Christopher, having curled himself up under the murunga tree, had suddenly fallen asleep. In his tightly clenched fists was a small Perspex brooch in the shape of a butterfly, the sort that was sold in the *kadés* that lined the seafront. The servant boy picked up the arrack and went inside, for he was certain he could hear shouting and crying on a very grand scale.

He had known her for over a year. Her name was Hildegard Rosenstall and she had travelled to the island from the Indian subcontinent where she had been living for some years. She was beautiful. And she was twenty years older than Thornton. Grace, looking as though she were on a saline drip, had the facts fed slowly to her.

"Now, Grace, take a deep breath. Slowly, breathe slowly," said Auntie Angel-Face. "Move away, everyone, she needs air!"

Frieda was crying because, well, because she was at an emotional point in her life, what with one thing and another. She felt incredibly sad and awfully tragic although she was not sure why. She hated atmosphere and there was certainly an atmosphere surrounding Thornton, and Grace. And almost everyone else. So Frieda was crying, buckets and buckets of tears.

"Will someone do something about Frieda, for God's sake?"

"Should we phone the newlyweds?"

"Innocent, don't just stand there!"

"Quick, get some ice."

All was confusion.

After the wedding night came the morning after. Understandably, no one had slept. The combination of alcohol and angst kept them all awake. All except Christopher, who stayed in his stupor unnoticed until the early-morning rain woke him, making him stumble, dry-throated, into bed.

"Poor boy," reported Jasper without making it clear which boy he meant. No one took any notice of him. No one took a swipe at him. Even Myrtle, his favourite, seemed incapable of paying him any attention.

"Hello, Shiny," he muttered, flying back into the trees.

Grace was still silent. Her anger was so great that it had rendered her speechless. The de Silva clan thought it was grief that robbed her of her voice. They had no idea that Grace had only two thoughts in her head. Should she kill Thornton? Or the Woman?

Thornton smiled quite a bit in those early hours. Beautiful, limpid smiles, but it was not working. He turned his eyes into dark pools of passion and sorrow. But that didn't work either. Jacob throbbed. He had turned into an engine of self-righteous speech. What on earth was it to do with him? wondered Thornton mildly. Not surprisingly Aloysius had reached for the bottle. This *was* a crisis. Uncle Innocent agreed, it was indeed a *crisis.* Uncle Innocent felt too many things, some of them to do with Hildegard herself, the hussy, but in the short term he felt he should show some solidarity with Aloysius and join him with the whisky and soda. The rest of them sided vociferously with Grace, whose beautiful teeth were clenched with rage.

Dawn came slowly. Rose-washed, delicate light, scented with the softness of rain. The heat of the day was slow to reveal itself, simmering, building up to its usual crescendo. Inside the de Silvas' house, outside on the veranda, and further back in the garden, however, the emotional temperature rose inexorably. Hildegard, her enormous eyes filling with tears, could stand it no longer. Thornton had begun to look like a little boy. He made her feel her age in ways hitherto unknown to her. There comes a time in a woman's life when her age begins to mean a great deal to her, and sadly this time had arrived for Hildegard. What could she have done? Her skin was still supple; her hair had no hint of grey. She had no children. Who would have thought this could have become a problem? Was every woman on this wretched island expected to be a sacred cow? Hildegard, her slim childless figure belying her age, wondered what she had done. They all clearly thought, as she had begun to feel herself, that she had seduced Thornton, instead of the reality, which was the other way round. Hildegard, whose eyes kept filling up, unaware of the effect it was having on Uncle Innocent, decided it was time to leave. She looked at Thornton for support but there was a vacant spot where Thornton's emotions should have been. So Hildegard left in a way that would be remembered afterwards, in silence and with dignified speed.

Thornton hardly noticed. He was feeling a little confused. Confused and with the beginnings of a serious headache coming on. He wished Frieda would stop weeping. It was getting on his nerves. He wished his mother would unlock her teeth. It was affecting the power of his smile. As for his eldest brother, he wondered again, what on earth *his* problem was? Still, he yawned, he was almost too tired to think. He had been certain he was in love but now, well, he couldn't be sure. His eyebrows shot up into a vulnerable position towards the top of his head. He felt tears of self-pity fill his eyes. Grace, noticing this, felt herself weaken. The family held their breath. And waited. It would be several days yet, but could the end be in sight?

"Quick," said Auntie Angel-Face in command again. "Prayma, tell the cook to make some food. Poor Grace has had nothing to eat."

"It's lunchtime already," noticed Mabel, surprised. "How the time has flown!"

"I don't think we should disturb the newlyweds, do you, Auntie Angel? Let them have a little peace to enjoy their honeymoon."

"Yes, yes, of course."

"A telegram will only upset them," shouted Uncle Innocent, wondering if he should catch up with Hildegard and offer her a lift somewhere.

Mabel took Frieda in hand and tried to staunch the tears, not in itself an easy operation, and Coco made some tea that no one drank. She had seen it done in the movies and thought she might try it herself. Jasper, feeling much better after a sleep, flew in and saw Myrtle more or less where he had last seen her.

"Hello, sister," he greeted her cheerfully, whereupon Grace, to whom this was absolutely the last straw, arose majestically and hurled her slipper with such force and fury at him that she caught him by surprise, sending him squawking out of the window, knocking over Aloysius's empty bottle of whisky in the process.

It was midday. The heat had at last revealed its hand. The de Silva family, those that weren't asleep, sat down to a desultory lunch. It was, they realised, somewhat with surprise, New Year's Day.

"Happy New Year!" said Uncle Innocent, experimentally, seeing how the words sounded and how they all reacted to them. He was trying to keep any lustful thoughts of Hildegard to one side, in order not to cloud the issues at stake. But he kept forgetting what these were and all he could think of were those enormous blue eyes. Uncle Innocent was a sucker, as clearly Thornton had been, for blue eyes. All this passion, he thought feverishly, it was too much for him at his age. Besides, he was worried in case Auntie Angel-Face got wind of his thoughts. Grace was bad enough at the moment without Angel-Face at it too. He poured himself a glass of cold water, clear, cleansing, life-sustaining liquid that it was, and retired to his bed for an afternoon rest.

9

The winds of change come swiftly. Seldom is there warning. No darkening of the skies, no cockcrow. Instead, suddenly, there comes a stirring breeze, a spiralling dust cloud, a change in things forever. January was cooler. The rains still fell daily, soaking into the ground with the parched and insatiable lust of many months. The island could never seem to get enough wetness, never quite quench its thirst. It breathed in the rain then paused while the forests grew, waiting for the heat to continue.

Grace, appearing to cope with the shock of Thornton's escapade, headed for the church. The family held their breath.

"My child," said Father Giovanni, "have they had carnal knowledge of each other?"

"No, Father," said Grace carefully. "Not to my knowledge. My son is headstrong," she ventured. "He is deeply sorry. He wishes to confess."

"Yes, yes, I understand," murmured the priest, frowning. He mulled over the recent events. "Would you say this young man was led astray? That he was gullible? That the woman was a corrupting influence, perhaps?"

Grace hesitated. Her anger with Thornton had not fully subsided. Where had she gone wrong? Should she have been firmer with him when he was a child? But he had been a wonderful child, thought Grace. She felt cornered.

Father Giovanni considered her. She was a fine-looking woman. An admirable woman, with an unfortunate, useless hus-

band. More importantly, Kollupitiya Cathedral was heavily sub-
sidised by the de Silvas. Christmas and Alicia's wedding had left
a warm glow in the church. And there was little doubt: Grace
had her fair share of troubles to bear. Looking at her face in the
candlelight, he thought, The poor woman deserves a break.

"Well, now," he said clearing his throat, making up his
mind swiftly, "he always was a headstrong boy, was your
Thornton." And he smiled at Grace. "Tell him to come and see
me in the mornin', will you?" he said. "And we'll see what we
can do to settle the matter."

At home, the family held their breath, but they were confident. It was just a matter of time. Annulments came only from
Rome, and the Holy City worked in mysterious ways. It would
not be hurried. There was nothing to do except wait. Twelfth
Night came and went. Myrtle noted the changes.

*January 15. Well they never do things by halves here. Naturally
we had to have two weddings! When the Golden Boy delivered his
trump card the expression on G's face was so funny that I had to go
out of the room because I was laughing so much. I had forgotten
what a temper she has. Illness aside, she became her old self when
it came to her darling son. A couple of pieces of her precious bone
china went flying in the process. Aloysius tried restraint but there
was no stopping G. I'm glad that everyone saw her true colours for
once. Innocent looked as though he was having some sort of fit. He
just stared and stared at the Woman! No one seems to know anything about this Hildegard, or where on earth Thornton found her.
In some gutter somewhere no doubt, although why she wants to be
married to him is a mystery to me. Can't she see how stupid he is?
Well, anyway, she's not going to be Mrs. de Silva for much longer
by the looks of things. I knew Thornton was a fool but even I
couldn't have anticipated such behaviour. They're all angry with
him, even Jacob. If anything could kill G off it's this. If Mr. B's
horoscope is to be believed, there's more to come!*

Grace appeared to have put aside her strange lethargy and depression. Uncle Innocent and Aloysius took to drowning their sorrows together, daily, Frieda was still crying intermittently despite all Mabel's efforts, and the bridegroom appeared to be in a state of confusion. He needed time to take stock, to confess to Father Giovanni. Had he thought about it, Thornton might have seen the desperation of Hildegard's love and the unsuitability of what he had done. But Thornton, as was becoming increasingly clear, had not been thinking clearly.

Everyone was preoccupied, leaving them unprepared for the next gust of wind. Quietly, unnoticed by anyone, except Grace, Christopher made plans to leave. Silently, without fuss, he went about his preparations. There was nothing to keep him here. No one noticed because what was there to notice? Only his mother, talking to him at odd, snatched moments, understood.

"What is there left for someone like me in this place?" he asked her bitterly.

He would be leaving in a few weeks. His ticket to the UK had arrived. He had confessed his plans to her.

"Things are getting worse here. I can't take any more," he told his mother, flatly.

Grace looked at the ticket. Colombo, Cairo, Genoa, Southampton. She handed him back his visa, his passport. He was exhausted by the effort of living. They both were.

"There's no justice of any sort," Christopher said. He spoke quietly. There was no sign of his usual anger. Perhaps disillusion was a quieter thing. "There's nothing left. The government is terrible. Wealth and religion and endless corruption have ruined my life," he said. "No one either notices or cares."

His voice broke. Grace nodded silently. She could not deny any of it. She would not argue, even if she had the strength. Nevertheless, she asked him, with infinite tenderness, "What will there be in England for you, Christopher? What comfort will you find there? Away from your own people?"

"At least I'll find justice there!" he said. "They have laws. Laws that work. They're English, aren't they? Decent English people. They care about the poor. They care about *their* people."

She said no more after that. It broke her heart all over again. He is young, she thought, he has ideals. Who was she to question if he was right? She did not mention Kamala. There was no need to say her name. Kamala moved between them like a glimmer of light, in the untouchable layers of their conversation. Kamala and Vijay. The long years of her mothering stretched behind Grace. She could not have foreseen any of this. She could not have foreseen her pain. Finally, hesitantly, it was Christopher who spoke of Kamala.

"There will never be anyone else," he said, so softly that she could barely hear him. He sounded lost and older than his years. "All that sort of thing is finished for me."

"You don't know that," Grace told him, quietly. She, too, hesitated. "One day, who knows? Don't talk in this way. Things happen. Unexpected things."

Please God, she thought. She wanted to say more. She wanted to tell him to be different from her. She wanted to say, make something of your life, Christopher. Don't waste it. You are not like me, you have more possibilities. But she was silent, afraid of hurting him further. She knew the dark scorched places in his life could not be eased, and that the hurt he felt would not be spoken of again. Both of us, she thought, have learnt to control ourselves. The light had moved, evening was almost upon them, she could only dimly see his face. Her heart ached for her youngest son, for his aloneness and for his courage. England would change him further. He would grow a new self; wear it as though it were clothes. She wanted England to work for him and because of this she wanted to make his leaving as easy as she could.

"If it is truly what you want," she said at last, her sense of hopelessness lengthening with the evening, "then go. I can't say I don't mind, because I do. But if it will help, then go."

She saw clearly what she must do. She saw that Christopher needed a last desperate leap in order to propel himself into his adult life and she acknowledged with sadness that her presence from this moment on could do no more than hold him back. This last act of her mothering was the most important. The time for *my* needs has passed, thought Grace. And she let him go.

The morning of Christopher's departure was dark and stormy. White topped waves scurried outside the harbour bouncing against the small boats that took the passengers out to the big ocean liner. Christopher had one trunk labelled with the name of the ship. "FAIRSEA," it said in blue and white letters. "SYDNEY," "COLOMBO," "CAIRO," "GENOA," SOUTHAMPTON," it declared. "DECK THREE. CABIN 432." Jacob stared at the ticket. "Passengers are expected to embark at 1400 hours for departure at 1600 hours."

Jacob was mesmerised. Never had he come so close to holding a ticket. He blinked owlishly at Christopher as though seeing him for the first time. Christopher, the runt of the litter, was escaping first, Christopher, the unexpected one, chasing the monsoons across the seas, getting away. Jacob was stunned. It should have been him. Whenever he had imagined this moment of leave-taking, he had been in the leading role. He had imagined himself waiting to climb aboard the motor launch that would take him to the ship. Looking very tall and serious, impressing the other passengers, his family, everyone, with his quiet reserve. But here instead was Christopher, unfamiliar in his new suit, surrounded by the family.

"Have you only one trunk?" asked Thornton, surprised.

Loaded no doubt with party political leaflets, thought Jacob.

"He's got an ocean-liner carrying bag," said Frieda. "I packed it this morning. It has got your favourite sambals and chilli pickles, Christopher. There are some ambarella fruit as well and a couple of Jaffna mangoes. Any more than that and they will spoil before you have a chance to eat them."

"I've put some rosary beads in a thambili, for you, darling," said one of the aunts.

"And a picture of St. Christopher as well," said Frieda.

She knew Christopher would not want it but would keep it because it was from her. At the last moment she gave him a framed photograph of all the family at Alicia's wedding.

"Well," said Jacob, trying to be magnanimous and show he did not care, "you're about to become a travelling man and embark on *life*."

Christopher, scowling and tense and with no sense of any new beginnings, suffered the wait while his family, together for the last time, solemnly wished him goodbye. First Thornton, his beautiful eyes filling with tears, no sign of Hildegard (where, wondered everyone, was she?), embraced him.

"Look after yourself, Christopher," he said. "I hope you'll be happy in England." He felt sad for the brother he knew the least, the darkly raging one, the one who made life harder for himself by always going against the flow. "I'll write to you. These are bad times we are going through," he said, thinking of himself a little too, for wasn't his own life undergoing a stormy patch at the moment? "I'll send you a poem of farewell!" he added.

Then Jacob embraced him and shook his hand as the English did. "We'll be meeting soon," he said cryptically.

Frieda demanded nothing, Frieda merely cried, making Thornton sigh heavily.

"When I have the schedule for my first concert tour I'll visit you," said Alicia, wanting to be different from the rest of them in her new married state. "I'll bring you some mangoes!"

Sunil had taken time off work. He alone looked relaxed and fresh. He kissed his brother-in-law on both cheeks with the genuine affection that touched everything he did, squeezing his shoulder, silently wishing him well. He knew the riots had affected Christopher deeply but he had never felt he could ask why. He hoped things would improve for him in England.

"I hope we'll meet again soon," he said smiling. "Take care of yourself."

Myrtle watched them all. Today she wore her predictions like a tortoiseshell ornament in her hair. Christopher, she knew, was only the first to go.

Christopher waited, enveloped by the smell of hot diesel and his family's good wishes, passive for once, silent as always, alien already. Until at last, the great horn blasting them back onto the motor launch set them waving. Until Frieda's arm ached and his mother's small strained tearless face became one with the sea of faces below, until he could distinguish them no more. In this way Christopher watched them slipping away as easily as the island itself with its coconut-dense edges, sinking into the sea. Slowly the waving became ineffectual and the enormity of the water a reality. Beyond the haze of sunlight, the ship turned from the safety of the coral reef, sounding its long last farewell home, before heading for the open seas. For Christopher, the mist forming before his eyes confirmed only that there would be no new beginning, no wonderful future ahead, but simply the restless movement and the endless cycle of his karma.

So Christopher was gone, flown the de Silva nest while Rome worked slowly behind the scenes for Thornton. The de Silvas, with their network of contacts in the Catholic Church, were able to call in a favour from a distant relative in the Vatican. Just two months short of his twenty-first birthday, Thornton's underaged marriage was ripe for annulment. Saved by a whisker, thought Jacob sourly. How did the boy do it? wondered Uncle Innocent, amazed.

"So *young!*" was on everyone's lips.

"What a waste! What a shame!"

Thornton the poet, the limpid-eyed heartbreaker, the lover of all the finer things in life, was left with no choice but to fall heavily and regretfully out of love with Hildegard. What a thing was this, thought Hildegard, weeping into the long hot nights. Packing her bags to return to a Europe she no longer had any taste for, running away as she had always run before. Vanishing (forgotten for the moment by all but Uncle Innocent), back to Europe where blue-eyed women cause less of a stir.

"Naughty boy," said Jasper, quietly.

Jasper was growing old, and no one heard him anymore. The rains had finished for the moment, the tropical vegetation grew and the shuddering awfulness of the *karapoththas*, the cockroaches, seemed everywhere. The imaginary leopard cub that had prowled the edges of the garden during Alicia's wedding had grown unimportant. Aloysius, aware of the distant rumble of violence, of Grace's unspoken despair, was quieter, stayed closer to home, drinking less and seldom organising any card parties. Christopher's absence had made more of a difference that any of them expected. There was a dullness in the air. The gelatinous heat shrivelled up the once green and pleasant parks. Who cared if the elephants had left the jungles? Who cared if they were dying in the towns? Elephants could not provide a national identity. Only language could do that. Language mattered more than anything else now. This was the thing to provoke bloodshed.

The de Silva children were adults now. Frieda stayed close to home. After that first mad dash towards emotional freedom she seemed to shrivel, minding her father, whose liver was not as it should be, and her mother, whose silent indifference frightened her. No one noticed the flush of youth slowly fade from Frieda's face. Thornton, too, was more cautious these days. Aware of the change in his mother, he was careful. Jacob had reluctantly found him a job at his office in the hope of keeping him out of trouble. Only Alicia seemed really happy. Sunil was in the Cabinet now and his dream almost a reality.

"If only they would have a child," Grace prayed, "their life would be complete."

Frieda, crying into her pillow at nights, dreaming of Robert Grant, thought, Alicia has everything except a child.

Alicia herself was puzzled by this absence.

"Why has it not happened yet?" she asked Sunil. "After a thousand days, why not?"

Sunil was not worried.

"There is plenty of time," he told her gently. "We're both still young. Don't worry. It'll be all right. Next year, when the rains come, you'll see!"

He was busy in the run-up to the general election. Rumours of dissatisfaction among the Buddhist monks simmered beneath the surface, and in any case Alicia had her first concert tour ahead. There was work to be done. So he told her: "There's plenty of time. Don't worry. Let's just enjoy our freedom while we can."

In his letters home to Grace, Christopher painted a picture of England that was difficult to believe. His letters were full of the cold.

"What on earth's the matter with Christopher?" asked Thornton irritably when he read them. "Why does he have to exaggerate everything?"

Christopher folded his disappointments in light blue aerogrammes, sending them home like small bullets of emotion. *Now that I am here I can see how wonderful it really is in Ceylon*, he wrote. *Our country has so much to offer, its past is so*

rich and vibrant. All we do is destroy it. Believe me, there is
nothing here for any of us. I don't belong here and never will.
There is no point in any of you coming. Better to stay and fight
for what is ours.

He wrote with an inexplicable longing, saying he missed the
heat and his home. He sounded confused.

Everyone here goes mad when the sun comes out. They talk
of nothing else. They sit in parks eating tasteless food. They
smile at the sun, yet their lives are ruled by the lack of it. And
when it rains, which it does nearly all the time, they talk about
the weather then too!

"Well," said Thornton, "Christopher has become like them.
He too talks about nothing else."

Jacob read the letters after everyone else had passed them
round, and was disbelieving. He did not want Christopher's
opinions.

"He's making most of it up. When has Christopher done
anything except complain? He's just showing off. It's fine for
him to go to England, but not us."

Jacob had still not forgiven Christopher for leaving before
him, for doing what he had planned for himself. He could not
understand these furious and confusing communications.
Soon I'll find these things out for myself, he comforted himself. Things won't stay this way forever.

It was true. Things don't stay the same, thought Thornton
joyously, coming home one afternoon.

"Look!" he cried, waving the newspaper noisily. "Look,
everyone!"

Finally, he had had a poem accepted in the newspaper.

"Hurrah for Thornton, dazzling smiler, dreamer of dreams,
and now, *poet*," said Frieda, seeing it. "His poem on the fishermen has been published at last!"

"What he knows about fishermen could be written on a
betel leaf," snorted Jacob.

"Still," said their mother encouragingly, "as everybody knows, it is not what you know but how you say it."

Thornton had indeed said it. Suddenly he had a whole new crowd of admirers to join the old followers. Grace roused herself and framed the poem.

"Good!" she said, determined to be cheerful. "Now you must write another."

But before he could do so, one of his new fans, an intelligent, funny, dark young orphan girl from the south, arrived like a laundry parcel tucked under his arm just as the new moon was appearing. Where he had met her was unclear, Thornton always being vague on these matters.

"Who cares anyway?" said Myrtle. "It's an omen."

"Oh no," said Grace, belatedly alert, anxiety gathering on her brow, "it's the End!"

"Good morning," said Jasper solemnly, and the girl jumped. And laughed, delighted.

"Oh, Thornton!" she said, excitedly. "I hope you've written a poem about him!"

Thornton looked at the girl with interest. A poem about Jasper? What a good idea. It's clear, decided Frieda, struggling with an instinctive hostility, and a heart that would not mend, this one is not good-looking enough for Thornton. It's clear, thought Myrtle, who could spot these things a mile away, that she is too clever for him. The girl's name was Savitha and she was always teasing Thornton.

"Oh please, smile at me," she cried, clutching her heart and pretending to writhe in agony. "I can't live without your smile. Your poems, yes, but not that smile!"

Thornton grinned. Grace, listening to them, glanced up in surprise. Jasper, watching them noncommittally, barked loudly, sending Savitha into hysterics.

"Imagine Jasper with a tail!" she cried.

"Jasper's tale," said Thornton, with a loud guffaw.

"Don't be rid-ic-ulous," said Jasper, with his usual random-ness, sending them into shrieks.

"Oh, don't you *see*?" said Savitha, hardly able to speak. "That's the title of your next poem, 'Jasper's Tale.'"

Of course, thought Thornton, amazed. So amazed in fact that he bent over and kissed Savitha. They were both taken by surprise.

Savitha's interest in Thornton expanded imperceptibly. Her friendliness began to extend to the rest of the de Silva family. She found them as enchanting as characters from a fairy tale. Fascinated, she looked a little closer and then she saw that all was not as it had first appeared. Thornton's mother was a very beautiful woman but something was definitely not quite right. There was an understated air of sadness to Grace that sur-prised Savitha. Ever since she had been a little orphan girl, dependent on her observational skills for survival, Savitha had taken a deep interest in other people. And, although she hid it well, she had the softest of hearts. So that now she asked her-self, why was Thornton's mother so unhappy? Why did no one else notice? She's desperate, thought Savitha, her curiosity increasing with every visit to the house.

"Can't you see it?" she asked Thornton, serious for a moment.

Thornton was staggered. What did she mean? His mother was, well, she was just his mother, wasn't she?

"Hmm," said Savitha. She wasn't so sure. "I think she's depressed, don't you? Every time I see her I feel she's on the verge of tears. She's lonely, too."

Thornton was both flabbergasted and silenced. He looked at his mother. She looked just as she always did. What was Savitha talking about?

"Perhaps," he said, struggling with the idea, "perhaps she misses Christopher. Although he did give her plenty of trouble."

"Oh, Thornton!" Savitha said, laughing again. "You're

hopeless. You're *such* a dreamer. Then again," she frowned, thinking her idea through, "maybe, this country *needs* some dreamers."

"How d'you mean?" asked Thornton, puzzled. He had thought they were talking about his mother. "D'you want me to write political poems, or something? Be like Christopher? Is that what you mean?"

The idea wasn't appealing. Savitha suppressed a smile. Thornton with his air of confusion looked like a little boy. The sight brought out all Savitha's developing maternal instinct. But being wise she waited. It was at this point that she noticed Myrtle properly, and for the first time.

"My God, Thornton. What's wrong with *her*?" she asked, truly shocked. What was the matter with the de Silvas that they could not see how much Myrtle disliked them?

"Myrtle does not like your family, one bit," she announced. "She shouldn't be living with you. Look how much she hates Alicia and Sunil. She's a jealous woman, isn't she?"

Once again Thornton was astonished. No one had asked him this sort of question, not his mother, nor Hildegard. Savitha made his family sound like a group of strangers. He had no idea how to respond.

Meanwhile, Savitha was indulging in a delightful little daydream of her own. The more she visited them, the more she was entranced by the de Silvas. She had never had a family in her life, let alone one as exotic as this. They were all so lovely to look at. Grace in particular looked as fragile as an orchid in a storm and Aloysius clearly adored her. Although, and here Savitha hesitated, puzzled, the other de Silva men were a different matter. Jacob's morose state was disturbing. He hardly responded when Savitha spoke to him. She didn't care much for him.

Three months passed. Savitha was a frequent visitor to the house. Thornton kept bringing her back. Frieda noticed and felt unhappy without knowing why. The two of them were always with their heads together, fooling about, and Frieda felt hostility bump against her every time she heard that laugh. What would Christopher make of these new developments? Myrtle noticed too and was uneasy.

What does this girl see in Thornton? she wrote in her diary.

Savitha was having a wonderful time. She felt as though she had strayed into a play. She wrote a funny article for the Sunday papers and it was published. She can write, thought Grace, rising from her trance, astonished in spite of herself. Savitha knew how to dig the knife into society. She had not got the orphanage school scholarship for nothing. The article was about the Westernised elite who had no love for their homeland. "Our Troubled Isle," she called it, and it was brilliant. Sunil was struck by it. Savitha had articulated everything he had always felt. She had stated boldly that the making of an empire had led inevitably to trouble. Several people wrote letters to the editor applauding it. Thornton was unprepared for this sudden catapulting into fame. He had only been mildly interested in Savitha until now. It had been *she* who had hung around, disturbing his tranquillity, worrying him with her questions, pushing against his contentment. Now, suddenly, Thornton began to see her clearly. He fixed her absentmindedly with an altogether different smile and the world tilted once and for all for her. Even Savitha had her weaknesses.

Grace, watching this small girl with a stirring of interest, noticed her reaction to Thornton's smile and smiled, too, in spite of herself. Myrtle, watching, knew exactly what would happen next. She wanted to laugh out loud, but something about Savitha made her wary. Instead she wrote her comments in her diary.

March 18. This latest is unpredictable. I've caught her watching me. I fear she's here to stay. At first I thought she'd tire of our pretty idiot. Then I expected G to frighten her off, but the creature is clever, she seems to have won G over. Still, I have to admit, it's very, very funny. G, not to mention the darling boy, are getting drawn into something beyond them. Must be karma!

"All the troubles with Hildegard for *this*?" she remarked casually to Grace one evening after dinner. Grace was silent, not knowing what to think. Some instinct told her Savitha might not be such a bad thing for Thornton.

"She's not as pretty as the others," she told Aloysius slowly. "Yet there's something about her. She forces him to think about things. She's good for him. I think she's falling in love, don't you?"

Aloysius did not care. He just wanted a drink. He thought the girl insignificant. Only Myrtle knew: the girl was not. Meanwhile Thornton, in the throes of some new confusion, was hooked. Perhaps it was her sharp intelligence, perhaps it was her humour and her constant enthusiasm. It certainly isn't her looks, thought Myrtle nastily, but the idiot's mesmerised, like a chicken before a rattlesnake.

Thornton immobilised! wrote Myrtle, in her diary. *Quite a sight!*

"Hello, Sa-Sa!" said Jasper who had mistaken her name. No one corrected him.

Savitha laughed delightedly, and Thornton laughed hearing her. She's mad, he thought. He had never met anyone as ebullient as Savitha before. Laughing all the time they were, those two, in those early weeks, before they dropped the bombshell, when Thornton, taking even himself by surprise, brought his second bride home to his mother. He had done it again! Savitha's dark face glowed with an inner light. For all her liveliness she was not used to being so impulsive. Have I really been thinking straight? she asked herself, head in a whirl. Then, before any of them had time to decide, it was too late and Aloysius, it appeared, was about to get his wish.

"A grandson at last!" he crowed. "A de Silva. A new generation on the way."

"Fool!" said Jacob, who had booked a passage to England in two months' time.

"When?" asked Grace. But she spoke softly, and she looked closely at Thornton, who was much more alert these days, and had just announced he needed a better job.

"It's exactly what we need, darl," Aloysius said, delighted. "To cheer us all up in this wretched country." He glanced quickly at his wife, for still at the back of his mind was the residue of the old anxiety.

Frieda wrote to Christopher the very next morning, her tears (she was uncertain whether from joy or grief) smudging the words.

Thornton seems very happy about it, she wrote. *Can you imagine Thornton as a father? Mummy doesn't seem to mind too much. In fact, I think she's secretly glad. Savitha makes her laugh, something Mummy hasn't done much since you left.*

The night of the announcement, Aloysius celebrated with a new bottle of whisky. Hang his liver.

"A new generation is not announced every day, darl," he said sheepishly when Grace glared at him. The father-to-be was missing. Where the devil is he? wondered Myrtle. Thornton returned triumphant with a new job offer. In his hand were the application forms for a passport.

"Idiot!" said Jacob angrily, unable to leave the subject alone. "Throwing your life away. Saddling yourself with a wife is bad enough, but a child as well? What sort of job is it anyway? What makes you think they want you in England?"

Far away in Delhi, sandwiched between Schubert and Beethoven, Alicia heard the news of the coming of the new generation and she wept. For the smallpox Sunil had contracted as a child had left a hidden mark on him. There would be no new generation for Alicia. That night her music floated

up towards the stars and her performance was filled with a
yearning that had never been there before. Soon she would
return home, in time for the general elections, to meet her
sister-in-law.

Something was wrong with Myrtle. It was obvious to Grace,
and to Frieda. But with Jacob's departure imminent there was
no time to find out what it was.

"He's off his food," said Jasper who seemed to have perked
up with all the recent activities. "Hello, Shiny?"

Myrtle was crying. No one knew whether it was the thought
of the New Arrival or Jacob's departure. An exhausted Alicia,
Sunil at her side, arrived to wish her brother goodbye. Frieda
noticed their sorrow had bound them closer together. Myrtle,
watching them, burst into tears.

"Good morning, Shiny," observed Jasper helpfully and,
when no one listened, made his now perfected devil-bird
sound.

"Hey, Jasp!" said Thornton, who was in the best of moods
these days. "Hey, Jasper, what's shiny?"

Jasper barked loudly.

"Jasper!" said Savitha. "Jasper, you are so cute! Oh, let's
call the baby Jasper, Thornton!"

Jasper stared at her silently. He had no loyalties.

"What is the matter with everyone?" asked Uncle Innocent
who had come down from the hills for Jacob's farewell.

"Silly old fool!" said Jasper, sailing out through the window, frightening the cook, sending her into a frenzy of waving
and screaming so that Grace had to be called in to speak sternly to him.

"Stop it, Jasper," said Jasper, enjoying himself hugely, running through his repertoire: barking dog, saw drill, crow caws,
Mozart, all in quick succession. So that Grace could not help
but laugh and Savitha clapped her hands with pleasure.

The line-up at the harbour was the same for Jacob's departure. Only Christopher was missing.

"We *will* visit you," promised Frieda. "When you're rich we'll come to see you and Christopher."

"Get a big house," said Thornton, laughing. "Because there will be a lot of us! Who knows, we might have twins."

Jacob sighed. Would he never be free of his siblings?

"Well," said Grace, taking comfort in the fact, "don't forget Christopher will be there too. So you won't be alone."

Why should I want to see *him*? Jacob was puzzled. We hardly spoke at home, what will be different in England? However, he did not say this. He was prepared to wait and see.

"Be good!" said Uncle Innocent. "Or if not, be careful!" he said, chuckling with delight. He wondered briefly if Hildegard was in England before hastily squashing the thought. Myrtle watched Jacob go. She was crying again.

"What the devil is wrong with her?" muttered Aloysius, irritated. Really, the woman had lived with them for too long. He wished Grace would get rid of her. She was no use in the house now that the children were all grown up.

"Don't forget to send me some shirts, putha," he told Jacob. "And some good whisky, and some chocolate for your mother," he added as an afterthought.

"Some bath salts too," said Auntie Angel-Face. "They put bath salts in the bath in the UK."

"But we only have showers!" said Savitha, amused. She liked Angel-Face.

"Well, we can smell them instead," said Angel-Face, confusing them with smelling salts. She was reading Jane Austen at the moment.

Looking at his mother's face, Jacob felt the stirrings of an old emotion from long ago. A leftover from those upcountry days. Savitha observed the family, her family now, and was silent, disturbed in a way she could not fully understand.

Certain things, unclear as yet, mysterious and interesting, were beginning to reveal themselves. Veiled in morning sickness, part of Savitha had begun to feel trapped. Sometimes, very occasionally, Thornton irritated her a little. His smile of course remained devastating, but certain things about him, certain *other* shortcomings, had begun to annoy her. Still, she brushed these thoughts aside, feeling the new generation turn restlessly inside her. Respect for the unborn subdued her for the moment. The harbour sounds were strangely haunting. Noises that spoke of unknown lands and other lives. Savitha shivered. What would it be like to leave? From the corner of her eye she saw Aloysius stub out his cigarette. He was looking edgy and uncomfortable. The smell of diesel made Savitha heave. Glancing at Grace she felt the moment stretch and magnify with unbearable poignancy. This is where Crown Rule has brought us, she thought. Dissipated by drink, full of suspicion, wanting to leave the country. Thornton was talking to Jacob, laughing at some joke of his own, ever-cheerful. In spite of herself Savitha felt her heart contract. She had married him impulsively, loving his beautiful face, his optimism. She had been right, she thought, this country needed dreamers like Thornton. What will we be like, she wondered, when we are old? Keeping her thoughts to herself, Savitha watched them all. Silence was soon to become her best tool.

There were twenty-one stormy days ahead before Jacob would leave behind the heat at the tip of the Bay of Biscay. Sweating in the coarse wool jacket of his UK-bound suit, wanting only to go, he had no clear memory of his departure. At last, was all he thought, at last. And then he was gone, with his two Jaffna mangoes and his packet of curry leaves, off to a *better life*. Following Jacob's departure Savitha wrote another article for the *Colombo Times*. It was an astringent little piece, cutting across social unrest and the looming elections. The article was about the rich stooges, as she called them, the nationalists who were forcing the Tamils to leave the country. They would go looking for a city paved with gold, taking all that was best in Ceylon with them. Savitha predicted there would be no rainbows, no golden treasures, and no happy ending, either abroad or on the island. It was a sharp piece on emigration, sending out a cry for island solidarity. The editor was struck again by the eloquence and wit of her prose. Grace, reading it, nodded. Once, long ago, she too had felt this way. Sunil read it and was amazed by her passion. He said nothing to Alicia, for Alicia, struggling with their joint sorrow, avoided Savitha of late. She was often at home, practising in between concerts, when Sunil was away canvassing for the elections.

It was July. The monsoons had broken again and the weather was tempestuous. Far out at sea, Jacob leaned over the side of the deck, looking out at the stormy inky water, longing for the voyage to end.

Which was where he was, on the morning of the general election in Ceylon. The island that was no longer even a speck on his horizon. The morning when Thornton, arriving at his parents' house for breakfast, leaving his wife still asleep in the one-bedroom flat that was their married home, looked down to find a gecko land on his shoulder.

"Thornton, master," said the servant, horrified, seeing him brush it off, "that is very, very bad luck!"

Grace, irritated, shooed the servant away and laid another place for her son.

"How is Savitha this morning?"

"She's still tired, after Jacob's leaving party," Thornton said. "I thought I would let her rest."

He was on his way to work but decided on the spur of the moment that he would stop off at what he still thought of as home, for breakfast. It was almost like the old days, only now

Thornton had got a decent job, thanks to Savitha's good influence. He sat down for a second breakfast and Grace smiled. She was pleased with the way things had turned out for him. Since the announcement of the new baby, he had changed. Although they had all changed, Thornton was the most altered.

"Your brother is so much more content," she often remarked to Frieda. "Less restless, happier, don't you think?"

And Frieda, agreeing, was glad it was Thornton who was the happy one.

On this morning of the election Alicia began her daily practice on the piano earlier than usual. She had slept at her parents' house because Sunil had been working through the night. It was an ordinary day with sunlight slanting down through the trees. Grace cut some flowers for the vases before the heat ruined them and entered the house just as Alicia began to play an old favourite, a Schubert sonata she rarely played anymore. The slow, lilting second movement of the andante was one that Grace had always loved. Pausing, she listened. The sounds pierced her heart and stirred up her buried grief. Looking around the table where various members of her remaining family sat, she allowed herself to be overwhelmed by sadness. Once she had stood in this very spot listening to this same piece of music, unaware of all that lay ahead. Lately, she had begun to bring fragments of certain images out into the open. Lately, she had felt able to do this without falling apart. Memory flooded out with the music. Vijay! Yes, she could say his name to herself at last but she no longer could recall his face clearly. He had been but a moment in her life, a flicker of light, going out like a shooting star. Doomed to fall. Yet the essence of him remained strong.

Alicia had reached the tricky part of the music, the part where she used always to go wrong, either stumbling over the chords or ruining the timing. Grace listened. How could C minor say so much? Today Alicia played with six years of experience, without smudging the notes, seamlessly shaping the phrases until it was no longer simply the melody they heard, but something more intrinsic, something more polished and complete than it had ever sounded before. Standing in the doorway, watching her elder daughter, seeing the young girl and now the woman absorbed into this slight figure, Grace closed her eyes. Even if she cannot have a child, she has her music. May it always see her through, prayed Grace, silently, as the andante was played out. No one heard the gate being unlatched. No one heard the knock on the door, or the simultaneous discordant ring of the telephone. No one bothered until a servant opened the front door and came looking for Aloysius.

"The police are here. They want the Master," the servant called, alarmed.

Frieda, coming out from the cool interior of the house, saw the small crowd that had gathered outside, saw her father's face, ashen and crumpled, heard Myrtle's cry, calling for Grace.

"Oh my God, my God! Grace, Grace, I didn't mean it!"

Someone was screaming, over and over again. Frieda could not recognise her own voice, as she cried out for Grace, saying it was not true. For how could it be true, for there was Alicia sitting at the piano as she always did, calmly playing Schubert, dressed as she always was. There was Thornton, for all the world still a bachelor, eating his breakfast of hopper and jaggery before he went out. And there were the crimson gladioli that Grace had just cut for the vase in the hall, indeed there was Grace herself holding the flowers, about to plunge them in cold water, so how could it be true? This unknown stranger, this white-clad messenger, telling them again and again things they could not comprehend, things that made no sense, words without meaning. Frieda, rooted to the spot, watched all this. But Grace, with her arms full of the dark red gladioli, seeing the piece of paper the policeman held out to her, even as the shutters slammed against the sunlight outside, Grace understood, instantly, turning, blinded by her understanding, towards her elder daughter. For as the last notes were played, as they fell into the cool light of early morning, she saw that Alicia had been widowed. Playing Schubert. Widowed by a single stray bullet meant for someone else.

Which was how it was that, watching flying fish on the high seas and the dawn rising over the horizon, Jacob travelled onwards in blissful ignorance of the bloodshed in his homeland. Twenty-one days is a long time for the dead to remain unattended. There were so many in this latest massacre. A prime minister with good intentions, a minister or two, standing in the wrong place, what did they matter, a few civil servants doing their jobs, counting ballots, perhaps if they had counted faster they might have been spared. A chauffeur, a servant boy bringing refreshments, another bringing a marigold garland. A saffron-yellow robe splattered red, strangely vibrant. Blue canvas chairs overturned, fallen onto spilt rice, a begging bowl of smoothest ebony. What did any of the flies care as they feasted in the sunshine, covering vast tracts of unexpected pleasure? Twenty-one days is a long time for the dead to lie unburied in such heat. By the time Jacob heard the news from home, in his little bedsit in Brixton, reading the letter in his father's beautiful handwriting, the first letter he had ever received from him, by the time he broke open the seal of the aerogramme, Alicia was already a widow of several weeks. The lid of the coffin and her piano simultaneously closed forever. All her life summed up in these simple gestures.

The recording of Alicia de Silva playing Mozart's Piano Sonata in A minor, K310, was in the shops in time for Vesak. Sales were good, considering a state of emergency had been declared and a curfew was in operation. Her delicate, tender touch was instantly recognisable. A music critic on one of the English newspapers, who had followed Alicia's brief career, picked up a copy of the recording. He wrote a glowing review about this unknown young artist. He wrote of "maturity and interpretation," "virtuosity" and "depth." Would there be any other albums, he wondered, Liszt, perhaps, or Schubert? Uncle Innocent bought a copy of the record and played it in his house on the tea estate, listening to the familiar sounds of his childhood when Grace's mother used to play this very same piece. The elderly doctor in the old hill station who had long ago loved Grace, and who had delivered Alicia and her siblings, bought a copy and listened to it in silence. Jacob bought a copy with some difficulty and listened to the sound of his sister from across the seas, unaware that his face was wet with tears. Christopher, on the other side of the river in Finchley, listened to it. It was music, he realised, that had filled his life and formed his childhood. Lately, he had successfully suppressed all thoughts of home, hoping to close all that had hurt him. He had joined the newly formed Tamil Resistance Party in London and written to the newspapers in protest against what was happening in his country. But he had distanced himself emotionally. The rage that flared so violently on the night of the riots of '58 had very nearly finished him and ever since he had been living in this little corner of London, in his cramped bedsit, he had tried to see things differently. He had thought he had hardened his heart. He *had* hardened it. Until tonight. Tonight he was caught unawares. As he listened to his sister's music, he heard again the other sounds he had tried to block out, saw himself struggling as his mother held him. Heard his own despair.

"It's my fault!" he had shouted. "She did nothing wrong. She was a Sinhalese!"

He heard his mother's voice, over and over again: "No, Christopher, it isn't your fault. She was simply in the wrong place at the wrong time."

Helplessly, for tonight he was defeated, Christopher rang Jacob. He hardly ever rang him but suddenly he needed the connection.

"Shall we meet up?"

Jacob sounded subdued. Christopher thought he could hear piano music in the background.

"OK," he said, quietly. "I'll come over to you. I'll bring some whisky."

Later, as they sat without talking, their loneliness blunted by drink, an unfamiliar connection rose between them. Mutely they accepted it. It was as though Grace was in the room with them.

"How many more lives will be ruined before there is peace?" Christopher mumbled.

In the orange glow of the electric fire Jacob shook his head. "I'll never go back," he said, finally. "I hate it there."

Thinking of the house where they had once lived, and the tea-covered hills with their many waterfalls, he began to see how impossible his hopes had been. Greenwood could never have lasted. Their youth, he saw in hindsight, had been a hollow promise. That was all. Now he didn't even have that. Finishing his drink, he stood up. It was late; he had work in the morning.

"I had better go," he said, reluctantly, "or I'll miss the last train."

Pulling on his coat he left. No, he thought, hurrying across the deserted street to the Underground station, he would never go back. He would never see his home again.

In his room, in the silence left by Jacob's departure, Christopher pulled out a battered suitcase from under his bed. Peering inside he found the cheap plastic butterfly brooch and the photograph, almost indistinguishable now, of a boy and a girl in the shadow of the sun. He placed the record carefully beside them; he would never play it again. Closing the suitcase, he fell onto the bed, clutching the handle, holding it tightly. It was his suitcase of lost hope. His life in pieces.

Alicia's pain sliced through the de Silva household, turning them mute. After the shock came a grief like no other. Then it retreated behind closed doors, horrifying glimpses, visible only occasionally. She was inconsolable. No one could have imagined such a complete disintegration. Like an injured animal she withdrew, leaving only echoes running through the house. Then one morning, almost twelve weeks after the funeral, a Buddhist monk arrived unannounced. After this latest massacre, and the involvement of the monks, the sight of an orange robe was enough to send most people into panic. The young Tamil servant girl, answering the knock, shrieked with fear. Myrtle, catching a glimpse of a shaven head, scurried into her room so that it was left to Grace to go to the door. The monk bowed respectfully.

"I have been sent here by a relative of Sunil Pereira," he told Grace.

In the mahogany hallway his saffron robe was frighteningly bright. Frieda gasped. Aloysius, hearing the Sinhalese voice, came in swiftly.

"What the devil do you want?" he asked angrily, in English. "We are Catholics here," he said. "We have no need for your services, thank you."

The monk bowed. He was a slight, youngish man, probably the same age as Sunil. Grace stared coldly at him.

"We are a house of mourning," she said quietly. "I'm sure you can understand. Our son-in-law is dead. Please, tell us what you want quickly."

The monk placed his hands together in greeting. "What happened was a tragedy," he began.

"Yes, we know," Aloysius said, sarcastically. "We don't need a bloody Buddhist priest to tell us that."

Grace laid a restraining hand on his arm. She did not want Alicia to hear him. The monk stood silent. Waiting.

"Why have you come here?" Grace asked.

"The man who is the uncle of Sunil Pereira sent me." The monk spoke softly, in halting English. "I have travelled up from Dondra. Mr. Pereira, the uncle, has had a dream."

Aloysius snorted and moved towards the front door. "Oh, get out," he said.

"No, wait," Grace said, frowning at Aloysius.

"Mr. Pereira insisted I come to visit you before any other misfortunes come."

"What more can happen?" Grace said quietly. "We just want to be left in peace."

The monk held out his hands, palms upwards. "Mrs. de Silva," he said, "I understand how you feel but I have come only to help. There is some sort of obstruction in your garden. The dead man's uncle keeps seeing it in a dream. He has been having this same dream every night since the funeral. Please let me help you, Mrs. de Silva. I have come with a boy to look for it, to dig behind the murunga tree. I have come to offer prayers. That's all."

"What *is* this nonsense?" Aloysius said loudly. "Clear off, men. We're not interested." He turned angrily to Grace. "He's just after money, darl," he told her pointedly.

Grace opened her mouth to agree but it was Frieda who stopped her.

"Oh please, Mummy, please let him. I'm frightened. What harm will it do?"

Grace hesitated, uncertain.

"I am not here for money," the monk said. He spoke firmly. "Just let me take a look in your garden. Then I'll go."

Grace looked at him; he's young, he doesn't look like an assassin, she thought. What harm can it do? Making up her mind swiftly, she nodded, and led the way into the garden.

The priest strode over to the murunga tree, as though he knew the garden well. Then, speaking in Sinhalese, he instructed the boy to dig under it. The de Silvas watched with a mixture of horror and fascination. By now the servants had come out and they too stood silently by the kitchen door, watching.

"Darl, he'll ruin the place," Aloysius said. "I'm going to stop this nonsense. We've had enough—"

Grace, her hand on his arm, mesmerised, held him back. A moment later the boy's spade appeared to strike against a root. Pushing him aside impatiently, the priest grabbed hold of the spade and continued to dig; then, bending down, he hollowed out the soil with his hands. They could see him tug at something below the ground. The servants gasped, crowding round as the monk with a grunt pulled up a long metal sheet. There was soil everywhere. He wiped the plate with the palm of his hand and the cook, seeing what he held, let out a wail of fear. The monk ignored everyone, continuing to polish the metal until it shone. Grace could see it glinting in the bright sunlight.

"This is what I meant," he said, walking towards her.

Even from this distance they could see the crude drawing of a man and a woman, etched on the plate, holding hands, garlanded by flowers, incised by lines.

"Here," the monk said calmly, showing it to Aloysius. "This is what Mr. Pereira's uncle saw in his dream."

No one spoke. Then the old cook who had been with the de Silva family for so long began to wring her hands.

"Oh missies, missies," she cried. "Who has done this terrible thing to this family?!"

"Someone put a curse on your house," the monk told them quietly. "On your daughter's marriage and on you. Only now can it be removed. I will bless this place with *pirith*. There will be no more deaths."

"Hello, Shiny," said Jasper, flying joyfully by, making them jump, seeing the metal plate glinting in the sunlight. "Hello,

Shiny," he said again, before disappearing into the mango tree, heavy now with fruit.

"Mummy," said Frieda, her eyes following Jasper, but Grace had turned and was walking swiftly towards the house.

"It's just a coincidence, darl," Aloysius called after her. "It's superstitious rubbish." But he sounded uncertain.

Myrtle was laying out the tarot cards when Grace burst into her room.

"Have you given up knocking?" she asked sharply, but she looked frightened.

"Why?" asked Grace, through gritted teeth, grabbing her cousin's arm, scattering tarot cards on the floor. "Why, after all I've done for you, do you hate us so much?"

"Grace," Aloysius said, appearing beside her.

Grace shook him off.

"Have I not loved you as my own blood relative?" she cried. "Did I not give you a home when you were homeless? Why have you wished my daughter, your niece, so much harm?"

"I don't know what you are talking about," Myrtle said. Her oily skin looked pale.

"We are a Tamil family," Grace continued. Her voice was beginning to rise. She hung on to Myrtle's arm, pushing her backwards and forwards. "We are just another Tamil family. Trying desperately to exist in the midst of *so* much ugliness, so much violence and hatred. Have you *no* loyalty, whatsoever, towards your own people? That you can only wish us ill? Tamils fighting Tamils, is that what this is? Or is it because she chose to marry a Sinhalese? Is that it? Tell me which it is?"

She let go of Myrtle, pushing her away in disgust. Myrtle laughed. The sound was ugly.

"*You*, a Tamil?" she asked, in a voice that sent a shiver down Frieda's spine. "*You*, Grace?" Her voice rose to a high-pitched whine. "No, no, no. Dear me, you're no Tamil!"

Frieda watched as Myrtle's face twisted and darkened. A nerve in her neck was pulsating. She looked as though she was about to strike Grace.

"You're a half-caste woman, my dear," she said triumphantly. "Your mother went off with a Burgher, didn't you know? Caused quite a scandal in the hills. Your father was so besotted with her that he took her back, pregnant and disgraced. Don't you know? You are no Tamil, my dear. You are the sort the Tamils need to be rid of."

"So," said Aloysius, advancing into the room. "So, your private grievances have evolved into politics, have they?"

No one heard Alicia's door opening.

"What would you like?" he went on, easily. "A pure Tamil state? Let's annihilate the others, shall we, keep the island for people like you and me? What d'you say? Let's get rid of these half-caste bastards, huh? Only trouble is the Sinhalese would like us out too. They want this place for themselves. There are more of them than us, so, what shall we do?"

He had moved close to Myrtle, his eyes fixed on her. With one swift gesture he swept the pots of powder, her diary, and everything on her dressing table, sending them crashing to the floor. Then, without taking his eyes off Myrtle, he put his arm around his wife.

"Get out," he told her quietly. "Pack your bags and get out. You are no different from the Sinhalese bastards. I can't have such a person in my house. I do not want you near my wife, soiling my home." He paused and took a deep breath. "I'm going to the club," he said, more quietly. "Pack your bags. When I return I want you gone, d'you understand?"

And without waiting for a reply, he walked out.

That evening, after Myrtle left and the Buddhist monk had gone, and the garden had been cleared up, Grace went to sit with Alicia in her room. She took a tray of food with her, to try to tempt her daughter to eat a little. She wanted to talk to her about all that had happened, to put the day and all its revelations into some context for both of them. But Alicia was not interested. Not in the food her mother had brought, nor in the events of the day. It had no bearing on her life. It could not assuage her pain.

"I had no idea," Grace said, looking at Alicia's pale face. "It was true. I did always feel different from Myrtle whenever we were together, but it was unimportant. I was so close to your grandfather, I used to feel sorry for Myrtle."

Alicia pushed the tray away.

"Whenever any of the servants commented on how very different we were from each other it would make your grandfather angry. I used to wonder why."

"I'm tired," Alicia said faintly. "I want to sleep."

She closed her eyes. She closed her mother out of sight. Politely, she dismissed Grace.

Thornton and Savitha arrived for dinner. Aloysius, coming in soon after, looked quickly at Grace.

"Has she gone?" he asked.

They told him that she had. He nodded.

"Good!" he said, pouring himself a glass of water.

Grace was astonished. Was that all he intended to say? There were so many questions she wanted to ask. Why was Aloysius not more surprised? Had he known about it all along? After they had finished eating she decided to walk in the garden for a bit. The day and all its implications lay heavily on her and she felt as though she could not breathe. She needed to talk to Aloysius but first she wanted to get her thoughts in order.

"I'm going to see if Alicia is all right," Frieda said. She had noticed that Savitha wanted to go into the garden too. She could not face going out with her sister-in-law.

Leaving Thornton talking with Aloysius, Grace took her

daughter-in-law out into the garden to see the spot under the murunga tree.

"You don't really believe in it, do you?" Savitha asked after they had stared at the spot in silence.

Savitha was swollen with the child, for her time was nearing, and she found walking difficult. So they sat on the garden seat within view of the coconut grove. Beyond it was the sea. Grace sighed. Although she felt exhausted, this moment in the coolness of the evening was strangely peaceful. The garden appeared transformed by the fading light, and the sound of the waves came towards them, rising and falling very clearly. Savitha sat quietly, her hands folded in her lap, carrying the new generation snugly within her. Thornton's child, thought Grace. Small fruit bats murmured quietly in the trees. Now and then they heard the rich, deep sound of a frog croaking in the undergrowth. A feeling of benevolence crept over Grace. Savitha seems so dependable, she thought. If I needed her help she would not fail me.

"No," she said aloud. "I don't believe in any of it. What hurts me is that anyone could have wanted to harm us so much. That one of our own, my own cousin, could feel this way about us, about Alicia."

She needed to hold the pieces of Alicia's broken heart together. It was the thing that interested her now. Savitha placed her hands on her stomach and felt the baby kick. Looking at Grace, feeling the flutter of limbs, she thought, I am loved. At last I have my own family. At last I too belong. She wanted to tell Grace that it did not matter that Myrtle was a relative, that hatred was present in the most unlikely places. But she did not feel it was her place to say such things.

"Alicia is very, very beautiful," she said instead. "Someone will love her again, one day. Wait and see. You must not despair. We are here, Thornton, me, Frieda, Aloysius. You are not alone."

In the quickening darkness, Grace looked at her daughter-in-law. In less than a month there would be a baby in the house. We *are* blessed, she thought, nodding. I love this dependable girl. My son will be safe with her.

Later when they were in bed, under cover of the darkness, she spoke to Aloysius.

"How long have you known?" she asked, hesitantly, staring into the night.

Outside, the frogs were croaking again and cicadas vibrated the air. He was silent for so long that she thought he had not heard her. Turning towards him she saw his face in profile. He was tired, she thought; wasted by drink. His hair was thinning. Grace hesitated, feeling her heart move. Then she did something she had not done for many years. She reached out and touched his face. Aloysius did not stir.

"I was never certain," he said at last, very softly. "There were rumours. A man at the factory told me some nonsense. I asked myself, who cares? Does the man whom she thinks is her father care? No. Well, neither do I. That's what I thought. Now go to sleep," he said.

And he kissed her forehead.

In London, the ex-Governor, reading about the recent violence on Ceylon, shook his head, saddened. He saw what no one else did: that a mantle of despair was settling like fine grey dust on the distant island, clogging the air, blotting out its brilliance and choking its people. And, as the dense rainforests turned slowly into pockets of ruins, and the last remnants of peace began to vanish, it seemed to those who loved the place that the dazzling colours of paradise would never be seen again.

10.

It was into this that the new generation dropped. All unsuspecting, bawling its head off, uncaring of any grief except its own. Red-faced in the heat of its passion, full of unspeakable need, huge tears rolling down its face, letting the world know about its hunger, its tiredness, its discomfort. Eyes screwed against the sun, fists clenched already in the grip of a mysterious discourse of its own. Then when its shell-shocked parents realised that dawn and dusk could occur in the same twenty-four hours without their once having closed their eyes, it stopped as suddenly as it had begun. And it smiled—a smile of such magnitude that it tilted the world.

"My God!" said Thornton, taken aback to find himself looking in the mirror.

Ah! thought Savitha. Here lies trouble.

She was looking at her husband's face. He wore a look she recognised but could not immediately place. Then she realised. It was exactly the way Grace looked at Thornton.

"Hmm," said Savitha, cryptically. "One in the family is quite enough."

In spite of the fact that she was hallucinating most of the time through lack of sleep, Savitha was maturing nicely.

"Yes!" Grace told Aloysius, with mild surprise. "I see the family resemblance!" She felt a little detached from the event. "Almost like Thornton."

For the new generation, that milestone for which Aloysius had waited with such eagerness, hiding a special bottle of

Scotch to wet its head, was not quite as he had imagined. Benedict Aloysius de Silva (as he was meant to be called) had not behaved according to plan. He was, in fact, a girl. Yes, yes, fooled you, fooled you, bawled Anna-Meeka de Silva, berating her exhausted parents, the visitors to the cradle, and anyone in fact who dared look at her.

"My God!" said Thornton again, having given in to his wife's fanciful choice of names, feeling the weight of parenthood press down sharply on him.

"My God! I've got a daughter!" Something stirred within him, some vaguely familiar feeling. Fragile and unexpected, it rushed towards him. Was this how his mother felt about them all? Rousing himself from the terrible events that had occurred, he found his carefree youth had vanished.

Perhaps, reflected Frieda, with amazement, he had been changing anyway. They had all changed, she realised sadly. While they were grappling with their sorrow, time had moved on. Frieda knew from his brief letters that Christopher had hardened his heart towards his homeland. She knew he would never return. What's left? thought Frieda. She was still lonely. Nothing had changed for *her*. Alicia was reduced to a ghostly presence in the house while Grace had become slower these days and easily confused. Their mother was growing old. The thought brought tears to Frieda's eyes. Myrtle, of course, had gone. Myrtle, who used at least to talk to Frieda, had moved back upcountry. No one kept in touch. Neither Aloysius nor Grace talked of what had happened and no one ever mentioned her name. The revelations of that day were buried once more. Often at night, after writing to one of her brothers or returning from Mass, having checked on her sister and her parents, Frieda would lie on her bed and return to her hopeless fantasies of Robert Grant. Their first meeting remained as fresh for her as though it had occurred yesterday. Distance had inscribed it with an unreal substance. She no longer cared about reality, she saw only what might have been. And now she added Catholic guilt to this. Remembering her past jealousy, Frieda chided herself inwardly. *Alicia has nothing either. It must be my fault, my life is my punishment,* she argued silently, grappling with her burden of guilt.

Thornton had no guilt. Guilt had never been his problem. His problems were different. His new daughter was barely six weeks old. Her smile pierced his heart, and when she cried he found he was paralysed with love and anxiety. He wondered if Savitha was up to the task of bringing the child up. Then he noticed something else.

"Savitha!" he said excitedly. "She is going to be really very clever!"

"Not the way she's going," said his wife, who planned to kill the child if she did not sleep tonight.

"How on earth will we give her the education she needs?" Thornton wondered. "She must be educated in *English!*"

Grace looked at the child; Thornton's child, her first grandchild. Things had not worked out in the way she had expected. There was no longer any music in the house. All that she had once hoped for, all that she had longed so ardently for, had gone its own way, the family she had nurtured was slowly being torn apart. Alicia hardly ventured from her room, and since Sunil's funeral, Aloysius had begun to drink again. There should have been no hope left. But somehow she felt closer to Aloysius than she had ever been before. Knowing what he had kept hidden for years had impressed her far more than the illegitimacy of her birth and a new gentleness crept into her voice when she spoke to him. Slowly beneath the surface, invisibly, the house was stirring. It had new life in it, vigorous and noisy. Grace felt it move impatiently. She felt it tug and pull at her and urge her to smile. It refused to take no for an answer. Grace looked again at Thornton. She felt a glimmer of amusement at the sight of her son's new life. Responsibility had settled on Thornton like thick tropical dust.

Unknown to his mother, other changes were occurring in Thornton. Sunil's death had affected him more than he realised. It had taken on a different, more sinister meaning. For Thornton, never having shown the slightest anxiety about the race riots, now began to listen daily to the news. How safe was this country for his daughter to grow up in? Should they too leave the island? Politics were pressing in on Thornton's life in a way it had never done before.

"Well," remarked Jacob, reading the news from home, and ringing up Christopher, "he's got his comeuppance. Time he joined the real world. He should try living here."

Christopher made no comment. He seldom wrote home. He had nothing more to say. Since Sunil's death he felt as though all ties with his family had been severed. It had happened slowly, but he felt there was no point in dwelling on the past. He saw it as a hostile place of no return. Only when he thought of his mother was he was filled with an unbearable anguish. Her grief still communicated itself to him subliminally even though Christopher no longer had the capacity to deal with it. She had let him go; she would always be with him but having learned to hide his hurt Christopher wanted no reminders. It had become easier for him to go to the pub than to write home. His only concessions were the occasional phone calls and spasmodic meetings with Jacob.

Thornton began planning. Panic had made him active.

"We can't bring Anna-Meeka up in *this* country," he declared, realising what Frieda had already seen coming. "Not with all that's going on. What on earth will her life be like?" It was clear, even at this stage, that nothing was too good for his tiny daughter. "We *must* go to England," he decided. "Anna-

Meeka can have a good education there. She is clever. She might become a doctor. Who knows?"

"Clever like her father, then," said Savitha who, having discovered the delights of sarcasm during the long sleepless nights, was beginning to sharpen her teeth. It seemed there might be a shift in their lives. For a moment it seemed as though there might even be a little hope.

"Hello?" said Jasper with what appeared to be false jollity, ruffling his feathers and preening himself.

He loathed the baby. She was larger than all the cats put together, and commanded more attention. Her screams confused him.

"Be quiet!" he said querulously.

Grace smiled. She had taken to waiting eagerly for their visits.

"You know," she told Frieda, "Savitha is exactly what Thornton needed. She is what we *all* need."

And she gently picked up the yelling child and carried her out into the great garden where Jasper sat sleepily in the murunga tree.

"Oh no!" said Jasper turning his back to them, but the baby stopped crying and began to laugh.

Savitha looked closely at Grace. Through her exhaustion (for the new generation had energy on its side), she turned her clever eyes on Grace. She watched as the baby was introduced to the servants, noticed how they carried her when she cried and listened as they talked to her in Sinhalese and in Tamil. Seeing the unshakeable affection for their mistress spill over and envelop Anna-Meeka, Savitha's admiration for her beautiful mother-in-law increased. Slowly, hesitantly, in the moments when the baby slept, and Jasper approached the house with caution, she talked to Grace.

"There are so many things that have to change," Grace told her. "The government should be focusing on these things, instead of being obsessed with eradicating the English language. There is so much superstition everywhere, crippling our lives."

"Oh, that's just ignorance," Savitha said, "that's what *that's* all about!"

"Take Myrtle, for instance," Grace continued, casually. "She should have known better."

Savitha hesitated. "Why was she so jealous?" she asked, at last.

"It's an old story," Grace said lightly. "From when we were young! She loved Aloysius once, you know." She paused, on the brink of saying more. "If we are ever to move forward, we must rid ourselves of all this useless superstition," she said, finally.

Savitha nodded, absentmindedly.

"Do you remember the eclipse?" Grace asked. "Everyone was frightened by it. People thought it was the cause of the riots!" She laughed, softly, her face sad.

"I remember," Savitha said.

"Someone I knew was killed on that night," Grace said.

She spoke faintly and Savitha, who had been daydreaming, glanced sharply at her. Grace's eyes were full of unshed tears.

"It was all such nonsense," she was saying. "But you couldn't convince anyone, even—"And she stopped speaking abruptly.

"Only education will sweep those devils out," Savitha agreed.

She didn't know what else to say. Averting her gaze, she waited. At last Grace nodded, smiling gently. A light breeze had sprung up, shaking some blossom to the ground.

"It needs to be offered to everyone or it simply won't work," Grace said.

Savitha was at a loss for words. She had lived most of her life with only her sharpness of mind and her passionate desire for the truth as her companions. She had lived for so long without love or family affection, without encouragement or good looks and she was unaccustomed to such intimacy. Her mother-in-law astonished her. We think in the same way, she told herself, basking in this unexpected affection.

"How wonderful to hear you say that," she told Grace.

"We were very privileged, you know," Grace said. "When Thornton was growing up, we had everything we wanted. My father always used to say we should put some of it back into the country. The country is like a garden. It has to be tended, he used to say."

It was dark now. The evening star was out. Savitha felt as though some danger had passed.

"It wasn't easy for Aloysius," Grace continued. "He was very handsome when I first met him. Like Thornton. But the British kept him in their pockets, you know. He used to tell me he was just their puppy, everything was fine if he did what they wanted. It wasn't any life for a man like him."

Savitha listened intently. She was slowly beginning to understand.

"In the end . . . all that eternal gambling, endlessly trying to prove himself . . . it was such a mess. Vijay . . . someone I knew, a long time ago . . . said it was because Aloysius had lost his way. He is a clever man. He could have done anything he wanted." She sighed. "It was all wasted. Then after Sunil's death . . ."

Her voice tailed off. One generation forever trying to put right the mistakes of another. All of them ground down and exhausted.

Later, when she was alone with her daughter, back in their little annexe, when Thornton had gone to meet a contact for the UK, Savitha mulled over the conversation with Grace.

"You must not be like them, Anna-Meeka," she told the sleeping infant, seriously. "You must be the one to change your family's history."

Perhaps, after all, Thornton was right and they should go to England. With the future here so uncertain, England might save them. Her daughter must learn to be resilient, Savitha sighed. That was what was important. The child stirred and sucked her thumb. Savitha gazed at the tiny dark lashes sweeping down from closed eyes.

"Your father is a handsome man, Anna-Meeka," she told the baby. "But he doesn't always know what's best. He's making plans for your future; he's full of ambitions. He wants you to be a doctor, to be famous, to be rich, God knows what he wants. Your Dada is bursting with love for you, but . . ." and she paused. She folded her lips together as though they were a paper bag, looking disapprovingly at the framed photo of her husband, hanging on the wall.

"You must do what suits *you* best," she said out loud, firmly to the sleeping baby. "I don't care what it is," she added, tenderly rocking the cot, "so long as you do it well."

Anna-Meeka grew rapidly. In no time at all she began to talk.

"Jasper!" she said as soon as she could. Both her mother and grandmother were delighted. Cautiously, for he was still uncertain, Jasper approached the house. Softly, fearful of the response, he made a whirling noise like the grandfather clock. Then, because the hideous screaming seemed to have stopped, he began to whistle his favourite bar from *The Magic Flute*.

"Look!" said Savitha to her daughter. "Jasper wants to be friends with you."

And indeed Jasper, whose affection had been only for Grace until now, began to follow the child around.

When she was two, Anna-Meeka began to sing. Savitha and Grace listened, entranced. Their friendship was growing, unnoticed by anyone. Something tender and unspoken, a thread of kinship, invincible and unexpected, surfaced and became stronger. Immeasurably and powerfully it arose. Effortlessly it linked them, for here were two generations of women springing from the same nation, their love for their family enduring and certain. Feeling some impermanence in the air, Savitha brought the child almost daily to the house in Station Road while Grace lived moment by moment, a hostage to fortune.

Thornton made his application to leave the island. The troubles had worsened and many Tamils were leaving Colombo. Thornton wanted to leave while they still could.

"Oh, not yet!" cried Grace, before she could stop herself. She hoped the little girl would have a few more years of sun, some time to grow with them, as a talisman for the future.

As her daughter grew, the change in Savitha became more visible. She had started out with fixed ideas but motherhood had begun its rich transformation. The sharpness in her face had softened and her passionately held values became more complex. These days she felt the insistent stirrings of some other inexplicable and complicated emotion. It gathered strength within her, glowing softly, as though being stored for what lay ahead. It coursed through her tenderly, drawing from the air what fragrance it could find, collecting up those everyday sounds, of bicycle bells and barking dogs, and shouts and bangs, and the sudden dull thud of a coconut falling in the grove nearby. And all the time, as the bright colours fixed themselves unconsciously on her mind, as the monsoons came and went, Jasper sat somewhere in the plantain tree, whistling small snatches of *The Magic Flute*, reminding them of a slowly receding era.

That year the rainy season was late. When it arrived the daily downpour seemed relentless. The child had grown like a plant. Looking at her daughter, Savitha knew she would resemble Grace; she would be beautiful. With unaccountable sadness, she knew that some day others would see this too and would remember Grace. At five, Anna-Meeka started school in the little convent next door to the cathedral where her silent aunt Alicia had been married. The nuns knew the de Silvas. They remembered Frieda, and they knew Grace. When Anna-Meeka began to learn to play the piano they were not surprised by her talent. They had all heard her aunt on the radio. Savitha was delighted; here were the signs of the family talent. Only Thornton was uneasy. Sunil's death and the change in his sister had affected him. He, too, had not touched the piano since that day ,and although he was pleased to let Anna-Meeka learn, he informed his wife it would be bad luck for her to follow in his sister's footsteps. Savitha was puzzled. She had not realised Thornton was so superstitious. She saw with amazement that many things had begun to frighten him. History frightened him. He did not want it to repeat itself. He did not want Anna-Meeka to go down that particular road. Thornton was no longer happy as he once was. The changes in him were imperceptible. It touched the luminosity in his eyes, dampening the glow of youth. He stopped dreaming and became anxious. As the hatred for the Tamil people grew he wanted only to leave. His brothers received the news of the family's unease in the thin blue-paper letters that arrived with regularity, difficult to comprehend and, very soon, impossible to connect with. What was there to say about the shortage of food, the lootings, the random destruction of property? How to explain that a pint of Guinness and a pie spelt happiness at the end of a long grey London day, when the thick fleece of clouds left no room for the sun?

As two more years went by, Thornton made his preparations. Civil unrest was no longer a rumour. It was a fact. Tamil youths were set upon in the street, a bus carrying Tamil students was fire-bombed, a sweep seller lynched because of his name. Trouble erupted at unexpected moments. An exodus to Jaffna was under way. Some Tamil families applied to leave for

Australia. In just over five years, as predicted, the jungle had crept into the towns. Grace could do no more than accept the inevitable. Alicia's arpeggios were a phantom presence; the bone china in the glass-fronted cupboards remained unused. Few people visited them these days.

At seven, Anna-Meeka was enchanting. Whenever Savitha brought her to see her grandmother the silent house at Station Road became filled with noise and laughter. She followed her aunt Frieda like a shadow; she loved it when her grandfather teased her. Grace's letters to her sons were full of all of this. They were interspersed with other disconnected things from long ago, from her memories of the House of Many Balconies with its faded water-lily gardens, for lately she longed to see the place again. She wrote telling them of the deaths of Uncle Innocent and Auntie Angel-Face. Did they remember Mabel? Her son had been born deformed, her husband taken by the rebels into the jungle. He was never seen again. Someone, a relative, found a bundle of his clothes, torn and mangled, left by the Mahaweli River. Jacob and Christopher, receiving this information, did not know how to reply.

Months went by. When Thornton received his visa for entry into the UK departure became a certainty. Seeing this, stirring herself, Grace began to give Savitha some of her precious china. She gave her the blue-and-white bowls, the tureens, some delicately painted teacups, a dinner service.

"It's for you," she said, pressing them on Savitha. "Keep it in memory of us." She wanted her little granddaughter to enjoy them in her new life in Britain. It was a gesture of acceptance of their impending separation; a torch to be held by Savitha in all the long lonely years of their coming exile, until Anna-Meeka would be old enough to receive her legacy. Then, with their departure hanging over them, with civil unrest reaching boiling point, Grace decided to visit her childhood home one last time. To show Anna-Meeka where her father had been born. Late in June, when the heat in Colombo was unbearable once more, and the sea breeze no longer strong enough to keep them cool, Grace and Aloysius, with Thornton and Savitha, with Anna-Meeka (now nearly nine), made the trip upcountry on the grand black-and-red steam train.

They left at night and travelled inland. They had booked a sleeper but Anna-Meeka was too excited to sleep. As the train climbed higher and higher, hooting its smoke along the narrow-gauge track, she sat humming to herself, first with Thornton and then Savitha, watching the dark ravines rush by, catching glimpses of the many waterfalls flash past in a gush of white foam. Towards dawn, the air cooled and all of them slept, exhausted. They did not wake again until the smell of tea assailed their noses. Hurrying to open the blinds, they saw to their delight and astonishment the bright green tea-covered hills, just as they had left them, swathed in veils of mist, rising softly all around.

"We're home," murmured Grace. "At last!"

"Oh, Jacob should be here!" Thornton cried.

Aloysius chuckled. "Look, darl," he said, "that's the place where they used to have the tennis tournaments, remember?"

"Meeka," Thornton said, excitedly, "I used to walk to school along this valley. Look! There's a cloud of butterflies. I used to try and catch them."

Grace nodded. Her eyes were shining. She remembered.

"Let's have lunch at the tennis club, first," she suggested. "Anna-Meeka, you'll be able to eat wild strawberries now, because they grow here."

Savitha watched, mesmerised. She had never been upcountry before.

"We'll take a taxi to the house," Aloysius cried. He was laughing with delight.

"Well, let's put our bags at the rest house, first," Grace decided. "And have a wash."

The air was thin and fragrant as they stepped off the train. Kingfishers darted through the trees.

"There must be a lake nearby," Thornton said. "Oh, I wish Jacob was here. And Alicia—" He stopped, abruptly. No one said anything. Grace glanced uneasily at Savitha.

"Come," she said firmly. "Let's get to the rest house first. Then we'll go up to the house."

"I hope it's how we left it," said Thornton, uneasily. "D'you remember how it was screened by the trees? I hope they haven't cut them down."

What had prompted them to look back? Jacob and Christopher, receiving a letter sent jointly to them weeks later, read it from their great impassable distance and were non-plussed. How could they feel the heat now, except as a distant memory? A strange paralysis had descended on these two brothers. Survival in this urban jungle with its cold wind tunnels and its incomprehensible communication took up most of their energy. How could they explain this to the mother who could not even see their greying hair? Their thoughts of the past were vague these days, insubstantial as breath on a cold morning on the way to work. They sat reading, brought together by the letter, somewhere in a cold winter pub. The task ahead, this thing called the *new life*, had not yet opened up. When it did, they would be unable to see its possibilities; they would notice only its limitations. So they sat, in their ill-fitting suits, holding their newly fractured lives, uncomprehending. They were in need of cherishing but this too was no longer available, and the likelihood of their recovery from such a brutal uprooting was a sad illusion. Somewhere in that pub, sitting close to the coal fire, the brothers read their mother's letter and struggled to imagine the rooms where they had once slept, with the painted walls scraped and broken by bullet holes, the polished green and pink glass smashed, the ropes swinging from light fittings, the chipped and dark-stained marble floors. It was time for another round of Guinness before reading the rest of the letter. Then, drink in hand, they learned about Jasper. Jasper, who should have lived to a ripe old age, shot for shouting at an armed soldier, while they were all away upcountry.

"Hello, sister!" he had shouted as, too late, the servant girl tried to stop the man from raping her.

Tucked away in the cosy pub, on that wintry evening, somewhere in the Borough of Southwark, halfway into their second round of Guinness, the brothers, reading of Jasper's fate, remembered and could drink no more.

ERRORS

11

August was mercilessly hot. It brought a rancid stench from dustcarts that mixed with the cloying sweetness of roadside shrine-flowers. Faded black umbrellas and orange robes walked the streets. Danger hovered in every alleyway. Fear hung oppressively around the city, turning what had once been lively and festive into dark suspicion. Gone were the days when the rich moved upcountry, opening their houses and their tennis courts, while their servants served soft drinks in tall bead-covered jugs. Gone were the days when the sound of rickshaw bells and horns and whistles and *baila* music from transistor radios filled the air. Once August had been the month of the Perahera, when shadow-dancers on the high trapeze pointed their elbows at the neon sky. But now all that was over. Carelessness was a thing of the past. Conversation in public was a dangerous thing, for language had become an identity card. No one was to be trusted. No one knew who might be listening. Anger filled the streets where once the shadow-dancers had walked. Anger was everywhere, simmering like the heat, unquenchable, taut, tar black and desperate.

This August was Grace's undoing. As she lay awake in the stifling heat, in a house grown empty, with a life that had shrunk to a husk, she listened to the night swelling in the darkness. Wherever Thornton and his family were, she knew it to be some other hour. What were they doing? Was it daytime in the place they were? Was the sun shining on them? They had left her. Now at last she understood what this meant. Before they left she had held herself together, wanting to be strong. Wanting to hold together these last precious moments so that later, when she was alone and Aloysius and Alicia and Frieda slept, and the sprawling house was silent, she could bring out the images of their departure. And look again at the faint imprints that were all that remained of the sad slow ebb of her life. It had been Savitha, almost completely silent for days, who had broken down with astonishing grief. Savitha, and then Thornton. Anna-Meeka had merely hopped from foot to foot, anxious to be gone, hoping that if they went quickly then no one would cry. Solemnly she promised Grace that she would look after her parents. Chattering brightly, on and on, wriggling and jumping up and down with suppressed excitement and worry, promising not to forget them all, to write often, and yes, yes, she would be good too.

"You won't cry, Granny, will you?" she had begged anxiously.

Grace had promised. No, she would not cry.

Now, staring into the unbroken darkness, the thin whine of mosquitoes just beyond the net, she heard a piano. The girl in the next house was playing a nocturne. Slowly the notes dropped like polished glass into the balmy air. Alicia slept in a room further down the hall, locked away, silent, impenetrable. Grace pictured her small form, crumpled among the white sheets, dark hair covering her face, sleeping just as she had as a child. Alicia had shown no sadness when Thornton left. No, thought Grace, recalling her daughter standing at the harbour in her widow's white, Alicia had nothing to say. She had witnessed too much. She was no longer reachable. Only Frieda, simple uncomplicated Frieda, with her abundance of tears, had hugged Anna-Meeka who, oblivious to the effect of her smile, talked on, telling her aunt kindly that they would be back soon, making it sound as though she was going to the market with her mother. In spite of herself Grace had smiled, even as she kissed her son goodbye, wondering if it was for the last time, remembering the small boy who used to walk home from school along the valley with its waterfalls, its blue-green tea-covered hills and its storms of butterflies. Remembering how he had played jazz late at night, his foot jammed on the loud pedal, until his sisters shouted at him, fearing he would break the piano, while Jasper, turning round and round on his perch, also shouted at him.

"Turn it down, old chap!" Jasper had shouted. "Be quiet!" he had said, making them all laugh.

And now, thought Grace, as the night jasmine uncurled itself, now what shall I do? Four thousand years of peace and an ancient god were no longer enough for a country brimming with violence. A sacred tree, a thin white thread around Savitha's wrist, what use were any of these things? The night was filled with doubts. Her son's discarded hat in the hall, Savitha's parcel of chilies, forgotten in her haste, Anna-Meeka's plastic doll, its blue eyes staring at the sky, all of these things with their touch still warm on them were more than reminders of her own grief. Seeing it from this great, terrible distance she knew it was a loss for the country itself. Other losses would follow. Irretrievably. But tonight was hers alone.

The sound of the piano had stopped, the lights had gone out, the garden was steeped in darkness, for it was a moonless night. Small rustling noises, soft murmurings filled the air. Frogs croaked intermittently. All these noises, thought Grace hearing them afresh, turning her despair against the wall, would never be heard by them again. Far away, as though in answer, in a distant part of Colombo, came the sound of heavy gunfire, muffling the constant rhythm of the sea.

Thornton looked out of the window and shifted his legs. Opposite him, Savitha talked quietly to Anna-Meeka. They were all exhausted. High banks of grassy slopes, scattered with buttercups, flanked the railway line; late summer in all its glory. Railway dust, golden and abundant in the wonderful morning sunlight, obscured the view. The sky was a cloudless blue. Looking up, Thornton could see a small glider rising up with the thermals. He watched it until it disappeared from view. Every now and then a neat patchwork of wheat-combed fields flashed by.

"Mama, I'm thirsty!" said Anna-Meeka in her sing-song voice, waggling her head from side to side. She stared at the man sitting opposite until he looked away.

"Why can't I have a drink, Mama?" she asked.

She scratched her head with an enthusiasm and a single-mindedness that did not seem quite possible. The sound of the train was different from the sounds she was used to. She swung her legs in time to its beat.

"My head is scratchy," she said, adding in a voice that carried clearly across the compartment, "Do you think I've got head lice? Or have they died because it's cold in England?"

The man opposite looked at her again and Meeka scowled at him. Someone else further along the carriage sniggered. Savitha spoke, aware of the man's glances, knowing he was listening. She spoke softly in Sinhalese. Anna-Meeka, ignoring her, continued to scratch her head. Thornton bent his handsome profile towards his daughter. He smiled at her.

"Leave your head alone, Meeka," he said softly. "Your mama will wash it with soap when we get to our place in London."

"Why is that man looking at me?" asked Meeka, losing interest momentarily in her head, fixing the man with a limpid unblinking stare.

"Anna-Meeka," said Thornton sternly, "don't speak so loud. These people *all* understand English here! We're not at home now."

He turned back to the window and the boat train, hooting

at a level crossing, passed swiftly through the sunlit country-side with its black-and-white cows, its green public footpath signs, its small farm outbuildings, hurrying and clattering into a small tunnel, speeding onwards to London's Waterloo.

In the taxi, sandwiched between her parents and the small amount of luggage they had brought, Meeka caught her first glimpses of the city. London encased in summer, lit by the afternoon sun, washing the embankment and the pineapples on Lambeth Bridge with its golden glow. London, that place her parents had talked about so much, bringing her here, they said, because here they could give her all the things no longer possible to give her at home. London, thought Meeka, enchanted by what she saw, was beautiful! Huge buildings, their tops dipped in light, their sides covered in grime, were everywhere. The traffic swished richly, silently, on thick rubber tyres, on roads without the smallest pothole.

Traffic that behaved, thought Thornton in amazement. No bullock carts, no horns, no open-topped vehicles with radios blasting or vegetables spilling out. Why had Jacob not written about the silence? It was hard to imagine his brothers here, in this huge city. He had not seen Jacob for thirteen years, longer in the case of Christopher.

Too big, thought Savitha, shivering a little, and too fast. She had been frightened for days. She felt beaten.

They were over the bridge now, passing Lambeth Palace.

"Where're yer from then, mate?" asked the taxi driver, sliding back the hatch, addressing Thornton looking at him in the mirror.

Thornton started. What had the man said? Was he talking to them?

So Meeka told him, in her clear sing-song voice, liking the man instantly, liking his funny way of talking, jumbling all his words up together, wanting to make him talk some more, wishing she could talk like him.

"We're off the boat train, mate!" she said copying him, liking the sound of his laugh.

"Blimey, you're a caution, ain't yer, luv? Mum an' dad'll 'ave ter watch it. Ye'll 'ave ter watch 'er, guv!" he said addressing Thornton through the mirror, winking at him.

"Yes," said Thornton not knowing what on earth this man was talking about, but willing, very willing, to be helpful.

"Yes. We have just spent twenty-one days at sea, so my daughter is a little tired. We are all looking forward to a rest on dry land tonight."

And he nodded his head politely. His wife, clutching her bags, frowned nervously and whispered something in the child's ear. The black cab, symbol of all they had anticipated for so long, crossed and recrossed the river in a cunning dodge of the one-way system and drove past the school where Meeka would be going before depositing them at last at their front door. They had travelled seven thousand miles.

Then this is what they found. A little ground-floor flat (the estate agent had called it a garden flat) in a block of dirty Victorian houses, on a wide tree-lined street close to the cricket ground. Thornton brightened a little when he saw this.

"Aiyo! There is no veranda," said Savitha, struggling to keep the tears from her voice. She wanted to go home.

"Carpets!" said Meeka, dancing down the hallway, having kicked off her shoes and socks. She did not like wearing socks.

The rooms were gloomy, for the house faced west, and although it was only four in the afternoon darkness threatened. The de Silvas prowled around the flat, released from the captivity of twenty-one days, uncertain what to do next. The beds had piles of thick blankets folded neatly, waiting to be made up. Heavy fusty curtains lined the windows, ready to be drawn, ready to block out anything that passed for light. Dotted around were small metal stoves that Meeka's Uncle Jacob had warned them about. He had found them the flat, and put in Aladdin paraffin heaters for when it got cold.

"It's cold now," said Meeka, laughing, throwing herself on the unmade bed in what was to be her bedroom, waving her thin legs up in the air, banging them against the wall. The cold was exciting, it made the air smell of all sorts of foreign exciting things, things she did not know about but wanted to investigate. It muffled the sounds around her. The silence had a texture to it that made her wish she had a piano to play.

"There's a note here from Jacob," shouted Thornton from the kitchen. "He's coming over tomorrow with Christopher and he's left some food in the fridge."

"Yes," said Savitha pursing her lips together, showing the first spontaneous emotion since they had embarked on their journey, so that Meeka, sensing some interesting drama, put her legs down and sat up.

"Hmm, that bastard! Couldn't he have met us at the docks?"

She spoke softly, and Thornton, not hearing, replied, "Come and see what he has left in the fridge! All sorts of things. Butter wrapped in paper and fresh milk! Come here, Meeka, putha."

Curiously, Meeka went to see the strange cheeses, bread and something called liver pâté. Thornton set the yellow Formica table, found an old teapot, and pulled out the packet of tea they had packed. It was, he noticed, with a stab of quickly suppressed homesickness, from the valley where he had been born. For a moment Thornton struggled. The distance seemed infinite. His mother was no longer a bus ride away. How had the past arrived so quickly? Grief, unexpected and sharp, tightened around him. There was a bottle of milk with a shiny gold lid on it, a box of dark chocolate. A feast.

"No, wait," said Savitha suddenly. "Wait, I'll get one of our teapots."

She unpacked one of their boxes, pulling at everything, so that the smells of sandalwood and ginger tumbled out and moved around the room. The sun had vanished. Had there really been sunlight when they were on the train? Or had they imagined it? Anna-Meeka shivered. The tune in her head had gone. It was suddenly too cold and her mother looked small and pinched. Her mother looked as though she was about to cry.

"Can I have some rice?" Anna-Meeka asked firmly. "Rice with *malu* curry?"

The brothers arrived the next day. Memories followed them into the room. Distance framed their childhood, sharpening its focus. Sentiments rushed in like warm air, for the moment anyway. Then Thornton smiled. No surprises here of course, nothing to write home about, thought Jacob, wryly. Everything was as it always was, in that respect at least. There were other shocks. In that swift first greeting, Jacob and Christopher saw their mother sharply defined in Thornton's face. Had he always looked like her? wondered Christopher, momentarily taken aback. He felt the angry stirring of emotions he thought he had left behind. Home tugged insistently. For a moment no one could speak. Savitha had been cooking, it was not much, but the smells were of home. Even twenty-one days and an expanse of water had not altered the smells they once knew. Christopher looked closely at his sister-in-law. The last time he had seen Thornton he had been in the thralls of Hildegard. Savitha seemed very different from *her*. Well, well, well, thought Christopher, so the film star played it safe in the end. I wonder what this one's like. His lips twitched. Savitha, serving them tea in their mother's bone china, realised that no one noticed or cared.

"Here," said Thornton, "have some of the *vadi* Frieda made."

Somehow the sight of Frieda's present, prepared for this exact moment, made him unable to say more. Anna-Meeka looked at her father curiously. He was behaving in a very odd way. Was he going to cry? She helped herself to the *vadi*, ignoring Savitha's frown. Christopher was the first to recover. He considered Thornton with satisfaction. He's much blacker than me, he thought, trying not to laugh.

Thornton was thinking too. He's fat, he thought, mildly surprised, and not so black! And there's something different about him. What is it? Christopher, noticing the look, patted his stomach and grinned. He *was* indeed fatter. The lean hurt look had left him, vanished into an unattainable past; the despair so transparent at Kamala's death had hardened into something else entirely.

"Hmm," muttered Savitha, folding her lips. She had just noticed a bottle of whisky in her brother-in-law's coat pocket. But Christopher, giving her a challenging look, burst out laughing. It seemed Thornton had found himself a conventional woman. It was only to be expected. The old spark of jealousy, never fully dampened, flared up momentarily. Thornton *always* managed to get everything he wanted: an education, a wife, a child.

"I need a drink," Christopher said out loud. "I need a drink to get through this bloody reunion."

Thornton frowned but Christopher, ignoring him, turned to Savitha.

"I say," he said, "give me a glass, will you? I want to drink to your arrival!"

And he took the bottle out of his pocket and offered it to his sister-in-law with a mocking bow. In spite of himself, Thornton was surprised. How had Christopher, always so silent at home, become this confident?

"Can I have another *vadi*?" asked Meeka, getting bored with the atmosphere. She helped herself to three.

"Anna-Meeka!" said Savitha. She spoke more sharply than she meant because she was embarrassed. "Don't take *three*. What's the matter with you, child?"

"I'm hungry," said Meeka, stuffing *vadi* into her mouth quickly.

Hmm, thought Jacob who had been observing it all from a point of some detachment, I can see there's going to be trouble here. He blinked owlishly, hoping the new arrivals would not cause him any headaches. He knew what Thornton was like. Did Savitha know about Hildegard?

"Do I look like my photographs, Uncle Christopher?" asked Meeka suddenly, smiling up at him, sensing her mother's dislike.

"More tea, Jacob?" asked Savitha sweetly, holding out her hand for his cup.

Looking around at his family, Thornton was confused. They seemed strangers. It made him weary. Jacob looked disapproving. Thornton hoped they would not start any unsuitable stories from his past. There was the child to think about now. What did any of his brothers understand about family life? Christopher was not listening to any of them. He was looking at Anna-Meeka, seeing her properly for the first time. But she's wonderful, he thought with delight. How on earth did these two idiots produce her? She should be *mine*!

"How many years is it since you three met?" asked Savitha for something to say, as if she didn't know.

There was nothing impressive about the de Silva men, she decided. There were too many of them, in her opinion, crowding into this small sitting room, standing all together, just like a clan. Savitha wrinkled her nose with distaste. It was clear they needed their mother to keep them in order. Silently, Savitha gave them more tea.

"I love London! I can't wait to go to school here," said Meeka. And she danced between them and their long shadows.

They tried to pick up where their letters had left off.

"So poor Jasper's dead," Christopher observed.

"Jasper!" cried Meeka, delighted, wanting to talk about him.

Yes, that's it! thought Jacob, who had been puzzling over it. The child reminded him of Jasper. Something about the way she fixed them with her eye, something about her darting movements. It was worrying. They would have to be careful, speak guardedly if necessary.

But something had changed overnight. Summer had moved swiftly, even as they slept, into a landscape chilled at the edges and tinted with the subtle unmistakable smell of autumn. The early-morning sunlight on the grass looked damp. Surely it was not possible? Thornton ventured timidly out into this cataclysmic change. The breeze was sharp and unwelcoming. He walked on the neat grey paving slabs carpeted by golden plane leaves that fell at his feet. His feet, too, seemed to belong in some strange land, clad in unfamiliar shoes, walking on unfamiliar missions.

"How do I get to South Walk?" he asked the girl in the library. The girl's hair fell like a curtain of gold, ramrod straight, silky as the cashmere sari his wife had worn on their wedding day. Tossing it back from her face, moving threads of it from her mouth, she laughed a little.

"South Walk? Do you mean Southwark?" she said.

She was unprepared for his smile. Lighting up the corners of her desk, alighting on her card indexes, softly tinting the long high windows until it seemed as though strains of some unidentifiable music filtered through them.

Why, it was sheer poetry, thought the girl, confused, watching as the smile hovered over the bunch of ochre-pink chrysanthemums. She had bought them on impulse, at the tube station that morning, never knowing how the day, this ordinary day, would present itself to her, like a bunch of glorious late-summer flowers. Exactly like the flowers, changed by the light, so too was her day altered by that smile. Sensing this, Thornton felt gladness flutter faintly, a small bird of continuity, the feathery down of hope, in his heart. Clearing a path through the leaves he headed for the river and his interview.

Later, returning home in the gloom, marvelling at how swiftly the night descended, he told Savitha he had got the job.

"Now at least we will have a proper income," he said proudly.

Savitha did not answer. She was preoccupied with the jar of seeni sambals from home, a casualty of the journey, covered in white inedible fur. She had been saving it for this very occasion and now she had no contribution to the celebration. So she was silent. The journey had left her disorientated and defeated. She had not expected to feel this way. In the short time that they had been here her homesickness had increased rather than lessened. She carried it heavily in her jacket, bound tightly in place by her sari, wrapped close against her breast, out of sight from the rapidly cooling air. The kitchen smelt of paraffin.

"I must trim the wick," said Thornton, thinking over his day, remembering the girl with ramrod hair, smiling so that Anna-Meeka, watching him curiously, asked, "What are you smiling about, Daddy?"

Tomorrow was the beginning of the new school term. Meeka had already visited her school. It was nice. There was a carpet in the headmaster's office but nowhere else.

"Because of the mud," the headmaster had said. "It would be too difficult to keep a carpet clean."

Meeka knew about mud. Mud came with the monsoon. But then the rains went away, and so did the mud. Was it going to rain here all the time? Was it going to rain and be cold at the

same time? When? When was this going to happen? The headmaster had smiled.

"Her English is very fluent," he said to Meeka's mother.
"We'll try her in the top class to start with." Then he had
turned to Meeka. "The weather is wonderful this year in
England, Meeka. It is what we call an Indian summer."

He had gazed gently at the child seeing the brightness within her face. He hoped she would settle but he could see it
would not be easy. She was rather exotic for this part of
Brixton, he thought. And so he chose her class with care.

The night before her school term started the brothers called
round. Anna-Meeka had gone to bed, much to Christopher's
disappointment. She was still exhausted from the journey.

"Here," said Christopher, pushing some money into
Savitha's hand. "Buy her some chocolates from me."

"Now, you must be firm with her," Jacob began when they
sat down to eat. "You know Brixton is a dangerous place. The
area is full of working-class people. You'll see what I mean
after a while."

"What's wrong with working-class people, ah?" asked
Christopher challengingly, helping himself to Savitha's excellent fish curry. At least the conventional woman could cook, he
thought. He paused and glared at Jacob.

"Don't start, men," Jacob said hastily, catching Savitha's
eye. "I'm talking about the child's education. It's important
that she only mixes with the right people."

Christopher opened his mouth to speak, then changed his
mind and laughed instead. Without waiting to be asked, he
helped himself to more rice. Once again Thornton was struck
by his brother's lack of manners. At home they had waited to
be served. But Christopher seemed to have forgotten his
upbringing. It made Thornton uneasy. And added to his homesickness.

"I say, Anna-Meeka is very clever," he told them, changing

the subject. "Ask Savitha. She's a little difficult, you know, but clever all the same."

They ate in silence.

"She will probably study medicine one day," he added casually.

Jacob glanced up. He had heard all about his niece from Frieda's letters. He could tell they all thought the child was some sort of genius.

"I've lived here longer than you," he said, at last, finishing his food and taking a gulp of water. He had not eaten anything so spicy for a long time and it was burning his mouth. "This isn't Colombo, you know." He hesitated, wanting to find the right words, trying to make Thornton understand. "Don't have too many hopes, men. In *this* country ambition alone isn't enough. You need much more than ambition here."

Unable to say what was needed, he paused. "You have no idea what being a foreigner in Britain is like, men," he said, adding confusingly, "Even going to the moon means nothing here in Brixton. Have you heard of the Swinging Sixties, for instance? Hah?"

Thornton looked at him blankly and Jacob nodded at him grimly. It was patently clear that the Swinging Sixties had not entered Thornton's consciousness yet, much less Meeka's. As far as Jacob could see, hell was merely in abeyance.

"Wait, men, I tell you, things aren't that easy," he advised.

It was perfectly clear to Jacob, from the little he had seen, the child would need a firm hand. Well, he decided, conscious of unspoken hostilities, he would say no more. He had given them fair warning and in any case it was only marginally his business. Christopher stretched his legs and yawned. Then he gave a small whistle of admiration. He had enjoyed eating the chili-hot curry. Thornton scowled at him.

"Look—" he began angrily, but Jacob held up his hands. He had not meant to start any arguments.

"I'm only here in an advisory capacity, men," he said, backing off. "I promised Mummy I'd keep an eye on things. Until you settle down, that's all."

It was time to leave. He hoped he would not be needed too often. For Jacob was a busy man. His time was strictly limited as, unknown to any of them, he had recently acquired a girlfriend and therefore had various plans of his own.

When they left Savitha cleared the dishes.

"At least they liked the food," she said finally.

Twenty-one days at sea had left her longing to cook with ingredients from home. But she felt exhausted and confused with the effort. She felt utterly tired in a way she never had before. And worse, she felt an alien among the de Silva brothers. Struggling with these emotions she told Thornton crossly, "In future, don't start talking about Meeka to them." Adding, "What do they know about children?"

Thornton grunted. Although he agreed with her he would not admit it. The discussion over Anna-Meeka's future worried him more than he was prepared to say.

"We are here because the predictions of war have become an actuality," he reminded Savitha. "Anna-Meeka will have every opportunity in this country. She *will* become a doctor, I tell you."

Savitha folded her lips. Worry buzzed around her head, moving pointlessly, like flies. Had they taken so momentous a step too lightly? Should they have waited a little longer? Surely only time could tell how clever Anna-Meeka *really* was. Time was what they all needed.

"It's too early to say what she'll become. We're from another culture; we have to settle first," she told Thornton. She did not ask how long this might take. She did not want to think of that. "I want her to be happy," she said slowly. "That's what's important. I can't bear it, if all we've done is bring her to an unhappy place." She struggled to express her own hopes for Anna-Meeka in the face of Thornton's confusion. "I want her to sing again," she said abruptly, feeling her eyes prick with unexpected tears. "She used to sing all the time. I don't know if you've noticed but she stopped as soon as we were on the boat."

"Sing?" asked Thornton, looking at her amazed. "Why of course she won't stop singing! What are you talking about? And if she studies hard and becomes a doctor, of course she'll be happy." He frowned, feeling both annoyed and uneasy. Savitha had a knack for unnerving him.

"Perhaps she'll want to do music," Savitha said tentatively.

She knew nothing about music. All she knew was that the nuns in Ceylon had said her daughter was musical. They had told Grace that Meeka had a very good ear and could play any tune she heard. Savitha had caught the tail end of Alicia's performances, in the days when music had still filled the house in Station Road. Now she hesitated.

"She may be as musical as Alicia, you know?" she said.

But at this Thornton shook his head vehemently and stood up.

"No, no," he said firmly. "Not music, men. Let's not talk about that. Think of my poor sister's life now, will you? She has nothing now the music's gone. Not music, Savitha. For enjoyment, yes, but not in any other way. If Alicia had had another profession, if she had been a doctor, she would be working now, going out, meeting people. She would be able to—"

He broke off and clamped his mouth shut. Savitha fell silent. She had never understood why Thornton connected Sunil's death with Alicia's music.

It was not the time to argue. It was up to the child, to show them what she really wanted. So thought Savitha as she embroidered her daughter's name on her socks and her PE clothes. So thought Savitha as she checked on the sleeping child, removing the new school tie from her hand, only to have it tucked under the pillow again by Thornton when he looked in on her later.

It took nearly three weeks to reach them. The servant brought in the post while they were having breakfast. There were four letters. The sight of them filled the day with translucent light. Which one should they open first?

"Thornton's," said Frieda.

"No, let's see what the little one makes of the place," chuckled Aloysius.

I start my new school TOMORROW! Anna-Meeka had written. *And I'm going to make lots and lots of English friends. Please could Auntie Frieda send some more vadi so I can give some to them.*

The child seems a bit of a handful, wrote Jacob. *Thornton is right to be worried. I told him he'd need to be firm with her. This isn't Ceylon. Things are different here.*

"Nonsense!" laughed Frieda. "Thornton will never be able to refuse her anything."

"Savitha will have to keep them all in order," chuckled Grace.

"Why are they so worried? She's in England," Aloysius said. "It's the children in this country who we should worry about. What's the matter with that boy?"

The little one is an absolute delight, wrote Christopher. *So clever, so inquisitive, so funny, so like Jasper really! As for Thornton and his wife, I can't imagine what they have in common of course. Meeka is certainly the best thing this family's ever had! She'll be the one to succeed in life, where all of us failed. She should have all the opportunities we did not. As far as I can, I shall make sure of that.*

Christopher has changed, wrote Thornton rather non-committally. *I've no idea what has happened to him but he is very strange. He seems fond of Meeka, which is worrying too. I hope he won't start talking politics with her.*

"Oh listen to this," read Frieda, laughing, "they're squabbling over Anna-Meeka already!"

I haven't heard Frieda laugh for such a long time, thought Grace, glancing at the empty place set for Alicia. Her elder daughter seldom arose before the afternoon.

"She'll shake them all up," said Aloysius, enjoying the conversation hugely, glad to see Grace look so happy.

He misses them too, thought Grace. Aloysius looked frail. He had developed a persistent cough and was easily tired. After Sunil's death his hair had whitened dramatically. These days, he drank less, and because of the intermittent curfew seldom went out.

"D'you remember how we used to be?" she asked them both, smiling a little. "All together, in this house, milling around, coming and going, talking, arguing. Remember how this place was filled with music?"

They nodded, remembering. It was hard to believe.

"No one could keep the boys in for long," Frieda said, wistfully.

"And then Thornton went and married that woman, Hildegard," Aloysius reminded them, shaking his head.

They burst out laughing. They could laugh about it now.

"Mummy, you were so angry," Frieda told her. "We thought you'd be angry forever!"

"Poor Hildegard," agreed Grace. "I wonder what became of her."

What's become of any of us? she thought later when she was alone. How have we come to this? What would you make of me now, Vijay, if you were here, if you could see me? Could you have predicted any of this on that terrible night before the eclipse? Now you are all gone, Sunil, my sons, and Alicia too, in her way.

Outside a few monkeys chattered angrily in the trees. They had taken up residence in the small coconut grove nearby. The owners of the grove had tried and failed to have them caught. The monkeys were raw-faced and defiant. They were outlaws.

There was a rumour they had a fever-carrying disease and the owners of the coconut grove were frantic to have them caught before they bit someone. But the monkeys did not care. They laughed and pulled faces at the passers-by. A man had been sent from the army barracks to scare them away. He had fired a shot but they had simply raced off, swinging across the branches as they ran. The army man had lost his temper. Not wanting to be beaten by monkeys, he had fired away at them all morning but with no success. All morning he stood in the raging heat firing into the horizon, unable to see the pointlessness of it. Those who saw him dared not laugh for he might have turned the gun on them.

"Fools," said Grace, closing the shutters against the noise.

"I will write to them," decided Frieda. "I will tell them about the monkeys."

She would not tell them about the Tamil boy who had died yesterday in the centre of Colombo. He had strapped some explosives to his chest and blown himself up at the Fort. Six other people had died with him. The boy had been the same age as Anna-Meeka.

"I'm ready!" said Meeka, coming into her parents' bedroom in her school uniform. White shirt, navy blue pleated skirt, sweater, long white socks, new polished shoes. A huge chorus of birds had woken her. The sounds were very different from the birds she knew; softer, insistent in a different way. She hummed quietly to herself.

"I can't do my tie," she said holding it out.

It was five-thirty in the morning. A chink of light showed through the dull mustard curtains. Thornton woke with a start. The street lights had not been turned off yet. He waited for the barrage of sounds to assail his ears, the crows, the servant girl using her coconut scrapers, discarding the shells one by one hollowly on the ground, the sound of the fisherman crying "*malu, malu,*" dogs barking, bicycle bells, whistles. He waited for the lurking heat outside the darkened room to come in, ready to pounce at the merest hint of movement, making itself felt, flooding the room with sweat. He waited, his heart pounding, but all he could feel, all he could hear was the sound of his daughter's humming. Close by, Savitha was snoring gently. Thornton had been dreaming of the girl with the ramrod hair. She had been smiling at him, moving threads of gold away from her mouth. He had been showing her around the Fort before the curfew, they were eating *thosai* and drinking king coconut. The girl kept smiling, telling him how wonderful his poems were, and Thornton was just reaching out to touch that great shining mane of cashmere gold with his long sensitive fingers, when Anna-Meeka woke him. He groaned, pulling the eiderdown away from his chin. Could a man not have a bit of peace, even in his own bed?

"Can you do my tie," said Meeka firmly, tugging at the bed covers, soaking him in cold air, determined.

The dawn chorus had got louder and she hummed louder too.

"It's five-thirty in the morning!" said Thornton, squinting at his watch.

Regretfully, promising to return at a later date, he put Miss Ramrod away. You understand, he told her, it's nothing personal, nothing to do with how I feel, but it is just not possible to have any conversation when my daughter is around. She is a fearsome presence, you know, a barrier to all carnal pleasure. Miss Ramrod smiled, still removing hair from her mouth (how much hair did the girl have? Thornton wondered fleetingly), and swiftly faded. She knew when she was beaten.

Later, even Meeka could smell the change in the air; a subtle shift here and there, some traces of dew on the uncovered earth, soft mist on the horizon. Thornton, walking her to the new school, bleary-eyed from his early start, felt it and was pierced with a sharp longing for the hills of his childhood. Meeka felt it and associated it forever with the first day of term, new pencils, ruler, rubber, resolutions. All across the street were children walking to school, calling out to their friends, laughing, chewing bubblegum. Meeka was entranced by them. She skipped along beside her father, singing softly to herself. At the gate her father kissed her goodbye. He smiled, a tall handsome man, waving to his daughter as she disappeared into the crowd. Several mothers noticed him and would look for him again in vain. Tomorrow Meeka would walk to school alone.

But, in spite of the early start, in spite of all the eager anticipation, the day did not go well. She could not remember when it began to go wrong. Was it during break when she could not drink the cold milk they were given? Was it the awful lunch, which for some reason was called "dinner," or perhaps it was when she called the "dinner ladies" the servants and everyone shouted at her? They had offered her something they called pineapple but it had borne no resemblance to any fruit she knew. Clearly the pineapples that grew in England were a different kind. Perhaps it was simply the fact that she had no one to talk to all day, no one to have as a best friend that had made the day go so badly. This very first day at her new school in England, which she had longed and waited for, from as far back as she could remember. In the afternoon she wondered what her granny might be doing, in her beautiful house by the sea. She had wanted to tell someone about her granny, but there was no one to tell. The tune she had been humming repeated itself over and over again in her head. It reminded her of the sea she had left behind.

When the bell finally rang, she was lost in thought staring at the floor, watching it dissolve before her eyes, for something was wrong. No, thought Anna-Meeka, *everything* was wrong, from the way she spoke, to what she said, and how she looked.

It dawned on her at that moment, in a flash of piercing insight, with belated astonishment coming from the morning's solitude, that she was very different from these large, fair-skinned children.

Savitha was waiting at the gate. Anna-Meeka could see her sari, tea-green and yellow, through the railings. She was standing alone, away from the other parents. She looked cold. Meeka swallowed. Her mother looked wrong too, as well as unhappy.

"Did you enjoy your day?" asked Savitha.

"Yes," said Meeka, walking hurriedly on, pulling her by the hand, moving as fast as she could from the school building, the teacher on playground duty and all the throngs of children.

"I'm hungry," she said. "Can I have some rice when we get back?"

She had nearly said "get back home," but somehow, what with one thing and another, the word "home" was beginning to confuse her too.

12.

There was nothing to be said. They were here to stay. Having finally unpacked all their luggage, Savitha threw away the things that had mould on them or were broken or stained by all the blood-red spices. The moment the trunks were opened, great clouds of powdery smells were released into the air, leaving traces of pungent condiments. She sat with the old newspapers that lined the trunks, reading about events from months ago. Already the paper was torn and yellowed. Here was a photograph of the murdered Prime Minister; there was another of a saffron robe splattered with blood. A review of a piano recital said the air-conditioning had failed that night but the Beethoven was unbelievably beautiful. A report of the New Year's festivities stated they were sub-dued. Like us, thought Savitha.

She felt desperate. Her loneliness frightened her. Being on her own in the house for many hours, with nothing to do and no one to talk to until Meeka returned from school, her thoughts circled around the past. She had often been lonely in the orphanage, but she had been younger and in those days she had been fearless. This feeling was different. Ceylon appeared to belong in another life. Savitha felt as though she had been cast adrift, abandoned in ways she had not thought possible. All that she had lost appeared before her, vast and incommu-nicable. Anna-Meeka no longer wanted Savitha to walk her back from school and Thornton, when he returned from work, was too exhausted to speak much. Savitha watched as her once cheerful family became slowly more preoccupied and with-drawn. She was bewildered and wanted only to spend her days dreaming of the time when she used to pick her daughter up from school in Colombo, returning home after a hot dusty train journey with Meeka in her white school uniform, a hard white hat keeping out the sun. In that other, extinct life.

"Mama!" Anna-Meeka would yell as soon as she came into view at the school gate. "Can we go to Elephant House, and have a Lanka lime?"

They would walk towards the station, Savitha holding her sari high above the filth on the road, Meeka begging for some ambarella, or mango rolled in chili powder and salt, from some filthy fruit sellers. Why had her daughter always wanted to eat from the dirtiest stall? wondered Savitha, smiling at the memo-ry. How impossibly difficult it had been to drag the complain-ing Anna-Meeka onto the hot crowded train, to even find a seat.

But then, thought Savitha, dreamily, sitting on the carpet, watching the flames from the paraffin heater, the train would begin to move and there below them, a little way from the rocks, would be the sea. Miles and miles of endless golden sand, miles and miles of blistering beach. Only mad dogs would be out on it. And the sea would swish and the cool breeze would waft in through the carriage and Meeka would stop scowling and grin and sit there, with the sweat trickling down from under her hat, her sweet small face streaked with dirt, demanding to know when Thornton would be home to take her for a swim. Thus remembered Savitha, feeling the salty spray against her face, and the sense of bereavement all around.

Nevertheless, Savitha was nothing if not resourceful. She had not lived all her life in that convent orphanage without a strong feeling of self-preservation. She had, after all, that famously sharp mind of hers and she realised dimly that it was time to use it. One morning she came to a decision. She had, with some difficulty, made a cake. She had begun to understand that the Cambridge Certificate in English and those brilliant pieces to the newspapers back home were as nothing here in Brixton. Shopping for the sugar and the flour, the eggs, the butter, and then afterwards negotiating the unexpectedly well-trained traffic (would it suddenly lunge out at her, would a bullock cart appear from nowhere to knock her down and break her eggs?), all needed care and concentration. She was exhausted by the effort of venturing forth, of contact with people, even before she started baking. While she had been buying the ingredients at the corner shop, she had caught sight of a notice in the window. It said: "WANTED. SEAMSTRESS FOR PIECEWORK. SMALL FACTORY. FLEXIBLE HOURS. 195 RAILTON ROAD, SW9."

Later on, in the afternoon, and before Meeka came home from school (why *did* she insist on walking home alone?), she was going for a job interview. She had told no one. For who was there to tell? In any case her husband lived in a mysterious world of his own, and the child could not be counted on.

Sewing was something Savitha could do. Often during those Cambridge Certificate years sewing had been her recreation, her right arm occasionally turning the wheel of her Singer, her foot pedalling furiously. It was what she did when she had a lot to think about, and, without a doubt, she had much on her mind at the moment. Changing into her brightest red-and-orange sari, she left the house, caught a bus (so like the ones back home, but smarter, newer), and headed in the direction of Brixton. The bus drove past the arcade and a crockery stall caught her eye. It was piled high with a wonderful array of blue-and-white willow-patterned china. Another stall flashed by. It had trousers hanging up all over it, flapping in the breeze. Savitha wondered curiously what it would be like to wear a pair. The bus passed under the bridge. The stalls here were run by black people. Savitha watched them curiously. They sold a confusion of interesting vegetables. A streak of red, a splash of dark green leaves, the sun-baked saffron insides of fruit, all flashed past her, jostling happily alongside stalls of apples piled high, and tight pale cabbages. Savitha's heart missed a beat. These black people appeared to be conversing easily with the white people on the nearby stalls. Even from a distance she could see their ease of manner. The experiences of the past weeks had almost overwhelmed her, shutting down the desire for analytical thought, but sitting here on the bus, lulled by its rocking movement and without the fear of bombs or gunfire, Savitha felt a sudden unexpected interest in her surroundings. The bus stopped at the terminus and she walked, A–Z in hand, towards Railton Road. So many closed faces. Here oppression descended once again so that it was something of a relief to climb the narrow stairs of 195, past the dingy passageway with "Dora's Place" and "Sally" on the doors until at last she reached the door marked "Rosenberg's Retail Studio."

He's Jewish, thought Savitha, looking at the man, shaking his hand and looking at the rows and rows of women, mostly pale, one or two of them black. Fleetingly she thought of Hildegard. The room was huge and high-ceilinged with large windows divided into many panes of glass. The lower ones were covered over in white paint.

"We don't want distractions, do we!" said Mr. Rosenberg heartily, seeing her look at them.

"Come into my office," he said, shouting above the noise of the sewing machines, eyeing her up, taking in her sari, her open-toed shoes, her feet without any stockings. Clearly this would not do. He made a clucking noise.

"One o'clock until four p.m. Starting tomorrow, promptly," he said, standing legs apart, tilting backwards so as to balance the weight of his stomach. "You will have to wear trousers. D'you have any? Well, you'll have to get some. We can't have all this." He waved his hand in the direction of her sari. "It wouldn't be safe with all the machinery. Besides," he added jovially, almost as an afterthought, "there's no heating here in the winter so you will get a trifle cold!"

And he laughed a long, long laugh that followed her back all the way down the stairs, echoing out onto the street, ringing in her ears all the way to her front door.

Full of energy, she put some rice on to boil. Next she scraped two carrots and one of those peculiar things called parsnips. She fried some coriander and some cumin from her precious spice jar and then, as a treat, she added a little of the fast-diminishing dried Maldive fish, bought specially from Wallisinga & Sons in Pettah. The hot smell hissed and spluttered, filling the kitchen and swarming out through the extractor fan. Out it went through the communal garden, over Mr. Smith's vegetable patch and through his wife's kitchen window so that Mrs. Smith, sniffing the air, could not think what on earth to make of these new neighbours with all their curious smells. Savitha stirred the saucepan vigorously, adding onions, garlic and small chilies sliced diagonally, a dollop of tomato sauce, some chopped lamb, coconut milk and then the vegetables. There, it was done. She lifted the lid off the rice, fluffing it with a fork so each grain gleamed white, and the hot fragrant steam rose, engulfing her with a wonderful sense of comfort like no other. Meeka would be home soon. She would be pleased to have a bowl of hot rice.

While she waited she decided to reorganise the cupboard that held her collection of bone china, miraculously unharmed by the journey. But when she opened the cupboard, hidden memories tumbled out, competing with each other. In the flurry of leaving, Savitha had not paid much attention and only now did she see the extent of Grace's generosity. Her mother-in-law had given her the best, most treasured pieces of her china. Savitha gazed at them, unexpected tears springing up.

Some of the china was much older than the rest. All of it would need protecting from Thornton who, unused to the task, was clumsy with the washing-up.

"I want you to keep them for Anna-Meeka," Grace had said. It had been late afternoon, everyone, even the servants, had been resting. Savitha could still hear her mother-in-law's voice clearly, could see her standing in the shuttered dining room.

"It's all I can give her," Grace had said. She had smiled, but her eyes were unfathomable. "Everything else, the house, the land, all of it was sold off years ago, you know, Savitha. All I have of any value is the china."

And Savitha had answered, "It is enough. I will keep it safe, I promise. I am its custodian!" With new admiration she recognised Grace's courage. Dimly she saw what these treasures, taken for granted by her children, meant to her mother-in-law. Things of beauty in a hostile land.

"In my safe keeping," she murmured to the empty room. "Until Anna-Meeka is old enough to have them."

Loss scattered like drops of rain around her. She imagined the grand old house in the hills, not as she had witnessed it on that terrible trip, but as it must have been long ago, in its heyday. When the de Silva women, wearing gorgeous cashmere saris, ate Tamil sweetmeats piled on these Hartley Green plates, and drank tea from W. T. Copeland cups. Lost in her daydream, Savitha stared at the flamboyant Royal Doulton dinner service, the pale Wedgwood. Silent receptacles of memory; witnesses to a vanished way of life. Here were the tea plates on which Sunil had been served petits fours. The touch of his hands remaining long after he had gone. Here in the cupboard in Brixton. Who could have imagined such a journey? Holding the tea-rose cups high up to the light, Savitha felt as though she was cradling her own fragile existence. Fiercely, stacking the lily-of-the-valley tureens, she decided, I will *never* stop using them. I will *never* allow Meeka to forget her home. A faint scent of straw from the ship's packaging filled the air, engulfing her in a terrible wave of sadness. As if in response, the sun broke through a cloud, exposing the dirt on the windows from many years of winter neglect, now unreachably high.

She did not tell Thornton about her job until the next morning. If she had wanted to surprise him she did. She wore her new slacks and made the breakfast. It was a brave decision and at first Thornton did not even notice. He was looking very handsome in his new work suit. The table was set; all seemed normal. An English breakfast, with toast, marmalade, string hoppers, last night's lamb curry, tomato ketchup and a kettle of water for the tea. There were his mother's pink-and-white cups and saucers, gold-rimmed and delicate. As far as Thornton could see, everything was as usual. Why should he suddenly look more closely? Why should he have to keep an eye on everybody *all* the time? He knocked loudly on the wall of his daughter's bedroom.

"Meeka," he said, "Meeka, get up. You'll be late for school."

Letting out a small sound of fury, Anna-Meeka thumped out of bed and shot straight out of her room. She glared at her father who was about to bang on her wall again. Then she stopped, and stared at her mother. Thornton went back to his toast with its coating of thick-cut marmalade. He was reading the newspaper.

"There's something here about Ceylon," he said to his wife. "You know, you should start writing for the papers here." And he held out his cup for more tea.

"What are you wearing?" asked Meeka dubiously.

Savitha eyed her daughter. The good thing about Anna-Meeka, she decided with satisfaction, was that she *always* noticed everything. But she did not say this.

"Hmm?" asked Thornton, not looking up. "I'm wearing my new suit of course, for work. Now hurry up and get ready."

He picked up another of the newspapers he had bought that morning. He was trying to decide which paper to take regularly. Christopher had said he should only buy the *Guardian* but Thornton had no intention of taking his advice untested. He wanted to check out all the possibilities for his future poems. It would be a pity to lose the momentum he had almost gained back home. Meeka stared at her mother.

"Mama!" she shrieked, suddenly wide awake and horrified to see her mother's legs evident in this way. "You can't go out like that."

"Aha!" said Savitha triumphantly, waggling her head from side to side. "Good morning, everyone. So finally someone speaks! My husband is blind but thankfully my daughter has inherited her sight from me. Well, I'm exceedingly sorry, men," she said, addressing the dining room in general, "in case you're interested, I have got a job!"

And she went back to pouring the tea into their lovely bone-china cups. But it was not that simple. Whatever made her think it would be? Later on, even though she was busy, there was plenty of time for her homesickness to return. Mr. Rosenberg had put her in the corner of the room, a little away from the rising and the falling of machines, the movement of the pedals beating the air like wings and the sound of scissors against cloth. She sat working, her own rhythm out of step with the rest of them. A small exotic seabird, stranded on a narrow spit of land, her wings closed. Sewing together this thing called denim: piece against piece, raw edge against raw edge. She wore black slacks.

Outside, the last fragments of a late-October sunshine gathered together for one final salute, one last display of warmth of the Indian summer, turning the afternoon, pivoting slowly, lifting up the edges of the plane leaves so they gave the appearance of being young and tender.

The green is so different here, thought Savitha, raising her face to the last of the sun. Soft sap green, lacking the sharpness of tropical colour. Muted just like the birds in this place, she thought. Caught below the tideline of the whitewashed windowpane, Savitha could see very little, working silently, bent over the cloth, words running like music through her head. An idea for an article was taking shape but it was too early to say where it might lead. To a random harvest maybe, or nowhere, perhaps?

In the beginning the women she worked with had tried to be friendly, but after she had overcome the business of understanding their speech she could find no point of common reference between them. She had been coming to the sweatshop for nearly a month now. When they were not working furiously, racing against the clock, the women gathered together in groups for their break, going outside for a cigarette, catching the last of the glorious autumn light, chatting, laughing even. Savitha was astonished, what was there to laugh about?

In the end they left her alone, thinking her stuck-up, having their breaks without her, cigarettes and mugs of tea in hand. Their conversation drifted backwards and forwards and again Savitha noticed how easily the black women fitted in. They were always teasing Mr. Rosenberg. Savitha did not know what to make of this either and, with no one to confide in, began every evening at home to write some notes of her own. Thornton, pretending to read the newspapers, eyed her slyly and was relieved. He hated her working in the factory. It made him ashamed and angry.

"What would my mother say if she knew?" he was always asking her. "What would Frieda think?"

Savitha refused to comment. Privately Thornton felt very unhappy. The woman he had married was changing. We no longer laugh together as we used to, he thought, puzzled, feeling helpless in the face of Savitha's stubbornness. So that every evening, hiding behind his newspaper, he watched her as she scribbled furiously. Clearly she was going back to writing. With any luck she would leave this stupid job, get out of these completely unsuitable clothes, and go back to behaving as a wife and mother should. This flat is too small, fretted Thornton. We're all on top of each other here.

Savitha, unaware of any of this, continued to work out her own confusions. Yesterday afternoon, during one of the short and difficult-to-negotiate tea breaks, two new recruits were introduced to them. Indian women both of them, wearing baggy red silk trousers, their hair was heavily oiled with ghee and plaited along the length of their backs. Looped gold earrings and startling fluorescent bangles moved discordantly on their arms. Mr. Rosenberg introduced them first to the group and then singled out Savitha.

"There you go, Savinta," he said. "I've got a couple of your countrymen so you can be 'appy. Don't say I don't give you nuffin!" He laughed a little nervously. For "Savinta," as he mistakenly called her, was not like his usual ladies. With her silent efficiency, her fluent (though heavily accented) English and her inscrutable stare, she was a mystery to Rosenberg.

"She's a bleedin' snob, ain't she!" observed Doris, his longest-standing employee and foreman by default.

Rosenberg was inclined to agree with her. "Savinta" unnerved him.

"What's she got to be a snob about, then? She's no better than the others."

Having hired the other Asians with the hope they were as efficient as Savitha, he herded them together in a little bunch, away from everyone else.

"All together, keep you 'appy," he told Savitha, smiling with a heartiness he did not feel.

Savitha stared at him with astonishment. The women were *Indian*. What did Rosenberg mean? They were Indian coolies, probably from a plantation rather like the ones the de Silvas once owned. On that last trip upcountry Aloysius had talked about the ancient rulers who once lived in the palaces. Grace and Thornton had shown her the lakes where Grace's mother had grown the flamingo-pink lotus flowers. They had stayed at a wonderful rest house and listened to the roar of a nearby waterfall. The air had smelt of soft rainwater and tea.

"All this," Aloysius had told her, proudly sweeping his hand across the view, "all this belonged to us once, you know, Savitha."

The younger, idealistic Savitha had stared at the old filigree carvings, the sacred statues softened by lichen and daily offerings of flowers, and had argued hotly over the injustice of such privilege existing hand in hand with the coolies working on the hillside. But now, *now* she felt torn. Now she was no longer certain of those beliefs. Something puzzling was happening to her principles. More and more since her entry into this country, she found herself being crushed between her old socialist tendencies and a new uncertain alliance with the de Silvas' past. The women beside her were Indian peasants hardly able to speak English, staring at Savitha with unabashed curiosity, talking to each other in their own language, cocooned in a strange world of their own. Refusing, thought Savitha, furiously, *refusing* to speak in English! Who did they think they were, refusing to learn this beautiful language? Why weren't they trying to integrate? Hadn't the British been criticised for this very thing? She glared at them.

During their break the two newcomers sat huddled on the landing eating from their tiffin boxes. Savitha's mouth watered but still she refused their overtures of friendliness. Was she a snob then? Was this her secret weakness? She felt she had become like the people she had once despised in Sri Lanka. She had hated them for their airs and graces, their useless pride, their snobbishness. And here she was behaving in the same way. It distressed her that it seemed no longer possible to live up to her ideals. But I am not like them, she wanted to cry, confused and upset without knowing why. How do I make myself interested in what interests them? There is something wrong with me, she decided, finally, filled with a different kind of despair as she continued to drink the weak dishwatery tea provided by the establishment, concentrating, instead, on reading George Bernard Shaw's *The Intelligent Woman's Guide to Socialism and Capitalism.*

13

Coming back late one evening, on a night with a full moon, Grace smelt the lime trees growing beside the house. The rain had washed away the dust and crushed the leaves, releasing their scent into the air. The monsoon was almost over, but the heat had not become oppressive yet. She had been to evensong at the cathedral. Small flecks of light hovered around the statue of the Virgin. It was the first time she had ventured out in months; Frieda and Aloysius had not wanted her to go but the curfew had been lifted temporarily. She would have gone anyway, but they did not know this. She no longer cared about her own safety. There had been another letter from Savitha. Included with it was a piece of paper covered in badly drawn musical notations from Meeka. Thornton had scribbled a note at the bottom of the letter, saying he would be writing separately.

Savitha was lonely; Grace felt the loneliness struggle through the thin blue paper.

Winter will soon be here, wrote Savitha, *the light has almost vanished. You can't think what that means until you are threatened with its loss. I listen to the sound of sewing machines all day. They remind me of the wings of small birds. My thoughts are continuously of home. I think of you all the time. When will it be safe for us to return?*

"She has a job?" Grace said to Frieda, puzzled. "Sewing? But she can write so vividly, with such passion. Why isn't she writing her articles?"

Frieda was nonplussed. Savitha had always been a mystery.

Thornton has become very quiet. He misses you and he worries all the time about Meeka.

From this Grace deduced Savitha was worried about him. And little Anna-Meeka, what news of her?

She's grown a lot, wrote Savitha, proudly. Grace was thrilled.

She's changing fast, wrote Savitha.

Must be the better food, thought Grace.

I forgot to mention Thornton has managed to buy a piano. You knew how much Meeka wanted one? Well, now she's very happy. She plays it all the time, listening to the records we have and copying the tunes. She can play anything just by hearing it once! A few weeks ago we found a piano teacher as well. A Polish woman, called Mrs. Kay. Thornton asked her to put Meeka in for her Grade 4 exam. He thinks it will be a good thing if she could do some exams. But Meeka doesn't want to do exams, she says. Mrs. Kay says she only wants to improve on the Beethoven! Mrs. Kay says it's not such a bad thing, and it shows where her interest lies, whatever that means, but Thornton is furious. He thinks we are wasting our money and wants to find another teacher. Anyway, Mrs. Kay has been teaching Meeka to write music (see enclosed) and she's been writing down all sorts of things. D'you remember how she used to suddenly make up little tunes when she was at the convent? Well, she's still doing that. Her teacher told us that perhaps Meeka should study music theory instead. Thornton was disappointed, although he tried to hide it. You know he would hate her to try to be a concert pianist, but still, I think he would have liked her to show some sign of her aunt's talent. Anyway, yesterday Meeka was playing some of these "tunes" when Thornton came in. She told him, "This one is for Granny and Auntie Frieda. It's about the sea and about Jasper." Thornton didn't say anything, he just stood watching her and then he told her to go back to practising her exam piece.

"Hmm," mumbled Aloysius, jerking his head in the direction of Alicia's room. "That's different. *She* never did that!"

So you see how she remembers Sri Lanka, continued Savitha. *And every day,* she added in her postscript, *every single day we drink our tea from your beautiful bone china!*

Thornton's letter had arrived a few days later. Grace stared at the well-loved handwriting for a long time before she opened it. But then, in spite of everything she felt, somehow the letter had made her laugh, for Thornton was unable to hide his irritation with the world, especially his beloved daughter.

Anna-Meeka, he told his mother, *is trying to talk like the white children in her school! She has a piano now but she's very stubborn and she keeps changing the notes in the exam pieces she's supposed to be learning. I hope this isn't going to be the pattern with her other lessons because she has the eleven-plus exams to take soon. Christopher makes matters worse. He's forever encouraging her to do whatever she wants, telling her stories about me from the past, simply to annoy me. As for Jacob,* continued Thornton, his irritation gathering momentum, *I just don't understand him. We meet up but he has nothing to say of any interest. He's become very withdrawn since he left home.*

Walking in the garden that evening, when the heat had died down a little, Grace thought about her letters. Even after all this time some things did not change. Thornton and Christopher were no closer to each other. Their squabbles and their worries continued, regardless. She could see no problem with Anna-Meeka though. It was Thornton and Savitha who were the ones in need of attention. Yesterday Aloysius had written to his granddaughter, his hand moving shakily across the paper, telling the child things about their daily life in Sri Lanka, reminding her of her home, aware that he was unlikely to see her again. Watching him, Grace had felt bereft. A fatal gap had opened up between them all. The ship that had carried them away had left a space too wide, and impossible to cross.

Two nights previously the curfew had been lifted and there was life back on the streets, giving it a deceptive air of normality. But it would not last. Thin rice-paper clouds moved silently in the sky. The crescent moon glided through them. Beyond the lime trees a performance of Kathakali dancing was taking place. Grace could hear temple drums. Last week there had been another suicide bomb in the capital outside the Central Bank. It had killed fifteen people including the child who had carried it. There had been a piece in the paper by Amnesty International protesting against the use of children in war.

As she walked across the moonlit garden, Grace noticed the lights in Alicia's room were on. Turning, she looked at the gate, half expecting to hear the sound of Thornton returning. Of all the pointless things, civil war is the most pointless, she thought. Tonight she had knelt in the candlelit church and prayed for the country to unite, hoping that when it was all over there might be something left to unify. Through the branches of the trees she caught glimpses of her elder daughter moving in her room. There was no longer any trace of the girl she once had been. Christopher had called this place a poisoned paradise, and Grace, with Vijay so recently murdered, had agreed.

"But we cannot blame the land," she murmured to herself, as the garden shifted and settled into the night. The land in all its beauty was not at fault.

Like the garden, her thoughts moved restlessly. It would take five days for a letter to reach her children. Lately, a soft film seemed to be passing before her eyes, making writing difficult. Before long her father's blindness would be hers.

"Are my sons happy?" she had asked feverishly, when she prayed. Always, she came back to this single unanswerable question. Could they be happy having cut their connections with their homeland as though they were the ribbons that had stretched from the ship? Could they be happy at such a price?

A servant hurried through the trees. He wanted to warn her

he had seen a snake in the grass where Grace stood. "The moon was nearly gone," he said, shaking his head. "It's a time for serpents. Did you notice an offering to the gods was left outside the gate earlier?" The servant was frightened. It was not an auspicious thing to happen.

"Ignore it," said Grace. "Why worry about the serpents and devils when all the time the real enemy walks, unmasked, within our midst?"

Above her, the luminescent moon slipped silently behind the clouds.

"Well," asked Christopher, "what d'you think then?"

He placed two pints of Guinness on their table and sat down, pushing some loose change towards Jacob. Then he raised his glass to his lips with a smile of satisfaction. He had not had a drink since lunchtime. Jacob frowned. Somehow, since Thornton's arrival, he seemed to have got sucked into the habit of meeting his brothers for a drink at the pub. It was Christopher's fault.

"Let's introduce him to pub life," he had said.

Why do I always end up paying? thought Jacob irritably. What do they need me for?

"Haven't you been paid yet?" he asked.

"No, men, not yet. I'll buy a round next time. Don't fuss."

"That's what you always say," said Jacob.

"Yes, OK. Don't be such a bloody capitalist. I'll pay next time. Now then," he leaned towards Jacob, his eyes bright, "tell me what you think of our sister-in-law."

"Oh!" Jacob was not interested in Savitha. "She's all right, I suppose. At least she keeps Thornton in his place." He yawned. Then he remembered something else. "Are you seeing that woman in the leopard-skin coat?"

"What?" asked Christopher startled. "What d'you mean? Has Thornton been spying on me again?"

"Calm down, Christopher. Thornton will be here in a minute. It was the barman who asked me, actually. I hope you're not entertaining a call girl?"

Christopher stared at his eldest brother disbelievingly. Then he burst out laughing.

"You know your problem, Jacob," he said conversationally. "This country has turned you into one of the bourgeoisie. You were halfway there before you left Sri Lanka and this country has simply completed the job. Soon you'll marry someone safe, just like our dear brother, and that will be that." He paused for a second to take a great gulp of his drink. "And if *I* want to be seen with a prostitute," he continued challengingly, looking around for the barman, "that's up to me, no?"

Jacob winced. "Keep your voice down," he said wearily. "I'm sorry, Christopher, but you worry me. You're drinking far too much. What will they say at home? What will Mummy say?"

Christopher snorted. "You don't know what Mummy thinks? Let me tell you, she's not the person you think she is. Let me tell you—"

Jacob held up his hand. "Don't start getting excited about everything I say."

They both fell silent. Sipping their drinks.

"We have nothing in common," Christopher said finally, flatly. "You and I and Thornton." He spoke without heat, his face expressionless. "That's the truth of it."

"Whose idea was it to meet?" Jacob said, defensively.

"Mine," Christopher said, suddenly serious. "It's what Mummy would have liked. I suggested it for her sake. Not my own."

Jacob was surprised. England had changed his youngest brother almost beyond recognition. He had become confident. Or maybe he always was, thought Jacob, but we never noticed. Christopher drank too much and when he was drunk it made him want to pick a fight. Just like Daddy, Jacob sighed. Why was it that every time he had any dealings with his family it was always unpleasant?

"The only good thing about *him*," remarked Christopher catching sight of Thornton, "is Anna-Meeka. She should be my daughter!"

Thornton had told Savitha he would be late back. He had a feeling Savitha did not want Christopher getting drunk in their house. He also suspected Anna-Meeka listened in on their conversation. So he was happy to meet his brothers in the pub. Tonight he had come straight from work where, as usual, his day as a clerk at the Central Office of Information had been both confusing and tiring. He had not told anyone, but he would never like the job. He had not made friends but he did not tell his family this either. Picking up his glass, he went over to his brothers.

"Aha!" Christopher said immediately, in a combative sort of way. He looked alert and full of energy.

"God, Christopher," Thornton said mildly, sipping his beer, "where do you get your energy from?"

"How's my niece?"

"She's been asked to join the school choir," Thornton said, brightening up.

"Really? I say! This calls for a present." Christopher leapt up and went over to the bar to buy some chocolate.

"He told me he didn't have any money," Jacob said.

"Oh, he's mad," said Thornton. "Take no notice. I'm so cold," he added, distractedly.

Jacob considered him. Thornton looked unbelievably oppressed, weighed down and unhappy. The speed with which he had saddled himself with a wife so unlike him still amazed Jacob. A wife now working in a sweatshop, no less!

"How's Savitha's job?" he asked.

Thornton groaned.

"Tell her to give it up, men. How can you let her work there?"

"Shh!" said Thornton, for Christopher was returning. "Don't start *him* off, for God's sake."

Jacob shook his head. His family was a complete mystery. Thank goodness his new girlfriend was nothing like any of them. Christopher threw the bar of chocolate down on the table next to Thornton.

"For Meeka," he said. "Ask her if she's written another tune yet." He gave a short laugh. His brothers both looked like a couple of stuffed cats. "Cheer up," he said, "it might never happen!"

Half-term arrived. Meeka seemed a little happier at her school. Savitha noticed she had some friends now. There was a girl called Gillian and another called Susan. Meeka talked earnestly about them and Savitha listened, suppressing a smile. Thornton did not think it significant but *she* could see her daughter looked more confident, and had begun to sing to herself again. Thornton only wanted Meeka to work hard. Soon she would be taking her eleven plus and he wanted her to stop wasting time playing piano and get into the grammar school. He noticed Meeka was still adding bits to the sonatas she was supposed to be learning, trying to improve on Beethoven, he called it, disapprovingly. He noticed she was trying to talk in the peculiar way of the white children. He was not happy about this either. Nor was he pleased when she told him one evening that from now on she would be calling him *Dad* because Daddy was too babyish. All this added to Thornton's irritation. Only Savitha was simply glad her daughter was settling down. Once or twice she suggested Meeka bring a child home for a meal but Meeka mumbled something about the children not eating spicy food.

"What d'you mean?" demanded Savitha. "I can make them a cake. You like my cake, don't you?"

But no one came and eventually she forgot about it.

Savitha had decided to stay on at the sweatshop until she found a better job. They needed the money, and besides, the article she had been writing was developing nicely. She planned to polish it up and send it to a newspaper back home. Until then she would stay with Rosenberg. On the first morning of the holidays, she left Meeka alone in the house while she went to work the early shift. There was plenty of rice for lunch and there were two curries. She showed her daughter how to warm them. There were some sweetmeats and apples. On no account was Meeka to open the door to anyone. She could go down the road to the children's library to change her books but she was to come straight back. No dawdling, no going into shops, no buying sweets. Meeka nodded, keeping the gleam out of her eyes. Her mother wrote the phone number of her father's office, and Rosenberg's too. She then went to the bathroom and fussed around, changing her slacks, redoing her hair, looking at herself in the mirror, admiring her new coat. Meeka groaned inwardly. Would her mother *never* leave?

"I'm off now, Meeka," she called out finally.

Meeka, lying on her bed, legs waving in the air, put them down hastily. Savitha came into the room and gave her a kiss. She hesitated. A feeling of unease was beginning to form at the back of her mind. There was something a little unsleepy about the child. Savitha could not put her finger on it, but there was a tension, a feeling of excitement, running along the length of Meeka's sleek little body as she hugged her mother with slightly too much enthusiasm. Savitha looked at her.

"Are you sure you'll be all right?" she asked again, anxiously, feeling her way around the dark corners of doubt lodged in her suspicious mind.

"Yes, Mum," said Meeka obediently and she sighed, and she yawned and then she slumped back into bed for all the world as though she were dog-tired.

Savitha hesitated again. She looked at her watch. If she did not leave now she would be late for Rosenberg's. After all, there was not much that Meeka could get up to. Finally, satisfied, she picked up her umbrella, saying she would be back at two. And out she went, shutting the front door with a brisk little tug. A small slam, the sweetest of slams, the most beautiful sound in the world, thought Anna-Meeka, pausing a moment. Which was just as well because Savitha was back a moment later, having forgotten her lunch. But then finally she left, trailing a string of instructions behind her, unable to linger any longer.

"Yes," said Meeka. "Yes, yes, yes!" She went on saying it for a few moments after this second wonderful closing of the door. Just in case.

She counted to ten. (She had overheard someone saying there was safety in numbers.) Then, in a flash, she dressed. She forgot to do her teeth or wash her face, but still, she was dressed and her hair hastily combed. There was no time to waste. Her mother would be back by two. Pulling out a paper bag from under her bed, she went into the dining room to set the table for lunch.

It was quite chilly in the dining room. She had learned that you said "chilly" when it was cold and "cold" when it was freezing, unlike her father who said it was cold even when the sun was shining. So far, she noticed, no one at school said it was cold yet. Clearly it would get a lot chillier. It was from the dinner ladies, now her firm friends, that she got much of her information. All those bits that Gillian and the others failed to tell her, all the filler-in bits that were needed for daily life, came from these wonderful ladies. They told her she was a little horror, and, holding this new applauded status to her chest like a shield, she hoped finally to be accepted by the *boys* and get into the rounders team. It was a modest ambition but one that, so far, she had been unable to fulfil. When she asked Geoff why this was so, he had grinned and tweaked her hair. Then,

making a noise like a motorbike, working the imaginary han-
dlebars with his hands, he told her.

"Titch!" he said succinctly. "Everyone thinks you're a titch.
Won't catch the ball, will yer. That's wot. Won't run fast
enough!"

He grinned, not unkindly, for Geoff was the sort of boy
who was nice to his cat. Later, he offered Meeka some
Maltesers, but this was not enough for her. She took the
Maltesers of course, but she loathed and hated Geoff-the-mes-
senger. For a while she could barely talk to him. Luckily Geoff
did not notice.

One evening Meeka had asked her father if she was a
"titch"?

"What is that you are saying?" asked Thornton suspiciously, looking up from one of his newspapers (tonight it was *The
Times* and the *New Statesman*).

"What is that word?"

Meeka wished he did not talk so loud. Get so excited every
time she opened her mouth.

"Of course you are not small!" her father had said, outraged. "You are my daughter. You are *beautiful!*" Having
given his final word on the subject, Thornton went back to his
reading.

After some time Meeka decided to change tactics with
Geoff and the other boys. Suspecting rightly that he was the
most powerful one in the class, she decided to be nicer to him.
Since Geoff had never noticed she hated him in the first place,
this too was lost on him. The subject of rounders never came
up again but Meeka was merely biding her time. And that was
when she had her good idea.

Today, at twelve o'clock, she was having a party. She had
invited her whole class for lunch. She had given them invitations telling them it was her birthday. It was not her birthday,
but still, that was a small point. Her stepmother, she told them,

was a frightening woman. They would not want to meet her. But thankfully, Meeka assured them, she would be out. So would her father. They had left her to have her party in peace. Unfortunately the party would have to finish at two o'clock promptly, as her stepmother wanted the house tidied up for when she came home. The children were agog. Never had there been such interesting goings-on in their class.

Meeka began getting ready. First she stood on a chair and got Savitha's new cookery book from the bookcase. The *Good Housekeeping Book of Dinner Parties*. Prawn Cocktail, she was going to make prawn cocktail, without the prawn. Then she was going to heat last night's leftover rice. Last night's curries would also be reheated. There were crisps and fish fingers, which had been defrosting nicely under her bed for a couple of days but, because the money was running out, only a few chocolates. She had been saving her pocket money for weeks, ever since she had first had the idea of the birthday party, to spend on bits of food from the shop at the end of her street on her way home from school. There was nothing to drink, only water. She had, however, noticed her mother buying some limes last Saturday, and Meeka planned to squeeze these into water to make Lanka lime. It was all decided in her mind. She had two hours to get everything ready. It was a race against the clock.

Carefully, so as not to break it, she took out the special china. There was a lot to choose from. The cupboard gleamed with the most beautiful things: pink-and-white plates covered in rosebuds, blue-and-white dishes, small bowls, jugs and teapots. But it was at the back of the cupboard that she found the real treasures. At the back, tucked away behind the Whitefriars crystal glass, were small neat stacks of the oldest pieces. There were tureens with worn patterns, cups and saucers, a whole dinner service with delicate figures, dense foliage, ivy, ferns, passion flowers. Meeka picked out her especial favourites. Side plates, sugar bowls for the jelly that she was about to make, serving dishes for the curries, a tureen for the rice. She spread them around on the floor, vague memories like the music that lived constantly in her head, rose up to greet her. Here was a dish that her granny used to serve *bolo de coco* on; here was another that always had *pente frito* in them whenever she visited her grandparents in their beautiful house in Station Road. For a moment she longed to taste some *vadi* or some *thosai*. To smell again the rose water and cinnamon in Auntie Frieda's kitchen. Her aunt always had something sweet for her to eat whenever she visited and when she hugged Meeka she always smelt of rulang and cochineal. Meeka had loved visiting them, her grandparents and her aunt, in their house by the sea. In the excitement of being in England she had forgotten how much she loved the island.

Suddenly, with unexpected force, she heard the rhythmic sweep of the sea and her father's laughter as they ran the length of the beach together. She could almost taste the fried prawns they used to buy. The texture within the sounds in her head changed becoming slower and more intense and she heard her younger self, screaming with excitement, as her father chased her under a wave. Droplets of spray sparkled in the sunlight as she swam through the water. When they returned to the house in Station Road, Aunt Frieda used to dry Meeka off with a soft towel and then serve a delicious meal on the old pink-and-white plates. On one occasion, when Meeka was sitting on the veranda, a crow had flown down from the murunga tree, knocking over a dish and breaking it. Auntie Frieda had said that was exactly what Jasper used to do when he was young. Meeka had loved the stories of Jasper. Thinking of him, after so long, she wished suddenly that he were still alive. Her father, who used to tell her lots of funny stories about him, still found it difficult to talk about the way he had died.

The memory of Jasper made the music in Meeka's head

shift subtly, getting faster. Forgetting about her preparations, going into the sitting room, she lifted the lid of the piano. Then frowning with concentration she began to play. It was not quite right. She played the G minor scales, adding six extra notes. Then she went back to her piece of music and added the bit in Debussy to the end of it. Her music sounded a bit better, but was still not quite right. Perhaps it was the scale that was wrong? Her mother, who always encouraged her, had said, "Practice makes perfect, Meeka."

At the thought of those folded lips, a sudden twinge of unease gripped Anna-Meeka. Hastily, so as not to spoil the day in any way, she put the thought firmly out of her mind and went back into the kitchen. There was still an awful lot to do.

She set the table with the special white damask tablecloth, lemonade glasses, dishes, side plates. Then she made the jelly. When she poured the boiling water over the ruby-red gelatine, the bowl cracked and coloured water began seeping onto the draining board. Hurriedly she took some Tupperware from under the sink, hiding the cracked dish at the back of the cupboard. Again the feeling of unease washed over her, only this time it was much stronger. But it was too late to start worrying now, she told herself sensibly.

Soon the jelly was setting nicely in the fridge. The prawnless cocktails were done, arranged in long crystal glasses. Unfortunately there were only four. The children would have to share. Or have a teaspoonful each, so it would all go round. The recipe book asked for something called cayenne pepper. Meeka did not know what this was. It looked red and the book said it was hot. So she sprinkled some chili from her mother's spice jar. It looked so nice that she sprinkled a bit more on top. Gillian was bringing a birthday cake with candles. Meeka had told her there would be no cake because her stepmother would not bake her one. It was against her religion, she said. When Gillian's mother heard this her eyes filled with tears.

"Poor little mite!" she said to Gillian's dad. "Don't you fret, Gilly luv, we'll make her one. You can help me mix a Victoria sponge."

So Gillian was bringing the cake. Soon the table began to look wonderful. True, the jelly did not seem to want to jell and the fish fingers smelt funny and had crumbled but the curries were magnificent. Meeka had heated them as her mother had taught her, with a tiny bit of water on a low heat, scraping the non-stick saucepan with a fork, until the familiar smell rose invitingly. The rice too had reheated successfully. All that remained was the mess from the limes she had squeezed rather vigorously. It was a quarter to twelve. She felt excitement rise up like the smell of paraffin from the heaters in the house. The telephone rang. It was her father, checking she was all right, checking she wasn't lonely, checking she would take his library books back.

"And don't waste time on the piano before you finish your homework. Understand? You *must* do well, Meeka. Playing the piano all day isn't going to get you into the grammar school, huh?"

"Yes," agreed Meeka, hopping from one foot to another nervously. "Yes, yes, yes. Bye-bye, Dad."

Again she felt unease creep up behind her, trying, but not quite succeeding, to stifle her excitement. Then, just as she wondered, what if no one came, the doorbell rang.

By the time they got to it, the jelly was almost set.

"Oh good!" said Meeka taking it out of the fridge, bringing it to the table with a flourish, all semi-wobbly and red.

"Now," she said firmly, "if you eat some of this your mouth will stop burning."

The curries had proved too hot for the children, and the prawnless cocktail was too full of chili. But there was cake, Gillian reminded her, when she had become crestfallen. There

234 · ROMA TEARNE

was still the cake. Meeka brightened up and it was then, as Gillian and Jennifer and Susan began to stack the plates and the dishes and the cutlery in a great clattering heap in the sink, that she had remembered the jelly, jammed at the back of the fridge, against a jar of seeni sambal and jaggery. So it'll be all right, thought Meeka.

"Sweet things always take away the burning of a hot curry," she said, unconsciously quoting her mother.

The boys tucked in, jostling each other in their greed. Meeka's presents were piled on the floor. She would look at them later. Two girls had locked themselves in the bathroom and she could hear them giggling and flushing the toilet. Gillian opened the back door, letting in a thin stream of cold air. It was raining a little.

"Let's play murder in the dark," said Geoff, having had enough of the food. He was trying not to think about it, but he felt a little sick.

"No," said Gillian firmly. "We have to sing 'Happy Birthday' now, you idiot. The grown-ups will be here soon and we'll have to go home."

And she swept the remaining crockery into the sink, unfortunately dropping two cups on the hard linoleum floor. They broke into perfect halves and lay there, two generations of use, resting neatly by the plastic waste-paper basket.

"Oh, whoops!" said Gillian, smiling apologetically at Meeka.

"It doesn't matter," said Meeka. Being her parents' daughter, she was polite. Her granny and her mother had always said if a servant broke something one should never get angry. It was bad manners. "I'll clear it up later," she said airily.

She ignored the strange feeling in the pit of her stomach and the knowledge that somewhere in the distance, waiting at some traffic light, crossing some road, were her mother's feet marching determinedly home. An advancing army. She would have to work fast to get the place cleaned up. The truth was she wanted the children to go home. They had played pass the parcel. They had played musical chairs. Meeka had a feeling they might have scratched her father's record of a Mozart opera, but that at least could be hidden. It had been difficult playing musical chairs to Mozart, and even harder to play it to a Beethoven sonata.

"Don't you have any singles?" Marion asked her. "Any Beatles?"

"'Ow abowt the Monkees?"

Meeka had none of these wonderful, exotic things, none of this forbidden fruit. The questions served only to highlight her inadequacies. Old-fashioned music was all that was on offer.

"Cor! Yer mum 'n' dad are different, 'nt they?" Geoff observed.

"Thas cos they're foreign," said Gillian, loyally.

In that moment of careless innocence Anna-Meeka felt a great longing not to be foreign. What would she have to do to stand with these children and be counted as one of them? She paused for a moment, wondering about her choices. Change her parents? Stop them listening to this old-fashioned music? Never. Her father would never stop listening to it and going on and on about Auntie Alicia. He could be surprisingly stubborn. Even if, by some miracle, she worked on him, what good was that, there was still the matter of the funny way they talked. That will never change, thought Meeka sadly.

She played dead lions with the children, but now she was desperate for them to leave. She was tired and hot. There was so much clearing up to do. And all the time the army was nearing. Geoff was being very friendly. Sam seemed to like her too. Susan wanted her to be best friends, annoying Gillian, who felt, quite rightly, that it was she, after all, who had *discovered* Meeka. Meeka listened to this talk as from a great distance, thinking about the Hartley Green pieces of bone china on the kitchen floor, and suddenly, she was certain. She wanted them all to go.

But there was still the cake to cut and the candles to blow out. Gillian was calling them to the table. Meeka had never noticed it before but Gillian was really very bossy, and large. She had the beginnings of breasts. As if reading her thoughts, Geoff grinned.

"Bossyboots!" he said, and he winked at Meeka.

"When we get back to school," he said, "I'll pick you for the rounders team."

Meeka grinned. Her grin did not reach her eyes, but no one could tell. Only her mother would have known that it wasn't her usual smile, but her mother was not there, thank God. Not yet. Gillian lit the candles and they all sang "Happy Birthday" and Meeka grinned again, this time because Jennifer had emerged from the bathroom with a pair of Savitha's knickers on her head and was singing the loudest. She blew out all the eleven candles with one huge whoosh while the children screamed, "Make a wish, make a wish and it will come true!" before cutting deep into the soft sponge covered in butter icing and thick strawberry jam. And it was like this, caught in the stream of cold air from the open back door, caught like a rabbit in the beam of a headlight, so too was Meeka caught in the icy rays of her mother's astounded stare.

It was clear she had died and gone to hell. Such was the power emanating from that glowing, red-ringed stare that when the front doorbell rang a moment later, signalling the arrival of the parents, Gillian's mother and Geoff's older brother, Marion's dad, Meeka was still standing at the Mouth of Hell. She would stand there for a long time.

"*Lasciate ogni speranza, voi ch'entrate!*" intoned Jacob solemnly when he heard the story. "Abandon all hope, you who enter."

He savoured the words slowly, rolling the sounds around his mouth, delighting in the movement of his lips as he spoke. It was as musical as the warm Irish brogue of Geraldine, his new girl-friend. The richness of her voice was what had first drawn him to her, thick and sleepy as a morning under the crumpled covers on her bed, with him beside her. Geraldine was the best thing to have happened to him and the key to his future success. She was his inspiration, the person who for the first time encouraged him to do what he wanted. She was *the one.* With her beside him his business idea seemed almost a reality. It was almost time for her to meet his family. Although so far he had hesitated, had been unable to mention her name to any of the de Silvas. Partly, he supposed, this was because he needed to be certain this warm, hoarse-voiced relationship was going in the right direction. Although *mostly* he knew it was because his family were so peculiar. He never knew from one minute to the next what their individual or collective responses might be. He never knew what major crisis might be taking place among them. What *drama* was going on that might suck him in. A point perfectly illustrated tonight at this meeting in the White Hart pub.

It was an Emergency. Thornton had been the one to ring him up on this occasion, and Christopher, finding it highly entertain-ing, was laughing now. Thornton finished his account of Meeka's behaviour and Christopher was still laughing in huge phlegm-gathering shouts, his whole body rocking from side to side. He slapped his thighs, he clung to the table. When Thornton came to the part where Savitha, walking into the house, found her underwear on some white child's head, Christopher seemed to have a seizure. Thornton wrinkled his nose in distaste.

"Holy shit, men!" said Christopher wiping his eyes. "Holy shit! I'm going to buy the girl a birthday present!" And off he went again hooting like the Capital Express that travelled across the island twice a day. It was not *that* funny.

"*Lasciate ogni speranza, voi ch'entrate!*" said Jacob again, loving the music in the words. "Do you remember the language teacher we had, Thornton? Back home? What was his name, men?"

Thornton could not remember. There was a crisis in his immediate home, never mind "back home." His wife and daughter stood with horns locked, his mother's priceless china was broken, there was mess all over the kitchen and birthday presents that needed to be given back. It was not easy. His head ached.

"If you don't stop making such a noise," he told Christopher with uncharacteristic fury, "I'm walking out of this place."

He had come here for some peace, for a drink with Jacob, not to be laughed at. Why is this jackass here, he thought, resentfully, forgetting he had rung Christopher in the first place. Why is he poking his nose in my family affairs? Thornton glanced at Jacob for support but Jacob was not listening. Is he going off his head too? wondered Thornton, amazed.

"What do you care about some teacher at Greenwood School?" he asked, crossly. "How many years ago was Greenwood for God's sake?" Thornton shook his head in disbelief, lowering it into the foam of his Guinness. "Greenwood belongs in another life," he said abruptly.

A life that had contained his mother and had order in it. This life, thought Thornton raging inwardly, is filled with worry from morning to night.

But Jacob continued to stare into space dreamily.

"I can *still* remember that last afternoon as if it were yesterday," he told them both, proudly. "You and I walking along the valley towards the house. There were cream butterflies everywhere, d'you remember, Thornton? They were everywhere, streaming through the sunlight, in between the trees. You said the sunlight was dappled and you were going to write a poem about it! Then you picked some of the azaleas, even though I told you not to. You said they were for Mummy. Now what on earth was the name of the language teacher?"

A great longing, an unbearable sadness brushed lightly against Jacob. All at once, and with piercing sharpness, his forgotten ambitions, and Dante, and his teacher's name came back to him.

"Hugh Wallace-Smith!" he said triumphantly. "That's it!" Thornton ignored him. Living too long in the UK had obviously made Jacob soft in the head. I am alone, he thought. Alone, among aliens and fools. And he too felt the gentle hand of the past brush against him.

Christopher, seeing his brother's face, tried to control himself. The old childhood grievances quivered within him. What use were Thornton's good looks here in this country? Back home his looks had got him almost everything he wanted. Here they were all third-class citizens, good looks or not. Here they were nobodies.

But all he said was: "The girl is a rebel, men. She is courageous! I predict great things for her. Not your medical-school rubbish," he said scornfully. "My advice, dear brother, is tell your wife to stop her weeping and wailing. Tell her to stop her bloody shouting and throw her crockery in the bin. Then you must encourage the girl with her music. Let her write down those tunes in her head. She is the future, men. Let her do what she wants, otherwise, mark my words, you'll have trouble on your hands."

He laughed again in spite of himself, a wild rasping laugh full of admiration for Anna-Meeka, who should by rights have been his and not his pretty brother's at all. And he thought how strange it was, this feeling of kinship, this sweet tenderness he felt for his small firebrand niece, fighting her way through the jungle of her new life. How unexpected it was that, having folded away his old emotions, having given up on his passions, he should be reminded of them once more by this child. He had never thought he would feel this way again.

14.

Frieda brought the photograph in to show Alicia. She had no interest but Frieda pretended not to notice. Sometimes Alicia wondered why her sister didn't just give up.

"Look," Frieda said. "Alicia, do look. It's a photo of Anna-Meeka, in her new school uniform. She looks just like those photos of Mummy when she was little!"

Alicia did not care. The child was a stranger. She had been born in the most terrible year of her life. The child meant nothing to her.

"I was imagining how wonderful it would be to see them again," Frieda said, wistfully.

Alicia made no response. She was stretched on her bed, reading. That was all she ever did.

"Alicia, don't you want to do *something*?" Frieda asked, her voice strained. She did not say, "Don't just sit here reading, day in and day out, hardly going out, never showing any interest in anyone." She did not say, "At least you were loved, unlike me." She could not be so disloyal. But they had these non-conversations regularly.

Alicia waited patiently. Eventually Frieda would go off to finish some job or other. Eventually she would leave her alone. She knew they had expected her to "pull herself together" long ago. She knew they were at a loss, uncertain how to cope with her. Maybe they had hoped she would find someone else. The thought always angered her. Years had passed, his name was no longer mentioned. She no longer went into the room where the piano was. It was true, she did not go out much, but that was because she hated crowds. The problem was she had nothing to say to anyone anymore. They thought she was *still* thinking of him. Of course she thought of him, but not in the way they imagined. He had simply become part of her flesh and bones, her skin, her hair. He was in the air that she breathed. Everything was overcast because of it. Most of the last few years had been spent in a colourless vacuum. They did not understand this and so they were frightened of saying the wrong thing. How could she tell them all she felt?

"I'm going to Mass later," she said instead.

Mass was the only other thing she actually took pleasure in. It was the only music she could stand. But she did not tell Frieda this either. Nor did she invite her to accompany her.

"There's no service tonight," Frieda warned. "Don't forget there's a curfew. There was a suicide bomber in Kollupitiya."

Today was a bad day. Her sister was lost in another world, an unreachable, untouchable world. Frieda sighed. When Alicia had first been widowed she had blamed herself.

"I was jealous," she had cried in confession. "I wanted what Alicia had."

Afterwards, she had vowed to devote her life to helping her in every way she could. But Alicia did not want any of it. She doubted if Alicia even noticed her anymore. Slowly, as the years had passed, and her own desires changed, her guilt faded, replaced instead by an uncomplicated sadness for her sister. She looked after her parents. She talked to her mother; for the first time she had her mother's undivided attention, and she found that she was strangely content. In spite of all the trouble around her, in spite of missing her brothers and her niece, she was happier than she had ever been. For the first time in her life she felt more confident than Alicia.

Frieda gazed at the picture of her niece. Anna-Meeka had an air of determination about her. Frieda suspected she was not easy.

"I bet she's stubborn," she said, laughing a little. Then, when there was still no response, she went out, gently closing the door.

Anna-Meeka did not pass her examination. She did not get a place at the grammar school. Thornton was speechless. Jacob shook his head; things had come to a sorry pass. Christopher laughed his phlegm-choked laugh and offered Meeka gainful employment with the Socialist Party. Savitha said nothing. What was there to say? She had only just recovered from the birthday party. She needed to get her strength back before she could comment, plan a course of action, prepare for battle. Her batteries were flat. She had sent her article to Wickrem Fernando at the *Times* back home only to have it rejected by that island stooge, that corrupt man who was not prepared to stick his neck out and blow the whistle on Life in the Kingdom of the United. Well, that was that. Her writing was rejected, her crockery was broken and she had had enough of Rosenberg and his damn sweatshop. Discarding her slacks forever in favour of her national dress (she should never have succumbed to such a betrayal), clutching her Cambridge Certificate and her newspaper cuttings, she marched on those now famous feet over the bridge to Millbank and into the Department of Environment, in search of a new job. If Thornton could do it then so too could she. Anna-Meeka, listening to those marching feet, that army of discipline moving off, kept silent, having only recently returned from the Mouth of Hell. Common sense told her to lie low for a bit. Instinct made her discreet.

Every afternoon after school, she went to the library, where a beautiful girl with ramrod hair and blue eyes worked.

"Is your dad called Thornton de Silva?" asked Miss Ramrod.

Meeka was wary. Was this a trap? Was her mother having her watched? These days she could not be certain. Only this morning at break she had said as much to Susan (they were going to be in the same class at the new school). So Miss Ramrod mentioning her father was understandably a little unnerving. Miss Ramrod smiled. Her hair smelt of hyacinths and winter.

"It's just that you reminded me of someone who comes in quite often. I thought maybe he was your father."

"Yes," said Meeka, deciding to take a chance. "Yes, he's my dad!"

And she loved the way she said it, like everyone else in her class. Just like Susan or Gillian or Jennifer, straight out and uncomplicated.

"He's my dad!"

Miss Ramrod smiled again. She moved strands of hair away from her mouth, and stamped Meeka's books.

"He's nice, your dad," she said softly.

Meeka was a little taken aback. Then she too smiled, throwing Miss Ramrod into an alarming confusion. The world tilted. Seeing a sliver of a possibility, the chance of an experiment, unable to resist, Meeka took it.

"We live alone," she said sadly, nodding her head, "me dad and me. Ever since me mum died, we've lived alone. That's why I'm often out on my own."

She smiled once more at Miss Ramrod, picking up her library books, ready to flee, congratulating herself on her performance. Then she noticed Miss Ramrod's eyes fill with tears. Was she that good? Obviously she was going to become an actress. Meeka couldn't wait to tell Susan and the others. Miss Ramrod was speaking again, so softly that Meeka had to bend forward to hear her, and again she smelt the hyacinths.

"Oh, poor man!" said Miss Ramrod. "Poor, poor man. He

must be so lonely." She looked at Meeka; the smile had vanished as quickly as it appeared. Poor little thing, thought Miss Ramrod, probably the child is lonely too.

"Give him my love," she said. "Tell him it's Cynthia from the library. He'll know me. You'd better go home now," she added, for the little girl was hopping from one foot to another. Meeka nodded. She was going to become an actress. Definitely.

Dinner that night was unusually silent. Everyone was preoccupied with their own thoughts. Savitha had got the job. Much to her surprise, her interview had been outstanding. Her future boss did not speak in the tongues of the local people but in the kind of English Savitha understood. He had quoted Kipling and welcomed her to the department. Savitha had squirmed with delight; at last, she had found an intelligent person to talk to. Someone she could share her love of poetry with. As she served up the food thinking about her boss, Mr. Wilson, the quintessential English gentleman (so different from that rat Rosenberg), she smiled silently to herself. They had talked about Swinburne at teatime and Mr. Wilson had offered her a biscuit from his biscuit tin.

Meeka watched her mother peering into the pot of lamb curry, delving into the rich umber juices, the curry leaves and the potatoes, smiling lopsidedly with concentration. Meeka watched closely; her large eyes were curiously bright and sharply focused. Had Jacob been there, he would have noted the resemblance; Grace certainly would have recognised it at once and Christopher would have been delighted. It was as though Jasper was in the room perched above them, watching with interest. Every time Savitha moved, her smile broadened in a peculiar way. Meeka glanced at her father but he was helping himself to dahl and raw coconut.

Thornton was busy thinking about *his* day. The office girl had come in, looking so thin, so pink-and-white and pantyhoseish, that everyone had commented. Thornton, never having registered her before, was startled. Belatedly he had realised she was looking straight at him. The boldness of the women in this country compared to those back home fascinated Thornton. Savitha was speaking and with a small jolt Thornton realised where he was. He glanced hastily around the room. Then he looked at Anna-Meeka. She was eating quietly, not talking too much for once. It occurred to Thornton that he was still very disappointed with her for not doing well in her exams. The headmaster had told them at the parents' evening how well she had made the transition to her new life.

"She's a perfect example of integration," he had said.

But he had not talked about her eleven-plus results. When Thornton grumbled to Jacob later all his brother did was shake his head.

"Find the money for a private school, men," had been his best suggestion.

Meeka, helping herself to a little more rice, tried to gauge the situation. A new tune circled around in her head. She wanted to play it on the piano after dinner. She knew she had been in the bad books for a long time, what with one thing and another, but she had an important announcement to make. Her father was quiet tonight. Even though he never said so, Meeka knew he missed her granny. She knew her mother did too. In fact, she was sure they did not like it here in Brixton. If only her granny lived in Brixton she was sure her parents would not fuss so much. Tonight, however, everything seemed fairly calm. Her father was not shouting or waving his hands about and her mother was smiling in a most peculiar way. Meeka wondered if her face would get stuck if the wind changed. She giggled. Instantly, both pairs of eyes were upon her, her father's suspicious, her mother's watchful. Oh Gawd! thought Meeka.

Thankfully, she did not say it. Instead she said what she had been waiting to say all evening.

"I'm going to be an actress," she announced, "when I grow up. I'm going to be like Julie Christie, and I'm going to dye my hair blonde!" She smiled her father's sweet smile, looking straight at them, piercing their hearts with love and fear and a longing to end this nightmare, leave it all right here on the Formica table and go back home. To take their darling daughter back to safety. Civil war or not.

"I think I have talent," she added, being her father's daughter and therefore certain. "And looks!"

Savitha gave a hollow laugh.

"We are going to put you in a private school to give you a proper education," Thornton said pompously. "Your mother and I are somehow going to find the money. Do you hear me?"

He had not meant it to come out like that, but there, it was out in the open. All his cards on the table. Meeka looked at her mother, but her mother's smile had vanished and she was frowning at her father.

"I went to the library today," she said, hoping to distract them. "After school. Cynthia said to say hello to you, Dad. She said you were nice. She's got blonde hair and you like her, so why can't I have it too?"

Afterwards, she could not understand what all the fuss was about. Why, for instance, her mother turned her mouth into a dark wrinkled prune and her father banged his fists on the table shouting in the "back-home" language that Meeka was beginning to forget. Would Cynthia, smelling as she did of hyacinths and winter, like the way her father had curry stains on his nice white shirt? she wondered. Anyway, she had one last thing to tell them. They were not in the mood at the moment. She would make it clear at some later date, when they were less excited. She was *not* going to any private school. There was no way this was going to happen. She would run away and live with Susan, or Jennifer or Geoff. Whatever happened, Meeka was quite clear about one thing. She was going to the local comprehensive school with her friends. In September.

September, however, was still a long way off. There was the summer to get through first. Their first summer in London; a slow, gentle summer of days that would be etched on their minds forever. They had been in the UK for nearly a year. All that angst, all that planning to get here, and now a whole year had gone so swiftly. Thornton looked out from his office window at the tube station with its stack of *Evening Standards* and its buckets of scentless, forced carnations. He watched the red London buses sailing close to the tops of the huge plane trees and he remembered the glimpses of sea that used to be his view. He sat dreaming of the early-morning swims with Meeka, the walk along the beach towards the crab seller and the snacks in greasy cones that burnt their hands. It seemed only yesterday that his small daughter in her checked cotton dress, a gap in her front teeth, would pull his arm as he nodded off on a rattan chair on his mother's veranda.

"Come on, Daddy, I'm bored. Let's go to the beach," she would pester.

And all the while his mother had watched them, standing in the doorway smiling, as luminescent tropical light slanted through the green glass of the skylight, gathering in iridescent patches, spreading on the cool marble floor. Alone in the office Thornton shook his head. Everything has changed, he thought, his beautiful face taking on the softness of loss.

They had come here for safety, to give their small daughter an education, a better life. But other things were happening to them instead. He was not prepared for any of it. Having grasped this thing called "The New Life" with both hands, his beloved daughter was now turning it into something he had not anticipated. I can see it, thought Thornton staring out of the window, they all think I'm a fool, but I can see where it's going. Straight to the dogs, that's what.

Yesterday he had finished early at work. He had forgotten to tell either Savitha or Meeka. He had intended to surprise them by being in the house when they returned, making one of his salads or doing the washing-up. With this in mind he had taken the tube, walked quickly past the park in Kennington, past the new corner shop just opened by an Indian family, past the library (it grieved him now that he had not even stopped here), such was his desire to get back before anyone else. As he turned into the street where he lived, he saw a group of children walking back from school, shouting and screaming, in that terrible unintelligible way he hated. One of the children was a girl with a skirt so short as to be almost indecent and hair like a bird's nest. She was throwing her school bag up in the air, dancing about, screaming louder than the others (singing quite beautifully, Thornton observed), making the other children laugh. It was only as she broke away from the group, taking her key out of her bag, that he registered who she was.

"Bye," said Meeka, waving at the little group, laughing so much that she could hardly get her key in the lock. "Bye, see yer tomorra."

Thornton hung back, skulking behind a plane tree. For a moment he felt ashamed to be stooping so low. It was early afternoon. The roses were just beginning to bloom. Thornton was shocked. Was this screaming harridan he had seen really Anna-Meeka? She had done something to her school uniform, turned it into a miniskirt. And there was something different about her face too, he thought, puzzled. She looked older, somehow. Why had her mother let her go to school like this? What sort of mother *was* Savitha? His own mother would be horrified if she could see the child of her favourite son looking this way. Thornton's anger rippled through the summer leaves of the plane trees. Unable to stop himself, he went to the main road in search of a phone box and some change.

"Hah! It's me!" he said as soon as the phone was answered. "What sort of woman are you, letting my daughter go to school dressed like a white child? Hah?"

Mr. Wilson, who had picked up the shared telephone, listened for a moment and handed it to Savitha.

"I think it's for you," he said with a small courteous bow.

"Yes?" Savitha. "Oh yes, what can I do for you?"

"What *is* wrong with you?" fumed Thornton, unstoppable now. "You have no standards. Money, money, money, that's all you think of. Why don't you stay at home and look after our daughter, huh? She has turned into a slummer!"

"Yes," said Savitha. She nodded earnestly. "I quite agree. You'll need to look into the source of it. Try finding the original file. It's probably in the archives somewhere. Go back to the beginning, I think."

She put the phone down with a firm little click,

"I'm sorry," she said to Mr. Wilson, who, being the perfect gentleman, would never have dreamed of asking her a single question. "We have some trouble with our plumbing."

And off she went, to wash her hands in the ladies' lavatory.

Thornton's eyes bulged. What was he to do? His wife did not seem capable of a coherent conversation. His immediate worry, however, was his daughter. All he had wanted to do was to come home early and surprise them both by being there, clean the house, wash the bloody china, read a newspaper or two. Now here he was, a wreck, outside the phone box on the Vassal Road. He searched his pockets in vain for some change, wondering if the pubs were open yet or whether to go back and confront Meeka, or phone that idiot wife of his again.

This was how Cynthia found him. Fortunately she had finished work early, ramrod hair swinging, short exquisite miniskirt that showed off a pair of gorgeous long, long legs, pretty pink lips, pretty handbag, pretty everything it would seem. That's how Thornton saw her.

"You have arrived at a moment of crisis," he said, going towards her.

Having played rounders all afternoon, Anna-Meeka was starving. She heated some leftover chicken curry. Then she made a sandwich, adding some sliced raw green chili, some tomato ketchup and some crisps. But before she ate it, just in case her mother came home early, she rolled her skirt down from the waistband, combed her hair and plaited it just as she had done before going to school that morning. One thing Anna-Meeka de Silva had learned over the months was the golden rule of not cutting it too fine. Since the fateful day of her disastrous birthday party she knew always to leave plenty of time for clearing up. She removed the traces of the day from her appearance, washed the eyeliner from her lashes and cleaned her teeth for good measure. Then, and only then, did she eat her sandwich. There were two letters on the mat, both blue aerogrammes. One was for her parents and the other was addressed to her in her grandmother's frail handwriting. Meeka opened it slowly. She had not written to her grandparents for ages. Somehow there was never enough time.

Her grandmother's face rose clearly from the paper. Guiltily, she wished she had kept in touch more. She had promised never to forget them all, never to forget her home, but she had forgotten. Her grandmother did not reproach her.

My darling Anna-Meeka, she had written. *I have been thinking about you a great deal, as have your grandpa and your aunties. We've all been wondering how your music is coming along, whether you are still making up your tunes or whether you are busy with exams. I long to hear you play. There is no music here.*

*Yesterday I walked to the end of the garden to the bench
(near the coconut grove, d'you remember where I mean?).*
Meeka paused. Of course she remembered. *You can hear the waves from there, although you can't quite
see them. I tried to pretend you were down there on that little
stretch of beach, with your daddy. That soon you would both
walk up the hill, laughing and shouting, being starving hungry!
D'you remember how Auntie Frieda used to scold your daddy for
not wiping the sand off your legs? My darling Anna-Meeka, how
I miss you all.*

Grace's voice came over the seas to her, carrying with it the
traces of coconut polish and heat. It brought with it the memory of an almost forgotten language. She made it clear she
thought Anna-Meeka was wonderful. Once when Meeka had
told her she wanted to be famous her granny had nodded in
agreement. She hadn't laughed, or folded her lips, as Meeka's
mother would have done. She had not knitted her eyebrows
together like her father. She had simply looked delighted, saying she was *sure* Anna-Meeka could do whatever she wanted
to. Thinking about her now, wishing also that she had made
another sandwich for she was still hungry, Meeka vowed to
write more often to her.

It is late afternoon now, Grace continued. *The servant is
out in the yard at the back shaking out some mats. I can hear
the coconut man throwing the coconuts to the ground. Do you
remember the thambili you used to love? And the coconut
sambals?*

Meeka stopped reading for a moment. A strain of music ran
through her head, borne on a distant sea breeze. It mingled
with the harsh staccato of the crows, cawing in the afternoon
as she fell asleep. Grace's loving voice rippled softly. The voice
drifted on, telling her of her aunt Frieda and her grandpa.
More trouble was brewing on the island.

It is a good thing, she wrote, *your parents have taken you to*

England. You will be safe there, safe from the terrible violence and corruption of our own people. In England, she continued, *there is justice. Still, no matter what, Ceylon is still your home, the place where you were born. There is something magical in that because it's where you will always belong. One day, Anna-Meeka,* wrote Grace in her tired handwriting, *I hope you'll be able to return home safely.*

Meeka read swiftly, skipping these boring parts of the letter. She agreed with her grandmother (dare she call her "Nan" as Gillian and Susan did?), England was fab. Then she saw that Grace had saved the most interesting bit of news for the last.

Your Auntie Alicia is coming to England. I have written to your mummy and daddy separately. We have been able to buy her a ticket at last.

Meeka gave a shriek of excitement. Her memory of her aunt was vague, but because of her tragic past she remained an exotic figure in Meeka's imagination. There was the music and the fame of course, and then there were the shootings.

Tomorrow, thought Meeka, I'll tell them about it at school. She frowned, thinking furiously. It would go something like this: "The gunman entered my nan's house. He overturned the grand piano, killed a few servants in the process and smashed all the bone china. Then . . ." Meeka paused, her mind racing, "he shot the mynah bird and shot my uncle Sunil too. Everyone screamed; there was blood everywhere. My dad came in like the man from U.N.C.L.E. and wrestled the gun from the man's hand, but he killed my mum by accident. All this happened long before he married my stepmother Savitha, of course."

Such was the drama of her story that Anna-Meeka's eyes shone with emotion. It was how Savitha, opening the front door just then, coming in cautiously after work, fearing God knows what in this madhouse, found her daughter. Standing in the kitchen talking to herself.

"What?" demanded Savitha, her eyes darting swiftly around the room, searching for the hidden children, the broken crockery, the mess, the God-knows-what. But all she could see was Anna-Meeka, standing alone, looking very sweet, her hair plaited, her uniform immaculate, and a few crumbs of food on the table. Savitha, shuddering, peered suspiciously at her daughter.

"Where's your father?" she asked.

Meeka shrugged. How was she to know where her father was? Didn't her mother know she had been at school? Was she keeping tabs on her father too? Perhaps he had been having a party. The thought struck Meeka as funny. She opened her mouth to say something and then she remembered the *news*.

"Mum! Mum!" she said. "Auntie Alicia is coming. She'll be here soon."

God, thought Savitha in a panic, I better start cleaning this filthy house now! But all she said was: "Has she got a visa, then?"

Thornton lit a cigarette. Then, with a gesture of exquisite courtesy, he placed it gently between the pretty lips of the stunning Cynthia Flowers.

They were sitting in the White Hart and Thornton was watching Cynthia Flowers sip her Babycham in its delicate glass. The frisky fawn, etched on the side of the glass, looked so much like her that he felt a poem coming on. A feeling of well-being drifted over him. It had been some time since he had felt the urge to write any poetry. Cynthia Flowers, frisky as her Babycham Bambi, saw the light in his eyes and the glow surrounding his beautiful face. It had all been her doing, she thought later, the poor man had been in such a state when she happened upon him. What could she do but take him to the pub? It had taken her some time, to find what the problem was. It was his daughter of course. How he loved her! Heavens, thought Cynthia, he must have really loved his wife. The child was probably a daily reminder of this lost love. Cynthia Flowers was too sensitive a person to ask him exactly how his wife had died. How could she ask when the man was in such pain? She had not yet begun to feel jealous of the dead woman. Not yet. So she did what she was very good at. She listened.

"In Ceylon," Thornton said, angrily, "girls don't behave this way."

Cynthia Flowers, her rosebud mouth very pink and kissable, asked, "Where is Ceylon?"

"It's a little island," Thornton said, used now to explaining where it was to the English. "A small piece of the world, shaped like a teardrop."

"Oh!" exclaimed Cynthia, covering her kissable mouth with her hand, giggling. "Is it that bit of land joined to India?"

Thornton sighed and shook his head, momentarily distracted.

"No, men. If it was, the world might take more notice of what's happening there."

He went back to the problem in hand. The child did sound a *bit* of a handful, thought Cynthia. With the wisdom of her twenty-two years she decided she probably just needed a little mothering. Having listened carefully, Cynthia suggested Meeka come to the library to see her after school. Perhaps she could get her interested in reading the children's classics.

"You are so wonderful!" said Thornton draining his pint, looking thin and interesting. "You have given me hope again. That I might save my child from these slummers!"

Cynthia gave a small gurgle. "I just want to help," she said, downing her Babycham with such speed that all the bubbles went down the wrong way making her laugh some more. She really could not help it. The early-spring evening glowed with promise. Dappled sunlight fell across the empty pub tables even though there had been no sun a moment before. It lifted the smoke in the air in shafts across the room and out through the windows which seemed high and majestic and wonderful.

Walking home, full of Guinness and largesse, thinking about the sonnet he would write, Thornton realised it was getting late. Letting himself into the house he felt a sudden urgency for the lavatory. Savitha, hearing this, thought, Yes, he's been to the pub again. Meeka, also hearing the sound of the flush being pulled, thought, Oh good, he'll be in a happy mood now. Then she remembered the *news*.

"Auntie Alicia is coming to England! She'll be here soon."

Thornton sat down heavily at the table. He was hungry.

"What's to eat?" he asked Savitha, feeling suddenly exhausted.

"Drunk!" said Savitha triumphantly, as though she had scored a hit. "I suppose you've been drinking with those brothers of yours? Like father like sons, is it?"

"I am not drunk!" bellowed Thornton, glaring at Savitha's retreating back and at his daughter's grinning face.

"What's wrong with you?"

Then he looked at his daughter again. She seemed normal enough.

"What are you wearing?" he demanded, confused.

Meeka, still in her school uniform, was doing her homework.

"What do you think she is wearing, you stupid man?" asked Savitha. "They don't wear saris to school in this country, you know."

Thornton's eyes bulged. He wondered again if his wife was going mad. For the first time in his life he wished he had had a son.

"My father was right," he informed Savitha. "Only now do I understand him. A man should have sons."

Anna-Meeka giggled.

"Respect," declared Thornton. "Without sons you cannot get respect."

He glared at Savitha, who looked as though she was trying not to laugh. Here he was in a household of bloody women all laughing, all completely mad. The feeling of well-being had vanished, along with the inspiration for his new sonnet. There it was. He sighed again and began to eat the rice, the fried green beans and chili Savitha had put in front of him.

15.

After the rebellion, nearly a hundred thousand people were thought to be dead or "disappeared." A stillness fell over the island. It was the lethargy that only follows great violence. The heat in the south had intensified. There was no sign of rain. Everywhere, buildings were deserted, looted, burnt. Those who dared ventured onto the streets. There they found the bloodied remains of unidentified corpses, strewn at the crossroads. In the sprawling white house on Station Road the shutters were closed against the heat and the gunfire. Someone had thrown a brick against one of them and now and then a hinge creaked in the slight breeze. A thin sliver of light knifed through the gap, streaking across the floor inside. Otherwise all was quiet.

The manservant who had been a mere boy on the night of Alicia's wedding came to see Grace. Word had come to him, he said, that someone had been murdered in his village. Murdered and strung high on a tamarind tree. The murdered man was young. He had swung for hours. No one dared touch him or take him down. No one dared even come out of the houses. The shadow of the dead man moved slowly across the ground. Backwards and forwards, backwards and forwards it swung. Carrion crows circled overhead. Silent, at the ready, waiting to swoop, in one graceful spread of talons and wings. Finally a woman, holding a blanket, screaming, inconsolable, racked with grief, had run out. Others followed; they had taken the body down for her. It was her son.

"I don't know if the victim is my brother," the manservant said. "We have not seen each other for nearly a year. After I left home we drifted apart," he told Grace. "Once we lived together, sleeping close to each other." The murdered man's mother had gone mad, it was rumoured. "I need to go to my village, to see if it is my mother. If it is my brother," the manservant said.

Grace watched him go. He took nothing with him, no clothes, just himself. Grace watched his slim figure in its flapping white sarong walk out into the blinding heat, a fluidity of light around him. He looked like the distant figure from her past, a symbol of all she had tried to protect and all she had lost. Her thoughts moved slowly, backwards and forwards, like the shadow of the dead man. The many aspects of her life no longer surprised her. Only her capacity for loving remained constant. Untainted by time.

"Imagine that poor woman!" she told Aloysius later, visibly upset by the manservant's story. "Her son's age is immaterial. He remains her child, you know. Her feelings for him will be as strong as they were on the day he was born."

Aloysius listened without comment, head bowed. He looked defeated.

"However old she is, she is still his mother."

Aloysius nodded. He went over to check the telephone but it wasn't working. It hadn't been working all day. Sometimes they would go for days with no phone. The last letter from England had been delivered over two months ago. Savitha would still be writing. She always wrote regularly, especially as she was so much happier in her new job. It was the fault of the post they had had no letters. There was a rumour circulating that it was censored. Other things were happening. Often the generator was broken, often they could not even tune into the World Service. They were cut off from the rest of the world, with only each other for company.

"There is nothing more we can do," Grace told Aloysius.

"Savitha will be Thornton's rock," Aloysius reassured her. "His and Anna-Meeka's. And the boys will have each other."

This was how they comforted themselves. Outside, the sun was like a drum beating in a cloudless sky. The heat stretched tautly over the skin of the drought-ridden garden. The cook, scraping coconuts in the yard, saw something tossed over the wall; it landed among the hibiscus bushes and fell with a soft thud onto the ground. It was a woman's arm, severed at the elbow, charred at the edges, congealed and black.

"We can't go on like this," cried Grace. She sounded hysterical. "It isn't safe here for the girls," she told Aloysius. "They must leave."

"I'm not going anywhere," Frieda said instantly. "I'm not leaving you. We are in this together."

But Grace could not rest. "They must go to England. I cannot bear it," she begged Aloysius. You must do something. Alicia has suffered enough; Frieda, you must have some sort of life."

It was not that easy. The smell of human flesh burning through the night filled the streets, and here and there across the city pyres, piled high with bodies, were openly set fire to. The elephants were not just out of the jungle, the elephants hardly existed anymore. Aloysius, silent for so long, found a link from the past. Dodging the curfew he went out. Someone he knew, he told Grace, returning late that night, owed him a favour.

"I've managed to buy a passage to England," he said. "But it is only one ticket. What shall we do?"

"Send Alicia," said Frieda instantly. "Send her. It might be what she needs. I don't want to go. I will never leave. Don't waste time asking me."

Who would have said it of Frieda? No one had seen the colour of her stubbornness before. It encircled them like steel cables.

"She is the strongest of us all," Aloysius said when they

were in bed at last. "All these years, we hardly noticed her in the business of our lives, but Frieda is *our* anchor."

Alicia did not want to go either, but Grace gave her no choice. A week later, they bundled her up and sent her out onto the harsh indigo sea. Sailing out towards safety. This time, Grace was dry-eyed.

Their second summer was hotter. London sweltered in a heat wave. The garden at the back of the flat in Brixton was a mess of builders' rubble and years of weeds. In July Thornton began to clear it; the sun had given him heart. He would grow a lawn, he decided, and pomegranates, he told his wife. It would be a welcome for his sister.

"How long do you think this weather will last?" asked Savitha, surprised to find herself laughing. "Haven't you noticed they don't have pomegranates in this country?"

Still Thornton worked on the garden, after he finished at the office and at the weekends. It was light now, long into the evening, a soft violet light, mellow and very beautiful. They had not noticed this before. Last year they had only been aware of the cold. Now, already, they saw shades of colours and splashes of loveliness in this place. One evening, after Savitha had washed her soft-paste porcelain, her blue-and-white willow-patterned dishes, she stood watching her husband turning the soil and clearing the ground as though he had been a gardener all his life. Afterwards, sitting at the kitchen table, with the sound of Meeka playing the piano, she wrote her weekly letter home to Grace.

It is astonishing, she wrote, her admiration reluctant, but growing daily. *Here is a man who had not polished his own shoes until a year ago and now he talks of growing potatoes. Here is man who, in spite of all the odds, is trying to adapt.*

She paused, watching Thornton moving between his rose bushes. Since their marriage she had grown to understand him better. Once, this handsome husband of hers had wanted for nothing. And in those halcyon days the world had fallen at his feet when he smiled. The careless abundance in his life had attracted her. Now, without his family, Thornton had grown smaller and needier. His good humour was fading, he felt diminished. This move had affected them all but *his* unhappiness was the most apparent. She did not tell Grace any of this, but she let her admiration show.

Watching him as he gardens, she wrote, instead, *I see he has inherited your green fingers, your ability to make something of chaos. I wish you could see it!*

Savitha stared at what she had written. She knew now, in the face of Thornton's unhappiness, what she had been uncertain of before. She knew she loved him, but she knew also that he was flawed. Raising her face to the soft summer warmth, feeling how her skin had aged since only a year ago, she thought, And I am the stronger of the two of us.

He's looking forward to Alicia's arrival, she continued. *As we all are.* And she sealed up the letter.

Privately, Savitha wondered how Alicia would cope away from her mother. She had never been close to Alicia. There had never been the time or inclination on either of their parts. Perhaps, she thought, the time had come for that now. The sound of the piano stopped. Meeka had finished practising. Thornton came in with a handful of runner beans.

"If only she did her homework as well as she played the piano," he said disapprovingly, "she would be the best in her class."

"Perhaps we should be encouraging the music instead of all these other subjects she has no interest in?" Savitha said, risking his annoyance.

"Don't start," Thornton said, his good mood evaporating. "There's absolutely no future in it. She'll never make a concert pianist, she's not good enough."

Savitha sighed. She heard Meeka heading towards the kitchen, looking for food. How her daughter was changing. These days she seemed to be eating all the time.

"I'm starving!" announced Meeka, coming in in a great hurry. "We had roast beef, mashed potatoes and gravy for school dinner today."

"What's all this school dinner?" growled Thornton. "It's called lunch." He washed his hands. "I'm just going to the library before it closes," he added. "I want to get a book on potatoes."

And off he went, escaping with a splash of aftershave before his daughter could question him more closely or, worse still, insist on coming with him.

Savitha watched him go. Who would have thought it possible a year ago? Who would recognise them now? They were carving a little path for themselves, cutting a small road of near contentment. Bravely. Things are not so bad, she told herself. Many times in the past months she had badly wanted to go back. At nights, often after reading Grace's letters, knowing Thornton's unhappiness, she had wanted to admit defeat, return. Her homesickness had not disappeared, she doubted it ever would, but she knew now that they would stay. Besides, even if they could, there was no life in Sri Lanka for them. Something had gone terribly wrong. Their own people had changed beyond recognition. Their easy-going, gentle temperament had been transformed into an unscrupulous cunning. Some implacable force had taken root within them.

That July, Mrs. Smith next door began to speak to Savitha. First they had smiled at one another and then slowly, when she saw the de Silvas in the garden, she had come over with little gifts. A few plant cuttings, a packet of seeds, some radishes from her husband's allotment. Shyly, for she was on uncertain ground, Savitha accepted. One day Mrs. Smith made a remark about Mr. Smith. Spontaneously, understanding the grumble,

Savitha laughed. They had become friendly after that, the two of them, with caution acting as a fence between them.

At the end of July, as the summer holidays began, Meeka was once more left alone in the house. Thornton and Savitha gave her instructions on what she could and could not do. "I'll just keep an eye open," said Mrs. Smith to Savitha. And she winked knowingly. She did not call Savitha by name. She was not sure that she could say it right. Also, as she told her husband, it seemed disrespectful somehow. Savitha was a proper lady in Mrs. Smith's eyes. Savitha, liking this small formality between them, felt glad of Mrs. Smith's eye.

Meeka did not care. She knew her mother and Mrs. Smith were friendly but, well, Mrs. Smith could not stand at her window all day, could she? So Anna-Meeka joined forces with Gillian and Susan and Jennifer, and roamed the streets of London whenever she could. It was 1966. It was still possible to dodge the ticket collector and ride the tube, round and round the Circle Line, on a ten-pence ticket. They went with Jennifer's gramps to the old pie and mash shop on Coldharbour Lane and ate jellied eels washed down with cider when no one was looking. They walked along the embankment eating ice creams, and they ran amok in the British Museum. All in all they had a wonderful time. It was in this way that Anna-Meeka began to understand the city, this adopted home of hers. She was certain she would never love another place in quite this way. The smell of the Underground soot and the sight of the river from the top of a double-decker bus were part and parcel of her life now. Sri Lanka was nothing to do with her. It belonged to some other life.

By the time her parents returned home in the evenings she was lying on her bed with the huge sash window open, reading. The librarian had taken a great interest in her and was forever finding her more and more books to read. When she was not reading, the thing she enjoyed the most was the piano. She played it endlessly, her head constantly filled with the sounds of the sea. Sometimes these textures were stormy and full of tempo, sometimes intense and melodious, but always at the very heart of her music was the sea, in all its endless vast expense of water. She played with great concentration. Mrs. Kay, her piano teacher, had left before the school holidays. She had moved out of London. Before she left, she quarrelled with Thornton.

"Your daughter is very musical," she had told him. "She needs nurturing. Music isn't about mechanically sitting exams."

Meeka, listening outside the door, could tell Mrs. Kay was angry.

"Thank you very much," Thornton said. He was polite but firm. "My daughter's music is a hobby."

Mrs. Kay gave up. She had taught Meeka to transcribe the short pieces of music she was always making up and she had taught her how to see the sounds as notation. She had refused to allow Meeka to play only her examination pieces, insisting she learned other pieces, tackled more challenging music as well. She did all this with an air of furtiveness.

"Get rid of the scaffolding, Anna-Meeka," she would say. "Just show me how you build your musical house! You don't need so many notes to do that."

Meeka had enjoyed those lessons. She had enjoyed the way Mrs. Kay listened so seriously to what she played, her head tilted on one side. Mrs. Kay never called these snatches of sounds "tunes." She gave then names like "Study" or "Scherzo." And now she was leaving, Meeka didn't want another teacher.

"I don't need any lessons," she told her parents. "I can teach myself."

She mastered the B minor scales. She was learning harmonics, and the results for her theory exam when it came showed she had got a distinction. Uncle Christopher bought her a wad of manuscript paper so that she could write down her pieces. The slow shift, the modulated harmonics and tender tones that she sometimes, accidentally, achieved were what she loved most of all. Thornton, returning from work on these warm summer evenings, hearing these tunes from afar, paused for a moment. Savitha listened as she opened the front door.

Then, as the summer turned a corner, Alicia arrived. Thin, beautiful Alicia, frail as the stalk of a lotus flower, silent and unhappy. She came with letters from home, and dust in her heart, shaken by so many days at sea, disorientated and utterly alone. The brothers were shocked. Savitha felt as though she had brought the island with her.

Jacob found her a bedsit in Highgate and Christopher bought his sister a record player and some records of her favourite pianists, some orchestral pieces, some opera. Savitha made her new curtains and Thornton had picked all the roses from his garden for her. They greeted her helplessly, for what could they offer Alicia from their own robust lives, what could they say that would give her comfort?

From the very first moment Savitha could see that it was not going to work.

"Alicia doesn't want to be crowded by all of us," she told Thornton.

What she meant was that her sister in law did not want to be friendly towards her. Well, that's that, thought Savitha, folding her lips. She doesn't like me. She shrugged her shoulders. Savitha did not like to waste energy. But she was sorry for Alicia all the same.

"She needs more inner resources," she told Thornton, firmly. "It's now eleven, nearly twelve, years since Sunil died. Someone should start talking to Alicia about him."

Thornton looked uncomfortable.

"She needs to move on," Savitha added earnestly, wishing only to help. "Perhaps London will give her some distraction."

Thornton refused to be drawn. Alicia's grief frightened him. "Why don't you take Anna-Meeka with you to see her?" Savitha persisted. "It might cheer her up."

But Anna-Meeka, too, was strangely reluctant to visit her aunt. She hated the closed windows, the drawn blinds, the hot radiators. The summer days beckoned. Outside were children's voices, a ball being kicked, an aeroplane droning. What was the matter with her aunt that she always had the heating on? It isn't cold, thought Meeka, astonished. It's absolutely sweltering! Savitha noticed her daughter trying to wriggle out of these visits and wished there was something she could do that would help Alicia. Thornton, disturbed without knowing why, made no comment. Weeks went by. Christopher's record player remained untouched.

"You must try to help her," Savitha said, again. "Her grief has become stuck. He would not have wanted this for her."

"I can't," said Thornton, fearfully.

Then one afternoon, almost a month after her arrival, as Thornton and Meeka walked up the stairs to Alicia's room, they heard the sounds of Mozart's Sonata in A. It cascaded towards them. Thornton, caught unawares, lost his footing on the step.

"Who's playing it?" he asked, shocked.

Meeka paused too, and held her breath; the notes seemed to catch in her throat, crystal clear and bell-like. She was transfixed.

"Is it Auntie Alicia?" she whispered.

Thornton shook his head. "It's a recording," he murmured. "I didn't know she still had it. Your aunt's recording. Before Uncle Sunil died."

They stood outside listening. The music ran on, lifting this ordinary summer's day, turning it into something suffused with light. The sound resonated in their ears. It wrapped itself around their limbs. It poured from the high, bleak window on the landing, seeped out from the cracks under Alicia's door, it propelled Anna-Meeka forward so that she felt as though she were flying, until at last, looking at her father with astonishment, she cried, "She plays wonderfully!"

16

A nd then, without any warning, Jacob, the eldest de Silva, the circumspect man, that dependable custodian of all their moral dilemmas, found he had a small problem of his own. Just when he had thought life could have no more surprises, suddenly he saw he was wrong. Thinking of this delicate matter was enough to bring the blood surging to his face. Jacob's problem showed no sign of going away. If anything it seemed to be getting bigger. He went to see Thornton, wanting to discuss it with him, but the child was always present, listening. Snooping around, smirking just like her father used to, unaware, like her father, of her capacity to create havoc. And in any case, thought Jacob unhappily, if it wasn't the child, it was the mother. Prowling around the kitchen, sharp eyes on the alert. Thornton's family, thought Jacob shuddering, was a nightmare. So he arranged to see both his brothers in the pub instead. Not that *that* made it any easier.

"I don't know how it all happened," he said when they were settled in their usual corner by the window at the White Hart. It was Christopher's turn to buy a round, which for once he did without a murmur. Jacob was sweating, whether it was because of the heat or the thing he was about to tell them was difficult to gauge. Christopher was unusually solicitous; perhaps he too was affected by the potency of the moment? He hoped Jacob did not disappoint. So often his family made a drama when there was no drama to be found.

"Wait, wait, men," he said. "Wait till I get the drinks. Same again?"

"Yes, yes," said Thornton expectantly. He wished Jacob would get on with whatever it was.

"I don't know how it happened," said Jacob when they were all settled again.

"Shit, men!" said Christopher losing patience. "Get on with it!"

"Shut up!" said Thornton, but Jacob was not listening to them. He was thinking back to the beginning.

Was it that night when she had nibbled his ear? Which night was that precisely? She nibbled his ears most nights. That was, he supposed, the problem. No, the problem was, well, in truth the problem was . . .

"She's in the family way," he said, being unable to think of a better way to put it.

"*Who?*" asked Thornton and Christopher in unison.

"Geraldine," said Jacob, forgetting they had never heard of her before.

"Who the fuck is Geraldine?" asked Christopher.

Such was Jacob's state of mind that he let this go.

"We'll have to get married," he said, demonstrating his resourcefulness.

"Have you got someone pregnant?" asked Thornton, catching on.

Christopher, who had been staring incredulously, burst out laughing. Both his brothers were at it now, breeding like rabbits! Mr. Enoch Powell had better watch it, he thought. There seemed an army in the making, with the de Silva family alone.

But he didn't say that. Thank God. Although he did think it was hugely funny.

"You need a whisky, men! A celebration whisky! Unless you are thinking of an abortion?" he paused, interested.

"Sit down for God's sake, men, and stop shouting," said

Jacob nervously, looking about. "You don't understand. She's Irish!"

"*Irish!*" said Christopher loudly. "*Irish?*" This was getting funnier and funnier. "In that case you've had it, men. No chance there." He clutched his neck and made choking noises. "Better accept fatherhood graciously. I believe it's not too bad," he added, glancing slyly at Thornton.

Thornton could not understand what all the fuss was.

"Now listen," said Jacob, rousing himself, "this is the plan. We'll announce the wedding first. Write home; tell everyone, her people too. Then we'll say she is pregnant. So the baby can be born early. You know what I mean?"

He appealed to Thornton. Thornton knew exactly what he meant, but Christopher was annoying him. Why couldn't the silly bugger stop sniggering like a smutty schoolboy?

Unfortunately there was more to come.

"But why on earth do you want to get married? That's for the bourgeoisie. What's the matter with you, Jacob? Why are you so spineless? This is the age of free love. What's wrong with you, men? You're like an old woman from back home. Stand up for freedom!"

Christopher would have gone on longer but luckily he needed a pee.

"So," said Jacob with some relief when he had gone, "that's settled then. We're getting married. Now you must bring Savitha and Meeka to my place to meet her. Meeka can be the bridesmaid," he added, regretting this almost the instant he had said it.

Tonight, he would write to his parents. "I won't say anything about the baby just yet, so I don't want you to breathe a word to Mummy either."

"What?" said Christopher, coming back after his pee. Unfortunately his flies were only half done up. "Mummy won't care, men. Don't you know she isn't like that? Don't you know she doesn't give a damn for stupid bourgeois conventions? Don't you understand? Don't you know? . . ." He stopped. It was clear they did not.

"What?" said Savitha when she heard. "*What!*" and she laughed.

"Yes," nodded Thornton, "I promise you, it's true. She's called Geraldine and she's in the family way."

"Blimey!" said Savitha, forgetting herself entirely and using the favourite word of the messenger boy at work. She couldn't stop laughing.

Thornton's eyes bulged. Meeka, standing on one leg outside the door eavesdropping, was amazed. Her mother was being surprisingly *with it*. Meeka was bursting with a hundred questions. What was this Geraldine like? And why, if she was in the family's way, did she not simply get out of it?

Meeka herself was always getting in the way, always being told, "Get out of the way, Meeka." She would like to meet Geraldine. But even more she couldn't wait to see Gillian, Jennifer and Susan. She could hear herself tomorrow recounting the developments when they all went for a wander on the District Line.

"My uncle is marrying an Irishwoman called Geraldine," she would say. "Unfortunately she is in her family's way but I am going to be the bridesmaid and I will be telling her what to do about keeping out of it."

That's what she would say tomorrow, when they were out on their jaunt, and as always everyone would be impressed.

When it finally occurred, the meeting had all the ingredients of failure. Had he been a betting man Jacob would have recognised this. Savitha and Geraldine entered the ring slowly with lowered heads and Meeka entered at a trot. Christopher came along for amusement only. Alicia came but only stayed for a few minutes. She had discovered some small solace in the long walks she went on daily and wanted to be somewhere else entirely. Outdoors, not cooped up in the bare-boarded, damp house that Jacob rented along the Finchley Road. She left to go walking on Hampstead Heath.

It was a Saturday afternoon, a good opportunity for high tea, thought Savitha, who was rereading Jane Austen. She knew what *she* would have done in the circumstances. She would have made a cake of spectacular, unbearable lightness. All eggs, fresh lemons and air (imagine, she thought, they have three different sizes of eggs here, even the hens do as they are told!), and then she would have iced it, pink and white. Out would come the bone china, the pale green Copeland perhaps, as it was a special occasion, or even the Spode, for the rosebud teapot was so lovely. Anyway the point was she would have made an *effort*. She would have put on a *good show*. Here was the soon to be married Geraldine, born in the land of Yeats, lucky thing to have such a famous countryman, unlike Savitha who came from the land of peasants. But what did they find when they arrived, thought Savitha afterwards, what did they find? Only Irish filth!

"It's the best I could do!" said Geraldine apologetically. "You see, I feel sick all the time."

Shameless Geraldine, admitting the obvious within minutes of their meeting, throwing her large husky voice around, giving out private information then producing a Lyons Corner House cake, serving it on ghastly Swedish-style plates, producing some "fizzy" for Meeka in a tangerine bark-textured glass. Savitha wrinkled up her nose, declining the cake. Thornton ate some, nervous as a foal, forgetting to smile. Jacob ate a slice; well, he had to, didn't he? Meeka ate huge pieces of the rubbish; it looks so stale and flat, thought Savitha. Have any eggs been used at all?

Meeka didn't care; she just wolfed it all down, swinging her legs.

Poor little mite, thought Geraldine, bet the bitch doesn't feed her properly. Only Christopher was enjoying himself. Who would have said his family could be such fun?

"I say, Meeka," he said, "what d'you think of this cake?"

"'S good," said Meeka with her mouth full, helping herself to some more.

"Meeka," said Savitha warningly, "that's enough now. You've had six pieces." And she wrinkled her nose.

"But Mum," wailed Meeka, "I'm starving."

Christopher drank mug after mug of weak tea (there were not enough hideous teacups to go round). It's clear Geraldine doesn't know how to make tea either, thought Savitha. What's Grace going to make of her new daughter-in-law?

"We're planning to go home after the baby arrives," said Jacob, looking self-conscious. Geraldine dimpled and patted her stomach archly.

"Baby? What baby?" asked Meeka between mouthfuls, wriggling on her chair.

Everyone ignored her. The talk turned inevitably to what was happening back home. A general election was coming up. Christopher had no faith in it and argued hotly.

"It will take more than a bloody general election to stop this war now. That damn Sinhala government is completely corrupt. There'll never be socialism in that bloody country with those Western boot-licking bastards."

Does he have to swear? thought Savitha with distaste. Though she agreed with him she was not prepared to say so.

Christopher helped himself to a swig from his hip flask.

"Can I try some, Uncle Christopher?" asked Meeka idly, sending him into a spasm of laughter.

"Not on this occasion, putha," he said, winking at Geraldine. "This is mother's ruin!"

"*Christopher!*" said Thornton and Jacob.

Meeka, opening her mouth to ask another question, caught her mother's eye and changed her mind. Geraldine stood up. She'd had enough.

"I'll make a fresh brew," she smiled.

That's just what it is, thought Savitha.

"You look like your daddy," said Geraldine, smiling at Meeka. The child was on to her seventh piece of cake; did her mother never feed her?

"Mum doesn't like interfering with nature," Meeka said suddenly.

Geraldine was taken aback. She looked at Anna-Meeka with narrowing eyes. What was the child trying to say? Had her sister-in-law-to-be been talking about abortion? How dare she, thought Geraldine hotly. The child shouldn't be here, listening to adult conversations, repeating things. It wasn't right. Jacko had warned her to be careful. Look out for trouble, was what he had actually said, watch what you say to her and watch your back, she's like her mother.

"She doesn't want me to have a brace," added Meeka, but no one heard her.

"More tea, Thorn?" Geraldine asked, coldly.

What's all this "Jacko" and "Thorn"? wondered Savitha, annoyed, wanting to go home immediately. Who *was* this impostor from the Isle of Poets?

On the tube home, for once, they were in agreement: the afternoon had not been a success. United in the face of change, they considered Geraldine.

"What does he see in her?" asked Savitha. "What on earth will your mother make of her?"

Thornton shook his head. He made a hissing noise through his teeth. "Of all the women in this country!"

"Did you notice, there wasn't a single book of Yeats poetry in the house?" When she got home Savitha intended to look up her favourite Yeats poem.

Thornton the poet did not mind about Yeats. He had other doubts.

"Her ears are pasted to her neck. It's an old Tamil saying. Never trust a person with pasted lobes. And she's dirty," he pronounced fastidiously, as the tube passed from Belsize Park to Chalk Farm. "Why couldn't she comb her hair?"

He was thinking most specifically of Cynthia Flowers and the curtain-of-gold. The lovely Cynthia, who probably awoke each morning, rising like Venus, majestically with her perfect hair. All over her mouth, thought Thornton, remembering her mouth. Yes, yes, he thought, imagining her sleepy mouth, imagining her first thing in the morning. He went into a small delicious daydream. So, no, Geraldine was not a bit like Cynthia Flowers.

Meeka watched her father. He had his silly look, all soft and furry at the edges. She wondered what he was thinking. She opened her mouth to ask him when she caught sight of her mother's reflection in the tube window. Her mother had folded her lips again. It was a good sign, Meeka knew. Her mother was thinking furiously and was displeased with someone other than Meeka for a change. As far as Anna-Meeka could see, this was as good a moment as any.

"Is she going to have the baby before they get married?" she asked. Loudly.

September came in with heavy rain. What had started out as a desperate bid for freedom was now filled with dissatisfaction. When her aunt Alicia had arrived, trailing her sorrow like a thin chiffon scarf, the summer had seemed full of possibilities, but now it was over. Anna-Meeka had her way and was accepted into the comprehensive school. She was not unhappy, but you could not say she was particularly happy either. She no longer had any piano lessons and the music lessons in school were useless too. The teacher was often absent and supply teachers, who had little interest in music, took the classes. There was not even a piano in the classroom. Soon after Christmas, her aunt Geraldine had had the twins.

"Cousins!" Uncle Jacob had said, expecting everyone to be as proud as clearly he was.

"What a riot!" Meeka muttered with the cynical onset of adolescence, not wanting to visit.

Two identical boys, screaming shrilly. Michael and Patrick, fair as their mother, blue-eyed like her.

"What a waste," was Savitha's only comment. "Why waste blue eyes on boys!" She said nothing of this in her letters to Grace, to whom she still wrote regularly.

More and more it was Frieda who replied. Grace was having trouble with her eyes, and found it difficult to write.

We are trying to get her to see a specialist, Frieda wrote. *But she keeps saying she doesn't need to, or she will when the war is over. She walks into things around the house all the time. I fear her sight is getting worse. Anyway, I have made an appointment for next week without telling her, so I will let you know what happens. She has become much frailer since Alicia left. Almost as though she was holding on for Alicia's sake. She hardly goes out anymore.*

They had been shocked when they heard, unable to imagine what Grace must be like now. Thornton tried phoning. His mother sounded just the same in the few minutes' conversation before the lines went down.

In the end Jacob did not go back with the twins. They were so small and the Foreign Office had issued warnings of the dangers of the war, so they sent photographs instead. Jacob looked haggard and overworked. The twins were a handful, and Geraldine was bad-tempered and depressed after the birth. Although she still had her hoarse Irish brogue, his wife was almost unrecognisable. She no longer nibbled his ears under the covers. In any case, no sooner had his head touched the pillow than it was time to get up again.

"At my time of life, fatherhood is hard work," he admitted to Thornton, adding, somewhat reluctantly, "Maybe you did the right thing, men, by having Anna-Meeka when you were young."

Anna-Meeka had become quieter. She too had changed. School and her friends absorbed all her attention. Her grandmother, her aunt Frieda and the island seemed a long way away. The war was remote from her daily battles over her schoolwork, her hair and the length of her skirt. Soon her parents' curfew was far more important than any news from back home. Besides, her relatives got on her nerves.

"Moan, moan, moan," she told Gillian wearily. "We're *here*, aren't we? What's the use of thinking about a place we can't live in any longer? Why do they go on and on about Sri Lanka?" she groaned.

Gillian was mystified. Meeka's family had always puzzled her.

"Every single time they get together that's all they talk about," Meeka told her. "They are so unbelievably boring, so utterly predictable!"

Gillian was forced to agree.

Even Aunt Frieda's letters, thought Meeka, are no longer interesting. Feeling uncomfortable and guilty, without even realising it, her own letters to her grandmother gradually petered out.

One evening, Jacob, in his new busy life as a family man, rang to say he had some news.

"He's coming over at the weekend to tell us," announced Thornton.

"What now?" asked Savitha, laughing. "Let me guess, the Impostor's pregnant again?"

"Oh, Mum," wailed Meeka, "they're not bringing the bloody twins, are they?"

"*Anna-Meeka!*" said Thornton shocked. "Anna-Meeka, don't let me hear you use language like that again. They are your *cousins*! This is Christopher's doing, men," he said, turning to Savitha. "He's always trying to undermine me, d'you see?"

"Dad!" said Meeka, wishing her uncle Christopher was here. He was the only one of her relatives she could stand.

Jacob and Geraldine arrived with their news. Geraldine carried one twin and her rolls of new baby-fat. Jacob carried the other.

"We've been saving up for the lease of a corner shop," Geraldine told them proudly. "Your brother is about to become a businessman!"

"My God!" said Thornton, his voice edged with what sounded dangerously close to envy. "An Asian businessman. You'll be rich."

"Well," said Christopher when he heard, "he always had a tendency towards being a capitalist bastard!"

Christopher refused to get excited about Jacob. His whole family was a disappointment. All, that is, except his delightful niece. In any case, he was off to Trafalgar Square to join a huge Amnesty International demonstration. Did anyone want to go with him?

The twins were crawling now, and Anna-Meeka loathed them. She had been the only child for so long that there was no room in her life for these large bawling infants. One twin crawled up to her when she was playing the piano and bit her leg, making Geraldine laugh her belly-rumbling emerald laugh. Meeka was silent, rubbing her leg, her smile not quite reaching her eyes, swearing silently to herself, saying nothing.

Watching her daughter, wryly, Savitha noticed that she no longer said everything that came into her head. Lately she had begun keeping her thoughts to herself. She is growing up, thought Savitha with a twinge of fear.

It was the end of the decade.

17

Ohe morning, before he went to work, Thornton received a letter. It landed gently on the mat.

"Nice stamp," said Meeka, glancing at it. "Who do we know in Lausanne?" She was late for school.

"Have you seen this?" her mother called out from the kitchen. She was reading a copy of a newspaper over breakfast. The paper was still called *The Colombo Times* but Ceylon was now renamed Sri Lanka. "The news is terrible! Those bastards in the government are reducing the numbers of Tamils going to the universities now."

Meeka winced, wishing her mother would not shout so much. Thornton shook his head.

"I saw it," he said, surreptitiously pocketing the letter, thinking no one had seen it. He was not expecting any letters, but instinct made him secretive. "There'll be rioting again," he said.

"It's odd," Savitha continued. "We haven't heard from Frieda for a while. D'you think we should phone them? See if your mother is all right?"

"Leave it till the weekend. She gets alarmed when the phone rings. Anyway, I think it's just the usual story of the post not getting through. We'll phone on Saturday."

"Don't forget, it's parents' evening tonight."

"I haven't," said Thornton. "Tonight we decide the future!" he added, trying in vain to raise a smile from his daughter.

Anna-Meeka scowled at them both and, picking up her lunch, went out. Thornton followed her. He often walked part of the way to her school before branching off to catch the tube. It was a situation that annoyed Meeka intensely. She would have preferred to walk by herself. She would have liked to wander across Durand Gardens alone, taking in the early-morning mist over the little park, peering in through the lighted windows of the big tall houses, dawdling. Another school year was under way. September was over and October was here again. This time it was not the Indian summer of their arrival. Looking back, Meeka remembered her younger self with embarrassment. She remembered wanting to feel the cold. Now it was cold all the bloody time. And she had nothing to look forward to anymore.

They passed Philippa Davidson's house. Philippa was in Anna-Meeka's class. Mr. Davidson was standing by his bright red two-seater. He was laughing with Mrs. Davidson. Oh yes, very funny, thought Meeka sarcastically. What a bloody funny morning. She imagined the Davidson family, from the time they woke up. Laughing while they cleaned their teeth, laughing as they dressed. Oh my God, how they laughed as they had their breakfast! She could just imagine it. Mr. Davidson did not spill his tea all over his jumper or eat too fast and dribble marmalade on the tablecloth, and Mrs. Davidson did not shout at him about some bastard in the government. She was sure Mrs. Davidson didn't even know the word "bastard." And Philippa? She probably had her head in a school book, shining hair tucked behind her ears, a dimple flashing on her cheek as she looked through her homework.

Seeing Meeka as she passed, Philippa turned and waved. In a friendly way.

"Hello, Meeka!" she said. "Hello, Mr. de Silva."

Meeka scowled, mumbling reluctantly.

"Pretty girl," observed Thornton as the two-seater drove off. "Why don't you make friends with her?"

Meeka scowled harder.

"Don't walk so fast," Thornton said mildly. "You're not late."

They parted at the top of the Clapham Road, Meeka turning with a sigh towards school, her father heading towards the tube station.

The tube was crowded and Thornton could not read his letter. Then when he got to work his boss was waiting for him, her face thunderous. Now what have I done? wondered Thornton wearily.

When he had sorted out the problem and apologised again, it was almost time for his tea break. The women in the next office fussed over him, plying him with chocolate biscuits and tea. It was nearly lunchtime before he next remembered the letter, but then Savitha rang.

"Alicia phoned after you left," Savitha said, sounding harassed. "I didn't have time to talk to her. The sink is blocked, and Meeka's forgotten her maths homework, again."

Thornton opened his mouth to speak. Savitha's voice buzzed angrily in his ear.

"What was I supposed to do? I was already late. I couldn't take it in. She had to hand it in today or she'll be given detention. We've got a parents' evening. I hope you haven't forgotten. I hope you're not planning to meet your brothers?"

Thornton's head was beginning to ache. Savitha was like his boss. She could stretch a single complaint into a thesis.

"No, no," he said, wearily, "I haven't forgotten. I'll get back early, and I'll ring Alicia, see if everything's all right."

Alicia had been to a concert the night before at the Royal Albert Hall. The first concert she had been to in fifteen years.

"It was so wonderful," she told Thornton, astonished.

As they spoke he could hear music in the background. Alicia was playing another record.

"I sat in the front row listening to the Berlin Philharmonic! The choral part was unbelievable," Alicia told him.

Thornton was taken aback. Alicia sounded animated. He made a mental note to tell his mother.

"We're ringing home this weekend," he told her tentatively. "Why don't you come over?"

After he had finished talking to Alicia he rang Jacob to tell him their sister had finally gone to a concert. But Jacob was busy and could not talk. Then he tried ringing Christopher at work. Christopher had taken a few days off to go to a Communist Party meeting in Paris. He remembered his letter, suddenly, sitting snugly in his pocket, but by now his boss was hovering and, although he wanted to read it, he decided to wait. At lunchtime the office boy came to collect his pools money and stayed chatting to Thornton, and before he knew it the hour was over. Although mildly curious, he decided to save the letter for later.

The afternoon was long and tedious, an in-between afternoon, not quite summer, not quite autumn, not quite anything. Dampness hung around the trees. Thornton stared out of his window, rearranging his pens and sharpening his pencils, threading a new ribbon into his typewriter.

Of such moments, he thought, was his life made up. Trivial markers for the minutes, the hours, and all the days of what was left to him. In three weeks it would be the end of the month and he would get his payslip. Briefly, vistas would open up, things of beauty and pleasure, things that were the stuff of dreams. Like the bright two-seater convertible he had seen this morning. Last night, when they had gone to bed, he had asked Savitha, "Would we have come to England had we known what it really was like?"

Savitha had not answered and he realised she was asleep.

"I am tired," he had said, softly, into the darkness. "This endless to-ing and fro-ing every day to my prison in Euston Tower is killing me. What will happen to people like us, so far from home?" he had asked. But Savitha had slept on peacefully.

Looking out of his window he saw thin misty rain break into a shower, sending people scuttling across the street below. In a few short years Meeka would leave them. Already she was an alien being beyond Thornton's understanding, struggling through a private war of her own, wearing ridiculous clothes, speaking with that ridiculous accent, trying to be someone else. Staring at the heavy rain clouds, Thornton shook his head. I will grow old and useless in this tower, he thought, sadly. He still missed his mother. The truth was he had never really got over leaving her or his home. Her presence had given substance to his life; his old home had been his anchor. Without them he belonged nowhere.

I don't want Meeka to have the same fate, thought Thornton, watching the rain dislodge the dying leaves. He glanced at his watch. They had a parents' evening tonight. If only his daughter could have a respectable profession, become a doctor, earn a good salary, *then* she would be safe. It was the reason they had brought her here. It was his goal. Placing a piece of paper in his typewriter, he opened his shorthand notebook and began to work with renewed vigour.

He did not think of the letter again until he was on the tube, caught in the rush hour coming home. It was still raining when he arrived at the Oval and he stood for a moment in the draughty entrance taking the letter out of his pocket, but apart from being postmarked "Lausanne," there were no other clues. The space for "sender" remained blank. Something familiar about the handwriting puzzled him and made him nip quickly round the corner to a pub. It was five o'clock on a wet Monday in October. He would have to hurry if he was to get to Anna-Meeka's school in time for the meeting. Savitha would be waiting impatiently for him. Meeka would most likely be playing the piano. Thornton opened his letter.

It has taken me a long while to pluck up the courage to find you again, he read. *So much water has passed under the bridge.*

But I never forgot you. Then last year, I met a friend of your family and I found out you were living in London and had been for a few years.

Outside the rain intensified. Thick banks of clouds gathered, darkening the sky. A huge lorry had drawn up by the pub. The driver began depositing barrels of beer, rolling them along the pavement. Someone had left the front door open and a sharp wind rushed in, curling itself around the tables, bringing in the sounds from the busy road outside. A taxi, its engine running, stopped by the traffic lights, an ambulance sounded plaintively far away. Fragments of voices hurried past, rushing out of the wetness. Thornton heard none of this. He did not notice the people coming into the bar shaking themselves free of the rain, he did not hear them ordering drinks or see the pub fill up with voices and smoke. His drink remained untouched as he read Hildegard's letter.

For Thornton was suddenly back on the dance floor. All around, the lights were twinkling in the trees. His father's shouts of triumph as he won a round of Ajoutha, drifted across the veranda. He saw his mother, her head thrown back, laughing, while his sister tossed away her bridal bouquet, as her new husband helped her tenderly into the car. And then, thought Thornton remembering, there was the serious dancing with the curly-haired girl beside him. How they had outdanced everyone, laughing all the way into the garden across the lawn and under the tree where Jasper watched them curiously. While the first moon of the New Year rose and shone all over her golden hair. Uncle Innocent had been unable to take his eyes off her. And Thornton, that younger, dark-haired Thornton, dangling his cigarette from his mouth, ignoring her protests, had thrown her up in the air. Laughing and jiving.

I understand if you find this letter distasteful. I know you have a very different life now, a wife, a child, how old is she? Does she look like you, Thornton?

Again he heard the music. How they had laughed, thinking it a joke, marrying on the same day as Alicia. How careless of the consequences he had been. Where had that life gone? It had vanished without warning and he had never noticed. Every part of that foolish marriage had been his idea, but he had let her take the blame. Never once had he tried to contact her, never once had he said he was sorry.

If there is any chance of seeing you again, for the sake of old times, such a terrible cliché, I know, please tell me. I only want an hour with you, to see you one last time. I shall be in London next summer. I should be glad of that chance.

Thornton looked up from the letter. London, the pub, the evening, everything, seemed strangers to him. He had no attachment here, no relation. Anything might happen, his link with reality seemed suddenly to have been cut like a balloon at a birthday party; it had broken off and was flying free. He looked at his empty glass; he had drunk what was in it without realising. Somehow he was still here. How had he come from that life to this, crossing time zones, sailing past the equator, never questioning where it would all lead, never quite understanding his choices?

Outside the sky had been swallowed by the night. At home, Savitha would be wondering where he was. If he did not hurry, they would be late for the parents' evening. Buttoning his coat against the wind, he walked out, noticing the paleness of the faces around him, as though for the first time. Young and old, hurrying past. A longing so great, a need suppressed for years, rose up and engulfed him. At this moment he wanted nothing more than to go back to where he belonged. To the place where the sun, when it vanished from the day, left its warmth on the land, and the people walking on the street, the *ordinary* people, were of the same colour as him.

This is what I am now, thought Thornton, overwhelmed by sadness. This is what I will be always, no matter what, no matter how long I live. The old cries for home will stay with me forever. They can never leave me now. I will simply live with them. And yes, he told himself, I *will* see her. Digging his hands deep in his pocket, clutching his letter, he thought, I will see her one last time, as she asked. It's the least I owe her.

They were late and her mother was cross. Anna-Meeka stalked ahead not wanting to be part of their argument. The Head of Year was waiting. He was smiling thinly. They were the last parents.

"Fantastic!" muttered Meeka. "Just wonderful! I'm really looking forward to this."

"Science," said her father grimly, as soon as they sat down. "She must do science."

There were here to choose her examination options. Meeka could see he was still fixed on medical school. She stifled a yawn.

Thornton looked at his daughter. Still reeling with the shock of his letter, he scowled. Then he took a deep breath and forced himself to concentrate on the matter in hand. Since he had first sat on the end of his wife's hospital bed holding the newborn Anna-Meeka, gazing with delight at his responsibilities, none of his ambitions had wavered. Many generations of responsibility were in that gaze; many past histories of love passed down at that point; a father's to a daughter, a mother's to a son. It had been this way for Thornton as little Anna-Meeka lay gently sleeping in his arms. So Thornton's determination was not to be meddled with. He could not be budged from his resolution. Not after all this history.

"She must do science," he said again.

"Well, her test results throughout the last year are not good," said the Head of Year, puzzled, running his finger down the list of names.

"No, no, no. She has to do science to become a doctor." He

had planned her future, step by slow step. Didn't this man know?

The Head of Year was taken aback. He looked at Thornton. In all fairness to him, he had no idea what he was taking on here. He thought this was a simple parents' evening. He thought that in a few minutes they would be done and he would be able to go home. How was he to know that he was taking on a whole valley covered in mist and tea and an ancient family home with a lake and God knows what? How was he to know he was taking on Thornton's lost education? He had never even heard of Grace de Silva, for heaven's sake. How would anyone in this school, not far from the Brixton Road (he told his wife later as he drank a glass of Eno's to clear his stomach), how could anyone have known what this man wanted?

"They usually want their girls married off quickly, and sent back home to have babies."

Well, this one was different and it took a while before the Head of Year realised.

Savitha spoke next. "I don't care if she becomes a doctor or not," she said slowly, "but she must have some secretarial skills. Should everything else fail, you know, she doesn't make it to medical school, et cetera," Savitha waved her hand, "well, then I want her to be able to get another job. Perhaps she could do music as well."

"Well," the Head of Year said, looking doubtfully at the timetable, "she can't do both music and chemistry. They're on at the same time. So she'll have to choose. If she wants to do music at university we recommend she does one foreign language at least. Possibly two. Does she play an instrument?"

"What?" interrupted her husband, startled. "No, no, no. Nothing of the kind. We are going to fix private tuition in maths, physics and chemistry. No? So don't you worry about that, men. She will be fine. Just put her into the right classes. That's all we want from you."

Savitha folded her lips. She was not about to have a public argument with Thornton in front of a schoolteacher. Later on, when they were back in the house, that would be a different matter.

Where, for example, did he intend to find the money? How he was going to pin Meeka down for these private lessons, had he thought of that? The girl was only interested in playing the piano. It was the only thing she did when she was at home. Shouldn't she be allowed to study it?

Savitha glanced across at her daughter. Their arguments had increased with the onset of adolescence. It both puzzled and saddened Savitha. What a sight the girl looked. With her maxi-coat and her eye makeup, her nail polish and her dark hair all over her face. Straight out of the jungle, thought Savitha, half in despair, half inclined to laugh. What were they going to do with her? Here she sat, slumped on a chair, sulking as usual, trouble written all across her brow. Of course Thornton might be right. Anything was possible, but from where she was sitting she doubted there was a future in medical school for Anna-Meeka. Sex, thought Savitha, *sex* was what she saw. Sex would be the next problem. Undoubtedly. Which teacher would they consult then?

The Head of Year was an optimistic man. It was why the job suited him so well. He believed that for every problem there was a solution. Savitha could see he had no concept of the misty hills, those tea-covered valleys or the boys' school her husband had once attended. She doubted if he ever drank his tea from delicate porcelain cups placed on fragile saucers. No, Savitha could see he did not have a clue. So she let him get on with it. Sitting back on the loose-weave blue office chair, crossing her saried legs, she waited.

"Anna-Meeka," said the Head of Year kindly, a smile crinkling the corners of his eyes, "we've done all this talking but we haven't asked the most important person what *she* wants from these next two years. Given that your parents want you to stay on, which subjects would you like to take?"

"Dunno," said Meeka, glancing across at her parents.

There was a silence. In that moment, unexpectedly and without warning, she saw them as if for the first time, from a great distance. They looked so small and defenceless sitting bolt upright in this unfamiliar place. Her father was wearing his psychedelic tie but the expression on his face did not match it. His face, she saw with surprise, looked closed, stubborn. And sad, somehow. Her mother wore open-toed sandals and socks under her sari. She too looked wrong. Like the time outside the school gate long ago, Anna Meeka saw, her mother looked cold and confused. How *old* they looked. How unhappy. She had not noticed this before. They had changed, she thought, in slow revelation. Suddenly, with blinding clarity she saw them as she never had before, their faces dark and troubled, and in this colourless room, their love for her so utterly transparent, so desperately clear.

A piece of music lodged in her head played over and over again. All day long the sounds had run on in this way, like slow-moving water, gathering and growing within her. She could think of nothing else. It engulfed her, flooding her senses, leaving no room for anything else. It seemed to hold all the colours from their discarded life, all the dazzling brightness they had once taken for granted. It was filled with the sound of the sea. She wanted to get home quickly, to write it down on the manuscript paper her uncle Christopher had given her. She wanted to play it in order to understand more clearly the subtle shifts and changes, and what difference these enharmonics made to the whole. She needed to sit quietly at the piano and let the sounds come to her, flow through her fingers, correcting themselves as they fell into the early-evening air.

"Dunno," she told the Head of Year. "I want the science option, I s'pose. Like my dad says."

18

T here's a visitor here to see you!" Frieda said, unable to keep the pleasure from her voice.

Her mother was sitting by the window looking out towards the garden, waiting for Aloysius to arrive with the newspapers. Every morning he insisted on going across the street to the hotel where he had a glass of whisky. Then he brought back the newspaper to read aloud to her. Grace never complained, although Frieda was aware she worried about her father's safety. Slowly, over the last few years, her parents had grown closer. Aloysius had changed after Grace's glaucoma had been diagnosed. These days he gambled and drank only moderately. Although physically much frailer than his wife, he did what he could to ease her path into the darkness, reading endlessly to her, writing her letters and taking over whenever Frieda went out. In the years since Alicia had left, the three of them had become a tightly knit unit.

"Guess who's here, Mummy?"

Grace turned towards her daughter's voice. When she spoke her own voice was strong and full of life. Her face remained beautiful. Only her sight, realised Ranjith Pieris, shocked, only that has gone.

"Hello, Mrs. de Silva," he said, taking her outstretched hand, "d'you remember me?" adding, as she struggled to rise, "Please, don't get up. I'll sit here by the window with you."

"Of course I remember you," Grace said, radiant with delight. "Of course!" And she clung to his hand.

"You were Sunil's best man. How could I forget you! Where have you been all these years?"

"I've been in Canada, until just two weeks ago, and now I'm on my way to the embassy in the UK. I couldn't leave until I'd seen you all once more." He would not let go of her hand. "How are you? How's . . ." he hesitated, "Alicia?"

So they told him. Over tea, on Aloysius's return, they told him all the news.

"She stopped talking," Grace said quietly. "D'you remember how she cried? How she could hardly stand up at the funeral?"

Ranjith nodded. He had been one of the pall-bearers.

"We could hardly hold her down," Frieda murmured. "We thought she would hurt herself." She shuddered. The monsoon rain had fallen, soaking into their grief.

"Afterwards the doctor had to sedate her for days," Grace said. "Only it wasn't much good. Her pain broke through." Black, terrible, rain. "And then, after that, only silence."

Ranjith nodded. He could guess how it must have been. He had been about to leave the country when Sunil had been killed.

"I stayed because of the funeral."

He had visited the house, again and again. But Alicia had been unable to speak. He had gone then, as planned, moving from embassy to embassy. Wandering the world, not wanting to come home. They had not seen him for years.

"I'm going to England now," he told them. "For four years."

"Oh, but you *must* meet them all," Grace said joyously. "Can we send gifts with you?"

"Of course, of course. No problem!" Ranjith said, delighted. "You don't know how much I have thought of everyone here, over the years." He hesitated. "I was at the ballot counting when it happened, you know," he said very softly. "I *saw*

Sunil being machine-gunned down." He shook his head, unable to go on. They had known that it had been Ranjith who called the ambulance. "When I accompanied the policeman back here, I could hear the piano."

"She was practising," Frieda said. "I remember it too."

Schubert, thought Grace. But she didn't say so. She remembered the Schubert, even now. But she had not known it was Ranjith who brought the news.

"How could you," Ranjith said. "You were too distraught."

He had lived with the guilt of being the one that survived, he told them. All these years, he had lived with this thought. They were silent. They had not spoken so openly for years.

"If Alicia will see me," he said, "of course I'll visit her."

"She still won't say his name," Frieda told him. "But she is happier in England. Strange, Thornton says she likes being left alone. There's nothing to remind her, I suppose."

"Maybe we should have sent her away long ago. Soon after it happened," Aloysius said.

"No." Grace shook her head. She was certain of it. "No, no. She was not ready for that. We sent her at the right time."

They talked late into the afternoon. Many things, previously unsaid, were uncovered. Frieda watched her mother's face brighten and become animated. The sun moved slowly across the sky and the servant brought in lunch. They ate rice, seer fish and murunga curry, followed by fresh pineapple and a slice of Frieda's cake. It was while they were drinking tea that a dull thud was heard. The house shook briefly. There was a harsh crackle of breaking glass followed by a moment's silence.

"It's another bomb," Aloysius said. "Another suicide."

The sky was a hard cut-glass blue; the afternoon's heat merciless. In a moment the air filled with sirens and distant screams.

"They'll put the curfew on again," Aloysius observed. "You'd better go, Ranjith, while you can."

"We'll write our letters tonight," Frieda promised. "And get a parcel of things together for you to take. I'll see if I can get some ambarella for Savitha."

In the four years she had spent in Highgate, Alicia had made no friends. She kept away from Savitha. Savitha was the one who had had the child, the husband. She was the one with a life. They had never been close. Thornton, once her favourite brother, was greatly changed, preoccupied with concerns of his own, and often bad-tempered. Alicia referred to this change in her letters home.

They are very different now, she wrote. *You would hardly recognise them, Mummy. I feel as though I will never have anything in common with this new generation of de Silvas. I can't even tell the twins apart and as for Anna-Meeka I have the strong feeling she doesn't like me much. I don't blame the child; she used to remind me of things I'd rather not think about.*

It was the closest she had ever come to speaking of the past. Regret lurked in the letter.

Thornton seldom brings Meeka to visit me any more, she continued. *I think he's embarrassed by her sulkiness. Last Saturday I went over there to deliver your latest parcel. I could hear Anna-Meeka playing the piano. I didn't recognise the music so I stood outside their front door for ages without ringing the bell. I suppose it was one of the pieces of music she makes up. It was strange but also very beautiful, and quite complicated. Not at all the sort of thing I'd expect her to be capable of, given her limited musical knowledge. I was reminded of Elgar and also Benjamin Britten and it made me feel bad that I'd never shown any interest in her. Still, it's too late now. When I rang the doorbell she stopped playing immediately and when I went in there was no sign of her. Savitha told me she had gone to finish her homework but I think she didn't want to see me.*

Apart from her solitary walks and occasional visits to concerts, Alicia's letters to her mother had become the only other regular feature in her life. As usual it was Frieda who wrote back, answering for the three of them, sending the news. Then, one day, Frieda's letter had news of a different kind.

Guess who's going to London? she had written excitedly. *It's someone you know! He's a big shot in the government. Can you guess?* Frieda had chosen her words carefully. *He was Sunil's closest friend.*

Alicia stared, her throat constricting. The name sat on the page branding itself into the flimsy blue paper, the "S" and the "u" and all the other letters falling into their place, making up his name, with such a sense of rightness, such a sense of loss that time itself stood still again. Somewhere in her head were the harsh sounds of weeping. Beyond this, she knew, terrified to read any further, were all the memories she dared not look at. She paused. Her hands were shaking. Often in the past she had wanted to end her life. When she first arrived in England she had come close to doing so. No one had known and, somehow, she had not. But her depression rarely lifted. The endless years of her widowhood stretched before her.

On an impulse, later that day she wrote back to Frieda. Yes, she would meet Ranjith.

Yes, she thought, that's him.

And she turned to the waitress and ordered a pot of tea for two. Ranjith Pieris had not changed much. He was a little greyer, perhaps, smaller than she remembered, but he still had the same smile, the same round face. There was an air of carefulness about him, a hint of authority, revealing itself as he threaded his way across the room. He was looking for her. She had suggested they meet in the British Museum for tea among the potted palms, behind the Sphinxes. Alicia loved the Sphinxes, the great dark obelisks, the ancient gods. Often before a concert she would while away an hour or two in their enigmatic presence. Like them she too waited for the end of time. The women in the café knew her now, knew all she wanted was a pot of tea, or at most an egg-and-cress sandwich. She looked as though she might have been somebody once, they decided. It was hard to say why. Perhaps it was in her face, perhaps it was the way she moved, or maybe it was simply that she never seemed to notice anything: their glances, the glances of others, the occasional smiles of curiosity.

She must have been lovely too, they remarked, this enigma-of-the-café.

"She's *still* lovely," said the chef. "With those large eyes, those high noble cheekbones!" he said, half in love with her.

But Alicia never smiled. She always looked cold, even in summer. Like some small bird, a sparrow who had strayed in for a crumb, a sliver of something, but who knew it could not settle here, she came and went. They watched her before going to take her order, gazing at the soft fineness of her faded sari. She was so unlike the other Asians that came in. Their resident sparrow. Belonging to the museum, coming early, staying late and always, so the invigilators reported, always wandering through Egypt.

Today seemed at first to be no different. She came in quietly.

"Ah," the waitress murmured, "she'll be wanting egg and cress, a glass of water, and then her tea."

She had her book with her; it fell open at the page she wanted, marked out by a blue aerogramme. Today, although she opened her book, she seemed restless, searching the room, her eyes a great beam of light moving up and around, first to one side and then another, pausing always by the entrance to the café. From this, they deduced, she was waiting for someone.

Ranjith Pieris saw her a second after she had ordered the tea and broke into a smile. She's aged, he thought, shocked, moving towards her. And he folded her in his arms tenderly, with something of the love for them both, Alicia and his dead friend.

"Alicia!" was all he could say; too much clamoured for attention between them. They stood, their hands tightly clasped as they once had when he visited her backstage after a particularly fine performance. It had been on the occasion of Alicia's engagement. Ranjith had come with Sunil, bringing flowers. She had teased him then, saying it was his fault for introducing Sunil to music. Their children would blame him, she said, when they were old and quarrelling with each other. Now he knew they were both remembering these words as they stood among the tables, with the china clattering and the tea urn bubbling, and the voices of tired children clamouring for a drink.

"Let's have some tea," said Alicia. Agreeing to this meeting had shaken her but it was nothing to how she felt on coming face to face with Ranjith Pieris. Knowing this, Ranjith sat down with her holding her hand, and drank the tea and talked of other things easily, letting it run on, about the troubles on the island.

"How's Jacob?" he asked. "And Thornton? What's Christopher up to?"

Alicia smiled and shook her head. "Where do I start! How long are you in England for?"

"Four years," Ranjith said. "Plenty of time to meet up. I'm staying with Robert Grant in Canfield for a while, just until I find my own place. D'you remember Robert Grant?"

"Ah," said the café staff to each other, "the little sparrow has found love!" They meant no harm; it was just the way it looked from where they stood serving teas.

"Who?" asked Alicia gratefully, for he was pressing on her wound and the floodgates trembled. They could spring open of their own accord at any moment she knew. "I don't know the name."

"Yes," said Ranjith, still holding her hand, giving the café staff hope. "Yes, you played at the party for his father at the Governor's house. Remember? The night of the riots that Christopher was involved in?"

"Oh! Yes," she said too quickly. Now she remembered. "Robert Grant, was that his name? Didn't he use to be Thornton's friend?"

"Everyone was Thornton's friend," Ranjith said, smiling broadly.

"Well, you should see Thornton now," Alicia warned. "I don't think he has any friends. He married," she hesitated, not knowing how to describe Savitha. "He has a beautiful wayward daughter," she said instead.

"Remember Hildegard?" Ranjith said.

"Oh Hildegard! Mummy saw her off pretty quickly!" and Alicia laughed softly, thinking, yes, there were other, good things she could talk about after all.

"Thornton is very different, now," she said. "His daughter's changed him. He's very serious. Bringing up Anna-Meeka is a serious business!"

Ranjith looked at her with amazement.

"It's true," Alicia said.

"Oh, I want to meet all of them again," Ranjith said delightedly. "And the wives, tell me about the *Irish* one. She's had twins, hasn't she?"

He looked at Alicia, searching her face for the clear-sighted girl he had once known. Wondering, fleetingly, what had happened to the music.

They talked and talked. About Grace and Aloysius and Frieda. And the light coming in from the high windows, curved and elegant, faded to a thin rosy glimmer until the bell heralding closing time rang, and rang again. The staff in the tea room clattered away the cups, and saucers and plates, until, at the third and final ring of the bell the huge fluorescent lights flickered off. They left through the side entrance. Maybe the sparrow will be happy now, the staff said again, taking off their aprons, hoping it was so. And the Sphinx slept, and the obelisk slept, and all the ancient gods from the Middle Kingdom slept, while the tiny magic eye of the security system kept watch over all of history and its memories trapped like so much dust in the fine midsummer air.

"She seemed diminished," Ranjith told Robert Grant later that evening. He had arrived at the Grants' country home in Canfield by train after saying goodbye to Alicia. Dinner had been served in the elegant candlelit dining room, for Robert now lived in grand style, although traces of the boyish youth still remained, nurtured by his wife, Sylvie, even as he rose up the political ladder. During the week he stayed at a flat in London, working, dining afterwards at the Athenaeum Club, rarely coming home. Tonight, however, was an exception. Tonight he was home in honour of Ranjith, the new Undersecretary of State for the Sri Lankan government.

"Tinpot Undersecretary!" Robert had greeted Ranjith teasingly. He was fond of Ranjith, having spent some happy times in Sri Lanka with him when he was not with the de Silva family.

"I had no idea any of them were here," he said as they paused over the port and the golden bowl of summer fruit. "Why on earth didn't they contact me?"

Ranjith shrugged. How to explain the fierce pride of the island's elite, their sense of loss since war broke out?

"You must understand, Robert, Sri Lankans are complex. You fellows on the outside see Sri Lanka as an appendage of India, but you know, it has a legal code introduced by the Dutch. And then of course it had the British." He sighed. "Two thousand years of Buddhism interfered with, gone wrong. God, what a mess! There's a lot of despair among the old, wealthy Tamils. Shame too, over the way things went when the British left." He paused, searching for the right words. "The personal tragedies of the de Silvas are mirrored all over the island, you know," he said, at last. "There's been a huge loss of dignity, a sense of alienation. Everyone there is depressed to a greater or lesser degree. It wouldn't have occurred to any of them to look you up. They were too busy surviving."

The telephone rang and Sylvie went to answer it. Robert poured more port into Ranjith's glass.

"Is anybody taking care of Alicia?" he asked.

Ranjith looked at him sharply. Sometimes Robert had no imagination.

"She has everything except the one thing she can never have again, Robert."

Robert was silent. He remembered how beautiful he had thought her.

"Schubert," he murmured. "I remember her playing Schubert."

"Yes."

"One of the sonatas? Which was it?"

"She was very talented," Ranjith said.

They were both silent.

"What about the other sister, what was her name?"

"Frieda? Oh, Frieda's wonderful," said Ranjith warmly.

"Ah yes. Frieda. I remember!" Robert smiled. "I met her first, did you know?" He would like to meet them all again. "And Thornton, beautiful, charming Thornton. I can't imagine him with a daughter!"

Ranjith laughed. Neither could he.

"Look, I'd like to see them again," Robert said. "Can you organise something?" He thought for a moment.

"The garden parties will be starting up soon. Your embassy people will be invited, I expect. Why don't you bring the de

Silvas? Come to supper afterwards. Sylvie would love to arrange it, wouldn't you?" he said, turning to his wife, who had walked back in.

"Yes, of course," agreed Sylvie. She was happy for Robert to indulge in a little flash of nostalgia. Theirs was a marriage of great good sense.

So it was decided. Those de Silvas who wished it would come as Ranjith's guests. Which was how Alicia, Christopher, Jacob, Thornton and their families received invitations to attend a garden party at Buckingham Palace.

19.

Garden party?" asked Geraldine, pausing as she strapped the twins into their pushchair. "To be sure, I'll not be going to any garden party." She snorted. "The very idea of it! What in the world are you thinking of, Jacko?"

She had been unable to find any smart clothes to fit her since the twins were born, and they were three now. Besides, why should she have anything to do with that stuck-up bloody de Silva family?

"Not your little brother Thornton, of course," she added, dimpling. "Ah sure, he's sweet. And not Christopher, he's just like a naughty boy." No, it was Savitha she could not stand. "Little bitch," she said richly. And the daughter was no better.

"Stuck-up cow. With her '*music*'!" said Geraldine. "I know the girl hates m'darling boys."

So, no, Geraldine was not going to any feckin' garden party.

"Good!" said Savitha, satisfied. "Then I'll go."

It would be a chance for her to see how the rich lived. She wasn't clear whether she meant Ranjith and those from the embassy, or the British aristocracy. She asked her boss for time off.

"We're going to a garden party at Buckingham Palace," she said, as though taking time off for the dentist.

Her boss, that delightfully old-fashioned Mr. Wilson, bowed low and called her Lady Savitha.

"You're all damn hypocrites, men," Christopher sneered. "Of course I'm not going. Who d'you think I am? That idiot

Ranjith *knows* I'm a Marxist, a man for the underdog, a man of the people. Anyway," he continued loudly, "as it so happens I shall be selling the *Socialist Worker* in Trafalgar Square on that afternoon." He grinned at Thornton's surprised look. "No, men, the short answer is I'm not going. You couldn't lend me ten pounds, could you? I'll pay you back next week?"

"All right, if I must," said Alicia, reluctantly.

"Oh no," said Meeka in despair, "what on earth shall I wear?"

It was all very well for Thornton; he just went down to Burton's and pointed. Then he came home again and had a shower. With his looks, all he needed was a shower.

"Who's paying for all this?" asked Savitha, whose own wardrobe was proving problematic.

Every time she decided on something to wear she was met with shrieks of horror from Anna-Meeka. Really, they're both a pain, thought Savitha, groaning inwardly. What was *wrong* with a yellow sari, red jacket and a yellow cardigan? Was she meant to freeze? Did the Queen freeze? No, of course not. Neither would Savitha then. What was wrong with this family?

"I'm beginning to wish I hadn't been so eager to go," she said out loud.

But what could she do now? Everyone at work knew. They wanted a daily progress report on the state of her wardrobe. Her nickname, Lady Savitha, seemed to have stuck. Secretly she was enjoying all the attention.

Meeka began sorting her clothes out. There was her long patchwork skirt, her skimpy cheesecloth shirt and a fringed shawl. Thornton's eyes bulged at the sight.

"Are you planning on seeing the Queen dressed like that? Are you planning on completely disgracing your father then?"

Savitha waited until he had finished shouting. Then she spoke, quietly.

"You're wearing a sari," she declared. "It is time to begin

wearing your national dress. You're a Sri Lankan girl and you're old enough now. What better occasion than this? We'll go to Soho to choose one."

She spoke firmly. Meeka opened her mouth to protest but no protest emerged. It seemed she knew when she was beaten. Thornton looked at his wife with amazement. She had turned her lips into a folded paper bag again.

Ranjith sent them personal invitations. Included were two stickers with large yellow crosses on them, to be placed on the windscreen (both front and back) of the car. It would allow them through the traffic lights at Trafalgar Square, and through Admiralty Arch, and on into Birdcage Walk. Meeka stared at the stickers.

"Where's the car?" she asked, aghast.

"Where's your bloody CD number plate, men?" laughed Christopher, when he was told.

Thank God *he's* not coming, thought Thornton distastefully. But there was still the matter of the car. Meeka in wild despair (they simply *must* go now, how was she to face her friends if they didn't?) suggested her father learn to drive.

"Don't be foolish, child," said Thornton, forgetting himself. He was already under too much pressure from Savitha.

Geraldine, taking the twins to playgroup, hearing of the latest crisis, was glad *she* wasn't going. The zip from the last pair of jeans she would ever wear had finally given up the ghost and broken today.

"It's the end of an era," Geraldine told the boys with a flourish of her hand. Tomorrow she and Jacko would be signing a contract for the lease on a newsagent's shop along the Finchley Road. One door closes, another opens, she sighed, throwing her jeans away. What did she need a garden party for? She would be stocking her shop with important things like Andrex while the rest of the de Silvas were wasting their money on a stupid fantasy.

In the end Thornton resolved the problem by walking into the taxi rank along the Brixton Road and ordering a taxi for the great day.

"Where to, mate?" asked the man in the office.

"I beg your pardon?" said Thornton, confused.

"Where to? Where do you want the cab to take you?"

"Oh, I see," said Thornton, relieved. "Buckingham Palace, please."

"Did you 'ear that, Steve? This coloured bloke who's just came in ordered a cab for next Thursday to take 'im to Buckingham Palace!"

"Yeah?"

"Yes," said Thornton, looking worried.

"Perhaps 'e's going to see the Queen, Bill. Charge 'im double!"

The de Silvas handed their invitations to the footman.

"Dr. and Mrs. de Silva, and Miss de Silva," announced the footman. "Mrs. Alicia Pereira."

Thornton was thrilled. He did not show it but he was. The footman had called him *Doctor.* He walked along the red carpet looking down at his feet, veiling the pleasure in his eyes.

"Where are you going?" hissed Savitha, pulling at his arm as he veered slightly off to the left.

"Dad!" said Meeka, and she giggled. "Now you're a doctor I don't have to become one!"

Savitha's lips twitched.

Outside a small group of musicians were playing something she recognised. Meeka began tapping her foot. She felt uncomfortable in her sari; it threatened to unravel at any minute, all six yards of it. Serve her mother right if it did. What a fright she must look. Even Uncle Christopher had given her a funny look. Luckily none of her friends had seen her. There had been another almighty struggle this morning over her mother's cardigan. Meeka had ranted and raved.

"Like mother, like daughter," Thornton had complained, wearily.

Glancing at him, Savitha noticed a piece of paper sticking out of the back of his collar.

"Go and check your father," she whispered urgently to Meeka. "I think he's got the label hanging from his collar! Quickly, Meeka, go, before anyone sees him!"

Anna-Meeka went over to where her father stood gazing at the lawns that sloped down to the water. She tried to walk like her mother and her auntie Alicia, without tripping up.

It was in this way that Ranjith Pieris first saw them. Father and daughter, arm in arm beside the lake in the grounds of Buckingham Palace. Meeka, her head thrown back, laughing at Thornton for wearing a price tag when he went to see the Queen. All around them was the gentle murmur, the subdued hum of voices. A pair of swans flew smoothly overhead. Women in pastel silks, the ribbons on their hats fluttering gently, stood tall as beanpoles. Men in morning dress, their laughter deep-throated and benign, balanced delicate cups of tea and plates of tiny cucumber sandwiches or bowls of strawberries and cream. Music played.

"So, Thornton," said Ranjith, coming up unnoticed, placing a hand lightly on his old friend's shoulder, "we meet again. After how long? Now tell me, who's this beautiful woman you are with?"

Meeka grinned. She looked around for her mother but her mother was staring at her cup of tea. Savitha turned the saucer over and peered at it and then she held it up to the light.

"Look at Mum!" Meeka said suddenly, tugging at her father's arm. "Any minute she'll turn the cup over and the tea will spill all down her sari!"

Thornton frowned, ignoring her.

"Chi, Ranjith!" he said.

And he smiled his old smile, reminding Alicia of those distant days. The music changed tempo. Visitors queued in the marquees for another cup of delicious Fortnum & Mason's tea.

Crown Rule! thought Savitha, looking at the royal crest. Somehow the thought had lost its sting in the face of so much elegance. Grace had sold a dinner service with the de Silva crest on it to pay for Alicia's passage to England.

"This is my daughter, Ranjith," said Thornton, barely managing to keep the pride out of his voice. "Meeka, this is an old friend of our family."

Meeka looked at the man. "I'm sorry," she said giggling, "but I think my bloody sari is about to fall off!"

"Chi!" said Thornton, annoyed, losing his feeling of pride. And forgetting for a moment where he was, he glared at Meeka. Why did the child have to *say* such things? He looked around for Savitha to take her off his hands, hissing at her, but Savitha, deep in a blissful dream, was ignoring him. Ranjith Pieris was entranced. He could not take his eyes off Anna-Meeka.

"Goodness me," he said admiringly, "she's a younger version of Grace!"

Thornton took a deep breath. He wanted to tell Ranjith that having a daughter was not an easy business. No one, he wanted to say, not even Savitha, understood the things that could go wrong.

"I'm starving," said Meeka, interrupting his complaints and smiling his smile. "I'm going to get a sandwich, with Auntie Alicia." Picking up her sari with the unconscious elegance of many generations, she walked away.

"Yes," Ranjith agreed watching her go, puzzled by Thornton's new capacity to worry. "Of course there'll be problems, but still, what an extraordinary thing it is, to see your mother, in such an unexpected place!"

He laughed with sudden joy at the thought of Grace here in the grounds of this quintessentially English garden, with its skylarks, its delicate flowers and its understated beauty.

She's lovely, thought Robert Grant, and no, Ranjith was wrong, Alicia was not diminished at all, just a little lost, and *still* so lovely. Feeling his heart constrict with pity, he went towards her. She was standing with her niece and for a split second Robert was taken aback. Turning, Alicia saw his mistake and she too smiled.

"Yes," she greeted him, before he could speak, "she looks like Mummy, doesn't she? Meeka, this is an old friend of our family, Robert Grant. Robert, my niece."

Meeka gave an exaggerated sigh. The place was crawling with "old" family friends, and she didn't want to speak to any of them. Her aunt had been telling her about a recent concert she had been to. It had been a rare moment of connection, but the old man had interrupted them. Bloody nuisance, thought Meeka, peevishly.

Savitha, watching from a safe distance, could see exactly what was going on in her daughter's mind. She folded her lips. It was safest to keep well away. She was having a wonderful time and planned to buy some new china tomorrow. Would the woman in the arcade know where she might get some Wedgwood like this? Savitha would be quite happy with seconds provided they were papery thin. She wondered if anyone would notice if she turned her plate over again and had another look at the mark.

The afternoon wore gently on. At some point the music stopped and the sound of clapping rose in the air. It floated across the lawns, delicate as willow on leather, overlaying the distant hum of London traffic. Then, magically from nowhere, the royal party entered. Meeka watched, mesmerised. But the Queen was so small, she thought, amazed. And was that *really* Prince Philip, looking exactly like his photograph? The guests with green tickets joined a privileged curtsying queue. A small Asian woman, the High Commissioner's wife, was talking to Princess Anne.

"She has done a lot for the Girl Guides," whispered Ranjith.

"Look, the Queen Mother has a plaster on the back of her calf," Meeka said, delighted without quite knowing why.

"Will you have dinner with me?" Robert was saying to Alicia, hoping she would not refuse.

"Yes," said Alicia, breathlessly.

Ranjith turned to look at Thornton's daughter again.

But she's beautiful, he thought with wonder. Really, he chided himself, what is wrong with me?

Everything seemed a little flat after the garden party, like a calm sea, but without the sun on it. Thornton went back to work, travelling the lift to the top of his glass tower. In a few weeks he had agreed to meet Hildegard. They had been in contact several times by letter and had planned to meet at Liverpool Street station. There were other things on Thornton's mind too. Ever since the garden party several people had remarked on Anna-Meeka's appearance. Even Jacob had brought up the subject.

"Isn't it time the girl was introduced to a suitable young man?" Jacob had asked. Adding caustically, "Before she finds something unsuitable herself"—knowing Meeka, it *would* be unsuitable—"bringing it into the house of her own accord?"

Thornton groaned. "What am I supposed to do?" he asked. "She needs to pass her exams and get to medical school. I can't think about a suitable boy just yet." This child of his had been nothing but trouble. "Why can't she show some interest in her schoolwork? In physics and chemistry? Why is the only thing that interests her the piano?" He was working himself up into a fury. "You're good at giving advice," he said, bitterly. "Send her to private school, find her a husband. Make sure she has a career."

"But Thornton, the two things are not incompatible," Jacob told him, earnestly. "Women can have a career and marry, you know. Look at Geraldine, she more or less runs the shop, you know."

Thornton had no wish to look at Geraldine. The idea of broaching the subject of a suitable boy with his daughter filled him with fear. He imagined Meeka with that big mouth of hers, hooting with laughter at the very idea. Popping a Rennie into his mouth, he hurried home to see what Savitha would say.

"I know we didn't have an arranged marriage," he began, sitting in the kitchen, watching Savitha prepare the food. "But we were living at home then. Here you don't know what sorts of fellows there are." He paused and cleared his throat.

"So, what are you planning then?" asked Savitha, when he recounted the conversation.

"Planning, planning?" Thornton said, instantly furious. "I'm not planning anything, I'm *asking*. Can't you tell the difference?"

Savitha folded her lips. Years ago, when they were still living in Sri Lanka and Anna-Meeka was a baby, she had had a discussion with Grace. Long before the subject had even entered Thornton's head, her mother-in-law had told Savitha something she had never repeated to anyone else. She had never forgotten the story. It had made a deep impression on the romantic Savitha, who wanted a love match for her only daughter. Something complete and perfect, something everlasting, was what she wanted for Anna-Meeka. She had decided this many years before. She did not want a marriage chosen by horoscopes or planetary influence. She did not want a marriage founded on superstition or the time of her birth. It was all such nonsense; she wanted her daughter to marry for *love*. One day she hoped Meeka would find happiness with a person of her own choosing. Savitha had no intention of voicing any of this and there was little use telling her besotted husband anything at the moment. In any case, she knew, he was simply frightened; he did not want Meeka to get hurt. Well, there's nothing we can do to stop that, thought Savitha. So instead, to take his mind off his worries, she said experimentally, "Well, she has been menstruating for two years now, so you better start looking straight away!"

Thornton spluttered. He turned red. Who would have thought he would develop a temper in early middle age?

"Aiyo!" he shouted, with disgust. "When did you become so coarse, woman! You're just like Christopher."

Savitha turned her back to him. Her shoulders shook with silent laughter.

"What's the problem?" she asked. "Do you think it's not about sex then?"

Anna-Meeka walking into the room just at that moment confused Thornton further. He glared at her. Meeka raised an eyebrow.

"Mum, he's flipped," she cried. "Being called 'Doctor' by that footman in Buckingham Palace has affected him!"

Savitha burst out laughing. Oh good, thought Meeka, at least we've got a happy mood in the kitchen. She wondered if this was the time to talk about the skirt she wanted to buy. Increasingly she was becoming interested in the differences between her parents' wishes and her own desires.

But the moment was not right. The garden party had had a profoundly disturbing effect on Savitha. She had gone to the arcade in search of the papery bone china she had seen at Buckingham Palace, but instead all she found was a crude imitation of the real thing. She would find nothing like it ever again. The day itself and all its luxury had vanished, but the feeling of elegance was still with her. It lingered elusively in her mind in the weeks that followed, surrounding her like a mist of

fireflies. Everything seemed to be touched with this new discovery. Nothing was real any longer; all was insubstantial. For
on that afternoon, in the palace grounds, Savitha had caught a
glimpse of something different, something that had been completely invisible until now. It gave context to this thing they
called Empire and to the people who once had ruled their
country. With a shock she realised that only by leaving her
home could she have seen any of it. For distance, thought
Savitha, was what had been needed, distance had sharpened
her perspective, revealing many hidden truths. Distance had
brought her to this point. Here it was then, unchanged by the
centuries, distilled down and concentrated. On a perfect June
afternoon, with the roar of traffic a faint smudge beyond the
palace walls, with the sun so gentle, and the flutter of well-
pressed linen all around, here, in this privileged corner of
England, was the thing she had until now only intuited.
Forcefully, she glimpsed it; effortlessly, she understood. Never
had she had this capacity to connect in such a way before.
Never would she see it so clearly again. For history, thought
Savitha, *history* was what made you what you are. History was
what made you feel at ease with yourself. History gave you a
solidity, a certainty, in everything you did. She had thought
they were escaping to a place they could call their own, but
now, she saw, this could never be.

In that moment, all her ideals, all her hopes for their life on
foreign soil, seemed as nothing. We are nobody, she thought
with silent pain. It was so simple. We are displaced people.
They had no history left, for carelessly they had lost it along the
way. Escaping with their passionate ideals, they had arrived
here. Hoping. Hoping for what? Acknowledgement perhaps?
Understanding, maybe? But she saw it was for *them* to understand. We belong nowhere, thought Savitha in despair. No
longer certain, she hesitated, wondering what she might do. She
was halfway through the journey that was her life, middle age

beckoned; the monsoon heat was seven thousand miles away. Suddenly she felt a great longing for the connections they had shed so lightly, the old certainties of her youth, the simplicity of it all. Looking at her daughter's young face, seeing the struggle ahead, saddened, Savitha kept her own counsel.

The summer wore on but it was disappointing; low clouds crossed the Atlantic, the sky was overcast. The promise of June would not be delivered. On the news it was reported that suicide bombing continued in Sri Lanka. Two British journalists, sent to cover the war, had been captured and were reported missing. Outside in Thornton's garden, rain splattered the roses to the ground. Late one evening, a telegram arrived. Grace had died peacefully in her sleep.

20.

From the bedroom window the view into the garden was mysterious. Overgrown honeysuckle and roses tangled with each other, forming a rough, dark tunnel. Thornton had not engineered this; it had just grown that way. As he glanced out while straightening his tie, combing his hair, brushing his jacket, he thought, I must cut it back. I must clear the space. But he did nothing. So the tangle of roses and honeysuckles flourished, mixing and knotting across the kitchen wall, scrambling the sash window, making it almost impossible to open. Overnight Thornton had aged. Everywhere he looked he saw his mother's face, heard her voice, felt the loving touch of her hand on his life. Like rivulets joining a stream, her presence threaded through everything he had ever done. Instead of growing closer to the others, Jacob, Christopher, Alicia, he retreated into a private grief. Like a man with third-degree burns, any bandage, any sign of containment was too painful to bear.

None of the de Silvas could go back for the funeral, none of them could organise their papers in time. There was also a nagging fear they might not be allowed re-entry into Britain. Instead they gathered at the Catholic Church in Highgate for a Mass, loosely together in spirit, bereft and silent, each with memories of their own. Sons, daughters, grandchildren, they were all present. Jacob, remembering his mother's face as he waved goodbye, felt his alienation with piercing sorrow. He had always felt he was the one on the outside, emotionally absent from his family. In the end his mother had never seen his wife or his sons. It had always been this way, thought Jacob, genuflecting. When the telegram had come, he had cried out to Geraldine, "What more could I have done?"

Standing with his head bent, listening to the words of a discarded liturgy, Jacob recalled his last walk across the tea-covered valley towards the House of Many Balconies. It was always the last day at Greenwood School that he remembered. "Everything finished that day," he had cried, when the telegram came.

He saw now, with the clarity brought on by her death, that he had blamed her for the loss of his hopes of a university education. But he had loved her, he told Geraldine. For all that he never showed it, he had loved her. And he had always done whatever she wanted, whatever was needed, without complaint.

"She was lonely," he said. "Like me, she was lonely." One of the aunts, he told Geraldine, had said their mother had loved a man from a lower caste. "If it was true we never saw any sign of it. The main problem was always my drunken father."

"It's not your fault," Geraldine had consoled him. "*They* were the ones who stopped you going to school. It wasn't fair, what they did. You were clever."

He had got away, although he did not belong here either. He would spend his days sitting forever behind the till of his corner shop. Looking around the church at his family, he felt a great weariness descend upon him. His youth had gone. Until this moment he had hardly noticed it. Jacob was not a political man. He was not like Christopher. All he had wanted was to study, to live and to die in the place where he had been born.

Alicia knelt in the pew behind Jacob. She had thought she had no tears left but she had been wrong. With her mother went the last of her youth. The incense in the church reminded her of the radiant day when she had married. The church in

Highgate was a modern one; the stained-glass windows were not as beautiful as the one in Kollupitiya. But the sun still filtered in through them. They stood for the Creed. Sunil. She could say his name, at last. On this day of her mother's funeral, something that had been stuck in Alicia for years seemed to loosen. Like grit it was falling away. She had done nothing with her life. How her mother had worried over her. Sunil would not have wanted her to live like this. Earlier that day Alicia had spoken to Savitha and a small barrier had come down for the first time.

"I never considered her feelings, once," she had cried.

Savitha had held on to her, saying nothing, comforting her with silence. A strange peace descended. Savitha had astonished Alicia. It was time to bury the dead. Next week Robert Grant was taking her to dinner. She was not certain why she had agreed. Suddenly, Alicia was aware of the need for connection. It was now nine o'clock in the morning. Across the world, in the afternoon sunlight, her mother's body was being placed in the ground. "Dust to dust," Father Giovanni would be saying.

Looking around the church, seeing the stunned faces of her family, Alicia was overwhelmed with love. It was many years since she had felt this way.

Christopher, shuffling his feet, did not weep. He was damned if he would weep in front of Thornton. Late last night, after all the others had made their phone calls, after all of them had done their weeping and wailing, Christopher had rung Frieda. Privately. His grief had always been a private thing. He had declined staying for the meal Savitha had cooked, declined talking on the phone with the rest of them. Instead he had walked home across London and made his own phone call.

"It's me," he had said, offhand, not wanting to say much.

"Christopher?" Frieda had asked.

Her voice had come across the ocean, faintly and somehow

young. She sounded strained and bereft. It had caught Christopher off guard, reminding him of his mother's voice. She had even said his name in the way his mother used to. With a questioning lilt. It had been Christopher's undoing.

"Don't worry," he had said. "I know how you suffered. I was there. I knew about Vijay."

Frieda had talked over him, trying to comfort him, not understanding a word he said.

"Your secret is safe with me, forever," he had said. "I *saw* what happened to you. It was the same for me." Then he had mumbled something about being the son most like her. "Not like Thornton," he had told Frieda. "Not like that idiot."

Taking Communion in Highgate, he remembered planting the jasmine bush, silently keeping his mother's secret, never uttering a word when the others had talked about the change in her.

"The body of Christ," the priest said.

I have only ever loved two women in my life, thought Christopher. There will never be another one.

Meeka, dressed in a pale sari, knelt in the pew opposite, her long hair falling across her face. She moved slightly, pulling at the silk, struggling with its length, wishing she had never agreed to wear it, wishing she had resisted her father's insistence. Turning, she caught Christopher's eye and hesitated, uncertain, not knowing if she should smile at him, her face unusually solemn.

But she's here, thought Christopher, astonished. Couldn't they see? Their mother was here with them, in this church. By some miracle she had come back. And she was young again. He stared at his niece. This is the one who will carry the de Silva name forward, he thought, clenching his fists. It must all come right with this child.

Anna-Meeka felt guilty. She remembered her grandmother of course, but time had blunted her memories. So many years had passed since she had lived that other life. She wished she could shake it off. Why on earth did her parents keep looking back? It only brought endless misery. She was here to support her father. *His* grief frightened her. Fear tightened her chest, made her hands cold. It made her feel a child, just when she had decided she would never be a child again. Maybe, she thought, waiting for the priest to clean the chalice, she should work harder at school, try to become the doctor her father wanted her so passionately to be. At this moment she was prepared to do anything for him to stop this grief. She fidgeted, distress crawling across her back, black-beetled and slow. Feeling disconnected, glancing at her mother, she noticed Savitha had a peculiar expression on her face. Meeka pressed her lips together. It was too much. Her mother looked so funny that tears of hysterical laughter filled Meeka's eyes.

Savitha felt apart from the de Silvas; she was not a Christian, she was a Buddhist. Churches gave her no comfort. She understood more than any of the de Silvas about karma and the cycle of cause and effect. The link that joined all their lives would exist through Anna-Meeka. While the de Silvas were only just beginning to see this Savitha had known it long ago. It was her job to anchor her daughter until she grew up. I am the custodian of their history, she thought, listening to but not understanding the Mass.

Ranjith could not take his eyes off Anna-Meeka. So much life in the midst of all this sorrow, so astonishingly beautiful. What was a man like him to a girl like this? He doubted she so much as noticed him. Watching, he saw her determination, mistaking it for certainty, forgetting the difference, forgetting his own youth. Watching her, Christopher felt her struggle and was filled with love.

Aloysius and Frieda simply waited for the day to be over. It was the longest day of their lives. There had been more bombs in the centre of the city and another member of the Cabinet had been assassinated. Frieda prepared the food silently. She needed something to do. In the middle of the preparations, unannounced, Myrtle had arrived. Frieda, trying to stay calm for Aloysius's sake, had been thrown. Myrtle had not brought a suitcase with her.

"Don't worry, I won't be staying," she said before Frieda could speak.

Frieda looked around wildly. Her father was resting.

"I'll go, if you want," Myrtle said, looking uncertain. "I had to try to get here. I wanted to speak to Aloysius. I wanted to tell him that I'm sorry."

She looked about to cry. Frieda was shocked.

"I know, I know, I'm the Devil from Hell, but she was my only relative. I tried to write to her afterwards but I never managed it. Don't think things have been easy for me either. I just wanted to say goodbye. But I'll go if you want." She managed to sound both upset and belligerent.

"Would you like a cup of tea," Frieda asked, helplessly, not knowing what to do. Her mother, she knew, would not have borne a grudge, but her father was a different matter.

"I'll see if he's awake," she suggested, uncertain.

Myrtle looked terrible. Her skin had darkened, her hair was white and she looked as if she had not slept for days. Aloysius was not asleep. He had been lying in the shuttered room watching the sunlight flicker through a gap in the wood. A bee-eater chirped in the trees outside. Everything around him looked as it always had. Only he had changed forever.

"Let her stay," he said heavily, when Frieda told him. "If she wants evidence of what I feel about your mother, then she'll get it. If not, she should not have come. I don't care either way."

Frieda's eyes filled with tears. She had been crying on and off during the last few days and she was exhausted. Her face was swollen with grief. She missed Alicia and Thornton desperately. She wanted Jacob with his sense of duty to help her to carry this new burden. She had never felt so alone in her life. Her father had been unable to eat or sleep. She was frightened that he too might suffer a heart attack. She had summoned the doctor several times in the last few days to sedate him. Frieda gave him another pill and tried to make him go to bed but she knew he would not sleep until later. Then she went back to talk to Myrtle.

"Please," she said, "have some tea."

Myrtle stared at her vacantly. "How are you?" she murmured. And then when Frieda remained silent, continued, "It's so strange. I half expect to see her come in."

Frieda's face quivered. She didn't have the strength to deal with her aunt. But after that one remark, Myrtle seemed more interested in telling Frieda about her own life in the years since she had left Station Road.

"They are playing merry hell in Jaffna. No one here has any idea of the things going on there."

She told Frieda about the shortage of food and the people who disappeared suddenly in the night, children plucked from their beds, boys on their way to school, old men who had connections with the Sinhalese.

"People are suffering," Myrtle said. "Your mother would have been shocked."

She paused and neither of them spoke. In a few hours they would have to leave for the church. Frieda felt faint with the strain.

"She was better than me, you know," Myrtle said at last. "Your mother."

The sound of distant gunfire added to the unreality of the moment.

Then, quicker than she could have anticipated, it was over. The cars arrived and Frieda brought Aloysius out into the bright, terrible heat. A peacock cried plaintively in the garden next door. The air was still; even the branches of the coconut trees were motionless against the dazzling, weightless sky. A few neighbours had come out onto the road to watch as Grace's coffin, surrounded by flowers, was borne swiftly away.

Afterwards, because of the curfew, those mourners who had come from afar left hurriedly. All that remained in the soft, sad, afternoon light was the scent of jasmine. Evening approached and the sea sighed.

"Nothing has changed," said Aloysius, "except me. And for me everything has finished."

After he had thrown the first handful of earth he had spoken briefly to Myrtle. "Thank you for coming," he had said, simply. "She would have been glad of it."

Myrtle had cried, embracing them both. She had given Aloysius a small photograph, taken many years ago, of a young and happy Grace, standing with her father in the garden at the House of Many Balconies, smiling into the sun.

Towards nightfall, the others rang again. Thornton had been unable to say much. Frieda had dreaded speaking to him, aware that he would be the worst of all. Incoherent in the end, he had handed the phone to Savitha. In all their lives together, Frieda had never known him be like this.

"Is he going to be all right?" she asked, frightened.

"Yes, yes." Savitha's voice came back to her with its own echo. "Don't worry, he is strong. As long as he has Meeka he will be all right."

Anna-Meeka, sounding restrained and distant with her strange English voice, spoke next. "Hello, Auntie Frieda," she said. "How is Grandpa?"

I no longer know her at all, thought Frieda. She has become someone else entirely.

Christopher didn't ring until much later.

"Meeka looks very much like Mummy, men," he said, awkwardly.

He spoke first to his father and then to Frieda. But when he heard Frieda's voice he had begun to cry. He had cried and cried for so long that she began to worry about the cost of the call. Then Frieda asked him something she had vowed never to ask any of them.

"Please come home one day," she asked. "When this war is over, come home."

And Christopher had cried, wretchedly, "I will, I will."

After the phone call, Aloysius went to bed. He was beyond speech and his eyes were bloodshot with exhaustion. Frieda gave him something to help him sleep. He had been drinking all day and she was worried about him. She closed up the house and moved some of the flowers into the hall where it was cooler. Glancing around, she caught sight of Jasper's old perch. It stood motionless against the skylight. No one had thought of removing it in all these years. Hesitating a moment, she went into her mother's study. Everything was as usual. Her diaries were stacked on shelves; photographs lined the walls, Thornton's published poems, Alicia's press cuttings, books and papers. Grace's glasses lay uselessly on her desk. Through a blur Frieda saw her mother's inner life spread out as though she might return to it in a moment. Grief struck her forcefully, sending her hurrying out to pour herself a glass of whisky, the first in her life. Tomorrow, she thought, tomorrow was time enough to start going through her mother's papers.

Distance distorted their grief. Thornton placed his sorrows out of sight, pressed like flowers within a book. Meeka, racing through her scales with impatience, reminded him of all that was best in his misspent youth. He had begun to understand that Grace would be with him forever. She was a collection of perfect things in his imperfect life. He closed his mind and refused to speak of any of it. He had almost forgotten he was to meet Hildegard. Cutting three roses, telling Savitha he was visiting Alicia, he left the house.

Summer was almost over. It was an unremarkable day of the palest blue, with a touch of autumn in the air. Catching sight of his reflection in the tube, he saw a man reaching early middle age carrying roses. How strange it was, he reflected sadly, to be travelling across London clutching yellow roses on his way to meet Hildegard after all these years. He could not remember the last time he had carried flowers for anyone. Idly, he wondered what she was like. They had corresponded a little since that first letter and he had told her of Grace's death. There was, he felt, a certain reluctance on his part to put too much down on paper, in case it might be miscon- strued. Better to say whatever they wanted when they were face to face.

The train lurched and rattled, emptied of almost all its pas- sengers, carrying Thornton with his reflections and his roses and all the uncertainties working in him as though he was a young man again and his mother in the house in Station Road waited for him to come home.

He did not see her. He was too deep in his melancholia, lost somewhere in the scent of the flowers that rested beside his cup of tea. The station café was a transient place of unhappi- ness and filth. Platform announcements cross-hatched his thoughts. The tea was watery. It smelt of detergent. Thornton sat as though he were resting after a great journey. Exhausted. Nearby sat an old, very large woman with thinning grey hair. A tramp. She coughed once or twice raspingly and Thornton glanced up only to look away again. The waiter began to sweep away the rubbish under the tables. A train rattled past, the café filled and emptied of people. Thornton sighed, staring into space.

Just like a ghost couple, thought Hildegard, sadly. Here,

then, was her heart's desire, while she was changed beyond recognition.

"Look!" she tried to say. "It's *me*, Hildegard. Can't you see?"

He could not see. Hildegard sat, stunned, her throat constricted. Like quicksilver, like the music his sister made, her passion had always run too fast. I was always out of step, she thought with despair, willing him to look at her again and see the woman he had once loved. Wanting him to recognise her. And even then, she thought, although my body was lithe and supple, and I could dance with the best of them, outdance him even, although I was pretty and golden-haired and Uncle Innocent loved me at first sight, it was never any use. I could never be one of them.

After a while, having looked at his watch several times, when the tea was cold and undrinkable, and the sound of rain on the high wrought-iron roof rattled like a thousand grains of rice, Thornton grew increasingly restless. Meeka was having a private lesson in physics at six o'clock and he wanted to be back to check she didn't miss it. Savitha, who took a dim view of the lessons, would not fuss if Meeka stayed at her friend's house. Where was Hildegard? he wondered, irritated. She might have rung him at work if she had changed her mind. Pushing his half-drunk tea away in distaste, he rose.

Well, he thought, frowning, glancing at his watch again, I at least have kept the appointment.

He had wanted to make his peace with her; he had been willing to talk. But she had changed her mind obviously. Enough, he had waited long enough. Pushing the flowers into the rubbish bin he strode hurriedly away.

Robert Grant stared at the ceiling. A thread of light from the street lamp moulded itself against the cornices, sharply defined in the darkness. A slight breeze moved the curtain and the thin line changed and swelled. It was raining again. The leaves were singed with brown. Autumn was on the march. With the children back at school he would be able to spend more time at work. Sylvie would busy herself waiting patiently until he finished work and came home. Now you can relax, supper will be ready in a minute, she would say, turning the side lamps on in the large drawing room, humming to herself as she moved plates and glasses about, lifting the casserole out of the Aga, pleased he was back. Sylvie asked so little. And here he was betraying her in this old-fashioned way.

Beside him Alicia slept. Soundlessly, hardly stirring, limbs curled towards him, dark hair covering her face. If he moved his head and lifted it slightly towards her, took in the faint perfume of her long hair and listened, he could hear her even breathing, could see her small body rising and falling underneath the covers. Robert stared at the line of light across the ceiling. Every night this is what he saw.

Every night, he thought wryly. Every night! If only it was. He loved her. It was the simplest feeling in the world, and yet unbearable. He would have thrown everything away for her. Every last thing he had worked for, his children, his work, everything he possessed was a pale shadow beside Alicia. Had he loved her all those years ago, when he had first heard her play the piano at the Governor's house? Since meeting her again the constant restlessness that had dogged his life had gone.

It seemed such a short while ago that he had taken his leave of her in Sri Lanka, dodging the monsoon, laughing as he went, putting the de Silvas out of his life. The trees in their garden had been strung with coloured lights in preparation for the wedding. He had been vaguely aware of Grace's watchful eyes and he had told himself firmly that he was glad to be sailing away. He had not dared to think of what might have been had Alicia met him first. And now, there was no one he could ask, no one he could share this love with.

She did not want it. She took from it only the barest crumb.

There is nothing of me left, she had said candidly, lifting her small face towards him. Not wishing to deceive him, not once, not even for a moment. Such was her honesty. He had only himself to blame. He glanced at her as she slept. Though she was no longer young, her skin was silky to the touch, glowing against the whiteness of his hand.

Anyone who knew him would have thought him crazy. Risking all he had, not thinking about his children, his reputation? If the papers got hold of the story it would be the end of his career. Caught by his conflicting desires, his thoughts circled round and round his head, like the endless wheels of a train, the street lamps kept on shining, and his heart kept on beating and Alicia went on sleeping, while the thread of light on the cornice marked the hours and the minutes ticking relentlessly towards the dawn.

21

No one had seen it coming. In one stroke, all that had been established lay shattered at their feet. They would never find it again. Time moved slowly for the de Silvas. Their last great realisation had shocked them. Life would not be what they had dreamed. Since his mother's death, since his failed attempt to meet Hildegard, Thornton had withdrawn quietly. Savitha watched him tending the garden. She served him hot rice in his mother's tureens, gave him cups of tea in her bone china, but there was nothing else she could do. She could see what she had always suspected: without their mother's influence the de Silva family was disintegrating. In spite of a drunken husband, in spite of the war, Grace had kept them together, while she, Savitha, could not even control her daughter. One end-of-summer evening, soon after the funeral, while Thornton cut the grass, Savitha sat at the kitchen table and began writing a letter to Frieda. All letters home were now written entirely by Savitha; Thornton simply sent his love.

He's all right, Savitha wrote, knowing Frieda worried about her brother. *We talk less but I expect that would have happened anyway. When you have been married for as long as we have, silence hardly matters. I know what he's thinking, anyway! You mustn't worry. Of course your mother's death was a shock, but living here has made him strong. I've been having dreams about the day we left Sri Lanka. You have no idea how frightened we were that morning when we said goodbye. Everything frightened us then, leaving you was terrible of course but the huge ship frightened us and the sea was so enormous. I thought we would drown. We were terrified! So we talked more. We are no longer like that, we are resilient. We have lost something else. Perhaps it's our innocence.*

She paused, not knowing how to go on. Not knowing how much Frieda would understand. It had taken the garden party to mark their dislocation. *You see, Frieda,* she continued, struggling to explain herself simply, *I have discovered that being part of an empire means you lose your individual and collective identity.*

Savitha stared at what she had written. Frieda would think her mad. Meeka had begun to play the piano. It was something she had been tinkering with for days. Recognising it, Savitha raised her head absent-mindedly and listened. The music travelled under the closed doors, reminding her of something familiar yet elusive. It drifted softly across the house, very sweetly and melodiously. Meeka played a chord and then a series of arpeggio. Her hands ran across the keys, pausing, and the music changed texture, its modulation rising slowly. Savitha held her breath without understanding why. Thornton, pausing as he cut some roses, heard it faintly and hummed absent-mindedly. The piano needs tuning, he thought. Frowning, Savitha went back to her letter.

We no longer know who we are, or what we want. Our sight is impaired and our anger too great.

She sighed. What was the point? Frieda would not see beyond her grief and the civil war that had taken her family away. With Grace gone there was no one else Savitha could speak of such things to. But she did mention Christopher. She had begun to understand Christopher better, she told Frieda.

He saw what the war would do long before anyone else. How it would destroy everything of value and wrench us apart. It has taken too many people away, dispersing the richness in the place, robbing it of its talent. Christopher saw that. And because he can't do anything, because he is a man, he drinks to forget this betrayal.

We are from the same place after all, she decided, pausing, thinking about Christopher, remembering Sunil, the other person who had tried to do the impossible alone. The piano music had changed into a minor key.

Things will only change slowly, she continued, hoping Frieda would understand, *and probably not in our lifetime. Fairer societies do not come overnight.*

"Is that Frieda you're writing to?" asked Thornton, coming in with some vegetables from his plot. He went over to the sink and turned on the tap. The scent of newly cut grass wafted in through the kitchen door.

"Close the door," said Savitha. "It's getting cold." Autumn was heading towards winter.

"Send my love, will you?" Thornton said. "Say I'll write as soon as I can."

His face was silhouetted against the fading light. He looks tired, she thought. His mouth was stern, disapproving. Pity clutched at Savitha's heart. She saw clearly what Grace had always known. I have come all the way from the orphanage in Dondra to this place, she thought, but I am so much stronger than he is. Sighing, she added Thornton's love and sealed her letter. Then she stood up. It was time to cook the evening meal. The piano music was reaching its end. For the moment, the green of the island retreated from Savitha's mind and instead the twilight of the late evening was filled with the tender sound of swallows.

It had started with her clearing Grace's room. Tidying up the papers, putting them in order. There were still letters to be answered. For a long time Frieda had been reluctant to do anything. Every time she went into her mother's room she simply cried. She was too apathetic to care. In this way eighteen months passed before she could face it. Then, one afternoon when Aloysius went for his walk to the hotel and she was a little stronger, she forced herself to begin sorting out Grace's things. Aloysius would not look at them. He was very frail now but he remained stubborn on the subject. Frieda let him do as he pleased, staying out even when she felt it was not safe, and drinking. It was all that was left and she had not the heart to stop him. She had given up worrying about the curfew and the bombs. They were part of daily life.

It was while she was sorting out the photographs, making them into piles, some for Thornton, some for Alicia, others for Jacob, that she found the photograph. Sitting back on her heels, Frieda glanced at it. She did not recognise the tall, slight man in the sarong. A few yellowed jasmine flowers fell out of the envelope along with it. Idly she turned the photograph over.

My dearest love, Vijay, Grace had written. *October 8, 1950.*

Frieda looked at the picture, puzzled. Vijay? She did not know anyone called Vijay. She put the photograph aside, meaning to ask her father when he came in, but then something made her reach for Grace's diary. What had they been doing in October 1950?

Today is June 23, Grace had written. *Three years and one day since Vijay died and I have been unable to write until now. A thousand days and nights have passed since that terrible night. Somehow I lived through all of them. Smiling on Alicia's wedding day. Dealing with the family, Thornton's crazy marriage. It's a small miracle that I managed to survive. Through the skin of my teeth and in spite of Myrtle's inquisitive stare, I have survived.*

Frieda read swiftly.

Only two of them know what I have been going through. Christopher and Aloysius. Who would have thought it possible, that my drunken husband, the man who wasted my money, who gambled away my home, should have kept me sane through these terrible days! Even though I have betrayed him with another man.

Frieda gasped. In an instant her world seemed to have turned upside down.

Nothing will bring Vijay back, nothing can change the past and yet, in spite of everything he knows, Aloysius does not judge me. How can this be? All he wants, he tells me, over and over again, is that I can be happy again. Poor Aloysius. I never knew how much he loves me. I will never leave him, never, never. We have both suffered enough.

The sound of her father returning made Frieda jump. Shutting the diary, she hid it quickly. The palms of her hands were sweating and she was breathing rapidly. It was the servant's day off and Aloysius would want a cup of tea.

Later on, after they had finished their evening meal, she read to Aloysius from *A Tale of Two Cities*. But all the time she was distracted by the words she had read about a man whose existence she had not known of until this afternoon. *My mother?* she thought incredulously. The past rolled like thunder. She sensed a passion she had never experienced in her own life. I always lagged behind, she thought, behind Alicia, behind Thornton, behind all of them. Life has passed me by. There had been the business of Robert Grant but she could no longer even remember his face. She was impatient to get back to the diary.

Aloysius had had enough of Dickens. Frieda switched on the radio so he could catch the evening news. The Sinhalese newsreader warned the fighting was very bad in the Batticaloa area. The Tamils were bearing the brunt, being stopped suddenly and hauled away at roadblocks, never to be seen again. The sky had begun to darken; the evening was over.

"Look," Aloysius said, with pleasure. "Your mother's jasmine bush is opening its flowers. She must be thinking of us!"

The air was fragrant with perfume as Frieda stared out into the garden, seeing it with her mother's eyes. Her mother as she had never known her. A sentence repeated itself in Frieda's head.

Until everyone can have the same opportunities, Grace had written, *until we stop this cruel caste system, until everyone is given the same chances, my dearest Vijay will have died in vain.*

Tomorrow, Frieda decided, I will go to the orphanage and offer my help. I will see what I can do to give some Tamil child another chance.

Anna-Meeka failed her physics, her maths and her chemistry A levels. Biology was a borderline pass.

Her father, sounding like a reversing lorry, shouted, "Retake! Retake!"

But in the end even Thornton could see it was useless. Anna-Meeka did not have the makings of a doctor. Savitha, watching her daughter slowly turn into a bad-tempered beauty, was at a loss as to what they might do for the best.

"Perhaps you're right," she conceded reluctantly. "We should think about introducing her to someone from Sri Lanka."

It was Saturday afternoon, and as usual Meeka had gone to her friend Gillian's house. She was meant to be revising for the retakes. Thornton gave the grass its last cut for the year and came in for his cup of tea.

"I can't do any work," he said, abruptly. "I'm too upset by her results. After all our hard work, after the struggle we had to get to this country, she's ended her schooling with no career. She won't become a doctor now, men."

He sat at the kitchen table, defeated. Savitha said nothing. She too was upset, but for different reasons. Anna-Meeka's wanton behaviour was what confused her.

"How's she going to manage when we die?" Thornton asked belligerently. He waggled his finger at Savitha. "She has no brothers, no sisters. She can't go back home. So who will look after her? At least if she had become a doctor she could have got a job anywhere in the world."

Savitha closed her eyes. She was tired of listening to Thornton and worrying about their daughter.

"Well, you're not a doctor and we managed," she ventured. "I told you, you should have let her do her music. Maybe she could have become a music teacher."

Thornton snorted. "How much money d'you think she'll make as a music teacher, for God's sake?"

"Stop shouting, she'll be back in a minute."

If Anna-Meeka were to hear them there would be another one of their eternal arguments. Savitha was sick of them. Gone were the days when they could tell Meeka what to do. Gone was that sweet smile. These days Meeka was eager to pick them up on more or less anything they said.

"She has no respect," Thornton fumed. "In Sri Lanka, girls have respect for their elders."

What d'you know about the girls in Sri Lanka? thought Savitha, wearily. But she didn't say this. Nor did she tell him that only the other day she had noticed Ranjith Pieris staring at Meeka a little more intently than he needed to.

Meanwhile, the subject of their concern was standing on the corner of the street talking to a group of teenagers from school. She was carrying a pile of books.

"Where's you been, Meeka?" one of them asked her.

"None of your business," said Meeka, tossing her long mane of hair and laughing. "I've been revising for my retakes."

The group gave a disbelieving guffaw. "That's what you tell your parents, Meeka, not us!"

Meeka smiled demurely. "Must go," she said, "talking of parents! I'm late and they'll kill me."

"Oy, Meeka, what's that on your neck? You got a love bite, or 'ave you been bit by a snake?"

Anna-Meeka, ignoring them, was running towards her house. Her father was sitting drinking his tea. He looked nervous and her mother looked cross. She guessed they had been having an argument. She took a deep breath. There was simply no easy way to do this.

"I've got a job," she said, bending her head low for the shrapnel which would soon be whizzing around the small kitchen. "It's at the hairdresser's. They're going to train me while I work. Then when I'm older I can set up a salon. So you don't have to worry about my future anymore."

She had expected disapproval, but to her surprise Thornton had looked merely crushed, and although her mother had glared at her and folded her lips, she too had said very little. This silent disapproval had been unnerving but the relief of leaving school was so great she didn't care. She had given up trying to please her parents. When she was not learning how to cut or shampoo hair, she spent her time daydreaming. Music continued to fill her head. The sounds followed her everywhere, faint echoes that haunted her waking moments and sometimes also her sleep. She listened to Elgar and to Vaughan Williams and she listened to Benjamin Britten's *Curlew River* until she knew it by heart. She spent all her money on cassette tapes which she listened to on a pair of headphones. It made it impossible to hear her parents' complaints.

One evening, on her way home from work, she bumped into Philippa Davidson. Why did she have to meet her when she smelt of shampoo and hairspray, looking her worst with nothing to say? Oddly enough Philippa did not seem to notice. She appeared really friendly. Meeka listened curiously as Philippa Davidson told her she was going to university. Of course, thought Meeka a trifle sourly. Clever, sorted-out Philippa was going to read English at Oxford. Meeka could not think of anything to say in response, but Philippa, hardly noticing, promised she would not lose touch.

That winter Meeka began to write a new piece of music. Every evening after work she would sit at the piano and work on it. Occasionally Savitha would stop what she was doing and listen. Her daughter's music was strangely beautiful. It always reminded her of home, fleeting images and snatches of conversations, memories from that distant life, all just out of Savitha's grasp. When she tried to talk about this to Thornton he would shake his head and refuse to be drawn. His daughter was eighteen; he had given up.

A new pattern began to emerge. Most evenings, after Meeka had spent some time at the piano, the three of them would eat their meal of rice and curry. They no longer laughed or argued as they used to. Then when the plates were cleared and if it wasn't too late, Meeka would go round the corner to Gillian's house. No one stopped this newfound freedom. No one dared.

"Don't be too long," her mother would say.

Her father would look at his watch, pointedly. "Shall I come and meet you?" he would ask tentatively each time.

And each time, Meeka would tell him, easily, "There's no need, Dad. Gillian always walks me back."

She was never very late and they knew Gillian, so they said no more.

One night after dinner Jacob phoned unexpectedly and Thornton went to meet him at the White Hart. It was the first time in months that Thornton had seen him.

"Don't drink too much," Savitha warned, but she spoke mildly.

"No, no," Thornton said. And he went out.

It was with a sense of relief that he began to recount the changes in his daughter to Jacob.

"She's always out," he said, "visiting that friend of hers,

Gillian. She's completely dropped her studies. Even Savitha can't understand it. Can you believe it, a de Silva working as a hairdresser? After all we've been through to get her to this country."

"Forget it, Thornton," Jacob said, shaking his head. "Haven't you noticed? Everything's changed. All the old values are slowly being lost. The young people from our country just want to integrate with these white fellows."

He looked at his brother not unsympathetically, for he knew how ambitious he had been for Anna-Meeka. Coming here had been a gamble, they had always known that. Jacob himself was not without troubles of his own.

"It isn't any easier for me," he said. "The twins are fighting with next-door's children. Aiyo, they're all ready to start a war! Geraldine just laughs and says boys will be boys, but I'm worried about where it will lead." Really, Jacob was appalled. "I've got the Irish situation right on my doorstep, you know, men."

Lately, now that he saw less of Thornton, Jacob had come to feel a lingering affection for his brother. Looking at Thornton's whitening hair, he felt as though he was watching the tide go out. Helplessly, unable to stop it. He himself was completely bald.

"Meeka has grown up here, Thornton," he said consolingly. "You can't expect her to obey you as though we were back in Sri Lanka. She is part of this system. I told you long ago, women here are different. They do what they want. Look at Savitha. Does she listen to you? Remember when she got that job in the factory?"

Thornton could not deny it. His brief sense of relief had passed. He moved restlessly, wanting to get back and check that Meeka had returned home safely. They finished their drinks and parted. Walking back, crossing Vassall Road in the moonlight, Thornton passed a young couple caught in an embrace. Dimly as he passed, he registered the girl's slender form and her long dark hair. Thornton sighed deeply and continued quickly down Southey Road, towards home.

At the end of January the weather got colder and snow threatened. Ranjith Pieris came to say goodbye. He was returning home. Savitha gave him some parcels to take back for Frieda and Aloysius. Meeka was nowhere to be seen. Later that evening, not long after he had left, Anna-Meeka came home from the hairdressing salon to find her mother cooking a chicken curry. Her father was reading the *New Statesman* and did not immediately look up. Meeka did not mind. She went over to the newly installed radiator and began warming her hands.

"I'm cold," she said.

"Well, why don't you wear something warmer?" Savitha told her, bringing a bowl of rice to the table.

Meeka gave her mother an odd look. Savitha brought a dish of ladies' fingers to the table. Seeing it, Thornton gave a sigh of pleasure.

"Ah, *bandaka*," he said. "Good!"

Meeka grinned. The grin did not quite reach her eyes.

"I've got some news," she said.

"Don't tell me you're leaving that bloody hairdresser's at last?" Thornton said, mildly.

Savitha looked sharply at her daughter. Some strange premonition made her heart miss a beat. Meeka was shivering with suppressed excitement.

"Mum, Dad," she announced, hardly managing to contain herself. "Guess what? I'm getting married in the summer!" She held up her hand, anticipating their questions. "He's from Calcutta," she said. "And his name is Naringer Gupta. He's a *doctor* and he's dying to meet you!"

Alicia opened her letters over breakfast. Robert poured her some fresh orange juice and signalled the waiter for more coffee while watching her surreptitiously. She looked relaxed. It was the first holiday they had had together. The last few years had been very difficult for him. He was absent as often as he dared but sometimes he suspected Sylvie knew what was going on. He had wanted to confess and leave but Alicia would have none of it. She did not want Robert to hurt Sylvie more than they already did. Every time Robert brought up the subject of his wife, Alicia appeared on the verge of flight. So this was how they had lived for nearly four years. He did not like it, but he did not want to lose Alicia either.

A week ago they had arrived by water taxi from the airport. Alicia had never been to Venice. Robert wanted to show her his favourite city. Sipping his coffee he reflected on the previous day. They had had an astonishing night. He had booked tickets for *La Clemenza di Tito* at La Fenice. It had been a wonderful performance. On their return to the hotel, whether as a result of the music or not, Alicia had gone to the grand piano in the reception area and without any warning played Mozart. Robert had been speechless. Alicia had stumbled a little but the receptionist and a few Americans who were present had burst into spontaneous applause. Afterwards, without a word, she had taken Robert's hand and led him upstairs to their room. They had made passionate love to the soft sounds of the water lapping outside. This morning the Grand Canal sparkled and shone as though studded with diamonds. Robert felt a lightness in his heart. A change had occurred. It made him afraid to breathe. The day stretched before him. He felt full of optimism and youth.

Alicia was frowning as she read Frieda's letter.

"Now what?" said Robert.

The de Silvas had such colourful lives compared with his own.

"Frieda is thinking of adopting a Tamil orphan." Alicia said. She began reading aloud from her letter.

"*I've decided to try to help a Tamil child. They are in a des-*

perate state. If they go back to the North they will simply get sucked back into the insurgent movement, which will mean certain death. I've been visiting the convent for some time. The nuns are very grateful for any help they can get. Of course I haven't said anything to Daddy as yet. He's very frail and I don't want to upset him unnecessarily. I wanted to ask you what you thought about the idea. This house is too large for the two of us. Mummy would have approved, don't you think? Remember how she used to help the nuns?"

"Well," said Robert. "Why not? She is a remarkable woman. Why not?"

"Mmm," Alicia said uncertainly, "I suppose so. She was wonderful with Anna-Meeka when they lived there. She was wonderful with me too," she added softly.

Robert nodded. He wondered how much Alicia had told Frieda about him. For all their differences, he knew the sisters were closer than was at first apparent. There was only so much Alicia divulged to him and there were some places where he felt unable to intrude, but he was certain Frieda knew. Alicia was opening her other letter.

"It's from Thornton," she said, surprised.

The waiter brought them more coffee. Outside, coins of sunlight danced a ballet on the water. A *traghetto* packed with businessmen was crossing the canal. Robert felt impatient to show off the city to Alicia.

"Does he know you are with me?" he ventured.

Alicia shook her head, briefly. Then she began to read her letter.

"Oh no," she said suddenly. "Oh my God, *no!*" She looked at Robert, horrified, her mouth moving soundlessly. Then she threw her head back and began to laugh.

"Now what?" Robert asked again.

"Oh, Robert," said Alicia. "Oh my goodness, Robert, you're not going to believe this!"

Robert smiled. It was good to hear Alicia laugh.

"Honestly, that *girl*!" Alicia continued, barely able to speak for laughing. "Would you believe, Anna-Meeka has just announced she is getting *married*. To an Indian! Thornton is beside himself!"

So that was that. She was getting married and the de Silvas were in uproar. The telephone lines were almost on fire.

"Well," said Jacob when he heard, "why are you so surprised? At least she told you before she did it!" Try as he might, he could not resist the dig.

"Has Princess Meeka blotted her copybook then?" asked Geraldine, picking up one of the twins and kissing him.

"*An Indian*! But why an Indian?" asked Savitha flabbergasted.

Her daughter's foolishness amazed her. Meeka glared at her mother and self-righteous rage kicked in.

"Mum," she shouted, belligerently. "He's a doctor! What's the matter with you? He's *not* English. What's your problem? I thought you'd be pleased."

Savitha was speechless in the face of this new development. She stared at Anna-Meeka helplessly.

"You better get used to it, Mum," Meeka was saying. "We're getting married *anyway*."

What was wrong with her parents? she asked Gillian in despair. "They've spent my whole life telling me how they hated *all* my white friends. Now I'm marrying someone like them but they're still not happy. And he's a doctor, for God's sake! You'd think my dad would be happy, wouldn't you? What the hell *do* they want?"

Gillian had no idea. Meeka's family had always been a mystery. "What will you do?" she asked.

"Get married, of course," Meeka said, shortly. She wished for the umpteenth time she had parents like Gillian's. Nice, quiet English people. The sort of parents she deserved. "I'm worried Naringer will think they're freaks. He hasn't even met them yet. God knows what sort of a wedding we'll have at this rate."

"We'll help," Gillian said, consolingly. "Mum and I'll help."

Meeka nodded her thanks absentmindedly, remembering her birthday party.

"Did they really know nothing about Naringer?" Gillian asked admiringly, unable to let the subject alone. Her friend always lived so *dangerously*.

Anna-Meeka shook her head again. "D'you like him?" she asked, suddenly.

Gillian nodded, cautiously. Her own boyfriend seemed dull by comparison. "Yeah. A bit quiet, but, yeah."

They were both silent.

"What's happened to Geoff?" Gillian asked, offhandedly.

Meeka swallowed. Tears of self-pity pricked her eyes. Geoff was English. He was training to be a plumber. *He* was not a doctor. Couldn't her parents *see* she had made the best possible choice?

"All I ever do is try to please them and this is the thanks I get." She looked at her watch. "I gotta go," she said. "I'm meeting Naringer at the tube station."

Naringer was sheltering from the rain. He was tall, and from a distance he looked handsome. Only on closer inspection, however, was it was possible to see the scars left by a heavy crop of chickenpox scabs. He had been born on a barge that glided along one of the many canals towards the Hooghly River. His family had been better off than most. Their barge was top-heavy with bamboo. They had poled it inch by inch through a mass of purple water hyacinths. The humidity, the factory smoke and most of all the rains were part of Naringer's memories. His mother had nine of them to feed and never enough money. His father existed on rice with chili and onion for flavour, followed by strong tea. But somehow Naringer had attended school. His mother, unlike others, had not sent for him halfway through his school day. Most of the boys left early to help with the business of making a living. Naringer had his mother to thank for a different fate.

When he was seventeen he moved into the centre of the city where he worked running a rickshaw from the arcades of Chowringhee along the length of the Lower Circular Road. At night they choked on the acrid fumes from the street campers that flickered among the filthy bodies. Somehow, call it karma or luck, Naringer managed to escape. By the time he had got a scholarship for the university he was much older than the other students. Introverted and hard-working, intensely proud of all he had achieved, Naringer shed his relatives. All except his mother. He would not forget his mother. He had never told Meeka this, but one day he intended to take her back to Calcutta to look after his mother and to live among the purple hyacinths.

Anna-Meeka approached him with a frown.

"What, no is-smile?" he asked mildly. "I have been waiting at this is-station for ten minutes and you can't is-smile?"

"Shh!" Meeka said. "Don't talk so loudly, and don't say is-station. It's *station*."

"Ah! Fine mood, fine mood," Naringer said humourlessly, waggling his head, drawing her towards him in a tight embrace.

The rain increased, forcing them further back into the station.

"You are very beautiful woman," Naringer told her seriously, pinching her cheeks together with his hands. *Grammar*, thought Meeka, but she said nothing. She wondered if Naringer was too tall for her. He began to kiss her neck, pushing her hair back. Meeka shivered. Naringer's hands were everywhere, like an octopus. Standing in the shadows of the tube, she wriggled uneasily. Supposing someone she knew saw them?

"So?" he said finally, disentangling himself from her. He rolled a cigarette. "How's the father?"

Meeka didn't answer and Naringer glanced at her indulgently. He hoped the parents weren't going to cause trouble. He had never met any Sri Lankans before. When he had first met Meeka, coming in again and again to have his hair cut, he had thought she was from north India.

"North Indian girls are very good-looking," he had told the blonde girl who had first cut his hair.

The girl had giggled and passed the compliment on.

"I'm Sri Lankan," Meeka had said with her posh accent.

"Where all the fighting is taking place? *That* place?" Naringer had said, surprised. They were difficult people, he suspected, small-built, unlike Indians, he thought wryly. Nothing special.

Meeka was smoothing her hair. She looked at Naringer. In spite of her edginess her good mood was almost restored. Seeing this, Naringer took her hand and planted another kiss on her head.

"Come on," he said, "why don't I just call on your parents now?"

He was unprepared for her screech of horror.

"Are you crazy?" shouted Meeka. "Don't even suggest it. Oh my God! Are you *mad*? You've no idea what they're like. I've got to prepare them first. It could take weeks."

"You stupid bastard," Christopher told Thornton, when he was told the news. This had all happened when he was away in France. "I knew it, I knew it. It's all your doing. *She's* trying to please *you*, you idiot."

Thornton did not hear. The shock had affected his hearing.

"Your mother must have felt like this," Savitha said.

Thornton did not care. He was not interested in anything anyone said, or felt. He was beyond mere speech.

"I'm worried about him," Savitha said, ringing Jacob up for a rare conversation, wishing she had not said that about his mother. "He went out to the off-licence earlier and now he's drinking, whisky."

Meeka, coming in just at that moment, put an end to this conversation.

"Hello!" she called. "Anyone home?"

It felt as though this was a war zone. No one spoke. Savitha folded her lips and waited.

"I want to talk to you, Anna-Meeka," Thornton called hollowly from the sitting room.

Having got himself into a state, having had all his dreams shattered, having declared war on his only daughter, Thornton was torn. Love and rage combined to form a lethal cocktail. He glared at Meeka. She was wearing black stilettos and a pale green dress. Around her neck was the gold chain her grandmother had given her long ago. Her hair gleamed (she had presumably done something to it at work), and Thornton stared at her as though seeing her for the first time. He had no idea where she had come from. The sleek young woman in front of him was a total stranger. He realised she was talking.

"What?" asked Meeka, again.

She kicked off her shoes and faced him patiently. With a great effort Thornton pulled himself together. I must be calm, he thought.

"When are we to see this man, then?" he bellowed.

He could not bring himself to say his name. Savitha, hovering behind the door, came in quickly. Thornton had not slept for days. It's too much, Savitha thought in alarm. An old feeling, some long-forgotten emotion attacked her. Her husband looked terrible.

"You need something nice to eat tonight," she said.

Going back into the kitchen, she took out her spices and roasted a tablespoon of coriander. She rinsed the Venetian glasses. Then, glad that the arguments seemed to have ceased for the moment, she went shopping. It was a Saturday afternoon. I'll make a crab curry, she thought, slipping out quietly.

Outside on the street, Mrs. Smith from next door was posting a letter into the pillar box. Mrs. Smith hesitated. She did not want to look as though she was spying. Savitha smiled uncertainly; neither knew what to do.

"You all right, luv?" Mrs. Smith asked, plucking up courage.

"He's an Indian," Savitha blurted out, before she could stop herself.

Her voice wobbled dangerously. Mrs. Smith nodded, kindly; she had heard everything of course, through the wall.

"We know nothing about Indians," Savitha said, trying not to cry.

Having started, the relief was enormous. Mrs. Smith nodded again. It was as she suspected. Swiftly she decided to take a chance.

"Why don't you come in and have a cuppa?" she asked.

Mrs. Smith's kitchen was nothing like anything Savitha had ever seen. It was filled with clutter. Even though she was upset, Savitha could not fail to notice the dresser filled with crockery. They were the sort of thing Geraldine bought and Savitha disliked. Somehow, in Mrs. Smith's cosy kitchen, they didn't look so bad. There were newspapers and knitting patterns strewn about. And balls of wool. A half-finished child's pullover lay on a chair.

"For our grandson," said Mrs. Smith apologetically, scooping it up. "Sorry about the mess."

Savitha was shocked. In all the years they had lived next door she had not even known Mrs. Smith had grandchildren. In the corner of the room, facing the window, was a large white seagull. Catching sight of Savitha, it opened its beak and gave an ear-splitting screech. Savitha jumped.

"Don't mind Jonathan," Mrs. Smith chuckled. "He's recovering from a broken leg."

In spite of her own state of shock, Savitha was astonished. Over a pot of tea, hardly aware of what she was doing, Savitha began to tell Mrs. Smith what was happening.

"If only we had consulted the horoscopes and found a decent Sri Lankan man," she said. "You know, my husband and I don't really believe in that sort of thing, but you know, we're in a foreign country. We should have protected ourselves. I think that was where we went wrong."

Mrs. Smith's eyes were round with wonder.

"He's a Hindu," Savitha continued. "And Meeka says he's a doctor."

Mrs. Smith nodded sympathetically. "It's nice for us," she said suddenly, "having you living here. But I can see, it can't be easy for any of you. You've got two places in your head to deal with, luv. See, my husband came from Bournemouth and he finds it hard enough! I always tells him, think how hard it must be for them."

Savitha was lost in thought. Mrs. Smith stirred her tea.

"She's beautiful, your Meeka," she ventured. "She could have anyone!"

"What's the use, being beautiful," Savitha reflected sadly, "if she behaves in this terrible way? It was the way she deceived her father that's upset him, more than anything else. All those lies about visiting Gillian, keeping it secret. For four whole months!" Savitha folded her lips, tightly. "We know nothing of this man, other than he's a doctor."

She paused and they drank their tea in silence.

"She's a difficult girl, you know," she continued. "She gets obsessions. Sometimes she plays the piano for hours and hours, forgetting to eat, forgetting the time. What kind of wife will she make?"

"We love hearing her play that piano," Mrs. Smith smiled. "Mr. Smith always switches the radio off to listen to her."

"I don't know what to do," Savitha confessed.

Mrs. Smith poured out another cup of tea for her exotic guest. She was having a wonderful time. Then, boldly, she put her hand over Savitha's.

"Get her to bring him over," she said confidentially. "Get the lad in the house, take a look at him. He mightn't be so bad. She's a clever girl, your Meeka, I'm sure she's not doing anything stupid. And she loves you all right, don't forget that. My Mr. Smith always says there's no knowing how things will work out."

Savitha was startled. Mrs. Smith sounded as though she really cared, and Savitha felt her eyes brim with tears. She had held herself together for so long, she had tried to be strong, but the effort had made her terribly tired. Sipping her tea, staring at the worn linoleum floor, she felt an unexpected sense of belonging, here, in this messy kitchen. Mrs. Smith was not like Savitha's boss. She could not quote Yeats or Tennyson, nor did she have any exquisite bone china, but there was something very sweet about her nevertheless.

"Thank you," she said, standing up with quiet dignity. "Thank you for the tea, and for being so kind to me. You're absolutely right. We must see him."

"Righto," said Mrs. Smith cheerfully. "Good luck, ducks," she added, forgetting herself. "All is not lost!"

And she let Savitha out.

Naringer planned his visit. It had taken two weeks but at last the invitation had come.

"Will I have to discuss my thesis with your father?" he asked.

Meeka looked at him sharply but he was not joking. She wanted to laugh. Naringer's visit coincided with the return of Alicia from Italy. Alicia wanted to see her niece to congratulate her on her news and, she told Thornton firmly, she was not prepared to judge Anna-Meeka.

"Let's give it a chance, at least," she told him calmly.

Savitha was taken aback by such decisiveness. "What?" she asked, momentarily distracted.

Alicia, when she arrived by taxi, had an air of well-being about her. Thornton wore his new suit, causing Meeka to stare at him with irritation.

"What's the matter with you, Dad? Why d'you need to dress up?"

Thornton said nothing. He was no longer shouting but his silence was worse. It made Savitha even more nervous.

"He's in a hell of a rage," she confided to Alicia. "I've never seen him like this."

"I'll tell you what's wrong with him. He's feeling ashamed," said Alicia, shrewdly. "Never having had an education, he finds, on top of everything else, he's going to have a son-in-law who's a doctor and this worries him. If only Daddy had educated them, Thornton wouldn't have become so obsessed with Meeka's education."

Naturally Savitha knew exactly what Thornton was thinking. *She* knew how his mind worked, but she had not expected Alicia to be so astute. She looked at her sister-in-law with new respect.

"You know he asked me if he should send for the Greenwood crest, so he could wear it on a blazer for the wedding!"

"Oh, poor Thornton," said Alicia, laughing lightly.

Naringer arrived for lunch and, for once, Meeka helped her mother with the preparations. She *looks* nice, anyway, thought Savitha, hiding her unease. Alicia joined them in the kitchen and an unusual calm fell on the household as the three women worked together preparing the food. Only Thornton continued to look terrible. He had started early on the bottle of whisky and Meeka, cautiously calling a truce, waited on him, filling his glass with ice. In spite of her own rage, her father's expression made her want to cry. Naringer declined any whisky and asked for some soda water. Thornton, keeping his face neutral, poured him some.

"You're a doctor, Meeka tells me," he said casually, not noticing his daughter's grin.

"Yes. I've just finished my is-studies at Imperial College," Naringer told him.

Meeka scowled.

"After we get marriage I'm going to is-start a job in Oxford. That's why we wanted to get married this is-summer."

Thornton swallowed hard and loosened his tie. Then he poured himself another whisky. Over lunch Naringer talked about things Thornton could not understand. He talked about drugs and chemical formulae, using words Thornton had never heard before.

"Are you going to be a GP?" Thornton asked him, looking important. "Or a hospital doctor?"

Naringer looked blankly at him.

"No, no, no," he said, understanding. "I'm not a *medical* doctor! I'm a Doctor of Philosophy."

There was a short disconnected silence while Thornton digested this.

"So you're *not* a doctor, then?" he asked, finally, his face bleak.

"Yes, I *am*!"

No one said anything. Alicia offered Naringer some more iced water. Savitha served her husband more rice. Naringer was eating heartily; Thornton hardly at all. After a while the conversation resumed and Naringer continued to talk about his research. Meeka, watching her father nod his head wisely, knowing he didn't have a clue, suppressed a giggle.

"I wish he'd stop being so stuffy and make a joke," she whispered to her aunt, when they were making the tea together. "I wish he'd say something funny like, 'Has anyone noticed Naringer's ears are pasted?'"

Alicia flashed her a smile and squeezed her hand, encouragingly.

"Give him time," she said. "Your father's a shy man, Anna-Meeka."

After lunch Alicia had a surprise for Meeka. She smiled at Naringer, handing her niece an envelope.

"It's your wedding present," she told her. "Go on, open it!"

Inside was a small key tied with a pink ribbon.

"I'm having it delivered to your new home," Alicia said, delighted by Anna-Meeka's expression. "I know it's totally impractical, *but* that's what wedding presents should be. Your grandmother would have wanted it for you. She believed wedding presents should be fun!"

Meeka stared. No one spoke. Never had her sister-in law looked so radiant, thought Savitha.

"Well?" said Alicia. "Aren't you going to say anything? Don't you know what it is?"

But Meeka, already having guessed, flew to her aunt, crushing her in an embrace.

"What is it?" asked Naringer, mildly interested.

"It's a piano!" shrieked Meeka, coming alive, dancing around the room.

"But you have one already," Naringer said puzzled, pointing to the one in front of them.

"Ah, Naringer," said Alicia, "this one isn't any old piano. *This* is a Bechstein Baby!"

"Yes," sang Meeka, "yes, yes!" and all the tension of the past weeks, her father's expression, the sunshine outside, all these things, made her eyes shine with unshed tears.

Well, well, well, thought Savitha, with the faintest flutter of hope.

The wedding took place at Our Lady of the Rosary, along the Brixton Road. There was no nuptial Mass because

Naringer was a Hindu. Suddenly, it became a jolly affair. Everyone rallied round. Gillian and Susan, Jennifer married now and pregnant, even Philippa Davidson, down for the weekend from Oxford, came. So it was a big wedding after all, not by back-home standards, not like his sister's wedding, thought Jacob, but huge for Lambeth.

Christopher came, shaking his head with anger. "Just look what she's gone and done," he said to Alicia. "Thanks to her stupid father."

Christopher would not have come if he did not love the girl so much. "What the hell do I want with weddings?" he asked, loudly.

He had spotted the groom. "Weddings are a state-organised form of capitalism suitable only for the bourgeois bastards," he told Naringer, pointedly.

He started handing out Socialist Party leaflets until the priest told him to stop. Christopher let out a short barking laugh and went outside for a cigarette. The truth was he was deeply upset by his niece's choice of husband.

"She's my niece," he told the photographer waiting for the bridal car. "She could have made something of her life, but no, she has to marry a doctor, to please her bloody father!"

The photographer smiled thinly.

"She's very talented. I used to hope there was a chance she would escape from drudgery. I told them to encourage her music, but no one listens to me."

In the distance coming slowly towards them with a streaming ribbon was the wedding car. Nodding hastily, the photographer went to meet it.

On the morning of her niece's marriage Frieda was tending her mother's grave, taking fresh flowers to it, talking to her of what was happening so far away.

"She has grown up," said Frieda. "Imagine! Alicia says she

looks *just* like you, Mummy. She must be so beautiful. Thornton's broken-hearted. No one will be good enough for Anna-Meeka."

It was the hot season and the air was very still and golden. A large lizard darted jerkily across the ground, reappearing against the white marble of Grace's headstone. Frieda stood, head bowed, thinking of her niece and her brother's broken heart, imagining her mother's voice chiding them. Anna-Meeka was still young; she had time on her side. Wait, her mother's voice seemed to say. Wait. And it seemed to Frieda that the jasmine bush she had planted waited, and the crows perched on the telegraph poles waited, and the land, war-torn and exhausted, waited for the rains to come, as Anna-Meeka de Silva was married on that summer's day in the church on the Brixton Road.

Savitha sat in the front row with an enormous orchid caught in her hair, hoping her sewing of Meeka's jacket would not unravel. Christopher, drinking from his hip flask, glared at anyone who looked at him. Thornton walked his daughter up the aisle. How lovely she looks, thought Robert Grant. He was looking at Alicia. The lightness in her face was his doing; *he* had given her something. Alicia was looking at her niece, remembering that other wedding long ago. Only now could she face the memory of it without flinching.

Thornton took his place next to Savitha. He felt defeated. The church was full of family friends, far more than they had expected. Mr. and Mrs. Smith from next door, smiling broadly and nodding their approval, the office girl from Thornton's office now married with two children, all the girls from the typing pool, little Cynthia Flowers no longer so little (she had found another sort of love, less exciting, more stable and the baby was due in a month) and Mr. Wilson, Savitha's boss, standing at the back. Savitha had worn the orchid specially to impress him. Then, before they knew it, it was over.

"You look great, Meeka!" shouted her friends.

"Be happy, darling," cried Alicia, wiping her eyes.

"Well, what happens now?" asked Geraldine.

Time was money; the twins had been babysat for nearly four hours already. Silly cow, thought Savitha, looking at Geraldine, why can't she wash properly? But then her daughter was gone, with a quick flurry of hugs and confetti, in her father's arms fleetingly, all those years of goodnight kisses distilled into this public moment, and Savitha, glancing at her husband, thought with shock, How frail he looks.

22

It had not worked out as Frieda hoped. Perhaps it was too late for a new beginning. The Tamil boy did not want what she could offer. He had seen his father's throat slit and their sub-post office in Jaffina burnt to the ground. His sister had been raped and shot, together with his mother. One by one he watched them die. Frieda's kindness had no real bearing on his life. Kindness was like chocolate. It could not satisfy hunger. Kindness only made him rage. The Tamil boy tore through the house like a hand grenade. Frieda saw that the laws governing his small life could only work if he had his own victim. The Tamil boy was eight, but he had lived several lives already. He went back to the orphanage. It was the best solution. The Devil was the best painkiller. The Devil danced inside him, telling him that love was safer at a distance.

Aloysius began to complain of stomach pains and the doctor had him admitted into hospital. Frieda rang Thornton and Savitha. She heard their desolation even before she gave them the news. It matched her own. Aloysius was eighty-four. His liver had finally given up. In the early hours of that morning, at the beginning of a rose-pink dawn, surrounded by the sounds of police sirens, he had died. Only his younger daughter and an empty glass were at his side.

"No," Frieda told them. "I am not leaving. Not now. This is where I belong."

She found it difficult to express her feelings. She had never been good at that. But she felt one of them should remain and, she saw, with exceptional insight, she was that one.

After the wedding the Guptas moved out of London, into a suburb of Oxford where Naringer had a job. He had fallen in love (he supposed it was love) with Meeka swiftly. She was beautiful in the way privileged Asians were, although of late he was beginning to see how odd her family was, full of inexplicable habits, full of pride in the things they might have achieved rather than what they actually had. They talked constantly about Meeka's grandmother as though she was a legend, as if she was still among them. He could not understand this. They were all uneducated, without a single university degree between them, but even though he had married Meeka, he sensed his father-in-law disapproved of him.

The move out of London had come as a shock for Anna-Meeka too. She got a job in a hairdresser's salon but the women she met there were not like the Londoners she had grown up with. She gave up the job and found she was both lonely and bored. The de Silvas came to visit. Christopher was the first, a bottle of whisky in each pocket and a carrier bag filled with books and flyers. Meeka was overjoyed to see him. Ah yes, thought Christopher, I'm not surprised.

Naringer was at work.

"Good!" said Christopher.

That settled it. He opened one of his bottles of whisky and poured himself a celebration drink.

"Uncle Christopher," said Meeka laughing. "It's not lunchtime yet!"

"Now don't turn into your bloody parents, please, putha!"

Meeka played the piano for him. She had just written another piece of music. "Listen to this one, Uncle Christopher." She had no one to play to since her marriage. Naringer did not like music. "Listen to the tone of this piano. Isn't it beautiful?"

Christopher closed his eyes, enjoying the smoothness of the whisky as it slipped down his throat. You are too, he thought grimly. *And* talented, and you had your whole life in front of you. So why the hell did you marry this cloth-eared, humourless man? For once, Christopher refrained from comment. Instead, he suggested they go for a walk.

It was cold and windswept outside. Once this village must have been small and pretty and well planned. Now it had grown like a weed into a long shapeless sprawl, full of sixties houses and ugly estates. There was a supermarket, a petrol station and a row of indifferent shops. Women with pushchairs bent double in the cold sharp wind, red-and-blue plastic bunting flapped unhappily over the car showroom. A few of the shops had started putting up Christmas decorations. Seeing this, Christopher snorted.

"Capitalist bastards," he muttered.

Meeka slipped her arm through his and hugged him. She was surprised at how glad she was to see him.

"Is that a library?" asked Christopher, suddenly alert.

And he darted in. Pulling out some Socialist Party leaflets from his pocket, he began to pin them on the public noticeboard. Then he went over to the desk and placed some on the counter. An elderly man was having his books stamped. Christopher gave him a leaflet, winking at the girl behind the desk at the same time.

"Uncle Christopher," said Meeka, tugging at his arm, laughing a little, "Uncle Christopher, what are you *doing*? Come on, let's go. Dad would be mad as hell with you if he could see you now!"

"Your father is an idiot, putha," said Christopher, belching loudly. "Don't talk to me about him."

The librarian was approaching. "Shh!" she said loudly.

"I'm sorry," Meeka apologised, suppressing a giggle. "We're just going." And she dragged her uncle out before he could reply.

Outside it had begun to drizzle. The sky was an opaque impenetrable layer of clouds. Nothing except the bunting and a few sticklike trees moved. No birdsong, no flowers, nothing.

"Oh God," said Christopher, unhappily, "I hate this weather. I hate this bloody place. I want to go home. Come on, let's find a pub."

Naringer hated the visits from his wife's relatives. Coming home late, hoping for a quiet end to the day, his heart would sink at the sight of the lighted windows and the strains of music. Always the damn music. He knew that if the visitor was Christopher, he would probably be drunk. He would give Naringer a book on the political crisis in Sri Lanka or the theory of socialism or some other rubbish. Then, although he said it was a gift, Christopher always somehow managed to extract money from him for it.

"Why does he think I want these books?" Naringer would ask irritably afterwards, when Christopher had gone. "What's the matter with him? Doesn't he know the East is always in crisis? It's a Third bloody World, innit?"

At first Meeka tried reasoning with him. Christopher, she told him, was only being friendly.

"Then why does he charge me for them?"

Meeka laughed. "He's probably short of cash!" she said.

Thankfully, Meeka's parents preferred the Guptas to visit them. In the early days she only went with Naringer, but it was soon clear he was bored.

"They are all is-snobs," he told Meeka.

Meeka made no comment. She began going home alone. Christopher, turning up, watched with interest.

"That husband of hers is a bloody cold fish!" he remarked to Jacob. "How long do you give this marriage then?"

Nobody was prepared to bet on it. The unsuitable, hasty match continued to baffle them. Thornton in particular was non-committal. Lately he had settled on an unspoken truce with his daughter and did not want to spoil things. Whatever disappointment he felt he had learned to keep to himself. Only Savitha knew of it. Only she saw how the events of the last year, the marriage and Aloysius's death, had aged him.

So a quieter, less robust Meeka, more subdued than before, came home to eat her mother's comforting boiled rice, her crab curry and her *brora*. To be served string hoppers by Savitha in her grandma Grace's bone china, and to listen to her father play his recording of *The Magic Flute*. Then, barely a year into her marriage, she discovered she was pregnant and everything changed. Little things about her husband that irritated her floated like scum to the surface. The way he sneezed for instance, wiping his hands all the way down his trousers.

Disgusting! she thought. She began to hate the way he prefixed the word "is" before anything beginning with "s."

"I will drive you is-slowly to the is-station," he said.

It made her want to scream. She decided she did not much like his mouth either or the way he spat into the washbasin every night before they went to bed. She made a list of her dislikes. Her husband, on the other hand, hardly speaking, hardly noticing, took to coming home early to prepare the meals she did not cook. He suggested that now that she was about to become a mother, she should start wearing a sari again. Meeka stared at him. Was he mad?

A strange in-between time began. Meeka did what she pleased. Sometimes she cooked. Sometimes she went into the town window-shopping, half-heartedly gorging on ice cream, dimly aware of an increasing well of loneliness. The one real pleasure she had was in playing her piano. During the day, when Naringer was at work, she lifted the lid and the rich dark tones poured through the tiny house, but at night, when he returned, the house was silent. She began to phone her mother more often. Savitha, aware of her daugher's need, knowing that many changes lay ahead, talked to Anna-Meeka endlessly in a way she had not done since she had been a little girl. What she had been waiting for was emerging slowly. At last, her daughter was growing up.

For Meeka, however, time ceased to have any meaning. She existed in a somnambulant state with the piano and her conversations with her mother as her anchor. Thornton, noting the frequency of the phone calls and his wife's laughter on the phone, was surprised.

"What's the joke?" he asked Savitha after a particularly long conversation.

Savitha folded her lips and refused to speak.

"Heh?" persisted Thornton. "What's she say?"

"Nothing," Savitha said, suppressing a laugh.

"What about that husband of hers?"

"What about him?"

"Well, you know his ears are pasted. That's not a good thing. In Jaffna—"

"Yes, yes, I know. In Jaffna they say you can't trust a man with pasted ears."

Savitha was laughing openly. Thornton gave up. I'm glad they're getting on so well, he thought, a little jealously. His poor, dead father had been right. Women were all the same in the end. Mistaking his daughter's state of mind for contentment, he was marginally relieved. At least, he thought, Meeka is settling down. Maybe the fellow with the lobeless ears isn't so bad after all.

"Pregnancy!" he declared, folding his newspaper. "I told you, didn't I, that's what she needed. No?"

Savitha grunted. It was not the new baby she was waiting for. It was something more elusive, something she was not prepared to discuss with her husband.

As the summer wore on Meeka began to garden. She bought climbing roses and honeysuckles, clematis and foxglove seeds. Next she bought an ornamental cherry. Soon her garden began to take on the appearance of a tumbling chaos of greenery. The month of October drew to a close. Meeka's baby was born just as the leaves began to fall, during the November rain. A little girl with dark eyes that shone like beacons in the night. She called the baby Isabella. Her parents filled her house with flowers. Savitha made tiny clothes, sewing soft cotton cloth by hand. Thornton was starry-eyed and ready to forgive Naringer, almost prepared to call him by his name. He was unable to keep away from his precious granddaughter. Christopher snorted and, as a joke, sent the baby her own book on imperialism. He meant it as a warning for her parents.

Jacob visited once but he was busy. These days Jacob was trying to distance himself from his family. They were too difficult and his hands were full with Geraldine and the twins. Geraldine wanted them to go back to Ireland. She hated it here in England and continued to dislike his relatives. In the end, thought Jacob, Anna-Meeka is just another ordinary Asian girl, marrying, having children, living an unremarkable life. What a disappointment!

"I have become a realist," he told Christopher privately.

"Don't you mean a capitalist, men?" was all Christopher said in response.

Jacob shook his head at the predictability of the remark. He no longer got any pleasure from the trips to the pub. He was tired of Christopher's drunkenness.

"Thornton's become a different person," Jacob told Geraldine, determined to slowly distance himself from his brothers. It was, he felt, best all round.

Alicia, abroad for the third time in a year, sent Anna-Meeka music by Saint-Saëns and an exquisite christening gown. She seemed happy.

I have a wonderful little flat overlooking the canal, she wrote to Savitha. *And there's even a piano. Would you believe, I've started playing again!*

Frieda, working in the orphanage and unable to send presents, phoned the new mother. Ranjith Pieris, hearing the news, had visited her and sat for a long time talking about the past. He had looked so desolate that Frieda had asked him to stay for dinner.

But they could not flourish. Too much had grown the way it wanted. Too much needed cutting back. It would need more than pruning shears, it would need an axe. Savitha, baking her cake, icing it with royal icing, finishing it off with pink rosebuds on top, travelled up by train from Paddington and watched. Thornton watched without knowing what it was exactly he watched. He took his wife's word that changes were afoot and came with his spade to dig a hole, to plant an apple tree and a rose bush.

Before the baby was born Naringer had been optimistic that Meeka would change. That change had not come. Except when his mother-in-law was visiting, the house was filthy; there were soaking nappy buckets, piles of unwashed dishes, and terrible meals. Naringer placed a statue of the goddess Kali in the hall; it stared at him every time he came home from work. On a bad day he confused Kali with his wife. He felt he was carrying them both on his back. He felt the filth in the house was worse than the stink of Calcutta. He was drowning in it. There was only so much a man could take. Naringer was a man of science. He had a logical mind and he was able to admit defeat. It was probably the saving of him.

One afternoon he returned home early and packed a bag. He found his passport. He informed Anna-Meeka he was leaving. He had had enough. He was going back to the purple water hyacinths that grew beside the canal where he had been born. Savitha, feeling as though she had been waiting for a bus to arrive, now stopped waiting.

"Well, it's no loss," said Christopher when he heard.

"She'll find someone else, soon enough," Jacob said consolingly.

And Geraldine, putting aside years of grievances, agreed. "Poor thing, it'll be tough to start with, but she'll manage," she said, thinking how large-hearted and forgiving she was in spite of how she had been treated by this wretched family. Thinking of all the things she might have said, thinking what a stuck-up little madam Meeka had always been, thinking how the girl's husband must have suffered (no one, after all, had asked *him* for his side of things), thinking how Savitha ought to feel shame but being Savitha she would not.

"Poor love," said Mrs. Smith when she heard. "Give her a hug from me when you next see her, ducks."

Meeka had a vague idea of what was being said about her. She felt the pity, but a glimmer of something else, some small defiant spark, began to glow within her. She painted the inside of her house a sparkling blue. She painted gold stars on the ceiling. It reminded her of the ruined chapel in the House of Many Balconies. Her parents were regular visitors now, along with her uncle Christopher. Even Uncle Jacob came on one occasion to help. Her aunt Alicia, having acquired a contentment hard to believe, sent her loving messages, telling her to play the piano as much as she could. What a change is here, thought Savitha, must be a man somewhere.

Meeka was grateful for any support. Her brief and confusing married life receded. All that remained was the piano, its black lacquered presence impossible to ignore. It stood now in a room stripped bare of distractions, its polished surface reflecting moments of passing light. Savitha, watching her daughter as she played, listened to the music from her childhood float tenderly across the house. Listening, she was glad that at last they were close. It had taken many years, but they had come through. Her daughter was happier than she had seen her for years.

When Isabella was two Savitha and Thornton squabbled about going back home for a holiday.

"Are you crazy?" bellowed Thornton. "There's a civil war on, people in the government are still being assassinated, there is still a curfew, it isn't safe to walk on the streets. And you want to go back now?"

But Savitha longed for the sun. She longed for her home. It was *still* her home. Nothing had changed that. Nothing would. It was something deep and necessary, something connected with the land itself. Try as she might, the longing had never gone away. She had swaddled her homesickness within her for too long. Meeka was a single mother but stronger, better able to cope, argued Savitha. And Isabella was an easy baby. But Thornton continued to refuse to go. He would not risk their both leaving Meeka.

"What if we can't get back? What if we're *both* killed? Who will Meeka turn to?" Their little granddaughter would be without grandparents.

In the end Savitha, agreeing with him, bought just one ticket. She would travel alone, she would visit Frieda, take her all their news. It would be a short trip, she would return in two weeks' time. One evening, a week before she was due to leave, she baked a cake. It was the best cake she had ever made; the icing was pink, and the rosebuds were perfect. She placed it on her mother-in-law's Hartley cake dish. She washed the Venetian glasses, the plates and the cutlery. She covered the leftover curry and swept the kitchen. Her husband smelt of whisky. What on earth was he reading now? He was getting old. It has not been easy for him, she thought, with unusual softness. Even though he would not go back, even though he always said there was nothing to go back to, he felt their losses keenly.

She would not be away for long. She knew he could not manage without her. Tomorrow morning, she told herself, she would go to her daughter's bright blue house and take the cake for her little granddaughter. Savitha smiled to herself. The child was exquisite. When she returned to the island, she would buy Isabella some sovereign-gold bangles.

Tomorrow, she thought with eager anticipation, she would see Anna-Meeka and the baby again. Savitha's heart lifted with joy. Telling her husband she was going to bed, she stepped out of her shoes. And out of her life.

Sitting on the InterCity train, with Isabella beside her, Anna-Meeka watched the fields rush past raked bare by the beginnings of autumn. A simple wreath of white roses had gone before her. A piece of music she had never heard before filled her head. Softly, gathering momentum, it rose above the darkening sky. Struggling to make sense of her grief, she heard it very clearly, cascading around her on this, her last journey to see her mother. The light outside cast long, luminous shadows across the thinning trees. Abandoned farm buildings with darkened windows sprang swiftly into view only to vanish again over the crest of a hill. In the twilight flocks of birds stretched endlessly; dark semiquavers across the telegraph poles, poised and motionless as though waiting to be played. They were heading south on a long flight back to find the sun.

BEGINNINGS

23

T ime passed. many springs, many summers, many years passed. The weeks and the months ran seamlessly into each other and in this way eighteen years went by. With time, the house on the estate where Anna-Meeka lived became shabby, its pebble-dash dark and discoloured. There was never enough money for whitewash but it did not matter. Anna-Meeka grew Albertine roses and ivy across the worst of it. The newness of the estate wore off but her own garden remained a tumbling mass of green in summer and untamed branches in winter, tapping against the windows. Like the garden, tended for so long, so too was Isabella nurtured.

Many voices came down to her, Grace's voice and Savitha's and Thornton's. All this Meeka gave Isabella.

Before Savitha died, soon after Isabella's second birthday, she had made a cake. It was from an old recipe. She had made it with rulang and sultanas, raisins and pumpkin preserve, rose water and many eggs. It had been found the next day, resting on a blue-and-white cake stand.

Sometimes on a warm summer's night as Isabella slept, Meeka caught the scent of jasmine growing beside the open window. It had been her father's favourite flower; and also, surprisingly, her uncle Christopher's. Fragments of memory, like shards of mirror glass, illuminated her thoughts and in these moments it seemed to her that other sounds, other voices, other hands, invaded the music she played. She played her piano nearly all the time now.

Thornton de Silva died in the fourth summer of Isabella's life. He collapsed on the way to the library and never returned to his council flat in Balham. An elderly friend of his, a woman, rang Meeka. Such a shame, the neighbours said. What a pity he refused to go and live with his daughter, but he would not leave London. What a lovely man, they said. Such a stunning smile.

All through what was left of that summer and during the winter storms that followed, Meeka played Schubert. After her father's death she gave up the job at the hairdresser's and began to teach the piano. This way she was always at home when Isabella returned from school. After she had finished her lessons, she would play her old favourites. She played Beethoven; she played Schubert; she played John Field's nocturnes. Then, softly, she played something of her very own. As yet it had no name. Filled with a new maturity, it carried within its haunting melody those things she had glimpsed many years ago in the head teacher's office. Isabella, drawing on the floor, raised her head and listened.

Frieda de Silva, thin and silver-haired, stooped and sad, lived alone on the island. Like her mother before her she had glaucoma. She lived in the house on Station Road, surrounded by photographs of her absent relatives, in rooms shuttered from the sunlight, with a garden a wilderness of neglect. The house no longer had music within it and the piano ivory had become yellow and broken as ancient teeth. Grace's presence lay silent across the threshold of every room. Frieda wrote when she could to her niece. She told her about the nuns at the orphanage and about Ranjith Pieris, killed by a car bomb as he crossed the road. She wrote of the waste of a whole generation. Ranjith had begun to depend on her, she said. It was a long time since she had felt this kind of affection from a man.

After her father died Anna-Meeka toyed with the idea of visiting Sri Lanka with Isabella. But the war frightened her.

She was settled at last and could not bear the thought of being disturbed. With the loss of her father she became reclusive. Small things made her anxious. Once she thought she saw Naringer Gupta in the street. It was her constant fear that he would return and claim Isabella, but Naringer had vanished long ago, back to his water hyacinths.

Nine more years went by. Alicia in Venice, where she now lived, had a bad fall. Isabella was eleven at the time. They had not seen much of Alicia although she never forgot birthdays and Christmas. Isabella loved the presents she sent. Her great-aunt wrote telling them about the concerts she held in her flat and the musicians she entertained. After her fall she became bedridden. Then as Christmas approached she caught an infection and was rushed by water ambulance to the hospital, too late. She died five days into the New Year.

One day, not long after they heard the news, a visitor arrived. He was an elderly gentleman. Winter cut sharply across the air, the evening sky was yellow and icy. Leafless trees dotted with abandoned birds' nests stretched across the horizon. Christmas was over, spring still an impossibility. The visitor stayed to dinner. His name, he told them, was Robert Grant. He had been a very old friend of Alicia's. He had wanted to tell them about himself.

"No one knew," he said. "She was the most important person in my life."

Robert Grant wanted to know about the rest of the family. He had lost touch with them all. Isabella, who had adored Christopher, told him what had happened. He had been staying with them when he collapsed last year.

"He was like Aloysius, I suspect," Meeka said. "He was an alcoholic. There was nothing we could do about it. He died as poor as a church mouse having spent all his money on drink."

"He used to turn up with two bottles of whisky and drink

the lot!" said Isabella. "He'd swear a lot and call us putha, and tell us all about his political rallies. Then he'd start calling Grandpa Thornton an idiot and Mum used to get upset."

Meeka smiled. "They never got on, you know," she said. "God knows why. Christopher used to say my father was an idiot but it wasn't my fault!"

"He kept saying he wanted Mum to do something wonderful some day," Isabella said. "He didn't know what but he always told her she would be the one to keep the family name alive! Didn't he, Mum?"

"Yes," laughed Anna-Meeka. "I think he secretly wanted me to be a famous concert pianist like Auntie Alicia. But I was never good enough. It's all down to you now, Isabella, I'm afraid!"

Robert shook his head gently, smiling.

"I am glad to have met you, Isabella," he said. "And when the war is over, Meeka, you must visit Sri Lanka. Take Isabella, show her your home, and give her back that part of her history. It belongs to her too. It's important you do."

He left them, disappearing into the night, an old man now, but still with a trace of boyish charm.

Meeka continued to teach the piano. She had lost touch with all her old school friends years ago and had not been back to London since her father's death. Only her daughter, her music and the garden held her, only here were the threads that anchored her.

Jacob de Silva, having sold his shop, moved to Ireland with Geraldine. Jacob never kept in touch. He had finally broken with the de Silvas. After Thornton's death he had felt no need for any connection with his niece.

"Too many years have passed," Meeka told Isabella whenever the subject of returning to Sri Lanka came up. Her childhood and its unwitting choices continued to cast their long shadows over her. Memories drifted aimlessly, mingling with the sounds of the piano. They mixed with the sunshine on yet another ordinary summer's day and greeted Isabella as she walked up the garden on her way home from school.

So they did not go back. And the past with its stone gods and its impossible dreams remained untouched, like unused sheets on a bed. Occasionally, the island appeared on the news as a small item. Western reporters did not go there much, not after the planes were blown up on the tarmac of the international airport. Ceasefires came and went, human rights organisations protested about the atrocities, but largely this was a forgotten war within a flawed paradise, with nothing to offer that warranted salvation. So that the violence breeding more violence locked into the land and the island waited while a force worked invisibly.

At eighteen, Isabella was offered a place at Cambridge to read English. Anna-Meeka was filled with pride. Suddenly, she saw that from now on she would be alone.

"Oh, Mum!" said Isabella. "The terms are short! I'll be back sooner than you think. And next year we *must* go back to Sri Lanka. I'm going to make you! You need to see the place again. We'll go together. I'm going to write about the war. I'm going to make people notice what's going on there."

Looking at Isabella and seeing her younger, stubborn self, Meeka was glad. Soon it was time for Isabella to leave. On her last night at home Anna-Meeka sat on the end of her daughter's bed thinking how well they had done together.

"You should go out more, Mum," Isabella told her. "Instead of just playing the piano all the time. Go out and make some friends for heaven's sake! I wish you would meet a nice man. Perhaps if we go back to Sri Lanka you will meet someone like Auntie Alicia's Sunil."

"Oh God! You sound like your grandfather," said Meeka. "That's just the sort of thing he would have said!" She laughed, for she could not have Isabella worrying about her.

But then, on a light summer evening when it was least expected, fate stepped in and took a hand in things.

It began with Philippa Davidson, who had been at school with Meeka. Philippa did not think she would meet anyone of interest on a Saturday walking through the centre of Oxford. Hordes of shoppers, youths munching burgers, tattoo artists peddling their skills, buskers with their sleeping dogs, homeless beggars, just like Calcutta, thought Philippa Davidson. She had never been to Calcutta. It was at that moment that she saw Meeka (hadn't she married someone from the very place?) walking towards her totally unchanged.

This was not strictly true of course, she thought later. Of course Meeka was changed, but she was also entirely recognisable. And just as lovely.

Philippa was on her way back from the covered market. She was carrying a shopping bag full of fresh fish and cheeses. She was en route to the French baker for her walnut loaf, for she was having some friends to supper. She was flabbergasted to see Meeka.

"It is you, Meeka, isn't it?" she asked, peering at her, standing in the middle of the street with the man selling mobile-phone covers and the buskers' dogs sniffing around. Her dimple flashed in and out and she tucked her hair behind an ear, showing a small pearl earring. Afterwards Meeka thanked God for that dimple. It was the only bit of Philippa that she recognised.

"I can't *believe* it's you!" said Philippa, and she bent and kissed her on both cheeks with a gesture of such genuine warmth that Anna-Meeka was taken aback. She had never really known Philippa.

They had coffee together. Philippa insisted on it. There was so much to talk about.

"You must come to supper," exclaimed Philippa, halfway

through their conversation. "Now I've found you I don't want to lose you again!"

Meeka was startled. The last time they had met was at her ridiculous wedding. Remembering how she had shown off, Meeka winced. What, she wondered, had happened to Philippa's parents and the wonderful sports car? She didn't ask. She was cautious. Philippa too was remembering. She remembered Meeka's dazzling father. Everyone had known how much he adored his daughter. What a stunning pair they had made. How ordinary her own family had seemed by comparison, how boring!

"You were the most exotic girl in our year," she told Meeka. "You never gave a damn about anything. I so envied you!" She laughed with delight, remembering.

Anna-Meeka stared. What on earth was Philippa talking about? She had been filled with angst, riddled with uncertainties and unhappy.

Pippa, as she called herself now, lived with her two cats in a wonderfully neat little village near Oxford. Anna-Meeka wondered why had she never married, or had children. Pippa answered all these questions with an open friendliness that drew Meeka instantly to her. She had cut her long straight hair. It was still blonde but now it had help from a bottle. Meeka could tell; she had not been a hairdresser all those years for nothing. They were the same age but Meeka looked ten or even fifteen years younger. Neither of them cared. It was as though all the indifference of their childhood had dispersed. Or maybe it was simply that Anna-Meeka was ready to give it room. Whatever it was, something affectionate rose up between them. Although Pippa lived alone she was very sociable. Her friends were a constant presence in her life, dropping in, teasing her, inviting her to the opera and crying on her shoulder. Meeka, listening to her stories, was mesmerised.

"Oh well," said Pippa easily, "I don't have a lovely family like yours. I don't have a *daughter.* So my friends are my family."

Meeka was staggered. Pippa Davidson smiled at her. She had no idea she used to make Meeka feel inadequate. She had always liked her. Seeing the loneliness that lurked in her old friend's face, Pippa's heart went out to her. If she was puzzled by the change in the once headstrong Anna-Meeka she kept these thoughts to herself. Instead, with characteristic generosity, she decided to take Meeka under her wing.

"Do you still play the piano? I remember you were brilliant at music," she said.

"It was the only subject I was any good at," said Meeka ruefully. "I was rubbish at everything else!"

"Come to supper on Saturday," Pippa said. "I want you to meet a friend of mine, whom you might find interesting."

"Who?" asked Meeka suspiciously.

"His name is Henry," Pippa said. "And he teaches here at the university. In between conducting the Birmingham Symphony Orchestra. Wasn't your aunt a concert pianist or something?"

Meeka looked wary. She felt cornered. Later she rang Isabella and told her.

"Well, why don't you?" asked Isabella. "Go on, Mum. Go out for once! Get dressed up. You look great when you do. For goodness' sake, what have you got to lose? If she's an old school friend, what harm is there in it? He might be interesting. You can talk about music. You'll *love* that."

Meeka continued to make excuses but Isabella would have none of it.

"Ring me tomorrow and tell me all about it."

Meeka sighed. Her garden was looking wonderful. Years of planting and pruning had given it a wild, magnificent look. She would have liked to stay at home and enjoy it. But she went all the same, dragging her heels a little, because she had promised, and heard Henry Middleton's laughter drifting through the open French windows. Some laugh, thought Meeka, hesitating at the front door, instantly wanting to go home. She might even have done so, had it not been for the fact that Pippa opened the door so quickly.

Well, thought Henry, what have we here? Where's this one from?

Life for Henry Middleton had not been without its struggles. It had tried to knock the edges off him but with little success. Henry always resisted. When his wife left him for a wealthier man, taking the contents of the house with her in an enormous removal van, he stood in the empty drawing room and observed the sunlight flickering on the bare floorboards. When he discovered the note informing him their joint account was now empty he had laughed out loud. His laughter echoed hollowly through the empty rooms. The day she left him he found his love melting away like the snow that covered the ground. But he was not an ungenerous man, far from it. He was not a man to bear a grudge. So when she invited him to visit her in her new home he did so without bitterness, driving through the gilded gates, made, it seemed, for giants, to wish her well. Having tried marriage and failed to understand it, he decided it was not for him. If at times he was lonely, if there were moments when he wondered what it might be like to find a love of his own, he brushed these thoughts aside, considering them sentimental. Instead he concentrated on distractions, of which there were many, for Henry Middleton was a man that women liked. For eleven years he had lived like this, the life and soul of many dinner parties.

"Henry's such fun!" his friends said. "We *must* invite him."

"There's someone we want you to meet, Henry!" they cried.

"You're sure to like her. She's pretty."

And Henry would turn up for supper wearing his outrageously colourful clothes, laughing his delightful laugh, looking deep into the eyes of whoever it might be this evening, flattering her with his attentiveness, *enjoying* her. Although always, on the next day, or the day after that, he would drive her regretfully home, for had he not eschewed love forever? So, as the beginnings of middle age turned his hair to silver, he hid his loneliness with perfect ease, for Henry Middleton had many good friends. Pippa Davidson was one of them. She was always trying to find someone for him. She told him nothing about Anna-Meeka before he met her, wanting an element of surprise.

"Where did you find *her*?" he asked afterwards, not being one to beat about the bush. "She doesn't look too happy."

Pippa had been surprised by Meeka's silence. Perhaps she had disliked Henry, she thought. Or maybe it was simply that she was shy.

"Sulky," Henry observed, with a short laugh.

She was not his type. Yet something about her interested him. Perhaps it was those dark eyes. So, thinking it best to keep these thoughts to himself, he found a way to bump into her in the music section of the lending library where Meeka had said she often went. This happened several times in a casual, oh-my-goodness-fancy-meeting-you-again, sort of way. Meeka believed it to be a coincidence. She was not interested in him. She did not have any interest in men. Once bitten, twice shy, she believed. Henry, on the other hand, was enthusiastically friendly, and in a desire to make himself more interesting invited her to have coffee with him so that he could tell her a somewhat exaggerated version of his life. He meant it as a joke, these stories of his conquests (the Greek, the German, the two Italian students, to name but a few), but Meeka, he noticed, was mesmerised. Although she had no personal interest in him, she listened. How did he do it? Henry sighed. It was hard to explain. With his engaging approach to life, having caught her attention Henry felt it was his duty to entertain her.

Eventually, on their third encounter it was assumed he would come over to her house for supper.

He hadn't learned much about her as yet, so throwing caution to the wind he went. But first, being an excellent cook, he offered to bring the pudding. He made a fruit salad in an old chipped blue-and-white china bowl. It had belonged to his mother and would have been worth something had he not chipped it (but then Henry was always careless with the washing-up). He wore a shirt that matched his eyes, which were of a particular sharply defined blue. It was a glorious evening; the spring flowers were out as he set forth on his adventure, whistling to himself. The estate where Meeka lived was thrown into sharp contrast by the light. When he found number 11 Henry was pleasantly surprised. The house stood on the curve of a cul-de-sac covered in a bower of greenery. Bluebells lined the path. Small delicate flowers sprang up everywhere. His own shop-bought offering seemed out of place. Bending low under the branches that would soon cascade with roses, he found the front door and was charmed. It was painted dark green; a wind chime moved gently in the breeze. Dimly, through the glass, he saw the outline of a grand piano. Someone began to play a slow three-octave scale. It rose to the top without a pause before descending. Henry hesitated, listening intently. Then he rang the bell.

"Goodness!" he said joyfully, by way of greeting, handing Meeka the flowers. Then he laughed uproariously as though at some joke of his own. Meeka frowned. She recognised that laugh but could not place it.

"Well," said Henry, conversationally, "we could stay out here all evening, or you could ask me in?"

And then he handed her the bowl of fruit salad, stepping inside unasked and making for the piano.

"Can you *really* play this thing," he asked, teasingly, "or is it just an ornament?"

For a moment it was as though someone had put the clock back and Meeka felt she was riding the District Line on the Underground in the school holidays with Gillian and Susan and Jennifer.

"Oh, get lost!" she said crossly before she could stop herself, making Henry roar with laughter.

It was not an auspicious start. Things could only get better. Isabella, when her mother rang her the next day, was outraged. She thought Henry sounded like a madman.

"What d'you mean he offered you lessons? How dare he be so condescending just because he's a conductor," she said, appalled by such arrogance. "Who the hell does he think he is? I've never even heard of him."

Too late, Meeka wished she had kept her mouth shut. Something about Henry, his ridiculous boasting ways, his impossible clothes, or maybe it was simply his irritating laugh, stirred a half-hidden memory. There was a vague familiarity to his behaviour.

A few nights later Henry appeared unannounced just as Anna-Meeka was about to eat supper. He looked enquiringly at her and, rather reluctantly, she invited him to join her. He had been away for a few days rehearsing Mahler in Birmingham.

"It's coming on nicely," he said, yawning, helping himself unasked to some raw carrots.

Then he opened his bottle of wine and went in search of two glasses. Meeka frowned. Once again, his behaviour stirred a long-forgotten memory. Who did he remind her of?

"It's hard work but exciting," he shouted from the kitchen.

"Make yourself at home," Meeka said, irritated.

"Thanks," Henry called out.

He brought in two glasses of wine. "Here," he said, not noticing the look on her face, "try this."

Meeka ignored him.

"I've got an incredible first violinist," Henry told her, tucking into the salad. He cut himself a piece of bread. "I've coaxed her to come over from Berlin," he said, talking fast with his mouth full.

Again Meeka frowned. Naturally the violinist *would* be a woman.

"Her name is Greta. I've been wanting to work with her for a long time."

He grinned at Meeka, who listened while trying hard to look uninterested. There was nothing she could contribute to the conversation. Suddenly a feeling of shame enveloped her. She felt hopelessly ignorant. With a flash of insight she understood how her father had felt when she had first brought Naringer home. It had been the way she felt whenever she used to meet Pippa. Then suddenly she remembered Alicia's recording.

"Would you like to listen to my aunt's recording?" she asked when she could get a word in edgeways.

To her surprise Henry was instantly enthusiastic. At first they were both silent. Alicia's magic touch was unchanged by time. When it was over Henry hummed a few bars, drumming his fingers absentmindedly on the arm of his chair. Meeka said nothing.

"Beautiful," murmured Henry. "I'd like to hear her play Beethoven. With a talent like that why on earth didn't she go back to it? That last movement was superb!"

"It wasn't that simple," Meeka said at last. "She loved my uncle Sunil. Life wasn't worth living after that."

"But you said she was all right later on?"

"Oh yes. Much later. She found someone else. She used to play for him."

"There you are then!" Henry said, satisfied.

Meeka was sitting beside a small table lamp, half in shadows, not looking at Henry. "I think," she said hesitantly, "everything that was happening in the country at the time was too much to bear. You know, the Sinhalese discriminated against my father's people. They had been wealthy once but then overnight they were nobody." She struggled to explain herself. "After my uncle was killed the whole family was petrified. That's why my parents wanted to leave. They were frightened for my future. They stayed frightened for the rest of their lives. Not understanding anything about this country. England was too much. In fact . . ." She paused. She had never had this kind of conversation with anyone before. "I could have helped more, but well . . ." She shrugged. "All I was interested in was integrating with the other children. Making friends, losing my accent! Without meaning to I broke their hearts, I suppose," she said softly. "Leaving Sri Lanka unsettled them more than they realised. My mother used to say the civil war was the invisible story of the British Empire."

"They certainly paid a high price," Henry said quietly. "I wouldn't blame yourself. You were just a child."

Meeka glanced at him sharply, uncertain if he was laughing at her. But Henry was looking a little solemn. With the oddest expression in his salt-blue eyes.

The next day when he visited Pippa, Henry could talk of nothing else but Meeka.

"Why does she act as though she's crushed?" he asked. He had a funny feeling Anna-Meeka was different underneath.

"Well," said Pippa doubtfully, "perhaps she *is* crushed. Have you thought of that? Being an immigrant in the sixties, and having parents who never fit in couldn't have been easy for her. I think she struggled with them." She paused.

Henry didn't seem to be listening.

"She was telling me about her aunt," he said. "You know she was a professional pianist? Then her husband was killed and she never played seriously again." Pippa shook her head. She had not known any of this.

"We didn't have a lot to do with each other at school," she said. "Meeka was awfully pretty and very remote."

Still is, thought Henry.

"You should have seen her father. He was very handsome. He adored her of course."

Of course, thought Henry, drumming his fingers. Pippa looked at her friend. Usually within days of meeting someone new he was bored. She was delighted to see him so preoccupied. Henry, unaware of her thoughts, was whistling absentmindedly under his breath. He whistled a few bars from *The Magic Flute*. Fully alert to all possibilities, he was making plans.

He decided to move things along, pull Meeka's leg a little, see what happened. With this in mind, throughout what remained of the spring, he conducted his investigations. Being Henry he went about it in his own way. He told Meeka stories about his former wife, hoping to keep her keen.

"She was very blonde," he said, closing his eyes with what appeared to be ecstasy. "And stunningly beautiful."

Meeka glared at him. Sensing he had got her attention, he told her about his last girlfriend.

"Francesca was really talented," he said, shaking his head as though with amazement. "I was staggered the first time I heard her play the flute."

Anna-Meeka narrowed her eyes. As far as she could see, *all* Henry's women were either goddesses or geniuses. What was he doing spending time with her?

"Well, why doesn't he bloody well go back to them?" snapped Isabella crossly when her mother rang her.

Meeka vowed to show no interest. Henry Middleton was getting on her nerves; she began to feel the stirrings of summer within her, smell the warm air. Henry had better watch out, thought Pippa Davidson, wondering what the devil he was up to. Like the cow-parsley that seeded itself, Henry seemed to be everywhere. Snooping into Meeka's life, invading her space, smitten. Watch out, Henry, thought Pippa, don't overdo it. Remember they don't usually understand your humour. But Henry Middleton didn't care. That was part of his trouble. And possibly also his charm.

A few months went by. It was high summer now, and the roses were out. Every time he saw Meeka, Henry was aware of experiencing all sorts of interesting emotions. Sally Dance, the well-known archaeologist, thought it hugely funny when she heard. She was one of Henry's closest friends. She had thought he had been a bit silent for some time. Now she knew why.

"Henry's met his Waterloo," cried Sally. "She looks young enough to be his daughter!"

"I hope he doesn't annoy her," said Pippa. "You know what he's like."

"Oh I know. I think he's trying to be endearing," said Sally Dance. "Why are men so clueless!"

"She sounds weird," said Henry's ex-wife, when she heard. "I think she's after his money."

The cat was well and truly stalking the pigeons. On close observation Henry could see that Meeka was thawing out nicely. He was pleased to see more than a hint of spirit whenever he teased her. Good, he thought. Good, good.

"I'd tone down your past," advised his lodger Dill. "Women don't like to hear about old girlfriends."

But Henry grinned, unrepentant. Careful, Henry, thought Pippa again. She didn't say it but, more and more, she felt he was pushing his luck.

"What *is* the matter with him?" she said to Sally. "This isn't how he usually behaves. He's not *that* funny."

Sally Dance agreed. "I think he's scared," she said shrewdly, enjoying it all. "He's scared he's falling for her!"

No one knew what might happen next. Only time would tell.

Henry too was surprised by how much he was enjoying himself. He waited, as one waits for a train that's late. He was discovering there was more to Anna-Meeka than even he had first thought. He began to visit her once a week, in the evening, a bottle of fine wine tucked under his arm. Bringing his stories with him, ready for more sport.

"I bumped into my ex again, today," he told her cheerily, pouring out some wine.

"Really?" asked Meeka, covering her glass with her hand.

Henry didn't seem to notice.

"She's invited me to one of her big dinner parties. Aren't you having any more wine?" he asked again.

Oh my God! thought Anna-Meeka, staring at him. She'd remembered! Henry was showing off like her father. Unaware of her thoughts, Henry continued.

"She has these black-tie dinners about once a month," he was saying. "She always wants me there."

As for that laugh, thought Meeka. I know exactly who his laugh reminds me of. And she remembered how her uncle Christopher had behaved at her wedding.

"Henry," she said, experimentally, "I know you were very hurt when your wife left you, but, you know, I think you're simply stuck in your own groove."

Henry was taken aback. He poured himself a drop more wine.

"What was that you were playing, when I came in?" he asked, changing the subject, knowing she was reluctant to talk about her music.

So, she composed music. As well as playing the piano. Hmm, he thought. That night, just before he left, shamelessly, he stole some of the sheet music lying around. He wanted to take a good look at it without Meeka knowing. The next day he examined her composition. Pursing his lips, he sat down at the piano and played a few bars. He raised an eyebrow, playing slowly, groping his way, trying to illuminate the texture of the music, to understand the underlying structure of the composition. He could hear a number of voices, rising together and falling away one by one. Thinking about the music, following Anna-Meeka's score, he made a few notes in red ink. Then he played it again, bringing out the tenderness within the melody. The sounds dropped note by note into his mind. Poco vivace and exuberant at first, then drifting into a brooding C minor. He could hear her voice through his fingers; her presence in the music. He felt a strong sense of her personality, lifting off the manuscript. The sunshine from the window fell softly like candlelight against the piano keys. There were small particles of dust moving slowly in the light, but Henry never noticed. He wore a strange lost smile of appreciation. An inner world of extraordinary integrity and balance was being revealed to him. The music came to its gentle insistent closure; after the last chord he did not take his hands away from the keyboard. He did not stir. It was as though he was under a spell. Staring out of the window, his face unusually serious, he wondered what he should do. Suddenly he was a little frightened. There was no doubt in his mind: the music was astonishing. She had not studied composition, her notations were not always correct. Yet the structure was clear. There was a tension within that went all the way through the piece, a connection that never once let up. Still Henry hesitated, not wanting to do the wrong thing.

"Beautiful," he said, sotto voice, playing some of the phrases again and again, listening to the cadence and resolution, the way it developed both emotionally and intellectually.

"Early twentieth-century English composers," he mumbled to himself.

And someone else. Messiaen, he thought, shaking his head, amazed. Probably she didn't even realise it. An extraordinary woman, he thought. So much locked away, undiscovered.

What on earth was she ashamed of that she wouldn't speak to him about it? He wondered how much more she had written, knowing it was too soon to ask. Lost in thought, he began to play once more. Then he reached for the phone. What he really wanted was a second opinion.

Two days later Henry visited Meeka again. He had several plots to thicken. On this occasion he recited poetry to her. Browning and then Tennyson, and after that Yeats. Yeats always came last in his opinion. Meeka flattened her ears as a cat might flatten them when it was confused. Heavens! she thought, remembering her mother had been crazy about Yeats. What would she have said if she heard all this? Henry, observing her reaction, smiled with secret satisfaction. The thaw had settled in nicely. Of late his eyes were the colour of blue lagoons.

"Oh no!" said Sally Dance seeing the seriousness of what was happening. "I do hope he doesn't get hurt."

"Listen, Henry, don't keep mentioning your ex," urged his lodger. "She won't find it amusing."

But Henry didn't seem to hear. He was preoccupied with thoughts of his own and was just off for a swim. At his age, he informed his lodger, he needed to keep himself in trim. Besides, it was time to invite Meeka to his house, for a candlelit supper.

Sally Dance and Pippa offered to bleach his tablecloth and make him a summer pudding.

"We'll eat alfresco," he declared, "beside the fountain and next to the statue of Venus."

Lavender grew among the rosemary. The scents mingled with the Dijon Rose petals falling softly onto the ground like confetti. Henry placed the speakers outside. They would listen to Bach, he decided. The backdrop was perfect.

Then disaster struck. Just as he was chopping the garlic for the *melanzane alla parmigiana*, the doorbell rang.

386 · ROMA TEARNE

"*Caro* Henry. *Ciao, caro!*" said a voice.

Shit! thought Henry. Shit, shit! It was Francesca the flautist.

"*Stai bene*, Henry?" she said, slinking in.

Francesca followed him into the kitchen.

"How sweet, you make-a my favourite dish-a!" And she started nibbling the cheese.

There was nothing for it, Henry gave her a large grappa and lured her into his study upstairs.

"Now you just stay here, Francesca," he said. "I shan't be long, well, not too long. I'm sorry to keep you out of the way like this, but I don't have much time. It's just a business meeting, that's all, you know what these musicians are like . . . I must go," he added, as the doorbell rang. Hastily (he could smell the oven from where they stood), thrusting the bottle of grappa into Francesca's hand, he rushed downstairs, taking care to close the study door, remembering to check his face for lipstick. He felt unaccountably hot.

It was an uneasy evening. Meeka had brought a dish that was perfumed with almonds and rose water but Henry's food was burnt and the wine corked. He opened another bottle. Every time he glanced up at the house he could see Francesca prowling around. The light was on. What on earth was she doing? Henry reached for the bottle of newly opened wine, helping himself liberally.

"My goodness, is that the time?" he asked, yawning loudly, glancing at his watch.

He had an early start the next day. Meeka agreed; it was time to go home. She had not drunk much but she decided to use the bathroom before she left.

"No!" shouted Henry, adding more quietly, "It's just that the bathroom isn't awfully nice, I mean, the light doesn't work." The bathroom light had just come on; he could hear Francesca flushing the toilet.

"Don't worry," said Meeka, "I don't mind."

"No!" said Henry, standing up in alarm, barring her way back into the house. "No, I mean, why don't you wait until I take you back? You can't be that desperate? Can you?" he pleaded.

Anna-Meeka was looking at him strangely.

"Henry," she said patiently, as though she were speaking to a child, "may I use your bathroom please? You needn't worry, I'm not going to pinch anything."

Pushing past him she went into the house. Henry watched her go. Francesca, all kitten heels and not much else, watched from above as Meeka went, head down, determinedly up the stairs.

"You *are* an idiot, Henry," said Pippa, shaking her head at his nerve. Why did he always ruin everything?

Sally Dance couldn't stop laughing. "I could have told you that would happen," she said, wiping her eyes. She could hardly speak. "Oh, Henry! She must have been livid!"

Henry did not bother to answer her. He was still clearing up the mess. The *melanzane* was everywhere.

"I've had enough," said Dill the lodger. "There are too many women in this bloody house."

Henry said nothing. He would have to repaint the wall.

"I've told you," said Isabella down the phone, "the man's a madman! Get rid of him." Her mother was hopeless when it came to men. Perhaps she ought to come home and sort it all out. No wonder Grandpa Thornton used to worry about her so much. "Get rid of him, do you understand? I'm going to ring you tomorrow to check you have."

But Isabella had worried too much. She had forgotten how stubborn her mother was. She had forgotten what happened when her mother made up her mind. She had not heard her grandma Savitha on *that* subject. Anna-Meeka unplugged the telephone. She closed the curtains, and turned out the lights. Then she settled down to wait. Had her father been alive, had her mother been there, had her uncles been around, they would have instantly recognised the look in her eyes.

That October was the best ever. From Broad Street, behind the high blue-crested gates of the college, Michaelmas spread its autumn crocuses. The air thickened with damp bonfires and the beginnings of river mist. The Oxford skyline was tinted once again in gentle late-afternoon light, while the college walls near the Martyrs' Memorial in St. Giles shed their crimson foliage leaving a pencilled scribble of bare branches across the yellowing stone. Bicycles, moving like furious insects, crossed and recrossed cobbled streets, and evensong in the cathedral swelled with its term-time choir. Henry Middleton had had an astonishing summer. When he was not mowing Meeka's lawn or tying her unruly honeysuckle back, he was playing on her beautiful piano. He took her punting on the river. He poured the finest champagne into his mother's old crystal glasses and toasted her health. He pedalled across Oxford with flowers for her. He invited her to listen to him conduct Mahler and then he took her to dinner to meet his friends. He watched her smile. And he felt his heart turn over with a long-forgotten emotion. Sally Dance and Pippa were delighted. Like the roses, Henry was flourishing. Isabella watched her mother with amazement; she had never seen her look so happy. She thought Henry was *so* sweet.

"Oh Mum, he's *lovely*," she said in astonishment. "He's such a tease! And crazy about you."

The house just now was filled with life. Cars parked outside, visitors came and went; Meeka and Henry played duets together on the piano laughing, and arguing with one another.

During the second week of term Henry Middleton took Meeka to a piano recital. In all her years living near Oxford,

Meeka had never once ventured inside a college. Henry was
delighted to be the one to take her. She had met the concert
pianist Carl Schiller at a party with Henry. Now he had come
to Oxford. Their footsteps crunched on the gravel. The
women all wore black. Pippa Davidson was excited. Sally
Dance had come too. She would not have missed tonight for
the world. Isabella had come home for the weekend. She and
Henry had become the best of friends. Several of Henry's
friends were present, including the music critic Adrian Taylor.
Henry introduced Meeka to him. Even Dill the lodger came.
He was glad Henry had painted the wall on the landing. It
looked as good as new. Only a slight mark remained. Dill fancied that sometimes, depending on the light or the time of day,
it glowed like an old war wound.

"Wear one of your saris," Henry had said. "The blue-and-
gold one, the one your aunt Alicia gave you."

He had been unusually insistent. So Meeka wore the blue-
and-gold sari.

The air quivered with a sense of expectancy. Meeka, sipping
her wine, watched the audience as they arrived. She noticed
Henry looking around the room and wondered when his
Venetian friend or his former wife would pop up. But Henry,
it was clear, was playing safe tonight. Sally Dance had brought
her man with her. He grinned at Meeka.

"How're you getting on with Henry then?" he asked loudly. "I hear he's behaving himself these days!"

"Shut up, Matthew," Sally hissed. When all was said and
done, Henry was still her friend, even if he sometimes made
mistakes. Besides, she did not want to ruin his big evening.

"What's happening?" asked Matthew, who had no idea why
he was here.

"Shh!" said Sally Dance. "You'll see in a minute."

Soon the auditorium began to fill up. Meeka gazed in
delight at her surroundings, unaware of Henry's anxious

glances as he introduced her to some of his colleagues, some members from his orchestra, a journalist and a producer from Radio 3. A flash went off nearby and Meeka blinked. Conversation spun in the air. There were so many people who knew Henry. She lost track of how many hands she shook or how many of these women were Henry's old "friends." She wished she had not worn her sari. She almost wished she had not come.

"Stop fussing, Mum," said Isabella as though she had read her mind.

Suddenly, for no reason, Meeka thought of her grandmother. The sari she was wearing had belonged to her once and she took some small comfort, a feeling of who she was, from the thought. Pippa Davidson, glancing across at Meeka and Isabella, was reminded of the dashing Mr. de Silva. The family likeness was very apparent tonight. Sally Dance was busy watching Henry, magnificent in his dinner jacket.

"He's as nervous as a cat," she whispered to Pippa. Henry was fidgeting.

"I'm not surprised," Pippa whispered back. "It's making me nervous too!"

Sally giggled.

"Stop it," Pippa said. "I can't bear this suspense."

The last of the audience took their seats. Then suddenly the lights were dimmed. Swiftly, with the speed of tropical darkness, silence descended in tiers around the room. Only a small spotlight illuminated the grand piano. Carl Schiller, fine-boned and delicate as porcelain, came onstage. He bowed once and sat down, pausing, looking down at the keyboard. In the dark his hands glowed white. All around the room the silence was velvet. Meeka felt her hands become moist with sympathy. Was this how her aunt Alicia used to feel when she had played in public?

Carl Schiller began to play. His slender fingers formed a chord, they ran headlong across the keys, clear and unhesitating. The sounds fell into the darkened room, parting the silence as though it were an overgrown path. They cascaded in a waterfall of notes, overlaying each other, dissolving gently, phrase echoing phrase. Fluid, haunting and unending. He played with a piercing yearning, turning inexorably, just as you thought he might pause, into a minor key and then back again, before being lifted by the music somewhere else entirely. The sounds moved across the room, unstoppable now, effortless and breathtakingly lovely.

A soft rustle went through the audience. Whose music was this? How astonishingly beautiful! How it sparked, how it lilted, how it turned on a chord, unpredictable and always with the melody never far away. A distant voice from long ago returning again, when it was least expected, brushing lightly against them.

Here was how it was, the music seemed to say. Of these things were our lives made. Here was the substance of our sorrows and our joy. Exactly like yours. How we laughed, and how we loved, in the place that was once our home. With its coconut palms, its sun-washed beaches, its ancient tea-covered hills. This land of ours where all our earliest desires are housed, and which, however far we may roam, will remain with us forever. For like you, we carry our youth in our hearts.

On and on the music flowed, brimming over in the oak-panelled room, telling of these things; new longings joining the others that the centuries had absorbed. Pressing insistently into the memory of this new space, crossing continents, moving boundaries, connecting. In a language without barriers, in ways that could no longer be denied.

In the darkness, above the familiar sounds, Anna-Meeka looked at Henry Middleton. He sat with her hand tightly in his, watching her, no longer able to hide his tenderness, his pride in her. Wishing that her father, and her mother, and her grandmother, all of them, all those people he had only heard about, could see just how long the journey had been, how far her music had brought her.

And, thought Meeka, looking at him now with eyes that shone, for all his paleness and all his Englishness, still, his ears were not pasted. His lobes hung freely! Happiness welled up in her, rising from a new depth. How pleased her father would have been. For what difference was there in the end? she wondered, smiling at him. There *was* no difference. People were people. Only their fears had made them struggle. And then, suddenly, she knew. In that moment, as the sounds of her music, submerged for so long, cascaded around her, she knew. With all the clarity that had been missing on the evening in the head teacher's office so many years ago, she knew what she must do. She needed to see her home once more. She needed to see that long-forgotten place, with its sweet, soft sound of the ocean, its wide sweep of beaches, and its clear tropical skies. That place, lodged forever within her heart, where the heat of the day glistened and trailed far into the night. Where her aunt Frieda waited so patiently with her moth-dusty sorrow for the past to be dispelled. For clearly she saw it, in spite of the shock, she saw that the things that had been mislaid, the history that had been buried and the memories no longer spoken of, all these things, were somehow being given back to her. And she saw too, at last, that here within this remarkable Englishman, with his sense of the ridiculous, his understanding and his love for her, was something of her beloved family. Returning again.

Far away in the distance, as a dream realised at last, came the rush of thunderous applause, rising and falling like surf-green waves, crashing against her and catching the dazzling sea light.

ACKNOWLEDGEMENTS

I would like to thank my agent Felicity Bryan, for her unfailing encouragement and kindness to me; Kathy van Praag, also, for her endorsement of the book; and of course Clare Smith, my inspired editor at HarperPress.

Thanks to Michele Topham from the Felicity Bryan Agency for her hours of endless discussion; and to Mally Foster and Annabel Wright from HarperPress for their humour and support throughout.

Also to Richard Blackford, who talked to me about musical composition; Maureen Lake, my long-suffering piano teacher; my friends Tessa Farmer and Jane Garnett, who read the manuscript in single, swift sittings; and my brother-in-law Paul, who pleased me by laughing uproariously while reading the manuscript but then informed me it was my spelling that amused him.

I would like to pay special tribute to the rest of my family, to whom this book is dedicated. Like the passengers of a very large and boisterous ocean liner ploughing the seas, it was they who provided the environment in which I could write.

Thank you.

ABOUT THE AUTHOR

Roma Tearne is an artist and author. Born in Sri
Lanka and raised in Britain, she completed her
MA at the Ruskin School of Drawing and Fine
Art. She has been artist in residence at the
Ashmolean Museum at Oxford University and
is now writer in residence at the Tate Modern in
London. Her debut novel, *Mosquito* (Europa
Editions 2008) was nominated for the Los
Angeles Times Art Seidenbaum Award for First
Fiction. She lives in Oxford, England.